KU-576-255

'The novel's beauty, wisdom and heartbreaking honesty lie in examining the small details of two seemingly different lives with equal amounts of compassion and detachment'   *Globe and Mail*

'Brutally wise, viciously funny and at times unflinchingly cruel'
                                                          Sunday Telegraph

'*The Post-Birthday World* is a novel which refuses to moralise or suggest there are easy answers: "You'll make the best call you can in the moment, and then you deal with the consequences." And its concluding chapter, where both strands of the narrative seem (at least until its final lines) to merge, is a skilful stroke. This is writing at its finest imaginative, compassionate, funny and inventive and not to be missed'   *Canberra Times*

'Shriver writes with elegance and a loaded intensity . . . she is a brilliant, witty storyteller and the book is utterly compelling'
                                                          Weekend Australian

'As fresh and biting as an arctic wind . . . Shriver is honest, but never judgemental about her characters' flaws'
                                                          Sydney Morning Herald

'Provocative. . . . *The Post-Birthday World* is . . . as unflinching as they come'   *International Herald Tribune*

'A tour de force'   *USA Today*

'A wise and moving novel, touching us most deeply when it shows us how finite our lives are, and how infinite we want them to be'   *Daily Telegraph*

'A playful, psychologically acute, and luxuriously textured meditation on the nature of love'   *The New Yorker*

ALSO BY LIONEL SHRIVER

The Female of the Species
Checker and The Derailleurs
Ordinary Decent Criminals
Game Control
A Perfectly Good Family
Double Fault
We Need to Talk About Kevin
So Much for That
The New Republic
Big Brother

THE POST-BIRTHDAY WORLD

LIONEL SHRIVER

THE BOROUGH PRESS

The Borough Press
An imprint of HarperCollins*Publishers*
1 London Bridge Street
London SE1 9GF

www.harpercollins.co.uk

This paperback edition 2015
1

First published in Great Britain by HarperCollins*Publishers* 2007

Copyright © Lionel Shriver 2007

Lionel Shriver asserts the moral right to
be identified as the author of this work

A catalogue record for this book is
available from the British Library

ISBN: 978 0 00 757803 0

This novel is entirely a work of fiction. The names, characters and incidents
portrayed in it are the work of the author's imagination. Any resemblance to actual
persons, living or dead, events or localities is entirely coincidental.

Set in Minion by Palimpsest Book Production Ltd, Falkirk, Stirlingshire

Printed and bound in Great Britain by Clays Ltd, St Ives plc

All rights reserved. No part of this publication may be
reproduced, stored in a retrieval system, or transmitted,
in any form or by any means, electronic, mechanical,
photocopying, recording or otherwise, without the prior
permission of the publishers.

MIX
Paper from
responsible sources
FSC
www.fsc.org
FSC® C007454

FSC™ is a non-profit international organisation established to promote
the responsible management of the world's forests. Products carrying the
FSC label are independently certified to assure consumers that they come
from forests that are managed to meet the social, economic and
ecological needs of present and future generations,
and other controlled sources.

Find out more about HarperCollins and the environment at
www.harpercollins.co.uk/green

'Nobody's perfect.'

—KNOWN FACT

For J.

chapter one

What began as coincidence had crystallized into tradition: on the sixth of July, they would have dinner with Ramsey Acton on his birthday.

Five years earlier, Irina had been collaborating with Ramsey's then-wife, Jude Hartford, on a children's book. Jude had made social overtures. Abjuring the airy we-really-must-get-together-sometime feints common to London, which can carry on indefinitely without threatening to clutter your diary with a real time and place, Jude had seemed driven to nail down a foursome so that her illustrator could meet her husband, Ramsey. Or, no—she'd said, "My husband, Ramsey Acton." The locution had stood out. Irina assumed that Jude was prideful in that wearing feminist way about the fact that she'd not taken her husband's surname.

But then, it is always difficult to impress the ignorant. When negotiating with Lawrence over the prospective dinner back in 1992, Irina didn't know enough to mention, "Believe it or not, Jude's married to *Ramsey Acton*." For once Lawrence might have bolted for his *Economist* day-planner, instead of grumbling that if she had to schmooze for professional reasons, could she at least schedule an early dinner so that he could get back in time for *NYPD Blue*. Not realizing that she had been bequeathed two magic words that would vanquish Lawrence's broad hostility to social engagements, Irina had said instead, "Jude wants me to meet her husband, Raymond or something."

Yet when the date she proposed turned out to be "Raymond or something's" birthday, Jude insisted that more would be merrier. Once returned to bachelorhood, Ramsey let slip enough details about his marriage for Irina to reconstruct: after a couple of years, they could not carry a conversation for longer than five minutes. Jude had leapt at the chance to avoid a sullen, silent dinner just the two of them.

Which Irina found baffling. Ramsey always seemed pleasant enough company, and the strange unease he always engendered in Irina herself would surely abate if you were married to the man. Maybe Jude had loved dragging Ramsey out to impress colleagues but was not sufficiently impressed on her own behalf. One-on-one he had bored her silly.

Besides, Jude's exhausting gaiety had a funny edge of hysteria about it, and simply wouldn't fly—would slide inevitably to the despair that lay beneath it—without that quorum of four. When you cocked only half an ear to her uproarious discourse, it was hard to tell if she was laughing or crying. Though she did laugh a great deal, including through most of her sentences, her voice rising in pitch as she drove herself into ever accelerating hilarity when nothing she had said was funny. It was a compulsive, deflective laughter, born of nerves more than humour, a masking device and therefore a little dishonest. Yet her impulse to put a brave, bearable face on what must have been a profound unhappiness was sympathetic. Her breathless mirth pushed Irina in the opposite direction—to speak soberly, to keep her voice deep and quiet, if only to demonstrate that it was acceptable to be serious. Thus if Irina was sometimes put off by Jude's manner, in the woman's presence she at least liked herself.

Irina hadn't been familiar with the name of Jude's husband, consciously. Nevertheless, that first birthday, when Jude had bounced into the Savoy Grill with Ramsey gliding beside her—it was already late enough in a marriage that was really just a big, well-meaning mistake that her clasp of his hand could only have been for show—Irina met the tall man's grey-blue eyes with a jolt, a tiny touching of live wires that she subsequently interpreted as visual recognition, and later—much later—as recognition of another kind.

Lawrence Trainer was not a pretentious man. He may have accepted a research fellowship at a prestigious London think tank, but he was raised in Las Vegas, and remained unapologetically American. He said "*con*troversy," not "con*tro*versy"; he never elided the K-sound in "schedule." So he hadn't rushed to buy a white cable sweater and joined his local cricket league. Still, his father was a golf instructor; he inherited an interest in sports. He was a culturally curious person, despite a misanthropic streak that resisted having dinner with stran-gers when he could be watching reruns of American cop shows on Channel 4.

Thus early in the couple's expatriation to London, Lawrence conceived a fascination with snooker. While Irina had supposed this British pastime to be an arcane variation on pool, Lawrence took pains to apprise her that it was *much* more difficult, and *much* more elegant, than dumpy old eight-ball. At six feet by twelve, a snooker table made an American billiards table look like a child's toy. It was a game not only of dexterity but of intricate premeditation, requiring its past masters to think up to a dozen shots ahead, and to develop a spatial and geometric sophistication that any mathematician would esteem.

Irina hadn't discouraged Lawrence's enthusiasm for snooker tourna-ments on the BBC, for the game's ambiance was one of repose. The vitreous click-click of balls and civilized patter of polite applause were far more soothing than the gunshots and sirens of cop shows. The commentators spoke just above a whisper in soft, regional accents. Their vocabulary was suggestive, although not downright smutty: *in amongst the balls, deep screw, double-kiss, loose red;* the black was *available.* Though by custom a working-class sport, snooker was conducted in a spirit of decency and refinement more associated with aristocracy. The players wore waistcoats, and bow ties. They never swore; displays of temper were not only frowned upon but could incur a monetary fine. Unlike the hooligan audiences for football, or even tennis—once the redoubt of snobs but lately as low-rent as demolition derby—snooker crowds were pin-drop silent during play. Fans had sturdy bladders, for even tip-toeing to the loo invited public censure from the referee, an austere presence of few words who wore short, spotless white gloves.

Moreover, on an island whose shores were battered by cultural backwash from the States, snooker was still profoundly British. The UK's late-night TV may have been riddled with reruns of *Seinfeld,* its cinemas dominated by *L.A. Confidential,* its local lingo contaminated—*chap* and *bloke* giving way to *guy.* But the BBC would still devote up to twelve hours of a broadcasting day to a sport that most Americans didn't know from tiddlywinks.

In all, then, snooker made a pleasing backdrop while Irina sketched the storyboard of a new children's book, or stitched the hem on the living-room drapes. Having achieved under Lawrence's patient tutelage a hazy appreciation for the game, Irina would occasionally look up to follow a frame. More than a year before Jude ever mentioned her husband, Irina's eye had been drawn to a particular figure on screen.

Had she thought about it—and she hadn't—she had never seen him win a title. Yet his face did seem to pop up in the later rounds of most televised tournaments. He was older than the preponderance of the players, who tended to their twenties; a few severe lines in the long, faceted face could only have scored it beyond the age of forty. Even for a sport with such an emphasis on etiquette, his bearing was signally self-contained; he had good posture. Because to a degree snooker's rectitude was all show (Lawrence assured her that away from the table these gentlemen didn't incline towards Earl Grey and cucumber sandwiches), many players grew paunches, their complexions by thirty hard-living and haggard. In a game of finesse, their arms often went soft and their thighs spread. Yet this character was narrow, with sharp shoulders and slim hips. He always wore a classic starched white shirt, black bow tie, and distinctive pearl-coloured waistcoat—a signature perhaps, intricately over-woven with white silk thread, its filigree reminiscent of certain painstaking fills in her own illustrations.

When they were introduced in the Savoy Grill, Irina didn't recognize Ramsey from TV. He was out of context. Brilliant with names, faces, dates, and statistics, Lawrence quickly put to rest her nagging puzzlement over why Jude's husband seemed familiar. ("Why didn't you *tell* me?" he'd exclaimed. It was a rare day that Lawrence Trainer was obsequious.) *Ramsey Acton* immediately pulled down a whole file on a man apparently an icon of the game, albeit something of a holdover from the previous generation. Borrowed from American basketball, his handle on the circuit, "Swish," paid tribute to Ramsey's propensity for often potting so cleanly that the object-ball never touched the jaws of the pocket. His game was renowned for speed and fluidity; he was a momentum player. A professional for twenty-five years, he was famous, if one could be famous for such a thing, for *not* winning the World Championship—though he had played five championship finals. (By 1997, that was thirty years, and six finals—still no championship.) In no time Lawrence had nudged his chair closer to Ramsey's, engaging in an exultant duet that would brook no intrusions.

Irina had mastered the basics: right, you alternate potting a red with potting a colour. Potted reds stay potted; potted colours return to their spots. Reds cleared off, you sink the colours in a set order. Not so difficult. But if she was always a little unclear on whether the brown or the green went first, she was unlikely to engage a pro in engrossing speculation on this matter. By contrast, Lawrence had mastered the game's most obscure regulations. Hence as he waxed eloquent about some notorious "respotted black," Swish bestowed Lawrence with a handle of his own: "Anorak Man." The gentle pejorative was clearly coined in affection. To Lawrence's satisfaction, Anorak Man would stick.

Irina had felt excluded. Lawrence did have a tendency to take over. Irina might describe herself as retiring, or quiet; in bleaker moments, mousy. In any event, she did not like to fight to be heard.

When Irina locked eyes with her friend that evening, Jude's rolled upward in a gesture a mite nastier than *Oh, those boys being boys.* Jude had met her husband during her journalism phase, when she'd been assigned a puff piece for *Hello!* in the 80s, and Ramsey was a minor pinup star; in the interview, they'd got hammered and hit it off. Yet for Jude what had probably started out a meagre interest in snooker had apparently slid to no interest in snooker, and then on to outright antagonism. Having made such a to-do about how Irina must meet *Ramsey Acton* only to display such annoyance, Jude must have routinely hauled her husband out and plunked him next to the likes of the adoring Lawrence in order to get her money's worth, or something's worth anyway.

Lawrence utterly neglected the woman he called his "wife" to others but whom he had never bothered to marry; Ramsey was better brought up. Shifting towards Irina, Ramsey firmly turned aside any more snooker shoptalk for the night. In a thick South London accent that took some getting used to, he commended her illustrations for Jude's new children's book, extolling, "Them pictures were top drawer, love. I was well impressed." He had a way of looking at Irina and only at Irina that no one had employed for a very long time, and it frankly unnerved and even discomfited her; she constantly cut her own gaze to her plate. It was a bit much for a first meeting, not presumptuous in a way you could quite put your finger on but presumptuous all the same. And Ramsey was lousy at casual chitchat; whenever she brought up the Democratic convention, or John Major, he plain stopped talking.

Quietly, Ramsey picked up the bill. The wine, and there had been a lot of it, had been pricey. But snooker pros made a mint, and Irina decided not to feel abashed.

That first birthday, his forty-second, as she recalled, he'd seemed perfectly nice and everything, but she'd been relieved when the evening was over.

Irina collaborated on a second children's book with Jude—the overt manipulativeness of the first, along the lines of *I Love to Clean Up My Room!*, appealed to parents as much as it repelled children, and had ensured that it sold well. Thus the foursome soon became established, and was repeated—often, for London circles—a couple of times a year. Lawrence, for once, was always up for these gatherings, and from the start displayed a proprietary attitude towards Ramsey, whose acquaintance he enjoyed claiming to British colleagues. Irina grew marginally more knowledgeable about the sport, but she could never compete with Lawrence's encyclopedic mastery, so didn't try. Tacitly it was understood that Jude was Irina's friend and Ramsey Lawrence's, though Irina wondered if she wasn't getting the short end of the stick. Jude was a little irritating.

The dinner that began the second year of their rambunctious foursome landed once again on Ramsey's birthday. For secular Westerners ritual is hard to come by. Two birthdays in a row sufficed to establish standard practice.

Self-conscious that Ramsey always footed the bill on his own birthday, the fourth July, in 1995, Irina had insisted on hosting the do. In the mood to experiment, she prepared her own sushi-sashimi platters, to which she'd noticed that Ramsey was partial. Unlike those precious restaurant servings of three bites of tuna and a sheet of serrated plastic grass, the ample platters of hand rolls and norimaki on their dining table in Borough left no room for the plates. She would have imagined that someone like Ramsey was used to being feted, and worried beforehand that her hesitant foray into Japanese cuisine wouldn't compete with the flash fare to which he was accustomed. Instead, he was so overcome by her efforts that for the entire evening he could hardly talk. You'd think no one had ever made him dinner before. He was so embarrassed that Irina grew embarrassed that she had embarrassed him, exacerbating the painful awkwardness that had come to characterize their few direct dealings with each other, and making Irina grateful for the boisterous buffering of the other two.

Ah, then there was last year. She and Jude had had a huge row, and were no longer speaking; Jude and Ramsey had had a huger row, and were no longer married. Though seven years was brief for a marriage, that was still a mind-boggling number of evenings in the same room for those two, and they were surely only able to stick together for that long because Ramsey spent such a large proportion of the year on the road. Had it been left to Irina, at that point she might have let their fitful friendship with Ramsey Acton lapse. She'd nothing in common with the man, and he made her uncomfortable.

Yet Lawrence was determined to rescue this minor celebrity from that depressing pool of people—sometimes an appallingly populous pool, by your forties—with whom you used to be friends but have now, often for no defensible reason, lost touch. He might have slipped in the rankings, but Ramsey was one of the "giants of the game." Besides, said Lawrence, "the guy has class."

Shy, Irina pressed Lawrence to ring, suggesting that he make a half-hearted offer to have Ramsey over; it was pretty poor form to ring someone up and ask him to take you out to dinner on his own birthday. Yet she expected Ramsey to decline the home-cooked meal, if not the whole proposition. A threesome anywhere would feel unbalanced.

No such luck. Lawrence returned from the phone to announce that Ramsey had leapt at the opportunity to come to dinner, adding, "He sounds lonely."

"He doesn't expect another sushi spread, does he?" asked Irina with misgiving. "I hate to seem ungenerous when he's picked up so many checks. And last year was fun. But it was a lot of work, and I hate to repeat myself." Irina was a proud and passionate cook, and never bought plastic bags of prewashed baby lettuces.

"No, he begged that you not go to so much trouble. And think of me," said Lawrence, who did the washing up. "Last year, the kitchen looked like Hiroshima."

Hence the fare had been, to Irina's mind, rather ordinary: an indifferent cut of venison cubed in red-wine sauce with shiitake mushrooms and juniper berries, which constituted an old standby. Yet Ramsey was as effusive as before. This time, however, Irina wondered whether it was really the menu that captivated their guest. Perhaps in order to add one note of novelty to a meal she'd prepared several times, before he arrived she had dragged out a sleeveless dress that she hadn't worn in years. The garment had almost certainly slipped to the back of the wardrobe because—as she discovered once more—the straps were a tad long, and kept dropping off her shoulders. The soft, pale blue cotton sized with latex stretched smoothly across her hips; the hemline was high enough that she had to yank it down her thighs every time she sat down. She'd no idea what had got into her, swanning around in such provocative gear before a man fresh from divorce. At any rate, it wasn't the venison that Ramsey kept staring at all night, that was for sure.

Mercifully, Lawrence hadn't seemed to notice. What he did notice was that Ramsey wouldn't leave. Even with snooker icons Lawrence's social appetite was finite, and by two Ramsey had exceeded it by a good measure. Lawrence vigorously cleared the plates, and washed them loudly down the hall. As the censorious clank of pots carried from the kitchen, Irina was stranded with Ramsey, and panicked for lack of subject matter. Granted that Ramsey was overstaying his welcome, but she wished Lawrence wouldn't do that with the dishes! Whenever they did get the ball rolling in the living room, Lawrence would interrupt the flow by brisking in to wipe the table, or to prize off melted candle wax, never meeting Ramsey's eyes. Oblivious to his host's rudeness, Ramsey refilled their wine glasses. He didn't collect his cue case, and then with obvious reluctance, until after three.

Thus the whole last year the trio hadn't reconvened, as if Irina and Lawrence needed that long to recover. But Lawrence didn't hold a grudge, agreeing with Irina that sometimes Ramsey's social skills were as inept as his snooker game was elegant. Besides, Lawrence was well compensated for his lost sleep with free tournament tickets throughout the following season.

It was July again. But this year was different.

A few days ago Lawrence had rung from Sarajevo to remind her that Ramsey's birthday was coming up. "Oh," she'd said. "That's right. I'd forgotten."

Irina chided herself. She had not forgotten, and it was foolish to pretend that she had. The slightest abridgments of the truth with Lawrence made her feel isolated and mournful, far away and even afraid. She would rather be caught out lying than get away with it, and thus live with the horror that it was possible.

"Going to get in touch with him?" he asked.

Irina had been chewing on this matter ever since she learned that Lawrence would be at a conference on "nation building" in Bosnia and wouldn't return until the night of July 7. "I don't know," she said. "You're the one who's big buddies with Ramsey."

"Oh, I think he likes you." But Lawrence's tone imparted moderation, or even reservation, as in "I think he likes you well enough."

"But he's so odd. I have no idea what we'd talk about."

"The fact that they're thinking about dropping the bow-tie rule? Really, Irina, you should call, if only to make an excuse. How many years have we—"

"Five," she said morosely. She'd counted.

"If you let it go, he'll be hurt. Before I left, I did leave a brief message on his cell-phone voice mail to apologize that I'd be in Sarajevo this year. But I let it slip that you were staying behind in London. If you want that badly to get out of it, I could always call him from here, and say that you changed your mind at the last minute and came with. You know, happy returns, but what a drag, we're both out of town."

"No, don't. I hate lying for petty reasons." Irina was uneasy with the implication that she didn't have a problem with lying for substantial reasons, but further qualification seemed tortuous. "I'll ring him."

She didn't. What she did do was ring up Betsy Philpot, who had edited Jude's and Irina's collaborations at Random House, and so knew Ramsey somewhat. Not having worked together for a couple of years, Betsy and Irina had morphed from colleagues to confidantes. "Tell me that you and Leo are free on the sixth."

"We're not free on the sixth," said Betsy, whose conversation never ran to frills.

"Damn."

"This matters why?"

"Oh, it's Ramsey's birthday, when we've had this custom of getting together. Except now Jude's history, and Lawrence is in Sarajevo. That leaves me."

"So?"

"I know this sounds vain, and it could be all in my head. But I've wondered if Ramsey doesn't—if he isn't a little sweet on me." She'd never said so aloud.

"He doesn't strike me as a wolf. I'd think he's nothing you can't handle. But if you don't want to do it, don't."

9

For Betsy, another American, everything was always simple. In fact, her cool, compass-and-ruler approach to circles that others found difficult to square had a curious brutality. When Jude and Irina had fallen out, she'd advised with a savage little shrug, "As far as I could tell, you've never liked her much anyway. Write it off."

Irina wasn't proud of the way she "dealt" with this quandary, meaning that she didn't deal with it at all. Every day in the countdown to July 6, she promised herself in the morning to ring Ramsey in the afternoon, and in the afternoon to ring him in the evening. Yet propriety pertained even to night owls, and once it passed eleven p.m., she'd check her watch with a shake of the head and resolve to ring first thing the next day. But he probably slept late, she'd consider on rising, and the cycle would begin again. The sixth was a Saturday, and the Friday before she faced the fact that a single day's notice so obviously risked his being busy that to ring at the last minute might seem ruder than forgetting the occasion altogether. Well, now she wouldn't have to face down Ramsey Acton all by herself. A flood of relief was followed by a trickle of sorrow.

The phone rang Friday at nearly midnight. At this hour, she was so sure that it was Lawrence that she answered, "*Zdravstvuy, milyi!*"

Silence. No returning, "*Zdravstvuy, lyubov moya!*" It wasn't Lawrence.

". . . Sorry," said an airy, indistinct British accent after that embarrassed beat. "I was trying to reach Irina McGovern."

"No, *I'm* sorry," she said. "This is Irina. It's just, I thought it was Lawrence."

". . . You lot rabbit in—was that Russian?"

"Well, Lawrence's Russian is atrocious, but he knows just enough—he'd never manage in Moscow, but we use it at home, you know, as our private language. . . . Endearments," she continued into the void. "Or little jokes."

". . . That's dead sweet." He had still not identified himself. It was now too awkward to ask who this was.

"Of course, Lawrence and I met because I was his Russian tutor in New York," Irina winged it, stalling. "He was doing his doctoral dissertation at Columbia on nonproliferation. In those days, that meant you needed to have some Russian under your belt. These days, it's more like Korean. . . . But Lawrence has no gift for languages whatsoever. He was the worst student I ever had." Blah-blah-blah. Who *was* this? Though she had a theory.

A soft chuckle. "That's dead sweet as well. . . . I dunno why."

"*So*," Irina charged on, determined to identify the caller. "How *are* you?"

". . . That'd depend, wouldn't it? On whether you was free tomorrow night."

"Why wouldn't I be free?" she hazarded. "It's your birthday."

Another chuckle. "You wasn't sure it was me, was you? 'Til just then."

"Well, why should I be? I don't think—this is strange—but I don't think, after all these years, that I've ever spoken to you on the phone."

". . . No," he said with wonderment. "I reckon that's so."

"I always made our social arrangements through Jude, didn't I? Or after you two split, through Lawrence."

Nothing. The rhythm to Ramsey's phone speech was syncopated, so that when Irina began to soldier on, they were both talking at once. They both stopped. Then she said, "What did you say?" at the same time he said, "Sorry?" Honestly, if a mere phone call was this excruciating, how would they ever manage dinner?

"I'm not used to your voice on the phone," she said. "It sounds as if you're ringing from the North Pole. And using one of those kiddy contraptions, made of Dixie cups and kite string. You're sometimes awfully quiet."

". . . Your voice is wonderful," he said. "So low. Especially when you talk Russian. Why don't you say something." *Summat.* "In Russian. Whatever you fancy. It don't matter what it means."

Obviously she could rattle off any old sentence; she'd grown up bilingual. But the quality of the request unnerved her, recalling those porn lines that charged a pound per minute—what Lawrence called *wank-phone.*

"*Kogda mi vami razgovarivayem, mne kazhetsya shto ya golaya,*" she said, binding her breasts with her free arm. Fortunately, nobody learned Russian anymore.

"What'd that mean?"

"You said it didn't matter."

"Tell me anyway."

"I asked you what you had in mind for tomorrow night."

"Mm. I sense you're having a laugh."

But what *about* tomorrow night? Should she invite him over, since

11

he liked her cooking? The prospect of being in the flat alone with Ramsey Acton made her hysterical.

"Would you like it," she proposed miserably, "if I made you dinner?"

He said, "That's bleeding decent of you, pet." The curious little endearment, which she'd only encountered once before when collaborating with an author from way up in Newcastle, was somehow warmer for being odd. "But I fancy taking you out."

Irina was so relieved that she flopped into her armchair. In doing so, she pulled the cord, and the phone clattered to the floor.

"What's that racket?"

"I dropped the phone."

He laughed, more fully this time, round, and the sound, for the first time in this halting call, relaxed her. "Does that mean yes or no?"

"It means I'm clumsy."

"I never seen you clumsy."

"Then you've never seen me much."

"I never seen you enough."

This time the silence was Irina's.

"Been a whole year," he continued.

"I'm afraid Lawrence wouldn't be able to join us." Ramsey knew that, but she'd felt the need to insist Lawrence's name into the conversation.

"Rather put it off, so Lawrence could come as well?"

He'd given her an out; she should jump at it. "That doesn't seem very ceremonial."

"I was hoping you might see it that way. I'll call by at eight."

For the most part, other people took couples as they found them: you were, or, at a certain point, you weren't. At its most torrid, your love life was merely titillating to others, and the done-deal nature of established couples like Irina and Lawrence was doubtless a big bore. Romantic devastation occasioned, at most, an onlooker's tinny sympathy or schadenfreude. Romantic delirium was even worse. Newly in love, you expected to draw envy or admiration, but were far more likely to attract a finger-drumming impatience for you to get over it. Of course, people did have opinions, about whether you were suited, or probably fought; almost always your friends—that is, friends of the couple—liked one of you more. But these opinions were cheap. They cost nothing to hold, and nothing to change.

Some friends regarded Irina-and-Lawrence as a factual matter, like the existence of France. Others relied on the couple as a touchstone, proof that it was possible to be happy; the role was a burden. Irina had a few companions who'd little time for Lawrence, and found him paternalistic or gruff; they regarded Lawrence as a friendship tax, the cost of doing business. But one way or the other, she didn't care.

Love having come to her neither easily nor early, Irina accepted the fact that any minor contribution she might make to human affairs would have nothing to do with unprecedented achievement in courtship. No one would ever recount the peaceable, convivial union of a children's book illustrator and a think-tank research fellow as one that launched ships or divided nations. No modern-day Shakespeare would squander his eloquence on the ordinary happiness—if there is such a thing—that percolated within a modest flat in Borough through the 1990s.

Nevertheless, Irina regarded her relationship with Lawrence as a miracle. He was a devoted, funny, and intelligent man, and he loved her. She didn't care if feminists would have maintained that she didn't need a man; she did need a man, more than anything on earth. When Lawrence was out of town, the flat seemed to generate an echo. She would not, any longer understand why she was here, in both the general sense of alive, and the specific sense of on a Georgian square just south of London Bridge. Many were the solitary evenings that she might have worked late in her studio, but the opportunity would be wasted. She would walk from room to room. Pour a glass of wine and leave it standing. Drizzle the stainless-steel drain board with corrosive to remove the lime scale. (So mineral was London's tap water—reputed to have cycled through more human bodies than any liquid on the planet, and leaving a white, crusty ghost behind every evaporated drop—that it might have stood sheerly upright on the counter like the Cliffs of Dover without a glass.) But suddenly the energy required to wipe the glop away would elude her. She would go to bed, and wake to a reek in the kitchen from the chemicals left to seethe.

Shameful or not, having a man who loved her and whom she loved in return was the most important thing in Irina's life. It wasn't that she didn't have strong and abiding subordinate affections, for Irina was far more sociable than Lawrence, and had put much effort into building a whole new set of comrades when they moved to London in 1990. Yet there were hungers that friends could never satisfy, and when you made the slightest bid to get them to feed this particular appetite they ran a mile. Moreover, it wasn't that she cared nothing for her "art," even if two histrionically self-involved parents in film and dance impelled her to couch the word in sour quotation marks. The illustrations, when they were working, were a joy. But the joy was greater when Lawrence eased up behind her while she was drawing, and purled peevishly in her ear that it would be nice to eat.

Monogamy had been effortless. Over nine years, Irina had been attracted to one of Lawrence's colleagues from the Blue Sky Institute for exactly half an hour—at the end of which the man rose for another round of drinks, and she noticed that his backside was pear-shaped. That was that, like a scratchiness in your throat when you don't end up coming down with a cold.

The period of solitary confinement while Lawrence was in Sarajevo had passed less painfully than most, but it is in the nature of the absence of pain that one fails to take note of it. Though she commonly prepared time-consuming meals for Lawrence without complaint, it was still festive to get out of fixing complete dinners with vegetables and grains. Alone, Irina had taken to skipping the whole nonsense altogether and working through the dinner hour. At around ten p.m., famished and pleasantly tired, she'd been downing a large, gooey slice of Tesco chocolate-cappuccino cake, whose very purchase was out of character; now on the eighth day of Lawrence's Bosnian departure, she was on her third box. Later she played the sappy music that Lawrence detested—Shawn Colvin, Alanis Morissette, Tori Amos, all those girl singers recently in vogue who deployed excessive vibrato in the exaltation of gloom, or to declare brassily that they had no need for men and you knew they were lying. Unsmitten by Lawrence's disapproving glare—his mother was an alcoholic—she'd been pouring herself a tiny nightcap before bed. Lawrence would never have countenanced cognac more than once a month. But he might have appreciated that the fumes of brandy swirled into heady reflections on how lucky she was to have found him, how eagerly she looked forward to his coming home.

In all, then, the week had been self-possessed. She'd allowed herself the little indulgences of the unwatched, including the gradual, contemplative incineration of a secret packet of cigarettes. But she'd made headway on her drawings, and a woman of Irina's slight dimensions could afford a little cake. In two days, it was back to trout and broccoli, and she'd be sure to air the living room of its incriminating nicotine taint.

Thus when Irina woke that Saturday she was startled to discover that her smug self-possession had cracked like an egg. It was ridiculously late, after eleven, and she would normally arise by eight. Groggily she reconstructed that after that disquieting phone call with Ramsey, she had not, as she ought to have, cradled the receiver and flossed. There was, she recalled, a second brandy. In the kitchen, the chocolate-cappuccino cake was decimated. That's right, she'd stood fretfully at the counter, slicing smaller and smaller pieces until there was nothing left. And oh dear, she had cranked up the volume of *Little Earthquakes* so high that a downstairs neighbour had arrived at the door in a bathrobe to complain. There would be hell to pay if Lawrence got wind of that, since he had only last month banged on the door below to get them to "put a lid on the salsa," and he "didn't mean the kind you dump on tacos, either."

Befuddled, Irina put on the large stove-top espresso pot. Armed with a second cup, in the studio she could do no more with the half-finished drawing than stare. It was not possible to work. Clearly her finite reserve tank in Lawrence's absence would last exactly eight days but not ten. Suddenly a whole lonely day and night and day again threatened only a debauched wooze of back-to-back fags, entire bottles of brandy, and endless fingerfuls of crass commercial icing whose main ingredient was lard.

Leaving for Borough Market, where she always shopped on Saturdays, she slammed the door resolutely behind her. Irina was going wobbly, and Irina had to be contained.

At the bustling covered market near London Bridge, the crowd was as ever abrasive with American accents. While it was irrational to bristle at the company of compatriots, one of the traits that Americans seem to share is a common dislike of running into one another in foreign countries. Perhaps it was having that mirror held up, reflecting an image so often loud, aggressive, and overweight. Irina didn't have a big problem with being American herself (everyone has to come from somewhere, and you don't get to choose), although, a second-generation Russian on her mother's side, she had always presumed her nationality to have an opt-out clause. Maybe she winced a bit at the familiar skirl piping from

Monmouth Coffees ("La-a-a-rry, they're out of decaf Guatema-a-la!") because she enjoyed the feeling of Britain being somewhere else, a sensation increasingly difficult to preserve in a town colonized by Pizza Hut and Starbucks. When she overheard another Yank inquire about the location of *South-wark Street,* with a hard R, it was hard not to feel tarred with ignorance by association.

On the other hand, out from under Lawrence's influence, Irina sometimes indulged in what she privately termed *mental kindness.* The exercise had nothing to do with how she acted; as a woman who had grown up treated rather badly by classmates, she had developed a chronic horror of treating anyone badly herself. It didn't have to do with what she said. It had to do with what went on in her head. There were merits to being nice in your *mind*—to hearing a fellow American mispronounce *Southwark* and deliberately choosing to think, *Why don't Brits cut us a little slack? Americans would never expect a Londoner to know that* Houston *was pronounced* Hyooston *in Texas, but* Howston *in Manhattan.* Surely that beat grumbling sotto voce, "You stupid twat." Of course, you could empathize or denounce your heart out within the privacy of your thoughts, and neither improve anyone's day nor injure their feelings. Still, Irina was convinced that what went on in her mind mattered, and silently cast strangers in the gentlest possible light as a discipline. If nothing else, internal generosity made her feel better.

Mental kindness was not a concept she had shared with Lawrence, who was more apt to indulge in the likes of mental laceration. He was awfully hard on people, especially anyone he considered of inferior intelligence. His favourite word was *moron.* That harshness could be contagious; Irina had to guard against it. However, she should really exercise *mental kindness* first and foremost on Lawrence himself.

For one thing, Lawrence liked to keep his life simple, restricted to a few close friends and mostly to Irina, period—who had extravagantly benefited from admission to his tiny pantheon of the beloved. Scornfulness was a form of population control. Since you couldn't invite the whole gamut of your acquaintances from your vegetable seller to your plumber for tea, you needed a filter. It just so happened that Lawrence's filter was made of very fine mesh indeed.

For another thing, Lawrence was a genuine example of what was once standard-issue in the States but had latterly become an endangered

American type: the self-made man. Lawrence clung fiercely to his condescension because his fingernails were sunk so precariously into the cerebral heights of a lofty British think tank. His upbringing was anything but intellectual. Neither of his parents had more than a high school education, and growing up in Las Vegas was hardly propitious preparation for earning a doctorate in international relations from an Ivy League school. A childhood of crass casinos had left him with a terror of being sucked back—into a world of lengthy debates over the quality of the eggs Benedict at the Bellagio. So all right, he was scathing, and sometimes had to be encouraged to give other people a break, to emphasize their finer qualities and to forgive their flaws. But it behooved her to see Lawrence's tendency to pillory as itself such a flaw, and worthy of her own forgiveness.

She purchased Italian black kale, smoked boar sausage, and a malicious fistful of chilies from flirtatious vendors who didn't know her name but had come to recognize her face. All too aware that going through the placid paces of marketing was slapping a superficial gloss of normalcy over an alarmingly unstable foundation, Irina also bought an armful of rhubarb to keep herself gainfully occupied when she got home.

Restored to the flat, she set about industriously constructing two rhubarb-cream pies, one for the freezer and one for Lawrence's homecoming. She increased the recipe's measure of nutmeg by a factor of five. A reserved woman of moderate inclinations to all appearances, Irina expressed an insidious attraction to extremes through decorative matters like seasoning, and few diners at her table suspected that her flair in the kitchen owed largely to a better-than-average mastery of the multiplication table. Fortunately, the fiddly lattice tops concentrated a mind that kept fragmenting like the fine strips of crust. Her hands weren't precisely shaking, but they moved in spasmodic jerks, as if under strobe. (That cognac—surely there hadn't been a third?) Lawrence wasn't coming home a moment too soon. She strained against it on occasion, but maybe she needed his stern regimentation and sense of order. Without Lawrence, Irina would obviously turn overnight into a chain-smoking, cake-hoovering, brandy-addled hag.

The pies came out beautifully, the egg and sugar bubbling through the lattice into brittle browned hats, the acidic sting of rhubarb spiking the air throughout the flat, but pastry only saw her through to about five What's more, while the pies were in the oven, she did something she very rarely got up to in the last few years, since Lawrence anyway, and once the pies were cooling, she did it again.

Six o'clock. Irina wasn't prone to dithering over her appearance; most of her clothes were offbeat secondhand items from Oxfam outlets, for during their tenure here London had officially topped the charts as the most expensive city in the world. Ordinarily allowing fifteen minutes to dress was ample. Two hours was ridiculous.

Yet this evening, allowing a mere two hours was cutting it close.

The bed grew heaped with discarded blouses. Flailing in and out of frocks, she recalled a charming project from a few years ago titled *I've Nothing to Wear!*, about a little girl who hurricanes through her entire wardrobe one morning, flinging outfit after outfit from her chest of drawers. Lines from the book returned: "I do not like the button holes, I do not like the collar! If I wear the polka dot, I'll bawl and shriek and holler!" The narrative arc had been predictable (big surprise, the little girl finally chooses to wear the first thing she'd put on), but the clothing flying through the air had a Futurist energy, and the illustrative opportunities had been rich.

Yet contrary to feminine convention, Irina was striking pose after critical pose in the full-length bedroom mirror with an eye to looking as dowdy as possible. While early in this melee she had toyed with the notion of the pale blue sleeveless that last year had threatened to keep Ramsey in their living room all the way to breakfast, she'd immediately chucked the idea. Was she insane? Instead she rummaged through the wardrobe's nether regions for the longest skirts, the crummiest fits, and the least becoming colours she could find. Alas, Irina didn't own a lot of ugly clothes, a lack she'd never before had occasion to rue.

This exercise in perversity was a waste. Ramsey was sure to select a ritzy restaurant where her few flashier garments would not look out of place. Lawrence always wore the most slovenly gear he could get away with, and on the few occasions she dared to don something chic he grew flustered: "It's only a Blue Sky cocktail party. No need to make a big *deal* out of it."

Calling time in this sartorial musical chairs, the intercom buzzer blared. Like a kindergartner lunging at the nearest empty seat, she was stuck with the outfit she had on: a straight-cut navy skirt that did reach

18

nearly to the knee, though with that ubiquitous latex sizing its cling to her hips was woefully snug. At least the short-sleeved white top didn't expose bare shoulders; better still, multiple launderings had worn a small hole in the neckline, lending the outfit a satisfying shabbiness. In fact, the ensemble was gloriously dull. Blue and white had the sexless connotations of sailor suits or high school football colours, and she fisted her dark hair into a hasty ponytail without using a comb. However, slipping into the only shoes that would go, she was exasperated to note that the high-heeled white sandals—broken down, ten years old if a day—tightened her calves and emphasized her slender ankles. *Nuts,* she concluded. *I should have worn slacks.*

Determined that she would *not* have him up for a drink, she grabbed the receiver and shouted, "Be right down!" and clattered out the door.

Out front, Ramsey stood propped against his opalescent-green Jaguar XKE, smoking a cigarette. Irina wouldn't, of course, encourage anyone to smoke, but the habit suited him. On the phone his silences gaped, but in person he could fill the gaps with reflective exhalations. Leaning but perfectly straight, Ramsey himself resembled a snooker cue set against the car; his limbs reiterated the same attenuated taper. Saying nothing— what was *wrong* with the man?—he took her in as she strode from the step, inhaling the image along with a last drag. Flicking the half-smoked fag to the gutter, he sidled beside her without a word, ushering her to the passenger seat. His hand hovered near the small of her back but never quite touched her waist, as a parent keeps an arm at the ready with an unsteady toddler who wants to cross the room without help.

Nestled into the bucket seat not even having said hello either, Irina was visited by a sensation that she'd first experienced in high school, after her mother—grudgingly—had acceded to braces, and the hateful hardware had come off. It had taken a long time for it to sink in that boys suddenly seemed to find her a draw, and in truth this elevation of status from over twenty-five years ago had still not sunken in. Still, there had been certain evenings like this one, when she would be ushered into a young man's car. The feeling was not of being attractive precisely, but rather of *not having to entertain.* It was breathtaking: to be ensconced in another person's company, yet to be relieved of the relentless minute-by-minute obligation to redeem one's existence—for there is some sense in which socially we are all on the *Late Show,* grinning, throwing off nervous witticisms, and crossing our legs, as a big hook behind the curtains lurks in the wings.

Hands clasped calmly in her lap as the Jaguar surged from the kerb, staring serenely ahead as it lurched to a stop at the light, Irina realized that right at this moment the fact of her presence alone was its own redemption. Though she'd agonized over how to carry a conversation with Ramsey Acton, he was already exuding the purr of the supremely contented, giving every indication that he would remain just as contented for the rest of the night should she continue to say nothing.

"Sushi?" he asked by the third intersection.

"Yes." It was marvellous: she needn't defer graciously to whatever plans he had made, or effuse about how Japanese was just the thing. *Yes* would suffice.

As the Jaguar thrummed over Blackfriars Bridge, Irina unwound her window. The air was the temperature of bathwater whose heat was beginning to fade, but still warm enough for a lingering soak. The midsummer evening was light. Lambent vermilion flared in the windows of tall buildings and made the whole city look on fire. Stained glass flamed in St. Paul's, as if the Nazis had successfully bombed the cathedral after all. Sheets of incendiary sunlight flashed across the Thames, like an oil slick to which some rascal had touched a match. Meanwhile, the Jaguar communicated every little bit of gravel to the bucket seat like a pea to a princess.

"These days, everyone wants to drive so high up," she said at last. "Those SUVs. When I was growing up, all the cool people tucked down as close to the road as possible."

"I'm yesterday's man in every way," said Ramsey, "if you believe my press."

"If they mean your taste in cars, I'm all for it."

Commonly she didn't give two hoots about cars. But she liked this one—that it was a classic from 1965, but unrestored, with its leather upholstery well worn; that it was *valuable* rather than merely expensive. Ramsey's driving was aggressive, full of accelerating thrusts and sudden downshifts. In contrast to the delicate articulation of his body, a refinement in his face, a social deference or even shyness, and a conspicuous fluidity of motion, all of which legislated toward a subtle collective effeminacy, Ramsey drove like a man. Although his rash weavings in and out of lane and close shaves with adjacent bumpers would ordinarily have made her edgy, the manoeuvrings were precise, boldness twinned with calculation perfectly replicating the authority with which he negotiated a snooker table. She trusted him. Besides, if Irina theoretically believed that modern women should be independent and forceful, all that, the truth was that old-fashioned passivity could be sumptuous. Total abnegation of responsibility presented the same appeal of sleep, and the ecstasy of surrender helped to explain why once a year, for fifteen minutes a go, Irina fell in love with her dentist. If the active deliciousness of being ferried about and paid for was little observed of late and potentially on the way to extinction, it was all the more intoxicating for being retrograde.

"So what you done today?" asked Ramsey.

"I made pies," said Irina festively. "They're therapeutic."

"Why'd you need therapy?"

"When Lawrence is away . . . I can get a bit out of kilter. You wouldn't think it, but I have another side, and—it has to be controlled."

"What happens when it ain't?"

Silence best implied that they were both better off not finding out. "So what did you do today?"

"I practised a bit, but mostly agonized all afternoon over where to take you to dinner." From most men this would have been flattering horseshit, but Ramsey had a funny naïveté about him, and was probably telling the truth.

"Are you satisfied with your decision?"

"I'm never satisfied." As he tossed his keys to a parking attendant, Irina waited for Ramsey to open her door. The queen-bee routine wasn't like her, but sometimes acting out of character was like breaking out of jail.

The Japanese would put the emphasis of *Omen* on the second syllable, but the name of the restaurant still exuded a foreboding. Omen was small and exclusive-looking, their table more exclusive still, up a few steps at the back and on its own. If Irina had dreaded being cooped up with Ramsey in the mortifying coziness of her own flat, Omen's premiere seating was no less claustrophobic. When Ramsey reached to pull the curtain, Irina asked could he please keep it open, "for air." With an expression of perplexity, he obliged. They'd only read through the starters when a young man skipped up the stairs to their table, clutching a menu.

"Oi, Ramsey!" the young man whispered, as one feels compelled to in Japanese restaurants. "Could you give us an autograph? That's right, just across the top there, like." He had slid his menu beside Ramsey's chopsticks.

"No problem, mate." Ramsey withdrew a slender gold ballpoint from his inside pocket; everything he owned seemed to reiterate the taut, sleek design of his body, and the signature itself was spidery, like his fingers.

"Blinding! Pity about that kick in the Embassy," the fan commiserated. Given Ramsey's involuntary wince, the "kick" must have been in the teeth. Leave it to strangers to blunder across your raw nerve. "Would've had the frame and match as well!"

"Everybody gets kicks," said Ramsey, shrugging fatalistically about the tiny grains of chalk that can send the cue ball veering off its trajectory. What an odd profession, in which one can be undone by a speck.

"Cheers, mate!" The fan waved his menu, which Omen would now forgo, and nodded cockily at Irina. "You snooker blokes get all the lookers! What's left for us?"

"That's why you wanted to close the curtain," said Irina. This wasn't the first time that Ramsey had been hit up for an autograph when they'd been on the town, and usually Irina had found the adulation fun. Just now, she felt possessive of his company during an evening that had recently yawned before her, and now seemed short.

"Too late; cat's out. Jude, now—she hated autograph hounds something fierce."

"The interruption?"

"That bird not only hated snooker fans, she hated the *idea* of snooker fans," he said, wiping his hands on a hot towel. "To Jude, snooker players were like schoolboys who can stand ten-p pieces on their end at lunch. Fair play to them, and no harm done, but you don't ask for their autograph."

The waitress took their orders; feeling extravagant, Irina added à la carte additions to the deluxe sashimi platter of sea urchin and sweet shrimp.

"If Jude thought snooker was trivial," Irina resumed, "why did she marry you?"

"I'd money and stroke, and she could hold my occupation in contempt. Best of both worlds, innit?"

"Didn't she think it was nifty, you on TV, at least at first?"

"Yeah, no mistake. But it's queer how the thing what attracted you to someone is the same as what you come to despise about them."

Irina dangled a translucent slice of cucumber. "If Jude's relationship

22

to my illustrations is any guide, you've got a point. You do know what she said?"

Ramsey tapped a chopstick on the table. "I wager she wasn't no diplomat. But you ever wonder if one or two of her observations weren't spot on?"

"How could I think what she said was 'spot on' and still keep working at all?"

"She did think your composition was brilliant, and that your craftsmanship was class. But there was something, in them first few books, a wildness—it's gone missing."

"Well, you don't just go put 'wildness' *back*. 'Oh, I'll add a little wildness!' "

He smiled, painfully. "Don't get your nose in a sling. I was only trying to help. Making a hash of it as well. I don't know your business. But I did think you was right talented."

"Past tense?"

"What Jude was on about—it's hard to put into words."

"Jude didn't have a hard time putting it into words," Irina countered bitterly. "Adjectives like *flat* and *lifeless* are very evocative. She put her sniffy disapproval into action, too, and commissioned another illustrator for her preachy story line. I had to toss a year's worth of work."

"Sorry, love. And you was bang on—what we was talking about, it's not something you can add like a pinch of salt. It's not out there, it runs through you. Same as in snooker."

"Well, I guess illustration isn't as fun for me as it used to be. But what is?"

Her degenerative expectations seemed to sadden him. "You're too young to talk like that."

"I'm over forty, and can talk however I please."

"Fair enough—you're too beautiful to talk like that, then."

Lawrence was wont to describe her as *cute,* and though Ramsey was a bit out of order the more serious adjective was refreshing. Self-conscious, Irina struggled with the oily strips of eel. "If I am, I didn't used to be. I was a scrawny kid. Knobby, all knees."

"What a load of waffle. Never met a bird what wasn't proud of being skinny."

"But I was also a klutz. Gawky, ungraceful. Do you think that's boasting, too?"

23

"It's hard to credit. Wasn't your mum a ballerina?"

Irina was always amazed when anyone remembered biographical details mentioned years ago. "Well, not a performing one, after she had me. Which she never let me forget. Anyway, I disgusted her. I wasn't limber. I couldn't do splits or tuck my heels behind my head. I could barely touch my toes. I was constantly knocking things over." Irina talked with her hands; with a smile, Ramsey moved her green tea out of reach.

"Oh, it was worse than that," she went on. "I guess plenty of kids aren't Anna Pavlova. But I had buck teeth."

Ramsey angled his head. "Looks like a fine set of chops to me."

"I don't think my mother would have sprung for them, but luckily my father paid for braces. Really, my front teeth weren't just a little crooked. They hung out of my mouth and rested on my lower lip." Irina demonstrated, and Ramsey laughed.

"Well, you helped explain something," he said. "You're not—aware of yourself. You *are* beautiful, and I hope you don't mind me saying so. But you don't know it."

Abashed, Irina reached for her sake cup only to discover that it was empty; she pretended to take a slug. "My mother's much more beautiful than I am."

"Even allowing that were ever true," he said, signalling for another round of sake flagons, "you must mean she *was*."

"No, is. At sixty-three. In comparison to my mother, I'm a schlub. She still works out on a bar, for hours. All on three sticks of celery and a leaf of lettuce. Sorry—half a leaf."

"She sounds a right pain in the arse."

"She is—a *right pain in the arse*."

Their sashimi platters arrived, and the chef was such an artist—the spicy tuna was bound with edible gold leaf—that eating his creation seemed like vandalism.

"Me," said Ramsey, surveying his platter with the same respectful look-don't-touch expression with which he'd met Irina by his car, "I watch buff birds strut the pavement, first thing goes through my head ain't, 'Blimey, love a bit o' that, 'ey!' but, 'Bloody hell, she must spend all day in the gym.' I don't see beauty; all I see is vanity."

"Great excuse for skipping sit-ups: oh, I wouldn't want to look 'vain.'"

"No chance of that, pet."

Irina frowned. "You know, something changed when that tin came off my teeth. Too much changed. It was sort of horrifying."

"How's that?"

"Everyone treated me like a completely different person. Not just boys, but girls. You've probably been good-looking all your life, so you have no idea."

"Am I?"

"Don't be coy. It's like me pretending to be ashamed of having been skinny." Worried that she was encouraging something that she shouldn't, she added, "I only mean, you have regular features."

"Grand," he said dryly. "I'm overcome."

"I'm convinced that decent-looking people—"

"I fancy *good-looking* better."

"—All right, then, *good*-looking people. They haven't a clue that how they're treated—how much it has to do with their appearance. I even bet that attractive people have a higher opinion of humanity. Since everybody's always nice to them, they think everybody's nice. But everybody's not nice. And they're superficial beyond belief. It's depressing, when you've been on the other side. You get treated like gum on somebody's shoe, or worse, like nothing. As if you're not just unsightly, you're unseeable. Ugly people, fat people, even people who just aren't anything special? They have to work harder to please. They have to do something to prove out, whereas when you're pretty to look at you don't have to do anything but sit there and everybody is plumb delighted."

Irina wasn't accustomed to talking so much. Early in that speech Lawrence would have interrupted that she had made her point, so enough already. When Ramsey said nothing to shut her up, he induced the little falling sensation of anticipating resistance and meeting none, like unexpectedly stepping off a kerb.

"Having buck teeth in junior high," she rounded up unsteadily, "must be ideal preparation for getting old. For pretty people, aging is a dumb shock. It's like, what's going on? Why doesn't anyone smile at me at checkout anymore? But it won't be a shock for me. It'll be, oh that. That again. Teeth."

"Rubbish. You'll still be ravishing at seventy-five."

"Dream on, buddy," she said with a smile. "But *you*—you have that telltale face of a boy all the girls were a-swoon over in high school. Grammar school," she corrected.

25

"Hate to disappoint you, sunshine, but I didn't go to grammar school. Secondary modern. I failed the eleven-plus."

"That must have been painful."

"I wasn't fussed, was I? I aimed to be a snooker player. Jesus God, I bunked off school more than I went."

"Still, I can see it. You were the kind of kid that the eyesores like me would all have hopeless crushes on from the back row, while you went out with the only girl in class who'd had breasts since she was ten." The image came readily. Maybe it was the Peter Pan effect of playing games all day, but Ramsey still looked adolescent. Even his hair, turning less grey than white, gilded in candlelight to surfer-blond.

"I may have had my options," he conceded. "But only in hindsight. In them days, girls scared my bollocks off. I'm thirteen, right? A bird named Estelle, a year or two older, takes me to her room and pulls her shirt off. I stare at her Beatles posters—anywhere but at her chest—mumble something about snooker practice, and scarper to the push-bike. I hadn't a monkeys' what I was meant to do."

"You left her there, standing in her room, with her shirt off? I bet she loved that."

"Seem to recollect she never spoke to me again."

"But you figured it out eventually. What to do."

"Matter of fact, I'm not sure I have done."

"I could steer you toward a few birds-and-bees how-tos, but I should warn you they're mostly targeted at ages five to eight."

"To be honest, the most erotic memories of my life ain't of shagging at all," he reflected. "I did have a girlfriend in senior school, you was right about that. And she did have breasts, but they were small. Small and perfect. We was inseparable, and I wager the rest of the school assumed we was bonking our brains out. We wasn't. Denise was tiny, and dark-haired, like you. Quiet. She spent every night she could get away at Rackers, the local snooker club in Clapham, watching me cane fellas twice my age for a fiver a frame. I'd give her the dosh to hold, and my coat, and she knew the signal for 'the competition's getting bolshie, so do a runner sharpish.' She liked to chalk my cue."

"Sounds metaphorical."

"Well, there's something to be said for getting your cue chalked, full stop, and not in any filthy sense. When I cleared up my last frame, I'd walk her home. She'd carry my case. I'd hold her hand. We always walked through Clapham Common and stopped midway at the same bench. We snogged there, for hours. It sounds innocent; I reckon it was. Them kisses, they were so endless, and each one so different . . . I wasn't really busting to do anything else. I didn't feel cheated. Though best nobody warned me that at sixteen I was experiencing the highlight of my erotic life. I still have dreams about Denise, and that bench on the Common."

Irina felt the squirm of an emotion that she was reluctant to name. In the early days with Lawrence, they, too, had whiled away hours on the battered brown couch in her apartment on West 104th Street, giving each other mouth-to-mouth. But those memories had grown too precious. At some indeterminate point in perhaps the second year they lived together she noticed that they no longer kissed—really kiss-kissed, the way Ramsey meant, even if they still pecked good-bye. It probably wasn't fair to blame it all on Lawrence, but Irina couldn't resist the impression that *he* had stopped kissing *her*. They had a robust sex life, and it seemed insensible to focus on the deficits of sensory window-dressing. Yet lately when she watched actors smooching in movies, Irina felt a confusing admixture of alienation—what obscure anthropological custom is this, the pressing of lips?—and jealousy.

"Kissing," she ventured wistfully. "It's more emotional than sex, isn't it? Especially these days, maybe it means more."

"I'd not want to do down shagging, but snogging might be more fun."

In the subsequent conversational lull, Irina bore down on her sashimi platter, now pleasantly vandalized. The creamy slabs of fish lolled indolently from her chopsticks, their fleshy texture indefinably obscene. The taste was clear and unmuddied, a relief after nine days of chocolate-cappuccino cake, whose clinging coffee icing left a residual sludge.

"So how long you been married?" asked Ramsey formally.

"Well, technically," she admitted, nibbling a giant clam, "we're not."

Ramsey clapped his chopsticks to his platter. "But the bloke calls you his *wife*!"

"I know. He says he's forty-three, and too old to have a 'girlfriend.' "

"So he marries you, don't he? Seems sloppy."

"Lawrence hates pomp. Anyway, these days your only real security is good intentions. You can't *get* married in the same way you used to, not since the advent of ready divorce. So it doesn't matter. I know how he feels."

"He adores you," said Ramsey. "It's one of the things I like about visiting you two. You and Lawrence, you're like—Gibraltar."

"What about you? Going to try again?"

"Figure I about packed it in."

"Everyone says that after a divorce, and it's always nonsense."

"Fair enough. But it's crap of you to try and rob me of such a comforting fancy."

Her loyalty to Lawrence firmly reestablished, Irina could afford to be nosy. "May I take that to mean that you aren't seeing anyone?"

"Not so's you'd notice."

There was no reason to be pleased. "But aren't snooker players constantly hit on by groupies? Like *Estelle,* who drag you to their rooms and tear off their shirts?"

"It's not as bad as football; snooker is massively a blokes' sport. But it's not so different to school. I got"—he paused decorously—"options."

"Did Jude leave you feeling burnt?"

"Jude left me *knackered.* Nil was never enough. We buy a house in Spain; it should have been in Tuscany. I mean, good on her, she's a bird what has high expectations of life, and that's brilliant. Honest to fuck, it's bloody brilliant. Still, when you're bollixing them expect- ations—when all you got to do is walk into a room to make your wife want to top herself from disappointment—well, it wears you out. Can't say as I've totally recovered.

"Jude got *ideas* of things," he speculated. "When real life didn't come across she kept trying to yank reality round to the idea 'stead of the other way round. Know what I'm saying? Snooker trains you out of that. After every shot, it's a whole new frame. You live with the balls the way they lay, and not the way they were a minute ago when you had the whole break planned out. She'd an *idea* of what it would be like to write children's books, which didn't include rejections or crap sales or having to compromise with illustrators like you. You know, she pictured touring libraries and reading aloud to gobsmacked six-year-olds, all big-eyed with chins in their hands. Fucking hell, she should have played snooker, if that's the sort of crowd she wanted. For that matter, I'm afraid she started out with a right unrealistic picture of living with a snooker player. The lonely humdrum of me being on the tour most of the year was a shock. So she rides me to come back to London between tournaments, meantime having worked up this notion of me, this airbrushed photo like, and then when I do what she asks and Actual Ramsey rocks up, she just acts ticked off.

"I reckon the short of it is," he said, ordering a fourth round of sake, "it's got to be perfect, or I'm not interested. Like you and Lawrence."

For years Irina had imagined that only the presence of Jude and Lawrence had made it possible for her to while away so much as ten minutes at table with Ramsey Acton. Yet apparently since 1992 those two hadn't been facilitating Irina's tentative relationship to Ramsey. They'd been getting in the way.

Thus by their shared dish of green-tea ice cream, the occasion had taken on the quality of a school holiday. Lawrence would be appalled. If Lawrence were here, he'd have been nursing his single Kirin beer through his chicken teriyaki (he hated raw fish), frowning at Irina's second sake, and by her third publicly abjuring that she had had enough; a fourth he'd not merely have discouraged but would have vetoed outright. He'd have been disgusted that she accepted an unfiltered Gauloise at the end of the meal, waving the smoke from his face and later recoiling from her breath in their minicab home—"You smell like an ash can!"—as if, had she forgone the fag, he would ever think to kiss her in the back of a taxi. It was nearly one , and he'd long before have pulled back his chair and stretched with theatrical exhaustion because it was time to leave. He wasn't obsessed with germs, but she had a funny feeling he wouldn't have liked the fact that she and Ramsey were sharing the same bowl of ice cream. Of this much she was certain: were Ramsey to propose to them both, as he did to Irina while she regretfully stubbed out her Gauloise, that they head back to his house on Victoria Park Road to get stoned, Lawrence would have dismissed the notion as preposterous. He might have smoked a bit back in the day, but Lawrence was a grown-up now, Lawrence didn't do drugs of any description any longer, and that meant, ipso facto, that Irina didn't do drugs, either.

Then again, Lawrence wasn't here, was he? That was the holiday.

So what if she said yes, and then confessed to Lawrence on his return from Sarajevo that she had stumbled off to Ramsey's to get stoned? He'd rebuke her for acting "juvenile." He'd remind her that she always clammed up when she got high—recalling the last time they'd tried marijuana back in '89 on 104th Street, when she'd gawked silently at the paisley wallpaper for three hours. Curiously, the one thing Lawrence would fail to observe would be that she was (or so it was said) a handsome woman; that while Irina was married in all but law, Ramsey had been divorced for eighteen months and had made a point of the fact that he was available; that going back to his house at this hour, to smoke dope no less, could therefore be dangerously misconstrued. Why was that the one thing that Lawrence would never say? Because it was the main thing. And Lawrence was afraid of the main thing. He had a tendency to talk feverishly all around the main thing, as if bundling it with twine. Presumably if he talked in circles around the main thing for long enough it would lie there, vanquished, panting on its side, like a roped steer.

Nonetheless, an acceptance of Ramsey's outré invitation would emphatically entail keeping the end of their evening a secret from Lawrence. Though Irina had always considered secrets between partners perfect poison, she nursed a competing theory about *small* secrets. She may have sneaked a cigarette or two not so much because she enjoyed the nicotine rush itself, but because she enjoyed the secret. She wondered if you didn't need to keep a few bits and pieces to yourself even in the closest of relationships—especially in the closest, which otherwise threatened to subsume you into a conjoined twin (who *did not take drugs*) that defied surgical separation. The odd fag in his absence confirmed for her that when Lawrence walked out the door she did not simply vanish, and preserved within her a covert capacity for *badness* that she had treasured in herself since adolescence, when she'd occasionally flouted her straight-A persona by cutting school with the most unsavory elements that she could find.

"Sure, why not?"

As she negotiated the steps from their nook in high heels, each stair took such acute concentration that putting one foot before the other was like reciting a little poem. Again, that hand hovered at the small of her back, not touching.

Outside, she thought that there ought to be a word for it: the air temperature that was perfectly neither hot nor cold. One degree lower, and she might have felt a faint misgiving about not having brought a jacket. One degree higher, and a skim of sweat might have glistened at her hairline. But at this precise degree, she required neither wrap nor breeze. Were there a word for such a temperature, there would have to be a corollary for the particular ecstasy of greeting it—the heedlessness, the needlessness, the suspended lack of urgency, as if time could stop, or should. Usually temperature was a battle; only at this exact fulcrum was it an active delight.

They strode the pavement a few millimetres closer than was quite the form. Fault, maybe nothing that evening had had anything to do with fault, but as for that short stroll down Charing Cross, she would feel sure in recollection that she was the one who'd walked fractionally too close to him.

Yet by the time the attendant retrieved the Jaguar, Irina was flustered. The easy flow of conversation in Omen had gagged to a dribble, their former awkwardness with each other restored in force. This was nuts. She'd had too much to drink (that was four *large* sakes). She couldn't even remember what it felt like to get stoned, which precluded wanting to. She'd left the rhubarb-creams cooling on the counter, and needed to get the pies in the fridge. She was tired—or ought to be. Lawrence might ring; with no answer at two, he'd imagine something terrible had happened. Yet last-minute extrication would seem cowardly, and conclude Ramsey's birthday on a note of rejection. Well, she could tell Lawrence if he rang that they'd hit one of those ludicrous traffic jams you found in London at the most improbable hours. Sometimes when you make a mistake, you just have to go with it.

The mood in the car was sombre. Rather than jaunting off to party, Irina might have been one of those rigid British kids of yore being dragged off to sit the eleven-plus, which could determine whether she ended up conducting heart-bypass surgery or scrubbing public toilets.

Most of Ramsey's colleagues were raised in down-and-dirty enclaves like East Belfast, or the rougher bits of Glasgow. When snooker players from dodgy parts began to pull in winnings, the first thing they did was move out. But Ramsey was raised in Clapham, then properly rough-and-ready, but now a fatuous, self-congratulatory area full of pokey but surprisingly expensive terraced housing that would merit the label "twee." Perhaps to maintain his proletarian street cred, once Ramsey had taken a few titles, the first thing he did was move to the working-class heartland of the Cockney East End.

Of course, you could hardly call it suffering. He owned a whole Victorian house on Victoria Park Road, the southern boundary of

31

Hackney. Irina had been to the house a handful of times when collaborating with Jude, and it was here they had come to the verbal blows that severed the friendship. High on a kind of bloodlust, Jude had impugned a great deal more than Irina's illustrations, castigating her for being such a "doormat" with Lawrence and deriding an enviable domestic contentment as "sleepwalking." All because Irina had dared to suggest that Jude's latest narrative, *Big Mouth,* was a little obvious (of her story— about a dog that barks all the time and no one can abide, until while he's barking he inhales a tossed ball and can't bark anymore, and then the whole family adores him—Irina had remarked, "Even kids will be able to tell that you're just trying to get them to shut up"), not to mention illogical ("But Jude," she had submitted tentatively, "if you inhale a ball you don't stop talking, do you? You choke to death"). Jude had accused Irina of being "passive-aggressive," a term widely misappropriated of late to mean "aggressive," and cited her literalism about the ball as typical of the stodgy, hidebound universe that Irina had come to inhabit. As the Jaguar surged into the drive, the memory smarted.

Irina didn't play the princess, and opened her own car door. Yet following Ramsey up the shadowy steps of his stoop still took on the sinister portent of a fairy tale, as if she were entering Oz or the castle of Gormenghast, where different laws applied, nothing was as it appeared, and the walls of libraries would fold back to reveal secret dungeons. She could hear the narrative of the last two minutes in that waltzing, emphatic cadence with which people compulsively read to children: *Irina climbed the big steps to the tall man's dark manor. The giant door creaked open and then closed behind her with a* boom *and a* click.

Too late, the little girl remembered that her mother had warned her never, ever to get into a strange man's car! True, Irina's mother had never warned her not to go into a strange man's house, especially when not safeguarded by her stalwart friend Lawrence. But that was because her mother had never imagined that her daughter was a moron.

The interior was still appointed with Oriental carpets and dark antiques, but some of the more valuable-looking pieces that Irina remembered were missing. For women, marriages foreclosed often resulted in an accumulation of booty; for men, these failed projects of implausible optimism were more likely to manifest themselves in material lack. It was hard to resist the metaphorical impression that women got to keep the past itself, whereas men were simply robbed of it. Here, a darker rectangle on the rug marked where the leather sofa once rested, and four deep depressions in the carpet evidenced the departure of a thick pink marble sideboard that Irina had once admired. Ghostly white squares on the cream-coloured walls hovered as the ultimate in abstract expressionism, whereas the original artwork that had once adorned the ground floor had been far more conservative. Yet Ramsey could afford to replace whatever Jude had made off with. Either he was attached to the image of himself as an ascetic, or keen to keep a grievance visually fresh.

Ramsey poured two generous measures of cognac. Jude having absconded with the sofa and armchairs, there was nowhere to sit. Said Ramsey, "Let's go downstairs."

Ah. The dungeon.

Irina trailed him to the basement. Ramsey switched on the lamp over his snooker table, which imbued the expanse of green baize and its gleaming mahogany frame with a sacred aspect, bathing the rest of the cavernous room in the subdued, worshipful glow of a cathedral. Dark leather couches lined his private parlour like pews, and Irina sipped gravely from her snifter as if from a communion chalice. This was the heart of the house, doubtless where Ramsey spent most of his time. The rack of cues caught the lamplight. A cabinet held dozens of trophies; in a row, six upright crystal runner-up platters from the World Championship grimaced across the top shelf like bared teeth. The walls were adorned with glassed posters of tournaments and exhibition games, from Bangkok to Berlin—décor that Jude had graciously allowed her ex to keep. Chances were that Jude had rarely ventured here, and Ramsey's option on repairing downstairs had probably facilitated the marriage's lasting a whole seven years. Irina felt admitted to a sanctum of sorts. The close, golden lighting, the otherworldly sumptuousness of the leather upholstery as she sank into it, and the plush, regal crimson pile under her sandals all enhanced the sensation of having entered a secret magic kingdom through a wardrobe or looking-glass.

Ramsey retrieved a medieval-looking wooden box. Though Irina had herself narrowed the distance between them on Charing Cross those few scandalous millimetres, he assumed a seat on the far opposite side of the couch, pressing into the arm. Reverently, he withdrew a packet of Swan papers, a one-sided razor blade, and a pewter pillbox, upending the box to spill its dark, dense lump onto the table before them. After slitting a

Gauloise with the blade, he laid tobacco along a fag paper. Flicking his slender silver lighter, he wafted the hash over the flame, pinched a soupçon of softened resin, and sprinkled its grains evenly across the joint. The black specks dropping from his fingertips recalled dark potions that had sent Sleeping Beauty to her long slumber, or felled Snow White to the cold ground.

The joint he passed on to Irina, extending his arm since she was so far away, was exquisitely slim and uniform, tapering to a fine point. She acceded to two tokes, shaking her head strenuously when offered a third. Ramsey shrugged, and polished off the rest himself.

To whatever degree she had dreaded from Ramsey the long associative rambles that cannabis can induce, much less the whooping giggle-fits the drug seems to elicit only in movies, her foreboding was misplaced. Ramsey stood from the couch and proceeded to ignore her. He opened his case, assembled the cue, and centred a frame of balls. He broke delicately on the left-hand side. When he pocketed a loose red with a deep screw, the white cannoned into the cluster, scattering the reds into easy pickings.

Like the dope, the exhibition was juvenile. He'd asked her to his house, and had therefore some obligation to play the host. Dragging her to his basement for this display was the kind of childish bid to impress you should really have got beyond by forty-seven.

Be that as it may, Irina had only seen Ramsey play on TV, and in three dimensions the twelve-by-six-foot table yawned much larger than it appeared on screen. Up close, the accuracy of his shots, the surety of their selection, and the unearthly precision with which every pot set him up for the next ball seemed inhuman. As he swung from shot to shot, Ramsey's black silk jacket wafted in the breeze from the open windows on the light well. The balls appeared to roll sweetly to their appointed pockets of their own accord, passing one another and missing by a hair, but never touching unless Ramsey planned to capitalize on the contact. The luminous balls as they swept the baize were mesmerizing; the colours seemed to pulse. The breeze lifted the fine hairs on Irina's bare arms, the air once more neither warm nor cold. The marijuana resin seemed mild, and Irina wondered why she had let herself get so tied up in knots over the prospect of such a commonplace narcotic's effects.

Ramsey had racked up another frame and Irina had taken an abstemious sip from her snifter, when—something happened. The dope, it turned out, was not mild. After only two tokes, it was not mild by a mile. The neutrality of the air gave way, and under the plain white blouse her breasts began to heat, like seat-warmers in expensive cars. Irina rarely thought about her breasts. Lawrence had cheerfully admitted that he "wasn't a tit man," and since her de facto husband never lavished them with any attention—never even touched them to speak of—Irina saw no reason to pay them any especial mind herself. Now they seemed to be rebelling against the neglect, for an infrared of her body would portray them in the molten vermilion that earlier that evening had flamed in the windows of St. Paul's. Aghast, Irina was half-convinced they had begun to glow, and wrapped her arms across her chest, as she had the night before when risking, "When we talk, I feel naked" in Russian to Ramsey on the phone.

This feeling, of being wired with electric coils that some mischief-maker had switched on high, proceeded to spread. Her abdomen throbbed, sending waves of alarming warmth up to her diaphragm and down her thighs. Irina was chagrined. This was not a sensation that a decent woman had any business suffering in company. Though she conceded that her entire torso probably wasn't blinking bright red like a railway crossing, she felt sure that her transformation from primly dressed illustrator to human torch would, in however insidious a fashion, begin to show.

Irina slowly turned her head to face the snooker table with trepidation, since in her untoward condition it seemed safest not to move a hair. Yet Ramsey appeared oblivious. His face was suffused with such restful concentration that she wondered if she'd done him a disservice; it looked bad, of course, like showing off, but surely this was just what he did when he got stoned, headed downstairs and shot practice frames, and this is exactly what he'd have done had Irina declined to come back to the house. He had yet to flick her sly, covert glances after a dazzling shot, to confirm that she'd been paying attention. After all, Ramsey's faultless cuing had been heaped with all manner of praise since he was about eight years old, and it was not for his snooker game that he craved admiration. Funny that it had taken until this very moment to notice—and not in that clinical sense in which she had detailed it to herself before, the way a witness describes particulars like hair colour and height to the police, but really notice-notice—that Ramsey Acton was a rather striking man.

35

A quite striking man.

In fact, he was devastatingly—vertiginously—attractive.

It would not have been objectively apparent, although her eyes may have widened, bulged a bit, blackened in the centre. But however imperceptible its exterior manifestations, inside the turn she took was anything but subtle.

If Ramsey didn't kiss her, she was going to die.

"Fancy trying a shot, to get the feel of it?" Ramsey proposed pleasantly, keeping the table between them. It was the first thing he'd said in half an hour.

As a girl, Irina had been wary of surly schoolboy cliques lurking down hallways, certain to make callous remarks as she passed that she had a face like a donkey. She'd experienced her share of test anxiety all the way through to university, and often blanked on answers she knew. She had tended to get fretful when boyfriends drove over the speed limit. Ordinarily she would be able to recall, albeit not at this moment, her anxiety that Lawrence wouldn't ring again after the first time they'd slept together. In her professional life, she was all too familiar with the inclination to put off opening a publisher's envelope, which might contain a clipped request that she please collect the fruits of six months' labour from their crowded offices without delay. In London, she had been through her share of IRA bomb scares in the tube, though after so many hoaxes the chances of blowing up then and there had always seemed distant.

Point being, like most people, Irina was no stranger to fear. She knew what other people were referring to when they used the word. But until 2:35 on the sixth—nay, now the seventh—of July 1997, she may never before have been seized by raw, abject terror.

Summoned, Irina obeyed. Her will had been disconnected, or at least the petty will, the small, bossy voice that made her put dirty clothing in the laundry basket or work an extra hour in her studio when she no longer felt like it. It was possible that there was another sort of will, an agency that wasn't on top of her or beside her but that was her. If so, this larger volition had assumed control. So eclipsing was its nature that she was no longer able to make decisions per se. She didn't *decide* to join Ramsey at the table; she simply rose.

As she negotiated her way to Ramsey's side, her sense that at any moment she might fall over did not seem to have been occasioned by high heels, hash, or cognac. The precariousness of her balance was in her head, like an inner-ear disorder. Apparently aircraft pilots can grow so discombobulated that they have no idea which direction is up or down. Especially before the advent of navigational instruments, many a pilot in a fog had turned his nose into a dive and ploughed straight into the ground. Even in today's era of reliable altimeters, an amateur can still grow so convinced of his internal orientation that he defies the readout on his panel and flies into somebody's house. When one cannot trust so primitive an intuition as which direction is up, surely one's moral compass was equally capable of fatal malfunction.

As she drew towards Ramsey—whose figure was now traced by a thin, white edge, as if scissored from a magazine—the whole evening snapped into place. He had taken deliberate advantage of the fact that Lawrence was out of town. He had dazzled her with fine dining, and slyly introduced racy, sexual stories from adolescence. He had *got her drunk,* for centuries a grammatical construction beloved of women who are loath to take responsibility for doing the drinking. In kind, he had *got her stoned.* He had lured her to his house, where he put on a display of prowess at his snooker table that she might be blinded by his celebrity status. And now this "fancy trying a shot?" gambit took the biscuit. Ramsey, naïve? It was Irina who was naïve, a flighty, airheaded fool who was dropping into her seducer's arms like an apple from a tree.

The revelation of Ramsey's chicanery came too late. She couldn't take her eyes from his mouth, and those grey-blue irises of a wolf, which Betsy had assured her that Ramsey was not. Standing sacrificially at his side, Irina presented herself for slaughter.

He handed her a cue off the rack, saying, "I've set up a shot, that red to the centre pocket." Irina thought, *You've set something up, buster, that is for damned sure.*

Ramsey arranged her cue in her right hand. Leaning over the table, he demonstrated the proper position for sighting the shot. She did as she was told. As he murmured about how you had to "hit *through* the white" and not "pull back after contact," she inhaled his breath, aromatic with brandy and toasted tobacco. When he reached behind her to adjust the angle of her cue, their fingers touched.

Yet in defiance of his own instruction that you mustn't "pull back after contact," his hand reflexively recoiled. When he urged her to move her grip further down the butt, he declined the pedagogic option of shifting her hand with his own. Turning her face to his, Irina was startled to confront an expression of idiotic innocence.

Irina finally twigged. Alex "Hurricane" Higgins? Ronnie "the Rocket" O'Sullivan? Jimmy "the Whirlwind" White? Without a doubt, many a snooker player was a rogue. They drank, they smoked, they whored; they never thought twice about "shagging another bloke's bird." And fair enough, Ramsey hoovered fags, had a taste for weed, and was no stranger to the bottle. But on one point he and his notorious competitors decisively parted ways. *Ramsey Acton was a nice man.* Maybe he did find her fetching; she could hardly hold that against him. But Irina had described her relationship as sound, satisfying, and permanent. And Ramsey was Lawrence's friend.

If anyone was kissing anyone tonight, she would have to kiss him.

Even putting the momentous matter of Lawrence aside, the prospect was fraught. Ramsey might never have thought of her in that way at all. At the very least, she risked the mortification that Estelle must have felt when she tore off her shirt and the teenage Ramsey Acton fled in dismay to his bicycle.

Still, it could have been a small decision. Drunken, addled revellers often do things late at night for which they apologize in the morning with a reductive titter. But the minimizing of such moments was a matter for other people. For Irina knew with perfect certainty that she now stood at the most consequential crossroads of her life.

"I almost forgot," she said with a shaky smile. "Happy birthday."

❖ chapter two ❖

At the rattle of the key in the lock, Irina felt her pulse in her teeth.

"Irina Galina!" It wasn't precisely a sobriquet. In a nod to the rhymey assonance of the Russian language, Irina's mother had chosen Galina for her middle name, and Lawrence loved the boisterous, comical cadence of the double-barrel. Yet tonight his pet handle rang from the hallway with a grating singsong, as if she were an adorable Muppet on *Sesame Street* and not a grown woman.

Dropping his luggage, Lawrence poked his head into the living room. In a stroke, her heart fell. She thought, *I have never before looked into that face and felt absolutely nothing.*

The first time Irina ever laid eyes on Lawrence—having found her posting for Russian tutoring on a Columbia message board, he'd made an appointment for his first lesson—she opened the door of her West 104th Street apartment with an imperceptible double-take. She wouldn't pretend to love at first sight, but she did register a familiarity, as if they had met before. Though his trim physique was buried in flannel and drooping denim, the face was arresting: sharply cut, cheeks hollowed from overwork, forehead curdled, deep-set eyes as big, brown, and imploring as a bloodhound's.

Even then, Lawrence liked to think of himself as a self-sustaining unit, like a geodesic dome whose moisture infinitely recirculates and waters its own crops. Irina did soon grow to appreciate that Lawrence was an enterprising young man who had bootstrapped himself from the moneyed equivalent of trailer-park trash to the Ivy League. But what tore at her sympathy that first afternoon was the immediate apprehension that he was starved—that emotionally he was like one of those wild boys raised by chimps, who'd been subsisting in the forest on roots and berries. That first impression had never left her, of pleading and raw need, of an undercurrent of desperation of which Lawrence himself was unaware. Even the cockiness with which he had leaned, smirking, against the door frame had proven simply heartbreaking in the end, since his improbable incompetence at Russian justified no swagger. Over the proceeding years her sympathy had only deepened.

Now, bitterly, with one sweep of the front door, the compassion was spent. To the degree that Lawrence's face was familiar, it was killingly so—as if she had been gradually getting to know him for over nine years and then, bang, he was known. She'd been handed her diploma. There were no more surprises—or only this last surprise, that there were no more surprises. To torture herself, Irina kept looking, and looking, at Lawrence's face, like turning the key in an ignition several times before resigning herself that the battery was dead. Strong, unapologetic nose: nothing. Boyishly tousled hair: nothing. Pleading brown eyes—

She couldn't look in his eyes.

"Hey, what's up?" said Lawrence, kissing her perfunctorily with dry lips. "Don't tell me you're just sitting here, not even reading."

Just sitting here was exactly what she'd been doing. Her own mind having converted overnight into a home entertainment centre, she'd felt no need to reach for a book. In fact, the prospect of reading anything as demanding as a cereal box was risible.

"Just thinking," she said weakly. "And waiting for you to come home."

"Well, it's coming up on eleven, right?" he said, returning to the hall to cart his bags to the bedroom. "Almost time for *Late Review*!"

Lawrence's voice died quickly and left dead air, as if the very acoustics of their home had gone flat. Irina struggled to right her posture, but kept sagging into the cushions of her chair. She heard bustling from the bedroom. Naturally the instant he arrived he had to unpack. Always this tyrannical obsession with order.

When he shambled back to the living room, Irina couldn't think of anything to say, and she wasn't accustomed to having to "think of" something to say to Lawrence.

"Okay," she croaked. As if contaminated by Ramsey's syncopated syntax, Irina's timing was off, and her response to Lawrence's proposal was minutes late.

"Okay, what?"

"Okay, let's watch *Late Review*."

There was too much space around their words. Irina visualized this ragged discourse as a mismatch of type-sizes and prints, like a kidnapper's ransom note snipped jaggedly from different headlines. That she and Lawrence had ever carried a competent conversation now seemed incredible. She wondered what they used to talk about.

"We've got another twenty minutes," he said, splaying on the couch opposite. "So how's tricks? Anything new?"

"Oh," she said, "nothing much since we last spoke." Behold, her first lie. Irina had a queasy feeling that it wouldn't be her last.

"Didn't you have dinner with Ramsey? Don't tell me you chick-ened out."

"Oh, right," she said thickly. She was no good at this. She was already botching it. Of course she'd have to give an accounting of last night. But the mere sounding of Ramsey's name gave her palpitations. "Yes, we did that."

"So how was it? You were worried that you'd have nothing to say to each other."

"We managed," she said. "I guess."

Lawrence was beginning to look irked. "Well, what did you talk about?"

"Oh, you know—Jude. Snooker."

"Is he entering the Grand Prix this year? Because I thought I might go."

"I have no idea."

"I wondered if his ranking's slipped enough to have to play the qualifiers."

"Beats me."

"Well, you can't have talked that much about snooker."

"No," she said. "Not so much." It was as if she had to hoist every word from her mouth with a forklift.

"Did you at least get any good gossip?"

Irina tilted her head. "Since when did you care about 'gossip'? That is, about what's going on in someone's heart, and not in their head?"

"I meant like, is it true that Ronnie O'Sullivan has checked himself into rehab. What's your *problem*?"

"I'm sorry," she said, and meant it. She had not, overnight, turned into an ogre, and she gazed at her partner mournfully. It was obscene,

41

though, that he couldn't tell the difference the moment he walked in the door, if a flicker of nervousness ran through her that maybe he had. Since Lawrence avoided *the main thing* like the plague, the fact that he hadn't remarked on her lacklustre response to his home-coming was if anything a red flag. It was hardly subtle: so far this conversation was reminiscent of a prison visit. They seemed separated by a thick pane of glass, and spoke haltingly as if through receivers. After all, Irina had broken a law of a kind, and had just begun her first day of what could prove a very long sentence. She added pitifully, "I made you a pie."

"I had a snack on the plane . . . Sure, why not. A small piece."

"Would you like a beer with that?"

"I've already had a Heineken . . . What the hell, let's celebrate."

"Celebrate what?"

"The fact that I'm back." He looked wounded. "Or didn't you notice?"

"I'm sorry," she said again. "Yes, of course. That's what the pie is for. To welcome you home."

In the kitchen, she leaned her palms against the counter, dropped her head, and breathed. It was a relief to escape Lawrence's company, however briefly; yet from the fact of the relief itself there was no escape, and it cored her.

Leadenly, Irina removed the pie from the fridge. Chilling for under two hours, it wasn't completely set. With any luck the egg in the filling had cooked thoroughly enough that the pie's having been left out on the counter for a full day wasn't deadly. Well, she herself wouldn't manage more than a bite. (She'd not been able to eat a thing since that last spoonful of green-tea ice cream. Though there had been another cognac around noon . . .) The slice she cut for herself was so slight that it fell over. For Lawrence, she hacked off a far larger piece—Lawrence was always watching his weight—than she knew he wanted. The wedge sat fat and stupid on the plate; the filling drooled. Ramsey didn't need admiration of his snooker game, and Lawrence didn't need pie.

She pulled an ale from the fridge, and pondered the freezer. Normally, she'd join him with a glass of wine, but the frozen Stol-ichnaya beckoned. Since she'd brushed her teeth, Lawrence needn't know that she'd already knocked back two hefty belts of neat vodka to gird herself for his return. Spirits on an empty stomach wasn't like her, but apparently acting out of character could slide from temporary liberation to permanent estrangement from your former self in the wink of an eye. She withdrew the frosted bottle, took a furtive slug, and poured herself a better-than-genteel measure. After all. They were "celebrating."

Lawrence was too polite to object that she'd served him a slice much bigger than he'd asked for, and exclaimed, "*Krasny!*"

"That's 'red,' you *doorak*," she said, in the best imitation of affectionate teasing she could muster. " 'Beautiful' is *krasivy*. Red Square, *krasnaya ploshchad, da?*"

Ordinarily Lawrence's tin ear for Russian made her laugh, but there was an edge on her voice that made Lawrence look over.

"*Izvini, pozhaluysta,*" he apologized correctly. "*Konyeshno, krasivy.* As in, *krasivy pirog*"—she was amazed that he knew the word for "pie"—"or, *moya krasivaya zhena.*"

For pity's sake. Even in Russian, he called her his "wife." The term had never before struck her as cheeky, but it did now.

And it was typical, wasn't it, that he could only call her *beautiful* in Russian. In English, she was *cute,* a safe, minimizing adjective that could as easily apply to a hamster as to a "wife." It wasn't fair to be irritated by a perfectly lovely compliment, but the resort to speaking in tongues when coming anywhere near emotional subject matter was painfully reminiscent of her father. A dialogue coach for mostly B-movies, her father was a master of accents; his work ran along the lines of coaching the man who did the voice of Boris Badenov in *Bullwinkle* on how to thicken his consonants with Soviet wickedness. He could switch readily from Chinese "flied lice" to Irish brogue, and she supposed it was all very amusing. Except that he had never told her he loved her, or was proud of something she'd accomplished, unless rolling his Rs like Sean Connery or lapsing into a Swedish lilt—*I lahf me leetle dahter, jaaaaaa!* She'd adored all the voices he'd employed reading her stories when she was little, but as she grew older the charm wore off. Why, he was born in Ohio, but even his Midwestern delivery sounded like one more accent.

Besides, Lawrence may have used Russian as a device to arms-length sentiments that might sound embarrassing in English, but it was also their private argot, and right now it was too much. It was too intimate. It hurt. "Thank you," she said firmly in English, and brought the Russki speak to a close.

Lawrence tried, with one more line, to keep it going. "*Tih u-sta-la?*" His minor-key delivery was wrenchingly tender, and Irina bowed her head. She hadn't touched her pie.

"Yes, I'm a little tired. I didn't sleep well." She hoped this didn't count as her second lie. Arguably "not sleeping at all" fell under the subhead of "not sleeping well."

"Something on your mind?" He had noticed. He was fishing.

"Oh, maybe it was the sushi. Only takes one piece of dicey tuna. My appetite's off. I'm not sure I can eat this."

"You do look pale."

"Yes," she said. "I feel pale." Not wanting to appear too conscious of the time, Irina surreptitiously glanced at the watch on Lawrence's wrist. Damn. Still five more minutes before *Late Review*.

"So, how was the conference?" It was disgraceful, how little she cared.

He shrugged. "A junket, basically. Except for the fact that I got to see Sarajevo, a total waste of time. Too many UN wonks, and NGO losers. You know, you need a police force. Well, duh. At least my budget didn't have to cover it."

"God forbid you should come back having learned something you didn't know already, or having met someone you actually liked." The sentence escaped her mouth before she could stop it. She tried to gentle the barb with a smile, but from the expression on Lawrence's face she might have slapped it. "*Milyi!*" she scrambled; "dear" sounded warmer in Russian. "I'm just razzing you. Don't look so serious."

She had to stop this, the compulsive criticism. What ever happened to *mental kindness*? For that matter, what ever happened to plain kindness? Lawrence had been out of town for ten days, and everything she'd said since his arrival had been either flat-out mean or insultingly fatigued. Another man—whoever that might be—would have taken issue with the dig. But Lawrence didn't like trouble, and reached for the remote.

Irina considered the word. The fact that Lawrence so frequently reached for *the remote* seemed apt.

More criticism.

When BBC2 came on, Irina was so grateful for the distraction that she could have kissed the tube. Ordinarily, in front of the TV Irina sewed on buttons, snapped beans, but now she focused on the screen with what she hoped was a look of rapt fascination.

She was rapt, and she was fascinated all right, but not by *Late Review*. Because Irina was seeing things. Really, it was like being possessed, or schizophrenic. Figures grappled in the shadows. Behind the TV, a man and woman grasped each other so tightly that it was impossible to tell

44

which arms and legs were whose. Their mouths were open and fastened. When she glanced to the left, the same man flattened his lover against the wall, raising the woman's arms overhead and pinioning her wrists to the plaster as he buried his face in her neck. If Irina cut her eyes a few degrees to the right, there they were again, disrupting the drapes, as the taller figure pressed the woman so fiercely against the window frame with his pelvis that her tailbone must have hurt. (It still hurt, but only a little. The soreness on Irina's tailbone was from the side of the snooker table. The abrasion might have been worse had they not sunk in tandem to the floor.)

These figures that had invaded her living room, Irina hadn't invited them, nor bid them to make such exhibitions of themselves against her walls. (And on her carpet. She glanced down, and there was the same immoderate couple. He was on top. Slight enough that the woman could still breathe, the man was still heavy enough to pin her. She couldn't get away if she wanted to. She didn't want to.) In their defence, the visitors were *only* kissing, but if a qualifier like *only* applied to kissing like that, one might as well say that Jeffrey Dahmer had *only* murdered and cannibalized people or that Hitler had *only* tried to rule the world.

The hallucinations were an affliction. She was trying to watch television with her partner, to have a convivial slice of pie and a quiet nightcap—though Irina's vodka seemed to have evaporated, and she couldn't remember drinking it—and here were these *people* in her home who couldn't keep their hands to themselves, and who induced her to keep squeezing and kneading against one another the muscles of her inner thighs.

"You might not be keen on the subject matter," said Lawrence. "But that still looks worth seeing."

Irina tore her eyes from her shameless guests. "What's worth seeing?"

"*Boogie Nights!*"

Gamely, she ventured, "Well, I wasn't big on *Flashdance,* but I didn't mind *Saturday Night Fever.*"

Lawrence looked incredulous. "How could you have listened to a fifteen-minute discussion of that movie and still think it bears any relation to *Saturday Night Fever*?"

Irina cringed. "Oh. What's it about, then?"

"The porn industry!"

"I was a little distracted."

"A *little*?"

"I told you I was tired."

"Being short of sleep might take the edge off, but it doesn't send most people's IQ plummeting to below fifty."

"Just because my mind wandered doesn't make me an idiot. I don't like it when you do that. You do it all the time, too. You're always telling me I'm stupid."

"On the contrary. I'm constantly trying to get you to have faith in your own opinions and to be more forceful about them in public. I'm constantly telling you that you *are* smart, and very perceptive about the world, even if you don't have a PhD in international relations. Sound familiar?"

Irina hung her head. It did sound familiar. Lawrence could be tempted to use the M-word on Irina, but he used it indiscriminately on everyone sooner or later, so there was no purpose to taking it personally. And he had, he was right, many times urged her to be more outspoken about her views around his colleagues' dinner tables.

"Yes, you're usually very supportive," she conceded.

"Why do you keep trying to pick a fight?" From Lawrence, this was brave.

"I don't know," she said, and with genuine puzzlement. She truly did not understand why, when she had such a powerful motivation not to rock the boat, she would keep being so provocative, or, on an evening when she was desperate not to attract close examination, she would behave in an erratic, irritable fashion sure to bring maximum scrutiny to bear. Did she *want* him to know? Maybe she was forcing him to play a parlour game, like Botticelli: *I'm a famous person, and my name begins with big scarlet A.*

Are you dead?

(As of tonight? To my marrow.)

Are you female?

(All too female, it turns out.)

Where *were* you last night, at five in the fucking morning?

(Only yes-or-nos. That question is cheating.)

You're one to talk about cheating!

Or maybe Lawrence was supposed to play hangman on the back of his conference programme, and, since he would never in a million years guess that she'd have chosen F-A-I-T-H-L-E-S-S H-U-S-S-Y, proceed to noose himself, letter by letter?

They finished watching *Late Review*. As if having given up on her ability to absorb the most primitive factual aspects of the novel and West End play the panel went on to assess, Lawrence didn't solicit her opinion for the rest of the show. He turned off the television, and as the tube went black Irina thought, *Come back!* Commonly vexed by its incessant prattle, tonight she could have watched TV for *hours*. Instead of getting ready for bed, Lawrence plunged back to the sofa; horribly, that clap of his palms on his knees meant he wanted to talk. Irina tried to fill the yawning silence with encouraging little smiles, though just what she was encouraging remained obscure. Apropos of nothing she said, "I'm glad you're home," an assertion that, while it unquestionably did constitute Lie #3, she did not throw out as duplicitous cover. Rather, she wanted it to be so, and half-hoped that if she said she was glad he was home emphatically aloud she could make it be so.

"And?" he said at last. "What else is new?"

Irina looked at him blankly. Did he suspect something? "Not much that I haven't told you on the phone. Work," she said starkly. "I got some work done."

"Can I see it?"

"Eventually . . . When I'm finished." She didn't want to show the new work to Lawrence. She wanted to show it to Ramsey.

Giving up, Lawrence rose with his face averted, and she could tell he was hurt.

They chained the door, closed and locked the windows, drew the drapes, took their vitamins, flossed, and brushed their teeth. A rote regime repeated every night, on this one it took on a murderous monotony. Though having missed a night's sleep and so exhausted she was dizzy, Irina dreaded going to bed.

Methodically, they removed their clothes, and hung them on hangers. Irina couldn't remember the last time that she and Lawrence had torn off each other's garments and thrown them to the floor, in a frenzy to contact bare skin. You didn't have to do that, when you shared a bed for years, and it would be wildly unreasonable of her to sulk over the matter. Everyone understood: that's what you did at "the beginning," and she and Lawrence were in the middle. Or she had thought for ages that they were in the middle, though you couldn't read your own life like a book, measuring the remaining chapters with a rifle of your thumb. Nothing prevented turning an ordinary page on an ordinary evening and suddenly finding that you weren't in the middle but at the end.

Irina cornered the rumpled white blouse onto the hanger with more care than the rag deserved; the little tear along the collar was longer now. The navy skirt was stretched; at least she'd had the presence to glance in the mirror when she came home, and yank the button round to centre it at the back. For the first time in a day she had combed her hair, which had flown into such disarray that she'd looked electrocuted.

But she hadn't had the presence to take a shower. She'd returned to the flat with so little time to spare. Even then, it had been hell to tear herself from the Jaguar. Climbing the depressingly steep learning curve that apparently attends the sordid departure, she'd refused to kiss Ramsey good-bye in front of this building; a neighbour might see. What little time that remained to prepare for Lawrence's arrival she'd squandered on vodka, and on standing in the living room in a state of paralysis, hands held out from her sides as if afraid to touch a body that had suddenly developed a vicious will of its own. But now she risked having left an incriminating odour on her skin, if only from a peculiar excess of her own perspiration.

The real telltale reek arose from these thoughts in her head. They were rancid.

She was naked now, but Lawrence didn't give her a glance. That was normal, too. You got used to each other, and the nude body lost its surprise. Still, it saddened her that her experience was of not being seen at all, much as the cool boys in seventh grade had looked straight through her before she got braces. On the other hand, maybe she did the same thing to Lawrence, whited him out with an *oh, that*. In the privacy of his obliviousness, she took the time to look for once, to really look at and see her partner's bare body.

He was fit. From a military regime of spending his lunch hour at a sports club near the office, his shoulders rounded with muscle, and his thighs were solid. His penis even at rest was a better-than-respectable size. Granted, gentle love handles swelled at his waist, but she couldn't ride him about a mere couple of pounds comprised entirely of her own pie. Besides, she gladly pardoned his minor flaws—flat feet, a thinning at the temples— for they had entered into a contract of sorts, which she could have recited like the Lord's Prayer: *Forgive me my defects, as I have also forgiven your deficits.* After all, her breasts were beginning to droop; she now awoke with little bags under her eyes; the hieroglyph of a lone varicose vein on her left calf warned cryptically of untold decrepitude to come, and she could soon have need to cash in on his own forgiveness in buckets. It was a shame that he held himself in a defensive hunch, since if Lawrence simply stood up straight he'd cut a fine figure of a man for forty-three. Most women Irina's age were obliged to overlook far more than slight swells or flat arches, and nightly bedded butterball guts, hairy shoulders, double chins, and bald pates. She was lucky. She was very, very lucky.

So why didn't she feel lucky?

"Read?" she proposed.

After ten days, he should have said no. After ten days, he should have slipped a hand around the small of her back, and clapped his mouth on her neck. "Sure," he said, kicking the duvet to his feet. "For a few minutes."

Irina had no idea how Lawrence could dive straight from a steady drone of "nation building" to *The End of Welfare*. In his place, she'd be desperate for an antidote, a sumptuous reread of *Anna Karenina*, or a cheap thriller. But then, since Lawrence's professional bread-and-butter was so dry that it was more like plain charred toast, she had no real understanding of wanting to spend your life blathering about "nation building" in the first place. She obviously wasn't a serious person. Still, she wished he'd leaven his life a bit. Back in the day he hadn't been averse to James Ellroy, Carl Hiaasen, or P. J. O'Rourke. Ever since becoming a fellow at Blue Sky, he was consumed with making every moment count. But towards what?

Irina settled on the adjacent pillow with *Memoirs of a Geisha*. She could take her time with it, since there was no chance that Lawrence would want to read the novel next. It was about submission, and weakness, and servitude. It wasn't about overcoming disadvantage, the way Mr. Think Tank defeated his vulgar Las Vegas upbringing (as Lawrence would say, he was "a phoenix rising from the trashes"). It was about living with disadvantage and even capitalizing on it. The book was too much, she realized, about women.

They didn't touch. Settling in, Lawrence rested his right leg against her left; Irina rearranged her leg to restore the distance. She turned a few pages, but the couple from the living room was back again, groping across the type. Preemptively, Lawrence switched off the lamp, right at the point that Irina had finally managed to digest an entire sentence. He might have asked.

There was a formula. Lawrence had assured her that all couples do it the same way pretty much every time, even if you make a stab at creativity at "the beginning." She had no idea how he'd come to this conclusion. This was a man who, left to his own social devices, would talk about safe externals like the election of New Labour for hours on end, so it was awfully difficult to picture Lawrence inquiring of colleagues over drinks, "Do you always use the same position when fucking your wife?" Nevertheless, he was probably right. You sorted out what worked, and it was too much bother to keep concocting some new twist on what frankly admitted of limited variations. Also, once you did get into a— she saw no necessity for calling it a "rut"—a set and roundly successful sequence, if then you suddenly started rooting around down there with your mouth, say, when for years that hadn't been part of the programme—well, it seemed weird, didn't it? Like, what is this, why are you doing that. Not only weird, but alarming. And the last thing that Irina wanted to be on this of all nights was alarming.

Besides, she didn't object to doing it the same way every time; sameness wasn't the problem. (Before last night, there hadn't been a problem, had there, or at least not one that seemed pressing. Whatever her modest dissatisfactions, their redress could always be deferred to the following night—be deferred indefinitely, come to that. Anyway, why not count her blessings? Hadn't she come—how many women could say this?— hadn't she come *every single time* that she and Lawrence had made love?) The problem—that is, if it was a problem—was same-what.

As always, Irina turned on her right side. As always, Lawrence did likewise, and fit himself behind her, slinging his left arm around her waist and nestling his knees in her crooked legs. Together they formed two Zs, a comic-book symbol of sleep. And on the evenings they had given each other the signal—a leonine yawn, a mutter about having had a damned long day—sleep was just what they would do, too. But Lawrence *had* been gone ten days, and ran his hand tentatively over her rump. "Are you feeling okay?" he whispered. "You said something about bad fish."

Unless she was about to tell all, and at such a bewildering juncture that she was still not sure what there was to tell, she could not seem cold to his advances. That would be a giveaway, wouldn't it, that something was wrong. She had to act normal.

"I'm fine," she said (Lie #4, and this one was a whopper). Truly wishing that she could give him the reassurance he deserved, she clasped his left hand as it wandered uncertainly across her hip—it seemed lost—and pulled his arm between her breasts.

Lawrence's arm felt like a two-by-four. His proximity may not always have stirred a rapacious lust, but the snug of his chest against her back had always provided a deep animal comfort and sense of safety. Now it made her feel trapped. When his pelvis worked gently against her tailbone (against that very abrasion from the snooker table), his erection had the pesky quality of a poking finger.

This was terrible! *What had she done?* Had Lawrence ever lain beside her only to experience the limbs of her body as pieces of timber, only to regard the press of her flesh as a "trap" and her own polite knocking at the sexual door as some bothersome nag, nag, nag, she would shrivel up inside to a black, fisted dried currant.

With practiced dexterity and Irina's numb cooperation, Lawrence slipped in from behind. It was, they had both agreed, a nice angle. But Lawrence may have had an angle on intercourse in more than one sense. Before the protocol had settled, they'd tried the usual assortment of positions. But it hit her now—how awful, that it had taken last night, of all things, to notice—that amid the several options available nothing had obliged them to choose this posture in particular and stick with it. Moreover, the selection of a front-to-back configuration as the only way they would make love for, prospectively, fifty-some years was Lawrence's doing, and the choice wasn't an accident, it wasn't arbitrary—it wasn't just how they ended up making love, willy-nilly, the way she had ended up wearing that navy skirt and raggedy white blouse to dinner last night, because that was the outfit she'd been trying on when the buzzer sounded. They'd been doing it for nearly *nine years* this way and she should never have allowed this position for more than a time or two and now it was too late to object and that was tragic. She had passively capitulated to Lawrence's weakness, to his real weakness and not the kind of weakness he feared, like atrophied pectorals or abdication in an argument about appeasement of the IRA.

This was what the coward in Lawrence had opted for: That they never kiss. That they never look at each other. That he see only the blurred profile of her head; that she always stare at the wall. That she never be permitted to meet those imploring brown eyes and watch them get what they begged for. Though in the West 104th Street days they had lit candles on the bed stand, now it was always dark, as if for good measure—as if being faced toward white plaster weren't impersonal enough. The irony was that Lawrence loved her. But he loved her too much. He loved her so much that it was scary, and he would no more gaze into her eyes while they were fucking than stare into the face of the sun.

Per custom, after a couple of minutes Lawrence reached quietly for her nether regions, circling and homing in on central command. His earnest manipulations were never quite right of course—never quite, exactly right. But to be fair, there was something inscrutable about that recessive twist of flesh, if only because the clitoris was built on an exasperatingly miniature scale. For a man to get a woman to come with the tip of his finger required the same specialized skill of those astonishing vendors in downtown Las Vegas, who could write your name on a grain of rice.

Because one millimetre to the left or right equated geographically to the distance from Zimbabwe to the North Pole. Little wonder that many a lover from her youth who had imagined himself nearing the gush of Victoria Falls had, through no fault of his own, been paddling instead the chill Arctic of her glacial indifference. To make matters worse (and again the distinction was a matter of a hair's width), the dastardly little scrap was capable of inducing not only bliss but blinding pain—total-turnoff, back-to-Go-do-not-collect-$200 *pain*—and how could anyone negotiate such a perilous node with any confidence if he didn't have one? She had sometimes thanked her lucky stars that she was not a man, faced with this bafflingly twitchy organ whose important bit measured not a quarter of an inch across, when chances were that the woman herself couldn't tell you how it worked. It would have been unreasonable, therefore, to take issue with the disappointment of a tad off this way or that, and given that the whole project was fundamentally impossible, Lawrence was surprisingly good at it.

Tonight, however, Irina couldn't catch the wave. Too much of her attention was focused on trying not to cry. And the truth was that she was fighting her own pleasure. For once, the off-ness, it didn't have to do with his middle finger being just a smidgen too far down. It was wrong; it felt wrong, even wrong as in morally wrong. But if she didn't come, Lawrence would know she hadn't come, and more to the point he would know that, while he was in Sarajevo, something had happened.

It was even more wrong, what she did, to get where she had to go; it was fiendish.

Irina had indulged her share of fantasies. She had imagined "a" man doing this or that, or even, though she had never admitted as much to anyone else, "a" woman; there were only two sexes, after all, and to keep yourself amused you had to use all the combinations at your disposal. Yet these throwaway figures were always faceless, like mannequins with the heads lopped off. She had never before conjured one man, a real man, a man you could ring on the phone, with an address, a preference for hot over cold sake, a long face, and a black silk jacket. A tall, willowy man, with thin lips and grave eyes and a mouth of such infinite depth, with such an inexhaustible array of recesses, that kissing him was like touring the catacombs of Notre Dame. Last night it had felt less as if she'd slipped her tongue into his mouth than as if her entire body had crawled into the maw. It was a whole world, his mouth, a whole unsuspected world, and kissing him occasioned the same sense of discovery as sliding a clear drop of plain tap water under a microscope and divining whole schools of fantastic fibrillose creatures, or pointing a telescope at a patch of sky pitch-dark to the naked eye and lo, it is spattered with stars.

She had *only kissed him*. So why was the modesty of her transgression such negligible solace? The skirt had twisted, but she'd kept it on. The blouse had ripped that little bit further, but she'd never let him lift it. *Let* him? He hadn't tried. He had, to do Ramsey justice, tried only to stop. Which she should have also, she should have tried to stop, but she didn't try, did she, or hard enough, because she hadn't stopped, had she, and when you try hard enough you succeed, don't you? You succeed. It was true that she hadn't pulled his T-shirt from the waist of his trousers and smoothed up the flat of his bare stomach to the mounds of his chest. But she'd wanted to, and now there was no stopping her mind, her wretched, unprincipled mind, from making up for lost time. She hadn't unclasped his thick leather belt, with its heavy pewter buckle. She hadn't unfastened the button at his waist, or edged the zip, tooth by tooth, to its nadir. He had said, "We can't do this," in defiance of the fact that they clearly could because they were. Sometimes, more accurately, "We shouldn't do this," a point on which their agreement remained shamefully theoretical. Later, plaintively, a helpless railing at the gods for smiting the poor man with what he most perfectly could not resist and most certainly ought to: "But I *like* Lawrence!" Nevertheless, if firmly belted, buckled, buttoned, and zipped away, the captive baton that had rounded neatly against the socket of her hipbone had given every indication that, if the spirit was reluctant, something else was very, very willing.

Still, she hadn't fucked him, had she? She hadn't fucked him, because that would be wrong. But she'd wanted to. She wanted to fuck him. She wanted to fuck him more than she had ever wanted to fuck any man in her life. She wanted to fuck him, and not "make love" to him either, she wanted to fuck him. It was all that she could do to keep from shouting as much out loud, and Irina gnashed a bit of pillowcase between her teeth. She was dying to fuck him. She could see it. She could almost feel it now. She *could* feel it. It was not only one of the things she wanted, it was the only thing she wanted, to fuck him. That was the only thing in the whole bloody world she wanted and she would always want it, too, not just once, but over and over, to fuck him. And she knew that she'd do anything, give up everything, humiliate herself to fuck him and if he ever refused her she could see herself begging, on her knees, *begging* him, please—

"Wow," said Lawrence.

Irina was covered in sweat, and it took a minute for her breathing to steady, and for the nuclear mushroom behind her eyes to recede. A considerate man, Lawrence was usually into ladies-first, but her enthusiasm had spurred him; he, too, had finished, whenever that was, and she hadn't noticed.

"I guess you really missed me," he said, giving her a final squeeze.

"Mmm," she said.

Sleep remained at bay, even as Lawrence began lightly to snore. Irina was disconsolate. Lawrence didn't know, and he never had to know. Not about last night, and not about tonight, either. But she still held herself accountable, and not only for her perfidy on Victoria Park Road, but for the more considerable infidelity a few minutes ago in her head. That was the whole theory behind *mental kindness*, wasn't it? That on any Judgment Day worth its salt, you wouldn't merely be confronted with whom you insulted or what you stole, but with the whole unspooled videotape of your tawdry little mind from birth to lights-out. Before tonight, Irina had never pictured fucking another man—not a real man, a man they knew. Now not only had she kissed another man while her partner was trustingly out of town, but tonight she fucked him. Forget clinging to cheap literalism. She had cuckolded Lawrence in his own bed.

Nothing could ever be the same again. How pathetic, that at Omen she had worried about "vandalizing" a deluxe sashimi platter with extra

54

yellowtail, while remaining coolly oblivious to smashing up nine years' worth of mutual devotion in a single reckless night. With one kiss, she had sent the greatest achievement of her life crashing to the floor in a million pieces, like the countless vases and crystal pitchers that she had clumsily upset as a girl. At forty-two, she was still clumsy, but worse, brutally so, purposely so. Yet maybe there was justice after all. As Lawrence slumbered faithfully beside her, she looked at the soft shadow of his face on the pillow, and felt stone-cold. While bull-in-a-china-shopping through this weekend, she had broken not only their covenant, but her own heart.

A grown woman should be able to stop herself. Adulthood was about thinking things through. Now she hadn't looked before she leapt, and everything was ruined. She had *kissed her life good-bye.* Even as she whipped herself for being an awful, empty, selfish shrew undeserving of the abiding love of an intelligent, loyal man like Lawrence, she was afflicted again by visions, of the black belt, the silk jacket.

For forty-two years, Irina had lived with the consequences of everything she had ever done. She'd taken her punishment for spitefully hiding her sister's ballet slippers the night before a recital. When Columbia had accidentally added an extra zero to her cheque for tutoring undergraduates and she spent the money, she'd paid back every dime when they caught the error, taking out a loan on her credit card at 20 percent. She had faced down the disagreeable results of every confidence betrayed, every hurtful remark blurted, every poorly drafted illustration irrevocably published for the world to see. Surely it was asking little enough, this once, to turn back the clock—not years or anything, nor months nor even weeks, but barely a day. Once again they would lean in tandem over the snooker table, inches apart, as Ramsey demonstrated how to brace the cue. Drifting uneasily to sleep, Irina looked temptation square in the face, smiled bravely, and withdrew.

▣ chapter two ▣

To Irina's mind, it was the most underrated of symphonies: the jingle of the ring, the hard rasp, the clop of the bolt withdrawing, open-Sesame. The soft brush of wood against carpet. Engrossed in her reading, she had turned down Shawn Colvin, the better to keep her ear cocked. Curled impatiently in her armchair, she had more than once brightened in a false start as neighbours tromped past the flat and on upstairs. At last there was no mistaking the bold assertion of dominion, of access, of belonging, into their escutcheon. These were the unsung peak moments of domestic life: those Pavlovian leaps of the heart on an ordinary night when your beloved walks in the door.

"Irina Galina!"

Still in the hallway, he missed the flush of her smile, though there would be others. Only Lawrence would be able to redeem a middle name otherwise a mocking misnomer. Galina Ulanova was the Bolshoi's prima ballerina in the 1940s, and Irina's squat pliés (before her mother gave up on her altogether) had conspicuously failed to live up to her namesake. She'd always hated that name, until Lawrence converted it first to joke, and then, if only because she now associated it with his voice, to joy.

"Lawrence Lawrensovich!" she cried, completing a responsive ritual that never grew tired. As for the sardonic patronymic, his father's name was Lawrence also.

"Hey!" He kissed her lightly, and nodded at the stereo. "The usual tear-jerking soundtrack."

"That's right. I do nothing while you're gone but sob."

"What are you reading?"

"*Memoirs of a Geisha.*" She teased, "You'd hate it."

"Oh, probably," he said airily, returning to the hall. "What don't I hate?"

"Come back here!"

"I was just going to unpack."

"*Sod* unpacking!" While Lawrence maintained a militantly American vocabulary as a point of pride, Irina appropriated British lingo whimsically, and even, after seven years here, as a matter of right. "You've been gone for ten days. Come back and kiss me properly!"

Though Lawrence duly dropped his bags again and U-turned to the living room, his expression as she looped her wrists about his neck was perplexed. He tried for a closed-mouth kiss, but Irina was having none of that, and parted his lips with her tongue. So rarely had they locked mouths in these latter years that their tongues kept smashing into each other, as at ten she would bumble into partners during a pas de deux. Unpracticed, he pulled back prematurely, stringing spittle between their lips—not cinematic romance. Lawrence glanced at her askance. "What's got into you?"

She would rather not say. She was not planning to say, and didn't. "You call me your 'wife.' Well, that's what husbands do, when they come home. They kiss their wives. Sometimes they even enjoy it."

"It's coming up on eleven," he said, launching back down the hall with his bags. "Thought you might want to watch *Late Review*!"

He was a hard case.

When Lawrence sprawled on the couch after unpacking, she took a moment to study his face. The feeling it induced was gratitude, if only for her own restraint. Last night had been close, as close a call as ever she had encountered, and a fleeting shadow crossed her mind, of that other life in which she could only look at Lawrence in guilt and shame and frantic desperation to cover her tracks. The contrasting cleanliness would have been even more refreshing had she intended to tell him everything, but she and Lawrence had been leaving something out—it was hard to identify what—for long enough that to gush that she had nearly kissed Ramsey Acton last night and then thought better of it would have been dangerous, however wryly she recounted the moment. To recount it wryly would entail a gross distortion anyway, and unless she related the crisis as the Gethsemane it had been there'd be no point. Fully truthful, she'd make him anxious, and create a wariness of Ramsey forever after. It was Lawrence's friendship with Ramsey as well as her own with Lawrence of which she had been mindful when she'd wished the snooker player happy birthday and then excused herself hastily, in a panic, to the loo.

Curiously, contemplating Lawrence she felt less the recognition of when they met than the mystery of his eternal *un*familiarity. There was a discomfort in Lawrence that his bluster would disguise, and in truth she was never quite sure what really went on in his head. As striking as the planes in that drastic face, they were like theatre flats that shut you from the pulleys behind the scenes. She even thought tentatively, *He looks a trace melancholy.*

There was no doubting that Lawrence's was a beautiful face, or better than beautiful; *fascinating.* The kind you could dive into like dark water and get lost. She felt privileged to be allowed to study it, and to follow the unexplained clouds as they crossed his countenance and then dispersed with the changeability of island weather. It was peculiar how the more you got to know someone, the more you grew to appreciate how *little* you knew, how little you had ever known—as if progressive intimacy didn't involve becoming ever more perceptive, but growing only more perfectly ignorant. To whatever degree she had been assembling a vivid portrait of Lawrence Trainer's nature, its refinement was all about deconstruction. She would no sooner limn this or that quality than rub it out for being wildly inaccurate or cartoonlike in its simplicity or exaggeration. He was kind; no, sorry, he was savage. He was selflessly devoted to her; to the contrary, he held something back in a way that was decidedly selfish. He was sure of himself; uh-uh, how could she buy into that superficial confidence when it was obvious that he was achingly insecure? At once, Lawrence *was* kind, he *was* devoted, and some portion of that assurance drove to his core. Were her mental picture of Lawrence an illustration on her drawing table, it would after over nine years appear a messy smudge of erasures. Maybe by the time she was eighty-five she would approach the limit of having absolutely *no idea* who Lawrence was, when before she might have listed out "character traits" as if together they amounted to a man. Maybe arriving at this state of being stymied was an achievement. Maybe to live successfully alongside anyone was to come to understand not how much he was like you but how much he was not-you—and hence to allow, as we do so rarely with one another, that the person sprawled across from you on the sofa is actually there.

"What are you looking at?"

"You."

"Seen me before."

"Sometimes I forget what you look like."

"Been gone ten days, not ten years." Lawrence glanced at his watch. It wasn't eleven.

"You haven't asked me how it went last night, with Ramsey."

"Oh, right. I forgot." She sensed Lawrence had not forgotten.

"We had a much nicer time than I expected."

"Talk about snooker? At least I've primed you enough that you should have been able to keep your head above water."

"No, we hardly talked about snooker at all."

"What a waste! Who else do you know who's a professional snooker player? You could have at least gotten the dope—the literal dope—on Ronnie O'Sullivan."

"Ramsey's not only a snooker player. He's a person." Deftly, she chose *person* over *man*. "He seems more at ease one-on-one."

Lawrence shrugged. "Who isn't?"

"Lots of people." She could see that Lawrence was jealous. But she wanted to laugh. Lawrence was jealous over *Ramsey*. Lawrence had title to Ramsey, and her evening with his snooker buddy was meant to have been awkward. Irina had been sent on a mission to maintain Lawrence's own friendship with Ramsey by proxy, but was supposed to learn her lesson along the way: that she and Ramsey were chalk and cheese, and that she was incapable of engaging in the jubilant snooker banter that only Anorak Man could furnish. Ramsey was meant to have learned his lesson as well: that while Irina might be nice to look at, shapely legs know nothing of Stephen Hendry's renown for mastery of side pockets, and at the end of the day her partner was much more fun. Alas, these lessons had not proceeded as their architect had planned.

Of course, the evening had been plenty awkward, leaving her unnerved, even shaken, but also intrigued. What *was* that, what had happened? Whence this improvident urge to fasten her mouth on the wrong man? After Ramsey had given her a lift home—the ride having proceeded in petrified silence—she'd battened herself into the flat, flipping the top bolt, drawing the chain, and leaning with her back against the door, palms pressed flat, as if something were trying to get in. Breathing a bit too heavily still, she had assured herself that the high voltage in that basement snooker hall must already be dissipating to static electricity. Brushing her teeth before bed, she'd envisaged the relief of waking prudently by herself in her as-good-as-marital bed this morning—having done nothing disreputable, nothing that she had to hide from Lawrence or might be tempted to divulge in a confessional rush, after which he would never quite trust her again. Surely once she was straight, sobered up, and well rested, her scandalous impulse while leaning over that fancy match-grade snooker table would shrink to drunken, stoned idiocy, to mere naughtiness, to a delusional infatuation that—there is a God—she'd had the eleventh-hour sense to squelch. In the plain light of day, she would take the strange evening under advisement, as testimony that she should stay away from drugs, that she should drink moderately, that she missed Lawrence and needed to get laid. Over coffee, she had told herself, rinsing her mouth, you'll shake your head in dry amusement and go *ha-ha-ha*.

Yet sipping her cappuccino this morning, she'd regarded her near miss with awe and respect. It hadn't shrunk. To the contrary, what had appeared beforehand as a merely diverting flirtation on Ramsey's part, one that could prove embarrassing or inconvenient for Irina, had only grown larger as she approached it. Last night had been like groping about in a fog and expecting to bump into a low stone wall, and instead banging her nose smack against an Egyptian pyramid. Whatever she had run up against on Victoria Park Road, by accident, in innocence, and however wisely she had about-faced and soldiered in blind lockstep in the opposite direction, it was big. Briefly, a whole other life had opened up before her, and the fact that she declined to avail herself of it could not eradicate the image.

One other memory had haunted her all day. At the end of that lift home, Ramsey had drawn into the lay-by in front of this building. He should have kept the motor running, to indicate that at three he had no expectation of being asked up "for coffee". Instead he switched off the engine, and sat for what seemed a terribly long time—though it wasn't—hands at rest in his lap with a dead quality. They were exquisite hands, with long, sinuous fingers and slender metacarpi, more those of a musician than a sportsman. Yet they lay on his thighs with corpselike inertness, the delicate dusting of blue cue chalk creased in his cuticles, lending them a ghoulish hue. He stared straight through the windscreen, his face, too, at rest, almost empty; he might have been contemplating a list of groceries to pick up on the way home at a twenty-four-hour Tesco. Irina as well made no move to get out of the car.

But that wasn't the memory that lingered so. After a beat, they had both resumed animation, and Ramsey got out. Irina remained seated, because she could tell he preferred to come round. He was a gentleman. He opened her door with the gravity of a chauffeur ushering the bereaved from a hearse. As ever, that hand hovered at the small of her back as she walked half a pace ahead. Yet as she rooted for her keys and proceeded to the door, she turned to find him still standing in the street—as if to take the next step onto the kerb was to cross a line in the sand. Since he remained ten feet away and gave no indication of coming closer, that took care of any discomfiting question of a farewell peck on the cheek.

The two matching Georgian squares on which Lawrence and Irina lived were registered buildings, and in order to so much as change the outside colour of the window frames from black to white their management company had to ask permission from the National Trust. (They said no.) So pristinely preserved was this estate that production companies like Merchant-Ivory often used it as a backdrop for historical films. Thus while standard aluminium London street lamps glared a rude orange, the lantern to Ramsey's left was an iron reproduction gaslight from the nineteenth century. The bulb was flame-shaped, its glow antique. Cast in this theatrical light, golden on one side with his other half in shadow, Ramsey himself could have been acting in a period drama; his uncompromising verticality seemed a posture from an earlier age. Tall, gaunt, and darkly clad, his figure evinced a brooding solemnity she associated not with *Snooker Scene* but Thomas Hardy.

"Good-night," she said. "Thank you for dinner. I had a lovely time."

"Yes," he said. From lack of use and too many cigarettes, his voice was dry. "I did as well. Thank you for joining me. Good-night." He stood there. "I'd say, 'Safe home,' but it looks like you're going to make it." A flickered smile.

She should have shot him a returning smile, and let herself inside. She didn't. She looked at him. Stock-still before the kerb, Ramsey looked back. Unlike the pause in the car, really only a moment, this suspension was a solid fifteen seconds—which once you have already exchanged "good-nights" has the touch and feel of about a year and a half. Something unsaid passed between them, and if Irina had her way it would stay unsaid, too. Forever. She turned to the door with the resolve of capping a jar of something tasty that is not very good for you, like lemon curd, after having sampled a tantalizing half-spoonful—turning the lid tight, slipping the jar onto a high shelf, and closing the cupboard.

Irina blurted unthinkingly to Lawrence, "I have a confession."

The look of instant wariness on his face announced that Lawrence liked everything to be *fine,* thank you very much, that Lawrence didn't care for "confessions," and that Lawrence might even have wanted, if necessary, to be lied to. He could seem so industrious, but in some respects he was a lazy man.

"When we finished dinner—" she continued in the absence of any encouragement. "Oh, and you'd have hated it—"

"Do we have *anything* in common?"

She laughed. "I like *Memoirs of a Geisha* and sushi. You don't. Anyway, it was still early when the check arrived—" It hadn't been remotely early. Irina was damned if she understood this compulsion to revise the irrelevant side details that didn't even matter whenever you were tinkering with *the main thing.* "So Ramsey asked if I wanted to go get stoned, and, I don't know. I said sure."

"You hate getting stoned!"

"I clammed up, as usual. I wouldn't do it often. I don't mind it once in a while."

"Where?"

"Where what?"

"Where did you get stoned?"

"Well, not out on the street in Soho. Obviously, we went back to Victoria Park Road. I've been there often enough, with Jude."

"They're divorced."

"I happen to know that."

"So you didn't go back there with Jude."

"Oh, never mind! I only had two tokes, and then he played a million practice frames and totally ignored me, and then rode me home. I just thought you'd be amused. In fact, I was sure you'd say I was 'juvenile.' "

"You were juvenile."

"Thanks. That was obliging." She had wanted to—to tell him something else of course, but like the deluxe sashimi platter there were no substitutions.

"Nuts, I don't want to miss the beginning." Lawrence reached for the remote.

"We've five minutes yet. Oh, and I almost forgot!" She sprang from her chair. "I made you a pie! Would you like a slice? Rhubarb-cream. It came out fabulous!"

"I don't know," he said, peering at her with the intense examination to which she had subjected Lawrence himself not long before. "I had a snack on the plane. . . ."

"I bet you spent all your free time in the hotel gym. And we're celebrating."

"Celebrating what?"

"That you're *home*, silly!"

His head tilted. "What's with you tonight? You're so—bubbly. Sure that dope's worn off?"

"What's wrong with being glad you're back?"

"There's glad and glad. It's late. You don't usually have this much *energy*. Not sure I can keep up."

"*Tih ustal?*" she solicited, in their tender minor key.

"Yeah, pretty whacked." His eyes narrowed. "Have you been drinking?"

"No, not a drop!" she declared, wounded. "Though speaking of drops, would you like a beer with your pie?"

"Whatever you're on, I guess I'd better have some, too."

Scrutinized for signs of inebriation and disgusted with herself for having overimbibed the night before, in the kitchen Irina poured herself an abstemious half-glass of white wine. She pulled out the pie, which after chilling for a full day was nice and firm, and made picture-perfect slices that might have joined the duplicitous array of photographs over a Woolworth's lunch counter. She shouldn't have any herself; oddly, she'd snacked all afternoon. But countless chunks of cheddar had failed to quell a ravenous appetite, so tonight she cut herself a wide wedge, whose filling blushed a fleshy, labial pink. This she crowned with a scoop of vanilla. Lawrence's slice she carefully made more modest, with only a dollop of ice cream. No gesture was truly generous that made him feel fat.

"*Krasny!*" Lawrence exclaimed when she set down his pie and ale.

"That's 'red,' you *doorak*," she said fondly. She always found Lawrence's incompetent Russian adorable. Maybe because he was otherwise so sharp, and an Achilles' heel was humanizing. Besides, his tin ear for Russian was a useful leveller. Without it, a PhD might have made her feel stupid, but he always humbly deferred to her mastery of the tongue. " 'Beautiful' is *krasivy*. Red Square, *krasnaya ploshchad, da?*"

"Konyeshno, krasivy!" He *knew* she was charmed by his mistakes, and this one was so primitive that he probably made it on purpose. "As in, *krasivy pirog"*—she gave his memory of the word for "pie" an appreciative nod—"or, *moya krasivaya zhena."*

He mightn't have legally married her, but whenever Lawrence used the word *wife*—which sounded more cherishing in Russian—Irina basked in the pleasure of being claimed. She understood his superstition about the institution. Sometimes when you tried too hard to nail something down you crushed it. Still, there were scenes in *ER* when a man would exclaim over a stretcher, "That's my *wife!"* and Irina's eyes would film. The word went to the centre. "That's my *partner!"* would never have made her cry.

Tucked into her armchair, Irina forked a first bite of pie with a sensation that all was right with the world—or her world, the only one that mattered at the moment. The creamy filling was balanced perfectly between tart and sweet, and struck a satisfying textural counterpoint with the crisp lattice crust. *Late Review* had just run its opening credits. Germaine Greer was on tonight, an articulate woman who had once been a knockout but who had aged honestly and was still classically handsome. She was that rare animal, a feminist with a sense of humour, who stuck to her guns but was not a pain in the ass. Moreover, this fifty-something writer radiated a compensatory beauty of wisdom and personal warmth. Germaine gave Irina hope for her own future and broadly bolstered her pride in her gender. The waft from the open windows was the ideal temperature, and for the time being Irina was able to put out of mind when last she reflected on that precise fulcrum of the neither too hot nor too cold. She was not a faithless hussy. Lawrence was home, and they were happy.

Yet Irina had once tucked away, she wasn't sure when or why, that happiness is almost definitionally a condition of which you are not aware at the time. To inhabit your own contentment is to be wholly present, with no orbiting satellite to take clinical readings of the state of the planet. Conventionally, you grow conscious of happiness at the very point that it begins to elude you. When not misused to talk yourself into something—when not a lie—the h-word is a classification applied in retrospect. It is a bracketing assessment, a label only decisively pasted onto an era once it is over.

She didn't intend to be dire, or to detract from her pleasure in

Lawrence's return, Germaine Greer's astute commentary on *Boogie Nights,* and the splendid rhubarb-cream. In fact, Irina reasoned that, for so much of the world to be roiling with war and animosity, there must be an international deficit of compelling men, BBC2 reception, and pie. Still, there was a weed in this garden, or none of her self-congratulation would have made itself felt. She had only been alerted to her own happiness by a narrow brush against an alternative future in which it was annihilated.

Whatever it was, that crossroads last night was one of the most *interesting* junctures she had arrived at in a long time, and the only person with whom she really wanted to talk about it was Lawrence, the one person with whom she couldn't. The singular prohibition didn't seem fair. On the other hand, it probably was. A don't-make-waves constitution was one of the things that she and Lawrence, perhaps tragically, had in common. Irina didn't like confessions, either—that is, other people's—and Irina, too, wanted everything to be fine. For her to be able to introduce with the gravity the subject deserved, "I almost kissed Ramsey last night; I didn't, but I wanted to, badly, and I think we should talk about why I might have wanted to," without all hell breaking loose would have required a kind of work during the last nine years that they both had shirked. She hadn't made the bed for that honesty, so she couldn't lie in it. Or she had to lie in it, in the other sense of the word. That they could not hunker down right now and turn off the TV and come to grips with what exactly had happened last night was a grievous loss. At once, there seemed some sneaky connection between the fact that they couldn't talk about it and the fact that it had happened at all.

"That looks worth seeing," said Lawrence. "Though you might not be keen on the subject matter."

"Why, do you think I'm a prude?"

"No, but porn isn't up your alley."

"*Boogie Nights* doesn't look like pornography. It isn't *mention versus use.*"

A logical fallacy, *mention versus use* entailed doing the very thing that you were pretending to eschew—for example, asserting, "I *could* say that's none of your business," when what you're really saying is, "That's none of your business!" As it applied to a panoply of ostensibly above-board and purely academic British "documentaries" on whoring and blue movies, *mention versus use* provided respectable cover for the standard sensationalist come-on of T&A—using *tut-tut* to disguise *tee-hee*.

"It's opening next week. Let's go. . . . So!" she said gaily, switching off the TV. "Tell me about the conference."

Lawrence shrugged. "A junket, basically. Except for the fact that I got to see Sarajevo, a total waste of time—"

"Yes, you say that about every conference. But what did you talk about?"

He looked agreeably surprised. "A lot of this 'nation-building' stuff has to do with the police. Whether you include the assholes, or ex-assholes—if there's such a thing—and take the risk of giving them power and guns, or shut them out and take the risk of their still having power and guns and making trouble on the side. And, you know, whether you can impose democracy from without, or if it only sticks if it's organic, so that no matter what kind of constitution you ram down their throats, as soon as your back is turned everybody reverts to type. In Bosnia, of course, there's this big question of now NATO is in, how to get us out. Once you build up institutions all founded on the power of an international force, it's sort of like setting a table and then seeing if you can rip the tablecloth out from underneath without breaking any dishes."

Irina often drifted off when Lawrence talked about international relations—one of the things that Lawrence might say "all couples did," since it was tempting to succumb to the hazardous impression that, whatever your partner was nattering about, you knew it already. This time she'd paid attention, and had been rewarded. Oh, she didn't much care about Bosnia, a morass she had never understood. But he was so good at cutting to the chase; in his work, Lawrence's very speciality was *the main thing*.

"That's a nice image," she said.

"Thanks," he said shyly. She should compliment him more often. Nothing meant more to him than her smallest kind word, and it cost her nothing.

"Was *Bethany* there?"

He put a look on his face as if he had to search the crowd in his mind, though he'd said on the phone that attendance was scant. "Mmm—yeah."

"What was she wearing?"

"How'm I supposed to remember that?"

"Because my guess is, not very much."

"I suppose she was *tarted up,* as you would say, as usual."

"Someday I'm going to get you to admit that you find her attractive."

"Nah," he dismissed. "Never happen. A little trashy. Not my taste."

Another fellow at the institute, Bethany Anders was a nicely put together little floozy with a brain. Tiny and almost always kitted out from head to toe in black, she wore leather microskirts and boots, patterned stockings, and voluptuous cowl collars; she'd a penchant for sleeveless blouses that displayed her shapely shoulders even in the dead of winter. Lawrence was right that her face looked a bit cheap; she wore stacks of makeup, and had big, pouty lips. Yet while this variety of feline prowled the alleyways of most big cities, they were not a dime a dozen in the think-tank biz, whose few female denizens inclined towards frump and paisley shirtwaisters. So in the halls of Churchill House, Bethany stood out. Rather than act cool and distant, whenever Bethany crossed paths with Irina she was overfriendly—more grating than acting chilly by a yard.

It was thanks to *Bethany,* whose name Irina routinely pronounced in goading italics, that Lawrence was taking over a portfolio at the institute that nobody else wanted. Formerly a bastion of Cold War strategizing, after the fall of the Iron Curtain Blue Sky was overloaded with experts in Russian affairs. (With the fall of the Soviet Union, Irina, too, had experienced a sudden drop in status. Abruptly among the diaspora of one more harmless, economically flailing dung heap, she missed feeling dangerous.) Wanting to distinguish himself, Lawrence had been hitting the books on Indonesia, the Basque Country, Nepal, Colombia, the Western Sahara, the Kurdish region of Turkey, and Algeria. Having written extensively on Northern Ireland (whose pasty politicians must have clamoured to be interviewed by a fox in stilettos), *Bethany* was teaching him the ropes, since to everyone else at Churchill House during an era of grand Clintonian optimism her pet subject was dreary, morally obvious, and tired beyond belief. If Lawrence wanted to research dumpy old terrorism, he was welcome to it.

Irina had misgivings about Lawrence taking on yesterday's news, and some portion of her resistance concerned *Bethany*'s tutelage. But at least "Dr. Slag," as Irina had dubbed her (or, in American, Dr. Slut), stimulated an elective jealousy that bordered on entertainment. The steadfast

Lawrence Trainer was no more likely to stray than to walk out the door in polka-dot pyjamas, and Irina was safe as houses.

"I think she fancies you," Irina teased.

"Bullshit. She'd flirt with a doorstop."

Lawrence was intellectually brassy but sexually humble—hence his chronic poor posture. Irina could never get it through his head that she *wanted* him to be attractive to other women, that she found the prospect exciting. If he, too, felt a little stirring once in a while, that was only red-blooded, for surely she was not the only one who—

"Let's go to bed," she proposed, and picked up the pie dishes.

Lawrence grabbed the glasses, a last sip of wine left in hers as an emblem of renewed forbearance. "But I haven't seen your new work!"

"Oh, that's right—and I've been looking forward to showing you." For Irina, the greatest satisfaction of finishing a drawing was to unveil it to Lawrence, and once they dropped off the dishes she led him into her studio.

"You remember the project, right?" she said. "*Seeing Red?* A little boy lives in a world in which everything is blue. And then he meets a traveller from another land in which everything and everyone is red, and it freaks him out. Naturally by the end they're both thrilled to bits, and have learned to make purple. It's another predictable story line, but an illustrator's paradise. This afternoon, I got to red."

"God, these blue ones are unbelievable. Reminds me of Picasso."

"Well, I wouldn't go that far," she said bashfully. "Though it was challenging to get all those different shades in coloured pencil. There's a vogue right now in using the same materials that kids do, felt-tip markers, crayon—as if they could've drawn this, too."

"I don't *think* so." Lawrence cheerfully admitted to having no artistic talent, and his wonder was genuine.

"Voilà." She turned to the last drawing. "Red."

"Wow!"

Something *had* happened that afternoon. Perhaps owing to the pent-up feeling that issued from drawing for weeks in blue, the arrival of the crimson traveller had released something. Surrounded by indigo with a fine halo of luminous pink, the tall, spare figure was shocking. Almost scary.

"You're so great," said Lawrence with feeling. "I wish you could work with writers who were on a par."

"Well, I've been saddled with worse text. I'd even like the idea, if I thought it really had to do with colour. I used to pine as a kid to see a different one—a really new colour, and not another rehash of the primaries. Unfortunately, I get a creepy feeling that this story was bankrolled because of its *multicultural* undertones."

"Like, let's all fuck each other and make purple babies?"

"Something like that."

"This last one." Lawrence studied the fruit of an unusually feverish afternoon; she'd felt possessed. "It's got a completely different feeling than the blues. Even a different line quality, and the style is more . . ." Lawrence was no art critic. "Bonkers. Is that a problem? That it doesn't fit in?"

"Maybe. But I ought to redraw the first ones, rather than throw this one out."

"You're a pro, know that?" He ruffled her hair. "I could never do what you do."

"Well, I'd be hopeless at *nation building,* so we're even."

Her mother would be pleased: their set sequence of retirement was choreographed with the precision of dance. Yet the last step of their waltz toward slumber Irina was considering shaking up a bit. Add a little cha-cha.

Chewing on the matter, she tidied the bedroom. She'd been so exhausted when she came home last night that she'd flung her clothes on the chair. They lay in a crumple, and Irina felt a tinge of aversion for them. With a sniff she found that the navy skirt reeked of Gauloise smoke, and tossed it in the laundry basket. As for the shirt, that little rip at the neckline wasn't mendable, and she dropped it in the rubbish. She was relieved to get the garments out of her sight, much as her shower that morning had been elongated by an eagerness to wash something more than grime down the drain.

They both undressed. Granted, glimpsing each other's nude bodies no longer inspired raw lust, but a reciprocal ease with nakedness had a voluptuousness of its own. Which is why it felt especially queer when Lawrence climbed into bed and Irina's heart raced. Why did the proposal she was working herself up to seem so radical?

"Read?" Lawrence suggested.

"N-no," she said beside him. "I don't think so."

"Okay." He reached towards the lamp.

"Don't—don't turn out the light yet."

"Okay." He wore the same perturbed expression that had met her earlier insistence that he "kiss her properly."

"I was thinking—you've been gone—I was just thinking, I don't know, about doing it a bit differently."

"Doing—?"

She already felt foolish, and wished she'd never said anything. "You know—sex."

"What's wrong with the way we usually do it?"

"Nothing! Not a thing. I love it."

"So why change anything? Doesn't it feel good?"

"It feels great! Oh, never mind. Forget it. Forget I said anything."

"Well—what did you want to do?"

"I was only wondering if maybe, say, we could try it—facing each other for once." The whole *point* was to be able to look him in the eye, but now she was so embarrassed that she was looking anywhere but, and they weren't even fucking yet.

"What, you mean like, missionary?" he asked incredulously.

"If you want to call it that. I guess." Irina's commonly throaty voice had gone squeaky.

"But you said, ages ago, that missionary was lousy for women, that it didn't work, and you thought that was one reason a lot of women went off fucking altogether. There's no friction, you said, in the right place. Remember?"

"It doesn't, ah—no, it doesn't work without a little help."

"It's easier for me to give you—a *little help*—from, you know, behind."

"True. Oh, let's just—it's fine. Let's just—the way we've been doing it is fine."

"But is there something bothering you? About the way we do it?"

Obviously there was something *bothering* her, like the fact that she had not seen his face while they made love for at least eight years, but she couldn't bring herself to say so aloud. She could see that she was upsetting him, the last thing she'd intended. She wanted to make him feel welcome and warm and loved, and not suddenly anxious that all this time she'd been dissatisfied with their sex life but had been keeping her mouth shut. This was all wrong-headed and backfiring like crazy.

"Not a thing," she said softly, kissing his forehead and turning on her right side to snuggle her back against his chest. "I've missed you, and you feel wonderful."

"...Is it all right if I turn out the light?"

A slight collapsing sensation, in her chest. "Sure. That's fine. Turn out the light."

In the soundest of relationships, it is not always possible to organize epiphanies in concert. Lawrence could hardly be blamed if he failed to experience a burning desire to assault Bethany Anders the exact same evening on which Irina had fixated on Ramsey Acton's finely articulated mouth, that they might both turn tail in simultaneous panic and rush headlong into each other's arms. This was probably not the best of nights to upset the sexual apple-cart, and any fine-tuning of their proven method could wait for another time. Besides, this felt good. It did. Looking at the wall. In the dark.

One thing The Usual had to recommend it was that, with her face unobserved, her mind could more readily roam its most disgraceful corridors. She was not opposed, in the privacy of her head, to smut. Yet when Lawrence reached around to graze his fingers lightly between her legs, her mind remained static, and refused to generate any nasty little pictures. She couldn't get anywhere. Indeed, she visualized herself in a small, enclosed room, standing still. There was a door. There was a door that she could open if she were willing to. But it was not a good idea. Proceeding through this one doorway was forbidden. Slammed in her own face, the door recalled the expression gaining such favour in the States that it was becoming a pestilence: *Don't go there.* As time went on and Irina stood helplessly in the same desolate place—it was all dull clinical white, the walls, the linoleum, like some austere coital waiting room where no receptionist ever called her name—she began to realize that only by passing through that forbidden portal would she be able to come.

Lawrence's dedicated ministrations had grown so protracted that Irina was abashed. She felt fairly sure that he didn't mind giving her a helping hand, but it was taking too long, and she hated the idea of the procedure becoming tedious, in which case he might even lose his erection. Irina's fretting that her excitement was becoming a chore for him didn't heighten it any. This wasn't working. It was so weird. She'd never had any real trouble with Lawrence, but then she had never told herself, either, that she couldn't think about something she wanted to think about. The

71

problem was that door, that closed door, and since she refused to defy her own prohibition and push through it, Irina could contrive no means of bringing this dutiful stimulation to a graceful conclusion besides fakery.

She didn't overdo it. She didn't light into a reprise of the diner scene in *When Harry Met Sally*. In fact, with a soft, shuddering groan, she tried to imply that this was one of the quieter ones—and wasn't it. She worried that she had underplayed the performance to such a degree that it had gone right past him, until Lawrence moved a few times and pulsed; he must have been taken in, because he always waited.

To have got away with the sham was discouraging. After all these years he should know the difference. Now sexual fraud joined the list of other little white lies, like claiming to have forgotten about Ramsey's birthday, or pretending that it had been early in the evening when the bill arrived at Omen. And she had ruined a perfect record. Never again could she say to herself that she had come when having sex with Lawrence every single time. Now she knew how a pinball player felt on an unprecedented winning streak, when abruptly the ball drops, *clunk,* into the machine.

The deception was minor. If she had effectively passed a counterfeit note in bed, the denomination was low—at most, a fiver. Doubtless some women faked climaxes for years with their partners; one bogus orgasm over nine years of the real thing could hardly matter. So why did she feel so sorrowful? She should be jubilant. Lawrence was home. Moreover, she had been tested last night, and her fidelity had not proved wanting. But drifting uneasily to sleep, Irina couldn't be entirely sure if she had passed the test, or failed it.

❖ chapter three ❖

Spurning her few minutes' lie-in, Irina was first out of bed the next morning. The rev and horn blare of bumper-to-bumper traffic on Trinity Street had been driving her insane. The relief of being on her own while buying a *Daily Telegraph* up the street was all too brief. As she ground beans and waited for the milk steamer to spit, the monotony of their morning routine grated. For a moment it had been touch-and-go as to whether she would top up the steamer with bottled water one more time, or shoot herself. At least while she ran through these paces it was unnecessary to look at Lawrence, or talk to Lawrence. Over the *Telegraph* at the dining table, her eyes glazed once more; sexual intoxication had turned her into an overnight illiterate. An illiterate who never ate and couldn't work and slept little, so what *did* you do when you were smitten? You fucked. And that was the one thing she could not do, would not do. Even for a changeling, there were limits.

Lawrence the up-and-at-'em was dawdling. That toast was taking him forever. His coffee was getting cold. For pity's sake, if he wanted to read *The End of Welfare* he would concentrate better in his office. It was nearly nine o'clock! As she turned the pages of the paper, it was hard not to slam them. When the minute hand on her watch passed twelve, her chest burst with ludicrous, hurtful, and patently unjustifiable fury. It was Lawrence's right, was it not, to linger with his "wife" a few minutes before soldiering to an office where he laboured long hours? Had Lawrence ever sat at table enraged by her mere presence, crazed with a desperation to get her out of her own flat, she would die. She would just die.

Still, she couldn't contain herself. "After having been gone for ten days, I guess you have a lot of work piled up at Blue Sky." The sentiment might have come off as seminormal, save for the angry quaver in her voice.

"Some," he allowed. Since rising, she had been convincing herself that Lawrence didn't know her at all. A sudden vigilance suggested otherwise.

"I wonder if I feel like having another piece of toast," he supposed.

"Well, do or don't!" she exploded. "Have a piece, or don't have one, but don't faff about deciding! It's only *toast,* for God's sake!"

Numbly, he collected the dishes. "I guess I won't, then."

She winced at his sense of injury as if ducking an incoming boomerang. Apparently cruelty hurled at someone you love—whom you used to love until two days ago, or who at any rate didn't deserve it— has a tendency to whip back round and thump you on the head.

Finally Lawrence gathered his briefcase. Once he stood on the threshold, Irina flooded with remorse. Now that he really was leaving, she kept him at the door with manufactured small-talk, trying to be warm, to do a creditable impression of a helpmate who will be left alone the whole day through and is reluctant to say good-bye.

"I'm sorry I snapped at you," she said. "I'm getting behind on the illustrations for *Seeing Red,* and I'm anxious to get to work."

"I'm not stopping you."

"No, of course not. I don't know, maybe I'm premenstrual."

"No, you're not." Lawrence kept track.

"Peri-menopausal, then. Anyway, I'm sorry. That was totally uncalled for."

"Yes it was."

"*Please* don't hang on to it!" She squeezed his arm. "I'm very, very sorry."

His stricken mask broke into a smile. He kissed her forehead, and said he might ring later. All was forgiven. Patching over her outburst had been too easy. She couldn't tell if Lawrence accepted her apology because he trusted her, or feared her.

❖ ❖ ❖

She steered clear of the telephone at first, relishing the opportunity to think straight, or if not straight at least alone. Besides, Lawrence could always come back, having forgotten something, and she wouldn't want to have to explain to whom she was speaking. By nine-thirty, her timing was poor, but Irina couldn't be bothered with the niceties of Ramsey's night-owl hours when her whole life was falling apart and that was his fault.

"Hallo?"

Irina deplored callers who failed to identify themselves. "Hi," she said shyly.

The silence on the other end seemed interminable. Oh, God, maybe what was for her an exotic journey on a magic carpet was for Ramsey a casual grapple on the rug. Maybe he really was the ladies' man the magazines made him out to be, and she should hang up before she made a bigger fool of herself than she already had.

A sigh broke, its rush oceanic. "I'm so relieved to hear your voice."

"I was worried I'd wake you."

"That would involve my ever having got to sleep."

"But you didn't get a wink the night before! You must be hallucinating."

"Since I let you go—yeah. I been worried I am."

"*I* started to worry that—that for you, it didn't mean anything."

"It means something," he said heavily. "Something shite."

". . . It doesn't feel *shite*."

"It's wrong." What he must have intended as emphatic came out as helpless.

"Strange," she said. "Not long ago, I'd have been able to conjure your face pretty easily. Now I can't remember what you look like."

"I can remember your face. But there's two of them. A Before and After. In the After, you look like a different person. More beautiful. More 3D. More complicated."

"I've been feeling that way," she said. "Unrecognizable, to myself. It's not all to the good. I liked looking in the mirror and having some idea who was staring back."

Despite a nominal sexual rectitude, they had already developed the long, thick silences of lovers—those characteristic pauses whose laden dead air has to carry everything that has nothing to do with words. Lovers communicate not inside sentences, but between them. Passion lurks within interstice. It is grouting rather than bricks.

"Did you tell him?"

"I promised you that I wouldn't."

"I know, but did you tell him anyway?"

"I keep my word." With every second of this phone call, she was breaking her word. How confounding, that her hasty promise to Ramsey already weighed more than a decade's worth of implicit vows to Lawrence.

"I cannot—" He stopped, as if consulting a crib sheet. "Because of the snooker and that, you may've got the wrong end of the stick. But I don't fancy anything tatty. With me, it's all or nothing."

"What if it were all, then?"

"You got Lawrence." His voice was stone. "You're happy. You got a life."

"I thought I did."

"You got to stop. You didn't know what you was doing. You got too much to lose." The lines were dull and empty.

"I can't stop," she said. "Something has taken hold of me. Did you ever see *Dangerous Liaisons*? John Malkovich keeps repeating to Glenn Close, 'It's beyond my control.' He's almost sleepwalking into a catastrophic relationship with Michelle Pfeiffer, like a zombie or a drug addict. *It's beyond my control.* It's not supposed to be an excuse. Just the truth. I feel possessed. I can't stop thinking about you. I've always been a practical person, but I'm having visions. I wish I were exaggerating, or being melodramatic, but I'm not."

"The film, I've not seen it," he said. "Does it end well?"

"No."

"Sure there's a reason the film came to mind. What happens to the bird?"

"Dies," Irina admitted.

"And her bloke?"

"Dies," Irina admitted.

"Tidy. In real life, love, it's messier than that, innit? I think it's worse."

"There is, in the movie," she said, struggling, "a certain—lethal redemption."

"Outside the cinema, you can forget your violins. It'll kill you all right, but you'll still be left standing. Trouble off-screen ain't that you can't survive, but that you do. Everybody survives. That's what makes it so fucking awful."

Ramsey had a philosophical streak.

Irina had an obstinate one. "*It's beyond my control.*"

"It's up to me, then." The gentleness was forbidding. "I got to stop it for you."

Irina was glad she'd skipped breakfast, because she suddenly felt sick.

"I don't need anyone looking out for my interests. Lawrence has been doing that for years, and now look. I don't need taking care of."

"Oh, yes you do," he whispered. "Everyone does."

"You can't make me stop. It's not even your right."

"It is my responsibility," he said, capturing Malkovich's robotic tone in the movie he'd not seen. "I can see that now. I'm the only one can stop it."

Her tears were mean and hot. This was robbery. What she had discovered in that basement snooker parlour belonged to her.

"You said—yesterday." His temporal reference jarred. Their parting seemed months ago. "I woke something up in you. Maybe you could take what you found with me, and bring it to Lawrence. Like a present."

"What I found with you," she said, "was you. You are the present. In every sense. My 'waking up' with all three of us in bed together might feel crowded."

"Nobody said anything about bed."

"No one had to."

"We're not doing that."

"No," she agreed. "For the moment at least, we won't."

"*I won't be your bit on the side.*"

"I don't want to have an affair either."

"Then what do you want?"

At that instant, Irina might have been spirited blindfolded in a car, then released to a neighbourhood of London that she didn't recognize. How did she find her way home? It was an interesting area from the looks of it, so did she *want* to go home? She'd been kidnapped. Now Stockholm syndrome had set in, and she was fond of her captor.

"I want to see you as soon as possible."

Another roaring sigh. "Is that smart?"

"It has nothing to do with intelligence."

He groaned, "I'm dying to see you as well."

"I could take the tube up. Mile End, right?"

"A lady like you got no business on the tube. I'll call by."

"You can't come here. Yesterday. You shouldn't have come here, either. You're too recognizable from television."

"See what this is like? It's a horror show! Like an affair already, without the good bit."

"What's the alternative?"

"You know the alternative."

"That is not an option. I have to see you." A whole new side of herself, this wilfulness. It was heady.

"It's a long walk from the tube."

"I'm a sturdy creature."

"You are a rare and delicate flower to be kept from the randy, filthy eyes of East End low-life." He was only half-joking. "What about Lawrence?"

"He's at work. He rings here during the day, but I could say I went shopping."

"You'll have nil to show for it."

"A walk, a fruitless trip to the library? I could get my messages remotely from your house, and ring him back."

"You ain't very good at this."

"I take that as a compliment."

"Most of them office phone systems give a read-out of the number what's rung up. Your—" He was clearly about to say *husband*. "—Anorak Man got a memory for figures. Like my own phone number. I should get you a mobile."

"That's a nice offer, but Lawrence and I have already decided that they're too expensive. He might find it. I'd have a terrible time explaining why I had one. My, there are a thousand ways to be found out, aren't there?"

"Yeah. Even when there's nothing to find."

"Your birthday? You would call that nothing? If I were yours?"

"You are mine," he said softly. "Last night. You slept with him, didn't you?"

"Obviously I *slept* with him. We share the same bed."

"That ain't what I mean and you know it. He's been out of town. A bloke's been out of town and he comes home, he shags his wife." He went ahead and used the word.

"All right, then. Yes. If I didn't want to, he'd know something was up."

"I don't like it. I ain't got no right to say that, but I don't like it."

"I didn't, either," she admitted. "I only—got anywhere by thinking about you. But it was foul, imagining another man."

"Best you're in his arms thinking about me than the other way round, I reckon."

"Being in your arms and thinking about you appeals to me more."

"So when can you get your luscious bum to Mile End?"

The pattern was probably typical: you spent the abundance of the call talking about how you shouldn't be doing this, and its tail-end discussing the particulars of how you would. It would've been nice to feel special.

❖ ❖ ❖

On the tube, people stared. Both men and women. It wasn't her short denim skirt and skimpy yellow tee that were turning heads. She had a look. Her fellow passengers mightn't have identified the look per se, but they recognized it all the same. People had babies all the time, coupled all the time, yet the look must have been rare. *Sex was rare.* You'd never know it, from the hoardings overhead in this carriage— the bared busts promoting island holidays, the come-on toothpaste smiles. But the adverts were meant to torment commuters with what they were missing.

This was not a journey that Irina McGovern had ever expected to take. However firmly resolved to keep her skirt zipped, she wasn't fooling herself. She was taking the train to cheat.

With no explanation over the loudspeaker, the train lurched to a standstill. Sitting for fifteen minutes under a quarter-mile of rock was so commonplace on the Northern Line, the city's worst, that none of the passengers bothered to look up from their *Daily Mail*s. In relation to the eccentricities of Underground "service," regular riders would have long since passed through the conventional stages of consternation, despair, and long-suffering, and graduated to an imperturbable Zen tranquillity. One could alternatively interpret the passengers' expressions of unquestioning acceptance as sophisticated, or bovine.

Yet the train gave Irina literal pause. First Ramsey and now this very carriage was insisting, *You have to stop.*

Unbidden, a memory tortured from a few years before, when she and Lawrence had been sharing their traditional bowl of predinner popcorn. Recently moved into the Borough flat, they weren't yet in the habit of grabbing blind handfuls in silence in front of the Channel 4 news.

"Obviously, there are no guarantees," she'd mused, searching out the fluffiest kernels. "About us. So many couples seem fine, and then, bang, it's over. But if anything happened to us? I think I'd lose faith in the whole project. It's not that we'll necessarily make it. But that if we don't, maybe nobody can. Or I can't; same difference."

"Yeah," Lawrence agreed, tackling the underpopped kernels that she'd warned him could damage his bridgework. "I know people say this, and then a couple of years later they're raring to go again, but for me? This is it. We go south? I'd give up."

The feeling had been mutually fierce. For Irina, Lawrence had always been the ultimate test case. He was bright, handsome, and funny; they were well suited. They'd made it past the major hurdles—that ever-rocky first year, Lawrence's professional foundering before he found his feet at Blue Sky, several of Irina's illustration projects that never sold, even moving together to a foreign country. It should be getting easier, shouldn't it? Coming up on ten years, it should be a matter of coasting. They'd worked out the kinks, smoothed out serious sources of friction, and their relationship should be gliding along like one of those fancy Japanese trains that ride on a pillow of air. Instead, with no warning, they had jolted to a dead stop between stations, to stare out windows black as pitch. Overnight, their relationship had converted from high-tech Oriental rail to the Northern Line.

Why hadn't anyone warned her? You couldn't coast. Indeed, her very sense of safety had put her in peril. Ducking into that Jaguar in a spirit of reckless innocence, she wasn't looking over her shoulder, and it was the unwary who got mugged. That was exactly how she felt, too. Mugged. Clobbered. She might as well have taken that rolling pin on Saturday afternoon and bashed her own brains in.

Unceremoniously, the train shuddered, chugged forward, and gathered speed. Her respite, the Underground's graciously sponsored interlude for second thoughts, drew formally to a close. These other passengers had places to go, and couldn't wait indefinitely for a lone, well-preserved woman in her early forties to get a grip.

If Lawrence was indeed the test case, and thus to go terminal with Lawrence was to "lose faith in the whole project," she was hurtling through this tunnel toward not romance, but cynicism.

❖ ❖ ❖

It was really rather wretched, thought Irina as she scuttled with trepidation from the Mile End tube stop up Grove Road, that you couldn't will yourself to fall in love, for the very effort can keep feeling at bay. Nor, if last night's baffling blankness on Lawrence's arrival was anything to go by, could you will yourself to stay that way. Least of all could you will yourself *not* to fall in love, for thus far what meagre resistance she had put up to streaking towards Hackney this morning had only made the compulsion more intense. So you were perpetually tyrannized by a feeling that came and went as it pleased, like a cat with its own pet door. How much more agreeable, if love were something that you stirred up from a reliable recipe, or elected, however perversely, to pour down the drain. Still, there was nothing for it. The popular expression notwithstanding, love was not something you made. Nor could you dispose of the stuff once manifested because it was inconvenient, or even because it was wicked, and ruining your life and, by the by, someone else's.

Even more than that kiss over the snooker table—and the proceeding eighteen hours had effectively constituted one long kiss—today she was haunted by that deathly moment when Lawrence had walked in the door and she felt nothing. Its disillusionment grew more crushing by the hour. She wasn't disillusioned with Lawrence; it wasn't as if the scales had fallen from her eyes and she could suddenly see him for the commonplace little man he had always seemed to others. Rather, with the turn of a house key, every romantic bone in her body had been broken. Her faithfulness and constancy with Lawrence had long formed the bedrock of her affection for her own character. This was the relationship that had been torn asunder. The weekend's transgression had violated the fundamental terms of her contract with herself, and disillusioned her with herself. She felt smaller for that, and more fragile. She felt ordinary, and maybe for the first time believed the previously outlandish myth that like everyone else she would get old and die.

Yet as she advanced, a spell descended. Victoria Park had a fairy-tale quality, with its quaint, peaked snack-pavilion, its merry fountain splashing in the middle of the lake, the long-necked birds taking wing. Children patted the water from the shore. With every step through the park, the frailty that had hobbled her up Grove Road fell away. She felt young and nimble, the heroine of a whole new storybook, whose adventure was just beginning.

Moreover, as she drew closer to her turn onto Victoria Park Road, something alarming was happening to the landscape.

In 1919, on top of Copps Hill in Boston, a ninety-foot-wide storage vat for the production of rum burst its seams and sent 2.5 million gallons of molasses flooding onto the city. The wall of molasses rose fifteen feet high and reached a velocity of thirty-five miles per hour, drowning twenty-one Bostonians in its wake.

In much the same manner, a wave of engulfing sweetness was breaking over Victoria Park, lotus trees glistening with such a sugary gleam that she might have leaned over and licked them. The dark lake stirred deliciously, like a wide-mouthed jar of treacle. The very air had caramelized, and breathing was like sucking on candy. Without question, the vessel bursting its seams and coating the whole vicinity with syrup was that house.

Ascending the gaunt Victorian's steep stone steps, she felt a stab of apprehension. As of her callous apathy when Lawrence walked in last night, Irina's affections were officially unreliable. She was, after all, a shrew now, who shouted at hardworking wage-earners for wanting a piece of toast—a fickle harpy who took fancies one minute, and went cold the next. Ramsey had seemed all very fetching on Sunday, but this was Monday. There was no certainty that the countenance she confronted across this threshold would foster anything but more barbarous indifference.

Yet, today anyway, this apparently was not the case. That face: it was *beautiful*.

Slipping his long, dry fingers along the bare skin under her short-cut tee, he slid them round to the small of her back, where not long ago they had hovered so tantalizingly, not touching. She emitted a little groan. He swept her through the door.

❖ ❖ ❖

She barely beat Lawrence home. The answer-phone light was blinking. Yanking a comb through her tangled hair, she pressed "Please hang up and try again. Please hang up and try again"—pleasant but insistent, the British female voice pronounced "again" to rhyme with "pain." Through some peculiarity of Blue Sky's phone system, this was the recording that consumed the full thirty-second limit on the machine whenever Lawrence rang up and didn't leave a message. He seemed to have taken the woman's advice. As "Please hang up and try again" droned in a demented nonstop singsong, she counted: he had rung five times.

Behind her, the lock rattled, sending her heart to her throat. "Irina?" It had only been a day, but he had already dropped the lilting addition of her middle name. "Hey!" He dropped his briefcase in the hall. "Where have you been all afternoon?"

"Oh," she scrambled, "running a few errands."

Wrong. People who have lived together for years were never "running errands." She could have said she was at Tesco because they were low on Greek yogurt, or at the hardware store at Elephant & Castle because the lightbulb in the studio desk light had burnt out—*that's* what you say to the man you live with. Because Irina knew all about the exactingly particular nature of domestic reportage, her failure to heed its form was tantamount to wearing a sandwich board that announced in big block letters, BEHOLD MY CHEATING HEART. Then again, she may have envied many a talent—her sister's for ballet, Lawrence's for politics. But a knack for duplicity? She didn't *want* to get good at this.

"I thought you were all hot to trot to get some work done today."

"I don't know. It just wasn't flowing. You know how that is?"

"Since you're suddenly so secretive about your drawings, no I don't know." She followed him limply to the kitchen, where he fixed himself a peanut-butter cracker. His motions were jagged. Those five unanswered messages had stuck in his craw.

"Anything up today at Blue Sky?"

"It's mooted the IRA ceasefire will be reinstated soon." His tone was clipped. "But nothing that would interest you. . . . What are you wearing that getup for?"

She crossed her arms over her exposed midriff, a style that seemed suddenly too young. "Felt like it. It's started to bother me that I wear rubbish all the time."

"Americans," he snarled, "say *trash.*"

"I'm half Russian."

"Don't pull rank. You have an American accent, an American passport, and a father from *Ohio.* Besides, a Russian would say *khlam,* or *moosr.* Not *rubbish, da*?" When no longer trying to please, Lawrence's Russian improved dramatically.

"What's—" Yet another British expression, *What's got up your nose?* would only rile him further. "What's bothering you?"

"You took my head off this morning because you were so anxious to get to work. I called around ten, it was busy, and by ten-thirty you were already gadding about. As far as I can tell, you've been out all day. Have you gotten anything done? I doubt it."

"I'm a little blocked."

"You've never indulged in that arty-farty—*rubbish.* A real pro sits down and does the job, whether or not she *feels like it.* Or that's what you used to say."

"Well. People change."

"Apparently." Lawrence scrutinized her face. "Are you wearing *lipstick?*"

Irina almost never wore makeup, and wet her lips. "No, of course not. It's been, you know, a little warm. Just chapped is all."

When Lawrence left to turn on the Channel 4 news, Irina slipped into the loo to check her face. Her lips were a bruised cherry-red; her chin was rug-burn pink. Ramsey had needed a shave. Maybe she'd been lucky. Lawrence hadn't remarked on her chin, or detected white wine on her breath. They'd polished off two bottles of sauvignon blanc, while Ramsey had insisted on playing her a flecked video of some famous 1985 snooker match on his flat-screen TV in the basement—which could not compete with the sport on his couch. Though she'd only managed a bite of the smoked salmon and beluga, the fish might still linger, and she'd cadged more than one of Ramsey's Gauloises. Not taking any chances, Irina brushed her teeth. It wasn't her custom to brush her teeth at seven, but she could always claim to have burped a little stomach acid or something. Discouragingly, even when you didn't want to get good at this sort of thing, you got good at it anyway.

It wasn't like Lawrence not to sniff out the wine. He had a nose like a hound. That meant he may have noticed her chin, too, and the hint of smoked fish. In the living room, his concentration on Jon Snow was excessive.

"I'll have the popcorn in a minute!" she said brightly from the doorway. "And for dinner, how about pasta?" She'd forgotten to take the chicken out to thaw.

"Whatever." One more report on mad cow disease could not have been that compelling. The British government had been slaughtering those poor animals by the tens of thousands for months.

"I could make the kind with dried chilies and anchovies that you especially like!"

"Yeah, sure." He looked over and smiled, gratefully. "That would be great. Make it hot. Make it a killer."

Pasta was far more than she need have offered. He was already accepting crumbs.

▣ chapter three ▣

The bedclothes were seductive, but, with Lawrence up, the swaddling lost its appeal. The dream eluding capture had been unsettling—something about the Beatles in her bedroom, mocking her undersized breasts. Lawrence would sometimes let her sleep in, but whenever Irina arose and found him away to work she felt dolorous and cheated. So she crawled out of bed. Even if they didn't chat much in the morning, percolating side by side without having to talk was its own pleasure, and it was nice to begin the day as a team.

After trotting off to buy a *Telegraph,* she yawned back to the kitchen in painter's pants and a soft, floppy button-down, entering into the clockwork of their morning routine. Some people found the infinite iterations of home life tedious. For Irina, its rhythms were musical; the shriek of the grinder was the day's opening fanfare. She welcomed a refrain to which she could almost hum along: the gurgle and choke of the stovetop espresso pot, the roar and strangle of the steamer wand as she whipped the milk to froth. If duplicating the same proportions every morning lent her coffee preparation an inevitable monotony, she wouldn't opt for too little milk just because making her coffee badly was different. There was nothing tiresome about having established that, because Lawrence liked his toast on the dark side, the ideal setting on the toaster was halfway between 3 and 4. The properties of repetition, she considered, were complex. Up to a point, repetition was a magnifier, and elevated habit to ritual. Taken too far, it could grow erosive, and grind ritual to the mindless and rote. In kind, the pound of surf, depending on the tides, could either deposit sand on the shore, or wear it away.

While Irina was not averse to variety—sometimes the coffee was from Ethiopia, others from Uruguay—overall, variety was overrated. She preferred variation within sameness. If you were voracious for constant change, you ran out of breakfast beverages in short order. She had some appreciation for folks with a greed for sensation, who were determined, as an old boyfriend used to say, "to squeeze the orange" and press fresh experience from every day. But that way lay burnout. There were only so many experiences, really—a depressing discovery in itself—and surely you were better off trying to replicate the pleasing ones as often as possible.

Furthermore, she reflected, steaming the milk with her signature teaspoon of Horlicks (which rounded the edge off the acid), that impression of "infinite" repetition—of having coffee and toast *over* and *over* and *over,* numbingly into the horizon—is an illusion. Boredom with routine is a luxury, and one unfailingly brief. You are awarded a discrete number of mornings, and are well advised to savour every single awakening that isn't marred by arthritis or Alzheimer's. You will drink only so many cups of coffee. You will read only so many newspapers, and not one edition more. You glory in silent communion with your soul mate at the dining table a specific, quantifiable number of times— so inclined, you could count them—before, wham, from one calamity or another at least one of you isn't there anymore. (Not so long ago, Irina had feared a falling-out, one that would shake her faith in "the whole project," but that anxiety had been latterly eclipsed by the more powerful fear that Lawrence would die. Thus a growing sense of security in one realm begot an accelerating sense of menace in another, one in which "the whole project" was jeopardized in a more absolute regard.) Whenever Irina read those listings in news articles, of how many meals the average person totals over a lifetime, how many years he spends sleeping, how many individual instances he will go to the loo, she was never dazzled by all those digits, but humbled by their paltriness and finitude. According to the actuarial average, this was one of only seventy-eight summers that she was likely to sample, and forty-two were dispatched. It was shocking.

"Been out all last week," said Lawrence through his toast. "Work's really piling up. I'm going to have to get a move on."

"Don't bolt your food!" she chided. "And if you drink your coffee too fast, you'll burn your throat. Why not take it easy, read a few pages of *The End of Welfare*?"

"I concentrate better at the office."

"Wouldn't you like another piece of toast? It's that gorgeous loaf from Borough Market, and it doesn't last. Eat it while it's fresh."

"Nah," said Lawrence, wiping the crumbs from his mouth. "Gotta go."

"Did you see this mad cow article?" Irina was shamelessly trying to keep him home a few minutes longer, as she'd once wrapped around her father's ankle when he had another six-week shoot to coach movie dialogue in California and was trying to get out the door. "Now that the price of mince is down to 49p a pound, beef sales are starting to soar. Have you *read* about what CJD is like? But never mind risking a long, slow death as your brain turns to sponge if you can save a quid or two on dinner. It doesn't make any sense! At £1.39, nobody will touch the stuff because it might kill you, but at 49p no problem?"

"Pretty good deal! How about hamburgers tonight?"

"Not on your life. We're having chicken."

Irina saw him to the door, and managed to stall his departure with more small-talk until she bid Lawrence a reluctant *do svidanya*.

She tidied up and took the chicken out to thaw, fighting a customary desolation. Even Lawrence's standard weekday abandonment fostered a little grief.

Once settled in her studio, she had trouble focusing on the next illustration of *Seeing Red*. The impulse to make a phone call was insistent. Merely a courtesy call, of course. It was plain good form, was it not, when someone has treated you to a sumptuous spread, to thank him for his generosity? She could make it short.

The number in her address book was still under Jude's name. Her hand rested on the receiver for several seconds, her heart pounding. A *courtesy call*. She picked up the phone. She put it back in its cradle. She picked it up again.

"Hallo?"

She put the receiver right back down. He'd sounded sleepy. It was too early. And she'd thanked him already, Saturday night, at the door. How silly, to have roused him for nothing. How much sillier, that she was shaking. At least he'd have no way of knowing who rang, only to rudely hang up. He'd assume it was one of those computer-generated phone solicitations, or a wrong number.

Yet as Irina returned to her drawing table, it came to her with a nauseous lurch that he would know. He would know with absolute certainty who had rung, heard his voice, been stricken by an opaque terror, and thrown the receiver to its cradle as if it might bite. In many respects they were near strangers, so it was disconcerting to realize that he knew her that well.

The illustration went no better than before. Whatever had lit her up while she was sketching the arrival of the Crimson Traveller was withdrawing from reach. Yesterday's inspired effort was the best of the set so far. But no matter how many times she tried, she was unable to recapture the style that Lawrence had described as unusually "bonkers." If she couldn't get the same frantic, energized quality into the companion illustrations, she would have to throw the "bonkers" one away. It didn't match. It stood out. The first introduction of the colour red had seemed alarming, outrageous, electrifying. In each of today's abortive efforts, red seemed ordinary. Blending side by side with the blues, it made purple all right, but purple seemed ordinary, too. Though now expanded by a factor of two, the palette still felt cramped, and she pined for a Yellow Traveller to release her into the spectrum. She made a note of the idea for the author, that for children to come to a fuller understanding of the nature of colour, a Yellow Traveller toward the end would make sense. Maybe she could imply slyly that the addition would be popular with the Chinese.

Lawrence rang early afternoon. He often called for no reason, and the more spurious his excuse, the more she was charmed. "Hey, I tried you around ten, and it was busy. Talk to anyone interesting?"

"Oh, you must have tried me at perfectly the wrong point. I picked up the phone to ring Betsy, and then thought better of distracting myself, and put it back."

What a strange little fib. She might easily have been honest: she'd rung Ramsey to thank him for dinner, had obviously woken him, and, abashed, had simply hung up with what Lawrence would regard as her usual social maladroitness. Yet just now she resisted raising the topic of Ramsey in conversation. Ramsey had become—private. Whatever had passed between them on his birthday belonged to her, and she cherished owning something of which Lawrence was not a part.

"So how's it going?"

"Lousy. I keep tearing everything up."

"Give yourself a break! The one you did yesterday was tremendous. Maybe you should take the afternoon off for once. Go for a walk, go to the library. Head up to that place on Roman Road where you found all those cheap Indian spices. While you're at it, you could go smoke dope with Ramsey and giggle over his video of the Steve Davis–Dennis Taylor match of 1985."

She should have kept her mouth shut about that joint. "Very funny."

"Well, I'm not kidding about the match. You should watch a replay someday. It's the most famous in snooker. Did I ever tell you that story?"

Oh, probably, but if so, Irina hadn't been listening. How did so many couples grow deaf to each other? Since he would clearly enjoy recounting the famous showdown—again—she encouraged him.

"It was the World Championship at the Crucible. Dennis Taylor—this geeky-looking guy from Northern Ireland, with big dopey-looking horn-rims, right? Well, he'd been on the circuit for thirteen years before he won a single tournament. So Taylor was considered a laughable long-shot against Steve Davis. Who was, you know, God's gift to snooker by '85. Reigning champion, and regarded as unbeatable. The final was bound to be a whitewash.

"That's the way it started, too: Taylor went down seven–zip in the first session. But he rallied in the second, almost evening the score at nine–seven, and in the third session he also finished just two frames down, at thirteen–eleven. Still, all the commentators are saying, isn't it great that the poor schmuck won't go down without a fight. Like it's cute or something.

"But in the final session, Taylor pulls even, at seventeen apiece. First to eighteen, right? So eventually the championship goes down not only to the last frame, but to the *last ball*. The black, of course. There's this unbelievable sequence where Taylor misses a double, then Davis fucks up, too, then Taylor takes on a long pot and barely misses, thinks all's lost and mopes back to his chair as if his pet just died. But it's a thin cut, and Davis botches his opportunity, too, leaving a pretty easy black. When Taylor potted it for the title, the Crucible went bananas."

"So it's a David and Goliath story. Little engine that could."

"Yeah. And the broadcast of that last session set BBC records. Watched by eighteen million people. Biggest audience any British sportscast had ever garnered. Ramsey says those were the days. Snooker players were like rock stars in the 80s. They lived the life of Riley, and got away with murder, too. Lotta bad boys. Ramsey says the new crop of players is too boring, and that's why the audience has shrunk."

Ramsey says. Though he had generously lent the man out for one evening, Lawrence wanted Ramsey *back*. Like Dennis Taylor, she was disinclined to relinquish a valuable trophy without a fight. "On the contrary. *Ramsey says* that the new crop of players has gotten too *good*, and *that's* why the audience has shrunk."

"Same idea," said Lawrence. "*Ramsey says* that too good *is* too boring."

They both understood they meant good at snooker rather than good as in virtuous. Still, once they finished the call, the line stayed with her.

◨ ◨ ◨

The concept behind the holiday of Thanksgiving in the States is all very laudable. Nevertheless, it doesn't work. It is nigh impossible to sincerely count your blessings on the last Thursday of November because you're supposed to. The occasion is reliably squandered on fretting that the turkey breast is drying out while those last morsels on the inner thighs are still running red.

Yet thankfulness can descend unscheduled. When Lawrence cried "Irina Galina!" at the door that evening, and Irina rejoined from her studio, "Lawrence Lawrensovich!" she was grateful. When he told her about his day over peanut-butter crackers—his contacts had passed on a rumour that the IRA ceasefire would soon be reinstated—she may never have quite understood the fracas in Ulster, nor have kept up with whether its paramilitaries were or were not bombing the bejesus out of Britain these days, nor have comprehended why they would do such a thing in the first place, but still she was grateful—that Lawrence had work that fascinated him, whether or not it fascinated her. That he cared enough to fill her in about what he did during the day and respected her opinion. That were she to ask him, he would patiently explain the ins and outs of Northern Ireland in whatever detail she wished. That he would not take offence if just tonight she gave the exegesis a miss. When they settled in front of the Channel 4 news, she was grateful that she wasn't a dairy farmer, watching his herd go up in smoke. While she was confessedly growing fatigued with the mad-cow-disease story, by and large British newscasts were superior to their American counterparts—more serious, more in-depth—and she was grateful for that, too.

Preparing their traditional predinner popcorn, Irina was thankful for another routine of perfectly balanced variation within sameness. She had worked out the exact oil-to-kernel ratio that would maximize loft and minimize grease; after experimentation across a range of popcorn brands, she always bought Dunn's River, the least likely to prove dried out. One shelf of her spice rack was devoted to so many ethnic toppings— Cajun, Creole, Fajita mix—that she could serve a differently seasoned bowlful every day of the month. Tonight she chose black pepper, parmesan, and garlic powder, a favorite combination, and as they decimated the batch she was glad of a snack that you could gorge on that would not fill you up.

Picking up the remnants of cheese at the bottom of the bowl with a moistened forefinger, Irina considered that they were both in perfect health, and sometimes physical well-being could convert from the blank space between ailments to witting pleasure. Entering middle age, they remained a handsome couple; she'd survived a rash bout of chocolate-cappuccino cake, and she still wasn't fat. No one close to her had recently died. Lawrence, grumbling over when this protracted segment on BSE would ever be over, was conspicuously alive. Dinner—the chicken had been marinating in a deadly Indo-nesian jerk sauce all afternoon—would be smashing.

Nothing was wrong. Most of all, the air between them was clear. She may have kept quiet about a couple of purely interior moments with Ramsey Acton over the weekend, but she had granted herself permission this afternoon to hold those slight cards close to her chest. If Saturday night's disquieting temptation had sent a tremor through this flat, the earth had stilled again. It was surely not naïve to believe that neither she nor Lawrence was hiding any great secret from the other. Lawrence was not covertly gambling away their savings at OTB—if he said he went to the gym on his lunch hour, to the gym he went—nor was he going through the motions of heading to the office every day when in truth he'd been sacked months ago. Maybe she did sneak an occasional cigarette, but Irina was not popping amphetamines while Lawrence was at Blue Sky. She hadn't developed a furtive morning sherry habit, or a stealthy dependence on Valium. Lawrence did not harbour a whole other family in Rome, whom he visited while pretending to attend a conference in Sarajevo. So while it was possible that a pizza delivery boy would press the wrong buzzer, there was no chance that their doorbell would be rung tonight by a sullen teenager whom Lawrence hadn't admitted to siring years ago, who now wanted money. Irina wasn't brooding through the news over how to break it to Lawrence that her self-absorbed mother could no longer afford the upkeep of her house in Brighton Beach and would be moving into their spare bedroom next week. Lawrence wasn't brooding through the news over how to break it to Irina that after all these years he had come to the realization that he was gay. And on Saturday night, Irina hadn't kissed another man while Lawrence was away.

Some years thanksgiving arrives in the lowercase, in July.

❖ chapter four ❖

On one more exasperating afternoon in August, Irina thumbed through the illustrations for *Seeing Red* up until the blazing arrival of the Crimson Traveller, gripped the pages by the corners, and ripped them from her drawing pad. Not allowing herself to reconsider, she immediately tore them in half, and crumpled the uninspired blue pictures into the bin. Only the new ones had life. Only the new illustrations were tolerable to her: those visited by a tall, terrifying figure from another world, whose rash, outlandish hues would blow the mind of any stunted visual pauper raised in the cramped, confining spectrum of midnight to cerulean. How had she ever borne drafting those first nine workaday pictures without red? Nevertheless, she would craft the blue ones again. The redrawn blues would pulse with need, with longing and deprivation, with all of the dolour and ache that gave "the blues" its emotional and musical connotations.

Though she told herself that she was simply being professional, the impatient disposal was still unnerving. What else formerly of such value, on which she had lavished painstaking care, might she suddenly tear asunder and cart to the bin because it was "workaday" and "uninspired"?

Meanwhile, just as Irina grew more expert at designing excuses for why she was out when Lawrence rang, Lawrence ceased to solicit them. By the end of the month, when once again she barely beat him back to the flat, no "Please hang up and try agains" would await her on the answering machine. If she wasn't there, he didn't want to know, so perhaps he didn't want to know why, either.

She found his company unendurable.

Always a bit excessive, their dependence on television grew extravagant. Night after night they propped stuporously in their appointed seats, both glad of such a miraculous object—one that facilitated spending hours at a go in the same room without speaking, and at once cast this catatonic antisocial behaviour as perfectly normal. Nervous of coming upon such a black hole in the schedule that they might be forced to turn off the set—say, a deadly confluence of *World's Wildest Police Videos*, *Gardener's World*, and *House Doctor*—Lawrence took to returning daily from work with a video.

Irina failed to follow the most primitive plot twists in the movies he rented. The visions that had begun that first phantasmagoric Sunday evening had only multiplied, furnishing far more transfixing drama than anything Lawrence dug up at Blockbuster. And visions they decisively were, as opposed to fantasies. She didn't seem to concoct them like a fabulist, but to be subjected to them like Alex in *A Clockwork Orange*, arms bound, eyelids propped. She doubted she could stop them if she tried. But then—she didn't try.

There is a knock on the door. It is late at night. They have not been expecting a guest. Irina sags. She is heavy with foreknowledge of who has come calling, and of what the visitor will require of her. Limp in her armchair, she is slow to rise. She follows Lawrence to the hall. On the landing stands Ramsey Acton, ramrod-straight and stock-still. He would never have travelled with his most treasured possession outside its case in real life. But in this solemn passion play, he is gripping his cue, planting the butt on the lino like a staff. Clad in black, he looks Old Testament, like one of the prophets. His blue-grey eyes are harrowing. They do not light on Lawrence, but stare directly over his shoulder to Irina. Ramsey's refusal to acknowledge her partner's presence does not seem rude. By implication—whatever the reason for Ramsey's strange appearance at their door in a city where people do not customarily drop in on one another unannounced, much less at such an hour—it has nothing to do with Lawrence. Irina meets Ramsey's eyes. They are uncompromising. No one says a word. Ramsey doesn't need to. This is a summons. Should she fail to heed it, he will not be back.

London's night air is cooling at the close of summer. Irina takes her coat from the rack in the hall. Following Ramsey's gaze, Lawrence turns to Irina as she draws on her wrap.

94

He looks mystified. He has not seen Ramsey Acton for over a year. He has no understanding of why the man would show up like this with no warning. Yet it is too late for explanations. She is sorry. In the oddest way, for Irina this has nothing to do with Lawrence, either. She picks up her bag from its hook. That is all she takes. It is all she will ever take. There is every likelihood that she will never return to this lovely flat again. Brushing silently past Lawrence, she slips to Ramsey's side. His cool, dry hand slides around her waist. Finally Ramsey looks Lawrence in the eye. The one look transmits everything. All these weeks she has been petrified by the prospect of sitting Lawrence down one arbitrary evening and blurting what he most fears to hear. The hackneyed scene will no longer be required. Lawrence knows. He is reeling from learning too much too fast. His dizziness can't be helped. He will have all the time in the world to regain his bearings—to piece together painfully why she must have snapped at him over so minor a matter as toast.

Ramsey tosses his cue lightly into the air and catches it at a midpoint, where it balances. The cue has transformed from Biblical staff to an implement more playful, like the cane in a tap dance by Fred Astaire. Gracefully, Ramsey turns her from the door. They walk down the stairs.

The other recurrent vision was odder, because it never went anywhere. It just sat.

Ramsey and Lawrence are seated at the dining table in Borough. This is the same table at which they had consolidated the couple's resolution last year—Lawrence's resolution, really—that though their established foursome with Jude and her husband was no more, Ramsey would not be jettisoned from their friendship. How poignant: it is only thanks to Lawrence's insistence that Ramsey has been rescued from social oblivion. Irina would have let the man slip from their acquaintance altogether. As if she knew, and had been leading herself not into temptation by sternly lashing the object of her unconscious desire to a little raft and letting it drift downstream. As if Lawrence had known also, and had run off to scoop Ramsey's raft from receding waters as a gift for Irina—as if Lawrence were pimping for his own ersatz wife.

Wife. *The word forms the centrepiece of the mirage, like a bouquet on the table. Lawrence and Ramsey are sitting opposite, squared off. In the knock-on-the-door fancy, Lawrence seems irrelevant. In this one, it is Irina who doesn't pertain. She is standing, exiled to the hallway. This is solely a matter between two men. Though the scene's trappings are civilized—the dining table is a Victorian antique, the hand-sewn drapes are drawn and discreet—the feeling is Wild West, OK Corral. There could as well be a gauntlet on the table, and a pair of pistols.*

Lawrence's expression is tolerant. Whatever this is about, he will hear Ramsey out. Ramsey's expression is simple, open.

Ramsey says to Lawrence, "I'm in love with your wife."

This one line, that is the vision. It poses neither question nor solution. It merely frames a predicament. The scene stops there, for there is nowhere for it to go. Were the confrontation to carry on— Lawrence might say gruffly, "Well, that's tough luck," and Ramsey might return quietly, "Whose tough luck?"—the perfect impasse would remain. However little Irina herself "pertains," Irina and only Irina has the power to move this encounter beyond face-off, to advance the plot.

Especially this second scenario was sufficiently trite that it ought to have embarrassed her. But she wasn't embarrassed. It was too interesting. *I'm in love with your wife.* Irina wasn't Lawrence's wife. Yet the word arose in her mind's eye because it was true. Whatever the law might dictate, Irina was Lawrence's wife.

❖ ❖ ❖

In the days she'd been capable of focusing on more than her own misery, Irina had registered what the dramas and thrillers of the sort that Lawrence fed their voracious VCR were abundantly about. In the main, films place protagonists in a moral quandary, or test their mettle with trials by fire. Yet few members of the audience ever confront the cinematic dilemma in real life. Most people don't have to figure out how to blow the whistle on government conspiracies without getting themselves killed. Most people aren't pledged to take an assassin's bullet to protect the president. World War II is over, and the standard Western mother is not likely to have to choose between the lives of her two children in a concentration camp.

By contrast, there is one province in which, sooner or later, virtually everyone gets dealt a leading role—hero, heroine, or villain. Performance in this arena is as fierce a test of character as being tempted to sell nuclear secrets to Beijing. Unlike the slight implications of quotidian dilemmas that confront the average citizen in other areas of life—whether to report cash income on your taxes—the stakes in this realm could not be higher. For chances are that at some point along the line you will hold in your hands another person's heart. There is no greater responsibility on the planet. However you contend with this fragile organ, which pounds or seizes in accordance with your caprice, will take your full measure.

Irina had liked to think of herself as a decent person. Yet in this most telling of spheres her behaviour had grown disreputable overnight. While she might have preferred to regard her two-timing as "out of character," it is never persuasive to argue that you are not the kind of person who does what you are actually doing. Ipso facto, her furtive afternoons with Ramsey Acton were necessarily *in* character. For that matter, barring the onset of brain-wasting diseases like variant Creutzfeldt-Jakob, there may be no such thing as behaving "out of character." Should what you get up to fail to comport with who you think you are, something is surely inaccurate (and likely optimistic) about who you think you are. Since Irina had not consumed enough British beef to blame vCJD, she was not therefore "a decent person," but a duplicitous, traitorous tramp whose attachments were shallow, whose word, implicit or otherwise, meant nothing, and who was hell-bent on defiling the finest elements both of her life and in herself.

Yet every time her eyes found Ramsey's face—which had a delightful way of changing ages depending on the light; since over the course of five minutes it could flicker from adolescent devil-may-care to middle-aged gravity, then on to the fatalistic resignation of an old-timer, she often felt in the presence, cradle-to-grave, of a whole man—she felt *good,* and not the indulgent, petty feeling-good of eating chocolate. When he touched her—and he needn't cup her bare breasts or sidle fingers up under her skirt; holding her hand would do it, or resting his forehead on her temple—she experienced the sense of revelation that physicists must enjoy, when they believe they've finally put together that elusive theory of everything, located the one prion or quark that binds all matter. In the moment, it was impossible to conceive of this feeling as wicked. In Ramsey's arms, her attraction to this remarkable snooker player (of all things) not only seemed "good," made her "feel good," but seemed an attraction to *The* Good—to an absolute that made all life worth living, rejection of which would be both morally reprehensible and inhuman. Only back in the Borough flat, and confronted with a man who had bestowed on her nothing but generosity and did not deserve to be repaid for his devotion with coldness and perfidy, did Irina feel unclean.

❖ ❖ ❖

On the morning of August 31, Irina trotted once more numbly to the newsagent for a *Sunday Telegraph*. En route, she upbraided herself for imputing internal turmoil to strangers, for her fellow pedestrians seemed universally to look stricken. She allowed herself a touch of irritation at having to weave past so many laggards, trolling the pavements in a narcotic daze. More bizarrely, at the newsagent customers were murmuring to one another, as if all the rules of city life had been suspended for the day.

Alarming headlines were inconclusive, photos consuming most of the front pages.

Brow furrowed, Irina scurried back to their building, to find the girl from the ground-floor flat sitting on a lower stair with her head in her hands. Irina had never learned her name, but wasn't so devoted to the chilly etiquette of urban life herself, nor grown so callous in her recent self-absorption, that she would angle her way blithely around a crumpled fellow tenant sobbing her heart out.

Irina put a hand, just, on the girl's shoulder. "Are you okay? Do you need any help? What's wrong?"

Again, with London protocol so drastically revised that Westminster could as well have issued a decree, the girl didn't merely snuffle that she'd be fine, thanks, but began to gush. "My boyfriend doesn't understand! He's furious with me! He says I didn't even cry like this when his mother died. But I just can't *believe* it! I'm gutted! It's so *sad*!"

Irina shyly unfolded the paper in her hand, which she had halved not so much for ease of carrying as out of respect. "I'm sorry, I just got up, and the papers only . . ."

Overcome, the girl could now only nod. "B-both. Both of them."

This turn of the wheel wasn't quite in the same league as the collapse of the Soviet Union, but in Britain it came close.

"This is absolutely incredible." Closing the door, she hugged the headline to herself. "Diana!"

"What's that cow up to now?" said Lawrence. She knew he would light into one of his cruel imitations. *"Oh,"* he said in falsetto, lowering his head and batting his eyelashes, *"I'd love to help the underprivileged, but I just ate five jars of marshmallow fluff, and have to go throw up! While I'm stuffing my whole hand down my throat, could you tell those nice people that was not cellulite in my thighs? I'd just been sitting on a chenille bedspread! Afterwards, can I tell that story about Charles saying, 'Whatever love is'? Because with so many dresses I only wear once, it's important to keep the commoners feeling sorry for me!"*

"Are you quite finished?"

"Just getting started!"

"Because she's dead," Irina announced.

"Get out."

"She and Dodi Fayed were being chased by photographers and crashed in a tunnel in Paris." Irina delivered the news with spiteful triumph. Not often did she see Lawrence speechless (all he could manage was, "Wow. That's weird"), and watching him flounder was satisfying. "So maybe the next time you start to say something vicious about someone you hardly know, you should stop to think that any day you could find out they're dead, and consider how you'd feel."

Over the national keening of the next few weeks, Irina took the jarring death of the "people's princess" personally. In narrative terms, Diana's story had lurched from genre to genre. Like Irina's once-charmed romance with Lawrence Trainer, a fairy tale had soured to soap opera, and then hurtled towards tragedy.

❖ ❖ ❖

"You said you had something you had to talk to me about, and this had better not be just another girly mope about Princess Di." The merlot banged on the table, next to Irina's zinfandel. "For a schlep all the way out to the East End, I expect nothing short of scandal."

For some people keeping secrets was invigorating, but for Irina they were combustible; by September she was about to explode. Absent a therapist, the next best thing was plain-speaking Betsy Philpot. They'd arranged to meet at Best of India, a hole-in-the-wall on Roman Road. Betsy and Leo lived in Ealing, well west, and Betsy had resisted travelling across the whole of London with five Indian restaurants in her own neighbourhood. But Irina insisted that Best of India served distinctive dishes at reasonable prices; it lacked a liquor licence, but didn't charge a corking fee. An executive with Universal—recently acquired by Seagram's—Leo had just accepted a salary cut to stay on board. Glad to save a few quid on the wine, Betsy had relented. Besides, like most excellent company, Betsy was a gossip, and would have met Irina in Siberia if she had "something to talk about."

With the conventional obsequiousness of Indian waiters (a thin cover for contempt), the Asian uncorked the zin, then presented their poppadoms and condiment tray with a flourish. Irina made a mental note to avoid the raw-onion relish.

"Well, out with it," said Betsy. "Life's short, and tonight's shorter."

Irina hesitated. Obviously, it was dangerous to spill the beans to anyone who was friends with Lawrence as well. But to release the story into the world was also to relinquish sole proprietorship. When you let other people in on your business, you allowed them to have cavalier opinions about it; you might as well hand guests your prized original Monet miniature for a coffee coaster. Too, the moment she opened her mouth, her transgressions would become a matter of public record. Any prospective retreat would leave a slime trail.

"You're not going to approve," said Irina.

"I'm your judge and jury?"

"You can be moralistic." Though Betsy hadn't been Irina's editor for years, a shadow of hierarchy remained. Betsy wouldn't live in any fear of Irina's opinion of her.

"Excuse me, I didn't realize this was going to be a critique of my character."

"It isn't." Irina took a slug of wine. "I'm sorry, I shouldn't start defending myself against all the mean things you're going to say when you haven't said them yet."

"My guess is that you're the one who's been saying mean things, about yourself."

"You're right there—vile things." Another slug. "Anyway, back in July, something—happened to me."

"You know how when you're in the gym, and you have to do your sit-ups, and you go for water and retie your shoes? Putting it off never makes it any easier."

Crumbling her poppadom, Irina couldn't look Betsy in the eye. "I met someone. Or we'd known each other for years, but only *met*-met this one night." No matter how she told it, the tale sounded cheap. "I seem to have fallen in love with him."

"I thought you *were* in love," said Betsy sternly. Her own congenial marriage had the dynamic of a corporate partnership, and Betsy had more than once expressed a wistful envy of Irina's conspicuously warmer tie.

"I did, too," said Irina dejectedly. "And now, on a dime, I feel nothing for Lawrence, or nothing but pity. I feel like a monster."

"—Since when do you *smoke*?" Irina's British friends would have cadged one, but Betsy was a fellow Yank, and rather than slip out the packet of Gauloises, Irina might as well have tabled a Baggie of white powder, a used syringe, and a spoon.

"It's only occasional." Irina tried to direct the smoke away from Betsy's face, but the circulation system blew it back again. "Don't tell Lawrence. He'd have a cow."

"I bet he knows."

"I do the whole breath-mint thing, but yeah, probably."

"Oh, he *definitely* knows about the ciggies. But you have bigger problems to fry. I meant I bet he knows you're having an affair."

Irina looked up sharply. "I'm not."

Betsy examined her sceptically. "This is a platonic infatuation? You go to museums, and work yourself into ecstasies over a painting?"

"I've never been sure what 'platonic' means exactly. We, ah—it's physical, all right. But we haven't; ah, sealed the deal. I thought that was important." She was not at all sure it was important. Restraint has an eroticism of its own, and the agony of forgoing sexual closure had for weeks achieved a sweetness that bordered on rapture. If this was loyalty, what in God's name was betrayal?

"Has the nooky side of things been so bad, with Lawrence? Fallen off?"

"*Bad?* It's never been bad with Lawrence. We probably, or we used to until recently, have sex three or four times a week. But it's strangely impersonal."

"*Three or four times a week,* and you're complaining? Leo and I fuck about as often as we rotate our mattress."

"I never know what's going on in his head."

101

"Why don't you ask him?"

"I'm too afraid that he'll ask me what's going on in mine."

"Which is?"

The waiter arrived, and Irina coloured. The Asian surely assumed that loose Western floozies routinely conducted just this sort of seedy discussion over poppadoms.

"I think about someone else," she mumbled once he'd taken their orders. "It started out as a last resort, and now it's an entrenched bad habit. If I don't summon a certain other party in my head, I can't— finish the job."

"This *other party*. What does he do for a living?"

"If I tell you, then you'll know who it is."

"You're planning on getting through a lamb korma, a chicken vindaloo, and a side order of spinach and chickpeas without telling me the guy's name?"

Irina stirred a shard in the coriander chutney. "You'll think I'm nuts."

"You're projecting again. *You* think you're nuts."

"It's not that crazy. On the face of it, there's no reason that a children's book illustrator would have a whole lot in common with a think-tank research fellow, either."

"What, is this guy some working-class gardener or something?"

"He *wishes* he were working class. But he has plenty of money."

"Look, I'm not going to play Twenty Questions here."

Irina shook her head. "If we ever go public, Jude is sure to think we were running around behind her back while they were still married. We weren't."

"*Ramsey Acton?*" said Betsy with incredulity. "I'll give you this: he is good-looking."

"I hadn't even noticed he was handsome before; or only abstractly."

"This entire country has noticed your boyfriend's good-looking, as of the 1970s."

Their food arrived, and Irina helped herself to a tiny spoonful of each dish, which puddled in disagreeable pools of red oil on her plate.

"You know, you've lost weight." The observation carried a hint of resentment. Betsy, as they say, was *big-boned*—though she was pretty, and Irina had never figured out how to tell her that. "It's okay for now— you look hot as the blazes, frankly—but don't overdo it. Lose any more and you'll get waiflike."

"I'm not on a diet. I just can't eat."

"You're on the *luv* diet. Worth ten pounds. But don't worry—you'll put it back on at the closing end."

"Who says there's going to be an end?"

"Irina, get real. You're not going to run off with Ramsey Acton. Jude made that mistake; learn from it. Get him out of your system. For that matter—if you're telling me the truth—maybe you should get it over with and fuck the bastard. Stop building it up into such a big deal and find out one more time that fucking is fucking. On this score, most men are fungible. Then patch things up with Lawrence. As for whether you tell him about it and have a big cry, or shove it under the carpet like a grown-up, that's your call. But *Ramsey* is not a long-term prospect."

"Why not?"

"For starters? Take what you said, about money. Sure, Ramsey's made a lot of it. But according to Jude, it's all very easy-come. There's a corollary. She couldn't believe how little there was to filch when they divorced."

"She got a house in Spain!"

"Out of *millions*? I don't know how much you know about snooker, but these boys make do-re-mi hand over fist when they're on a roll. Why isn't there more of it left? I'm not only talking about finance, but temperament. You go all the way to Roman Road so you can bring in your own bottle of red. You're frugal. Ramsey? Is not frugal."

"It could do me good, to learn to splurge a little. It has done me good."

"Did you ever talk to Jude about what it was like to live with a snooker player?"

"Some," said Irina defensively. "She moaned a lot. But she was prone to. As Ramsey says, she's chronically dissatisfied. They were a bad match."

"And you're a good one? Go on the road with them, and you're stuck in hotel rooms, playing with the tea machine. But they don't want you to go on the road, not really. They like to play hard away from the table, too. And stay home, you're a widow for the season, sitting there wondering how much he's drinking, what's up his nose, and who's sidling next to him at the bar."

"That's a cliché."

"They always come from somewhere."

"Ramsey's different."

"Famous last words."

Irina sulked over her spinach, and threw back another defiant gulp of wine. When the waiter silently opened the second bottle, she sensed his disapproval.

Betsy wasn't finished. "If you're seriously contemplating a future with this character, can we talk turkey? Ramsey's, what, fifty?"

"He's only forty-seven."

"Big diff. Forty-seven, in snooker, is like ninety-five for everybody else."

"Ramsey says that, when he started out, plenty of snooker players were only reaching their prime in their forties."

"Times have changed. The superstars are all in their twenties. Ramsey's slipping. You can count on the fact that he'll keep slipping, too. Maybe it's eyesight, or steadiness of hand, or just starting to get burnt out despite himself, but he'll never get back to where he was. He's never quite won the World Championship, and he hasn't a snowball's of winning it now. The point is, you're getting the guy at the tail-end. It's not the fun part. Sometime soon he'll be forced to retire, unless he's willing to publicly embarrass himself. Snooker's his whole life, as far as I can tell. Retirement's not going to be pretty. When I picture it, cognac and long afternoon naps feature prominently."

"They almost always take up golf."

"Oh, *great*." Betsy heaped another spoonful of the neglected lamb onto her plate, eyeing Irina askance when she poured another glass of wine. "Listen, you must be having a rough time. But before you do anything hasty, try to be practical. Jude says he's neurotic."

"She's one to talk."

"I just want you to walk in with your eyes open. She says he's a hypochondriac. That he's superstitious and touchy, especially about anything to do with his snooker game. Expect snooker, snooker, snooker. You'd better like it."

"I *do* like it," said Irina. "Increasingly."

" 'Increasingly' means you didn't give a shit about it before. But I get the feeling it's not a fascination with snooker that's driving this thing."

"All right. No." Irina had never tried to put it into words, and had a dismal presentiment that any attempt to do so would prove humiliating. Nevertheless, she'd give it a go. "Every time he touches me, I think I could die. I could die right at that moment and I'd leave this earth in a state of grace. And everything fits. No matter how we sit next to each other, it's always comfortable. The smell of his skin makes me high. Really, breathing at the base of his neck is like sniffing glue. Slightly sweet and musky at the same time. Like one of those complex reduction sauces you get in upscale restaurants, which somehow manages to be both intense and delicate, and you can never quite figure out what's in it. And kissing him—I should be embarrassed to say this, but sometimes it makes me cry."

"My dear," said Betsy, clearly unmoved; boy, was that speech a waste of time. "It's called 'sex.'"

"That's a belittling word. What I'm talking about isn't little. It's everything."

"It *isn't* everything, though it seems that way when you're drunk on it. Eventually the smoke clears, and there you are, with this guy downstairs hitting little red balls into pockets the whole day through, and you wonder how you got here."

"You think it doesn't last."

"Of course it doesn't last!" Betsy scoffed. "Didn't you go through something like this with Lawrence?"

"Sort of. Maybe. Not as extreme. I don't know. It's hard to remember."

"It's no longer *convenient* to remember. Didn't you two go at it hot and heavy for a few months? Or you wouldn't have moved in together."

"Yes, I guess. But this seems different."

"It seems 'different' because right now you're up to your neck in it. And meanwhile, there are traffic bollards in your head to keep you from getting at what it was like in the olden days with Lawrence. My money says it wasn't different at all."

"You think everyone goes round in the same cycle. You get all very giddy and infatuated at 'the beginning,' and then inevitably the fire dies down to sorry little embers. So in no time I'll be having mechanical, impersonal relations with Ramsey three times a week instead of with Lawrence."

"If you're lucky."

"I refuse to accept that."

"Then you'll find out the hard way, cookie." Betsy's eyes sharpened when they caught Irina glancing surreptitiously at her watch. "I'll stand behind you whatever you do, because you're my friend. And I promise I won't say this again. Still, I'd feel remiss if I didn't at least say it once. Lawrence may not be God's gift to womankind. But—don't laugh, this isn't unimportant—he is a 'good provider.' He's *solid,* and I'm pretty sure he loves you like all get out, whether or not he's always able to show it. He's the kind of man you'd want around in a flood or an earthquake, or when some hood is breaking into your house. Icing on the cake, he's a caustic, irreverent son of a bitch, and I like him. I'm not saying that a girl doesn't gotta do what a girl's gotta do. Just because if you leave him you'll break his heart doesn't mean you shouldn't follow your nose— literally, from the sound of it. But I think you'd miss him."

"And, in the other event, wouldn't I miss Ramsey?"

"I don't doubt that cutting this thing off right now would probably feel like hacking off your arm. But it would grow back. You've been with Lawrence, what, ten years?"

"Close," said Irina absently.

"That's like a bank account, steadily accruing interest. You *are* frugal. Don't shoot your wad. You could blow your savings on some fancy, shiny gadget. Then when it jams, you'll be stuck with this glorified paperweight in your bed, and you'll be broke."

It wasn't nice, but Irina was no longer paying attention, and she asked for the bill. That's what happens when people give you advice that you don't care to take: their voices go tinny and mincing, like a radio playing in another room.

Betsy folded her arms. "Doesn't Ramsey live a few blocks from here?"

"Yes, as a matter of fact." Irina stirred her bag for her wallet.

"Next question." Betsy's eyes were flinty. "Are you or are you not walking back with me to the Mile End tube?"

"I might—take a cab."

"Swell. We can *share* one."

"Borough's not on your way."

"I don't mind the ride."

"Oh, stop it! Yes, if you must know, I am. We hardly ever get to see each other in the evening. I won't have long, either."

"Did you really want to see me? Or am I just a beard?"

"Yes, I *really* wanted to see you. Can't you tell? Two birds, one stone is all."

"So you drag me all the way out to the East End—"

"I'm sorry about that. I have warm associations with this place. We— well, the management isn't into snooker, so they don't know who he is. And I do like the food."

"That's funny. You didn't eat any."

"I told you, my appetite is crap."

"If Lawrence asks me when we wrapped things up here, I'll have to tell him."

"He won't ask." This was true, but there was something sad about that.

Irina tried to treat her friend, but Betsy was having none of it, as if refusing to be bought off. They split the bill. Walking down Roman Road, they said nothing.

At Grove Road, where Betsy would turn left and Irina right, Betsy faced her. "I don't like to be *used*, Irina."

"I'm sorry." She was fighting tears. "It won't happen again. I promise."

"You've got to talk to Lawrence."

"I know. But lately we can't seem to talk about anything."

"I wonder why *that* would be."

"He's such a purist about loyalty. If I ever allow that I've been attracted to someone else, he'll slam the door in my face. And I'd destroy his friendship with Ramsey. I don't think I can say anything without being sure what I want to do."

"Lawrence is a good man, Irina. They're thin on the ground. *Think twice.*"

❖ ❖ ❖

"You're panting!"

"I ran. We don't have much time."

"Get in here, pet, you'll catch your death. Your hands!"

They crossed the threshold, hips locked like freight cars. Closing the door with his back, Ramsey massaged her fingers with his own.

It was a minor malady, and common: Raynaud's disease, which sent the small blood vessels of the extremities into spasm at even moderately cool temperatures. Now that September had kicked in, the problem had returned. When it was diagnosed, Lawrence had suggested, for working in the studio during the day, a pair of fingerless gloves.

Not bad advice. But when she'd explained the ailment to Ramsey at Best of India last week, he'd instinctively reached across the table, working the corpse-cold flesh until its temperature conformed to the touch of a live woman.

A minor distinction, or so it would seem. Lawrence came up with a technical solution, and Ramsey a tactile one. But for Irina the contrast was night-and-day. Oh, she'd rarely complained. Big deal, she got cold hands; there were worse fates. Lawrence had even bought her those fingerless gloves, which helped a bit. But on some winter nights out her hands got so stiff that she couldn't turn the front-door key, and she'd have to knock with her foot. Yet not once had Lawrence massaged her fingers with his own until they warmed. He was a considerate man, ever drawing her attention to up-and-coming publishers, and she never lacked for little presents, sometimes for no occasion at all. But she didn't first and foremost crave professional advice, or thoughtful trinkets. She wanted a hand to hold.

"Brandy?"

"Oh, I shouldn't," she said, accepting a snifter. "I was on edge at dinner, and went through a bottle of wine like seltzer."

As usual, he led her to the basement, where they nestled onto a leather couch with the light over the snooker table switched on. The expanse of green baize glowed before them like a lush summer field; they might have been picnicking in a pasture.

"I feel awful," she said. "I told Betsy about us, and—"

"You oughtn't have told her."

"I had to tell someone."

"*You oughtn't have told her.*"

"Betsy can keep a secret!"

"Nobody keeps another git's secret like they do their own—and most people can't keep them. Not even you, pet, if tonight's a measure." He sounded bitter.

"I can't talk to Lawrence. You're hardly objective. If I didn't confide in someone I was going to go mad."

"But what's between you and me is private. You're turning what we got into dirt. What secretaries titter about over coffee. It's soiling."

"It's soiled anyway."

"That's not my fault."

"It's mine?"

"Yeah," he said to her surprise. "You got to decide. I might keep up with this carry-on, against my better judgment. If it weren't for one thing. Irina, love—*you're making a horlicks of my snooker game.*"

Irina wanted to pitch back, *Oh, so what?* but she knew better. "What do I have to do with your snooker game?"

108

"You've spannered my concentration. I'm lining up a safety shot, and all that's running through my head is when you'll ring. Instead of rolling snug up against the baulk cushion with the brown blocking the pack, the white ends up smack in the middle of the table on an easy red to the centre pocket."

"Oh, what a tragedy, that your practice game is off, when I'm repaying the kindest man in my life with duplicity and betrayal!"

Ramsey withdrew his arm coolly from around her shoulders. "The very kindest?"

"Oh, one of the kindest, then," she said, flustered. "This isn't a competition."

"Bollocks. Of course it's a competition. Naïveté don't suit you, ducky."

"I hate it when you call me that." The way Ramsey pronounced the anachronism (nobody in Britain these days said *ducky* outside West End revivals of *My Fair Lady*), it sounded like anything but an endearment. She hugely preferred *pet*. The northern usage may have been equally eccentric, but it was tender, and—pleasingly—she'd never heard him address as *pet* anyone but her. "I have so little time. We shouldn't waste it fighting!"

Ramsey had retreated to the far end of the couch. "I told you from the off. I'm not into anything cheap. We been sneaking about for near on three months now, and that'd be three months longer than I ever meant to smarm round behind a mate's back and roger his bird."

"But we haven't—"

"Might as well have. I had my arm up your fanny to the elbow. Tell that to Anorak Man and ask if it really matters that it's not my dick. Fifty-to-one odds he'd not shake my hand for being so respectful, but punch me in the gob. And I can't say I'd blame him. I'm bang out of order, I am, and so are you."

Irina bowed her head. "You don't have to try so hard to make me feel bad. I feel awful already, in case you were worried."

"But I don't *want* you to feel crap, do I? *I* don't want to feel crap. I don't want to think of you leaving here tonight and going to bed bare-arsed with another fella. I don't want to and I don't have to and I *won't*."

Irina had started to cry, but Ramsey made a show of hardness, as if her tears were a gambit. "If I was a bird, I'd be fancied a right mug. Letting some more or less married bloke mess about with me during the day. But I'm a bloke, so instead I'm a Jack the Lad. Hand in the knickers, and it costing me no more than the odd chardonnay.

109

"That's the way your man in the street thinks, but it's not the way I think, darling. *I* think I'm a right mug. You slink in here and rub up against my trousers like a cat itching her backside on a post, and then it's, Blimey, look at the time! And you nip out the door again—leaving me with the post. I got no moral objection to self-abuse, but it's well short of a proper good time."

"You shouldn't talk about us like that," she sniffled. "Or me like that. It's ugly."

"We been making it ugly! Bugger it, woman!" Ramsey socked a fist into his opposite palm. *"I want to fuck you!"*

Despite her miserable curl at the far end of the sofa, Irina felt a twinge, as if he had her on a string, and could tug at the tackle between her legs like a toy on wheels. Thus her pride at his declaration was dovetailed by resentment. It was all very exhilarating to have conceived a consuming infatuation against the placid backdrop of her reserved relationship with Lawrence. But there was no opting out; she could not nibble at sexual obsession when it suited her. The craving was constant, and with Ramsey now removed by three feet even the brief deprivation was unbearable. "I want to fuck you, too," she mumbled morosely.

"You treat me like a rent boy! It's been long enough. You rubbish me, and you rubbish us. You rubbish yourself. If you're right and Lawrence hasn't twigged yet, you can nip back to your happy home and stay. Or you can get your bum into my bed and stay. You cannot have him and me both. 'Cause I am shattered. I am half demented. Waiting for you to show tonight, I couldn't pot the colours on their spots, and I could pot the colours on their spots standing on a fruit crate when I was seven."

"Three months may seem like an eternity to you, but I've nearly ten years with Lawrence at stake here. I have to be sure of myself. There'd be no going back."

"There's never no going back! In snooker, you learn the hard way that every shot is for keeps. I got no time for prats who hair-tear about *Oi, if only I'd not used quite so deep a screw on the blue.* Well, you didn't. You potted the blue, or you didn't. You're on the next red, or you're not. You live with it. You make the best call you can in the moment, and then you deal with the consequences. Right now, it's your visit. You're in amongst the balls. You got to decide whether to go for the pink or the black, full stop."

"Is Lawrence the pink? Because I don't think he'd appreciate the colour."

Ramsey looked unamused.

"Sorry," she continued with a nervous smile, "it's just, *Reservoir Dogs* is one of his favourite movies, and there's this scene where Steve Buscemi whines about why does he have to be 'Mr. Pink' . . . Oh, never mind."

"I'm playing the Grand Prix next month," said Ramsey levelly. "I got to get tournament ready, and I got to be able to concentrate. In the best of all possible worlds, I'd ask you to come with me to Bournemouth. But that's obviously a nonstarter."

"Oh, but I would love to—"

"I mayn't have made world champion," he ploughed on, "but I been in six championship finals, and got an MBE from the Queen. That mayn't mean much to a Septic Tank"—he had taught her Cockney rhyming slang for *Yank*—"but it does mean something to me. I won't be treated like a toy by a bird who's snug as a bug with another bloke but needs a bit of buzz. And I won't play in a bent match. I'd never have played a single frame if I knew from the off that the trophy was pledged to another fella."

The monologue had all the earmarks of a rehearsed speech. But Irina was starting to get a feel for Ramsey, and she didn't think so. He was a performer, and his game was the soul of spontaneity. This show had taken an improvisational turn at her imprudent outburst about betraying "the kindest man in her life"—though her more considerable imprudence may have been impugning the paramount importance of *snooker*. Impetuously, he had gone with the turn and kept going. His voice sounded measured; the discussion itself was out of control. She could already sense where this was leading, and her cheeks drained. It was all she could do to keep from leaping across the sofa to clap a hand on his mouth.

"I don't want to see you again before the Grand Prix," he said. "And that'd be no love notes neither, nor blubbing on the blower. When I come back to London, I only want you to rock up on my doorstep if you told Lawrence you're in love with me, and him and you are finished."

If Ramsey was being melodramatic and had had a fair bit to drink, his it's-him-or-me ultimatum made unpleasantly good sense. Yet he couldn't resist taking his levelheaded proposal that one step further that would make it hasty, foolhardy, and scandalously premature: "And that

111

ain't all, *ducky*. When you leave Lawrence, if you leave Lawrence, you don't tuck in upstairs as my in-house personal slag. *You marry me.* Got that? *You marry me,* and toot-sweet. At forty-seven, I got no use for long engagements."

As proposals go, this one was less bended-knee woo than assault. His delivery had been cruel, his clear intention to make what was already a terrible choice only the more stark. There would be no "trial separation" from Lawrence, no sampling of Ramsey's wares like one of those small squares of Cheshire at Borough Market with no obligation to buy. On the other hand, no man had ever asked Irina to marry him before, in any tone of voice. His furious demand, flung at her from three feet like a wet rag, prickled the back of her neck.

"Ramsey—I didn't even marry Lawrence, after nearly ten years."

"*I rest my case.*"

❖ ❖ ❖

On return to the flat, Irina made little effort to disguise the fact that she'd been crying. Since it was past midnight in a town with cosmopolitan pretensions but provincial transport, the tube was shut. Flaunting the coldness of his newfound absolutism, Ramsey hadn't rung her a cab, but had abandoned her on his steps to make her way home however she saw fit. The *handshake* at the door was the limit, instigating such a torrent of sobs on her flight from his house that when she finally flagged down a taxi on Grove Road the cabbie had to ask her to repeat the address three times.

Ramsey was not the only one inclined to make a show of his indifference. Failing to comment on her puffy red eyes, Lawrence said stiffly in the living room, "It's late."

"I missed the tube. Took forever to find a taxi."

"You, spring for a cab? Since when do you not look at your watch every five minutes to make sure you can catch the last train?"

"Time got away from me. It's a Friday night, and the minicabs were all booked up, so I had to wait." As long as she was lying, she might as well go all the way, and disguise the fact that she had hailed one of those exorbitant black taxis off the street.

"Why didn't you call to let me know you'd be so late? I might be worried." He didn't sound worried. He sounded as if he'd have gladly paid a hoodlum to biff her over the head on the way home.

"Finding a working pay phone would have delayed me even longer." Her delivery was fatigued, and her heart wasn't in this.

"If you rang a minicab," said Lawrence, "you'd already found a working pay phone. And that's assuming that *Betsy* didn't have her cell." His pronunciation of *Betsy* cast doubt on whether Irina had seen the woman at all. Apparently one of the sacrifices of lying, however selectively, was the ability to tell the truth.

"Okay, I just didn't think of it when I had the chance. I'm inconsiderate." She added lamely, "Still, maybe it's time we broke down and bought mobiles."

"Yeah, that would be great. I could call you, or you could call me, and I'd have no idea where you were, and you wouldn't have to tell me."

Irina let the crack slide, as if stoically allowing a spewed gob of spittle to drizzle down her cheek. "If you must know the real reason I'm so late, we had a fight. Betsy and I. It took some sorting out." The amount of effort required to concoct this transliterated excuse was stupendous, and she wondered why she bothered. It was nearly two and for an ordinary girls' night out an improbably long evening.

"What about?"

Irina searched her conversation with Betsy for some scrap to throw him like a bone, but could find little to salvage. "I won't bore you, it was stupid. But you should know that Betsy's a big fan of yours. She thinks you're wonderful."

"Glad somebody does." Lawrence got ready for bed.

❖ ❖ ❖

During the ten-day countdown to the Grand Prix in Bournemouth, Irina might have been scratching wobbly *X*s into the stone walls of her gulag, marking the inexorable march of time toward her own execution.

Indeed, fantasies of death daily flickered through her mind. She wasn't so far gone as to contemplate sticking her head in the oven, but whenever she crossed Borough High Street the image descended of the lorry that was barrelling in her direction running the light. She rued the fact that the IRA had, as Lawrence had foretold, reinstated its ceasefire, making a spontaneous explosion in their local tube station just as she exited the lift that much more far-fetched. Walking beneath the scaffolding of the numerous luxury housing developments springing up in the neighbour- hood, she didn't exactly *wish* that breezeblock overhead would tipple off the slats, but she could still *see* it careen two stories to her skull. These morbid flights were silly, but like the visions of Ramsey at the door, the couples grappling on the carpet, the figments of fatal accidents were uninvited.

Also uninvited were the persistent daydreams of Lawrence going leadenly through her address book to inform Irina's friends of her untimely passing. Tentatively, Betsy would ask, "Has anyone told Ramsey?" Lawrence wouldn't understand why Ramsey of all people should be high on the list, especially when it had been pulling teeth to get poor Irina to go out to dinner with the guy on his birthday. Plain-speaking or not, Betsy would still be discreet, though she might volunteer to give Ramsey the black news herself. At the funeral, Lawrence would be flummoxed why Ramsey, of all the mourners, seemed the most distraught. Finally, something would click—that birthday; Irina's exasperating remoteness when he came home from Sarajevo; her mystifying short temper since, and unexplained absences during the day . . . Lawrence would be angry at first, but with no Irina to fight over anymore fury would rapidly fold into grief. Maybe at length, having loved the same woman would bond the two men, and cement their friendship. (Nonsense, but beguiling nonsense nonetheless.) You see, it wasn't that she wished she were dead, exactly. Rather, the only circumstance in which she could bear to have Lawrence informed that she was in love with another man was one in which she did not—nay, could not—witness the consequences.

Lawrence may have made dutiful visits to Las Vegas every three or four years, but his parents thought think tanks incomprehensible and pretentious, and he thought golf instruction aimless and vapid; the disconnect was total. His brother was a methamphetamine junkie always hitting his father up for money; his unambitious sister worked for Wal-Mart in Phoenix. Irina was not part of Lawrence's family; she *was* his family. Given the books-and-politics jaw that filled out his rare socializing, she was also his one true friend. The resultant responsibility had never weighed heavily in the past. Now it was crushing.

Still, not a day went by that she didn't stare down the telephone when Lawrence was at work, or finger a 20p piece when passing a phone box. The sensation was akin to that of a smoker who is trying to quit, when he eyes the one packet he has hidden for emergencies in that little magnifying-glass drawer on top of the OED, thinking, *Well, just one, just one fag wouldn't make any difference in the long run—would it?* Ramsey may have issued rash ultimatums over too much brandy, but were her quavering voice ever to emerge from his receiver he would surely loose a deep, soughing sigh of relief, and within minutes she'd be rushing towards his arms in Hackney.

Oh, probably. Ramsey's resolve would be as easy to break down as the fibres of a skirt steak soaked in a full bottle of Barolo. But a temporary fix wasn't the answer. She had a decision to make. As Betsy had observed, retying her trainers would make the exercise no less onerous.

To the naked eye, Irina's bereft afternoon ambles during this period— which had an insidious tendency to veer, once across the river, toward the East End—gave every appearance of maudlin self-pity. To the contrary.

She felt sorry for Betsy, now saddled with a secret that she didn't want, bound to make her feel a traitor in any future gathering at which Lawrence was present.

She felt sorry for Ramsey, who had merely taken a friend out for sushi in all innocence, and who couldn't have anticipated that with two tokes on a doobie his shy, demure dinner companion would transmogrify into a voracious sexual predator; who gave heartbreaking credence to "the code" between men about keeping your hands off *your mate's bird,* and despised anyone who broke it, not least of all himself; who was obliged at this very moment to focus all his energies on that £60,000 prize in Bournemouth, when his head was raging with anxiety that the sole object of his desire was even now rededicating herself to a safe, comfortable relationship with his rival; who meanwhile was helpless. The passivity of his romantic position would echo all too familiarly the last frame of six championship finals, during which he could only take limp sips of Highland Spring as the trophy he coveted most in all the world slipped through his fingers.

Most of all, of course, she felt sorry for Lawrence. When he didn't think she was looking, she had more than once caught an expression on his face like that of a small boy who had been abandoned by his mother at Disney World. It was infused with longing, bewilderment, and desolation. He was being punished, and he had no idea for what. Everything about him that his partner used to adore now drove her insane. She wouldn't speak two words of Russian to him anymore, and hadn't employed the tender solicitation "Lawrence Lawrensovich!" for months. Whenever he told her about his work, like that coup of getting his proposal accepted by *Foreign Policy*, she acted bored, and no longer even pretended to listen. When he brought home a photocopy of the published article, she left it languishing unread on the dining table until he sheepishly slipped it back into his briefcase. Even his walking into a room seemed enough to make her irritable and claustrophobic. Whenever he proposed that they go see *Boogie Nights* at the weekend, maybe take one of those long Sunday-afternoon rambles of hers together for once, or go to Borough Market for vegetables as a team, she shrugged the invitations off, or discouraged him with faux consideration that he must have too much work. While not long ago she had prepared delectable meals in order to please him, now she concocted, if anything, more elaborate fare, but he could tell that she was merely driven to escape his company for the kitchen. He could do nothing right, and lately there seemed little purpose in trying. Presumably she would explain when she was good and ready. Since every indicator pointed to the fact that the explanation was dire, he had a vested interest in delaying that juncture for as long as possible.

Among the principals in this drama—she'd no illusions about its being anything but ordinary, although all the earth-shaking experiences of life, birth, death, love, and betrayal, were technically "ordinary"— there was only one party for whom she had no sympathy whatsoever. Were her own affections constant, Ramsey would easily concentrate on the upcoming Grand Prix. Betsy would have shouldered only the manageable burden of Irina's sour thoughts about Jude Hartford. And Lawrence would be happy as a clam.

❖ ❖ ❖

Two nights before the tournament was to get under way in Bournemouth, Lawrence made a radical bid for quiet and switched off the TV.

"Listen, I know you're not that interested in snooker." Knees canted, arms thrown wide on either side of the sofa, his posture was confrontational. "But I thought maybe you were interested in *Ramsey*."

A wave of white cold washed Irina's face, leaving a prickling sensation along her hairline; she might have dived into an Arctic ocean full of pins. She wasn't ready for this. She'd wanted to have prepared something, a list of reasons or a speech. Even carefully composed disclosure would have been bad enough. Discovery was worse by a mile.

"Snooker's all right," she said faintly.

"I mean, his story *is* interesting, isn't it? First he's a prodigy, then he fades from view because prodigies grow up, and, according to legend, he fell seriously into the gutter. But he pulls himself together, and this time more from application than pure natural talent, he nearly makes it to the top. But not quite. Becomes the sport's ultimate also-ran. Six championship finals, never wins a one. So you've got this guy who's getting older, past his prime, never quite got his hands on the ultimate prize, and is beginning to slide. But it's all he knows, snooker. What does a guy like that do? When he's got nothing to look forward to but falling apart? Where's he going to find a fresh reason for living?"

The sweat rising from her breasts was rank. Lawrence may have historically avoided *the main thing,* but this sadistic cat-and-mouse wasn't like him.

"In something else, I guess," said Irina.

"Like, another sport? Go for a whole new game."

"As I understand it"—Irina amazed herself by still being able to talk—"retired snooker players often take up golf."

"But golf's got none of the elegance. None of the strategy, the scheming—thinking half a dozen moves ahead, plotting the big picture. Chess would make more sense, if he had the brains for it. Which he doesn't."

"Ramsey's not stupid."

"He dropped out of school at sixteen. Oh, he can go on for hours about the merits of a percentage versus an attacking game. But don't talk to him about New Labour having co-opted the Tories' agenda. I tried once; it was painful. And this is his country."

"There are different kinds of intelligence," said Irina blandly. She wished he would get on with it, and stop trying to be clever.

"I can see why snooker players gravitate to golf," Lawrence carried on, still taken with his coy conceit. "It's not direct combat. You take on an opponent by besting him side-by-side, by taking turns. When you're on the green, or at the table, your rival's hands are tied. It's polite—not gladiatorial, like soccer, or even tennis. Really, sports like snooker and golf are for pussies."

"Real men fight it out hand-to-hand?"

"Yeah. They do. But you couldn't call Ramsey a macho man."

"Are you saying that he's a coward?"

"Sportsmen seek out games that suit their natures. He's weak, so he's avoided a test of physical strength. And he's averse to head-on conflict—with another man anyway. In snooker, your opponent is an abstraction. The lay of the balls could as well be generated by computer. Ultimately, all snooker players are playing against themselves, their personal best. Now Ramsey is playing against himself and losing."

"In some contests," she submitted, "Ramsey keeps up his end pretty well."

"So, all this drama—it captures your imagination?"

"Yes, Ramsey captures my imagination," she said heavily, looking at her hands.

"Good. Because the Grand Prix is next week. Ramsey's in the lineup, and Bournemouth's only a train ride. Get a B&B, make an outing of it?"

"You mean," she asked, raising her gaze incredulously, "you want to go?"

"You don't sound very enthusiastic." At a stroke, his squared-off posture wilted, and he dropped his arms to his lap. "It's just," he continued morosely, "we haven't done anything in a while. Together. I've been to tournaments, but you haven't. And when you know one of the players, you have an angle, a—reason to care . . ."

Discreetly, Irina patted her forehead dry with her sleeve.

"A snooker tournament is very British," Lawrence added. "You know, it could be culturally enervating." His correction, "I mean—edifying," was embarrassed. Lawrence had resigned himself to being lousy at Russian. English was another matter.

"I'd be glad to watch the tournament with you," she said carefully, trying to breathe deeply, to slow her heartbeat. "But don't you always say that you can actually follow the frames better on TV?"

"Well, you miss the atmosphere. And I bet Ramsey would take us out."

All right, he didn't know. Yet on some instinctive level Lawrence was savvy enough to use Ramsey as bait. The vision of that threesome trying to soldier through an entire dinner—well, Irina hoped the horror didn't show on her face.

Lawrence added, "Also, Ramsey says he's optimistic, about the Grand Prix."

"You talked to him?" asked Irina sharply.

"Sure I did. Free tickets."

"So how is he?" With luck, her wistfulness was not pronounced.

"Damned if I know. The poor bastard may not be socially adept, but that call was the limit. For all the banter I got out of the guy, I might have been Inland Revenue. Maybe he's not comfortable on the phone."

"No, I bet he wasn't comfortable." Subtext-laden dialogue was great fun in plays, but in real life it was hideous.

"So what do you say?"

"If you'd like to do something together—wouldn't you rather it were just us two?"

"*Just us two* doesn't seem to do it for you lately. I thought maybe a third party . . . a little excitement . . ."

"I don't need that kind of excitement," she said in all sincerity.

"Never mind, then," he said glumly. "It was only an idea."

"Well, as you say—I'm not as big a snooker fan as you are," she said gently. "It seems a lot of trouble, going all the way to Bournemouth. But we could still watch the tournament together. The first rounds are broadcast late, aren't they? After eleven-thirty? Maybe get a bite out first. Make it a date?"

Lawrence perked up. "Okay. Would you like that?"

His expression of struggling hopefulness was soul-destroying. These days Irina's small kindnesses, to which Lawrence was now prone to attach exaggerated importance, seemed downright malicious, encouraging as they did an optimism that she might more decently quash. Hence Irina was mean when she was nice to him, and mean when she was mean. Since it didn't matter, presumably she was free to treat him however she liked. So this was "power." It was overrated.

"Yes, I would like that," she said softly.

Yet she thought, *Oh, how I would like to like that.* For a moment, Irina could feel the haunting presence of that other life in which the prospect of dinner out with Lawrence and a nestle in front of a snooker match presented itself as simply glorious.

❖ ❖ ❖

When Irina had suggested "a bite out," she had in mind the likes of Tas, a cheap Turkish restaurant a ten-minute walk up Borough High Street. But Lawrence wanted to make a grand night of it, and made a reservation at Club Gascon, whose prices had previously restricted their sampling of its Basque haute cuisine to special occasions.

Irina didn't select her most fetching of outfits (she reserved her really smashing garb for outings to the East End), but made herself presentable. Which is more than she could say for Lawrence. "You're going to wear *that*? Club Gascon is pretty posh!"

He was clad in the same uniform of baggy jeans and plaid flannel he'd worn when they met. She should have been accustomed to his chronic slovenliness, but now she was spoiled. Ramsey had impeccable dress sense.

Lawrence shrugged. "If I'm going to pay all that money, I want to feel relaxed."

Irina rolled her eyes. "You make me look like a twat! Here I am in a skirt and heels, and I walk in with a man dressed like a dog's dinner!"

"Oh, shit-can the Brit-speak, would you?" he grumbled, shambling back to the bedroom. "For one night?"

He reemerged in navy slacks and an aquamarine button-down. Years of living with an artist hadn't improved his sense of colour. "Those blues clash," she muttered.

"Blues can't clash," he said resentfully.

"I did the better part of a book in blue, and I assure you they can."

Lawrence powered toward Blackfriars Bridge, brow in a scowl, torso tilted as if fighting a heavy wind. His stride was short but his pace vigorous, and Irina had trouble keeping up on cobbles in heels.

Seated in the dark restaurant, with its knurling arrangements of exotic blooms, Lawrence griped that their table was cramped by other diners— "Not very romantic." Irina swallowed the advisement that a thriving romance could readily flourish at a lunch counter over corned beef hash. As she surveyed the extensive menu, her selection was hampered by apathy. When Lawrence suggested that they opt for the five-course prix fixe with matching wines—an extravagant sixty quid a head that was sure to get them both pole-axed before the Grand Prix back home—Irina said sure just to spare herself the effort of ordering à la carte. Getting well oiled for their sports date also appealed. If she weren't desperate to lay eyes on Ramsey Acton even on television, Irina would happily have drunk herself unconscious.

Orders taken, Lawrence moved his champagne-and-armagnac cocktail out of the way and leaned forward over the table. "So," he said intently. "How *are* you?"

Irina recoiled as if from a loaded gun. "Okay," she stonewalled. "The first illustrations for *The Miss Ability Act* seem to be coming out all right."

He stared her down a beat. Her expression was stolid. He leaned back. He sighed. "I hope you don't mind," he said, "but when you were out with Betsy the other night, I sneaked a peek at your drawings. They're pretty outrageous. Good outrageous, I mean. Still—don't you think those illustrations are a little *adult*?"

"How so?"

"Well—sensual."

"Children have senses."

"The protagonist is a gimp in a magic wheelchair, right? Not a vamp."

"Nothing about being disabled means you can't be beautiful."

"I thought characters in children's books were more supposed to be *cute*."

"Sleeping *Beauty*? In the classics, female protagonists had breasts, and were woken with kisses. They were smitten with handsome princes, and wanted to get married. It's only nowadays that children's books have been purged of sex, and the principals are consumed with learning that little Somali children are just like them, or with putting away their toys."

"But your illustrations are for 'nowadays.' "

"I'm sorry you think my work is unprofessional."

"I didn't say that. Just, what I glanced at seemed a little risqué."

"I didn't show any terrible body parts."

"You didn't have to. It's something about the line, the feel. The look on the gimp's face. I don't know how else to say it—it's lustful."

"I'm sure Puffin will let me know if they think my illustrations unacceptably lewd."

The white wine that accompanied the foie gras was late-harvest, the mournful, bittersweet colour of a day's end, that piercing golden bask over the landscape made all the more aching for the fact that it wouldn't last. The undercooked goose liver lolled on a bramble of presentational sticks like one of Dali's melting clocks. When Lawrence raised his glass, he couldn't think of anything to salute, and their flutes clinked against each other to nothing in particular.

"You know, this Asian financial crisis is galloping, and the baht is in freefall," said Lawrence. "I'm a little worried about our investments, but there's a bright side. Taking a holiday in Thailand in the next few months could be fantastically cheap."

"Why would we want to go to Thailand?"

"Why not? We've never been there. The beaches are supposed to be great."

"You hate beaches. And since when do you want to go anywhere that doesn't double as research? No terrorists in Thailand, are there?"

"Now that you mention it, I had thought about taking a trip to Algeria." He waited; no reaction. "That's fine with you. If I go to Algeria."

Lawrence's going anywhere would mean being able to see Ramsey with impunity, even at night. "Shouldn't it be?"

"It's only one of the most dangerous countries in the world right now. In that Islamic raid on Sidi Rais in August, three hundred villagers were massacred with machetes."

"Oh?" Her eyes clouded. "I missed that."

"How could you *miss* that?"

"It's not my business to follow that sort of thing, it's yours."

"The rest of the world is everybody's business! You *used* to take an interest."

"Algeria is no safer if I personally keep up with how dangerous it is."

"Anyway, I wasn't serious, about Algiers. I was serious about Bangkok."

As for demurring, *I don't think we should be making any plans, because I may be leaving you within days,* she wasn't there yet. "Maybe," she said dubiously. His disappointment was palpable.

His agenda for their evening having inspired such little uptake, Lawrence fell back on his stock default: terrorism. It was a fascination she couldn't fathom. Lawrence had had little or no experience of being victimized by terrorists himself. He hadn't lost his mother in Lockerbie. He couldn't trace his lineage back to Belfast. They'd occasionally been ejected from the tube over a scare, but nothing in their vicinity had ever blown up. His professional interests exhibited a curious arbitrariness; they came from nowhere, had no organic roots. Maybe having made himself up, rejecting the tat and anti-intellectualism of Las Vegas, lent his adult incarnation an inevitable artifice. On the other hand, maybe having lived for months with a woman whose head was roiling with God knows what, whose behaviour had utterly transformed, and none for the better, due to no transgression of his own that he could identify, whose comings and goings were so overtly suspicious as to encourage his darkest imaginings to run rampant, and—most importantly—whom he could no longer trust to be truthful, or even nice—well, maybe that was something like being terrorized.

"This decision to invite Sinn Fein into talks, not a month after the IRA ceasefire was reinstated"— he attacked his scallops as if they had delivered a personal insult—"I think it's hasty. They don't get punished for Canary Wharf and Birmingham, they get rewarded. Oh, sure, we'll take you back into the fold, never mind you broke the last ceasefire with no warning and caused millions of pounds in commercial damage! It's undignified, and overeager. Blair is sucking Sinn Fein's ass, and it looks bad."

"You don't think there's a place for forgiveness? For drawing a line and saying, never mind the past, let's start here, clean?"

"People who have acted in bad faith before are likely to act in bad faith again. You don't do yourself any favours by acting credulous."

"By that reasoning, you don't negotiate with terrorists, period."

"You probably shouldn't. You probably have to. But at the very least, a long probationary period makes sense. When you can't trust someone's word, make them prove themselves with what they do."

❖ ❖ ❖

They staggered through the last three courses as if dragging themselves around the final laps of a demanding jog. The meal was a waste. Lawrence was trying so hard, and wanted so badly to conduct a joyful, energetic evening, one that confirmed that Irina had simply been going through a moody, difficult period now emphatically over. Irina made an effort as well, she truly did, smiling during lulls, admiring each dish, racking her brain for topics, but they all seemed booby-trapped; even her speculation about Betsy's "business partnership" marriage felt laden with allusion. Somehow their incapacity to match the theatre of dining with theatre of their own revealed the whole restaurant business as a swindle. The cost of this meal could have kept a child alive in East Africa for a year, and they might have derived the same sustenance from a Big Mac.

Their separate bank accounts enabled Lawrence to pick up the bill. "Thank you so much for dinner," she said formally. "I had a lovely time."

"Yeah, it was great!" Lawrence exclaimed. "We should do this more often."

Thus they conspired: they had had a *lovely time*. Surely with so many good intentions applied on both their parts, so much high finance applied to the purpose as well, the occasion could not conceivably have come off as dumpy.

They hustled home, for the most perverse of postprandial entertainments.

❖ ❖ ❖

Lawrence switched on the TV just as the announcer introduced the players. Ramsey's loyal cult following screamed *Ram-see! Ram-see!* when he walked on. "You know, this we-try-harder Avis thing that Ramsey's got going," said Lawrence, bombing to the couch. "I wonder if it hasn't made him more popular. I bet that audience wouldn't go nearly as ape-shit if he'd won those six championships instead."

Riveted by that face, Irina merely grunted. The camera panned eight men in black T-shirts, each printed with one letter of G-O- R-A-M-S-E-Y on the front.

"Oh, man!" Lawrence cried when Ramsey's opponent was introduced. "What a rough draw. Stephen Hendry in the first round!"

The world's #1 was greeted with a lacklustre patter of polite applause.

"It's a real study, isn't it?" Lawrence continued. "Hendry's universally considered the best all-round snooker player in history. But listen to that crowd—they don't give a rat's ass! The better Hendry plays, the more the fans can't stand him. Maybe it's a working-class thing, that love of the fatal flaw. Most snooker fans are paunchy, hard-drinking wife-beater types who buy tickets every week but never win the lottery. I bet they can't identify with someone like Hendry, who hardly misses a shot. Where Ramsey makes a great poster-boy for the downtrodden—with that tragic inability to consolidate, *I coulda been a contendah*."

Suppressing her impatience with this incessant chatter, Irina said, "I don't know about all that. Hendry's trouble is he's not sexy."

Lawrence looked over. "You think Ramsey is sexy?"

Irina shrugged, eyes to the screen. "I don't know. That's his reputation." She scrambled for safe territory. "At least he's not a killjoy. Hendry isn't only boring for being perfect. He's a boring *person*."

Indeed, according to Ramsey, dreary excellence was only part of Hendry's problem. Away from the table, he was not a Great Character. A family man nearing thirty, Hendry had personally ushered in a well-behaved, biddable era of snooker in the 90s of going to bed early and eating all your vegetables, and so might be accused of single-handedly halving the popularity of the game overnight. His build was medium, his plain brown hair cut short. The expression on his doughy face remained strangely blank even after those rare shots he botched. His skin was pocked, his posture sway-backed, his buttocks protuberant. In interviews, he was well mannered, always giving his opponents credit for their skill. Hendry was a no-frills player, and the only thing he brought to the game was the game itself. He just happened to have won the same number of World Championship finals that Ramsey had lost. He'd racked up more than twice as many centuries as anyone in the history of the sport, and he collected titles like flannel did lint. Who gave a toss. Not this crowd, none of whose members had bothered to get T-shirts specially silk-screened to spell G-O-S-T-E-P-H-E-N.

Of course, Irina had no interest in Stephen Hendry, except insofar as he presented a barrier to her view of Ramsey's face, and she chafed whenever the camera wandered to Hendry's wooden countenance. She only had eyes for the tall, severe-looking character in his signature pearl-coloured waistcoat. When he found his opening in the first frame, he built his break with swift, cleanly cornered moves that earned the tribute from Clive Everton, "He doesn't hang about, Ramsey Acton!" It was like hearing voices. Everton seemed to be advising Irina personally that Mr. Acton would not wait on her verdict beyond this week.

As she leaned forward in her armchair, Irina's anxiety mounted with every pot. When Ramsey sank a spectacular long red, and then the white followed it agonizingly into the pocket for an in-off, she groaned so audibly that Lawrence looked over in perplexity. "Now, that *is* unfortunate," tsked the commentator.

"Notice how suck-ass shots are always *unfortunate* or *unlucky*?" said Lawrence. "The commentators are so decorous. *Unfortunate* is a euphemism for *incredibly stupid*."

A sound and even interesting observation, save for the fact that Lawrence had made it. Irina pressed her lips. Why couldn't he keep a lid on it and watch the match?

The second commentator, Dennis Taylor, intoned, "You can't afford mistakes like that, for you're letting another man in. Not when that other man is Stephen Hendry."

Snooker was all about taking advantage of opportunities that may never come your way again, providing it some romantic application. Thus Hendry began to demonstrate that a real champion needs only one chance. Ramsey's break of fifty-seven was respectable, but with seventy-five points left on the table, the frame was still up for grabs.

Alas, Ramsey's penultimate pot had cannoned the white into the pack, and the reds were spread like cherries for the picking.

As Hendry proceeded to clear the table with the dutifulness of one of those model children's book characters tidying up after dinner, Lawrence narrated. "You take these paragons for granted when they're in their prime. Oh, yeah, Stephen Hendry, Mr. Perfect, clinching another frame. And I'm rooting for Ramsey I guess, since he's our friend. But man, he really can't hold a candle to Hendry. There's never been a player like him, and may not be again. It's only when these perfect people begin to falter that everybody starts to appreciate them in retrospect. Like, gosh, I guess they really used to be fantastic; weren't those the days. Like, you never know how good you had it until it's gone."

Shut up, thought Irina uncontrollably as Hendry, with no need of the last seven points, left the final black on the table. *Just shut up.*

As the second frame commenced, Irina scrutinized Ramsey's comportment for clues to his frame of mind. Playing with unusual ferocity, he emitted a repressed fury, like the superficially normal-looking but secretly twitchy sort of character whom you bump against on the tube, and who before you can say *pardon me* will whip out a flick knife. He wore the same steely expression as when delivering his ultimatum that she had until the end of this tournament to make her decision. She wondered if he thought she was watching.

In accordance with this pent-up, explosive quality, Ramsey took on a ludicrous diagonal long-shot, and fired the white with such pace at the opposite corner that it not only knocked in the far red with a resounding crack but ricocheted higgledy-piggledy around the table, disturbing several other balls and banging three separate cushions.

Everton exclaimed, "No holding back on that one!" while Taylor chimed in, "Gave that some abuse!" Yet this was rash, uncalculated play of which seasoned commentators sternly disapproved. Everton grunted, "Some of the pots this man takes on I think are outrageous." When he added, "But you can't criticize when they go in," he meant that you can, too, criticize—that for a snooker purist, expedient ends never justify slapdash means.

"Has he been fortunate?" Taylor wondered as the white settled. Lawrence was right, of course, that snooker commentators wielded terms to do with good or bad *fortune* in a judgmental manner, one indicating that this sport, when properly played—the odd speck of chalk notwithstanding—should have nothing whatsoever to do with luck. To be *fortunate* was to get away with something that should properly have been punished.

In this instance Ramsey's reckless display of aggression *had* been punished. His position on the next shot left disgracefully to chance, lo, the route to the only colour available was solidly blocked by a stray red. He had, eponymously, *snookered* himself.

But as Irina gazed with yearning at the comely man trapped on the opposite side of the screen like one of C. S. Lewis's Narnia visitors banished to the other side of the wardrobe, and meanwhile Lawrence chided from the couch about what an unprofessional shot that was— honestly, what did we have commentators for, when we had Lawrence to endlessly chip in his two cents from the peanut gallery—the concept of the *snooker* took on a larger significance. The term referenced a configuration whereby an obstruction you don't want to hit—cannot hit, by the rules—stands between you and your object. Accordingly, Irina as well had *snookered* herself. Ramsey escaped his predicament by hitting an extravagant swerve shot. Yet she couldn't imagine any metaphorical equivalent to the swerve shot, a course of action that would put her back in contact with Ramsey Acton without smashing headlong into that innocently irritating fellow spectator on the couch.

"Well, he got out of that with panache," said Lawrence, "but he's not on a red—"

"Would you *please*?" Irina cried at last.

"Please *what*?"

"Just—keep it down, so I can follow this!"

"You usually sit there and sew or something," said Lawrence. "Since when did you get so involved in a snooker match?"

"It's *snooker*!" she exclaimed. "Not *snucker*! You've lived here for seven years, it's a British game, and if you're going to be a *snooooker* fan you should at least learn to PRONOUNCE it!"

Granted, Brits rhymed the game with *lucre*, whereas Americans, who employed the word primarily in the metaphorical sense that Irina had so recently appreciated, rhymed the game with *looker*. A minor distinction. What was not minor was her tone of voice, and on an evening they had resolved to spend as warmly together as possible. Irina was *bang out of order*.

Lawrence's expression fluctuated between injured, angry, and stunned.

Irina dropped her head in shame. She might have cared passionately whether Ramsey took the second frame a moment before, but now the soft, polite commentary emitting from the television merely underscored the contrasting incivility of her outburst. Heavily, Irina did the honours, and switched off the TV.

An opening line of dazzling originality might have made for more sophisticated dramaturgy. Yet at crucial turning points—when the otherwise laudable goal of sparkling repartee comes a distant second to clarity—one is apt to rely on the established codes of one's culture. Thus Irina fell back on the pat American prelude to cataclysm:

"We have to talk."

In his lacerating attacks on colleagues, his lashing contempt for the copious *morons* in his surround, Lawrence perpetually exuded a barely contained violence. While he had never struck her, she'd never given him reason to. Consequently, when Irina had contemplated the scene that now inexorably unfurled in their living room, it had crossed her mind that Lawrence could well be moved to take a hard swing at her jaw. Yet however much she had despaired that her partner was a known quantity—however often since July she had supposed that their lives together had gone flat if only because a relationship is among other things a research project, and now that she'd reached the end of her private doctorate on Lawrence James Trainer there was nothing left to find out—Irina was mistaken. Curling on the couch, he whimpered in a small, childlike voice that she had never heard before, "I had what I wanted more than anything in the world, and I messed it up."

Any images she might have conjured of being beaten about the head or slammed against the wall revealed themselves as the stuff of fantasy, not what she feared, but what she craved. Because what he did instead of hit her was far more brutal.

He cried.

▣ chapter four ▣

Through the bucolic afternoons of August, Irina laboured diligently in her studio. When Lawrence rang on pretexts, she was always touched to hear from him, but there was little to say. The work was going *okay*. Okay wasn't good enough. While she had reluctantly cast the drawing aside for its dissimilarity to its companions, she kept that illustration of the Crimson Traveller tacked above her drawing table as a reminder of an elusive quality that was retreating from reach. It had a fire to it, a vividness and excitement that none of her work had exhibited since. The pictures she drew lately were well wrought, and sometimes lovely. But they did not take her breath away. The Crimson Traveller had been a brief visitation, and he had not come back.

One afternoon when the drawing on her table bored her intensely, she slipped off to the bedroom to get a certain restlessness out of her system. It was rarely necessary to let off steam below the waist on her lonesome, given the regular schedule of passable orgasms that life with Lawrence afforded. But Irina was fidgety right now, and Lawrence wasn't here. Even if he were, she couldn't remember when they last had sex in the afternoon—abstention from which may constitute the definitive juncture at which courtship is over.

There is always a peculiar interim, in between the level-headed decency of daily toil and the dementia of private abandon, in which one resolves, while still of sound mind, to get off one's head. In kind, she had faced down many a deceptively tiny pill or blotted tab of paper in her youth, and decided, in a state of utter self-possession, to abdicate that possession —to invite irrational states like paranoia or unjustified exultation, to make straight lines bend. But to abdicate one's own sanity is not, strictly speaking, a sane thing to do, so at the point she decided to masturbate she had entered a nether-region one step from reason toward madness.

Irina was not entirely comfortable with this activity. Although releasing a little tension solo hardly equated to making it with another man, she had a feeling that Lawrence wouldn't like it. Cheating on Lawrence with herself seemed, in some respect she couldn't articulate, the ultimate adultery.

She had never asked if he indulged himself along the same lines; she rather hoped that he did. She knew so little about what went on in his head when they made love (little, hah!—she knew nothing). For his sake and theirs, best that he maintained a secret pornographic cave in it, shelved with lascivious videos that he could rent for free.

Besides, in her twenties the image of a man jerking off had been a chief turn-on. Why was that? Were her own sensations any guide, sex with another person was never quite right—never quite exactly *right*. She had loved the idea of it being exactly right—of a man blind with his own pleasure. And autoeroticism was the inmost sanctum, the veritable definition of the private. Any number of lovers from times past had proven game for all the standard variations and then some, but the one thing they never volunteered to do—with one memorable exception—was jerk off in view. Yet this was the initial discovery from which all sex hailed; it was the source. Most boys would have masturbated hundreds of times before they ever encountered a girl in the flesh, and adolescent wanking is famously hallucinogenic. The awkward fumbling that characterizes the abundance of cherry-losing episodes must be almost universally a disappointment in comparison. Even through adulthood, surely plenty of men continued to experience far greater ecstasy pumping over the toilet with make-believe partners than bedding real women with cellulite and an irritating compulsion to insert "actually" at the beginning of every sentence. Funny, that. Since the same might also be said of women, it was curious why anyone bothered with fucking at all.

Yet this afternoon as she lay atop the bedspread with her jeans pulled down, Irina's preparatory strokes were listless. She remained sane. So far this was every bit as dull as filling in the monotonous maroon bricks of her crippled protagonist's house.

She applied herself with more vigour, but succeeded in little more than making her labia sore. She could not shed a self-conscious embarrassment, the image of her body on the bed, hands clutched between her legs, the rumpled jeans, the tennis shoes scuffing the white chenille. She felt silly. There was something paltry about women, doing this—shamefully minor, fitful. She envied men the flamboyance of their display. They got to watch a part of themselves formerly small and shrivelled and drooping go all hard and big and high. They got to see their own excitement, red, aggressive, and bursting. They could hold it in their hands, seize it, squeeze the three-dimensional fact of their desire. A little snuffling and rustling on top of the bedclothes couldn't compare. Coming, men had something to show for themselves. It wasn't fair.

She needed to think of something, concoct some illicit pictures to get off, because otherwise she might more profitably apply these energies to scrubbing porcelain in the loo. Yet summoning any visions with a man in them left her unmoved. Somehow having sex with Lawrence night after night, daily seeing him naked on the way to a shower, had made an appendage, previously so exotic, infinitely accessible and therefore plain, like an arm or a toe. There was always that door in her head that she had refused, to this day, to open, but it had been locked tight for so many weeks now that the plaster seemed to have seeped into the cracks and now there was nothing available but a blank wall. She wondered idly what had lain behind it.

Giving herself permission to be very, very bad—and this exercise was pointless if she weren't allowed to be bad—Irina conjured what had become, in the latter years with Lawrence, an old standby: your basic open beaver, on which she mentally fastened her mouth. Yet even at her most intoxicated, a corner of her mind was eternally uneasy with this fantasy—not only uneasy, but confused by it. She had nothing against such people, of course, but she didn't consider herself a lesbian, and had never fancied another woman, much less fallen in love with one. Moreover, this latter-day proclivity made no historical sense. In younger days, her exclusive fixation on the penis had bordered on nymphomania. Were she to picture a secret assignation with a bona fide rug-muncher, she saw herself standing fully clothed, looking at some strange woman like a fence post, making nervous conversation about the hotel-room décor. Out of obligation, maybe she would try a closed-mouth kiss—which would be repulsively soft and too wet, and have the erotic effect of kissing overcooked okra. Gathering her things quickly, she would apologize profusely to this perfectly nice lady for having made a terrible mistake.

Further, the fantasy genitals were always floating in space; they had no larger body attached, nor a face. Though she was at last beginning to climb into a state that could pass for arousal, Irina's reverie was interrupted by an unwelcome revelation that came into her head like one of those crackly announcements on the Northern Line: she was simply imagining herself. Lawrence, by being both infinitely on offer in a physical sense and yet inaccessible in every other, had unwittingly turned his whole sex into a big bore. Because she was an incurable hetero after all, Irina McGovern's sexual universe had subsequently shrunk to Irina McGovern, period.

It wasn't enough. Her vagina coiled, shuddered, and relaxed. That was no orgasm. It was a stop, a thudding halt—as unceremonious as the jolt and sudden stillness of a train stalled under the Thames. No little mystified, Irina looked around the pleasant bedroom, and down at the jeans scrunched around her knees. She wriggled them up, fastening her belt buckle with a pragmatic that's-that. She hadn't come. Nevertheless, the afternoon's entertainment was over.

Strange, how upsetting that was. In her long resourceful private life, Irina had never failed to round off an occasion of this nature with satisfactory results, and she could first remember masturbating at the age of four. What a weird thing to have grown incompetent at. But whether the lesbo daydream was a visual objectification of herself or she really was a raging but repressed pussy-eating dyke, the fantasy was about as tired as the pale, flannelled denim of these secondhand jeans. It was all worn out.

Too disquieted to return to work, Irina treated herself to a walk instead, venturing toward London Bridge to head for the City. Ritually, she tsked at the proliferation of slick luxury housing developments that were ruining Borough's gritty Dickensian atmosphere, walking cautiously around scaffolding piled with teetering breezeblocks. Evading the bumper of a lorry that ran the light at Trinity Street only by running to the kerb full-tilt, she grumbled about the execrable standard of driving in this city. Londoners had no respect for pedestrians, and given the risks of strolling two blocks in your own neighbourhood you might as well have gone skydiving instead.

A more reflective state of mind soon descended. Bus-shelter adverts struck her as alien—the salacious appeals, the busty women promoting products. Nearly every campaign had something to do with sex, and for the life of her Irina couldn't understand why. The old in-out, it seemed so known and done before. What was the big deal? Groping couples seemed inexplicably occupied, and she wondered why they didn't go to the Imperial War Museum instead, or sit in the library to read books on Georgian architecture.

Lawrence's libido was strong for his age, and she was fortunate. Yet the hard truth was that on evenings he made it known through their codified stretch and yawn that tonight he'd rather go straight to sleep, Irina was often relieved. The sensation made her feel like her mother (who devoted herself to looking ravishing, yet seemed to regard sex itself as a messy annoyance; she preferred the perks—the power, the attention, and the envy of other women, not least of all her own daughters'). Irina's growing inclination to get out of the whole folderol duplicated the put-upon sexuality of previous generations, whose women purportedly regarded coitus as "a wifely duty," the onerous price of financial support. Imagine, she had risked all manner of punishment by climbing out her bedroom window in Brighton Beach at eighteen to seek out the dubious attentions of boys with pimples. Now that she could fuck her heart out by sidling three inches to the left on any ordinary evening, she'd rather skip it.

Maybe this was what it was like, getting older. You tired of sex, even of good sex, the way you'd tire of a good spaghetti carbonara if you ate it three times a week. Or maybe there was such a thing as *sexual laziness*, to which she'd fallen prey. In most regards she was industrious; she never purchased precut carrots. But ecstasy, too, was an effort.

Lost in contemplation, Irina looked up in surprise; why, she was nearly to the East End.

◼ ◻ ◼

On the morning of August 31, after comforting a disconsolate tenant on the stairs for twenty minutes to little effect, Irina returned to the flat, clutching the *Sunday Telegraph*. "You're not going to believe this! Diana!"

"What's that cow up to now?" said Lawrence.

Irina recognized the lowered head and first wicked bat of his eyelashes, and waved frantically. "Don't start! Not this morning! You'll regret it!"

"I'd love to help the underprivileged—"

"Stop it! Enough! She's *dead*."

As Irina read aloud the lead paragraph, she felt sorry for Lawrence.

This was not destined to be his news story. There was nothing to be but sad. Princess Diana mightn't have been very bright, but she didn't deserve to die. Aside from some questionable lesson about how maybe the paparazzi shouldn't be so zealous in the pursuit of celebrities, itself not a Lawrence-esque sentiment, no meaty moral emerged into which he might sink his teeth. Lawrence could only stand on the sidelines and be blandly sympathetic with everyone else.

Call her perverse, but for Irina feeling straight-up sad that something bad had happened came naturally.

■ ■ ■

It was difficult to think of anyone to whom Irina might comfortably confide, "I'm a little unnerved, because the other day I masturbated and couldn't come." The lone candidate was Betsy Philpot, whose candour bordered on uncouth.

Betsy and Leo had two kids, and unlike a certain layabout freelancer, both worked nine-to-five jobs. So Irina insisted on making the journey to Ealing. Betsy put up a half-hearted protest, then selected a curry joint two blocks from her house.

The trip out was the usual nightmare, and Irina was forty minutes late. When she lit into the travails of the Piccadilly Line, Betsy cut her off.

"Life's short, and tonight's shorter. Haven't you mastered London etiquette yet? *No one* wants to hear tube stories. You're here. Which, given the state of the Underground, alone proves the existence of God. Have a drink."

Often inclined to have just a *bit* more wine when out from under Lawrence's disapproving eye, Irina poured herself a glass of red that was conspicuously abstemious. Over poppadoms, she asked about Betsy's new publishing projects, the chances that Leo would keep his job, and the two boys' progress in school, meanwhile decimating the basket. "Oh, dear," Irina remarked, piling the last poppadom high with spicy raw-onion relish. "Maybe we should order another basket. You've hardly had any."

"That's because I've done all the talking."

"Fine by me," said Irina. "Honestly, sometimes I hesitate to see friends just because I can't imagine what I'd talk about. 'I finally found the perfect colour yellow for the rubber duck in the bathtub' doesn't make for sparkling repartee."

"There's always current events."

"If I want to talk about articles in the newspaper, I can stay home."

"Don't you and Lawrence discuss anything else?"

Irina frowned. "Not really. Oh, and TV. Lawrence can go on at length about the merits of *Homicide* over *Law and Order*."

"Don't you ever talk about how you feel?"

"What's to feel?"

Betsy cocked her head. "You're a robot?"

"Lawrence is interested in the world outside himself. What happens, what might happen, and how to stop it."

"What about you? What are you interested in?"

"Well. The same thing, I guess. I try to keep up."

"So you really do want to talk about whether the IRA ceasefire is going to hold."

"We could do worse. What else is there?" For the life of her, Irina couldn't understand why this sentiment came across as nihilistic, and she was glad to be interrupted by a waiter taking their order. She did ask for more poppadoms, as well as basmati rice, chapatis, samosas, a chicken vindaloo, and a vegetable side-dish.

"The army we are feeding is, I assume, camped outside?" Betsy had stuck with a lamb korma, period.

"I'm starving. I don't know why, but for weeks now I've been ravenous."

"You do look—healthy."

It was her mother's code word. "You mean fat!"

"No, a fuller figure suits you!" Betsy backpedalled. "Sometimes you look waiflike."

Betsy was right; Irina didn't want to squander their time on the IRA ceasefire. Between samosas, she hazarded, "Anyway, back in July, something—happened to me."

"You *did* find the perfect yellow for the rubber duck."

"I almost kissed someone."

"*Almost?* Honey, you really do need something to talk about."

"I didn't do it, but I was awfully tempted. I feel as if I narrowly averted disaster."

Betsy burst out laughing. "Irina, you're such a little straight-laced moralizer! I bet you're one of those people who finds an error on her statement in her favour, and immediately calls the bank."

"Don't make fun of me. I've never felt powerfully drawn to another man since Lawrence and I got together."

"That's astonishing."

"Loyalty starts in the mind."

"So you've sinned in your heart?"

"Jimmy Carter was onto something."

"Why didn't you do it? Might have been good for you. I've ended up necking at the occasional book launch with too much free wine. You sober up, can't meet the guy's eye in the hallway for a few days, and laugh it off. Keeps the blood running."

"Oh, don't pretend to be so hard, Betsy. It doesn't wash. This moment, it really bothered me. I didn't think it should be possible."

"How's the nooky side of things with Lawrence? Fallen off?"

"No, it's fine! Though routinized, obviously."

"Why 'obviously'?"

"Well, all couples pretty much do it the same way every time."

"How do you know?"

Irina stopped herself from saying, *Lawrence says so.* "Common knowledge."

"With Leo and me, nothing you do once every six months qualifies as 'routine.' "

"But do you really think it matters, that you don't do it very often?"

"Yeah," said Betsy gruffly. "It probably does."

"I'm not so sure. In fact, lately the rest of the world doesn't make sense to me. On TV, in adverts, in the movies, everybody's shoving their hands in one another's trousers. It seems so boring. Is this a terrible thing to say? Sex bores me."

"Whoa! Sure we're talking about real sex here?"

"Real sex over many years, yes. Most of the time frankly it's too much trouble. I'd rather go to sleep. But that's the way it must always get. You're all hot and bothered to begin with, and then the fire dies down, and what's going to make or break you isn't the spice in your bedroom, but whether you both like chicken vindaloo. In fact, I came across a study in the paper the other day that measured these chemicals that course through your blood when you fall in love? Apparently no one can maintain them for longer than about a year and a half."

Betsy squinted. "And I thought I was cynical."

"I'm not cynical, I'm pragmatic. I know you've been frustrated, physically, with Leo. But you have two wonderful boys, and you can carry a conversation. What more do you need?"

"I always thought you and Lawrence had more going for you than this." Betsy's tone was defeated.

"We have plenty going for us! And the sex thing is fine. There's only, well, one small disappointment . . ." Irina balanced a whole green chili on a small bite of chicken. "He doesn't kiss me. Hasn't for years."

Betsy stopped eating. "That's the one thing you've said that's alarming."

"It shouldn't be that important." *Ah.* The chili was like shooting up, and Irina's eyes watered.

"Meaning it is."

"No, meaning it shouldn't be, and maybe it plain isn't."

"Anything stopping you from kissing him?"

"No. I try sometimes. But it feels strange now. Radical."

"Kissing is radical. That's why it's important."

Irina smiled victoriously. "You said a few minutes ago that kissing colleagues at book parties was something you 'laugh off.' A few minutes ago, I should have kissed this other man on a whim if only to improve my circulation. Now a kiss is *radical*?"

"I never claimed to be consistent. But you're not, either. According to you, by not kissing this mysterious character you narrowly missed the end of the world, but when it comes to Lawrence, kissing is 'unimportant.' Can't have it both ways, cookie. And while we're at it, can we get back to the fun bit? Who was this guy you wanted to kiss?"

"You'll think I'm nuts."

"I already think you're nuts—for giving yourself such a hard time over something you didn't even do."

"You absolutely have to promise me that you won't tell Jude."

"Hold it. . . . *Ramsey Acton?*" Despite her incredulity, Betsy appended, "I don't know about nuts. He's damned good-looking."

"I've no idea what came over me. I'd never looked at him that way before."

"I've never looked at him any other way. To me, snooker is a big snore. But there's nothing soporific about that mouth. Sure you made the right decision?"

"I've never been so relieved as I was the next morning. I like a clean life. I hate subterfuge. I have nothing to hide from Lawrence, and I plan to keep it that way."

"Nothing whatsoever? That's hard to credit. And if it's true, it's depressing."

"Okay, I didn't tell him about that urge I had. It was just one of those funny what-might-have-been moments."

Betsy chewed on her lamb like an idea. "Have you and Lawrence thought about having a kid?"

"We have mixed feelings. The time's never seemed right."

"The time's never right. You just do it."

"So you think I need to mix things up somehow? I'm afraid I've given you a picture of us that's flat and lifeless. It's not; I'm just burnt out on sex. After all, fucking is fucking, and on that score most men are interchangeable. It's in other areas that they differ—whether they know something about the Western Sahara, or can rescue you from a fire."

"Do you remember what it was like with Lawrence, at the beginning?"

"Sure. It was great. We were so excited to be in the same bed that sleep seemed unbearably wasteful. But we've had that, and after a while you get something else. Something deeper and fuller, but without the edge. It's musical: the beginning is all treble, and the latter part of your relationship is bass."

"It can still be base—in the most sordid sense. Or do you think that's impossible? That no one 'keeps it.' That it doesn't last."

"I think it's pretty impossible. That's what everyone says, don't they?"

"You listen to everyone?"

Irina chuckled. "I'd never have pegged you as such a romantic."

"I'm not. In fact, I keep having the creepy feeling when I'm listening to you that in another conversation that's what *I'd* be saying. It sounds more disheartening in someone else's voice. It sounds fucking dark."

Irina gnawed a last edge of chapati. "But I love Lawrence. It happens to be a big round warm love instead of the sharp I-can't-get-your-fly-down-fast-enough kind. I don't see what's so dark about that."

"Have you thought about getting married? The occasion might do you two good."

"We could. Though I don't know what difference it would make."

"I've never known you to be so dismal."

"I'm not dismal! I'm perfectly happy!"

"Your perfect happiness bears a strange resemblance to other people's despair. This—moment of yours, with Ramsey. Think he noticed? He can be pretty dense."

"I had a powerful sense he felt the same way. Though later he'll convince himself it was all in his head. And we haven't spoken since. For that matter, I'm afraid to."

"Ergo, you're afraid of yourself."

"There's something about him . . . I felt something stir that night that had been hibernating for a long time."

"That's the healthiest thing you've said all night."

"I have to stay away from him."

"Maybe. But whatever's hibernating in there could stand to wake up."

Grateful that Irina had made the trip, Betsy picked up the bill, and the two women parted outside.

"You've got to talk to Lawrence," Betsy advised.

"Whatever about? Algeria?"

"No man would be thrilled to learn that his woman considers sex dull and she'd rather cop some Zs. If nothing else, you should get the son of a bitch to kiss you."

"Do you know how humiliating it is, to have to ask a man to kiss you? When he obliges, it's as if he's being a good camper."

"I know Lawrence, and he likes to play it safe. He's got a lot of intellectual bravado, but emotionally he lives in a fortress. You shouldn't let him get away with-it. Make him lower the drawbridge once in a while."

◼ ◻ ◼

When she finally got home, Lawrence cried from the living room, "It's late!"

She'd waited for an hour at the South Ealing station before the system deigned to announce that there would be no more Piccadilly trains this evening. "I missed the tube. Took forever to find a taxi."

"*You*, spring for a cab?" His tone wasn't chiding, but grateful. It was nearly two , an improbably long evening for a girls' night out, and his mind must have been churning with assaults, rapes, and train accidents. "Why didn't you call and let me know you'd be so late? I was worried."

"Sorry, I really should have. But finding a working pay phone would have delayed me even longer. Maybe it's time we break down and buy mobiles."

"Cells cost a fortune here. And I can't stand people shouting to their invisible friends down the street. You can't tell the difference between

139

CEOs and the homeless anymore. But didn't you find a phone to call a minicab?"

"I didn't want to confess," she said sheepishly. "I didn't have any minicab numbers on me, so I grabbed a black taxi off the street. I refuse to tell you what it cost."

"Fuck it," said Lawrence. "I make good money. I'm just glad you're all right."

Irina plunked down beside him on the couch, and Lawrence shot her a quizzical glance. Lawrence always extended on the sofa; Irina always assumed her armchair. She kissed him, with closed lips, but on the mouth. "I think you're wonderful."

"What brought that on?"

"Only that I don't tell you that often enough." When she braved an arm around his shoulders, his body tightened, and he looked crowded. After waiting a discreet beat or two, Lawrence disengaged himself politely and got ready for bed.

▫ ▫ ▫

Irina's killjoy pragmatism that Friday night had perturbed not only Betsy, but Irina herself. The fact that she considered her relationship with Lawrence a miracle did not comport with this appearance of reduced expectations. Irina had never bought into the notion that you "worked on" a relationship like a job, but there was something to be said for paying attention to each other.

Unfortunately for Irina's turned leaf, Lawrence was not himself still recuperating from a recent scare with a mouth. Though he acceded in principle to her fervent declarations that they should spend more time together, his affable cooperation never seemed to extend to a particular afternoon. She asked him three times if he wanted to go see *Boogie Nights,* but he had an article to finish. She invited him to come along on her trip to Borough Market, but he "hated shopping" and would rather catch up at the office. By the time she inquired if this Sunday he would join her on one of her long ambles through Hyde and Regent's Parks, she used the negative construction, "You wouldn't like to X, would you?" and her tone was forlorn. No, as a matter of fact he wouldn't.

Her physical advances were no more successful. When she sidled up to him in bed mornings, he wriggled and mumbled that he was hot. Her returns to his couch continued to feel like territorial incursions, and eventually Irina would retreat to her armchair. When she held his hand on the street, he'd have to scratch his nose. Her one request for sex face-to-face had been so unavailing that she was reluctant to try again, as she was also reluctant to demand, once more, to be kissed. You shouldn't have to ask, and it seemed too torturous for words to ask that she not have to ask.

Alas, she was treating the symptoms and not the disease. There was a reason he was discomfited by her sprawling across his chest, plopping on his personal sofa, clasping his hand, meeting his eyes during sex, and—most of all, strangely enough—opening her mouth to his. While one could conjure a variety of abstruse psychological labels for the underlying condition, the most succinct of them was *Lawrence*. Any ailment that went by so dense and complicated a name would not easily admit of a cure.

So Irina resolved to treat one symptom that had become a disease in itself: *television*. Lawrence turned on the news when he came home, kept all manner of rubbish nattering in the background through dinner, and then plunked in front of the box until they turned in. Holding hands was one thing; this time she was in for a fight.

When she announced that she'd like to experiment with keeping the TV off evenings, Lawrence was consternated. What, he asked, did she propose they do instead? Listen to music . . . read . . . , she proposed tentatively. Lawrence observed that he spent *all day* either reading or writing text, thank you very much, and he needed a break. Moreover, Lawrence didn't play an instrument, keep a woodshop, or build ships in bottles. What did she suggest, that he take up knitting? It was one of those funny existential moments when there simply seemed dismayingly few things to do in the world, period. Irina was at a loss.

"We could . . . talk," she submitted.

"We do talk. But talk is more words," he objected. "In the days before electricity, you got up with the sun, muddied around in the fields all day, and by the time you'd grubbed up something to eat, it was dark—that is, totally dark. There was nothing to do but sleep. Now even people like me who put in damned long hours have more leisure time on their hands—more light—than they know what to do with. That's what television is for. It takes up the slack."

"Television is words," she said meekly.

"Television takes *no effort*, and that's the point. I come home, I'm exhausted."

"It just seems tawdry. That noise all the time. We're not really together."

Lawrence relented—or pretended to, though in retrospect the experiment was rigged. For three nights running he put himself at her disposal, a nice way of saying that he dumped his full 160 pounds in her lap. The only diversion Irina could come up with was Scrabble, which Lawrence tactfully refrained from observing was still *more words,* and which, after he placed the Q on a triple-letter score two games in a row, he seemed destined to win by a humiliating margin. Defeated in every respect, on the third night Irina turned on the TV herself.

Thus it was all the more extraordinary when two nights later Lawrence turned it off. "Listen," he introduced, settling into a confrontational position on the couch. "I know you're not that interested in snooker. For that matter, you've never seemed all that interested in Ramsey, either."

"Snooker's all right," she shrugged, curious.

"See, the Grand Prix is coming up next week in Bournemouth, and I thought I might catch a round or two."

"If you're asking permission to watch television, I've given up."

"No, I meant go to the tournament."

"By yourself?"

"Not exactly. Ramsey would be there. Thought we might arrange a boys' night out—like you and Betsy."

"Why don't you want to go with me?"

"It's not personal! I could just use a little guy time."

"What's with this powerful interest in buddying up to Ramsey? You don't have much in common. He dropped out of school at sixteen."

"Ramsey's not stupid."

"Maybe not, but you couldn't call him an intellectual. I doubt he knows much about British politics, much less about the Tamil Tigers in Indonesia."

"I can talk about the Tamil Tigers at Blue Sky until the cows come home."

"With *Bethany,* I assume," she said too quietly to be heard, and when Lawrence asked her to repeat herself she said never mind.

"With Ramsey," said Lawrence, "I talk about snooker."

"Is that what he wants? He didn't talk about snooker with me."

"Look, I'd only be gone overnight, and you've been ragging on me to do something besides watch TV. Now I come up with something, and I get it in the neck."

Irina mumbled to her hands, gone icy again, "I've been looking for things for us to do together, and you're always busy. You hardly ever take a trip for fun. Now when you will do, you want to go alone. Why are you trying to get away from me?"

Softening, Lawrence knelt by her chair. "Hey. It doesn't make sense for you and me to go to a snooker tournament. You'd get bored. Besides, Ramsey'd be there. If you'd like to do something together—wouldn't you rather it were just us two?"

"*Just us two* doesn't seem to do it for you lately," she said glumly.

"Oh, balls. It just seems an awful lot of trouble to go all the way to Bournemouth for a game that's not up your alley. But we could still watch the tournament together. The first rounds are broadcast late, at eleven-thirty. Maybe get a bite out first. Make it a date?"

Irina perked up a little. "Okay. Would you like that?"

"Of course! And then if Ramsey makes the second round, maybe I will go to Bournemouth for a night. He sounded optimistic."

"You talked to him?" asked Irina sharply.

"Sure I did. Free tickets!"

"So how is he?" With luck, the wistfulness in her voice was not pronounced.

"He admitted he was lonely. Which considering the social life on offer for top-sixteen snooker players is strange in itself. But then he went on this long riff about how fortunate I was, having nabbed such a 'class bird.' It was kind of weird."

"Why weird?"

"Men don't usually say that stuff to each other."

"Well," said Irina. "Maybe they should."

◘ ◘ ▣

For their "bite out," Irina had hopes of making a grand night of it at Club Gascon, but Lawrence preferred to cheap it at Tas just up the street, from which they could more easily make it home in time for Ramsey's first round. She made it up to herself by dressing to the nines.

"You're going to wear *that*?" asked Lawrence. "Tas is pretty down-market!"

"Why do you get embarrassed whenever I look good?" She hadn't intended the question as rhetorical, but Lawrence thought introspection was for losers and she got no response.

A pleasant establishment with blond wooden tables, Tas had lighting too bright and service too prompt; it was one of those restaurants that you could stroll into and then find yourself back out on the pavement forty-five minutes later wondering what happened. "Not very romantic," said Irina wanly once they were seated near the kitchen.

"You're not into schmaltz anyway. The food's decent, and I'm hungry."

"So," she said with an intensity at odds with their rotgut red, "how *are* you?"

Lawrence didn't look up. "Okay," he said absently. "The fact that Sinn Fein's been asked into talks without so much as saying they're sorry is bad news politically. But I'm sure to squeeze some op-eds out of my indignation, so it's good for me."

Irina had asked how he was, not how his work was going, but for Lawrence these inquiries were synonymous. "I guess for you it's good when the whole world blows up."

"That's right!" he said cheerfully. "World's always going to hell anyway. Someone might as well cash in."

"I don't know why you're studying the menu. You always get the same thing."

"Lamb-stuffed vine leaves!" Lawrence had blind faith in the merits of repetition, and may never have reflected on its insidiously erosive effects. Little by little, the appeal of those vine leaves would abate. But Lawrence did not live in a world of subtleties or shades, and was certain to experience being sick of this order on a single evening all at once. He did not keep track of gradual disintegrations. For Lawrence, a leftover in the fridge was either fine or it was spoiled, while Irina could detect the incremental waning of flavour and the first faint whiff of corruption without having to meet a forest of mould to throw it out. In relation to food his black-and-white vision had negligible repercussions, but in relation to Irina his colour-blindness was potentially perilous. He wasn't *vigilant.*

As Irina soaked a square of spongy sesame bread in tahini dressing, she paused to consider the rashness of her sudden impulse this evening. It was true that Tas wasn't romantic, but when you did seek to arrange romance by design it was most apt to elude you. If nothing else, the quality of spontaneity could not be planned.

Meantime, Lawrence remarked, "I hope you don't mind, but I took a look at the drawings you're doing for Puffin. They look really— professional."

Irina sighed. "They're merely competent. Even Ramsey hinted that Jude might have had a point when she called my later work 'flat.'"

"Flat my butt. It's beautiful."

"It's not beautiful, it's pretty. I'm doing illustrations, but, sorry to be pretentious—not art."

"Why do you have to be so hard on yourself? I think everything you do is great!"

They weren't communicating. Lawrence tossed the human spirit into the same mythical grab-bag as elves and fairies.

Over salad, Irina mentioned, "You know, this Asian financial crisis may be bad for our investments, but it might have one upside. The baht is in freefall. Taking a holiday in Thailand in the next few months could be fantastically cheap."

"Why would we want to go to Thailand?"

"Why not? We've never been there. The beaches are supposed to be gorgeous."

"I hate beaches. And if I'm going to go abroad, I'd rather go somewhere that can double for research. Frankly, I've thought about taking a trip to Algeria."

"You are *not* going to Algeria!" Irina exclaimed.

"Why not?" His innocence was feigned.

"It's only one of the most dangerous countries in the world at the moment."

"According to whom?"

"According to *you*. I read that *Foreign Policy* article of yours."

"Oh, yeah?" he asked bashfully.

"You left it out."

"Took it from my briefcase is all."

"I thought you wanted me to read it."

"Okay." He smiled. "Maybe."

"So you can forget Algeria. I'll handcuff you to the bedstead first."

"Sounds fun."

If only he were serious. "As for Thailand . . ." Irina took the plunge. "I thought it might be a good place for a honeymoon."

"Whose?" he asked, in earnest.

Irina simply stared at him.

"Oh," said Lawrence.

"That's it? *Oh?*"

"I guess a 'honeymoon' would entail getting married first."

"That is generally a prerequisite." This wasn't going well.

Lawrence shrugged, expressing the same scale of emotion she might have raised had she successfully cajoled him into ordering something new off the menu. Not only the same scale, but the same emotions: scepticism, wariness, and dread.

"I guess so," he said. "If you want."

"If *I* want. Wouldn't *we* have to want?"

"It is your idea."

"We've lived together for over nine years. You couldn't call the notion bizarre."

"I didn't say it was bizarre. I'm just not especially bothered either way."

"*Not bothered.*"

"You're repeating what I say a lot."

"Maybe I'm wishing you'd say something else."

"Look. You know I can't stand ceremonies."

"Like beaches. And other people."

"Are we talking a white dress and reception? Because I've been to loads of weddings, and I've had it. Friends resent the plane tickets and hotel bills; the *happy couple* resents the catering. Both parties think they're doing the other a huge favour. The hoo-ha is over before you know it, and all anyone's got to show for it is a hangover. Weddings are a racket, and the only people who profit are florists and bartenders."

"Are you quite finished? Because I never said anything about a reception. A registry office and private toast with Korbel is fine by me."

"We could at least spring for Veuve Clicquot," said Lawrence, who had his standards. "But what's got into you? Sure, we could do it, but we could also skip it, right? Why not keep on the way we've been doing?"

"Why not order the lamb-stuffed vine leaves one more night?"

Lawrence looked baffled. Irina hadn't the energy to explain, since she shouldn't have to. Why get married? Because it would be fun. Because it was the very folks who claimed that they "couldn't stand ceremonies" who needed them, who without the barrelling intrusion of occasion would, metaphorically, order the lamb-stuffed vine leaves for eternity. Because—how could she say this, when it was Lawrence's place to say this to her?—he wanted to spend the rest of his life with the lovely, the nonpareil Irina McGovern.

146

"Never mind," she said wearily.

"What did you mean, about the vine leaves? They're great, as usual. Want one?"

"I've had them before, *bolshoye spasibo*." Some instinct dictated that she use the rather formal form of *thank you*.

▢ ▢ ▢

They got back home in plenty of time for the Grand Prix replays at eleven-thirty, and Irina made popcorn. She'd gone quiet, though Lawrence didn't seem to notice.

Having not laid eyes on Ramsey since that haunting birthday night, she was curious how she'd react to his face. When he entered the arena, she had to remind herself that she knew him. Ramsey looked older than she remembered, almost haggard. That night in July his face had been animated with adolescent mischief, especially when he'd spoken of Denise, his faithful girlfriend at sixteen whom he'd walk home from his Clapham snooker club, and they'd kiss on the Common. He'd once mentioned that Denise was the name of his cue, a fact that now left a peculiar residue of jealousy, though only a trace.

Surely it was a relief that her flush of forbidden passion did not return. She should be grateful to feel little more than vague good wishes for his performance. The fact that Ramsey Acton was an attractive man had been safely restored to the abstract. In tandem, she was plagued by an enigmatic sense of loss. Usually one rues the fact that a desire has gone ungratified. Yet maybe the commodity more precious than its fulfilment was the desire itself. This kind of thinking was subversively un-American; the Western economy thrived off of the insistent, serial satisfaction of cravings. Still, perhaps the whole tumbling cycle of wanting and getting was wrongheaded. Desire was its own reward, and a rarer luxury than you'd think. You could sometimes buy what you wanted; you could never buy wanting it. While it might be possible to squelch a desire, to turn from it, the process didn't seem to work in reverse; that is, you couldn't make yourself yearn for something when you plain didn't. It was the wanting that Irina wanted. She longed to long; she pined to pine.

His manner curiously leaden, Ramsey built his break with the dispirited lethargy of an underpaid labourer sandbagging a seawall. You'd never guess that this was a sport he'd hungered to play professionally since he was seven years old. Moreover, here was a player renowned for

147

audacity, yet who dawdled through several visits playing safeties, demurring from the very long pots for which he was famous. Although commentators conventionally commended discretion, the voice-overs were tinged with disappointment.

"That shot was well prudent, Clive," Dennis Taylor observed. "Still, the Ramsey Acton of the 1980s would never have been able to resist that far red to the corner pocket."

"What's wrong with Ramsey?" said Irina. "He seems so phlegmatic, so—apathetic. Do you think he's depressed?"

Lawrence grunted.

". . . What's a 'plant'?"

"Hitting another ball to hit the object ball," Lawrence said tersely.

". . . How do they decide who breaks first?"

"I think it's a coin toss."

"Is winning the break-off considered an advantage in snooker?"

"Irina, could you *please* keep it down, so I can follow this!"

"Well, how am I ever going to care about snooker if I don't understand it?"

"The best way to learn about snooker is to PAY ATTENTION TO THE FRAME!"

His abrasive tone jarred her from a larger complacency. Hitherto, it had not come home to her what, exactly, had happened this evening. She marched to the set and switched it off.

"Hey, I'm sorry I raised my voice, but why does that mean we have to stop watching the match, huh? Don't be a baby."

"I'm sure you'd like to forget, and however incredibly I almost did, too, but at dinner tonight *I asked you to marry me.*"

Lawrence crossed his arms. "So?"

"You neglected to say yes or no."

Clearly he'd say whatever would get the TV back on. "Okay."

"*Okay?*"

"Yeah. *Okay.*"

She plopped into her armchair. "That's my answer then. *Okay* equals *no.*"

"I guess you're not too great at math. I don't know in what calculus *okay* equals *no.*"

"I owe you an apology," she said. "You're a very traditional man, and I should never have taken it upon myself to propose. I should have waited until you're ready to get down on the floor with roses and a ring—though that would probably involve betrothal in a long-term-care home, when you're too old to get back off your knees without the assistance of a burly nurse."

"I don't get it," he said. "I said yes. Why are you upset?"

"I'm not upset." Surprisingly, she wasn't. "But you didn't say yes, you said *okay*. And no self-respecting woman is going to marry a man who says *okay*. If the prospect of marrying me doesn't present itself as the one thing you want to do more than anything in the world, then forget it."

"But it's fine with me!"

"*Fine*. See? The truth is that you couldn't bear taking off a whole Saturday afternoon merely to get married when you could be catching up at Blue Sky. Anyway. It's too late."

Lawrence may have been regretful about missing the Grand Prix, but he didn't wish to hurt her feelings. Thus he lavished some minutes on explaining his reservations about his own parents' marriage, his reluctance to change anything for the very fact of being so happy with Irina already, and his "willingness" to get married if that would mean something to her, totally missing the point, as ever, that the idea was for it also to mean something to him.

Meanwhile Irina stayed with this thought that by now a wedding was *too late*. There may have been a time to have saluted their having found each other, maybe to have invited their friends to the occasion, at whatever expense. But had that time ever arrived, it had passed. Like those embarrassing renewals of vows in middle age, now the gesture would only read, to themselves and to others, as a desperate effort to revive something that was therefore implicitly moribund. Which it was not. It was not dead or dying. It was simply quiet.

It was—what it was. Her relationship to Lawrence had gone the way it had gone, and there was no purpose in trying to wrench it into something else. It was contented, it was steadfast, it was companionable. She could trust him with her life; she *had* trusted him with her life. But tearful promises at the altar and that voracious desire to swallow a man whole that she had bumped into by sheer accident in July were not part of the package.

She let Lawrence babble on with all his excuses and apologies until he ran out, but remained firm in taking the whole proposition back, until he was indeed asking her to marry him, comically, on bended knee, while she was the one who adamantly refused. Finally she restored him to his couch, and insisted on making a new batch of popcorn, since the half-finished bowl had gone cold. Nestling into her regular armchair once the debacle seemed officially over, she was not even tempted to cry.

Maybe she should have been.

❖ chapter five ❖

By the time she got to the corner of what was, until two minutes ago, the street on which she lived, Irina had registered that her hasty departure was not well planned. This jacket was too light for the cutting October wind; the fabric wasn't waterproof, and it was raining. Her raincoat was still hooked on the hallway rack, snug in the possession of a man who had once held her in the highest esteem, and now had every reason to despise her. Whether he did or didn't they would both have agonizing leisure to contemplate, unless she turned around right now, damp with remorse, to beg his forgiveness, and swear that her dalliance with the improbable—no, Lawrence's word was "laughable"—romantic object of Ramsey Acton had been nothing short of an attack of middle-aged insanity.

Oh, maybe she was off her nut, Irina thought morosely, standing on the corner, though the light was green. But even insanity was *her* insanity, and commanded an imbecilic loyalty of its own.

The cold truth was—the light turned red again—she had no idea where she was going. Given the run of the balls in those first two frames, Hendry had doubtless defeated Ramsey, who would therefore have headed home if not last night then this morning. But she'd no notion how long a drive it was from Bournemouth to the East End. Besides, the poor man hadn't a clue that his would-be lover was brooding over his whereabouts while standing drenched and desolate on a Borough street-corner. Ignominiously defeated in the first round, Ramsey may even have headed to some grotty pub near the venue to drown his sorrows. She resolved to rouse him on the phone, though with an undertow of pessimism, for Ramsey could rarely be bothered to keep his mobile switched on.

By the time she spotted the phone box across Borough High Street, the light was once more red. At the risk of turning into a pillar of salt, Irina looked longingly back over her shoulder. In front of their building her eyes found no less than Lawrence himself.

"Where are you going?" he cried. "Do you even know where he is?"

"Don't worry! That's my problem!" she shouted plaintively. But having for so long considered her problems his as well, Lawrence could not *stop worrying* on a dime. In kind, since it was midafternoon and Lawrence had yet to eat, she had to keep herself under the circumstances—she was leaving him—from chiding on the corner, *Lawrence Lawrensovich, go make yourself a sandwich!* A deep-seated sense of being accountable for each other's crude well-being seemed to survive flagrant betrayal perfectly intact.

As if to demonstrate, Lawrence added, "You're getting soaked! You're not dressed for this! You'll get cold! And you don't even have your toothbrush!"

"I'll manage!" she asserted, knowing full well that Lawrence did not credit her with the wherewithal to negotiate the outside world without his help. It wasn't only that he was condescending; he wanted to be needed.

Short but effectively infinite, the single city block between them engendered the unbreachable quality of an airport security barrier, and recollected many a more cheerful parting when Lawrence had seen her off at Heathrow to visit family and friends in New York. He always stood on the opposite side of the metal detector, smiling and waving encouragingly until she'd retrieved her carry-on and had turned with a last returning wave to find her gate. Who was it who'd said not long ago, "Everyone wants to be taken care of"? Whatever his shortcomings, Lawrence had always taken care of her—to excess, but that could hardly qualify as a failing. Why, how extraordinary, for such a practical man, to routinely escort her all the way to Heathrow an hour and a half on the tube, and once she was safely rested in the care of British Airways to schlep an hour and a half back by himself. Those long homeward trips could only have been boring and sorrowful. His thanks? *We have to talk.*

For the second time in less than a day, Lawrence was crying. This frequency was so anomalous that it was strange she was able to tell in a downpour. But Lawrence's face ordinarily exhibited the jagged chiaroscuro of a woodblock print, its eye sockets dark, cheekbones highlit, the cuts from the nostrils to the corners of his scowling mouth sharp and severe. Now the portrait had melted, its slashing lines gone blurry and soft, as if the black ink were running in the rain. His commonly firm, pressed lips were parted and unsteady. When he waved good-bye one last time, he could only raise his hand waist-high, as if despite daily trips to the gym he hadn't the strength to bring it to his chest. The fingers waggled weakly, and Irina wished she were dead.

Ramsey. It was Ramsey who'd said that everyone wants to be taken care of.

She couldn't remember what Ramsey looked like. Nor could she remember why she was venturing out ill-clad in miserable weather when she had a nice warm home a few steps away, installed with a nice warm fellow. Presently her not-quite-affair felt like a book she had barely begun that she was free to put down. Irina didn't understand herself. Except that as a reader she was prone to dispatch books she'd begun. She was a thorough person. To have pursued those treacherous assignations for over three months, and to have so anguishingly revealed her errant desires to Lawrence, only to turn tail and say oh, never mind, let's have lunch, violated her conviction that you should finish any job you start. Anyway, she thought. *It's beyond my control.*

Irina waved forlornly back. Clutching her sodden jacket, she ran across the street, desperate to take herself out of his line of vision as a kindness.

The phone box reprieved her from the elements, but relief was short-lived. She only got Ramsey's voice mail, and her message bordered on incoherent—something like, "Darling, I've done it, I'm all yours now, but I have no idea where you are . . ." and without a mobile herself she couldn't leave a call-back number. Moreover, she worried that "I'm all yours now" sounded burdening. Lawrence had just this morning raised the issue of Ramsey's reliability. It was one thing to carry on with *another bloke's bird* on the sly, quite another to accept responsibility for the woman lock-stock-and-barrel with no invigorating rivalry to keep you interested. Lawrence's cynicism was infectious—especially once she'd rung Ramsey's landline in Hackney. No pick-up, and no answering service.

She could always ring Betsy for refuge, but the purpose of this rash departure wasn't to throw herself into an Ealing guest bed. Trying to be resourceful, she ducked into the newsagent for an *Evening Standard,* in which a small article in the sports section reported on the Acton–Hendry "upset" in Bournemouth. Why, Ramsey had beaten Hendry after all, in a closely fought contest that lasted four hours. She should have been there, clapping feverishly when he prevailed, toasting his achievement while tucked under his arm in a bar. Turning a blind eye to the article's snide quip—"While Ramsey Acton is mooted to be staging a comeback, Swish has been 'coming back' for the last ten years and so might reasonably be expected to have got here by now"—she seized on the fact that Ramsey's second round against Ronnie O'Sullivan was scheduled for tonight at seven-thirty. Even in a country passionate about sports, the Pakistani vendor may have been disconcerted by a customer moved to tears by snooker scores. She'd found him.

Irina bought a flimsy umbrella and managed to break only three of its eight spines while battling the wind on the fifteen-minute walk to Waterloo Station. Frugality so ingrained, it never occurred to her to take a taxi.

Struggling to decode a rapid-fire Cockney made all the more incomprehensible by sheer surliness, she gathered from the ticket seller that the next train to Bournemouth would leave an hour hence. Riddled with requests that the irritable man repeat himself, even this purchase left her dejected; it was just the sort of logistic that Lawrence always took care of. She retired to a hard bench, the high iron ribs of the railway station putting her in mind of having been swallowed by a whale, and breathed into her icy hands. Good Lord, she'd neglected to bring a pair of gloves, which for a woman with Raynaud's disease in October was a damned sight more foolhardy than leaving the flat without her toothbrush.

Now severed from the sustenance of one man and not yet entrusted to the safekeeping of another—for the moment, officially homeless— Irina was visited by a sensation both profoundly female and, for this day and age, deplorable. She felt *unprotected.* An independent income and separate bank account didn't make a dent in this impression of mortifying vulnerability. That she felt deserted was inane; she had walked out on Lawrence herself. That she felt a rising petulance toward Ramsey for having his mobile switched off was irrational; he'd no reason to expect her call. In her younger days, she'd have found being thrown on her own wits in a European city exhilarating. Older, she was wiser to the woes that could fall abruptly from the sky like weather, and all that feminist brouhaha aside, a woman was safer—plain safer—when she made a survival pact with a male of the species. The feeling on that bench was animal, of having done something biologically stupid.

It would have been sensible to ring Ramsey repeatedly until he answered. Yet she was low on change; ringing a mobile from a UK pay phone cost nearly a pound a minute. Besides, now she wanted to surprise him. Of course, underlying this impulse to "surprise" was fear—that Ramsey would not be pleasantly surprised. That he fancied her only so long as she remained unattainable. That his talk of marriage had been insincere, because that's what he thought every girl would want to hear. That he really was a feckless (Lawrence's word) sleazebag opportunist. That Irina had therefore just made the biggest mistake of her life.

On the train, where she sacrificed the small succour of her wet jacket in order to pile it on the next seat and discourage company, Irina's feeling of frailty gave way to a sense of security so sumptuous that she'd have been happy to never arrive anywhere, ever. She was cosseted on all sides by a snug rectangular box whose steady chug lulled her like a cot with rockers. Although in the *pre-birthday world* she'd sometimes squandered her solitude on concocting recipes that would employ wild garlic, right now her head swam with a great deal more than what to make for dinner.

To her astonishment, on the heels of *We have to talk,* no torrent of recriminations had ensued. Rather than take her faithlessness to task, Lawrence had assumed all the blame for their relationship's short-comings—head bowed, shoulders humped, knees pressed, while slow, fat tears dropped on his crooked wrists. His gentle, inward collapse resembled those skilful demolitions of large derelict buildings, whose charges are set in such a way that the bricks cave inward; aside from accumulating an elegiac layer of dust, surrounding structures remain unharmed. Since most self-destruction of the personal variety sucks everything and everyone in the vicinity into the rubble, the spectacle on the sofa was not only terrible to witness, but wondrous: an implosion so complete, which yet left his onlooker unscathed.

Why, at the start he'd been so loath to reproach her for straying that she was abashed, for it was never her intention to get off scot-free. But Lawrence insisted that their incremental alienation was all his fault. He loved her more than his life, but how could she appreciate the scale of his feelings, with the perfunctory expression he gave them? Long ago he should have asked her to marry him, and that was his fault, too. He knew he was too tight, too regimented—obsessed with order and control, with doing the same thing the same way day after day—and he had allowed them to get into a rut. They should have taken more trips together, hopped the Eurostar to Paris. He shouldn't have imposed so on her graciousness in the kitchen, and ought to have taken her out to dinner more often.

"But I loved making you dinner," she'd objected. "That wasn't the problem." Horribly, she was already speaking of their relationship in the past tense.

"What is it, then?"

"You stopped kissing me."

She had surprised herself. For months she'd been compiling cruel mental lists of her partner's deficits: he was harsh with other people, watched too much television, dwelt excessively on the cold externals of life like politics at the expense of the spirit. She was startled to discover that all along only one deficiency had mattered. One so seemingly slight, so remediable as well. Were Lawrence to lean to her lips, could she forget about Ramsey, would all be well? Except for the stark, dumb fact that she no longer wanted to kiss Lawrence. She wanted to kiss Ramsey.

Lawrence did not dismiss her lone complaint as minor. His parents, he explained, were never physically demonstrative, not with their children, not with each other. When prodded, he'd tried to remember to kiss her more often, and he wasn't sure why he never kept it up, because he liked it. But he'd grown shy. Strong emotion embarrassed him, and maybe frightened him a little. It made him feel weak. It didn't seem manly.

"Passion," said Irina, "is the manliest thing on the planet."

This was exactly the kind of conversation that the two of them should have been having, and could have been having, and that might have prevented her from closing those fateful few inches over Ramsey's snooker table in July. Now that they'd finally learned to talk to each other, it was too late.

Prepared for an onslaught of rage and vilification, instead Irina had been showered with generosity and remorse. By two, it had seemed only natural that they go to bed together. Though there'd been no question of sex, they slept naked in each other's arms, Lawrence never once complaining that he was hot.

Thus she woke in a state of complacency. She'd been braced for the worst, and now the worst—in its way, unexpectedly moving and lovely—was over.

Not so fast.

The night before, Lawrence had never asked the identity of his rival, though she'd been willing to reveal it. Perhaps Lawrence wasn't ready, and had to take his poison in small sips. But that morning he rose from the pillow in a single rearing motion that somehow recalled that oft-quoted *I fear we have awoken a sleeping giant* metaphor about the United States after Pearl Harbor.

"All right," he snarled. *"Who is it?"*

Irina pulled the sheets to her breasts. The name weighed so heavily in her mind, but when she croaked the syllables aloud it sounded flimsy.

"Ramsey Acton?" Lawrence employed the same tone of appalled incredulity as Betsy in Best of India. Twice didn't quite make a pattern, but the symmetry was forbidding. He bundled furiously out of bed. "Are you out of your *mind*?"

This morning, there would be no regrets that he hadn't taken her to Paris.

She'd sworn the night before, truthfully, that she and The Other had never had sex. Yet despite Lawrence's standard-issue masculinity, this formal rectitude made no difference to him. Her legalistic chastity had served only to make her feel better but protected Lawrence not a whit. Thus whipping on his jeans he growled, "Christ, you shoulda let him drill you a few times and gotten it out of your system. I thought maybe you'd found a *credible* alternative, and not some *loser*. This hare-brained infatuation won't last five minutes! He's not bad-looking, and he has a greasy, superficial charm. But Irina! You have *absolutely nothing in common* with the guy!"

"I wouldn't say that," she said quietly, drawing on her clothes.

"Then I will! You have no interest in snooker whatsoever! Do you just like latching on to a celebrity? Because if so, you could've done better. He's a has-been! You saw the way he played last night. He used to be considered daring, and now he's just reckless. Banging the cue ball around the table like demolition derby—"

"He wasn't himself. He knows I've been trying to decide what to do, and I think the situation's got him rattled."

"How *flattering*," said Lawrence. "But even if he keeps a hand in, how long will you be able to stand watching frame after frame? You know he's going to expect you to be all ga-ga and follow his every pot. Forget having your own life as an illustrator. You'll be his groupie! Is that what you want?"

"I guess I'd expect to keep up with his progress—"

"*Progress?*" Lawrence railed. "Try 'decline'! Do you have any idea what you're getting into? That man is *vain*. He used to be a star, and he'll expect you to treat him as if he's still a star. Not only will you become a portable brass band, but you'll have to collude in his self-delusion! He's a rampant narcissist, and you're looking at a lifetime of long-winded, backward-looking *snooker stories.*"

"I listen to you talk about Algeria. What's the difference?"

"Nothing short of enormous is what's the difference. You're an intelligent woman! You're used to being around people who care about the world and who read the newspaper. Think *Swish* has bought a broadsheet in the last *five years*? He probably thinks 'BSE' is an honorary award from the Queen! Before he dropped out of school altogether, he skipped most of his classes. Don't ask me, ask him—because he's proud of it! Sneaking off to that Clapham snooker club instead of learning to spell D-O-G. Truth is, I'm not even sure he knows how to *read*. I bet if you gave him one of those tests for whether you're compos mentis— who's the president of the United States and can you count backwards from one hundred—that chump would fail hands-down without the benefit of Alzheimer's! Irina—the guy is a *fucking idiot!*"

"He may not have a PhD from Columbia, but he is naturally bright." Some meagre defence of the man she loved seemed an obligation; later she could tell herself she tried.

"His head is full of little red balls, Irina. And *that's all.*"

"I thought you liked him," she mumbled.

"Liked. Yes. Past tense. If I ever see that bastard again, he's toast. He's taller than I am, but scrawny and weak." Lawrence formed a circle the diameter of a quarter. "His wrists are about this big around. I could deck him in three seconds."

"I don't doubt it," she said wearily, robotically making coffee.

"I *like* our Pakistani newsagent. That doesn't mean I'd want to spend night after night listening to the guy tell me about the exciting magazines he sold today. A little Ramsey goes a long way. Couple times a year has been plenty. One solid week of you-wouldn't-believe-the-angle-I-got-on-the-blue and he's going to bore you under the table."

The milk steamer gagged, its barrage of obliterating white noise only driving Lawrence to further raise his voice. "Know anything about what snooker players' lives are like? How much they're on the road? How many broads they plug? How much coke they snort? How much they smoke? How much they gamble? How much they *drink*?"

"Ramsey is pretty moderate, in context," she submitted numbly.

"Know anything about the 'context'? Jimmy White disappears on his wife for weeks on end going on benders in Ireland. Alex Higgins is so dissipated that he's reduced to suing tobacco companies over his throat cancer. Far from being the millionaire he ought to be, Higgins mooches off his few remaining friends for handouts, hustles amateurs in backstreet snooker clubs—and half the time still *loses*—and now has no fixed address!"

This went on for *hours*. It was clearly Lawrence's intention to wear her down, to convince her of the folly of her affections with what were, in fact, well-conceived debating points. But this was not a battle that could be won with argument. He might as well have been thwapping a rubber ball relentlessly against a squash court in the expectation of knocking down the wall. By the end he wilted back onto the sofa in the exhaustion of having played a marathon match. The wall was still standing.

❖ ❖ ❖

When Irina emerged from the cocoon of her carriage in Bournemouth it was already dark and closing on six-thirty In no mood to boldly make her way forth on foot with a skeletal map from railway information, Irina sprang for a taxi. When she named her destination, the chatty driver asked if she was off to the Grand Prix.

"Of course." Like lovers everywhere who cannot say the name of their beloved enough times, she volunteered, "Ramsey Acton is playing Ronnie O'Sullivan tonight."

"Swish has seen better days, ain't he?" said the cabbie. "But he's old guard, and it's bloody amazing the boy's still at the table. And his form's come on of late. I missed it 'cause I had a shift, but they say the showdown with Hendry last night was cracking. Ramsey snapped those balls like a whip, he did. To make your ears ring."

"I'm afraid I missed most of it, too," she said wistfully. "Which is too bad, because Ramsey's—a friend of mine."

"That the truth? Them snooker blokes got a fair number of friends, I wager."

"Actually, Ramsey's not all that social."

The cabbie compressed sure-you-know-Ramsey-Acton-and-the-Queen-herself-is-coming-round-to-my-flat-for-tea into a politic grunt. "The Rocket—now, that pup is cut from the same cloth as your Ramsey Acton. They say he's inherited the same touch. A momentum player as well. But the way the kid carries on, sure he didn't inherit the class. Swish is nothing if not a gentleman, and you never hear him question a call. But at the weekend you should have heard O'Sullivan go on about the state of the baize. Raised Cain with the ref over whether his toe left the floor on a long red. I wager the fella gets a right smart fine for the ruckus from the Association—not that he can't afford it. We all give the kid a break of course, his father in prison and all. Hard cheese. But you don't get a free pass on that excuse forever. Whole country's waiting for that lad to grow up."

"Ramsey says that O'Sullivan has unprecedented natural talent, but if he doesn't become more self-possessed as a person he'll never exploit it to the full." Irina was practising. This brand of banter was apparently the conversational bread and butter of her new life. Moreover, she should grow accustomed to the eccentricities of her paramour being up for knowing discussion among several million people.

"Seems to me I heard him say the same thing," said the driver. "On the telly."

She kept her inside track to herself for the remainder of the short ride.

❖ ❖ ❖

Irina entered the mammoth red-brick structure with a stab of disappointment. On television, snooker matches looked so intimate—the tables aglow in the dark, the balls pulsing with the warmth and vibrancy of an Edward Hopper. Though snooker had come into its own in the 80s as a high-stakes national sport, the game had gestated in a host of smoke-fogged local clubs in down-at-the-heel towns like Glasgow, Belfast, and Liverpool. These grungy bolt-holes were magnets not only for boys bunking off school but for men dodging wives, their fingers stained from hand-rolled fags, veins burst from liquid suppers, complexions pasty from curry-chip takeaways when the hall finally booted them out on the streets at two The sport's dark hint of deviance had given rise to the aphorism that a good snooker game is a "sign of a misspent youth." To Irina, snooker was old-world: funky, close, and low-lit. It was the Britain of flat, room-temperature bitter, threadbare velvet bar stools, greasy pork pasties, and thick, indecipherable accents.

Yet the cavernous Bournemouth International Centre was the stuff of Tony Blair's slick new ad campaign "Cool Britannia," which promoted the UK not as a poky empire in retreat, but as an MBA model of efficiency and progress. "Cool Britannia" bannered the island's impersonal chrome-clad wine bars, its thriving information-technology sector, its chichi restaurant fare of lemongrass Chilean sea bass. Bournemouth International was shiny and spanking new. Under glaring overheads, the lobby's floor was polished crushed marble, its ten-foot windows exposing the black expanse of Bournemouth Bay. At jarring odds with snooker's cozy, storied character, this venue had no memory, and no soul.

Irina bustled to the booking desk, only to learn that the evening match was sold out.

"Is there any way you can contact Ramsey Acton in his dressing room?" she asked. "I'm sure he could get me a seat if he tried."

"I wouldn't doubt it, madam," said the man. His brittle politeness made a mockery of good manners; the British often use decorum as a weapon. "But the players go on in a matter of minutes. You wouldn't want to disturb your man as he collects his thoughts."

Your man was only an expression, and Irina had to stop herself from insisting, *You don't understand, he really* is *"my man."* She struggled to keep her voice level. "I think you'll find that if you do contact Mr. Acton, he'll be very, very grateful that you alerted him to my presence. He's not expecting me, but he would be very pleased to learn I was able to make the match after all. The name is Irina. Irina McGovern."

Face set in stone, the ticket seller neglected to jot down her name. "I'm sure that *Mr. Acton* is grateful to be playing to a full house," he said, "and sorry that any number of punters in addition to yourself have been turned away."

Alas, her voice grew shrill. "*Mr. Acton* will be very, very cross to learn that you refused to apprise him of my arrival, and if you don't at least sell me a ticket—you *know* you have a few in reserve—I'm afraid you could get into BIG TROUBLE."

"Is that so," he said flintily. "I'm touched by your concern. But I reckon I'll take my chances, madam. Next?"

Threatening the man had been a mistake. Exiled from the counter, Irina began to sob. If it wasn't her habit to weep in public, she hardly made it a habit either of walking out on perfectly marvellous men and throwing herself at snooker players. Making a spectacle of herself was the least of her problems.

"Sorry—" The portly character with barbarously short hair looked like a bouncer, but his touch on her sleeve was gentle. "Couldn't help but overhear in the queue. As it happens, me mate was poorly this evening, and I've a ticket only bound for the bin. Would you take it? Never could bear to see a lady cry."

Irina wiped her eyes and accepted the proffered ticket. "Oh, thank you so much! You've no idea how important this is. You've saved my life. Can I pay you for it?"

"No, I won't take your money. Just chuffed it won't go to waste, like."

"Oh, it won't be wasted. I'm not just anyone, whatever that ticket agent thought." Unable to contain herself, she blurted, "Ramsey, you see—I'm in love with him!"

Her benefactor shot her a sad smile. "Wouldn't be the first one, sweetheart."

Irina chided herself: of course the man would mistake her for one more smitten fan. But then, according to Lawrence, that's precisely what she'd become.

❖ ❖ ❖

Irina followed the signs to Purbeck Hall, outside of which bookies had scrawled the odds for this match on a white board in felt-tip marker. Ramsey Acton paid five to one. (How awful, to have other people's lack of faith in you put in such brutal numerical terms.) Delightfully, she was directed to the second row, albeit right next to the burly young man who'd bequeathed her the ticket. She should have reasoned before she made a fool of herself that of course if he had a pair of tickets she'd be sitting beside the man for hours. She tried to shoot him the cordial smile of a normal person.

With game-show brassiness, an MC announced that the Rocket "needed no introduction" and proceeded to introduce him. Irina was familiar with the statistics. O'Sullivan had broken the very records—

fastest maximum break, fastest clearance, youngest winner of a ranking tournament—that Ramsey had set.

Ronnie emerged from the curtain, raising his cue high to his rowdy fans. In his early twenties, he was coarsely handsome, though not pretty. Pale with black, longish locks that were probably washed every day but somehow managed to look greasy, he had a loutish aspect, his face roughly hewn, his eyebrows lowering, every feature a tad too thick.

By now, Irina was well familiar with the Rocket. His background was colourful: O'Sullivan's parents ran a porn shop, until his father was put inside for coldcocking a black pub patron and his mother was incarcerated for tax evasion. While both porn and tax evasion paid well, his accent was impeccably proletarian; in post-match interviews, he asserted the likes of, "I shou-ah known beh-ah." (One of the luxuries of which the underprivileged were deprived in the United Kingdom was consonants.) As for Ronnie's game, it was swift, aggressive, and—when he was on form, which he wasn't always—impossibly perfect.

Lawrence detested him. Ronnie's tendency to boo-hoo when he lost a match, to go before the cameras in a state of crestfallen dejection and to forswear playing snooker ever again in his entire life in the spirit of taking his marbles and going home, was in Lawrence's view the conduct of a consummate baby. The ultimate unforgivable to Lawrence, Ronnie was an inarticulate yob, an *idiot savant*—"emphasis on the *idiot.*"

Ramsey's fatherly concern that the boy would never exploit his potential unless he shored up his all-or-nothing ego (Ronnie was either bloated on adulation like a succulent, or as wilted and bruised as a crushed petunia) was more complex. Famously gallant, Ramsey was averse to admitting to rancorous emotions like resentment, envy, or bitterness. But these would be apt. That taxi driver had iterated the collective consensus: in terms of technique if not temperament, Ronnie O'Sullivan was Ramsey Acton resurrected. As many a parent is ambivalent over a child's success, Ramsey was uneasy recognizing his own younger self sprinting around the table firing colours into pockets like mortars into enemy dugouts. Nobody likes to be replaced.

The MC introduced Ramsey "Swish" Acton; always being described as merely a "finalist" in six World Championships must have smarted. As the curtain parted, cheers rose from older members of the audience. In comparison to the roar from O'Sullivan's boosters, the duration of applause was noticeably shorter.

Nevertheless, Irina's heart melted. Crudely handsome maybe, but Ronnie O'Sullivan couldn't hold a candle to Ramsey Acton. In equine terms, Ronnie was a dray, while Ramsey was a racehorse—long legs lean as well-bred fetlocks, the edgy, pitched vibration that emanated from his figure that of a high-strung handicapper on tight rein. There was a classical refinement to his elongated face and an elegant, vertical grace to his bearing that O'Sullivan's vulgar and swaggering presence couldn't touch with a barge pole.

Irina's ferocious clapping failed to attract Ramsey's attention. She wasn't sure if she should be trying to catch his eye or not, for she was nervous of distracting him from the task at hand. The one thing that would never endear her to the man was damaging in the slightest his chances of winning a snooker match.

The lights dimmed, the crowd quieted, and the game commenced. Ronnie broke, dislodging a single red marginally pottable from the baulk cushion. Rashly, Ramsey took it on. Rash and brave are kissing cousins, and the red went in. Ramsey built a splendid break of fifty-six, although not quite ample enough to take the frame. Alas, once Ronnie returned to the table, he hogged it like a fatty at an all-you-can-eat buffet. After clinching the frame at seventy–fifty-six, the Rocket sank the final black, ricocheting the white around three cushions just to show off.

This was Irina's first live snooker tournament, and at first she missed the whisper of BBC commentary from urbane old-timers. There was a starkness to the contest unadorned with historical tit-bits, its shots not foreshadowed with, "Oooh, this is a tricky one, Clive!" The sound of the game was so different, with all the wah-wah quiet, the empty space. But gradually as the second frame got under way she began to appreciate the purity of the exercise without a murmurous voice-over telling you what to think—why this shot is problematic, whether a player has got position on the pink. Absent chitchat, the reverberation of the balls echoed for seconds through the hall, and reds rattled in the jaws before tumbling into pockets with the suspenseful resonance of a drum roll. The competitors gliding about the table in total silence provided the game an atmosphere less of sport than of rite, like the mystical, unfathomable progress of Catholic mass when still conducted in Latin. Following the game was a more demanding business sans Clive Everton's spoon-feeding. You had to pay more attention.

Irina was indeed having trouble paying attention. Lawrence's face in the rain that morning constantly interposed itself—that devastating wobble, the weak waggle of his farewell wave.

On stage before several hundred spectators, Ramsey did not seem to belong to her in any but the most fractional sense. The crowd made her both proud of him for being such a star, and resentful of these strangers for making him one—since apparently he was a toy she would have to share. She could lay claim to such a parsimonious slice of the man that his very attractiveness became a torture.

What was she doing here? Having wandered off by herself to the south coast of England, she felt like an impetuous grade-school runaway—who, with no source of food and nowhere to sleep, grows rapidly aware that the whole project is wrongheaded, but who insists on ploughing down the street with a stuffed bunny and fistful of Oreos until the cops scoop the kid into a cruiser. Maybe walking out this afternoon was an act of sheer bloody-mindedness, nothing more.

According to the monitor overhead, while she'd been drifting Ramsey had lost a second frame in a row. Irina forced herself to focus on the third frame. The pattern repeated itself: Ramsey built a substantial but less than consummate lead. Once the Rocket horned in, Ramsey spent the rest of the frame sipping Highland Spring.

Irina may have been in no mood for sport, but she gradually found the spectacle more engrossing. The two players' styles so mirrored each other that the match seemed the supreme expression of Lawrence's axiom that ultimately in snooker you "play against yourself." For if Ronnie O'Sullivan had ever studied anything in his life (which was questionable), he had studied Ramsey Acton's snooker game. Indeed, the match took on an Oedipal flavour, the son out to slay the man who sired him.

But in Oedipal contests, the younger contender reliably enjoys the advantage. Snooker was visibly fresher to O'Sullivan; he was more engaged by its vicissitudes, more gleeful over its command. By contrast, Ramsey looked faintly wearied by configurations that, although no constellation of snooker balls is ever, strictly, repeated again, he had broadly seen before— and before and before. His quiet, seemly satisfaction when a ball went in appeared subtly overshadowed by foreknowledge that there were more shots to come—more matches, more tournaments, more seasons— and the next mischievous sphere was not predestined to be so obliging. Wisdom and perspective are the compensatory comforts of old men, and little service the moment.

Thus Ramsey played fast; O'Sullivan played faster. Ramsey took on pots improbably long; O'Sullivan took on pots that were longer. Ramsey cracked in colours with the velocity of Mighty Casey at the bat; O'Sullivan upped the technological ante, and launched them to oblivion with the force of a particle accelerator.

Irina had given up trying to clap with extravagant pitch and pace to draw Ramsey's eye; her seatmate's concerned looks had made her self-conscious. The lighting on stage haloed the table and left the audience in murk; he couldn't see her. She scrambled for a Plan B. Presumably access to Ramsey Acton would be as blocked after the match as it was beforehand in the lobby. How would she ever get him the message that the woman he loved was within arm's reach? She'd no notion in which hotel he was staying, and that frosty booking agent was unlikely to volunteer an address.

At the interval, the score a discouraging four–nil, the players retreated to their dressing rooms, and Irina dared to pipe, "Ramsey!" But he was too accustomed to hearing his name called from an audience, and disappeared without a backward glance.

It didn't help that her seatmate was now convinced he had given away his extra ticket to a lunatic. As they both stood to stretch, Irina submitted with the lameness of the well-adjusted, "O'Sullivan's really on fire tonight."

"They say Ronnie's got more natural talent than the game's ever seen," he said, and promptly fled.

Irina plopped back down with an eye-roll. She'd already heard this old saw about O'Sullivan two dozen times. Was this what her future held in store? Fielding snooker clichés and anodyne statements of the obvious night after night?

At least Ramsey's assessments had more nuance. To wit, while the doughy World #1 Stephen Hendry and the slouching bad-boy Ronnie O'Sullivan might seem to vie for the title of Best Snooker Player Ever Born, Ramsey had observed that the two young men claimed distinctly different crowns. Where Hendry had mastery, O'Sullivan had inspiration; where Hendry went at the game like a job, O'Sullivan made it an art. Like a good schoolboy, Hendry seemed to understand the nature of geometry; like a riveting evangelical, O'Sullivan seemed to understand the nature of the universe. Hendry was all knowledge, O'Sullivan all instinct, and—however inexplicably—intuition is more captivating than intelligence every time. (Something clicked: no wonder Lawrence couldn't abide O'Sullivan.) Yet as Ramsey and his reincarnation returned to the stage, Irina registered a sinister corollary: intelligence is reliable, and inspiration, with no warning, can fail you.

This time, Irina didn't clap at all. She didn't feel like it. She rested her hands in her lap, resignation lending her deportment a measure of repose. This whole Bournemouth mission was turning out a fiasco, and giving over to point-blank disaster was relaxing. After the anguish of leaving Lawrence and the chill scuttle to Waterloo with neither gloves nor toothbrush, under a Tinkertoy umbrella in the rain, she would probably have to find a hotel room in the area and curl on a cold mattress by herself. Ramsey was perfectly wretched about retrieving his phone messages.

Maybe it was the fact that alone in the audience she *wasn't* clapping. Maybe Ramsey's sixth sense switched on at last. Or maybe Ramsey finally took advantage of the interval to retrieve his goddamned voice mail. For whatever reason, he turned to look squarely at the second row, sighting Irina McGovern as if lining up a colour with a pocket.

He smiled.

Now, in tournaments Ramsey smiled seldom. He was certainly not given to smiling when behind four–nil and being roundly beaten by his own double. But when he deigned to, he transformed not only his countenance, but his whole surround, so that the snooker table at his side seemed illuminated not by lights overhead but by the refractive radiance of his tall, white teeth. It was not merely a smile of warmth, of kindness, of gracious-ness, as given his reputation you'd expect, but it contained an element of the zany, the manic, the alarming. It was not, entirely, a nice smile. It was anarchic—and now freshly festive with indifference. After spotting a certain someone in the audience, Ramsey Acton couldn't be arsed whether he recouped his losses in this match, for it seemed that earlier in the day he had won a much more considerable contest.

Irina's returning expression was mild, though it might have appeared, in its very gentleness, a little smug. She leaned back in her seat, which suddenly seemed more comfortable, and crossed her legs. Her seatmate, who'd been flapping his programme in desperation to avoid talking to her, peeked at this erstwhile bint with new respect.

Ramsey's demeanour on the dais eased like a raw egg spreading on a plate. The high-pitched vibration that had jittered off his figure through the first session lowered to a steady thrum. In defiance of his famous fleetness, his motions grew dreamy, almost torpid. Ronnie broke, but this time when one long if notionally pottable red emerged from the pack, Ramsey coolly ignored it. He played a safety instead, landing the white behind the yellow so snugly that he snookered Ronnie from every red on the table.

It was like that. Ronnie loved to play fast, so Ramsey dragged the pace to a crawl. Ronnie loved to pot, so Ramsey paralysed the table with safeties. Once O'Sullivan's rhythm was destroyed, Ramsey began to bait the cocky parvenu by leaving tantalizing but frankly ridiculous balls available that he knew the boy could never resist. Ronnie tried for each of these unlikely shots and missed. Ramsey's masterful handling of not only the balls but of his opponent raised the question of whether Irina herself had been as astutely manipulated. If so, she could only admire him. Presently he was making his way about the table in the very same lithe, languid manner in which he negotiated her body.

In fact, by spotting her in the audience, Ramsey seemed to have discovered the female in the strategic respect. After all, when playing a younger, more vigorous revamp of your own game, you're not going to beat it with the fatigued forty-seven-year-old version. Ramsey would never defeat O'Sullivan with power and aggression, but with guile—with feline deviousness and cunning. With the kind of snooker that O'Sullivan despised. With the kind of snooker that *Ramsey* despised: slow, boring, and sneaky. Since Ramsey knew his own game, he knew what was wrong with it. He knew that momentum players get tripped up when they have to keep rising from their seats only to play a single shot and sit back down. He knew that the one side of the game he himself had neglected to practise as a young prodigy was safety play, which he had odiously shoved down his own throat in middle age.

After losing three games straight in this frumpy fashion to nearly level the score, Ronnie unravelled. He took on ever more ludicrous pots, and missed them more lavishly—while Ramsey grew only more coy. By the end of the session, it was Ronnie playing what Lawrence deemed "demolition-derby snooker," cracking balls every which way but in the pockets. Manly snooker was held up to ridicule, and girly snooker, at five–four, won the day.

As the lights rose, Irina's seatmate turned to her with a deferential nod. "So you're mates with Ramsey Acton?"

Irina messed with her wet jacket. "I thought I mentioned that in the lobby."

"So you did. Known him long, then?"

"Awhile," she said vaguely. The young man's sudden solicitousness was creepy. Lacking a powerful hankering after celebrity on her own behalf, Irina had an immeasurably small hankering after celebrity by association. She had no intention of plying scraps of inside gossip on Ramsey Acton the way some folks post letters from famous writers on eBay. Thus when her seatmate asked whether it was true that, having opposed Ramsey's becoming a snooker pro from his childhood, his parents had refused to attend a single tournament, Irina didn't parley, "Yes, and even at forty-seven that hurts his feelings," but claimed to have no idea.

The audience dispersed. Minions collected programmes and sweet wrappers, shooting her curious looks. Ramsey would be doing his interview with the BBC. Seat 2F was, as they say in the detective trade, her "PLS"—point last seen. Sometimes when two people are trying to find each other, the best thing one of you can do is stay put. She'd come a long way in every sense today, and the prospect of wandering the conference centre and forlornly failing to intersect with a certain snooker player only to end up in a Novotel whose room service had cut off at ten was unbearable.

The wait provided the leisure to fret over her appearance. Not wanting to subject Lawrence to watching her dress up for having sex with another man, this morning she'd grabbed her black jeans, woven velour sweater, and black tennis shoes—all of which she'd been wearing the previous afternoon. Had been wearing, in fact, for three days running, so the clothes were stale. The jeans fit her all right, but their cut was unfashionable; the sweater was huge. Worse, the dark, morose outfit had got soaked in the London downpour, and had only dried to the point that it made her itch. Evaporation had given her a chill, and she couldn't stop trembling. The clasp of her clammy hands looked jarringly pious. Grooming in public was frowned upon, but the urge to comb her hair grew obsessive.

She also needed to get her head showered in not only the literal but the colloquial sense. She needed to get a grip. She was waiting for Ramsey, but all she could think about was Lawrence. She wondered if he'd eaten anything. She wondered if he'd made himself popcorn, though he didn't know the right oil-to-kernel ratio or the ideal flame setting on the hob. She wondered if he'd changed clothes after standing out in the rain that afternoon. She wondered what it was like to walk out of a love nest, and back into a bachelor pad. Likely you didn't think in trashy expressions like *love nest* and *bachelor pad*. She fought the impulse to find a pay phone and ring home—how could Trinity Street not still seem like home?—and ask if he was all right, or grant him official permission this of all nights to pour a stiff second drink. She wanted to blurt into the receiver that she loved him, which under the circumstances was inane, or even insulting.

Fifteen minutes passed. The ushers might have shooed her away, if not for a seized quality to this remnant in the second row—the weird clutch of her hands, that huddled posture of the homeless—which made her seem, if not dangerous, at least *difficult*.

Unceremoniously, there he was. On stage. In the usual pearl waistcoat, though he'd taken off the bow tie. When he slung a black leather jacket over his shoulder, white-gold cufflinks caught the house lights. As her gaze rose, Irina realized that for her to be sitting alone in a deserted conference-centre auditorium in Bournemouth, it was absolutely crucial that at this moment she be flooded with love. If she was not head over heels for this man, she had no business in this incongruous setting, far from another man whose heart this very night was breaking in two. So when she did meet Ramsey's eyes, she checked and double-checked her reaction, like patting her coat pockets up and down in a gathering panic to find her wallet.

Pat-pat-pat. No wallet. He looked like a perfectly pleasant gentleman nearing fifty who just happened to be a total stranger.

With the same infuriating languor that had defeated Ronnie O'Sullivan, Ramsey headed for an aisle, and threaded down the row to sit beside her. He propped his long legs on the seat in front, and knocked his head back. He reached for and held her hand, sharing the armrest between them. His clasp was dry from cue chalk. He closed his eyes.

"Crikey," he said. "Your hands are cold."

"I forgot my gloves." She propped her legs in parallel and stared at the ceiling.

Ramsey continued to recline, motionless, holding her hand but without squeezing or fiddling with her fingers. If she didn't know better, she'd think he was praying.

"You're beautiful," he said.

"How can you tell? Your eyes are closed."

"I can tell."

"I look awful. I'm sorry." The knot in her stomach loosened a bit. She'd been braced for a frontal assault, tongue-down-throat. Passive hand-holding was just right.

"I'm not in very good shape," she said.

"I could see that. Straight away."

"I've been wondering if I should be trying to catch the last train to London, actually." Ramsey always made her say what she was thinking. Queer that felt so novel.

"Why aren't you?"

"You'd seen me. I couldn't."

"Still can. I'll give you a lift to the station if you like."

"I don't know if I've made the right decision." It would take some time for it to come home that she might never know.

"Sounds to me like you haven't made one."

"Oh, I made one. I'm here, aren't I?"

Ramsey opened his eyes, turning his head slowly toward her but keeping it rested on the seat, as if he knew that she could withstand introduction to the man with whom she was supposedly in love only by the smallest of increments. "Telling him—was it bad?"

"In some ways, not bad enough. Which made it worse."

"Did he get angry?"

"Not at first. Later, but he'd earned that."

"What'd he say when you clued him up it was me?"

"I think you're off his Christmas card list," she elided.

"I'll miss him, a bit," said Ramsey wistfully. "*Anorak Man.*"

"I've never felt this way before," she said. "I'm not the battered-wife type. But I really wanted him to hit me. Hard. It would have been easier."

"Sounds like he hit you in other ways."

"He hit me with the fact that he adores me, and that's not the kind of violence you can hold against people. He's a wonderful man. I guess I'd forgotten. This would be so much easier if he weren't a wonderful man."

"I'm a right wonderful man as well," Ramsey reminded her.

"I know. It's hell, frankly. And not fair. There are so few of you out there. I have an embarrassment of riches. It seems greedy. Other women would have every reason to feel resentful that I'm taking more than my share."

Tentatively, she rested the hollow of her temple against the ball of his shoulder. His white shirt was damp; it must have been hot, under the stage lights. As if soothing a skittish animal, Ramsey curved his arm around her, resettling her head carefully into the crook of his neck. Then he paused, letting her get used to the contact the way you let an unbroken horse accustom itself to the weight of a blanket before you add a saddle.

"This is going to sound stupid," she said into his stiff, open collar. "But I love him." She had to tell someone, even the worst possible person.

"I know," he said, and she admired more than she could say that he absorbed this without flinching, like taking a bullet for the president.

"I liked seeing you play," she mumbled. "I'm glad you won."

"I'm not fussed either way."

"But you're only *not fussed* about winning when you win."

He chuckled. "You got a good feel for this shite."

"That was sly," she commended, "the way you messed with O'Sullivan's head."

"He's dead easy to read," said Ramsey, closing his eyes again.

"Meaning he's just like you?"

"Like I was."

"Must have cost your pride," she said. "All those safeties."

"I passed Ronnie on his way out of his press conference. Looked at me daggers, he did. Said I 'played like an old lady.' "

An air of normalcy permeated the chitchat, as if the two had been debriefing after snooker matches for years. Not that it felt ordinary. It just felt simple.

❖ ❖ ❖

The white limo that drew up to the stage entrance brought back her childhood, when the family's economy exhibited the same all-or-nothing quality of O'Sullivan's ego. Her mother's ballet lessons were hand-to-mouth; the big infusions of cash were from her father's sporadic dialogue-coaching gigs. When one of these sleek white whales pulled up to their old apartment house on the Upper West Side to collect her father for the airport at five , she was awed as a little girl, and frustrated that it was too early for her friends to see. Older, she shared her mother's despair that the studio didn't have him take a taxi and issue a cheque for the difference, helping to cover next month's rent. A limo did nothing that a car couldn't, and had trouble turning corners at that; if one of the primary perks of being rich was merely looking it, the real benefits of wealth were thin on the ground. She couldn't help but be impressed by the fuss made over Ramsey, but she didn't want to be impressed by it.

As if to demonstrate not only money's limits but its sacrifice, the limo travelled the half-mile to the Royal Bath Hotel along the coast road, while Irina stared longingly at the beach, whose pure white sand glowed in the moonlight even through tinted windows. How much more delicious, to have strolled hand-in-hand beside the bay. But Ramsey required shepherding from the madding crowd, and a posh comportment was expected.

Thus far disheartened by the garish contemporary appointments of Ramsey's occupation, Irina was relieved when they arrived at the Royal Bath: it was old. Not to mention immense, white and lambent like the beach, bespeaking a bygone era of knee-length bathing costumes and parasols. One of those palatial institutions where it always seemed time for tea. Though the evening would not, however liquid in nature, sponsor a great deal of tea.

The hotel staff fell over themselves congratulating Ramsey on his victory over O'Sullivan. Yet offers to carry his cue case were unavailing; Ramsey's hands-off included Irina herself. *Denise* was destined to be the other woman in this relationship.

Ramsey issued her into a large suite on the top floor, which overlooked the bay. Checking out the view, she played the silky tasselled tie-backs on the heavy maroon drapes through her fingers. In the outer sitting room, the hotel had placed a birds-of-paradise bouquet on the mahogany coffee table, with a congratulatory card. When she excused herself to the loo, she rinsed her hands under gold-plated taps, wiping them on one of the fat white towels, in ostentatious supply. The terry-cloth shower curtain was embroidered with a colour reproduction of the imposing Royal Bath as seen from the beach. The hotel's opulence may have been at odds with the down-and-dirty ethos of Ramsey's sport. Yet from whatever rat-holes they had crawled, these days successful snooker players lived high. When she emerged, the manner in which Ramsey tossed his waistcoat on the brocade spread, then grabbed two champagne splits from the mini-bar fridge, which listed on a nearby card as £15 apiece, was decidedly blasé.

Ramsey stood beside the bed with his shirt half-unbuttoned to expose a triangle of his chest. Though women traditionally swoon over well-developed pectorals, it was the very subtlety of the slight mounds that Irina found mesmerizing, and that made her long to touch them. His hairless, creamy torso was that of a boy on the high school swim team.

As she kicked off her tennis shoes and slid onto the king-sized mattress, Ramsey shot her a sharp glance, glugging champagne into water glasses with all the ceremony of Diet Coke. "You came here with fuck-all? Not even a change of clothes?"

"What I had in mind," she said shyly, "more involved taking them off."

"Your message," he continued. "I sussed out that you left Lawrence. Not excused yourself for a dirty weekend. Am I getting the wrong picture?"

"No." Irina frowned. Why at this of all junctures was he looking for trouble?

"So why didn't you pack a bag? Since, unless I flatter myself, I assume you left for keeps, a great massive bag at that?"

Irina looked down. "Lawrence was there. I couldn't force him to watch me load up a suitcase—with clothes that he'd washed and folded. It was too mean."

"It's what was happening, innit? You was leaving him. When you don't take a fresh pair of knickers, you give him the wrong idea. Like, never you mind, mate, I'll be right back. Make him watch you bung in the frocks, he gets the message. This way the poor bloke can tell himself you'll rock back up any time now, 'cause you need your shampoo."

"I can buy more shampoo," she said warily, hugging her knees.

"You worry about being mean to Anorak Man. What about being mean to me?"

Irina's frown was now entrenched, and if she kept her forehead in this clutch for much longer she'd get a headache. "I just left another man for you. This very afternoon. I'm not sure how that's an act of cruelty, except to Lawrence."

He wouldn't let it go. "You walk out on a bloke, you get your theatre right. Your trappings. You stand at the door and you wave good-bye with a *bag.*"

Irina felt the rise of an emotion so rare of late that she almost didn't recognize it. But if she wasn't mistaken, that was rage. "I've had a hard

174

day, Ramsey. And that's by way of employing your famous British understatement."

"That match with O'Sullivan wasn't no doddle neither."

She straightened her back. "You played a *game* today. I left a *man*. A man who's been nothing but kind to me for nearly ten years. I'm not sure I'd put repudiating him in the same class as entertainment." There was an edge in her voice that she wasn't accustomed to hearing. It was interesting.

"I'm chuffed you hold my profession in such high regard."

"I didn't say anything about what regard I hold your profession in, high or low."

"I got the message."

"You're getting nothing."

Ramsey stood a good ten feet away, having already slugged his champagne. Irina was bunched on the bed. This was a game, too, not one she'd played before.

"Why are you doing this?" she said.

"Doing what?"

"You know."

"You should have packed a bag," he said.

"Doing that."

His expression resembled a dog's with a rope in its mouth. Pull on the other end, and he'd just tug harder. "I want to know why you didn't. It seems flighty. Not serious. Like you're not here. Like you're planning to go back."

Well, there had indeed been no purpose served by the one-hundred-mile journey from Waterloo if they could not close the last ten feet. Irina's body went limp. She dragged her legs off the bed like the overstuffed hold-all that, criminally, she'd neglected to pack. She pulled on her wet tennis shoes, which had shrunk in the rain and felt tight. They were unpleasant.

"This was a mistake," she said to the shoes, having difficulty tying bows through large, exasperating tears. "Maybe there's still a train back to London."

Wiping her eyes impatiently, she stepped towards the sitting room. Ramsey took an unsteady step to bar her way.

"Let me go," she said wearily.

For a moment he tippled on the brink. She could see the indecision in his face, as his mind prepared yet another belligerent assertion that she *should have packed a bag,* then, almost whimsically, thought better of it. With a fluidity that belied Lawrence's characterization of weakling, Ramsey reached under her arms and swept her over his head. Lowering her slowly, he slid her body against his until her mouth descended to within a hair of his lips.

"Are we having a fight?" She inhaled the champagne and tobacco on his breath.

He considered the matter. "No."

"Then what would you call it?"

"I don't see why we got to call it anything."

"How about 'wasteful'?"

Just before she kissed him, Irina had the presence of mind to flag the last five minutes for future reference.

❖ ❖ ❖

When she stirred the next morning, or what she took for morning, it was difficult to remember having sex the night before. Not because it had been drunken; she'd not even finished her split of champagne before they sank into bed. Rather, because something about fucking Ramsey was mysteriously unretainable.

Twisting to read the clock, Irina discovered that it was two Wakening, she grew conscious of her body as the worse for wear. Ah: the shank of last evening swam into focus. After the sweat had dried, Ramsey had allowed that after such a high-profile upset, he'd be expected to put in an appearance at the bar of this hotel, where most of the other Grand Prix entrants were staying. More's the pity for Irina's head, the bar had a late licence, and they must have spent a couple of hours schmoozing with Ramsey's colleagues downstairs. Irina hadn't eaten all day, and no one ever got around to food. After one night in Ramsey's care, she was already, as Lawrence would remonstrate, on the Alex Higgins diet.

Ramsey had spent the whole time in company with his arm around her, and Irina had relished the public claiming. Nonetheless, the rapid banter of the players and their managers, the clamour of Welsh, Scottish, and Irish accents, and the multiple allusions to notorious fluke pots all left her feeling in over her head, and she spoke little. Clinging to Ramsey without contributing much by way of conversation made her feel ornamental, and in dank jeans and an oversized sweater not much of an ornament at that. Resorting to Lawrence's brand of social survival, at one point she'd tried to engage Ken Doherty in a discussion about Northern Irish politics, since he hailed from the Republic. But Doherty had excused himself anxiously for another round as soon as he could drain his glass.

Ramsey himself was a surprise. He'd been so shy in foursomes with his wife the writer and Lawrence the think-tank wonk that she'd assumed he was socially quiet. Yet slumming with his own kind, Ramsey was garrulous, funny, and at his ease, leading the whole crowd in a rendition of some zany, interminable song called "Snooker Loopy." It had been heartening to learn that Ramsey had a reputation with his colleagues as a life of the party. But if last night was anything to go by, there was only so much party she could take.

It would be dark in four hours, and the day was already a washout. So Irina curled into Ramsey's alabaster chest and kissed the bridge of his nose to wake him. After all, when you couldn't quite remember what something felt like, the simplest way to refresh your memory was to do it again.

◧ chapter five ◨

By the time Lawrence would be getting to the corner, Irina had registered that his hasty departure in this downpour was not well planned. Perhaps clinging a bit after their confrontation over marriage last night, he'd lingered at breakfast, then grabbed a light jacket as he raced out the door. Snatching his trench coat, she ran downstairs, glad that Lawrence had missed the light and was still waiting to cross Borough High Street.

"Hey, Anorak Man! You're getting soaked!" she shouted from their step, waving the coat. "You're not dressed for this! You'll get cold!"

The light had turned, and he was late. "I'll manage!" he cried.

In her other hand she waved the clincher, a bagged ham-and-cheese beading in the rain. "But you forgot your lunch!"

After mutual hesitation, they both ran to the other, closing the block between them in a comic reprise of lovers dashing slo-mo through a field—only Irina wasn't leaping barefoot through clover, but scampering across gritty, wet London pavement in socks.

"Are you out of your *mind*?" asked Lawrence. "You're not wearing any shoes!"

"I have a nice warm home to go back to," she said, pulling off his jacket—an *anorak*, in fact—helping him into the overcoat, and handing off their sturdiest umbrella. "I can change my socks." After tucking the bagged sandwich in the ample pocket of the trench coat, Irina took the umbrella back, opened it, and set it in his free hand. She wiped off the droplets beaded in his eyebrows, slicked his matted hair back from his forehead, and smiled.

"Thanks," he said, holding the umbrella to shelter them both. With a look of having just remembered something, he leaned over and kissed her. It was a small kiss, closed-mouthed and chaste, but tender.

One of those many interstitial sequences that didn't tell well: *Lawrence left for work in a jacket that wasn't waterproof, and I ran after him in the rain with his overcoat and lunch.* Little wonder that Irina began dinners with friends like Betsy at a loss for stories. But these moments were the stuff of life, and they were the stuff of a good life.

Irina shivered back to the flat. Padding the hall to find dry socks while leaving wet footprints on the carpet, she reflected that the larger tale of their duo probably didn't *tell well,* either. The only unconventional element in their lives together was this stint of expatriatism, but with Americans in London a dime a dozen, *Several Years in the UK* would never make a best-selling memoir. They were not waiting for anything in particular to happen. Presumably Lawrence would continue to establish himself in the think-tank biz—make more money, perhaps join the rotation of talking heads on the television news. Presumably Irina would continue to reap muted acclaim; who knows, maybe she'd win a prize. Likely they'd move back to the US in time, but Irina was in no rush. They hadn't quite decided the question of childbearing, though whichever way they resolved the matter they'd not make history. Eventually they'd grow elderly and have health problems. In some ways, their lives together amounted to one big lamb-stuffed vine leaf. Why, look: the upshot of last night's marriage palaver was that they'd keep on doing what they'd been doing. *What a shock.*

She tidied the toast-and-coffee dishes, then fetched the post, sifting supermarket offers for bills. Rain splatted the windowpanes, but the building was old and solid and they'd never had a problem with leaks. Treating herself to an upward nudge of the thermostat, she slipped a cassette of Chopin nocturnes into the stereo and nestled into her chair at the dining table to write cheques. Her black woven velour sweater was a little dirty and oversized, but thick and soft. She felt *protected.*

Snug in the flat for the rest of the day while it bucketed outside put her in mind of camping in Talbot Park with her best friend at age fourteen. After their wiener roast, the sky had blackened; in high winds, she and Sarah barely managed to pole and spike the tent. Zipping the flaps as a torrent unleashed, the two girls had unfurled their sleeping bags and grinned. Only a thin nylon interface separated them from misery, its very tentativeness intensifying Irina's conscious gratitude for

179

refuge. They'd played gin rummy with a flashlight while the rain lashed their flimsy dome, the seams overhead barely beginning to glisten. Still, the seams gloriously held, the pelting resonating in their ad hoc home, replete with books, a transistor radio, and a thermos of minestrone. The overnight in Talbot Park was a touchstone of sorts. That evening she'd experienced an explosive joy for the simple fact that she was warm and dry.

For most Americans, the sensation of safety was an unmindful default setting, the least you could expect, or the worst. "Security" was often cited disapprovingly as the reason that some women stayed in bad marriages, implying, *security* meaning money, an arrangement just shy of prostitution. Too, folks who opted for *security* supposedly traded adventure and spontaneity for a spiritual subsistence that was pat and dead. But for Irina and Lawrence, achieving any semblance of security had been hard work. Safe haven was probably hard-won for most people, whose refuges were far frailer than they appeared—not so different from that Talbot Park tent, and as readily flattened by a gust of circumstance: a plant closure, a dip in the markets, a flood during the one month that the house was freakishly uninsured. It stood to reason, then, that *security* was a more precious commodity than its plodding reputation would suggest—and that it was profligate to treasure safety only in retrospect.

Not only had Lawrence earned a doctorate in international relations from an Ivy League school after growing up in a desert in more than one sense, but he didn't have a job out of school. For their first three years together he churned out applications to universities, journals, and think tanks galore while part-timing in bookstores. Here and there he'd have an article or op-ed accepted, but for the most part it was three solid years of rejection. He spent his weekends glowering at televised golf. For all that time, they had no reason to anticipate that at long last salvation in the form of a crisp, letterheaded envelope with postage stamps of Queen Elizabeth would ever perch in their mailbox. Meanwhile, every unexpected expense, even a broken toaster, prompted a crisis.

For her own part, the road to illustration had run neither straight nor smooth. Tormented over her buck teeth, Irina had been a reclusive child who often drew alone in her room after school. She'd kept a pictorial journal with printed captions since she was ten ("Irina has to tip-toe passed the stoopid studio or she'll get in big trouble"; "Mama's ballet students are rilly stuck up"), but narcissistic, self-dramatizing parents had left her allergic to the arts. So she hadn't gone to college at Pratt or Cooper Union but Hunter, capitalizing (a little lazily) on her background by majoring in Russian. She'd first earned her crust by translating dry Russian seismology texts, and tripped over illustration by accident.

In her late twenties, she'd been living with a brooding, volatile divorcé named Casper, a frustrated novelist (if there's any other kind) on the Upper West Side with joint custody of a seven-year-old daughter. Inspired by the library books he checked out for his little girl, like a legion of naïve novelists before him he figured that in comparison to literary fiction the children's market would be a cinch to crack. Since Irina had continued to draw idly in her journal evenings, he proposed that they collaborate.

Convinced that it was never too early to introduce kids to the "real world," Casper wrote a story about a little boy named Spacer (a less-than-apt anagram of the author's name) who wants more than anything in the world to win the sack race on Sports Day at his school. The boy practises and practises in his backyard (for Irina, drawing all those different sacks—not only the traditional potato sack, but duffels, sleeping-bag covers, those lovely white-and-orange carrier bags from Zabar's—had been great fun). But when the big day arrives, Spacer doesn't win the race. He doesn't even place.

Yet Casper refused to wrap up his tale with any tried-and-true moral, like it's not whether you win or lose. He was adamant the story not suggest that Spacer just needed to try harder, or that Spacer might prevail next year. Rather, the narrative underscored that Spacer had tried as hard as he could but his best wasn't good enough. Casper wouldn't allow that his protagonist was somehow a finer character for learning to lose graciously, nor would he let the poor kid off the hook by at least down-grading the importance of sack races in general. Casper's idea that you teach kids point-blank that sometimes you don't get what you want, *period,* was, um, sophisticated she supposed, but a little brutal. While she was also able to head off titles like *The Loser* and *Little Engine That Couldn't,* his final choice, *Sacked Race,* was no more inviting.

The text was roundly rejected. Yet to her astonishment, one editor at Farrar, Straus and Giroux expressed interest in the illustrator. Although the selective come-hither spelled the end not only of the collaboration but of the relationship, doodling on her lonesome with coloured pencils sure beat translating papers on plate tectonics.

It wasn't easy, though, and it still wasn't. For long periods she'd had to illustrate on spec, and several of these projects never saw the light of day. Even now, after eight published picture books, her work was not widely known. Only thanks to Lawrence's patient encouragement had she never given up.

Point being, there'd been nothing exhilarating about tippling on the edge of professional oblivion. More recently, there was nothing boring about being able to pay the phone bill. *Not* being able to pay the phone bill had been boring as could be.

But it was in the romantic realm that Irina was particularly flummoxed why anyone would exalt unremitting peril. What was dreary about being confident that on the average evening your partner would come home? Irina's most profound sense of safety hailed from the solidity of her bond with Lawrence, which she pictured visually as one of those sisal ropes that tether ocean liners—weathered a shade grey by the elements, but six inches thick and multiply wound on a one-hundred-pound brass cleat. Lawrence would never leave her. Lawrence would never cheat on her. Irina never rifled Lawrence's post or went through his pockets, not because she was gullible or afraid of being caught, but because she knew with certainty that there was nothing to find. In turn, she would never leave Lawrence nor, that bizarre brush with temptation in July notwithstanding, cheat on him, either. Barring an untimely car accident, that they would grow old together wasn't simply an aspiration; it was a fact. She'd bet the farm on it. Now, that was real *security,* regardless of whether Lawrence lost his job or her illustration prospects dwindled. She was damned if she understood why anyone would prefer to get up in the morning and confront the snarl, "All right! *Who is it?*" She failed to see the entertainment value in one of you flouncing out the door with no promise of ever coming back.

So, Irina considered over the electric bill, did their difference over marriage last night qualify as a "fight"? Funnily enough, she rather hoped that it did. Curious, this hunger she sometimes felt for conflict, since the odd affray seemed to lend their lives the grain and marble of fine red meat. Yet she could count the instances that she and Lawrence had conducted proper set-tos with fingers to spare.

There was memorable aggro over the coffee table of green Italian marble that she'd located at the Oxfam outlet in Streatham, whose installation Lawrence had resisted with disproportionate ferocity—

being convinced from her description that it was garish. Wilfully, she bought the table over his objections, though the deliveryman would only prop it in the lobby on the ground floor. Lawrence refused to help in protest, and alone she hauled the heavy slab to their first-floor flat stair by stair. Silently she slid it before his beloved sofa of a like shade. "Huh," he said sheepishly. "Kind of brings the whole room together, doesn't it?"

In kind, when he was offered the research fellowship in London, she was happy for him of course—but irked that she'd no say in the matter, regardless of her attachment to New York. But in short order she loved London, relished living abroad, and conceded cheerfully that he'd been right to accept the post.

Thus their few clashes had clustered around issues of dominion: who was the boss and of what. Resolutions involved the division of territory. Indeed, most couples seemed to carve up the world like rival colonial powers divvying the spoils of conquest. Much as Germany got Tanzania and Belgium the Congo, Irina ruled the aesthetic, and Lawrence the intellectual. She spoke with authority about the appalling lineup for the Turner Prize at the Tate Gallery this year, he with authority about New Labour's inconsistent immigration policies.

Granted, the perpetual peacetime that yawned before them was potentially stultifying. Yet with her parents constantly at each other's throats, Irina's childhood had been anything but oppressively serene. The hurtle of porcelain may have provided a brittle thrill, but now Irina and her sister would inherit only a few stray pieces of the cobalt china that their maternal grandmother had improbably wheeled out of the Soviet Union in a tea chest when fleeing Hitler's armies and all the way to a Russian enclave of Paris. Did their mother go to the trouble of shipping that tea chest when she emigrated to the US, merely to ensure that she and her husband would fling dishes of the finest quality? Imagine, that china surviving the clash of civilizations, but not one lousy marriage.

As for what Irina's parents fought about—money, of course; her father refused to sell insurance when dialogue coaching dried up just so Raisa could buy another $300 A-line from Saks. There were fights involving jealousy, although Raisa was generally enraged that, when she mentioned a handsome widowed father of a ballet student on costly calls to California, her husband didn't get jealous enough. They didn't like each other much. Since even minor disputes tended to expose this unpleasant truth, Irina resisted romanticizing the "tempestuous relationship" for its queasy injections of excitement.

She and Lawrence were contented together. If that was a problem, she could live with it.

◼ ◼ ◼

Lawrence phoned early that afternoon. "Yo, Irina Galina! I've got a surprise!"

"You just spent ten grand on an engagement ring."

"What, you trying to make my real surprise seem dinky?"

"No, I'm trying to turn a point of contention into a joke. And if you did any such thing, I'd have your head, *milyi*."

"Anyway, I checked last night's snooker results. Turns out that Ramsey beat Hendry by a frame. After a slow start, seems it was a great match."

"Which I deprived you of. All over the trivial issue of whether we should get married." But her tone was good-humoured.

"You can make it up to me," said Lawrence. "Ramsey's playing the Big Baby tonight in the second round. If we get the 4:32 out of Waterloo, we can just make it."

It was meant to be a lovely little gesture of inclusiveness, compensation for his lacklustre response to her marriage proposal. Curiously, her stomach tightened around her small lunch. "You mean . . . go to Bournemouth?"

"Yeah! You were hacked off when I wanted to go by myself, remember?"

Being hurt that he didn't want her along was quite a different matter from wanting to go. "Yes," she said faintly. "I remember. Though the weather . . ."

"*Eat* the weather," said Lawrence. "I tried to raise Ramsey on his cell, but it's switched off—so I couldn't get us comps. But I called to reserve tickets, and lucked out; there were only a few left. I found us a hotel in the area, so we can make a night of it."

"So, what . . . then we eat out?"

"Well, obviously we should see if Ramsey's free afterwards. He'd be offended if we came and then didn't try to hook up."

"Not necessarily," she said in a tone that Lawrence wouldn't have understood.

"Get a few things together, and meet me at Waterloo information at four-fifteen."

Lawrence could be a little bossy.

After her self-congratulatory reverie this morning she didn't want to be conjuring sharp thoughts like *Lawrence could be a little bossy*. Though she had a couple of hours before she needed to leave, the sudden change of plans put her in such turmoil that continuing to draw was out of the question. She hadn't seen Ramsey Acton since that disquieting birthday dinner in July, and she didn't want to see him.

Lawrence wouldn't care if she showed up at Waterloo wearing the same rumpled clothes she had on, but abruptly the jeans felt grungy, the voluminous sweater shapeless and unflattering. After burning through a variety of outfits before the mirror, she wondered whether rocking up at Ramsey's match in an alarmingly short skirt of black denim, which flared sassily from her thighs, and strapped 40s heels that with this skirt made her legs in black nylons look a mile high might be inconsiderate of a man who admitted that he was "lonely." But hey, it wasn't her fault if he couldn't find his own girl. Checking out the effect in the mirror before she dashed out the door, she thought, *Good God—I look like* Bethany.

She brisked to the station with their second sturdiest umbrella. At the information booth, for once Lawrence didn't ride her for dressing up, but whistled thinly through his teeth; he seemed to like it when she looked like *Bethany*. Having already purchased the train tickets, he imitated the Cockney ticket seller as they located the platform—"Aynt no trines bick to Loondun ofter tan-farty-throy, mite!" He had a good ear.

Once they were ensconced in the carriage and it lurched off, she was free to lie back and think of England. Out the window, poky houses with gardens the size of bathtubs gave way to sheep.

"Ramsey must be pretty pissed off with some of his press," said Lawrence. "The guy beats the #1 in the game, and the coverage was snide. This also-ran rep he's got—it's not as if he's a *loser*. To stay in the game for thirty years, you have to win a shitload of matches, even if he's never taken the championship."

"I'm still worried about his future," she said. "He can't keep playing forever, and then what's he going to do?"

"Long as his hands stay steady and his eyesight holds, nothing's forcing him to retire. Besides, he can always commentate for the BBC, do endorsements."

"I don't see him as a commentator. He can be awfully inarticulate in public. Product endorsements? Oh, great. When I picture his later life, it seems depressing. I think having *been* something is sort of awful."

"Has-been beats never-was."

"I know you have a thing for snooker," she ventured. "But I've still found your friendship with Ramsey hard to understand. You don't seem to have much in common with the man. You're used to being around people who read the newspaper."

"You don't get *male bonding*. And Ramsey tells great snooker stories."

"Don't those stories ever get tired?"

"Alex Higgins throwing his own television out the window? You've got to be joking."

◼ ◻ ◼

At the station in Bournemouth, Lawrence flagged a cab. While it was pleasant to be taken care of—not to have to bother her *pretty little head* about tickets, reservations, and taxis—passivity was enervating. Once they were off, too, Lawrence chatted up the taxi driver about the Grand Prix, while Irina sat silently alongside.

"Swish has seen better days, ain't he?" said the cabbie. "But he's old guard, and it's bloody amazing the geezer's still at the table—"

"Ramsey's not only got staying power, but Ramsey's got class," Lawrence proclaimed. "O'Sullivan's a whiner and a sore loser. Not to mention a moron."

Irina winced. For all Lawrence knew, the cabbie was an O'Sullivan fan.

"Hear him caterwaul in the first round, like?" the taxi driver rejoined; Lawrence was lucky. "Never stopped whingeing—about the baize, the calls, the kicks. Made the ref clean the ball twice, he did. Nothing's ever good enough for the Rocket."

"The guy's a prima donna, and he's spoiled. Sometimes you can be too talented. He's never had to work hard. When matches don't fall in his lap, he busts into tears."

"American?" the cabbie picked up.

"Las Vegas." Lawrence happily claimed the town he detested if it added colour to his bio, and leaned hard on his *R*s in a refusal to apologize for his accent. Since Americans in Britain were wont to feel cowed about their crass vowels and violent consonants, Lawrence's unadulterated pronunciation surely displayed a strong sense of self. But for some reason, his aggressive skirl grated on her ear this evening.

"You Yanks don't follow snooker much, am I right?"

Irina struggled forward. "No, in the US—"

"Not generally," said Lawrence. "But I love snooker. Makes pool seem like something you'd play in a sandbox. And we've gotten to know Ramsey a little over the years, you know, friend of a friend? Helps give me a feel for the game."

"You don't say. How do you find him, mate?"

"Great guy. Modest. Incredibly generous."

"Though he does have something of a chip—" Irina began.

"He has a sense of honour," Lawrence ploughed on. "A real man's man."

"From what I hear the bloke's not unpopular with the ladies as well," the cabbie leered. "Not quite the blade he once was, what with that grey around the temples. But you watch your woman about that fella. He's more of an operator than he lets on."

"I don't know about that. He was married for several years. To an insufferable twit, I might add."

When the cabbie let them off at the Bournemouth International Centre, Lawrence tipped him a whopping 30 percent—a benevolence that Irina knew full well hailed not from sympathy for hard-workers in service industries, but from gratitude that the driver had stooped to banter with his lowly passenger. Lawrence could come across as so brassy and arrogant, but in the odd excuse-me-for-living moment her partner's emotionally emaciated upbringing poked through like a bone.

Much like Lawrence himself, the conference centre was trying too hard. The bulky brick building's materials were ostentatious, and Irina wondered if its designers had any idea that their project was failed and ugly. The tall, tinted windows overlooking the bay, which made the long, ghost-white pedestrian pier extending into the water look not only enticing but permanently out of reach, somehow recalled Lawrence as well. He seemed to peer at his own experience like Alice in Wonderland, after nibbling the wrong side of the mushroom and now much too tall to fit through the door, looking longingly at the tiny garden. On outings like this one they tried to have fun, and every minute positively ached with mutual good intentions. Yet unselfconscious, fully inhabited joy mysteriously eluded the man, and Irina yearned to give it to him like a present, to give him nothing less than his own life.

A burly character with a buzz cut behind them in the tickets queue was looking impatient. Frosty at first—*sir* this, *sir* that—the booking agent had warmed to Lawrence's schmooze about the upcoming match, and was now conceding that, though the wager would pay little, he'd had to put his money on O'Sullivan. "Ronnie's the future, mate!"

"Listen," said Lawrence. "Any way you might get a message to Ramsey Acton?"

"This look like a Royal Mail office to you?"

"Mind if I go ahead, mister?" the man behind them finally intruded. "Just trying to return a ticket before it turns into a pumpkin."

"No problem, no problem!" Lawrence demurred frantically. "Just thought I'd ask. Thanks a lot," he said, in gratitude for tickets he'd paid for, adding to the beefy man in the queue, "And sorry about that, pal, really, sorry for keeping you waiting!"

He might have pressed his case about getting a note to Ramsey a *little* harder, and surely all that grovelling was unnecessary.

This compulsive criticism was out of control, and she had to stop it.

Purbeck Hall was spacious, so once they found their seats she could not fathom whence derived this sensation of explosive claustrophobia. It had been kind of Lawrence to buy her an overpriced programme, but she flapped it, reading nothing, just to keep from looking at his face. She couldn't suppress a feeling of constraint, as if she were tied up, and when Lawrence reached over to push a strand of hair from her eyes she battled a ludicrous impulse to slap his hand. Yet it was only when Ramsey strode on stage that Irina realized this trip to Bournemouth wasn't just a dubious journey in bad weather or a trip to see a sport she was tepid about when she'd rather stay home and work. It was a catastrophe.

A catastrophe, as in the definition of a collision: two objects trying to occupy the same space. As soon as Ramsey materialized, a feeling of wrongness permeated the hall, of an occurrence that shouldn't be physically possible, like parallel lines meeting, or attending your own funeral. Suddenly the occasion felt off, out of kilter, like that uncertain period that precedes full-fledged nausea when you don't yet accept that you're going to be sick.

Although she'd suffered that little dolorousness on seeing Ramsey on television last night and feeling no pang of desire, on balance her neutral response to his broadcast image had been a relief. Yet now that he was loosed from the cage of the screen, Irina's urge to reach out and rest her hands on either side of those narrow hips was overwhelming. As Ramsey assessed the lay of the balls after O'Sullivan's break, her mind's eye spontaneously fit her own hips into the cups of that barely broader pelvis. Over her own dead body, her head compulsively slipped two hands around the tight, delicately muscled back, up under the shirt, knuckles brushing the starched white fabric. Irina felt crazed. This wasn't supposed to be happening. That attraction in July, it was bad and traitorous and stupid and just the result of too much drink; but now she was stone-cold sober. July was supposed to be a one off. She couldn't have been more devastated if, after testing clean past the crucial five-year mark, a doctor had informed her sadly that a lethal cancer had recurred.

It seemed impossible that Lawrence couldn't tell. But he didn't appear distracted from the game by the fact that his partner was at this very moment having some kind of public sexual attack, with a flush rising—visibly, she was sure—from her clavicle to her hairline. She considered claiming to be suddenly indisposed and insisting they go straight to their hotel, except that now she'd laid eyes on Ramsey in the flesh—she thought that very phrase, *in the flesh*—it was too late.

Irina had sampled a smattering of illicit drugs in her youth, but she'd picked her spots—a few tabs of acid and mescaline, a little ecstasy and grass, the odd upper. She'd steered clear of heroin, crack, and crystal meth. Whether or not she'd prove susceptible to these more famously addictive substances, she theorized that for everyone there was that one high you couldn't refuse, for which you'd sell your soul—and anyone else's. There was no way of knowing which quantity would produce a permanent craving until you took it. As soon as you took it, even that single, investigative taste, you would have to have more. Thus the only protection from yourself in this instance was never to try it. Presented with a palmful of tablets guaranteed to induce her own customized version of consummate bliss, she would scatter the pills to the winds.

Yet here was Ramsey Acton, propped on stage like an upended capsule concocted in some back-room laboratory as the one substance on earth that Irina Galina McGovern could not resist. She'd had fair warning in July, sniffed a few heady grains from a split vial, just enough to know that this was the drug that she had been avoiding her whole life.

However much a mess, Irina didn't need the overhead monitor to keep track of the score. She could readily read the tide of play in the language of Ramsey's body.

He was winning. His cuing was a model of economy; not a muscle moved that was not in the service of the shot. At rest, he was exquisitely still, demurring from even pro forma sips of water. Last night on TV, he'd looked so lifeless; he visibly didn't give a damn. What he appeared to have clawed back for himself in the meantime wasn't so much his cueing skills per se, but the very quality that gave rise to them in the first place. He had made himself care. No mean feat, when she thought about it—to care violently about a bunch of little balls, and about whether in traversing a rectangular surface they bounced against one another in such a way as to land into holes.

Lawrence applauded frantically after every frame, obviously hoping to draw their friend's attention to the fact that a certain couple was in the audience. Irina's impulse was to the contrary, and she slumped in her second-row seat, praying that the stage lights didn't cast enough ambient glow to illuminate their faces.

At the interval, Ramsey's removal from her sight was a relief, for simply sitting in his presence was aerobic exercise. Despite a chill in the auditorium, her hairline was damp. Though Lawrence had piped "Ramsey!" as the players withdrew, their friend had disappeared without a backward glance.

"This is a fantastic match," Lawrence proclaimed. "I bet right now O'Sullivan's crawled back to his dressing room to bawl."

Irina looked at him oddly. It wasn't quite as if Lawrence were speaking a foreign language—she understood each individual word as it emitted from his mouth—but she could not make sense of them together. Heart skipping, skin slick, mind festering with so much soft-core porn that she could rent out videos, she was at an utter loss why Mr. Trainer seemed to be talking about, of all things, a snooker match.

". . . You look bored," said Lawrence, not concealing his disappointment.

"I'm not bored," she said honestly.

"Then, so far, are you glad you came?"

Irina crossed her legs. They were her best feature; Lawrence seldom admired them. "It's very interesting," she said, and meant it, too. But then, acid rain was interesting, and Srebrenitza.

As the cheers rose when the players returned to the stage, Lawrence resumed his feverish clapping. Irina patted her hands inaudibly together, for form's sake. Despite the moist mash of her applause, or perhaps because of it—as if Ramsey had a canine sensitivity to the very softest sound in the hall—before the lights had fully dimmed, he turned to look at the second row, sighting with the one-two of a knock-out combination first Irina McGovern, then Anorak Man beaming in the next seat.

He smiled.

But this was not the smile of ease, of expansiveness, of anticipatory triumph that one might expect from a sportsman in the advantaged position of four frames to nil. Slight and asymmetrical, it had an element of the wan, the bittersweet, the self-mocking and sardonic. Disconcertingly for a player enjoying such a dramatic lead. It was a fender-bender, a prang of a smile, crumpled, a little twisted. It was a smile of defeat.

As if determined to coordinate his game with his facial expression the way some women accessorize outfits with handbags to match their hats, Ramsey began to lose. It was dreadful to witness, like watching a compulsive gambler in the black squander his prodigious pile of chips until there's nothing left to bet besides his house. After Ramsey folded in five frames on the trot, Irina was left with the perplexing impression that not only was he losing on purpose, but that he was doing so to show off. The ritual sacrifice of his lead seemed to constitute the inverse of conspicuous consumption, the way some wealthy people try to impress you not with what they've got but with what they're willing to throw away.

Irina was unsure if she was supposed to be flattered. Ramsey had, after his fashion, given her the Grand Prix—though *normal* men would try to impress a girl by *winning* it, would they not? For all his appearance of gentlemanly containment, there was something flamboyantly self-destructive about Ramsey Acton that was downright childish, and won or lost what was she supposed to do with the Grand Prix?

Once the rest of the audience had cleared off in the desultory spirit of leaving a sporting event that had started out cracking but ended rather crap, Ramsey tooled coolly out on stage with his untied dickie bow stringed around his neck and his pearl-coloured waistcoat unbuttoned, hooking over his shoulder a short-cut black jacket whose leather looked thick enough to saddle a horse. After such a disgraceful performance, he should have been shuffling with rounded shoulders. Instead he peacocked towards their seats, wearing an unflappable expression that most people can only manage with dark glasses. The very ferocity of her annoyance angered Irina the more. The ex-husband of an estranged friend should elicit none but the mildest emotions of any stripe.

"Yo, Ramsey!" cried Lawrence, standing. "What happened?"

Ramsey exuded a ridiculous cheerfulness, moving with the celebrative lightness of a man who has just lost a great deal of weight. "I been at this donkeys' years," he said, squinting. "Sometimes I just lose interest. Can't predict it. And can't be helped."

"When you lose interest in snooker," said Irina, "do you get interested in anything *else*?"

"Whatever else would I be interested in, *ducky*?" He looked her in the eye.

"Listen," said Lawrence, his glance flicking from Ramsey to Irina with an ear-pricked, wind-sniffing alertness that one rarely sees outside of wildlife programmes. "We should probably check into our hotel. But according to the Internet, it's not far from here. You available for a bite to eat?"

"If I'd have won, an appearance at the Royal Bath bar would be expected. But losing makes the colleagues nervous—they're afraid they'll catch it like crabs—so I'm free. We can swing by your hotel in the limo, and then make a night of it." His grey-blue eyes glinted. "Sure I'm massive behind on Afghanistan."

If it was a joke, it was at Lawrence's expense. Before she fell in behind the two men, Irina muttered at Ramsey's side, "Since when have you ever even heard of *Afghanistan*? I bet you a hundred quid you couldn't find it on a map."

"I'm full of surprises," he said.

"You're full of something."

It was like that, and it had better stop being like that. Irina shut up.

Outside the stage door, Ramsey issued them into his limo, muttering in Irina's ear, "Nice gear." She ploughed gracelessly in front of Lawrence in order to insert him between her and the snooker player—scooting down the leather upholstery as if sternly sliding a wine glass out of her own reach.

When Lawrence gave the driver the address, Ramsey interceded. "Hey, Anorak Man, the Novotel's a tip! Why not let me get you a room in the Royal Bath?"

"Nah," said Lawrence. "I checked out their Web site, and it's out of our league."

"On me," Ramsey offered.

Lawrence stolidly refused Ramsey's generosity, and the limo proceeded to the Novotel. Irina fought a disappointment. They never stayed in upmarket hotels; the extra towels, terry-cloth robes, and gold-plated taps might have been fun. Her disappointment redoubled when they arrived— at an address that wouldn't have collected many snooker celebs in limos at its kerb. A doorman hustled out to ask the driver if he was lost.

After Lawrence checked them in, they skipped up the stairs (thin carpeting, gold-and-navy paisley) to give the room a glance. Lo, it was one of those overheated units with plastic water glasses, powdered-coffee sachets, bare bars of Ivory, and windows with brown aluminium frames that didn't open. The colour scheme was mauve. Lawrence hit the remote, flicked through the stations, and frowned. "No cable."

"No fresh flowers! No champagne! No fruit basket!"

"Hey—did you want me to take him up on it?"

"No, you were right. He's sure to pay for dinner, and that'll be pricey enough."

"Sometimes that guy throws his money around in a way that—I don't know. Some of us have to work for a living, right? And he doesn't have to call this place a dump. It's okay, isn't it?"

"It's fine," she said. "Bottom line"—a smile—"it's warm and dry."

"Too warm," said Lawrence, searching the walls. "And I don't see a thermostat."

"I admit it's a little grotty, but it's only for one night."

"Look, if you *want* to stay at the Royal Bath, I could afford it! Just say the word!"

"You mean, *we* could afford it. But we're not going to spend hundreds of pounds for wrapped soap."

Across the board of expenditures, their frugality was uniform. Taking one last look at the room whose air freshener was so rank that it made you want to smoke to cover it up, Irina wondered what kind of a splurge they didn't consider wasteful. It was only one night, but after a sequence of nights just like this one they'd be dead.

Waving at the driver to stay put, Lawrence held open the car door, so Irina had no choice but to slip in next to Ramsey. En route to the restaurant, she pressed her elbows to her waist and squeezed her knees together. Staring rigidly ahead, she might have been mistaken for a prisoner incongruously escorted to death row in a limousine. As the ungainly vehicle negotiated corners, her left arm would brush Ramsey's stiff leather jacket, administering brief electric shocks like foretastes of the chair.

Ramsey apologized that, the hour being late, they were "stuck with Oscar's," the Royal Bath's in-house restaurant, which wouldn't be serving after ten either, but would make an exception in his case. The hotel was making a mint off of snooker players this week, and had to make nice. Lawrence's terse rejoinder, "Of course," contained a hint of *Oh brother!*; maybe it was Ramsey's having to be special that rankled. That and the fact that they were not to avoid having their noses rubbed in the spectacle of the grand hotel they were missing. When they drew up to the imposing white edifice—five floors between two fairy-tale turrets, set back on landscaped grounds, and lit up like Disneyland—Irina refrained from remarking on its splendour.

After a doorman rushed to usher the snooker player from the limo, Ramsey held his hand out for Irina, who had a tricky time not showing so much leg in her short black skirt that it qualified as a different part of the anatomy altogether. The doorman gave her a discreet once-over, and shot Ramsey a nod of approval. Lawrence strode around from the other side and roughly grabbed her hand in a spirit that Irina did not especially like.

"Hard luck, mate," a bellboy called to Ramsey on the way in.

"Got nil to do with luck, son," said Ramsey. "Rarely does."

The dining establishment that they were "stuck with" was pretty flash, and Ramsey was right about the maître d' being willing to keep the kitchen open for select clientele. When Ramsey excused himself to change his damp shirt, Lawrence anxiously scoped out the few remaining patrons, all on dessert. "In no time we're going to be the only people here," he fretted. "We should go to an all-night diner or something."

"This isn't New York. There may not be any all-night diners in Bournemouth."

"At least we should just order an entrée, no extras, and get the check in advance."

"You mean *the bill*."

"Check, bill, who gives a shit? Think Brits don't still know you're talking about money?"

"Shh, calm down. You know very well that Ramsey's not going to ask for a carryout of meatballs and a glass of water. Why not relax and enjoy yourself?"

"Because it's rude! These waiters want to go home!"

"They may get overtime. The maître d' sure did; Ramsey slipped him something crisp. I didn't even recognize the denomination."

"Which is gross. Buying people like that."

"You're one to talk! The biggest tipper I know."

"I don't tip people to get them to stay up until three in the morning on my account, just in case I might want a second espresso."

"If we're here 'til three , I bet we're not drinking *coffee.*"

"That's another thing. Whenever we're out with Ramsey, you're pretty liberal with the booze. You should watch yourself."

"I haven't had a sip of wine, and I'm already criticized for drinking too much?"

"Advance resolve never hurts. . . . By the way, your hair's kind of a mess."

"Thanks for the boost of confidence. I thought you liked the way I looked."

"Well, sure. You look fine."

"Fine."

"Good."

"Fine or good? Which is it?"

"Okay, good!"

"So why does that make you mad?"

"I'm not mad, I'm just hungry, and I wish Ramsey would stop powdering his nose and get his precious butt back here before we have to order breakfast instead."

"I thought you liked him."

"I like him fine."

"*Fine* again. I thought you liked him a lot."

"Yeah, a lot, so? What's with you?"

"What's with you?"

"Are you having a row?" Ramsey inquired pleasantly, taking his seat in a freshly starched white shirt.

"No," said Lawrence.

"Then what would you call it?" said Irina.

"Why call it anything?" said Lawrence.

"How about 'daft'?" said Irina.

"Since when do you say *daft*?" Lawrence charged.

"What's wrong with *daft*?" said Irina.

"It's pretentious."

"What am I pretending to?" she countered. "Having lived in London for seven years? Besides, since when do you not have a taste for every synonym under the sun for *stupid*?" She'd tried to give the tease an affectionate cast, but it hadn't come out right.

"Sorry, but I'm feeling a bit left out," said Ramsey. "Oh, do carry on. But someone might clue me up on what the argy-bargy's about."

"The *argy-bargy*—if I'm allowed to say that—is about what all the best arguments are about: absolutely nothing," Irina interpreted for their host. "It's pure, like abstract expressionism. No vases or dead pheasants. Subject matter just gets in the way."

"Don't be glib," said Lawrence. "We were talking about something plenty substantive. I'm uncomfortable keeping all these restaurant employees after hours."

"I aim to make it worth their while," Ramsey said smoothly, perusing the wine list, "and yours, mate."

The waiter took Irina's order first, and she opted for the scallop starter, with wild bass and morels for the main course. Lawrence's face twitched when Ramsey duplicated the same order, down to the side of spinach. Though his self-denial would not let the help go home a minute sooner, true to his vow Lawrence refused an appetizer, and chose the cheapest, plainest dish on the menu, some kind of roast chicken.

Irina's chair had been placed in front of a leg of the round table, and to make herself comfortable she'd scooted to one side. Moving the chair toward Ramsey had been a mistake; she'd left her partner geographically odd man out. Yet now to rearrange her chair on the opposite side of the table leg would seem strange.

"An excellent choice, sir," the waiter commended when Ramsey selected the wine—ergo, it was exorbitant. Once the bottle arrived, Lawrence put his hand over his glass, and asked for a beer. It seemed churlish. When Irina and Ramsey cooed over the saffron cream on the scallops, Lawrence wouldn't taste one, but noshed antagonistically at a bread roll whose crust was so thick that he might have been gnawing on Ramsey's leather jacket.

Since Anorak Man was not playing his usual part of well-read snooker fan, Irina had no choice but to do the honours. After all, like many people with narrow specialities, Ramsey might have liked to express interest in professions like illustration or defence analysis, which were beyond his ken, but he didn't want to ask dumb questions. That left it to his guests to ask dumb questions of him. Since the sounds at the table had reduced to those of clanking silver and the click of Ramsey's cigarette lighter, the lamest of inquiries was better than none.

"Is snooker a very old game?" asked Irina. "And where does it come from?"

"Snooker is right recent. But it's a variation on billiards, which goes back to the sixteenth century. China, Italy, Spain, as well as Britain all claim they invented the game."

"Nice to be fought over," said Irina. This very evening suggested otherwise.

"Snooker grown out of a version of billiards called 'black pool.' "

"Like the coastal town?" asked Irina. "Is that what the place is named for?"

"Blackpool," Ramsey ruminated. "Maybe. Never thought of that."

"How could you dine out on stories about 'black pool' and not have thought of that?" asked Lawrence.

"'Cause I'm a poor dim bugger," said Ramsey affably, heading off that this was exactly what Lawrence meant. "As for where snooker came from, people say it was invented by Neville Chamberlain."

"At least there was one arena in which the guy had balls," said Lawrence.

Since snooker had surely been around for well over a century, the men were almost certainly referring to two different Neville Chamberlains, a generation apart. But Irina kept the tackless suspicion to herself.

For Ramsey, all that skipping school in Clapham had come at a cost. He looked blank. "Chamberlain was a colonel in the British Army, stationed in India. Them blokes must have got dead bored. Black pool already used fifteen red balls and a black. Chamberlain added the other colours, and invented new rules. In India, there's still a snooker hall in the Ooty Club at Ootacamund what's preserved as the cradle of the game. Always wanted to head there, I have. The table's meant to be the absolute business. They're right particular about who gets to play, but I wager they'd let Ramsey Acton hit a few."

"This'd be your idea of a pilgrimage?" asked Lawrence. "The *Ooty Club*?"

"You could say that," said Ramsey, unfazed by Lawrence's tone. "In the old days, balls were made of ivory. Had to be cut from the very centre of the tusk. Word is some twelve thousand elephants gave their lives for the glory of snooker. I got a set myself—cost a king's ransom, they did. Should stop by and take a look at them someday. Hardly ever play that set. But you get a click from the ivory, a ring, that modern balls can't match."

"Lawrence might find that fascinating," said Irina.

"I reckon the ivories are more the sort of thing an artist might fancy."

"I'm not big on pilgrimages," said Lawrence. "So feel free, Irina. Go see his etchings."

"Really, *Lawrence* is the snooker fan," she said firmly.

"Seem pretty interested yourself, love."

"Only up to a point," she said, softening a crust with the saffron sauce intently.

Ramsey glugged Chateau Neuf du Pape in both their glasses. The hand hovered over her setting—the slim wrist, the tapered fingers. Lawrence took a niggardly sip of lager. Ramsey lit another fag. Lawrence waved the smoke from his face.

"So what are balls made of now?" she proceeded in despair, like reshouldering a heavy suitcase when it was clear that no one else was going to help.

"Plastic," said Ramsey, spewing smoke. "It's thanks to snooker that plastic was invented. Changed the face of the world, this game did. Though some would say"—he clicked a nail against the Perspex salt cellar—"not for the better."

Lawrence squinted. "Neville Chamberlain invented snooker, and snooker invented plastic. Are you making this up?"

"I'm not that clever, mate. It's true. Them ivory balls were so bleeding dear that the sport was desperate for a substitute, and put out a reward, right? It was you lot got it sorted as well, back in the days you Yanks were always inventing shite. Manufacturing outfit called Phelan runs adverts offering ten large in gold for a ball you don't have to shoot an elephant to make—right inconvenient, you'd agree. Chap named John Wesley Hyatt in Albany, a printer, comes up with the first version by accident. Spills some printer's what-all that hardens like a treat."

"You mean, the way the telephone was invented," said Lawrence.

Since Alexander Graham Bell had nothing to do with snooker, Ramsey looked uncomprehending again. "Trouble is, them first plastic balls? Hit them together hard enough and they'd *explode*."

Irina laughed. Lawrence didn't.

"What I'd give to have a set of *them*," said Ramsey fondly. "Gives a whole new meaning to *safety play*."

"Lawrence! Finally snooker and terrorism intersect."

"Modern balls," said Lawrence with a steely quality, "are made of super chrystalate."

"Good on you!" Ramsey raised his glass (not that he appeared to require an excuse), and the arrival of their entrées suggested a change of course in more than one sense. "So, Anorak Man! What's up with the, you know, the politics and that?"

Irina wished that Ramsey were skilful enough to make his asking after her partner's affairs seem better than conversational duty. But then, Irina suspected that Ramsey had no earthly idea what a "think tank" was.

"This year, a lot of my work concerns Northern Ireland."

As if Lawrence had evoked a hypnotist's trigger to send his subject into a trance, Ramsey's eyes spontaneously filmed. Irina had seen it before: all over the world, the incantation *Northern Ireland* had magical powers. With the potential to put commercial soporifics out of business, the topic could drive die-hard insomniacs into a deep, dreamless sleep within sixty seconds.

"Now that he's got a ceasefire in his grubby hands," Lawrence continued obliviously, "Blair has dropped all the other preconditions unionists have demanded for letting Sinn Fein into talks—like an IRA weapons handover and a declaration that the war is over. Blair's concessions upfront could be harbingers of more outrageous concessions in a settlement down the road."

Ramsey looked up from his wild bass with a hint of panic. The pause in Lawrence's monologue seemed to indicate an apt juncture at which to pass comment. None was forthcoming.

"Concessions like what?" Irina felt like a young thespian's mother prompting her dumbstruck ward from the audience when the kid only has one line.

"*Obviously,* giving in on a united Ireland," said Lawrence, shooting Irina a what-are-you-stupid? look that she knew all too well. "Putting together some bullshit federation, or handing Dublin the power and London the bill. But there are other issues—prisoners, the RUC . . ."

Lawrence continued in this vein for some minutes, until Ramsey looked about to fall over. Whenever Lawrence talked shop, he used words like *dispensation* and *remit* and arcane phrases like *it isn't in Adams's gift*. He was proud of his mastery of fine points, but didn't seem to understand that for people like Ramsey you had to connect the dots, to tell a story—and to explain why of all people a snooker player should care.

"Alex Higgins is from Belfast, isn't he?" said Irina.

"Yeah," said Ramsey, with a glance of gratitude. "And just like Higgins, I always get the impression them Taigs and Prods wallow in the mayhem—that they don't want it to be over, that they enjoy it." Heartened, or a shade more awake, he braved another thought. "Still, the bleeding empire's over, innit? Might as well let them bastards have their freedom."

"Northern Ireland has nothing to do with colonialism!" Lawrence exploded. "It's about democracy! The Protestants are in the *majority*, and the *majority* want to stay in the UK. They don't *want* their goddamned freedom!"

Ramsey looked bewildered. "But—all them bombs and that . . ." It was for all the world like watching a small boy wander into traffic. "Why not give them IRA wankers what they want and wash our hands of the tip?"

Lawrence's eyes lit up like the twin headlights of an oncoming lorry. "That's exactly the reaction they're COUNTING ON! Why are all you Brits a bunch of SHEEP? This country stood up to HITLER! Your friend Neville Chamberlain may have been a craven suck-up, but Churchill had brass balls! London was half levelled by the Nazis and stood fast, and now with a few car bombs in shopping centres the whole country's ready to cave!"

Ramsey messed with the cellophane on a new pack of Gauloises. "Never understood the whole carry-on myself," he mumbled.

"It's actually pretty simple," said Irina, who wouldn't cite too many *fine points*, since she couldn't remember any. "Terrorists use your own decency as a weapon. You don't want people to get hurt, so you do what you're told. How the troubles play out is a test case for whether being an asshole pays off."

"Of course being an arsehole pays off," said Ramsey, shooting her another grateful glance. "Take Alex Higgins! Hardly wins any tournaments at all, and his two World Championships are ten years apart. Makes a packet mostly for being the most obnoxious, abusive, destructive, insulting, and all-round unbearable berk on the planet. You realize, don't you, there's not a hotel left in Britain will let him stay the night? He's

200

banned from Cornwall to the Hebrides! I wreck that many hotel rooms, there'd be five competing biographies of me as well."

"Actually, that's not a bad parallel—from what I understand," she added, with a deferential nod to Lawrence. "Remember all the traffic seizures on motorways last spring?"

"Got stuck on the M-4 on the way to Plymouth for the British Open for the better part of a bloody day."

"IRA hoax threats, but they worked. And remember how another IRA hoax threat delayed the Grand National in April? Well, giving folks like that what they want is like the management handing Alex Higgins two splits of champagne and a complimentary bouquet after he's trashed his hotel room."

Throughout this exchange—whose mysteriously ulterior quality made it seem a misuse, even abuse, of an issue that Lawrence cared about very much—Irina's shoulders had swivelled thirty degrees towards Ramsey. When she tried to yank them to a more neutral orientation, they seemed cast in this attitude in bronze.

"Northern Ireland's not boring," Lawrence insisted, as if the fierceness of his assertion could make it true. "The details may be hard to follow. But it's the biggest issue in this country, and other scumbags around the world will be watching closely how a settlement turns out. Sinn Fein walks away with that bouquet, plenty of other cities will go blooie. It just floors me how the British don't give a shit."

Meanwhile a chorus of song arose from the hotel's bar. Ramsey cocked a wan, private smile. Around the corner his mates were having a high old time, while he was stuck in this poxy restaurant in earnest discourse about *Northern Ireland*. As the throng at the bar grew more boisterous, Ramsey joined in on the refrain: "*Snooker loopy nuts are we / Me and him and them and me—*"

"What is *that*?" asked Irina, laughing.

"*With loads of balls and a snooker cue—*" The tune was as goofy as the lyrics, but Ramsey's voice was clear, and he had good pitch.

"That is—appalling!" cried Irina, wiping her eyes.

" 'Snooker Loopy,' " Ramsey explained, while his friends began yet another ghastly verse. "By Chas and Dave and the Matchroom Mob. Rose to #6 in the charts in '86, if you can credit that. Recorded as a promo for the championships. Sort of what the pair of you was saying about terrorism. It's horrible, it shouldn't have paid off, but it did."

"Where does the name *snooker* come from anyway?" asked Irina. She'd given up on reeling Lawrence into the conversation, when the line proved repeatedly to have not a live fish on the end but an old boot.

"It was slang for, what, *cretin* in the military," said Ramsey. "Some soldier in India slags off another player for being a right *snooker* when he misses an easy colour. Chamberlain intervenes all diplomatic. There, there, boys, sure we're all *snookers* in this game, we are. He says, so why don't we call the whole kit *snooker*. It stuck."

"The original colloquialism *snooker*," said Lawrence, "meant *neophyte*."

"*Neophyte*." Ramsey turned the word in his mouth like a fishbone. "Sounds like some new compound. 'Hey, you blokes still use super chrystalate, but my own balls are made of *neophyte*!'"

Irina laughed. Lawrence didn't.

◫ ◫ ◫

"You could have asked *me* where the name *snooker* came from," said Lawrence, marching up the stairs of the Novotel.

"I was only making conversation," said Irina.

"You sure made a lot of it."

"Somebody had to," she said, catching her heel on the carpet.

"You're drunk," said Lawrence harshly, never wont to employ colourful terms for inebriation—*blootered, legless, half-tore*. The unadorned *drunk* was never in danger of sounding adorable. "And I don't need you to interpret for me about politics." He jammed their key-card into the slot. "I think I'm pretty clear. That's my job, you know. My Russian may suck, but I don't need a translator in English."

"I was only trying to help. You sometimes forget whom you're talking to."

"Thanks for holding my professionalism in such high regard."

"I didn't say anything about how I regard your professionalism, high or low. It's just that you toss off *unionists* this and *unionists* that, when someone like Ramsey may not know a *unionist* from a hole in the ground."

"Well, that's pathetic," said Lawrence, letting the door slam behind them. "It's his country. And you've got to admit, his views on the subject display the instincts of a total pussy."

"He doesn't have any views. He's a snooker player."

"We're never allowed to forget *that*." Plopping on the bed, Lawrence

202

reflexively turned on the TV. "His rendition of 'Snooker Loopy' was incredibly embarrassing."

"No one else was left in the restaurant," she observed wearily.

"*As* I predicted," said Lawrence. "Bursting into song, getting sloppy drunk, overstaying your welcome, acting as if you own the place—pretty low-rent."

"That's how British celebrities are expected to act. We were tame, as these things go."

Irina's defence of their host was as pale as it was impolitic, and she wandered to the window, fiddling aimlessly with the polyester tassel on the tie-back. This hotel was nowhere near the beach, and looked out on a McDonald's car park whose bins were overflowing. Some glum consolation, bolts of satin brocade wouldn't have improved the fabric of the evening itself. You could feel lonely anywhere, verge on tears anywhere, even in a luxury hotel like the Royal Bath. If Lawrence hadn't been apprised at the station that the last train to London was at 10:43 , she'd have urged that they just go home.

"All this commercial buildup," said Irina. "But we're in Dorset. It's hard to remember that this is Thomas Hardy country. Moors and brooding and tragedy."

"I don't know," said Lawrence. "Many more matches like tonight's, and *Ramsey the Obscure* might start to have a ring."

The buzz that was beginning to ebb had little to do with wine. Irina felt vaguely guilty, but as she reviewed her behaviour couldn't locate an offence. She'd been attentive to their host, an obligation. She'd looked comely in public, but not trashy, which only reflected well on her partner. She'd been lively company, laughing at Ramsey's jokes, and it was only fitting to express enjoyment when so much money was being expended toward this end. There had been no hanky-panky, no footsie or fingers straying into the wrong laps. She'd been a good girl. She had nothing to be ashamed of.

Be that as it may, she knew perfectly well that you could follow proper etiquette to the letter and still violate a host of unwritten laws in that sneaky fashion that no one could nail you for. In some respects this was the worst rudeness, the kind that you could get away with because it wasn't in the book. Lawrence would never be able to cite her transgressions outright without sounding touchy or paranoid. He couldn't reasonably object to a flash in her eyes, or to a fullness to her laughter disproportionate to the small witticisms that gave rise to it. He didn't quite have the courage of his own perceptions to charge that while she *looked* rapt enough when he was talking and hadn't ever interrupted, his conversation had obviously bored her. As for the sassy black outfit, he would like to take his whistle at Waterloo Station back, or at least to ask the kind of question that Lawrence Trainer seemed constitutionally incapable of posing: *Did you really put on that short skirt for me?*

"How was that cake thing?" Lawrence grunted, scowling at the late-night replay of Ramsey's match on the BBC.

"It was good," she said to the window. Ramsey had ordered a flourless chocolate cake with raspberry sauce and pastry cream for the table. Like both bottles of wine, Lawrence had spurned the enticement. Which left Ramsey and Irina to fork tiny, sumptuous tastes from the same plate. There was nothing wrong with sharing a piece of cake. There wasn't. There wasn't, was there? "You should have tried it."

"I'd *had enough*," he said emphatically. ". . . You don't usually eat dessert."

"I didn't order it."

"Nope," he said gruffly. "I guess you didn't. And it takes a different sort of discipline to resist temptation that's plunked in front of you when you didn't ask for it."

Having skirted even that close to *the main thing*, Lawrence withdrew to the TV. "On replay, the second session is even worse. Ramsey was crucifying O'Sullivan before the interval. Then, wham. He tanked. Sometimes I don't understand these people."

"You do understand," she reflected. "That is, they *are* people. They're not machines. But they're trying to be. That's why the very best in the game, on a sustained level, are the likes of Stephen Hendry. People who are uncomplicated and a little blank. There's an absence about them that's mechanical. Really good snooker, perfect snooker, and maybe this applies to any sport, is all about defeating your own humanity. I was touched, in a way, when Ramsey imploded. When they're too good, I find it almost unpleasant. It isn't natural. It isn't warm-blooded."

Lawrence looked at her with curiosity. Applying this much consideration to a matter that had previously engaged her so little seemed to constitute one more infinitesimal, ineffable treachery.

The room lacked the panoply of props that one's own home affords— newspapers to flap, lampshades that need dusting, pepper grinders low on corns. Resorting to the only bit of business she could think of, Irina went for the comb in her handbag at Lawrence's feet.

"Your breath stinks," said Lawrence.

She wasn't near enough for him to tell. "I had one cigarette. Just one. Honestly, Lawrence"—she untwisted her hair tie—"it's like some moral thing now. As if we've gone backwards to the flapper days, when women who smoked were seen as loose. All this huffy disapproval seems to have nothing to do with lung cancer anymore."

"No tobacco is safe. And it makes kissing you like cleaning out the fire grate."

Since when do you kiss me anyway? She held her tongue, teasing out snarls in the mirror. Lawrence had been right, her hair was mussed, but he'd failed to mention that the escaping strands had sprayed into an impromptu disarray that was rather fetching.

"Speaking of bad breath," said Lawrence, "where did you put our toothbrushes?"

"*Bozhe moi!*" she exclaimed. "I forgot."

"I asked you to get some things together! No wonder I kept thinking something was missing. I can't believe you didn't pack a bag!"

"Well, we hardly needed anything—"

"All the more reason to remember what little we did!"

"I was in a hurry."

"I gave you plenty of time to get ready."

"I went back to work." The fib left her mouth with a dissonant twang, like a piano string snapping. She hadn't gone back to work. She'd spent two hours deciding what to wear.

"I could have used a fresh shirt." Lawrence sniffed his sleeve and made a face. "Ramsey must have gone through the better part of a pack, so this one smells like an ash can. And now you've got to take the train back tomorrow wearing *that*."

"So?"

"You'll have that I-was-unexpectedly-out-all-night look. As if you met someone and were up having wild sex."

"Little chance of that," she muttered.

"What's that supposed to mean?"

She almost said, *Never mind,* but pushed herself to say instead, "That you don't seem in a very good mood."

"I can't stand not brushing my teeth."

"I'll go downstairs and see if they sell a toiletry kit."

"Too late," he said furiously. "Nobody's at the desk. I can't believe you didn't pack a bag!"

Lawrence got up off the bed. She could see in his feint first in one direction, then the other, that what was upsetting him perhaps more than the prospect of furry teeth in the morning was the disruption of ritual. At last he moved decisively toward the bath, and Irina stepped in his path.

"Let me go," he said impatiently. "I have to take a leak." He seemed grateful to have seized upon a need.

Barring his way, Irina felt her humour teeter-totter, tipping first towards irritation: here she had done as he wished, gone to a snooker match, and put in an effort to make the expedition a success, and then he was a grouse most of the night for no good reason other than his worry about some strangers getting home from their restaurant jobs before midnight. She hadn't done anything wrong, and she didn't deserve this gruff, tough, angry treatment over two miserable toothbrushes and a spare shirt.

But under that justifiable vexation lurked a less defensible annoyance: that Lawrence, if not short, was not very tall. That Lawrence, if fit, was not finely streamlined; no number of sit-ups would sharpen an essential bluntness to his figure because that's the way his body was made. That Lawrence, if successful in his own realm, did not have an exotic occupation that would magically keep restaurant kitchens open all hours and land him in chic hotels. That Lawrence, if virtuous, did not exude an intoxicating perfume of dark-toasted tobacco, expensive red wine, and something else that Irina couldn't put her finger on and probably shouldn't. That Lawrence, if articulate, had a dumpy old American accent just like hers.

On the opposite side of the fulcrum lay *mental kindness*. In a way, it was Lawrence's very failings that she loved—or it was the overlooking of his failings that her love was good for. She would never forget the first time she noticed that his hair was beginning to thin, and the piercing tenderness that the discovery fostered. Perversely, she loved him *more* for having less hair, if only because he needed a little more love to make up for whatever tiny increment of objective handsomeness that he had lost. Thus this evening it was the very fact of his not being tall—of his having been, yes, a little boring at dinner, as well as wary and therefore less likable, not to mention harsh, judgmental, and impatient, with a small mustard stain on the collar of his trench coat, probably from that ham sandwich at lunch—the very fact of his *not* making the help jump for being such a celebrity, and *not* speaking in a disarming South London accent, and *not* sporting exquisitely tapered fingers but really rather stumpy, short ones like breakfast sausages—that tipped her to the sweeter disposition. She slipped her arms around his waist. Lawrence's returning clasp was ferocious.

❖ chapter six ❖

Fantasies were one thing. But throughout months of frustration and with so much at stake, Irina had accepted beforehand that finally fucking Ramsey Acton would probably prove anticlimactic. She'd been braced for awkwardness, even a tragicomic wilting at the gates. Reared overhead at the Royal Bath, Ramsey himself had said drolly before taking the plunge, "This is what's known in snooker, pet, as a 'pressure pot.'" Moreover, at the risk of tautology, sex was only sex—it got only so good, lasted only so long, mattered only so much. You still fretted afterward that you were out of milk, or hastened to turn on the news.

Truth be told, fucking had always been a touch disappointing—like so many experiences in life generally of which much is made, from island holidays (with biting black flies) to $300 French dinners (rarely surpassing a cracking bowl of pasta). Losing her virginity in particular had failed to live up to its billing. A lanky guitarist in a garage band, with entrancing long blond hair, Chris had been her high school boyfriend throughout her junior year; he was solicitous, patient, and, if not a novice himself, no rake. But when the big afternoon arrived, his mother safely shopping in Jersey, Chris had trouble getting in, and the condom was gross—its lubrication slimy, its latex the colour of moulted snake skin. Once he'd inched inside with all the romanticism of a carpenter working a dowel into a snug hole with a slather of axle grease, her deflowering was over in short order, and left her sore. The experience of entry had been neither here nor there; it was bigger, but still a penis didn't feel that different from a finger or a tampon. She'd anticipated a sensation more momentous, unimaginable. Not only did the real McCoy lie well within the realm of the known, but her imagination had done a more bang-up job. Having agreeably entertained herself in private, Irina had assumed that she would orgasm as a matter of course. No one had warned her that women had to learn how to come all over again—that for women coming through fucking was often work, sometimes so much work that the results didn't merit the effort. But since fucking for men roughly approximated what they did with the bathroom door closed, Chris only suffered the typical teenage difficulty of coming a little soon. Irina felt cheated. The exercise dispatched, she hadn't reclined in dreamy satisfaction, but had retreated up onto the pillows with sullen, barely disguised petulance. She'd been awaiting this for years, and now look: like so much else, sex was a sell.

Fair enough, she'd warmed to the pastime, systematically researching which positions accomplished at least a tiny amount of friction in the right place, abetting these calisthenics with sordid little stories in her head. The one upside of all this yeomanlike fucking was that she no longer brought unrealistic expectations to the erotic table. At best, sex with Ramsey would be nice. She hadn't presumed that she would come. After all, even tried-and-true sex with Lawrence had never lost a trace of effortfulness, of having to expend quantities of energy and concentration for a marginal reward.

So had Irina placed a premium on validating her worldview—if she cared more about being right than being happy, and there are plenty of such people—she'd have been disgruntled. Lo and behold, sex with Ramsey failed to live *down* to her expectations. Dazed and dizzy in those thick linen sheets of the Royal Bath, as if recovering from a head-on collision, she had the distinct impression that she'd never really *fucked* before, leaving her to wonder what it was all those years that she'd been doing instead.

"Come to think of it," Irina speculated in the crook of Ramsey's arm on perhaps the third day in Bournemouth (it was hard to keep track of time, which had grown fat, sluggish, and lazy like an overfed cat), "before your birthday, I'd never fantasized about fucking. It's always seemed, as an idea anyway, too permissible. Even when I was fucking, I was sneakily thinking about something else. Something more forbidden."

"Like what?" asked Ramsey.

Strange, but no one had ever asked her that before. With trepidation, she ventured, "Oral sex, sometimes."

"You mean, sucking cock," he corrected.

She laughed. "Yes, *sucking cock*. Though with a twist. I like the idea of being forced. I don't think women are supposed to admit things like that, but yes, forced—to drink it. In theory anyway. In my head. I don't know if I'd like it in real life."

"I had rape fancies for years," he volunteered cheerfully. "Had one about you last week. I *ravished* you. Up against a wall. Put up a right good fight at first, but in the end you was begging for more dick."

Emboldened, she went further. "For a while I found the idea of two men together exciting. Lately, with Lawrence . . . I shouldn't tell you this, it's too embarrassing."

"There's *nothing* you shouldn't tell me. Never forget that."

"All right. I've thought about women."

"Eating pussy? What's wrong with that? I think about eating pussy myself."

"You're a man. You're supposed to think about that."

"There's no *supposed to* in this business."

"I don't want you to think I'm a dyke. I just—ran out of other ideas."

"Only so many toys in the chest. I thought about blowing a bloke before."

"Really?"

"Really. Not many blokes would admit as much, but I wager the notion's not uncommon. Don't mean you want to do it with some real-life smelly tosser, neither."

"Thank you. That makes me feel better," she said, resting her head on his chest. "Funny thing is, after your birthday? When we couldn't? For the first time I fantasized about fucking. All the time. Every day. I started to feel a little crazy."

"So what do you think about now, when we're fucking for true?" asked Ramsey sleepily. It was early afternoon; he played his third-round match that night, and should have been at the practice table by now.

"I don't *think about* anything," she marvelled. "With you, I don't go elsewhere. If I fantasized when I'm fucking you, I'd fantasize that I'm fucking you. See, for the first time, fucking seems *outrageous*. You're going to put *that* in *there*? And there's something—primitive. So it doesn't seem like something you're supposed to do, but like something you *have* to do. As if I'm in heat. It's like rutting."

He chuckled, sliding a dry, tapered finger along her hip. "You're an animal, know that? A bloody animal. You act so Girl Guide and that. You bake all them pies. Nobody'd ever guess it to look at you. Except me. I could see it, even if you couldn't, pet. Keeping a beastie like you in the cupboard is a crime. Like them wankers who chain tigers in the back garden, and they get mangy and thin and depressed."

"Should report it to PETA."

"Peter?"

"Never mind."

❖ ❖ ❖

It wasn't only sex proper, either; it was everything. Sleeping, they had yet to hit on a position that wasn't so sumptuously comfortable that she wanted to cry. Kissing was like going for a swim, a tireless, gliding breaststroke in a sheltered pool. His skin was always cool, with the texture of kid, an apt word since his person seemed cryogenically frozen in adolescence.

Long, narrow, hairless save for a soft sprout of light brown furze in the underarms and groin, his body was neat and unmarked, as if Ramsey had been saved for her, sealed from tarnish in cellophane like polished silver. Snooker fostering an indoors life, his skin was an even cream from head to toe, with no shadow sock-line at his ankles, nor stripe under his watch. He had one of those rare figures that looked completely normal naked—sound, right, whole—whereas men often look incongruous in the nude, embarrassing or not quite themselves. Stripped, he strode their hotel room like a creature in its natural environment, and no more called out for cladding than a stag in the woods. That burnt-sugar scent was bewitching, and sometimes she would nestle down for a distilled whiff at the base of his neck like sniffing a hot oven ajar.

Objectively, Ramsey Acton was not the most handsome man in the universe. His hair was turning; his face may have transformed readily from age to age, but one of its modes was careworn. True, he was one of those irritating people who could eat and drink as much as he liked and never gain an ounce, and who retained a taut, articulated musculature absent a single sit-up. Nevertheless, he didn't display the bulkier masculinity vaunted in magazines. That was the point. He was not unbearably handsome to every woman; he was unbearably handsome to Irina. The slight curve of his buttocks, one of which would fit perfectly in the clasp of each hand, his attenuated toes and high arches and slender hips were all designed to satisfy Irina McGovern's personal, quixotic aesthetic. Ramsey Acton was a custom job.

Yet one aspect of this made-to-order sticky-trap was rather horrible. Fucking Ramsey and kissing Ramsey and sleeping with Ramsey, watching Ramsey stride naked from the bed to the minibar and letting Ramsey carry her around the room over his head, just as he had lifted her that first night, their close brush with throwing all this away like carelessly leaving a suitcase of money behind on a railway platform—well. It was all she wanted to do. She didn't want to eat, and she didn't want to illustrate children's books. She didn't want to meet her friends in Indian restaurants. She didn't want to watch *Panorama* expose how Her Majesty's Government had tried to cover up the truth about mad cow. For that matter, Irina posited to herself, puzzled, a little frightened even, it was entirely possible she would never want to do anything else but slide in and out of bed with Ramsey Acton for the rest of her life. Since she had always considered herself a woman with broad interests, concern for world affairs, deep affections for a range of friends, and a driving ambition to pursue her own career, the discovery that apparently all she'd really wanted all along was to get laid by a particular snooker player was a little bit grim.

❖ ❖ ❖

"Do me a favour," said Irina in the limo that night. "Don't go in the stage entrance." Frowning, Ramsey complied, though entering the conference centre through the main doors cost him signing some twenty programmes on the way in. "Put your arm around me." A gratuitous directive; aside from hasty trips to the loo, they'd been in physical contact of some sort since that first embrace in the Royal Bath, from simply holding hands to such a complex interlocking of convex and concave parts that together they formed once of those coffee-table puzzle cubes that exasperate dinner guests. So in a double clasp, a neat jazz syncopation of three steps of Irina's to Ramsey's two, they sauntered past the ticket counter, where Irina met the eyes of that snooty booking agent. He nodded, finally with a properly shit-eating deference rather than the kind that was secretly insulting. "Thank you," she whispered, flicking a slippery scarf of burgundy rayon back over the shoulder of the smart, slinky black frock Ramsey had also bought her that afternoon. "That made my night."

"At last a bird what's easy to please," said Ramsey, and showed her to her seat in a special section for family, managers, and guests. The view of the table was peerless. "Wish me luck." He kissed her long and deeply in open view. Others in the section cut sly, curious looks at the dark-haired woman in the first row.

Irina was apprehensive. They had taken too long shopping for her new wardrobe, leaving no time for Ramsey to warm up at the practice table. Although if he lost tonight she'd have Ramsey all to herself thereafter, she couldn't bear responsibility for a defeat.

Ramsey's opponent was John Parrott, a good-natured player from Liverpool who at thirty-three, chubby and moon-faced, with an aura of the two-car garage, seemed prematurely middle-aged. Thick black eyebrows forever shooting to his hairline in astonishment or ploughing noseward in despair, his elastic expressions so broadcast every nuance of the game that he was effectively a commentator for the deaf. (The MC introduced Parrott by his ostensible nickname "The Entertainer," though snooker was rife with fabricated sobriquets; flaks forced down the throats of fans improbable handles like "The Golden Boy" for Stephen Hendry or "The Darling of Dublin" for nice-guy Ken Doherty, which even an anorak wouldn't employ with a gun to his head.) Ramsey said Parrott was a capital fellow, with a dry sense of humour and an appealing streak of self-deprecation.

Indeed, together Ramsey and Parrott epitomized their sport's legendary decorum. Beyond a handful of raggedy debut shots, Ramsey's lack of preparation didn't seem to have done him much harm. In fact, she was pleased to note about his play a new ebullience. Hoping to prove a positive influence, Irina was relieved when at the interval he led by a frame.

During the break, a man in the row behind touched her arm. In his forties, he had a florid face creased from the overkill smile that he promptly unleashed, though his eyes didn't smile with it. Slightly longer hair than suited his age betrayed a vanity, and his tie was so loud it hurt her eyes. "Anybody ever warn you, love," he said, breath tinged with beer, "that our lad Ramsey is already married?"

Irina's mouth parted, and despite herself her colour may have dropped a shade.

Clapping her shoulder, the man laughed boisterously. "Only riding you, doll! Didn't your face look a picture now! I meant to snooker, missy. Snooker's his first wife, and make no mistake about it, snooker will be his last." He stuck out his hand. "Jack Lance. Match-Makers. I'm something between Ramsey's dogsbody and his mum."

Irina shook the hand, whose fingers sprang dark hairs. Underslept, she was slow to sort out that this was Ramsey's manager. Instinctive dislike battled the urge to make a good impression. "Pleased to meet you. Irina McGovern."

"American!" he accused.

"A congenital birth defect," she said. "It's not polite to make fun."

"So it ain't!" Jack laughed too hard, as if in amazement that a Yank had managed a bit of banter. "Just visiting, then. Seeing the sights? Westminster Cathedral? Big Ben? Pick up some candy floss on the pier?"

"No, I live in London. From which you may assume that I visit Big Ben about as often as New Yorkers take the ferry to the Statue of Liberty. Like, never."

Mercifully, Jack cut to the chase. "I didn't see your man at the practice table these last three days. Now, I can see how an attractive lady like yourself might make for a formidable distraction. But we wouldn't want our mutual friend to neglect his responsibilities, would we?"

She nodded towards the table. "He's winning, isn't he? What more do you want?"

"A piece of 350,000 quid." The smile dropped.

"I had no idea the purse was that big."

"You going to follow this sport with the pros, sweetie," he advised, "those are the first stats you master. Fastest break, lifetime centuries— Web site filler for fans."

"I'll work on it." Clipping her voice, she turned to face forward again.

"You work on Ramsey first," said Jack to her back.

"Sorry, I don't think we've met," said the attractive brunette to Irina's right, in the spirit of coming to her rescue. "You're Ramsey's friend, right?"

"Yes. Irina McGovern."

"I'm afraid we're backing different horses! I'm Karen Parrott. But John thinks so highly of Ramsey. Says it's gobsmacking that he's never won the World."

"Yes, I wish it didn't matter to Ramsey so much."

"Oh, it's all they care about," said Karen. "The Crucible, the Crucible. Almost has a religious ring, you reckon?"

"Yes, *the Crucible* sounds like a church, doesn't it?"

Karen glanced behind her; Jack Lance had left the section. "Sorry about Jack," she said quietly. "He's not a bad sort. But the managers either see the women as the enemy, or get matey on you and try to enlist you on the team. Either way, they're mighty proprietary."

"True, he didn't seem too happy about Ramsey's having found a *companion*. I guess he thinks he's made an investment, and that earns him a controlling interest. As you said, the players are like racehorses."

"Actually, it's more like a manager's got part-ownership of a trained seal."

Spotting Jack again, Irina asked brightly, "Do you come to all John's matches?"

"Crikey, not on your life! But this week I figured the kids would enjoy a trip to the seaside before it gets too nippy. Sorry to be a nosy Parker, but have you been Ramsey's—friend very long?"

"No, not long. Funny, I used to find snooker a little dull. But now I'm starting to get it. It's like a cross between ballet and chess."

"Throw in the Battle of Waterloo, and you've got something."

"It seemed like such a low-key sport at first—soothing. But sometimes it's incredibly exciting."

"Mmm-hmmm," said Karen noncommittally.

"So how often *do* you go see John play a tournament?"

"Oh, some years I'll go to Sheffield for the World. And maybe if he's in a final of a ranking event. Three times a year? Something like that."

"That's all?"

"Well, it's not quite like when you've seen one game you've seen them all, but . . . You'll see."

"So wives and girlfriends don't usually come along on the tour?"

"Sometimes," Karen said cautiously. "For a little while. Actually—a real little while. It's hard. There's no room for you. Boys, you know. Drink. And snooker. *Buckets* of snooker. It's all they talk about. Maybe you'll—feel differently," she added with gracious optimism. "But, uh, most of the girls burn out."

As the lights dropped for the second session, a small indentation dimpled between Irina's eyes. She hadn't thought things through. Vaguely, she'd envisioned accompanying Ramsey on his travels to a cornucopia of other lavish hotels; with equal vagueness, she'd pictured a comfortable domestic routine on Victoria Park Road, more or less a facsimile of her life with Lawrence, with better sex. Moreover, she had her own commitments that she was already neglecting. Oh, well. How much time could he spend on the road per year anyway?

❖ ❖ ❖

The debriefing in the Royal Bath bar after Ramsey's narrow victory over John Parrott was jovial enough. His colleagues were all curious about how Irina knew Ramsey; "We've both been divorced from the same woman" made a convenient shorthand. The while, Ramsey ensured that she always had a fresh drink (everyone was getting hammered), and that some part of his body was always touching hers (the barest contact sent her whole body humming like a toaster), although his grip on *Denise* in the opposite hand was discernably tighter. When John Parrott told the terrible tale of having the cue with which he had won the 1991 World Championship stolen from his car at Heathrow, Ramsey rejoined, "Serves you right, you tosser! I'd sooner lock a live dog in the boot than leave the cue behind in a car park." "Aye!" cried John Higgins, "sooner leave the wife in the boot!" and Karen chided with a biff, "Don't give him ideas!" Much merriment was derived from one of Ramsey's attacking pots that evening, after which the cluster had miraculously settled to leave a clear path for the pink to the corner pocket, "like the parting of the Red Sea!" Granted, after the third retelling Irina was unable to muster more than a polite smile. If it was one of those I-guess-you-had-to-be-theres, she had been there, and it didn't help.

So the banter was lively, but whenever being amusing escalated from option to obligation Irina grew dull-witted. Dazed by the superficial spangle of wordplay and silly stories, she began to crave substance, if not gravity. Talking to these people was like eating candy floss, until she didn't want more sugar but a steak. Midway through a *fascinating* twenty-minute debate over whether a draft in Purbeck Hall had made the top cushions too springy, Irina reflected that Ramsey's profession had little or no *moral content*. Oh, there were occasional issues of honour (calling the ref's attention to your own foul) or humility (that apologetic tip of the head when you fluke a pot). But in the main, snooker was about excellence for its own sake. The game's beauty, its limitation as well, was that it didn't matter. It didn't save Tutsis in Rwanda, or a farmer's beloved cattle from mad cow. Some nights Irina was sure to find relief in a world outside the news; on others she feared that she was bound to find the pageant frivolous and empty.

During a lull, she even resorted to Princess Di. While she'd been sad at first, a bit abstractly, as she would have been over the untimely demise of any young woman she didn't know, after weeks of mawkish public mourning Irina had reluctantly come to share Lawrence's view that the nationwide hair-tearing, breast-beating, and rending of garments was an exercise in mass hysteria, and that rather than represent a salutary emotional catharsis it demonstrated that the British had lost a grip— that there were, effectively, no real English people left. Yet as soon as the hallowed subject was raised in the bar, the company in unison composed their faces in stricken solemnity, leaving Irina to reconsider uttering the adjectives *maudlin* and *bathetic*.

A mention that her mother was born in the Soviet Union went nowhere; presumably, then, Russians didn't play much snooker. For any conversational tendril that curled beyond the purview of the snooker circuit died on the vine. While these characters had played across the globe from Hong Kong to Dubai, a typical international anecdote involved Alex Higgins playing drunk and shirtless in Bombay. Parrott regaled the bar with a tale about Zimbabwe, where the local butcher had stapled the cloth to the table; "You could see the staples jutting out!" collapsed the company into gales of laughter. By this point, Irina knew better than to press Parrott for his take on Robert Mugabe's plan to confiscate white farmland. Like Anne Tyler characters, these accidental tourists travelled in a hermetic capsule all done up in green baize.

So maybe it wasn't so surprising. But once she slid onto the brocade spread in the suite, one conspicuous omission came home: no one, not once, had ever asked what she did for a living herself.

❖ ❖ ❖

It was official: later that week, the fact that Ramsey Acton had hooked up with "a sultry Russian beauty" was published in *Snooker Scene*. The trashy little snippet got everything about "Irina McGavin" all wrong, but she cherished her copy as a keepsake.

Ramsey rolled on to conquer all the way through the semis. If his game had previously been missing some intangible final ingredient, Irina's arrival in Ramsey's life must have added that last half-teaspoon of cayenne that makes a dish sing. How often Irina herself had battled with a sauce as Ramsey had wrangled for thirty years with his snooker game, only at the last minute lighting upon the smidgen from her overflowing spice rack that suddenly bound a dissonant jumble of penultimate flavours into a triumphant melange. At forty-seven, Ramsey Acton appeared to have discovered love and mastery in a fell swoop.

When the winner of the other semi was a freak success, a weedy, green young player named Dominic Dale ranked #54, Ramsey regarded the final as a mere formality. Having once himself been a young, unproven player subject to blithe condescension from old hands, he should have known better. But one of the things you lose in the wisdom of age is the wisdom of youth. Education is not a steady process of accrual, but a touch-and-go contest between learning and forgetting, like frantically trying to fill a sink faster than it can empty through an open drain—which is why Dominic Dale and his ilk would eternally capitalize on the underestimation of their "betters."

After the final they dined at Oscar's, their planned celebration now downgraded to a quiet tête-à-tête for the licking of wounds. By now, she and Ramsey had established a ritual twin order of scallops with saffron cream, wild bass with morels, and a side of spinach.

"It stands to reason," Irina said over the starter, "that if winning the Grand Prix would mean something, then coming second in the Grand Prix means something, too."

Ramsey mashed a scallop vengefully with his fork. "It means I lost."

Irina rolled her eyes. "Inability to take satisfaction in anything short of total victory is a formula for a miserable life. When do you ever achieve total victory?"

"When you win the World at the Crucible," said Ramsey promptly.

"I think we should talk about something else besides snooker."

"What else is there?"

She examined his face. He wasn't joking.

During his winning streak, dinnertime conversation had ranged their lives like a great heath, stopping to examine every little copse and pool: Ramsey's growing concern that to break the standoff with his parents someone would have to die first; Irina's reasons for demurring from fine art; her sister's gushy manner as overcompensation for resentment ("Killing with kindness," she'd noted, "is still murder"); her ambition to finally visit Russia, and her odd regret that now she'd never experience the grisly Soviet Union proper; the comical lengths to which certain female fans had gone—sometimes dogging him from town to town for whole seasons—to get Ramsey into bed. Although there was one gloomy grove that Irina was prone to avoid—her anguish over how Lawrence was managing her desertion—in the main these rhetorical ambles had been bracing and far-flung. Now that Dominic Dale had, it was said, "played above himself" (a curious concept, in Irina's view—that you could ever play better than you knew how), Ramsey had fallen in a hole.

"We could talk about the fact that, while this is a very nice hotel, I'm looking forward to going home."

Ramsey looked up sharply. "To Lawrence?"

"No, silly. To Victoria Park Road. Remember that quaint establishment? It's called *your house.*"

"And when do you figure that would be?"

"Tomorrow, I assume."

"The Benson and Hedges Championship starts in Malvern tomorrow."

Irina's fork drooped. "Malvern. Where the hell is Malvern?"

"Don't you worry about where Malvern is. Jack's made all the arrangements."

"How long does that last?" she asked limply.

"Twelve days."

"Oh," she said. The saffron sauce didn't seem as lively tonight; maybe she was getting tired of it. "What's after—Malvern?"

"The UK, of course."

"Of course," she said faintly. "And how much time is there between this Malvern thing and the UK?"

"Mmm," he said, massacring his last scallop. "Between the B&H final and the first round in Preston? Three, four days. Have to check the schedule. Ask Jack."

"When do you take some time *off*?"

"Let's see," he reflected. "There's a week between the UK and the German Open in Bingen. Good fortnight at Christmas. And we haven't decided whether to enter the China Open this year."

"Tell me that the China Open is played in Leicester Square."

"Shanghai," he said breezily. "If we give it a miss, there's a handful of days to put our feet up at the end of February. But if we do go for Shanghai, it'd be daft not to do the Thailand Masters in Bangkok straight after."

"Maybe I'm missing something, but when is all this time off?"

219

"In May. After the World."

"May," she said heavily. "It's now October."

"There's the exhibition circuit after the tour's done, but that's up to me."

"Ramsey. I can't go with you to all these tournaments. I have work to do." Though he professed to adore her illustrations, Ramsey never seemed to take her occupation seriously as an activity as well as a product. Yet despite herself, she remembered with relief that she'd left her passport carelessly in her handbag ever since the last trip to Brighton Beach.

"But you got to!" he cried. "I'll not play for shite without you there!"

"You played *for shite* for thirty years without me there."

"If you must do, take the work along, then. We've loads of downtime."

Which they had thus far spent fucking, talking, drinking, and—well, fucking. Little wonder that Irina was sceptical of making time for long hours of drawing in hotel rooms. "Maybe," she said dubiously. "Do you always play this hard?"

"You should know. You and me's played powerful hard upstairs." He reached across the table for her hands. "See, when I leave for Bournemouth I haven't a baldy if I'll ever see you again. I reckon on balance, what with Lawrence being a decent, clever chap what's never raised a hand to you, why would you bolt for a ne'er-do-well snooker player? So I tell Jack to enter me in the whole calendar. I figure I'll need something to take my mind off you something desperate.

"Now I'm on the play lists. But that's not necessarily so terrible. I done this circuit all on my own since I was eleven years old. My parents thought a snooker player a bare notch above juvenile delinquent, and I'd to raise the entry fee for junior tournaments hustling middle-aged mugs at Rackers in Clapham. Got more than one hiding when they were none too pleased to lose a fiver to a cocky sprog as well. It's been a lonely life, whatever you read in them snooker rags. I never had nobody. Jude got so she hated snooker, hated snooker players, not to mention me, and sure as fuck hated parking her bum at any snooker tournament. I can't make you come with me, and I'll understand if you don't. But if there's any fairness in this life, I must finally be owed a bird what will raise a glass with me after six hours on the bounce at the table."

"I have a life, too," she said gently.

"Sure you do, pet." An offhand tone belied that he understood anything of the sort. "Take it one tournament at a time. But at least come with me to Malvern."

"All right," she said reluctantly. "But only Malvern."

❖ ❖ ❖

Spirited from the Royal Bath in another limousine while she was a little hungover, Irina never did sort out where Malvern was—aside from being somewhere in Worcestershire, of which she saw little enough during their play-all-night, sleep-all-day schedule that in her mind it remained not a county but a steak sauce.

Though she couldn't recall agreeing to accompany him to the UK Championship per se, she next found herself manifested in Preston as if by *Star Trek* transporter room. Nightly after the matches were played, Irina reported for duty at Squares, the massive bar around the corner from the Guildhall; apparently three or four rounds with the lads were included in her job description. She liked to think she was getting a bit better at snooker shop talk, but still found it draining. So she retired from one such session toward the end of the first week with equal parts self-congratulation and relief.

Yet on return to their hotel room, Ramsey began ominously, "You know, *ducky*. Speaking to the opposition, you got to watch your tongue. They may seem all very hail-fellow-well-met, but they're the competition as well. Best you never forget that."

"What did I say?" said Irina guardedly, swallowing *this time*.

"This palaver about the World."

"That you've lost six World Championship finals is a fact. It's not a deep dark private secret, but a detail on which Clive Everton comments every time you play."

"Coming from you, it means something different."

"Since you were eavesdropping on my conversation, did you hear what I said?"

"I wasn't *eavesdropping*. I *overheard*."

"I said it was common to interpret those six losses as clutching, as wanting it too much, or wanting it not enough, as collapsing under the ultimate pressure. In sum, as a character flaw. I said to the contrary you lost each of those matches for different reasons, and the impression of pattern is an illusion. I said sometimes you just don't make a shot because you don't make a shot, period. It doesn't mean that your mother didn't love you or you hate yourself or you're suffering from fear of success. Since what I said was distilled from listening to you go on at length over countless bottles of wine, I *thought* you'd appreciate my efforts."

"Nice try, ducky, but too sophisticated by half for this lot. All they hear is Ramsey Acton's own bird thinks he's washed up. It's like you was running me down."

"I wasn't running you down!" Irina wondered what happened when people who perceived imaginary slights on every corner were insulted for real. Nevertheless, hypersensitivity was ingenious as a tactic. An outraged reaction to the most harmless remark suggested that nothing short of apocalypse would ensue after a proper put-down, helping to ensure that before criticizing him sincerely she would think twice.

"The point is, you was focusing on the negative," said Ramsey. "On what I've not won. I might add, the *only* tournament I've not won. You got to understand, this game is half mind-fuck. When them blokes come to the table, I don't want them thinking, *Ramsey Acton, that old-timer, this'll be a cakewalk.* I want them dropping their trousers in fear. I want them remembering, this geezer's won near every ranking tournament known to man. If I'm intimidating that gives me the edge. They talk to the bird and she shovels out the excuses—like there's something what needs excusing—I lose the edge. I know you didn't mean to. But you done me a powerful lot of damage tonight."

"I was trying to be sociable," she mumbled. "I don't know these people. I don't know much about snooker. I was trying to get on. I want you to be proud of me. I never intended to embarrass you."

"I didn't say you embarrassed me. I said you damaged me." This was classic. He would press an advantage one step further than seemed necessary or kind—thereby, as the Brits might say, over-egging the pudding. Of a habit anything but sweet, Americans would describe it more brutally as *putting the boot in.*

"I'm sorry," she said. "Though I'm not sure what I'm apologizing for."

"That'd be a right crap apology, then."

Ramsey continued to stand aloof, several feet from the bed. Already a trademark of their relationship, there was either not a fag paper between them, or they were light-years apart. There was no in-between. With Lawrence, there'd been nothing but in-between, and this new inch-as-good-as-a-mile was difficult to adapt to. She was reminded of the game of trust popular in the 60s, in which you extended both arms and fell dead-weight backwards, expressing blind faith that your partner would catch you. Either Ramsey was right there, not allowing her to drop a half-inch, or he turned heel and she slammed smack on the floor.

"What am I supposed to say to these people?" she asked dismally. "I'll say whatever you want."

"That my form's coming on. That you never seen me play better."

"That sounds like something your friend Jack would put out in a press release."

"Fair enough. Then tell them I got a really, really big dick."

She looked up. He was smiling. His zip was down. He did have a big dick.

One flying lunge from six feet, and the confrontation was over. Her release from his displeasure was like finally being allowed to go and play after sitting in the corner in a dunce cap. For much like the unwritten etiquette of the telephone, whereby it is the caller's implicit prerogative to wrap it up, only Ramsey could end what Ramsey had started. Since Irina never started anything, that left Ramsey as the sole gatekeeper of their garden, from which she was cruelly exiled and into which she was graciously readmitted, at his whim.

◆ ◆ ◆

When the promised fortnight break finally arrived around Christmas, after Bingen am Rhein, Ramsey wheedled her into a getaway holiday in Cornwall—though by this point what she really needed to get away from was more holiday.

Their first afternoon on the rocky, desolate southwest coast, Ramsey led her to their rental car, and wouldn't explain. He drove to Penzance to a poky municipal building. Although she did remember signing something preliminary during a giddy three tussle in November, only when she read the placard did she realize what he was up to. "But I look a dog's dinner!" He said she looked beautiful, as always. "But I haven't bought you a ring!" Ramsey frowned, patting his pockets, then spotted a bit of flotsam in the gutter. He pressed her palm with a round piece of discoloured steel with two blunt prongs. "I reckon it's a radiator hose-clip," he explained.

"Ramsey, I can't marry you with some car-part off the street!"

"Pet, you can marry me with a twist-tie, or a knackered rubber band."

Look here"—he demonstrated—"fits just right. I'll never take it off, promise."

The official inside was irritable, perhaps having hoped to make it a short day and do some Christmas shopping; to Ramsey's obvious annoyance, the short, plump woman with bad teeth didn't seem to recognize who'd walked in. They filled out some forms. It was over in ten minutes. Ramsey had bought a ring; he assured her it wasn't at all expensive, and he was probably lying.

Although Irina hadn't dreamt of white tulle and three-tier cakes, this "wedding" had been no-frills by the most modest of standards. On the other hand, maybe it was the medium course that was squalid—having a cake but not an especially tasty one, springing for a dress but off the rack. She could see the merit in either blowing £20,000 on five hundred of your closest friends, or tying the knot on a rainy afternoon with a radiator hose-clip. Indeed, the latter approach had the benefit of focusing not on a single day, but on the rest of your life. Ramsey wasn't keen on *getting* married, but he was keen on *being* married, ultimately the greater compliment.

Irina walked out in a daze. She and Ramsey were married. They'd been together for less than two months.

After following her "husband"—it would take time to ease into the word—to the Regal Welsh Open in Newport, the B&H Masters at Wembley, and the Regal Scottish Open in Aberdeen, she would have been judicious to have resisted Ramsey's imprecations to keep tagging along and to have knuckled down to her own work. But he begged her so winningly. She was touched by his fervid gratitude to at last have company in a life that she could now appreciate had been gruelling and lonely. Colleagues were also rivals, and you could never be wholehearted friends with your structural foe. The connection between the two of them was so total, but also so fragile—on or off.like a switch—that she feared inserting whole fortnights of insulating separation into their idyll. Besides. She had never been to China.

Outwardly, Irina appeared a hopeless girlie pushover, standing by her man; in truth she was driven by the selfish, insatiable greed of an irretrievable junkie. She was shooting up with Ramsey Acton twice a day, and the prospect of going cold turkey for the length of an entire tournament was too desolate to contemplate.

Yet as many an addict must, she found that a floating, disconnected vagueness began to fog her head, especially on the rare afternoons that Ramsey tore himself away to hone his game. Alone, she no longer understood what to do with herself or quite who she was. Thus over Ramsey's protests she demurred from taking his surname, not from feminist zeal but because she could not afford it; the appellation *Irina Acton* would make official the very vanishing act at which she was already getting too much practice. She flapped magazines instead of reading books, sometimes poured a wine miniature from the minibar rather earlier than she should have, and awaited Ramsey's return with a jittery impatience peculiar for a freelance artist accustomed to working long hours on her own. Growing ever more adept at snooker banter—and at keeping her remarks sufficiently anodyne that she did not get it in the neck later in the hotel—should have been gratifying; it was actually disquieting. Her new expertise was grafted on, artificial. She was learning to talk energetically and at length when addressing a subject about which she cared little. Or she cared about snooker only because she cared about Ramsey, and the transitive relationship was weak. He'd been generous to include her so utterly in his world, but *in*clusion could slyly morph to *oc*clusion. Some days this warm envelopment into the snooker fold seemed a guise under which she was being steadily colonized, consumed, co-opted. *Irina McGavin,* famed new consort of snooker legend Ramsey Acton, was coming along great guns. *Irina McGovern,* illustrator of gentle enough success never to have made it into a gossip column spelled correctly, was in mortal danger.

▣ chapter six ▣

After returning with Lawrence from the Grand Prix in Bournemouth, Irina was haunted by a question that she'd wanted to ask for ages, but not having done so for so long made it harder to put. On the first night back home, when the two snuggled into bed, she couldn't enjoy their goose-down burrow, much less the subsequent sex—because the whole time she was working herself up to asking what she wanted to ask, failing to ask it, then berating herself for being such a coward now that it was time to sleep. It wasn't obvious why Bournemouth should have occasioned such a flaming recrudescence of an old curiosity, or why this line of inquiry seemed so frightening.

At length the embarrassment of her timidity exceeded the embarrassment of the question itself. Early the fourth evening she vowed that by lights-out she would put this *perfectly harmless question* to her partner, rehearsing the solemn covenant so fiercely through the preparation of dinner that she burned the garlic for the eggplant. She paid no attention to the Grand Prix's third round into which Lawrence predictably tuned after they ate. Anyway, Ramsey wasn't in it.

Locks. Thermostat. Floss—like a countdown. Lawrence plopped into bed and reached for his book. Irina slid next to him, exasperated with herself because her pulse was pounding and this was ridiculous.

"Lawrence," she said, too gravely; she had wanted to impart an air of idle musing. "I was wondering—what do you think about when we make love?"

Wrong! They never said "make love," which Lawrence considered sappy.

He turned his head with a slight jolt, taking longer than need be to mark his place. "Well, obviously about fucking you, what do you think?"

Her heart fell. Now she understood what she'd been afraid of. That he would lie. That, having lied, he would stick to his story, and she could never ask him again. She realized too late that she'd only have had a chance at getting a straight answer, an unsafe answer, by raising the matter breathlessly in the heat of passion (such as it was, facing the wall), and not during the prosaic lights-on of the night's last few pages.

Sensing her one and only opportunity slipping rapidly out of reach, she pressed, "You don't ever have sexual fantasies?"

"I wouldn't say I've *never* had a sexual fantasy, of course not."

"Then what are they about?"

He looked annoyed. "Sex, obviously!" If all this stuff was so *obvious*, it was a wonder that so many books and movies and sociological studies were squandered on its examination.

"But you never have fantasies while we're fucking? Only by yourself."

"I don't do anything *by myself*, I have you."

The lies were stacking. She did not believe that he practised perfect abstinence in a private regard any more than she believed that the only thing that turned him on was straight-up, by-the-book intercourse.

"Why," he added, "do you do anything *by yourself*?"

"Why would I?" she said, with a flash of defiance. "As you said, I have you."

Stalemate.

"You don't even—" she tried again. "For example, fellatio. Which we used to do, but sort of quit. The idea of that—doesn't appeal to you, in your head?"

"Oh, that's a typical adolescent thing. All boys are into it. It's a phase." Lawrence often took refuge in the general, in the hopes that you wouldn't see the tree for the forest.

"Do you wish we still did that?"

"Not really. It makes me feel self-conscious. Serviced. And it seems a little degrading. To you. I don't like that."

How very upstanding.

"But I'm getting the impression that you do have fantasies," he said. "When we're fucking. Since you assume I do."

"Maybe." She had instinctively withdrawn up on her pillows. While the conversation was technically about "intimacies," the distance between

227

their bodies was greater than usual, and they were not touching. "Once in a while."

"So what are they about?"

Enter the final answer to why she'd been leery of opening the pornographic Pandora's Box: that he would turn the tables. But, what—he would admit only to conjuring the kind of seemly relations written up in "marital guides" from the 1950s, and she would admit to fantasizing about eating pussy? She would regale him with an X-rated catalogue of sickness through the ages, thinking about a man jerking off all over her face or forcing himself into her mouth and making her drink come? *Get real.*

"Well—*obviously,*" she said, "about fucking."

"Why would you fantasize about something you're actually doing?"

"I don't know. Maybe it's not called fantasizing in that case."

"So why did you ask me that?"

"I was just curious," she said morosely. "People are different."

"I may have my eccentricities when it comes to how I'd sort out the Irish Question, but in this area I think I'm pretty conventional."

Surely it was more conventional in *this area* to be privately consumed with forcing your woman to eat come than it was to exclusively get off on the idea of standard coitus. Irina folded on her side, and Lawrence went back to reading. After a few minutes he turned out the light, and nestled behind her, running a tentative hand over her shoulder. "It sounded as if you were in the mood."

"Mmm," she hummed. If in some regards he was a total stranger, he was determined to remain one. Sexual fantasy was by its nature undignified, and—tragically—it was more important to Lawrence to be respected than to be known.

While Irina could never prove outright that his claim to what went on in his head during sex was cover, like many a poker bluffer he had a tell, which in this case was a certain belligerent barometer needle whose pressure reading sat stolidly at zero. Lawrence the person could go through the motions of cozying up to his lover, but his penis felt a million miles away and didn't like being lied for. No matter how insistently he rubbed against her buttocks, it refused to cooperate with its deceiving master.

"I must be tired," he said at last.

"That's okay. Maybe tomorrow," she whispered, and turned to kiss his forehead. She could tell he was unnerved. Throughout their years together, he'd never failed to summon an erection on demand, one reason that she was fairly confident that he did have fantasies, and bloody good ones if they did the trick every time. The lone exception was the very first night they slept together. The following morning, wearing only sagging briefs with crenellated elastic, Lawrence had shuffled out to her kitchen where she was preparing coffee, and looked dejectedly at his feet. "But I like you *so much!*" he said plaintively. Lifting his chin, she'd smiled and said, "I think that's the problem." Although sexual dysfunction wasn't usually subject to nostalgia, she cherished the memory. From Mr. Confidence, impotence had been a compliment.

Snugging his arm reassuringly between her breasts, Irina couldn't sleep right away. Why couldn't he be honest about what got him off? And why did she lie to him in return?

The self-evident answer was shame, but of a particular shade. Maybe what made "I think about you jerking off in my face" shameful wasn't its outrageousness but its comedy. Out in the open, it sounded silly. Tacky, and not even inventive enough to make it into the *Hustler* letters column.

More crucially still, perhaps the impulse to lie about what drove you privately wild (and Lawrence was not alone; previous lovers had shared what they "liked," but almost never what they honestly *thought about*) derived from a prudent desire to preserve the inexplicably mystical power of these sordid vignettes. You relied on those little stories, however risible they sounded when uttered aloud, as keys to the kingdom, and the idea of eroding those keys by exposing them to the acid of ridicule threatened banishment from your own pleasure palace. Reflected in another set of eyes as laughable, ugly, clichéd, or dirty not in an arousing way but dirty as in defiling, they might cease to turn the lock. Even preserved safely in her head, Irina's own fantasies had still systematically worn out, and lately she'd had a beastly time coming up with something new. (Whatever did one think about at eighty-five, having run through every orifice and excretion that the body affords? Even depravity is finite.) Little wonder, then, that Lawrence played his erotic cards close to his chest, or that at the very thought of disclosing those cards his penis had recoiled in horror. Still, she felt cheated. She would have found his fantasies exciting. If nothing else, she needed to borrow one.

▣ ▣ ▣

The following week, Irina insisted on attending a lecture Lawrence was giving at Churchill House. He was clearly pleased.

Before the small crowd, Lawrence looked striking in the suit he rarely wore, and having a partner considered an expert on world affairs was gratifying. He was so articulate and serious. In her humble seat near the back, she was proud of him with a determination.

Nevertheless, Lawrence was not a natural performer. The podium struck him midchest, and made him look short. He read verbatim from a prepared text, absent the biting asides that typified his conversation. The sentences were long and subordinated, and it was hard to follow the thread. Though he was a rash rhetorician at the dining table, here his points were qualified or hedged. She wished that he were able to integrate his irreverent, caustic character into his public persona—that he realized ideas were entertainment. It didn't help that his subject matter was the deadly *Northern Ireland.* More than once after a hypnotic sequence of buzz-phrases like *cross-border bodies with executive powers, confidence-building measures,* and straight-faced allusion to something called the *Decommissioning Commission,* which sounded straight out of Monty Python, she caught herself: for the last five minutes she'd been trying to envision the next drawing for *The Miss Ability Act,* and hadn't heard a word he'd said. She knew that the IRA had murdered nearly two thousand people, and that the prospect of such a "scumbag" strategy paying political dividends made Lawrence livid. Why didn't that passion translate into his speech? In some intangible way, the failure was of a piece with the fact that Lawrence adored Irina herself with all his being, yet couldn't quite translate that passion into bed.

After the lecture the applause was polite, the questions few. Only when one gentleman inquired after the possibility that a peace settlement would lead to the wholesale release of terrorist prisoners did the real Lawrence peek through. "Those dirt-birds?" Lawrence sneered. "Not a chance! Even Tony Blair will let them rot in hell." Irina smiled. This was the Lawrence she loved, and that one answer infused her subsequent kiss on his cheek and whisper "You were great!" with genuine feeling.

A reception followed. Mostly Lawrence's colleagues at Blue Sky, the attendees also included a few journalists and representatives from the Foreign Office and Irish Embassy. Irina had milled at similar gatherings before, and always felt a little in over her head. She may have been a newspaper reader, but these people were conversant with fine political details to a degree that made anything a children's book illustrator might contribute seem obvious and dumb. She might have been happy to volunteer that Tony Blair's cheesy "Cool Britannia" advertising campaign seemed unbecoming to the British; in a discussion about his Byzantine proposals for a "public–private partnership" in the London tube system, she was lost. When she got into a chat with some Foreign Office toff about Zimbabwe's programme to confiscate white farmland, she blanked on the name of the country's president in the middle of a sentence, which was enough for the dignitary, after filling in "Robert Mugabe," to excuse himself for a stuffed fig.

Everyone asked dutifully what Irina did for a living. She could see them struggling to come up with something to say about children's books, and in this august environment the titles she'd published—*Bubble Boy Goes Camping, The World of Buh*—sounded preposterous. Inquiring after a woman's career was an obligation these days, but after going through the painful exercise four or five times she came to wish that they'd skip it.

As a fallback, to rescue one think-tanker from flailing ("Do you use paints, or chalk?"), she managed to insert the fact that her mother hailed from the Soviet Union, at which point his face lit with gratitude. While Irina's answers were disappointing—no, her mother was not a politically motivated defector, but a displaced person from World War II; no, she was not even Jewish—his questions became confident and more relaxed. Mention of Russia also facilitated a segue into sharing deep concerns about securing the former Soviets' nuclear arsenal and chemical weapons, which was apparently these people's idea of a good time.

For pity's sake, they were supposed to be socializing! So why did no one in the room (well, the Irish Embassy folks excepted) dare to drink more than one glass of white wine? How about a few amusing anecdotes, a little playful, meaningless banter to lighten things up? Why did they feel obliged to be so weighty and grave, as if the fate of mankind would be imperilled if instead of anguishing over violations of the no-fly zones over Iraq they speculated on whether Niles and Daphne were ever going to get together on *Frasier*? After about an hour of this intellectually high-protein diet, the conversational equivalent of a sixteen-ounce porterhouse, her only remaining appetite was for sweets.

By happenstance, she discovered a magic bullet in her back pocket. Much as mention of *Northern Ireland* to Ramsey had triggered instantaneous narcolepsy, mention of *snooker* to these lofties brought their self-important discourse to a thudding halt.

"Is that so?" said a natty dignitary, after Irina said that she and Lawrence had gone to the Grand Prix last week. "Don't follow the sport myself. Will you excuse me?"

As the gathering grew smaller, one merciful moment of levity ensued when someone raised the subject of Diana. In unison, the group rolled eyes, and a wag christened the crash in that Paris tunnel "the death that wouldn't Di." It was an enormous relief to laugh.

Unfortunately, the reception's population was now sufficiently reduced that it would soon become impossible to avoid talking to *Bethany*. Thus far Irina had managed to position herself on the opposite side of the room from Lawrence's supple colleague, while cutting eyes covertly in the woman's direction. As usual, the pert little vixen was decked out in a perilously short skirt and tarty heels. She had a provocative habit of propping an elbow on a jutted hip, thus supporting her wine glass. The hand with the glass lolling so languidly that she might have dropped it, she leaned over the rim to take kittenish sips. It was much too chilly in late October to be wearing a sheer black sleeveless top that revealed a lacy bra underneath, but from the looks of those arms, *Bethany* spent hours in the gym every week, and must have needed to get her boredom's worth. The rippling shoulders and veined forearms reminded Irina unpleasantly of her mother, who had bequeathed to her a gut aversion to exercise fanatics of any description.

Alas, Bethany crossed the room first, and so got credit for being the friendly one before Irina had quite resigned herself to the inevitable. "Irina, *zdravstvuy*!" Bethany kissed Irina on both cheeks and continued in Russian, "I save the best for last!"

One of Irina's eyes began to twitch. Making her own bilingualism seem small beer in comparison, this to all appearances air-headed pixie spoke four or five languages. Bethany had explained her habit of talking to Irina in Russian as giving her welcome "practice," which was nonsense. Bethany was fluent, and she was showing off. Further, her appropriation of Russian felt impertinent. Once long enough from Brighton Beach, Irina had begun to regard Russian not as the language of 200 million Slavs, but as Lawrence's and her secret code, and now look: *Bethany* had cracked it.

Switching to English would seem standoffish. "*Privyet, kak dela?*" Irina said neutrally, reconciled to the fact that the rest of their chitchat would be in Russian.

"Wasn't Lawrence erudite?" Bethany effused. "Two years ago he would have mistaken Paisley for a pattern on drapes. Now, with Northern Ireland, he's knowledgeable about every twist and turn. And doesn't he look dashing! I rarely see him in a tie. I tell him, you should dress up more. He hides himself under a bushel, your husband."

At the word *moozh*, Irina flinched. But she wasn't about to tell *Bethany* that she and Lawrence weren't married. And somehow whenever Irina was at a loss for words, she blurted her most private reflections because she couldn't locate the public ones in time. Owing to this exasperating reflex, she was prone to share her inmost thoughts with total strangers, awkward misfits, and people she disliked.

"*Da*," said Irina. "But I wish he'd employ his sense of humour more in speeches. And talk a little more off the cuff instead of reading from a script. It's so dry."

"Oh, I think the political puzzle is anything but dry," Bethany differed. "And Lawrence's design of an agreement prospectively acceptable to both sides is very astute."

"Of course, I didn't mean that it wasn't a wonderful speech."

"*Konyeshno*," Bethany purred with a smile. "You know, with your background, you must be so excited about Lawrence going to Russia!"

"Russia? . . . Y-yes, of course I'm excited," Irina stammered.

"Lawrence is thrilled," Bethany added, eyeing Irina closely. "Are you coming, too?"

"I . . . don't know, we . . . haven't decided. What's the trip for again?"

"You know, this fact-finding mission about Chechnya. The funding came through from Carnegie over the summer. Lawrence has been working on his Russian in the office. I've tried to help over lunch at Pret A Manger, but as you know, he's hopeless! He's so intelligent, but in foreign language—"

"He's a *moron*," Irina finished fondly in English, slipping an arm around Lawrence as he approached. She always packed him a sandwich so that he could nosh at his computer after his workout at the gym. Since when did Lawrence eat out for lunch?

▣ ▣ ▣

As they walked home from Blue Sky, Lawrence said heartily, "Listen, thanks for coming. I know Northern Ireland isn't your favourite subject."

"I wouldn't have missed it," said Irina. "Though at the reception—

233

well, I don't know these people. I don't know much about politics. I hope I don't embarrass you."

"Of course not! Being with an artist makes me seem more interesting, whether or not you can blather about *decommissioning*. And you're smart. If that's not enough for any of those stuffed shirts, fuck them."

"I liked your speech."

"Bethany said you thought it was humourless."

"I didn't mean—!"

"No, that's okay. It was pretty humourless," said Lawrence jauntily. Engaging with such a robust ego was relaxing—like dining with tumblers that won't break if upset, and plates you can drop on the floor.

"I realize Northern Ireland isn't the stuff of stand-up comedy," she said. "But you might make the odd wisecrack. You're funny. You should use it. That's all I meant. I didn't mean to criticize."

"I don't mind if you criticize me," said Lawrence. "You're right. I should loosen up a little. Was there anything else?"

So she mentioned shortening his sentences, going lighter on the jargon, and trying to keep from scowling all the time. Unoffended, he seemed to take mental notes.

"By the way," he said, "I overheard some of your conversation, about PPP, and Iraq? I thought you held your own pretty well."

"Thanks. But I run dry on those subjects in two minutes flat. They have no idea what to ask about illustration. What else can I talk about with these people?"

"Standard fallback? Just tell them that I've got a really, really big dick."

She laughed. "*That's* what I was talking about. Use that in your speeches."

"My dick?"

"Metaphorically, yes."

By the time they arrived at Borough High Street, Lawrence's confidence in the triumph of his lecture had been restored. Yet if self-satisfaction was his natural state, humility underpinned it. His expectations of himself were reasonable in scale. He had not stumbled in his delivery. His ideas were sound. The attendance had been reputable. That was sufficient. He was not going to rail at the heavens if he hadn't, just today, changed the course of history, drawn prime ministers and presidents, and brought down the house with a standing ovation. Surely a key to contentment, he appreciated modest success.

Walking up to the flat, Irina was about to ask, "What's this about your going to Russia?" and, on impulse, didn't. As a matter of discipline, Irina didn't raise the subject for the rest of the evening, just to see if he'd bring it up himself. The funds had been approved back in the *summer*? And when was this trip to be? Would he ask if she'd like to go? Even if she'd never been there, Russia was a country about which she naturally felt proprietary.

As the night concluded, then the week, then the whole of November, all without a peep from Lawrence about a prospective visit to her motherland, discipline gave way to scientific experiment. At Christmas, when for once they begged off visiting Brighton Beach, Irina's original proposal that they honeymoon in Thailand got downgraded to a getaway in Cornwall. True, their ancient rental car dropped a hose-clip, and put Lawrence out of sorts; yet nothing about a little automotive breakdown prevented his using one of their long, coastal walks to broach the subject of an impending research trip. It was one thing to be independent, but independence could slyly morph to exclusion, and Irina felt shut out. Through the following months, his omission grew tumorous, and she would brush up against it like a lump on her breast in the shower. As many a woman has done to her peril, she told herself it was nothing, in preference to bravely palpating its dimensions, testing for a texture that might indicate a discrete, cystlike aberration, or a growth more invasively malign.

◆ chapter seven ◆

The British Open was played in Plymouth across the Easter holidays. Increasingly prone to hiding out in their hotel room, Irina often watched the news. Though she'd been unable to raise even an "Oi, that's a fair turn, innit?" from the snooker players down in the bar, every channel was chockablock with an occasion of "historic" magnitude: late into the night of Good Friday, politicians in Belfast had arrived at an agreement that would officially bring an end to the Northern Irish troubles, which had been festering for thirty years.

The signing of the Good Friday Agreement was not a salutary event in Irina's life. Yet it was certainly salutary for Lawrence Trainer, which the media moguls of the BBC and CNN were not about to let her forget. As a recognized expert at ready hand to London TV stations, Lawrence was *everywhere*. For days she couldn't switch on the set without confronting her ex, who pierced her with an expression that she interpreted as chiding. Lawrence was ambitious. Lawrence was well regarded. Lawrence was doing his job. Lawrence didn't drink too much and Lawrence didn't smoke too much—at all—and Lawrence didn't trot along in accordance with someone else's schedule and thereby demote himself from player to fan.

He looked handsome, the brown suit he wore in interviews bringing out the warmth of his umber eyes. His delivery was so self-assured that she had to wonder if he was doing better without her than she'd have expected—which was good, of course, very, very good, so why did his fine form make her feel forlorn? Quoting verbatim, he seemed to have memorized the entire document, and was ready with an opinion on its every aspect. That old dinner-table scorn emerged whenever the interviewer raised the issue of the agreement's wholesale release of paramilitary prisoners, a "get-out-of-jail-free card" with which Lawrence was utterly disgusted. "This means a raft of convicted killers," he told Jeremy Paxman on BBC2, "will end up serving a shorter sentence than they would for an outstanding parking ticket. But anything for *peace*, right? Justice is expendable."

Lawrence was popular with the media as the sole Cassandra in a chorus of Pollyannas. In their eagerness to see the back of all that mayhem, most commentators showered the agreement with flowers, and didn't examine the fine print. Only Lawrence noted that the supermajority required for passage of politically significant legislation in the assembly was a formula for deadlock, and that the biggest sticking-points in negotiations—revamping of the police force and paramilitary dis-armament—hadn't been resolved but put off for a very rainy day indeed. His lone voice of forewarning was drowned by drunken high spirits from every other corner, but seemed only the braver for flying in the face of prevailing winds. Whether or not he was right, she was proud of him.

Yet Irina had a sixth sense that it would really be better, wouldn't it— *anything for* peace, *right?*—if Ramsey were to miss altogether these appearances of his predecessor. Such premonitions descended often these days, leading her to elude any line of conversation in which Lawrence's name might possibly crop up. But since she thought about Lawrence often—how could she not?—and most of her stories from the last decade involved him in some way, that meant eradicating from her discourse many of the very confidences that drew her close to her husband. Perhaps too much caution was dangerous.

Since Ramsey was no more interested in the Good Friday Agreement than in the migration patterns of caribou, it had been fairly easy to deprive him of these newscasts, although on a couple of evenings she barely got the set off as he was inserting his pass key. One night when he was safely at the practice table, with Lawrence once more holding forth on ITV, she was overcome with such a melting tenderness that, though she knew it was silly, and self-dramatizing like her mother, she rested her cheek against the screen.

Her timing was poor. The remote was back on the bed when Ramsey walked in the door. Irina sprang from the tube, searched in vain for the power button that she'd never used, and grabbed a sock. "The screen was dusty," she said, hastily wiping it down. She got her hands on the remote, but too late.

"That's Anorak Man."

"You know, you're right!" she said brightly.

"You're not telling me you hear the voice of the bloke what you used to live with, and see his face big as life on the telly, and you don't recognize the git."

"Well, of course, now that I'm paying attention, I *recognize* him . . ."

"You knew he'd be on the telly, didn't you. That's why you pushed me to go and practise. It's called *appointment TV*."

"But Ramsey—Lawrence has been on every channel for a week!" Error.

"That so. And you been a faithful viewer. Funny you've not mentioned you seen him and that. Not once."

"Why would I? He's talking about the Good Friday Agreement, which puts you to sleep."

"'Cause I ain't *intellectual*. I don't care about *world affairs*. All I care about is *snooker*."

That's right would not exhibit the height of diplomacy. "You can't begrudge him a few days in the sun. Experts on *Northern Ireland* don't get many. And think about it—he must have to see your face pop up on television all the time."

"He doesn't have to watch *you* watching me on the telly, does he now?"

"No," she said. "He has to watch, in his imagination anyway, me fucking you blind every night instead. Who's got the better deal?"

Of course, that was only the beginning, and, like so many knock-down-drag-outs before it, this one carried on into the wee-smalls. But this time what stayed with her afterwards wasn't another self-admonition to conduct her life with Ramsey as if Lawrence Trainer had never been born, but the haunting image of those deep-set brown eyes, harrowing from the screen with reproach. What was she doing in Plymouth? Since when was her solution to too much time on her hands to jack up her consumption of *cigarettes*? For that matter, since when did she have time on her hands? Didn't she once have a horror of being idle? Puffin had been decent enough about giving her an extra six months to deliver *The Miss Ability Act* for "personal reasons," but shouldn't she save begging such indulgence for illness or emergency? Had she lined up her next job yet? Didn't she used to make sure there was always another project in the pipeline? And didn't she miss those feverish afternoons, when she was so consumed by an illustration that she forgot to eat? Nothing wrong with having a good time on occasion, but wasn't such absorption once, more than drinking and fucking and bantering about next to nothing with snooker players, her very definition of a good time? Somehow Lawrence had morphed from ex to alter ego, her good angel, the voice of her straight-A self.

His transformation was not altogether in her head. Maybe taking advantage of her carte-blanche access to Ramsey's laptop (which he mostly used for responding to fan mail on his own Web site) for this purpose was scurrilous, but Irina had established tentative e-mail contact with her former partner. She was careful to pursue the correspondence only when Ramsey was certain not to walk in; superstitiously, she changed the password on her Yahoo! account every week. Her notes were discreet, allusions to frequent "differences of opinion" arising in her new life left opaque. She kept from Lawrence just how debauched her average evening had grown, and to how many tournaments—like, all of them—she had accompanied Ramsey this season.

Of course, to regale Lawrence with the high times would have been cruel—the raucous songfests in bars, the amniotic oblivion of waking in Ramsey's arms. But what she most protected him from would have been far more hurtful. In defiance of Lawrence's bleak forecast that a life with Ramsey promised only dreary reruns of the same old snooker stories, what reliably kept the pair up until four in the morning was less often sex than *talk*. Ramsey listened; Lawrence had waited for her to finish. So driven was Ramsey to dissect *the main thing* that he might have learned the occasional value of the unsaid.

By contrast, discussions with Lawrence had always a strange tendency to truncate. When appraising an acquaintance, he would slap a hasty label on the subject of their speculation—"He's a fool"—like pasting an address on a parcel at the post office. *Whoosh,* it was down the chute; there was nothing more to say. With Ramsey, conversation only took off—and could wend on wing for hours—at the very point at which, with Lawrence, their earthbound craft had sputtered to a halt. Regarding other people, Ramsey was as fascinated by the *fine points* as Lawrence was by the minutiae of the Good Friday Agreement. So long as she steered her husband gently away from snooker, like guiding him around an open manhole, he displayed remarkably keen instincts about, say, her father, who, he noted, clearly hid behind foreign accents because he had lost touch with the sound of his own voice. Or Irina would remember how, when she was twelve, her mother had kneeled solicitously at the dentist's, murmuring tenderly that she'd never have conceded to these bothersome braces for cosmetic reasons, but only because Irina's dentist claimed that they were a "medical necessity." Ramsey exclaimed, "What a cow! Your mum would keep you from getting your teeth fixed if it was *only* so you'd be pretty?" Funny, Irina had never considered that snippet appalling before.

And while it was true that Northern Ireland plunged Ramsey into a coma, in relation to many other issues of the day he could profitably apply the same natural intuition about what made people tick, even if he had trouble keeping the facts straight. Lawrence had kept nothing but facts straight. Lawrence focused on the *what*, Ramsey on the *who*. For Ramsey, politics was about particular, barmy people getting up to no good. He said Milosevic had a face "like a baby what's just soiled his nappies—and is right pleased you've to clean up the mess." When two boys murdered several fellow students with their grandfather's shotguns in Arkansas, Irina was mystified; Ramsey said, "Well, in your country, they're not going to impress their girlfriends by getting high marks in English, are they?" Clinton's apology for slavery on a trip to Africa elicited a snort. "What's the use in apologizing for something you didn't do? That phony poser—he's busting with pride! When you're really sorry, you're ashamed of yourself." And a casual stroll by the television news could occasion comments surprisingly astute. "Sounds like Marvel Comics, don't it? Can you believe your president and the PM both say 'weapons of mass destruction' with a straight face?"

But then, the very, *very* last thing she would ever tell Lawrence was that even discussions of current events with Ramsey were funnier and more reflective than Lawrence's terse lectures while washing dishes, so her e-mails tended to be short. Lawrence's e-mails were even shorter. He did sometimes indulge in a savage diatribe on the subject of Ramsey. (Although out of spousal loyalty she probably should have told him to keep his disagreeable thoughts on her husband to himself, somehow she could never quite bring herself to disclose to Lawrence that she and Ramsey had married.) Yet his dominant running theme was that at all costs she must return to her work. He was right. Lawrence knew her so well. Like prodding her with clues to a word on the tip of her tongue— *It begins with I*—Lawrence could remind her who she was.

❖ ❖ ❖

Just as Irina was working up to a firm resolve to rededicate herself to her own occupation, the next tournament on the calendar would have to be the World Championship—the one tournament that Ramsey might most reasonably expect her to attend. Hence Irina acceded, but for the first time begrudged the gesture as a bridge too far.

In such hushed tones did players and commentators alike speak of "the Crucible" in Sheffield that she had pictured the venue for the championship as old and gilded, garlanded on its grand façade with stone-carved olive branches and cornered with gargoyles, its theatre ornate with velvet-lined boxes and glittering chandeliers. What a disappointment! The real thing was a hulking concrete affair harkening back no further than the architecturally inaugust 1960s. Its lino was gritty, its carpeting thin, the interior's overall atmosphere that of a failing comprehensive school. So even the building put Irina in a foul mood.

Now, by this time Irina had seen an awful lot of snooker. She had learned most of the fiddly rules, how a perfectly tied score was resolved by a "respotted black." Furthermore, when watching Ramsey himself Irina was implicitly invested in the results. Victory or defeat would determine whether later that night Ramsey would carouse in manic elation, throwing her in the air and jigging around their suite to Charlie Parker, or would brood through a room-service dinner and pick a quarrel. Nonetheless, a whole back-to-back snooker season involved *thousands* of frames. As fully as Irina might now appreciate the fact that no frame is ever perfectly repeated, after seven months of snooker OD they had started to look mighty goddamned similar to her. Slumping through the first few rounds of the World, she had to admit that she was bored. Not just a little bored, either. Unrelentingly bored, jump-out-of-her-skin bored, so bored that she wanted to kill.

Ramsey made it all the way to the final again this year, to Irina's exasperation, for in the privacy of her head she was now unapologetically chafing for him to drop out early so that they could please, finally go home. Be that as it may, when at the end of the match Ramsey extended his hand in congratulations to John Higgins and then accepted the seventh runner-up trophy of his career—not an elegant silver urn, but yet another clunky glass plate—no amount of grace could disguise a devastation that any decent wife would find anguishing in her own husband's face.

Here she was married to a man with a singular talent, the stuff of fanzine profiles and interviews on the BBC; strangers badgered him on the street. The whole world was entranced with Ramsey Acton's snooker game, with the notable exception of his wife. These days, rather than be captivated by his uncanny long pots, ingenious doubles, and dazzling plants, she reliably watched Ramsey's matches with eyes at half-mast. What most distinguished the man to others had become the very excellence that she not only took for granted, but could no longer see. As she threaded guiltily from the guests-and-family section to console him, a line from that seminal birthday dinner returned: *It's queer how the thing what attracted you to someone is the same as what you come to despise about them.* He was right. For now, she was merely bored with snooker. After another whole season of tagging along, she would come to hate it.

❖ ❖ ❖

As their limo at last headed back to Victoria Park Road in early May, Ramsey brooded. He was always touchy about coming in second, which fortified the popular myth that he didn't quite believe in himself, that whenever he was really up against it he was driven to lose. All he would say aloud regarded some vague intestinal complaint, though he was too shy to explain whether he was shitting too much or too little. Irina was beginning to find his bafflingly complicated relationship to his guts a little trying, and such bashfulness about the biological basics between spouses was ridiculous.

Much as she had pined for months to go "home," as she walked into Ramsey's gaunt three-storey house, Irina's heart sank.

Apparently the home for which she'd really been pining was the flat in Borough. She missed her mismatched Victorian crockery, her multiple rows of spice jars, her 1940s mixer lovingly retouched with green and manila enamel. Having forsaken her motley possessions made her feel like a wanton woman who'd walked out on a homely brood. Yet in mourning the familiar objects of her abandoned household—the stacks of great white pasta bowls, the Delft sugar bowl and matching creamer— she may have used them as mediums for a grief she could not yet afford to face in its animate form. For as she manifested her old flat in her mind's eye, it rang with the ritual rattle of keys in the lock; *"Irina Galina!"* echoed down the hall.

It was a brisk spring afternoon. When Irina suggested a walk in Victoria Park, she hoped it wasn't too obvious that, after carrying on so about longing to come back here, she was immediately desperate to get out. The ducks on the pond had bits of sticks and peanut shells stuck to their feet. After months of too much champagne and hour upon hour of dark, airless snooker matches Irina was exhausted and could think of little to talk about, other than the one subject that she should keep to herself. Ramsey was her husband. It wouldn't be considerate—or wise—to confide on the very day he swept her over his threshold that she was dolorous over another man.

"I'm dying to eat in tonight," she said by the snack pavilion. "Do you mind?"

"Sounds a bother," he said. "Shopping and chopping and washing up?"

"I've been yearning for one night of quiet normalcy."

"Like with *Lawrence*."

"Like with you, you dope. And you've taken me out every night since October. The least I can do in return is make you dinner."

Thus they wandered to the Safeway on Roman Road, drawing numerous salutations from passers-by. Sometimes the kindness of strangers was touching, but today she wished they'd leave Ramsey alone. In the vegetable aisle, as Irina was contemplating stir-fried eggplant with big hunks of garlic, Ramsey tossed organic broccoli into their cart. She'd nothing against broccoli, but it wasn't on the menu.

"You know, I do this dish with eggplant—aubergine," she began tactfully.

"Can't say as I fancy aubergine," he said, grabbing carrots and zucchini.

"For tonight—you have something in mind?"

He shrugged. "I stay in, I always eat the same thing: steamed vegetables on brown rice."

"But you're a *snooker player*!" she exploded in consternation. "When you people aren't throwing your money around, you're supposed to eat chips and beans-on-toast! Not macrobiotic goody-goody, it's all wrong!"

"Us *people*," he said flintily, "don't have to eat rubbish just to suit the stereotypes of punters like you."

Irina looked in exasperation at the packet of chilies in her hands. "I was going to make you kung pao chicken."

"What's that?" he asked suspiciously.

"It's hot."

"You mean spicy? I don't eat spicy. I never understood, why mix food and torture." True, he never ordered dishes with any kick. Even at Best of India, he'd always gone for the chicken tikka, a gloppy bastardization about as fiery as tomato soup.

"My mother claims that my unnatural appetite for hot food is defiant. She says that it all hails from when she put Tabasco on my thumb as a toddler, to keep me from sucking it. I sucked it anyway, though the Tabasco made my eyes water. Seems I got to like it."

Ramsey raised an eyebrow. "I can think of something else we can put Tabasco on."

"Mmm. Might sting a bit." Alas, no amount of flirtation resolved a clash in tastes whose disappointment for Irina was strangely piercing.

"Go ahead and make pow-pow chicken if you want," Ramsey urged. "I can do the vegetables and rice on my own."

"I'm not going to make myself a separate dinner." Putting the chilies resignedly back, Irina muttered, "*Bozhe moi!* My mother would have had better luck putting me off sucking my thumb if she'd coated it in steamed vegetables and brown rice."

When she picked up a litre of milk, Ramsey said, "I don't eat dairy."

Irina crossed her arms. "I've watched you eat dairy for the last seven months. Scallops with *saffron cream*? Did you think that Oscar's used blenderized tofu?"

"I eat out, I make exceptions."

"But you eat out every night."

"All the more reason that when I kip back home I knock off the cow. Otherwise there's nothing for the saffron cream to be an exception to."

Irina frowned. Such minor incompatibilities should be negligible in the face of true love; still she battled an absurd impression that Ramsey's dietary fastidiousness was catastrophic. "If you don't mind my saying so, you're kidding yourself, and you're a hypocrite."

"Blimey! Heavy hitting for Safeway."

"I have strong feelings about food."

"So you can understand as how I might have strong feelings as well."

"Most people do."

At last they were agreed on something. Yet to confirm that otherwise they were batting a perfect score of zero, she had to ask: "You do at least like *popcorn*?"

"Sticks in my gut. And tastes like polystyrene, don't it?"

"If you say so," she said miserably, and carted her four bags of Dunn's River kernels back to their shelf.

They strolled back down Roman Road with their boring groceries, each carrying excessive weight in one hand that they might hold hands with the other. "By the way," said Irina, "I suspect my mother's Tabasco story is apocryphal."

"*Apoca*-what . . . ? "

"Oh, never mind."

Ramsey dropped her hand. "It cuts me to the quick when you do that."

"Do what?" Irina stopped and turned to him. "What did I do?"

Ramsey rested his load on the pavement. "Whenever you use a word I don't know, or mention some news story that's passed me by—"

"You mean, like the death of Princess Di?"

Their eyes met, and they took the measure of each other. Ramsey only concluded after a beat that she was teasing, for the remark was right on the edge of something else. He put on an expression of shock-horror. "You mean, she's *dead*?"

Irina clapped his shoulder. "Sorry to break it to you."

"Why, my appetite's clean gone to shite, then," he said gamely, picking up the groceries and walking on. "We'll skip our tea and I'll blub my eyes out instead."

"At this point, weeping really won't suffice, friend," she said, falling into step. "Only suttee would make the slightest impression."

"Sauté?"

"Just a joke." She reached for his hand again, but he pulled it away.

"You done it again," he said sharply. "*Never mind*. It's condescending. I know you like my dick. But you seem to think my head's just a Global Positioning System for transporting it to your fanny."

"Look—you explain a joke and it's not funny."

"You think I'm a doughnut."

"What's a donut?"

"A Yank should know what a doughnut is."

"When an American says *donut* he generally aims to eat it."

"There now, see? Even if it ain't funny, you want me to explain myself."

"All right," she said. "*Suttee*. The custom in India whereby a widow throws herself onto her husband's funeral pyre to be burned alive."

"Bit over the top."

"Something like being buried with your possessions—a wife being one of them. It's a big feminist issue on the subcontinent."

"Fair enough. That wasn't so bad, was it? 'Cause for me it was interesting. And what about a-pack-of-whatsits?"

"Pack of . . . apocryphal?" She smiled and squeezed his hand. "More or less, a *pack of bull*. It means mythical."

"Why didn't you say *mythical* then?"

"Because if I change the word I'd rather use on the assumption you wouldn't understand it, that *would* be condescending. Still, I'm sorry. I don't think you're a *donut*. You live in a very"—she scrambled for a better word than *narrow*—"rarefied world. I may have a larger vocabulary than you do, because I went to college, and I didn't skip high school to hang out in snooker halls. But I also don't earn hundreds of thousands of pounds a year for my celebrated attacking game. As for current events, living with Lawrence I didn't have any choice but to keep up—because we spent virtually all our time together talking about politics. That's not a boast. It's actually appalling."

❖ ❖ ❖

Ramsey's huge old-fashioned kitchen retained its original Victorian fixtures, for he had purchased the house before London's scourge of "renovation"—the mysterious practice of facilitating a substantially higher price for a property because you had gone to the trouble of ruining it. Ramsey's cabinetry was solid oak, his old double-sink proper porcelain. The tiles were slate, the cold grey counters not crushed marble with epoxy resin but the real thing, and the massive Aga cooker was a museum piece. But Ramsey's meagre utensils comprised one dull knife and a wooden spoon; he had one small pot (rice) and one large (vegetables) and one of those rinky-dink basket steamers that were always losing leaves.

As she set about the dispiriting business of sawing broccoli into florets, Irina inquired further after the parameters of her new cooking regime: No butter. No cheese. No processed flour or grains. No red meat. No salt. No sugar.

"You say no sugar, but what do you think sauvignon blanc is made of?" she asked, nodding at his brimming glass the size of a goldfish bowl.

"All the more reason not to bung more in," said Ramsey, perched on a stool by the long wooden table.

"And what about soy sauce?"

"Soy sauce is the business."

"But soy sauce is chock-full of sodium, much more than a sprinkle of table salt."

Ramsey shrugged. "I like it."

"And I *like* Irish butter, parmesan, and New York strip!"

"Go ahead."

"We'll not sit down to separate meals. Before long we'd sleep in separate beds."

"How do you figure?"

"I can't explain, I just know there's a relationship. We have to be able to eat together. But where did all this ascetic nonsense come from? Were you kidnapped by a killjoy cult?"

As she hacked through the vegetables, Ramsey explained that in the early 80s he went through a crisis. As a teenager he was a prodigy, setting records left and right; when he first turned pro, he cut a swath through tournaments with the ease of an electric lawn mower. But then Steve Davis and Alex Higgins hit the circuit, and he was "caught between the stools."

"Steve Davis was kind of the Stephen Hendry of his day, wasn't he?"

"Right—dull as ditch water. The poncy, eat-all-your-mushy-peas sort of chap; plays terrible slow. I can't tell you how hacked off the punters got in them days, when Davis won another bloody World Championship. And on the other hand, there was Higgins. The Jack the Lad, the bad boy. Fast and nasty. More press off the table than on. Overrated in terms of product, but—a genius all the same," Ramsey begrudged. "Wearing all manner of paisley rubbish and silly hats. You know Higgins got a *medical exemption* from wearing a dickie bow? He passed off some waffle about having a *skin condition*!"

"Ramsey, the guy is now an inch from one of those homeless men in trash bags who wash in bus stations. Why does he still make you mad?"

"'Cause I *fell between the stools*!" (A mantra.) "I'd not coldcock opponents in the hospitality room nor play fancy dress to offend the refs. I couldn't compete with Higgins for being a rank shite, and didn't try. But I couldn't compete with Davis for boring, perfect git. If nothing else, I was a *mite* hip."

"We were talking about salt," said Irina. Pressing the dull blade into the carrots hurt her hand. "Surprise! Somehow we end up talking about snooker instead."

"Maybe I talk round the houses 'cause this period ain't my favourite to recollect. Dropped off the circuit. Drunk as a sack, most days. Lived on crisps, burnt through all the dosh. I've not got much time for blokes what think falling into the gutter takes talent. But I will say your Ramsey Acton don't do nothing by halves."

"So what pulled you out of it?" asked Irina warily. Men always seemed to tell tales of self-abasement with pride, and she delivered the cliché with a sour twist: "You finally *hit bottom*?"

"No such thing as bottom. Things can always get worse. No, what turns around any man, love?"

"Whole grains?"

"A bird, of course. Ariana. I told you about her."

When he'd first mentioned the woman in Shanghai, she'd found the name annoying. "You mean the dumb, long-suffering one."

"She sees me play at Pontins when I'm seventeen and never forgets it, right? So round about '85, Ariana finds me in a pub in Manchester giving the barkeep a bollocking over last orders. Sweeps in like an angel. Puts me on a strict brown-rice diet, and drives me to the local snooker club every day. It's a bastard, but I get my game back. Though I fancy it's never been the same as before. You never trust something you lose, even if you find it again. Like a bird, come to think of it. She messes about and comes back, you can kiss and make up, but you're never so cozy as you was."

Chopping with an eye only to dumpy old steamed vegetables was laborious. All the joy of cooking was gone if she couldn't add chopped chicken thighs, peanuts, and mounds of nefarious chilies. "Seems you have a history of women following you around and wiping your nose. Sometimes I get the impression that what you hold against Jude is she wasn't a step-'n'-fetch-it bootlick."

"What's up your arse?"

"For one thing," she said, leaning into a carrot, "it's *up my arse* that I'm making the crappiest dinner I've ever prepared in my life, mostly to service some superstition of yours that dates back to the 1980s. You totally ignore these nutritional edicts on the road, meaning most of the year. Why should I cook as if I'm at a Zen ashram just so you can touch base with a conversion on the road to Damascus with some ass-kiss vegetarian slag?"

"Damascus?"

"Never mind."

"Call it *superstition*, it's all the same to me," he said coolly. "When the season's through, I like to clean out the system. Purify. Find that a laugh if you like. Anorak Man would."

Irina stopped chopping. The remains of her appetite rolled off like her last slice of zucchini. This evening was signally failing to embody the "normalcy" she had craved. But normalcy as she once understood it was apparently a thing of the past. So far she and Ramsey had either been high as kites—on booze, on sex, or simply on each other—or anguishing over the latest dreadful abuse she'd visited on poor Ramsey without even noticing. In walking out on Lawrence she had unwittingly repudiated the steady-as-she-goes, and for the moment she was undecided as to whether swapping the glassy waters of popcorn-and-TV for the stormy swoop, lurch, and plummet of these last seven months was a criminal swindle or the biggest bargain of her thrifty life. In any event, once you were pitching down the sheer bank of a breaker in open seas, it really didn't do much good to contemplate whether it would have been wiser or more relaxing to be paddling in circles on a duck pond.

"It's disappointing for me!" said Irina, still holding the knife. "Find it pathetic if you want, but I like to feed people!"

"You are feeding me."

"I'm feeding you—yuck-nothing!"

"But it's what I want. So why's that not make you happy as Larry?"

"Because I like to make things. It's not so different from illustration—which I also *used to do* a fair bit in the *olden days*. I like to prepare dishes that are interesting and exciting and beautiful. This is the culinary equivalent of stick figures and lollipop trees!"

"So it's not really for me a jot. You cook for your private satisfaction, not to *feed people*. You want me to tell you how good it is and how clever you are."

"Oh, crap! You like to give your audience a good game, don't you?" Analogies to her own work clearly fell on deaf ears. "Well, making brown rice and steamed vegetables every night is like sinking the colours on their spots over and over again!"

"Sod it," said Ramsey, rising from his stool and sweeping all the vegetables Irina had chopped in a single motion with his forearm to the floor. "Let's go out."

Irina stood looking down at the litter of florets and arduously sliced carrots. She bristled at the waste. Still, her skin tingled. Hitherto Ramsey had picked all the fights, and it had been energizing not to sink into an injured little funk for once, but to get mad.

Ramsey raised her chin. "What's this really about? Can't all be broccoli."

Irina closed her eyes; her exhale shuddered. "Lawrence loved my cooking."

"Anorak Man's just the other side of the river," said Ramsey, pulling her hips to his. "I could drive you there in twenty minutes. I wager he'd be chuffed to see you. Tell him the whole lark's been a mistake. If we motor, we could get you back in time to stir up a right nice supper. With sugar and salt and stacks of red hot chilies."

This was hardly the first time Ramsey had made this generous offer, and had he done so from across the room it would have been a declaration of war. But his arms around her back made all the difference, and she looped his neck with her hands. "Don't be a *donut.* But let's sit down a sec. Pour me a glass of that sauvignon. There is one thing we have to talk about, and you're right. It's not broccoli."

They repaired to the snooker room downstairs and settled on the couch. Irina cadged one of Ramsey's Gauloises, spewing the smoke in a high stream that celebrated not having to endure Lawrence's disapproving glare, and putting from her mind that her daily intake, never in days past exceeding one or two fags at the most, had stealthily risen to half a pack.

"I can live without my clothes and household stuff," she said, tucked under Ramsey's arm. "But I've left a project unfinished. I've got to get my drawings and art supplies. So be prepared for the fact that I'm going to have to drop by and see Lawrence."

The arm around her stiffened. "Why see the bloke? He works, don't he? You still got keys? We can go together, and clear off all your kit whilst he's away."

"Look." Irina sat up, with the pretence of tapping an ash. "I don't want Lawrence to come back from work one day, and all this stuff has vanished without so much as how-do-you-do. It's too brutal. Besides . . . I want to make sure he's okay."

"How *okay* is the bloke going to be, if his bird's left him? Let him get on with it!"

"Hold on. You're not expecting that I'll never see him again, are you?"

"That's bang on what I'm expecting! You're the wife now, no mucking about!"

"It would be one thing if he'd beaten me or cleaned out my bank account"—she took a hefty slug of the sauvignon—"but he's been the soul of kindness and generosity, and I won't repay that with cold-bloodedly turning my back!"

"I'm getting well knackered hearing all about how *good and kind* Anorak Man was—if he's so bloody *good and kind,* go back to the gobshite!"

She stood up. "You know, *every* time we have a fight—meaning, three times a week—you raise the stakes to whether we're together at all. What was the point of getting married if it was only by way of presenting you with constant opportunity to threaten divorce? And it's cheating. You're like a poker player who bets towers of chips on every hand, so in order to call you the other player has to risk everything he has. Which, so long as we're on the poker allusion, also means you're *bluffing*!"

"Bollocks, I'm bluffing!" Ramsey cried, springing from the sofa and jingling his car keys in her face. "I'll drive you to sweet, adoring Anorak Man right now!"

"Which is all by way of not talking about one problem in particular!" Irina shouted back. "Like, I have to get my stuff, and I won't sneak into the flat behind Lawrence's back. Or: yes, I'm in love with you, but I never said I'd never see Lawrence again just to make you feel safe. No! We always have to address the big question of whether we're going to make it at all, so we never get around to the little questions that are the only ones you have a hope in hell of getting your hands on! It's childish, Ramsey! Can't get through those little questions and the big one is a *moot point.*"

"*Moot,* what's *moot*? You can stuff your *moot* right up your arse!"

She burst out laughing. Apparently domestic discord was a sport. She'd been hopelessly out of shape last autumn, but the muscles were starting to come on. Maybe the best hope for this marriage wasn't in gelling it into a harmonious aspic, but in learning to give as good as she got.

Ramsey lassoed her waist and swept her to the couch. "Let's go get you something bunged with chilies. That knocks your socks off. And everything else whilst we're at it."

"Best of India. I'll skip the main course and just eat pot after pot of *lime pickle.*"

As Irina lay across Ramsey's lap and caught her breath, he traced her moist hairline with a forefinger. "What's with this spicy-food lark? What's the draw?"

Head flung back, she pondered the matter. "I like playing a line— between pleasure and pain. Like cheeses so high that they almost taste awful, but not quite. And with chilies, it's also about sensation. Raw sensation. The extremity of it."

"Sensation, is it?" said Ramsey, sliding his hand under the waistband of her jeans. "I'll show you sensation."

They never did make it to Best of India that night. But lime pickle or no, Irina would be playing a line between pleasure and pain for some time to come.

❖ ❖ ❖

For Ramsey, to put any point of contention permanently to rest was to throw something perfectly good away. Thus the question of how Irina might retrieve the tools of her trade was anything but settled, and consumed virtually every evening for the next few weeks. Exhausted by reiterations of how she really *was* over Lawrence and multiple assurances that she *wasn't* conniving to arrange a romantic rendezvous and pain-staking postmodernist deconstructions of just exactly what she'd meant by wanting to find out if he was "okay," she negotiated a compromise: she would pick up her things at the flat on the Q-T while Lawrence was at work, but without Ramsey. Irina managed to impress upon him the horror all around if by any chance, however remote, Lawrence chose that of all afternoons to come home early, to find not only his estranged partner absconding with her possessions on the sly, but the scoundrel who had stolen her away. If she was appealing to Ramsey's cowardice, she was also employing a skill that, absent his acquaintance, might forever have lain dormant.

She lied.

In truth, she had quietly e-mailed Lawrence from Ramsey's computer. Their exchange was brief. Lawrence agreed to take an afternoon off, and meet her at the flat.

The irony of sneaking around to see Lawrence just as she had once sneaked around to see Ramsey was not lost on her. But there was no chance in hell that she was going to covertly disappear herself from Borough, leaving Lawrence to experience entry into his own home like a sock in the jaw. Besides, what drove her most powerfully to arrange a meeting with Lawrence she was reluctant to explain. Ever since coming back from Sheffield, burning through the fog of sexual intoxication, a vision in the back of her mind had grown steadily more insistent.

It is late. After eight or even nine. With no one to jump up at his return, to sally to the kitchen to make popcorn, he has no motivation to cut short his work, to which he has turned with a vengeance these last few months. Tonight, after lingering in the office, picking aimlessly through Web sites, at last he trudges the walkway along the Thames in the chill mizzle of a cold spring. Wearing faded black Dockers and a maroon-and-black striped button-down that Irina had always liked, he shoves his hands deep into the pockets of his 50s reproduction baseball jacket, a present for his fortieth birthday. Maybe this jacket ought to have become repugnant to him. Instead, all her presents, freshly finite, have grown more precious. He will persist in wearing this jacket to work well past the point that it's too warm for the season.

The lights of the South Bank across the river glimmer with all the Shakespeare and Pinter that he once yearned to make time for. Now he cannot imagine getting up the gumption to see a play. By himself— no way. The slope of Blackfriars Bridge feels steeper than usual. Off to his left, Tower Bridge twinkles in the distance. Its fairy-tale turrets used to look, if not beautiful, at least hilarious, and now just look hokey. If the walk also seems longer than it once did, he would have it take longer still.

Nearing the flat, he surveys the heavy postindustrial neighbour-hood with its Victorian remnants of red brick. He searches for his former sense of satisfied ownership, of having annexed a Dickensian domain far from trashy Las Vegas. To the contrary, he feels like a foreigner again, and wonders what he's doing here. Moving to Britain had seemed a well-calibrated adventure at first. The natives at least nominally speak English. An American can get the nuances and really come to grips with the place. Yet now Britain feels like any old somewhere else, somewhere he doesn't belong. He wonders if it's time to pick up stakes and move back to the States. He still prefers the company of Americans, who don't have broomsticks up their asses. And maybe shipping back to the US would keep at bay the confusing sensation he suffers almost nightly: an overweening ache to go "home" when he's already there.

He traipses to the first floor according to the Brits, which he insists on calling the second. He fumbles with his keys. The stairwell's timer-light is out. It was always Irina who nagged the management company to make prompt repairs. Inside, the flat is also dark. He forgot to open the drapes this morning. Without the street lamps glowing through the windows, he gropes for the switch. The flat is not strictly silent. Past rush hour, the traffic on Trinity Street is still thick. But the rev of engines and irritable honk of horns outside don't provide a reassuring sense of human bustle nearby. They merely press the existence of several million strangers he doesn't give a shit about.

Big surprise: he turns on the TV. Its yammer might have been a reminder of too many happier evenings squandered in front of the tube, but he is not a what-might-have-been kind of guy. BBC2 announces the upcoming broadcast of the World Snooker Championship in Sheffield. Most men in his position would hasten to change the channel. He decides to leave it on. He likes irony. He may even like to torture himself, though circumstance seems to be torturing him without his help. Besides, he doesn't consider keeping snooker in the background an act of maso-chism. He's staring reality in the eye. He may be running a distant risk of tuning into that miserable prick. But he's a strong man. He could look the miserable prick in the eye, too. There's always the danger that he will ram his fist through the screen. The satisfaction might be worth a few hundred quid. He likes the image. He saunters to the kitchen for a peanut-butter cracker.

He has resolved to eat proper meals with vegetables. Yet so far by the time he gnaws through a handful of these peanut-butter crackers, he can't get it together to steam broccoli. He stands over the cutting board to catch the crumbs. His eye roams the kitchen. The shelves by the stove are still lined with all those spices he hasn't a clue what to do with—though apparently a good third of the array is for sprinkling on popcorn. The spices will get stale. Meantime the long rows of jars make passable wallpaper. Of course, every room in the flat is impressed with Irina's hand. The only time he tried to participate in the décor was when he put his foot down about that green marble coffee table. Now look—he loves it. But it's in the kitchen her presence is the most insistent. Arcane condiments from the West Indies and Thailand, when all he needs is mustard. The counter-encroaching clutter of pasta-maker, food processor, meat grinder, when one sharp paring knife will suffice. He could pile all this junk into boxes. He won't.

He roams back to the living room with a beer, semireclining, as ever, on the green couch; he has yet to sit in her armchair. It's nice here. She did a good job, finding all this wacky secondhand furniture that somehow fits together, and for a song. What a cheapskate she was. Is? (That bastard is loaded.) If only he'd had advance warning, he'd have spent more money. On her. Gone places.

This is the stuff people think on deathbeds. You know, why didn't I max out my credit cards. Well, he's not dead yet. Just ailing. He'll get over it. These are still early days, and they have to be the worst. Think of it as any other discipline, like getting through all the other things you don't want to do—revising the article on the Ulster peace process for that fool at the National Interest, crunches at the gym. As he ponders, pretty much every task in his day falls into the category of what he doesn't want to do.

Christ, she must have spent a solid week sewing those drapes, with linings and everything. Never made drapes before, and they came out like a pro's. She was handy.

Oddly, he finds reminders of her more consoling than painful. Which doesn't make a lot of sense. He knows that he should be angry. He knows that he probably is. He knows that he would be better off if he hated her, not necessarily a lot but a little. But he doesn't want to and it doesn't come naturally and it probably wouldn't help after all. She's a perfect idiot, and that's a shame. But stupid is not the same as bad. Maybe that's a distinction he might have allowed a while ago.

He didn't used to think like this—about how he feels. He prefers to think about what he's doing, about what he's going to do. But Irina doesn't realize that not thinking about what you feel is not the same as feeling nothing. He doesn't like to embarrass himself, and he had thought she understood. Apparently not. Or maybe she just doesn't give a damn what he feels, though he has a hard time believing that. Anyway, as for this feeling crap, there is only one rule now, which he enforces with military discipline: he is at liberty to think about anything else he likes. But he is absolutely forbidden to imagine that she might come back.

The snooker is not very riveting. He can't tell if it's the match itself—Graeme Dott, who looks about four years old, and that weasel Peter Ebdon, who's always punching the air like an ass when he wins—or his state of mind. (Should Miserable Prick have been on air he might even have found the exercise in an-tipathy invigorating. Still, he is relieved to skip it. He was at the office for almost twelve hours today, and he's tired.) Faced with this sport, he may always flinch a bit from now on. But he doesn't see why he has to forswear snooker altogether. In fact, he resists its being taken from him along with everything else. Man, who would have guessed that such a harmless pastime would produce consequences so cataclysmic. Then, maybe if it weren't that lying, narcissistic prick, it would have been some other creep. He himself is reliable, smart, decent—even Irina would agree—but maybe that's just another way of saying that he's the kind of man that sooner or later women leave.

By the end of the evening, he has allowed himself one more beer. He resolves to cut his nightly consumption back down to one. He brushes his teeth. Her toothbrush is right where she left it. He has to remind himself to turn down the heat and chain the door, because these were Irina's jobs. But overall, the course of his evening has not really changed much since she split. True, he eats too many peanut-butter crackers and Indian takeouts. He misses her cooking, but not quite as much as she might expect. Food isn't that important to him, not nearly as important as it is to her. What he misses most of all— however sleazy this might sound—is her doing the shopping.

And there is one standard ritual that he's had to chuck. He tried going through the motions once, and it made him cry. So he can't eat popcorn. The picture of a grown man bawling over a bowl of popcorn was too humiliating to repeat. He'd added too much salt anyway. The bottom of the batch had burned; the pop under the lid had been dull and fitful. The grudgingly exploded kernels were tight, and stuck in his teeth. In his throat, more like it.

In bed, he reads a few pages, and considers jerking off. [It is here that Irina's imagination was stymied; she never did know what went on in his head when he got hard, and she still didn't.] *He decides it's too much trouble. He would have to go get a washcloth to keep nearby, or make a mess.*

He did plenty of work today, wrote a good ten pages on the piece for Foreign Affairs. *He put in a heavy workout at the gym, and skipped lunch. He should be pleased with himself. But the only thing that pleases him is that one more day is over.*

The etiquette of such occasions was obscure, but Irina stayed on the safe side and knocked. She had a key, and the deference felt unnatural. At the last minute, she hurriedly slipped her wedding ring into her pocket. She should break the news gently when the time was right—and when would the time be right? When Lawrence opened the door, she experienced a mild shock: she'd never apprehended him before as a solidly middle-aged man. The last several months may have taken their toll. Or perhaps they had enabled her to see him as the age that he actually was.

"Hi," they both said shyly. Lawrence kissed her uncertainly on the cheek.

"Coffee? Or would you rather start packing?" he offered.

"Let's have coffee first," she said, though she didn't want any. She trailed him to the kitchen. The flat was neat, and nothing had changed. Because this was his flat now, Lawrence would prepare the coffee. She hovered as he ground the beans.

Whatever he was saying, it was impossible to pay attention. The flat itself was too distracting. To enter these rooms was to visit not only the past but an alternative present, and their sheer physical reality exerted an alarming pull, tantalizing her with the ease with which she might simply hook her bag on the rack and never return to Hackney. The flat held a secret that she needed to crack. As Lawrence made small talk, something about a washer on the hot-water tap, her glance ping-ponged from the spice rack to the Spanish anchovies to his fast-forward older face, frantically taking the measure of how she felt. What had this life been like? Was it deficient in some way; had it all been a sham? No . . . Life in Borough was simply different than life in the East End. Known, but anywhere and anyone you stayed with would become that. She did not feel unhappy here; they must have had an agreeable life together. It was a tad stuffy, pent up, but the verdict of her first reentry was that she could have left, and could have not. What good was *that*?

"So," said Lawrence once they'd carted their coffee to the living room in the usual glasses, though Lawrence hadn't added quite enough milk to hers. "Are you all right?"

"I'm fine," she said.

"You look pale. And too thin."

"I'm underslept." Embarrassed by what this might seem to imply, she added, "The last few weeks. We've had some conflicts. It takes hours to hash them out." In fifteen minutes, she was already telling tales out of school.

Lawrence had a stricter sense of decorum, and didn't ask conflicts about what.

"You and I never fought much," she went on uneasily. "I'm not good at it."

His eyes sharpened. "He doesn't hit you, does he?"

"No, never!"

"If he ever lays a hand on you, I'll break his thumbs."

She smiled. "*The Hustler.*"

"Good pick-up. At least he hasn't turned you into a complete idiot."

She sighed. "Oh, go ahead, have fun. You've earned it."

"I've *earned* nothing, it was dumped on me. And it's not fun."

"I worry about you, Lawrence."

"What good does that do?"

"No good. But it would be appalling if I didn't. Don't you worry about me?"

"Habit's hard to break."

"Speaking of habits, before I forget." Irina rummaged her bag. "I got you a present." She handed him a plastic bag. "It's tiny and stupid."

Lawrence pulled out the packet of a dark red mixture and looked at it uncomprehendingly. "Hey, thanks!" he said. He had no idea for what.

"Popcorn seasoning," she explained. "One of your favourites. It's hard to find. I knew we were out"—the *we* was a slip, but correcting it would only make matters worse—"so when I came across dry garlic chutney in the East End, I picked you up a bag."

As he held the little packet limply in his lap, she realized that the gesture was misjudged. In her delight at locating the obscure masala in the Indian shop on Roman Road, she'd reminded herself that Lawrence's sudden allergy to popcorn had merely materialized in her imagination. Surely, she'd reasoned, he still ate popcorn with a beer every night, because such a routinized man would take solace in ritual, in sameness. But now she suspected her initial intuition that the snack had overnight become anathema to him was probably accurate. The dry garlic chutney clearly depressed him. When he put it aside on the couch she even wondered whether as soon as she left he would throw it away, maybe taking it immediately to the wheelie bins out back the way he would quickly dispose of a chicken carcass, lest it begin to reek.

She apologized, "It's amazing I didn't show up here with an armload of groceries and your dry cleaning."

"You're not responsible for me anymore."

"That's funny. I think I am. Once you assume a certain kind of responsibility, I'm not sure you're at liberty to give it back."

"Sure you can," he dismissed. "Look, I'll be okay. As for our splitting up, it's not so great. Not what I wanted. But I'll get over it. They say it takes about a year."

"You've never set much store by what *they* say."

"Yeah. Chances are that's horseshit." Despite his pretence of practicality, he was having trouble looking her in the eye. He trained his gaze forty-five degrees to the left of her face, as if there were a third person sitting at the dining table. "By the way, I had an option on going to Russia this last month. Big Chechnya project, but I passed."

"I'm surprised. Why didn't you go?"

"Don't let this swell your head, but—Russia's too wrapped up with you. Even the language. I figured I'd hear, you know, *Privyet, milyi!* on the street and mistake it for your voice. Maybe if we'd been able to go to Moscow together . . . Spilt milk, I guess. Funny, I thought I was really interested in the place. When the grant came through for the project, I was excited at first. But without this—association . . . Turns out I don't give a shit about Russia. Kind of weird."

"*Nu shto zhe tak,*" she sorrowed. Yet the language jarred, much like the dry garlic chutney, as staking a claim to an intimacy she had forsaken.

"You know, I knew you'd be back," said Lawrence. "Your illustrations of *The Miss Ability Act* are due at the end of next week, and you're a pro."

"You remember my deadline?"

"I remember everything that's important to you, and for you."

"I'm a little behind on that project," she admitted. "I got an extension."

"I've never known you to deliver a project late. But you can't have drawn much the last several months. Unless moneybags has bought you a new set of art supplies."

"No, it's been something of an impromptu holiday."

"Must have been some party. Your body's thin, but your face is puffy."

"I told you, I need sleep."

"And you're smoking."

"Just a little!"

"I can smell it." He pulled up short. This wasn't the direction he'd have wanted their meeting to go. "I know you think I'm oppressive. But I just want you to take care of yourself. That's all it's about. Not trying to *control* you or something."

"I didn't say that."

"Guess you could tell me a thing or two about snooker now!" he said with false heartiness.

She smiled with one side of her mouth. "More than I'd prefer."

"Be careful what you wish for."

"I didn't wish for snooker. It came with the territory."

"I'm damned what you did wish for, but that's my problem."

"I don't expect you to understand."

"Good. I don't." He seemed to struggle with something, and succeed. "You can't neglect your work, Irina. You'll regret it. Chuck me, but keep that."

"It's been a big change. I haven't reached an equilibrium."

"Are you going to all his tournaments?"

"So far," she said cautiously.

"If you don't watch out he will *eat you alive*." Lawrence assumed the voice of her conscience. That's the role he'd always assumed, so no wonder she'd fled. One's conscience is not always charming company.

"You should trust me," she said without thinking, since the repost was predictable.

"I did."

Irina looked down. "I worry that I'll never be the same again. I still don't feel *good*. As in constant. Trustworthy."

"I wouldn't have wanted you to stay with me out of virtue. As if you were doing me a favour." He shrugged. "You should have done what you wanted."

"What I *wanted* wasn't so simple."

"Sure it was." His face lurched to one side like water in a bucket. Other people would read the expression as snide, but Irina could see it for a wrench of anguish that he was trying to disguise. "You wanted to fuck me, or some other guy."

"N-o-o . . . One of the things I wanted was to be a woman who keeps her word."

"We never got married. You didn't break a promise."

"I think I did," she said. "And I've always hoped to be a woman who loves the same man for a long time. Now I can't have that anymore. Even if I stay with Ramsey until death us parts, I'll always have left you. At first I was upset about betraying you; now I'm upset about betraying myself."

He had never been comfortable with this kind of talk, and he still wasn't. "Don't give yourself a hard time on my account. I'm a *survivor.*" His pronunciation was bitter, like, look at the clichés you've reduced me to. In fact, this whole scene seemed suddenly to embarrass him as the kind of melodrama that in the lives of others drew his contempt, and he stood up. "Want to get to it?"

Irina slid her coffee onto the green marble coffee table. The little she'd drunk had soured her stomach. The picture of his pouring most of her Guatemalan dark roast down the drain after she'd left was unbearable. "I guess."

In the studio, several collapsed cardboard cartons leaned against her drawing table, atop which sat a roll of packing tape, a tape gun, and a black felt-tip marker, all still in their packaging from Ryman. There was a new portfolio for the drawings, too; he'd chosen an expensive brand.

"All these packing things must have set you back," she said. "You should let me reimburse—"

"Don't be stupid." As he briskly assembled a box, Lawrence's businesslike demeanour granted her permission to go about this task with a similar stoicism. If they got maudlin over every paintbrush, he implied, they'd be here for a week.

"Lawrence, I can do this by myself."

"It'll go faster with two of us," he said grimly. "Go ahead, get a move on!"

Irina rolled up her sleeves and focused on which materials she couldn't live without, and which, like the craypas, had been a passing dalliance she was unlikely to use again. Directed to whole shelves of pencils, charcoals, and coloured inks that had to go, Lawrence wrapped them into neat rolls of old *Daily Telegraph*s. He was an industrious man, even when going about the systematic destruction of his own universe. At length, they both seemed to take a perverse pleasure in being engaged in a project together again, and to grow wistful when the cartons were taped and labelled, the portfolios tied.

"Don't you want to take anything else?" He gestured at the prints on the walls.

Irina recoiled. "No!" The notion of removing a single element of his familiar landscape was horrifying.

"What about your clothes?"

"I don't know—there's nowhere to put them. You know British architecture, there are hardly any closets, and Jude absconded with her wardrobes. I've picked up a few things, and Ramsey has—a lot of clothes." Just then, the musical chairs of modern romance seemed if nothing else an organizational hash. Apparently the phenomenon most fuelling property demand in London was divorce, requiring two residences where once a single dwelling had sufficed. Wasn't monogamy more efficient? How many times in your life do you really want to buy a blender?

"He's something of a dandy," said Lawrence.

"I know you—you mean a faggot."

"Wish he were." He smiled. They were playing.

Irina wandered to the bedroom and flipped through her thrift-shop finery, shabby compared to the gear that Ramsey had bought her, at whose price tags he never glanced. In fact, she'd felt self-conscious showing up this afternoon in a blouse that Lawrence had never seen. As the primary launderer of the pair, he was the intimate of her every sock, and was sentimental about her most tattered tops. He'd spent £5 on a pre-treatment preparation for the turmeric stains on that faded blue polo-neck, when the shirt itself had cost £1.50 at Oxfam. By lavishing so much care on the garments, he had come to own them more than she did, and Irina closed the wardrobe empty-handed.

"One more thing," Lawrence raised in the living room, not looking up from last week's *Economist*. "Your mother. She's called several times now. I palmed off some excuse about our being too strapped to come to Brighton Beach last Christmas, but she's expecting us this year. You obviously haven't told her we've split up. I don't think it's in your interests that I do the honours. So get it over with."

"She likes you," Irina despaired.

"And I can't stand her, so? I don't want to have to field any of these calls again."

"I'll tell her." Irina's voice was steeped in dread.

"Now, is Asshole coming to pick you up?"

"No. I'm supposed to take a taxi."

"Supposed to. You're taking orders now?"

"I seem always to be taking orders from *somebody*."

Lawrence rang for a minicab, and negotiated with the dispatcher over finding a car with a large capacity trunk. (The exchange took longer than need be because Lawrence refused to say *boot,* and the dispatcher refused to understand *trunk*.) He carried the cartons downstairs, and wouldn't let her haul a one. He waited with her at the kerb, loaded the cab, and proffered a twenty to cover the fare.

She hesitated. Twenty quid was too much, and Ramsey was rich. But demurring might imply that she didn't need him now, or that the gesture hadn't touched her. She accepted the bill. They faced each other on the pavement.

"So far," he said, "do you think you're going to stick this out?" Something had changed. Lawrence was learning to ask about *the main thing.*

The three words were difficult to lift from her mouth. "I think so." Imagine how much harder it would be to tell him that she was married.

"Be careful," he said. He didn't mention of what.

"Careful would have been staying with you," she said wanly.

"Don't drink too much!"

"I won't."

"Get some work done!"

"I'll get some work done."

"And *stop smoking!*"

"*I shall always wear my hat,*" Irina sang from *Amahl and the Night Visitors.* The opera's responsive parting between mother and son (*Wash your ears! / Yes, I promise / Don't tell lies! / No, I promise / I shall miss you very much . . .*) had always raised the hairs on her neck.

"You should take that CD," said Lawrence. "You like to play it at Christmas."

Irina searched his face. *"Why are you so nice to me?"*

"You were nice to me for almost ten years," he said gruffly. "Why should that count for nothing just because it's not going to be eleven?"

◘ chapter seven ◘

Once the Good Friday Agreement was signed, Lawrence was called away almost nightly to rant about it on television. Naturally, awaiting his return, Irina tuned into whatever programme on which he was to appear. He looked handsome in his brown suit—unsettlingly so—and his accelerating lucidity on camera unnerved her as well. You'd never have guessed that a few years before this overnight celebrity was working retail in bookshops and parked blackly on weekends before televised golf. Although she wouldn't claim nostalgia for those dismal days, something was on offer when Lawrence was depleted or vanquished or sad that was simply not available when he was full of himself. And full of himself he certainly was. In making every effort to be "supportive," had she created a monster? The more dazzlingly self-sufficient Lawrence became, the less he seemed to need her. Hence in bolstering his self-confidence all these years she may have been systematically eliminating her own job, like a member of a special in-house task force on corporate downsizing, whose final undertaking is to fire himself.

So it was probably from this fear of becoming superfluous, and a nervousness about being demoted from equal partner to underling who microwaved dinner for the Great Man at midnight, that Irina found herself watching his interviews with a jaundiced eye. Lawrence was likely so negative about the agreement because he hadn't seen it coming; the very week before Good Friday, he'd predicted that the impasse over would keep the parties fighting it out for years. He hated to be wrong. She couldn't share his indignation over the prisoner releases. Their victims were dead; what more could be gained by keeping the culprits in jail? Lawrence scorned this kind of thinking, but weren't a few shorter sentences a small price to pay for an end to all that killing? She'd never say aloud anything so unkind, but when he quoted whole sections of the agreement verbatim, he sounded smart-alecky, like the kid with all the answers, whom his classmates despise.

Thus after several nights of the same drill, she treated herself to a channel on which Lawrence was sure *not* to appear—BBC1, currently broadcasting the British Open. As luck would have it, Ramsey Acton was playing. Ever since Bournemouth, Lawrence had been unaccountably less engaged by snooker; having thus seen precious little of the game for months, Irina had stored up an appetite for the sport. After so much sonorous pontificating about peace and paramilitaries, it was glorious to watch a man go about his business and keep his mouth shut. Since Lawrence had yet to raise the possibility of dining with Ramsey again, the odd televised tournament provided her only access to their old friend.

There was no doubt about it: Ramsey cut a fine figure of a man. She may never have precisely regretted not kissing him on his birthday, but as she followed his clearance of 132, Irina renewed her appreciation for the temptation. He executed a series of uncanny long pots, ingenious doubles, and cracking plants with mesmerizing grace and savoir faire. Despite his faultless performance, a subtle suggestion in Ramsey's demeanour—of bearing up more than bearing down, with the kind of courage that you see at funerals—reminded her of Lawrence in the bleak days of West 104th Street. Ramsey exuded a woundedness that made her want to reach through the glass and place a reassuring hand on his temple. So it was silly, she supposed, but Lawrence wasn't back yet, and Irina indulged herself by resting her cheek on the cold screen.

Only to spring back when Lawrence walked in the door. "The screen was dusty!" Hastily, she wiped the glass with her sleeve.

"That's Ramsey."

"Oh, you know you're right!" she said brightly.

"You're not telling me that you see a guy on TV who we've had dinner with a couple of times a year since 1992, and you don't recognize him."

"Well, of course, now that I'm paying attention, I *recognize* him . . ."

"So now you can stop recognizing him," said Lawrence. "The segment for *Newsnight* was prerecorded, and I'd really like to catch this one."

Without asking, Lawrence grabbed the remote and switched to BBC2. Irina's shoulders drooped. Ordinarily she kept up with current events, but honestly, tonight the idea of yet another newscast bored her speechless. So she wasn't being sardonic when she submitted, "But I don't care about *world affairs*. All I care about is *snooker*."

◘ ▣ ◘

By the beginning of May, Irina finally bullied her famous know-it-all partner into a Saturday constitutional. Their walks in Cornwall over Christmas had been overcast with her anxiety over his strange silence on some impending trip to Russia. Now that Lawrence hadn't dropped word-one for over six months, Irina was beginning to relax about the whole business. Dandering past Buckingham Palace (incredibly, still littered with withered floral tributes to Diana), she reasoned that the Russia gig must have been cancelled. Unfortunately, they had to cut short her favourite section of the walk, the circuit around Hyde Park and Kensington Gardens, because Lawrence had to find a loo—or, no, "had to take a dump," a vulgar expression that made her cringe. Indeed, he was jubilantly explicit about his evacuations, and though she was as keen as the next woman on intimacy, surely reports on texture and buoyancy qualified as *oversharing*.

Before they walked the last two blocks home, Irina noted that they needed a few things for dinner, and proposed a quick trip to the Tesco ten minutes south.

"Okay," said Lawrence. "I'll meet you back at the flat, then."

"Why don't you come with me?" While not rippling from a Nautilus like *Bethany,* Irina's arms were firm from routinely hauling forty pounds of groceries by herself.

"I hate shopping. You know that."

"It's not my idea of a party, either. Do you think you're above shopping? That it's woman's work?"

"Division of labour. More efficient."

"We're not a corporation, we're a couple. And I'd appreciate the company."

Scowling, Lawrence reluctantly joined her. As soon as they hit Elephant & Castle—decked with a giant plaster elephant like a dipso hallucination, a shopping centre of such suicidally depressing design that it was a wonder you didn't dodge customers plunging off the roof on a daily basis—he began to plough several feet ahead as if to disassociate himself from the enterprise. When she caught up with Lawrence at Tesco, he was wrestling violently with a shopping trolley. Unaccustomed to the acquisition of goods in this country, he did not understand that you had to slip a pound coin into the handle to release the trolley.

"What would you like for dinner?" asked Irina as she did the honours with the coin. For men, incompetence was a gambit: *I'm terrible at this; you do it.*

"Everything you make is great, Irina," he said wearily. "Whatever you want." Lawrence's idea of participation in meals was eating them. *Division of labour.*

Thus when she proposed, "How about kung pao chicken?" he answered, "Fine," flatly. Carte-blanche command over the menu may have amounted to a dumb kind of power. But power too readily ceded seemed worthless.

Picking her way nimbly between shoppers, Irina collected chilies, chicken thighs, an array of vegetables, as well as milk, cheese, ham, bread, and Coleman's mustard. But she was constantly losing Lawrence, who would either careen down the aisle when it was clear, or loiter behind sullenly, refusing to ask anyone to move out of the way. So far it was more trouble to shop with Lawrence than without him—which was, of course, the point.

"What's all this?" he complained as the trolley mounted.

"Your lunches, among other things. Where do you think your sandwiches come from, fairies?" The subject left a shadow. She wondered what happened to those sandwiches if he was really eating lunch with *Bethany* at Pret A Manger.

Their timing was poor. The after-work crowd had hit the shop, and the queues for checkout stretched fifty feet into the aisles. Lawrence kept looking at his watch, turning steadily purple. As they inched towards the front, he refused to crack a smile, even when she read off the supermarket's comically exotic flavours of crisps—"Chargrilled Steak and Peppercorn Sauce," "Creamy Chicken Pasanda and Coriander," "Slow-Roasted Lamb and Mint," "Peking Spare Rib and Five Spice"— which conjured a whole meal from a handful of carbs and twelve hundred calories in fat.

"How about 'Roast Turkey and Stuffing, Candied Yams, Overcooked Brussels Sprouts, and a Glass of Cabernet-Merlot' crisps?" she proposed. "Or 'Salmon with Rocket, Cheesecake with Coffee, and a Double Measure of Hennessy XO While Wearing a Red-and-Black Smoking Jacket and Watching Reruns of *Yes Minister*' crisps? I bet they could even add an ashy aftertaste of a postprandial fag."

Lawrence wasn't playing.

"Fuck," he said once they were finally outside again. "I'd rather starve."

"You would starve if I didn't wait in queues like that two or three times a week."

"I don't know how you stand it. If it were up to me, I'd live on peanut-butter crackers and beer from the minimart."

"Not living with me you won't. But don't worry, I'll never ask you again. Tesco is obviously too grubby for Mr. Fancy Conflict-Resolution Expert."

Hence the mood, on return to the flat, was a little sour. Yet long ago weary of her experiment, and now convinced that matter had been shelved, Irina decided it was time to put that vixen's mischievous rumour to rest.

"So," she said casually, deboning chicken thighs as Lawrence washed dishes. "I overheard a mention at Blue Sky a while back. Something about a trip to Russia?"

"Oh." He intently sudsed a water glass that only needed rinsing. "I thought I told you."

A piece of cartilage took similar concentration to cut out. "You know you didn't."

"Well—guess I was putting it off."

"I guess you were. How long are you going for?"

"About a month."

"A month!" Irina's knife paused. "When is this?"

"Couple weeks from now."

"When were you going to tell me, packing for the plane?"

"Tonight, actually, if you hadn't brought it up."

"That's easy to say now."

"I wasn't going to just disappear."

Ripping the skin off another thigh, Irina pondered once again how difficult she found it to simply say to Lawrence what she was thinking as she was thinking it. She pushed herself to ask boldly, "Have you not considered my coming along?"

"Nah," he dismissed, sloshing rinse water onto the floor. "You'd be bored."

"It's my country. Why would that bore me?"

"It can't be *your country* if you've never been there. And you've said yourself that you try to put as many miles as possible between you and your 'heritage.' "

"I try to put as many miles as possible between me and my *mother*," said Irina, chopping chilies. "And I've never bought her sentimentality about a place she left when she was ten. That doesn't mean Russia doesn't interest me."

"Forget it. Your coming along would cost a fortune. Hotels in Moscow are larcenous for foreigners—and don't imagine that you'd be considered anything but."

"I earn my own money; I could pay for it. Besides," she added shyly, carving out a pocket of chicken fat, "maybe I could get paid something for being your translator."

"The Carnegie grant covers the cost of a translator, who'd be more experienced. And we're trying to arrange a side trip to Chechnya. You'd never get security clearance."

"I wouldn't have to come to Chechnya. I could stay behind in Moscow."

"Irina, you're not thinking! You have work to do. This should be a great opportunity to bear down while I'm gone."

"I'm ahead of schedule for Puffin already, and I could bring my drawing kit along."

"You're not going to be productive holed up in some hotel!" said Lawrence, mashing peanut butter on a cracker. "And if you were, then there'd be no point in your being in Russia to begin with."

So far this conversation was reminiscent of the Peter, Paul and Mary ballad "Cruel War," in which a girl appeals repeatedly to her soldier lover to allow her to come with him into battle. She makes a variety of arguments, offering, for example, to tie back her hair and don a uniform to pass as his comrade. The refrain, *Won't you let me go with you?* is regularly followed by the mournful, *No, my love, no*—albeit mournfulness was noticeably absent from Lawrence's own discouragements. As Irina recalled, the girl's beseechings are all in vain, save the last—and she scrambled for the successful verse. *Lawrence, oh Lawrence!* (okay, the soldier's name in the song was Johnny, but the substitute had a ring) *I fear you are unkind! / I love you far better than all of mankind / I love you far better than words can e'er express / Won't you let me go with you?* Finally, soft and sibilant: *Yes, my love, yes.*

"But I love you," Irina blurted, realizing as she did so that sappy folk songs weren't an optimal source of inspiration when cajoling a wiseass like Lawrence Trainer. "I can't make you take me with you, and I'll understand if you don't. But I'll miss you. I don't want us to be apart for a month."

Alas, *Yes, my love, yes* was not forthcoming.

"I don't, either," he said. "Still, we both gotta do what we gotta do, right? And nobody travels on business with wives or girlfriends anymore. This'll be a boy thing."

"If it's a *boy thing*, does that mean that *Bethany* isn't coming?"

"Bethany's not somebody's wife. She's a research fellow."

Irina grabbed yet another fistful of chilies. "You mean she is coming."

"I don't know—maybe."

"You do too know! And maybe means yes!"

"What's it matter? She speaks perfect Russian—"

"So do I!"

"But you are *not* a fellow at Blue Sky, you are *not* up on the separatist war in Chechnya, and you are *not* covered by a grant from Carnegie!"

"You forgot to mention that I'm also not a slag." The pile of chopped chilies was now mountainous even by Irina's immoderate standards, and glistened with evil intent.

"Look, we'll be doing interviews all day, and you'd feel like a third wheel."

"You just want to have your own special thing!" Irina exploded. Briefly, the image beckoned of sweeping all the preparations for dinner dramatically onto the floor—but they were not that kind of couple. "You *know* I could come as long as we paid my way, and you've said that I'm pretty good at holding up my end of things with your think-tank cronies. But you won't let me because you want to have Russia all to yourself, so that it's yours and not mine!"

Propped against the counter, Lawrence blinked. It was not their habit to put subtext on the table, any more than it was Lawrence's habit to concede that there was one. "If," he said after a pause, "I would like to have my *own special thing*, what is wrong with that?"

"Nothing," she said defeatedly, surveying the makings of kung pao chicken with no appetite. "Except that the alternative would be to do something together, and have Russia as something we have in common, instead of a place you've colonized for yourself because you got there first."

"Irina," he said with unusual earnestness. "It's important that we both maintain our independence."

"I don't think that's our problem, *maintaining independence.*"

"I wasn't aware we had a problem."

"No," she said sorrowfully. "You wouldn't be."

If the purpose of spicy cuisine was to play a line between pleasure and pain, it was apparently possible to tip full-tilt over to pain, period. The chicken turned out hot beyond precedent, and neither managed more than a few bites.

◘ ◘ ◘

The fortnight's lead-up to Lawrence's departure for Moscow was civil but strained. Irina never took back what she said about his *own special thing* or softened her sense of injury over not being invited. When it was time for him to leave for Heathrow, they both agreed it wasn't *sensible* for Irina to accompany him to the airport. As he watched for his cab out a living-room window, Lawrence asked with seeming idleness, "So—do you think you'll see some people while I'm gone?"

"Sure, I suppose."

"Well—like who?"

Irina tilted her head quizzically. "Betsy. Melanie. The usual suspects."

"And I guess you'll see your editor. And that author you're working with."

"That's right." This was filler dialogue, and she was perplexed why he drew it out. He knew her friends, and as for which she elected to consort with in his absence, she'd be bound to tell him as these occasions arose when they spoke on the phone.

"Anyone else?" His expression was so anxious that she got it.

In another life, or in another relationship, Irina might have been able to reassure him expressly. But for the same reasons that Lawrence wouldn't own up to what he thought about when they had sex (whatever those were), she and Lawrence had never discussed what lay at the heart of that night in Bournemouth last autumn, much less the Gethsemane of Ramsey's forty-seventh birthday. Were they ever to do so, this was not the time and place—the air crackling between them for weeks, Lawrence's cab due any moment. Nevertheless, Irina did hold his eyes an extra beat, and imbued her response with a gravity that she prayed he understood: *"No."*

The flicker of relief in his face seemed to indicate that the interchange had been a success, though there was no way to know for sure.

◼ ◼ ◼

While Lawrence was in Russia, Irina was very productive. Because she was mad at him, she didn't pine, and never wandered the flat with that floating, disconnected vagueness that had sometimes afflicted her while he'd been in Sarajevo. She rose promptly with an alarm, tidying up the coffee grains after the pot was on, sweeping militantly to her studio with her cup. So dutifully did she toil over her drawing table that the illustrations for *The Miss Ability Act* were in danger of getting overworked, and she completed the project well before its due date. On long walks late afternoons, she didn't stroll so much as march. She made time to see friends two or three nights a week, injecting these evenings with such vivacity that Betsy remarked on her good form. She was careful to keep her alcohol intake moderate, and to eat sensibly, though couldn't resist the odd cigarette as a token of up-yours-Lawrence defiance.

In all, she was an efficient little mechanism, who had her own work and her own friends, and the fact that in Lawrence's absence she was *just fine,* thank you very much, provided a mean satisfaction. Still, there was a thin, brittle feeling to this just-fineness, as if she'd turned into one of those dry Scandinavian crispbreads that never have enough salt. If her evenings of a readily dispatched bacon sandwich were refreshingly simple, they were too simple. Maybe it was embarrassing for an emancipated woman of the 1990s, but Irina was possessed of a profound drive to do for someone else, and when it was merely a matter of taking out her own rubbish, acting on her own desire for an oatcake and slice of cheddar, half the time she couldn't be bothered.

When she masturbated on restless afternoons, the physical gratification was technically more pronounced than when she was forced to depend on Lawrence's poignantly flawed ministrations. Yet even here, the simplicity made for thin gruel. Maybe some measure of what made sex with someone else so much more interesting was what was wrong with it. The most thunderous orgasm still seemed trifling unshared, and unlike the drifting bask that followed on proper sex, in private there was no afterglow. She missed postcoital smugness—that unspoken mutual congratulation over a job well done.

Thus her very one-two-three competence at solitude throughout the month served only to demonstrate that, living by yourself, this was as good as it got, and that wasn't good enough by a yard. Returning from walks to an empty flat, she couldn't tell Lawrence about the irksome invasion of American evangelicals at Speakers' Corner in Hyde Park, drowning out the crusty soapbox socialists who, post-Blair, had become quaint, for-tourists-only anachronisms, like the classic red phone box. Untold, stories didn't seem quite to have happened. Inexorably, then, Irina was once again thrown back on her understanding of herself as a woman who craved, more than professional kudos, material prosperity, the respect of peers, or the camaraderie of close friends, *a man.* If that made her small-minded, biologically trite, unrealized as an individual, or lacking in self-respect, so be it.

Said man, however, was incommunicative, even for Lawrence. He blamed the sparseness of his phone calls on a hectic schedule, but their few conversations yawned with so many gaps of silence that she sometimes imagined that the connection had failed. Of course, Lawrence never liked talking on the phone, and if his discourse comprised meetings recounted or set-piece recitations of the historical justifications for Chechen secession, he always took refuge in facts. They were inept enough at addressing touchy subjects face-to-face, so the rift she'd opened between them over this trip was hardly going to be bridged in short, expensive phone calls from a Moscow hotel. At least he didn't take umbrage at her forceful iterations of how swimmingly her life was proceeding in his absence; why, she rather wished that he would. Times past, they had both had trouble issuing that most difficult of romantic licences: permission to have fun without you. For her own part, Irina had to make herself sound interested in his adventures. Why hadn't he wanted her along? Why was the stingy thrill of annexing *her* country for his own not outweighed by the benefits of annexing all that tundra for them both?

◻ ◻ ◻

The music of the front-door lock was off-key. The usual jingling symphony of his key ring jangled the still afternoon air; the rake of metal in the escutcheon was abrasive. Now accustomed to having the flat to herself, Irina felt invaded. It was Lawrence's flat, too, she told herself, and there was nothing presumptuous about his walking in without knocking. She waited for his traditional mating call—*Irina Galina!*—to resonate down the hall, but heard only a shuffle and slam. He lumbered into the living room and unshouldered his bags. Though washed out, he looked younger than she remembered, and he had definitely lost weight.

"Hey!" He pecked her cheek, and didn't meet her eyes.

For intimates even small partings are estranging, but for a moment the distance between them seemed so great that this might have been a first awkward platonic reunion after a harrowing breakup. "Hi," she said shyly, and offered, "Coffee? Or would you prefer to start unpacking?"

"Sure, let's have coffee first." He trailed her to the kitchen, looking around with the nervous curiosity of a guest who had only been here once before and did not quite remember the location of the loo. Doubtless he was just confirming with his usual paternalism that she'd hoovered the carpet. But idling as she ground the beans, he did seem distracted, making her running commentary about problems she'd been having with the hot-water tap feel like tiresome domestic prattle. Still, someone had to say something. For pity's sake, a month in Russia should hardly leave one at a loss for words.

"So," she said once they'd carried their coffee to the living room. Lawrence looked at his glass critically. He liked it with less milk. "Is everything all right?"

"Yeah, fine," he said.

"You look pale. And thinner."

"I'm underslept," he said. "The last few nights. The group's had some conflicts, over our sympathy, or lack of it, with the Chechens. It's taken hours to hash them out. As for thinner, well, you know the food in Russia."

"No, as a matter of fact I don't. I've never been there."

"I'm here ten minutes, and you want to fight?"

"I'm sorry, I didn't mean that to sound pointed. I don't want to fight. If nothing else, I'm no good at it."

"You got pretty good at it before I left." It was Lawrence who seemed to want to fight. He kept his gaze trained forty-five degrees to the left of her face, as if there were a third person sitting over at the dining table. He wasn't drinking his coffee.

"Well, you'll be pleased to learn that Betsy's on your side. She said, 'Hey, it's a business trip!' And pointed out that if I really wanted to go to Russia so much, I could pick up and go on my own."

"She's right."

"I know. It was annoying." She took a sip. "Though I doubt I'll go. *Ya nye khotela syezdit v Rossiyu. Ya khotela syezdit v Rossiyu s toboy.*"

"Irina, would you *give it a rest*?" he exclaimed.

She flinched. She'd tried to deliver the thought with conciliating tenderness. Yet in *I didn't want to go to Russia, I wanted to go to Russia with you* he could only hear nagging. "I'm sorry. Drawing is very involving in a way, but my work is all in a room sitting, and sometimes I envy your going interesting places and meeting new people."

"Well, that's not my fault. If you want a more adventurous professional life, do something else."

It was disconcerting; they were both basically saying the same thing, yet concurrence staunchly took the form of dispute. Even when she bowed her head and said, "I know it's not your fault. That's what I'm saying," they still didn't seem on the same side. She gave up, and changed the subject.

"By the way, my mother already wants to know if we're coming for Christmas."

"Oh, great."

"Of course, we could always go to Las Vegas instead . . ." Irina threatened.

"Anything but Vegas. I guess Brighton Beach gets us out of that."

"My mother likes you."

"I could be anybody so long as I tell her she's wearing a nice dress."

Irina felt a building desperation to provide him something positive to have come home to. So far he'd returned to a woman who was bitter about having been left behind, whose work was dull, and whose family was burdensome. But she could only lay her hands on the very sort of lame compliment that Lawrence had just pilloried: "Speaking of which, I like your new shirt."

The fact that he'd arrived wearing clothing that she didn't recognize had heightened his unfamiliarity when he walked in. The black crewneck with a slashing diagonal red line and punctuating white dot suggestive of Russian constructivism was more daring, and frankly more stylish, than Lawrence was wont to don.

"Oh, yeah. Got it in Moscow, at GUM."

"*You* went *shopping*? Without a gun to your head?"

"I don't see what's so suspect about that. I've bought things in my life."

"I didn't say it was 'suspect.' Just out of character."

"Well, I was ah, I was looking for something for you. In fact . . ." He got up to rustle around in his luggage, and came up with a plastic bag. He thrust it into her hands. There was no card. The present wasn't wrapped.

Giving anyone anything takes courage, since so many presents backfire. A gift conspicuously at odds with your tastes serves only to betray that the benefactor has no earthly clue who you are. Accordingly, showing up at the door with a package could be more hazardous than arriving empty-handed. Tendering nothing risks only seeming thoughtless or cheap. Barring the generic gratuity like a nice bottle of booze—and the neutral offering has its own pitfalls of seeming too impersonal or cautious—any present risks exposing the donor for a fool, and the relationship as a travesty.

But the choker she pulled from the bag was quite pretty—a band of black velvet with a delicate floral enamelwork in the centre. Its finely painted bouquet against a cream background was characteristic of a Rostov finift. So what was it about the gift that didn't quite work? The word? Given the prickly tenor of his homecoming, did "choke-her" sound upsetting? That was absurd. No, it was just this funny feeling that it could have been anything. See, Lawrence hadn't seemed impatient to give her the bag as soon as he walked in, nor had he made anxious inquiries about whether she liked it when she first pulled the choker from its tissue paper, and now he wasn't fussing over it to show her how to work the clasp. So she had a hunch that, perhaps bought in haste on the last day in order to give her "something," the present didn't mean much to Lawrence, in which case it couldn't possibly mean much to her. Even if the choker were expensive, Irina might have been more touched had he rocked up instead with a little package of Russian seasoning for their popcorn.

Oh, she was being unreasonable! Lawrence had been run ragged, and for him to have darted out for any token at all was sweet. She thanked him profusely, and put it on.

Irina followed him into the bedroom, where he took his bags to unpack, frustrated that it was only four-thirty, which precluded a reunion activity like a drink or dinner any time soon. Nevertheless, she was taken aback when Lawrence announced that he had a box of documents from the trip to haul to Blue Sky, and he was leaving for the office.

"Can't you do that tomorrow?"

"I've got e-mail to catch up on. Don't worry, I'll be back in time for dinner."

The box was heavy, and he decided to ring a minicab. Irina walked down with him to await its arrival at the kerb. She knew he was busy, and behind at the office. Still, there was something very, very wrong about his having been gone for a whole month only to flee after a single cup of coffee that he didn't drink. It was so wrong, so disturbing on a ground-shifting, tectonic level, that as soon as she started to think about it her mind shimmied over to whether to dress the salmon tonight with a vanilla sauce or sesame seeds and soy.

When the taxi pulled up, they faced each other on the pavement.

Displaying the sleeve-tugging insecurity that Lawrence couldn't abide, she asked, "You are glad to see me, aren't you?"

Yet rather than act annoyed, Lawrence looked into her face long and soberly, and for the first time since his arrival met her eyes. He wrapped his arms around her and pressed her hard against his chest. "Of course I am," he said. "Very glad."

She was so grateful for the moment of warmth that it seemed to wipe out all his previous combativeness in a stroke, and she touched the choker at her throat with a resolve not to find it meaningless but to treasure it always, because it was beautiful and because anything from Lawrence necessarily meant the world. Yet as he scooted into the cab and waved, assuring her that he'd be back by nine at the latest, she had the eerie impression of saying good-bye to him in a more profound sense than the one in which one commonly bids farewell to a man who will return a mere four hours hence for dinner.

❖ chapter eight ❖

For Ramsey, playing was work. Summers, he worked at playing. To celebrate his forty-eighth birthday that July, he took Irina on a trip to India to visit the Ooty Club, where he gave a spontaneous exhibition of trick shots on one of the world's first snooker tables. On their return, there was always something that beat labouring over a drawing in her stuffy garret—wine-soaked lunches, afternoon cinema, a spontaneous excursion to Dover. By the time the snooker season resumed in October, Irina had made pitiful progress on *The Miss Ability Act*.

Mindful of her springtime vow to knuckle down, she gave Bournemouth a miss, albeit with regret; if the Ooty Club was "the cradle of the game," Bournemouth was the cradle of their marriage. Yet the dislocated sensation that afflicted her on the road grew only more manifest in their large, empty home. She would pare her nails, sharpen pencils, fix tea. It's not so simple a matter for an artist—however she avoided the word—to "knuckle down." She'd make a mark on the paper and it was wrong and the paper was spoiled and she would have to start again. Grown accustomed to companionship morning to night, Irina had lost the knack of solitude.

If only for distraction from the harrying task of tracking down her peripatetic talent, which seemed to have wandered off like a naughty child, Irina filled the gaps in the furnishings left by Jude's plunder. Habitually, Irina headed down to the Oxfam shop in Streatham. Although while Ramsey was in Bournemouth she found several lovely pieces for a song, his Platinum MasterCard in her wallet undermined her satisfaction. Indeed, Irina wasn't cut out for wealth, and with money infinitely on offer found the world curiously cheapened. Negotiating an expensive city on a budget took ingenuity and cunning. Times past, snagging yellow-tagged supermarket mangetout in excellent condition for half-price had made her feel victorious. Now that their average weekly restaurant bill that summer must have been £1,000, how could she feel clever for saving 60p?

Ramsey rang every evening on his mobile from the Royal Bath bar, and she could hear the carousing in the background, the crooning and ballyhoo and clinking of glassware. When she'd been along for the ride, the swanning from hotel to hotel had seemed tiring and depersonalized; from a distance the tour inevitably appeared glamorous again. In the vacuum of the stay-at-home wife, she grew paranoid. Snooker players were dogged by packs of adoring fans, not all of whom were boys.

Ramsey's take on the Monica Lewinsky scandal across the pond was at least reassuring; the hoo-ha was rapidly advancing toward the impeachment of President Clinton. Unlike most Europeans, Ramsey didn't deride the American public for being unsophisticated about the perks of power. Nor did Ramsey trot out the hackneyed assertion of the day that must have disquieted American women coast-to-coast: *All men lie about sex, right?* Rather, Ramsey said that if you'll lie about sex, then you'll lie about anything, because if a man will lie to his wife, he'll lie to anybody. Too, Ramsey said that a man who would put such an august career on the line for the sake of a little "messing about" with a groupie was a gobshite.

Still, after hours of aimless snacking, fags lit and extinguished and lit again five minutes later, and dull, uncomprehending confrontation with blank sheets of paper, who could blame her for fleeing such a dismal life for the adoring companionship of a lovely man at the UK Championship in Preston in November?

Right before Christmas, she pulled three all-nighters straight to meet her extended deadline for *The Miss Ability Act,* more than once breaking down in tears. Irina conceded to herself on the way to deliver the portfolio to Puffin that perhaps the last ones were a little "hasty," but at least she got them in on time. Nevertheless, fatigue, insecurity, and a soiling sensation of having done a slapdash job on her homework was not the best preparation for Christmas in Brighton Beach, and for finally introducing her mother to not only Ramsey Acton himself, but to the fact of the man's existence.

❖ ❖ ❖

After Lawrence's chiding, Irina had headed off her mother's calls to Borough by ringing Brighton Beach frequently herself. She did hint that she had a "surprise" when announcing that "*we* are coming for Christmas," but demurred from identifying the constituents of the pronoun. Since there was no telling how her melodramatic mother would react to her having left dependable Lawrence Trainer for an impetuous snooker player, Irina decided to simply show up with Ramsey Acton at the door. It was a plan indicative either of a newly matured boldness, or of a regressively childish desperation to put off the unpleasant for as long as humanly possible.

En route to Heathrow in the Jaguar on December 23, Ramsey nipped and surged in and out of traffic with the usual nervy precision, and being whizzed about zip-zip-zip was thrilling. Yet by Hammersmith, she laid an apprehensive hand on his arm. "Now, you know that my mother is difficult," she said.

"You made that more than clear."

"And you know it isn't easy for me to visit her, at the best of times. And this isn't the best of times. That is, she won't be expecting you. She's obsessed with order, and people like that don't like being snuck up on. They like to know what's coming."

"So why didn't you tell her on the blower?"

"As I told you, there's a raw power in a person standing physically in front of you that brooks no argument—and that may shut her up. But I want you to make me a promise."

"Shoot," said Ramsey.

"Promise me that under no circumstances will you pick a fight. You can berate me up one side and down the other when we come back. But even if I get drunk and dance naked on a table, you will not, *will not* take it up with me in Brighton Beach."

"Why do you assume we'll have a row?" he asked, sounding wounded. Their every set-to had lodged indelibly in the part of Irina's brain that stored other major traumas, like car accidents and the deaths of close friends. Ramsey never seemed to recall having spoken a single harsh word.

"I'm not assuming anything," she said. "I'm asking you for a promise. Ironclad, pinky-swear. You haven't made it yet."

"Fair enough." He shrugged. "No rows. I promise."

Irina squeezed his arm and thanked him, but his assent had sounded ominously offhand. Like the inexpensive toys she used to get for Christmas from distant relatives, a promise cheaply given was prone to break the first time you played with it.

❖ ❖ ❖

At duty-free, Irina could no more stop Ramsey from springing for a bottle of Hennessy XO than she'd been able to discourage his purchase of first-class tickets. Indeed, turning a blind eye to the buckets of money that Ramsey threw at any problem or pleasure was becoming the norm. At first Irina had grabbed the odd lunch bill; lately she hadn't bothered. She didn't harbour any presumptuous notions about his funds being hers as well now that they were married. Still, Ramsey was rich, he enjoyed spending money on her, and it was amazing how readily a woman who once spooned out the Cajun seasoning at the bottom of the popcorn bowl to use again could adapt to plane tickets that cost—well, she'd rather not even think about it. And merely because those complimentary toiletry kits were, according to Ramsey, "the business." Never mind that for the price of a miniature spritzer of noisome cologne, foam earplugs, and two tablespoons of mouthwash you could probably put a down-payment on a small house.

On the plane, the service was solicitous, and they did get rather tipsy. Between queries about how he'd fared in the UK Championship, the flight attendant was forever asking if Ramsey wanted another box of chocolates or an extra blanket.

Extra blankets came in useful. Irina had always spurned that "mile-high club" nonsense, for she couldn't see the appeal of sexual intercourse atop the plastic toilet of a cramped airline loo that's wah-ing from a circulation fan and reeking of nauseous disinfectant. Yet somewhere over Iceland as they reclined under a mound of tartan synthetic it did seem wasteful to ignore the fact that Ramsey had a hard-on that could have doubled as a police baton for bashing anti-globalist protesters over the head. Once Ramsey loosened his belt, in their dark tent her hand traced the outlines of the most beautiful dick she had ever encountered. It was impossible to say why. Irina may never have been one of those women who find male genitals a little repulsive, but she had never, either, made great aesthetic distinctions between them. But this particular dick was unspeakably exquisite—smooth, simple, and straight, with testicles that snugged close to his groin with skin that was taut and talcum-dry. When Ramsey forced himself to the practice table in Preston last month, she had only to conjure the image of his erection that morning to emit a groan of such helplessness and urgency that the waitress in the hotel café asked if there was something wrong with the coffee. Frankly, she'd become a slave to that dick, and it sometimes alarmed her what extravagant sacrifices she might make or humiliations she might endure just to be allowed to touch it one more time.

They got Ramsey's shirt wet. Once he slipped under her skirt to return the favour, he chuckled in her ear, "I could wash my hands down there!" When he reached her cervix she managed to keep from crying out, but her eyes bulged and the rasp of her inhalation was probably audible. None of their little activities seemed to take very long and they were careful to keep covered, but chances were that the flight attendants knew exactly what was going on. Old Irina would have been mortified. Old Irina had never had a very good time on airplanes, either.

❖ ❖ ❖

As the front door opened, Raisa's outfit obligingly announced the fact that her personality as well was contrived and over-deliberate: a flaming red blouse over a snug black skirt, with a scarf, belt, and heels colour-coordinated in the same precise shade of blinding sun-yellow. It was flashy, it was Sunday-magazine-supplement sharp, and it was too much.

Ordinarily Raisa imbued her every sentence with an artificial enthusiasm, like a mortician pumping embalming fluid into a corpse. Yet she was so nonplussed to find a tall, narrow stranger beside her daughter that she failed to marshal her hallmark theatricality. She kissed her daughter with perfunctory distraction, then asked flatly in a normal-person tone of voice that Irina almost never heard, *"Eto kto takoi?"*

"Mama, I'd like you to meet my husband, Ramsey Acton."

"Tvoi muzh? *Bozhe moi, Irina, ty vyskochila zamuzh!"* She shot a sceptical glance at Ramsey's hose-clip, which he'd forbidden Irina to replace.

"You heard me."

"Tak!" Raisa exclaimed. *"Eto tvoi suprees!"*

"Ramsey, this is my mother, Raisa McGovern." Obscurely, Raisa had refused to relinquish her ex-husband's surname, to keep him and to get back at him at the same time.

"Pleasure," said Ramsey, kissing his mother-in-law with Continental elegance on both cheeks. He was just the kind of man Raisa would admire—graceful, kitted out in soft dark fabrics with expensive tailoring, albeit with that little dash of dangerousness in the leather jacket. Yet her clumsy, wallflower elder daughter had no business marrying such a striking older man. Raisa would be far more comfortable with a son-in-law in slovenly plaid flannel, whose comeliness was at best an acquired taste, preferably two inches shorter than Raisa's own stately height of five-ten, and with chronically poor posture. In sum, Raisa was far more comfortable with *Lawrence*.

"*Akh, izveneete!*" Having recovered a measure of her excruciating vivacity, Raisa ushered the two inside. "*Kak grubo s moei storony! Pozhaluysta, prokhodite, prokhodite! Dobro pozhalovat!*"

"Mama, Ramsey would feel a great deal more welcome if you'd speak *po-angliyski*. You'd never know it, my dear, but my mother has lived in this country for over forty years, and does speak English of a kind."

"*Rumsee? Rumsee Achtun, da?*" It was all an act, including that Slavically trilled R on Ramsey's first name. When she deigned to switch to scrupulously crummy English, that was an act, too. "I no can get over it! When you two marry? *Ee gdye Lawrence, Irina? Shto sloochilos s Lawrensom?*" As if Ramsey couldn't translate the word *Lawrence*.

"Lawrence and I have amicably parted ways. And please don't take exception to not being invited to the wedding. No one was. It was a registry-office job, just the two of us."

"This very sudden, *da?*"

"Yes, Mama," Irina lied; their first anniversary was last week. "Very sudden."

Raisa led Ramsey upstairs to deposit their luggage in Irina's old room, then gave him a tour of the house, which she'd bought for a pittance with the spartan proceeds of her divorce when her marriage finally went up in flames during Irina's senior year of high school. (The dowdy hovel's now being worth a small fortune was a fact about which Raisa was both smug and secretive.) She'd made a beeline for the increasingly Russian enclave, where she could live among *her people* and feel superior to the Jews at the same time. Presently, she'd be wanting to show off her studio to Ramsey, in order to impress upon her guest that she was not just anybody but an accomplished ballerina and famously strict dance instructor (Raisa boasted that her students were afraid of her) who still worked out at the bar indefatigably every day. Raisa was not going gentle into that good night, and Irina supposed, despite herself, that her mother's ferocity at sixty-four was impressive.

Exhausted at three London-time, after too much wine on the plane and too little sleep while meeting the deadline for *The Miss Ability Act,* Irina sank—insofar as it was possible to *sink* into such uncomfortable furniture—into one of the parlour's red velveteen chairs. Deserting a nice man for a raffish snooker player was sufficiently scandalous behaviour to cast her in the liberating role of black sheep. So why had she still felt bound by the convention of coming home for Christmas? Ramsey was the only man who had ever made her feel beautiful. Her mother always made her feel dowdy, unfit, and mousy by comparison. On the boardwalk, men still stared at Raisa's calves. While Irina was proud of her mother, in a way, there wasn't much point in presenting her husband with this statuesque paragon of muscle—with a slimmer waist, higher cheekbones, and more lustrous bound black hair—only to show herself up.

When the other two returned, Ramsey ran his hands over her shoulders and kissed the hollow behind her earlobe. Her mother's eyes sharpened. Raisa didn't approve of "groping" in public. No matter how obvious it appeared to Irina that behind that stern glance of reproach lay jealousy, Raisa herself would never recognize her sense of decorum as the bitter fruit of sexual neglect. In fact, because the unself-aware—which includes basically everybody—are impervious to uncharitable perceptions of their underlying motives, all these insights you have into people and what makes them tick are surprisingly useless. Censure registered, Raisa excused herself coolly to the kitchen.

As the matching red velveteen chair was insensibly positioned so that one of the shelves supporting Raisa's hideous porcelain figurines jutted into your neck if you leaned back, Ramsey pulled it four inches forward before taking a seat. As the legs sank into fresh royal-blue carpet, Irina's eyes widened in alarm. When soon thereafter Ramsey popped upstairs to the loo, she shot up and restored his chair to its previous position.

Ramsey returned, having retrieved the Hennessy XO. He looked at the chair.

"You don't know the drill," Irina whispered. "She'll go bananas if you make new depressions in the carpet!"

"I don't fancy learning *the drill*," said Ramsey, full-voice. He yanked the chair back out a good foot—that would make a second set of criminal indentations in the pile—and slid back into the seat with his long legs extended, as if hoping that someone would trip over them. He reached for his Gauloises. Irina made frantically slashing motions. With an eye-roll, he put them back.

Raisa entered with a tray, the presentation of which, with its glasses resting in filigreed silver holders, was the whole point, since nobody wanted any tea. As for the plate of Pepperidge Farm cookies, it was meant to cameo the fact that Raisa wouldn't have one. Setting the tray on the coffee table, she looked steadily at the legs of Ramsey's chair. Held any longer, her gaze would have set the carpet fibres on fire.

"So, *R-rumsee*," Raisa began after she'd poured a round. "What you do for living?"

"I'm a snooker player."

"*Snookers*," Raisa turned around in her mouth. "This—game?"

"It's a game," said Ramsey tolerantly.

"Card game? Like bridge?"

"The closest thing to snooker in the US is pool," Irina intervened. "You know, when you hit balls with a stick into pockets on a green table?" She rued the fact that her description made all forms of billiards sound inane, but there was no limit to the English words that her mother would pretend not to know. Why Raisa imagined that to live in a country for decades and still have little command of the language seemed charming was anyone's guess. Honestly, every day she must have walked around this house practising dropping her articles, expunging every form of the verb "to be," and converting each hard *Th* to *Z* and *W* to *V*: "*Zis— game? Vat you do for living?*" For a smart woman to maintain this degree of just-off-the-boat authenticity after forty-some years of Jehovah's Witness missionaries, *Reader's Digest* sweepstake mailings, PBS miniseries, and screaming ads for Crazy Eddie's would be hard work.

"You play this—*snookers*," Raisa directed to Ramsey, "for money?"

"*Da,*" said Ramsey. "I play *snookers* for money."

"But you only make this money when you win?"

"Spot on, Mum. I only get paid when I win."

"Ramsey wins a lot, Mama."

286

"So you no know until you play your—*snookers*"—Raisa never took her eyes off Ramsey—"if you have fat pocket or you have nothing." (*Nozzing.*)

"That'd be one way of putting it," said Ramsey neutrally; he seemed to be enjoying this.

"Mama, you don't get it! In the UK, Ramsey's famous. The pool analogy, it's not helpful. Snooker is a big deal in Britain. The players are superstars. They're on TV all the time. Ramsey can't walk down the street without five people asking for his autograph . . ." She was speaking into a void.

"You ever think, *Rumsee*, you get real job?"

"When hell freezes, I reckon." Playing his part to the hilt, Ramsey knocked back his cold tea, then reached for the cognac beside his chair. He peeled off the lead strip, popped the ornate cork, and poured a triple. "Can't see nipping off to an office or such. See, Irina and me fancy a bit of a lie-in mornings. As a rule, I'll have got so dishmopped the night before"—Ramsey took a demonstrative slug—"it takes most of the day to get my head right."

Raisa rose stiffly to remove the tea things.

"That's it, we're going to bed," Irina announced, massaging her temples.

"Oi, the party's just getting started!" cried Ramsey, laying on the South London with a trowel; *started* came out *stah-id*.

"For you maybe," said Irina. "This isn't my idea of a party."

❖ ❖ ❖

"Why didn't you back me up?" Irina whispered once they'd repaired to her old bedroom. "I say you're famous, and you leave me swinging in the wind! She probably thinks you've dazzled me with a few shiny trinkets and your posh clothes, so now I've deluded myself that I've married a celebrity instead of two-bit hustler!"

Ramsey rolled back on the bed and chuckled. "I was winding her up is all. Joke's on your woman, innit?"

"No, the joke's on me," she grumbled, nestling next to him. "But it may not matter. I think you already blew it. She expects a lot of brown-nosing, a real snow job. For my mother, to have flattery withheld is tantamount to being insulted."

"What am I meant to say, then?"

287

"Any man who walks in here is immediately supposed to start going on about how gorgeous she is and what incredible shape she's in and how it doesn't seem possible that she's old enough to have a daughter in her forties."

"Well, I wouldn't, would I? 'Cause she looks like a bloody cadaver!"

Irina sat up. "You don't think she looks pretty good? For sixty-four?"

"That bird looks every year of sixty-four and then some. She's so skinny she makes the skin crawl, and her face is hard—with that ghoulish smile what barely moves. Fair enough, she's her parts in the right place, and them parts are nicely wrapped. But she's sexless, pet. I'd rather shag a cold baked spud. Your mum's not got a patch on you, pet. Haven't you figured it out yet? Why she's always having a go at you, like you told me? She's scared of you 'cause you're *beautiful*. And she's made bloody well sure that at least you don't know it."

"Well, you never saw her in her heyday—"

"Don't need to," Ramsey cut her off. "You was *always* the bigger knockout. And don't you forget it."

Irina smiled and kissed him gratefully, but it was funny; she didn't want what he said to be true. Maybe she didn't see her mother quite objectively. Yet when she was a little girl her classmates were in awe of her mother, and could never fathom how a buck-toothed ugly duckling could have issued from such a swan—impeccably groomed, imperial in manner, and dressed like Audrey Hepburn. That was the picture of Raisa that she wanted to keep. The alternative vision of an emaciated, pinch-faced neurotic growing old alone was anathema.

❖ ❖ ❖

"No breakfast?" Ramsey asked the next morning, which was Christmas Eve.

Irina was perched at the kitchen table over the *New York Times* with a lone glass of coffee, whose bottom she had carefully sponged before setting it first in a saucer, then on a coaster. In preference to explaining that in this household eating was a sign of weakness, she waved him off with a mumble about not being hungry.

Naturally Raisa had been up since dawn, having already worked out at the bar for hours. She was still wearing white tights with cherry-red leg-warmers and matching ballet shoes, whose familiar tap on the lino brought back a whole childhood's worth of inadequacy.

Ramsey was having none of this austerity lark. When his mother-in-law asked if he'd like toasted black bread he said fine, or scrambled eggs, too, and he said brilliant, and he turned a blithe blind eye to her rising horror when he accepted sausage as well as a side of kasha.

"*Bozhe*," said Raisa as she rushed perkily around the kitchen pretending not to feel put-upon. "When I here just me, I go to shops on Avenue and come home with one little sack! Now, with man in house! Whole sack, gone, in one day. So nice, *tak mylo*, to have appetite in house again. Like your father, Irina—who eat like bear!"

"Don't worry, Mama," said Irina; the one advantage of her mother's sledgehammer subtlety, you never had to rack your brains to figure out what she was getting at. "If you'd like us to reimburse you for the groceries, I'm sure that can be arranged."

"*Chepukha*, Irina, I no mean that!"

"Sure you didn't."

Ramsey had gnawed through three pieces of toast before he noticed Irina's hands. "Hey, what's with the gloves?"

It was awkward to turn the pages of the paper. "You know, Ray-naud. It's frigid in here. It's always frigid in here, so I brought several pairs. Thought I'd save the red ones for Christmas."

"You make no notice, *Rumsee*," said Raisa huffily. "Irina wear gloves so her mama feel bad. Big making-point no work if we ignore her."

"But she's dead on," said Ramsey. "I'm freezing my bollocks off. Why don't we crank up the boiler?"

"Because you should see gas bill!" said Raisa, wiping counters feverishly. "*K tomu zhe*, little nip in air keep you awake. Good for circulation, *da*?"

"No, Mama"—Irina kept her voice flat—"my circulation is just what living in a meat locker is *not* good for."

"Wake up in morning and *exercise*, Irina, you stay warm all day!"

"What's the sodding thermostat set at?" Ramsey had removed one of Irina's gloves and was rubbing her chill fingers between his palms.

"Oh, something Arctic. It's in the living room." When he walked down the hall, she called after him, "But Ramsey—!"

He came back. "What's your sixty in Celsius?"

"Sixteen?" Irina supposed. "Maybe more like fifteen."

"That's bleedin' savage!"

Irina lunged after him and grabbed his arm in the hall. "Don't," she

289

whispered. "I had the presumption to boost it a couple of degrees once, and you wouldn't believe the row. It's not worth it. I can wear gloves. I don't mind."

"*I* fucking well mind." Ramsey strode back into the kitchen and announced as Raisa sponged maniacally around his half-eaten breakfast, "Tell you what. I don't fancy my lovely wife tricked out like an Eskimo just to read the paper." He fished out his wallet, and threw four $50 bills on the table. "That should cover a day or two of your gas bill, 'ey?"

"*Nyet,* this too much, you must take back!" Raisa protested, waving the bills. "No money for gas, you my guest!"

"Keep the change." Ramsey strolled off to the parlour, and Irina looked on in amazement at his brazen apostasy as he twisted the thermostat to 75.

❖ ❖ ❖

After breakfast, Irina showed Ramsey around Brighton Beach, disappointed when nothing about the area piqued his curiosity. His eyes searched blankly the line of shops under the el, their marquees printed in Cyrillic, their help-wanted signs in windows specifying, "Must speak Russian!" He was polite enough when she led him into stores full of imports from Israel and the Baltics, with their long counters of smoked fish and shelves of black bread. He did engage briefly when they stopped at a caviar store, where he bought two ounces of beluga for Christmas dinner in the spirit of generosity-as-act-of-aggression that was beginning to typify his approach to her formidable mother. Yet Ramsey Acton's point of entry into any environment was terribly specific. When his eyes swept her old neighbourhood, they were compulsively scanning, in vain, for a snooker club.

Irina picked up a few things to forestall (temporarily) her mother's resentment, making small-talk with the cashiers. For over a year she'd spoken so little Russian, a language that allowed for the torrential emotions that English was too angular to express. Lawrence comprehended more than he could speak, and she missed rolling through a Slavic diatribe about London's larcenous water bills and being roughly understood. Ramsey often asked her to "talk Russian" in bed, but to him the susurrant murmur was gibberish.

They had arranged to meet her mother for lunch at one of the boardwalk's outdoor cafés, in December zipped up with plastic sheeting.

When they arrived, Raisa was already regally seated at a prominent table. Her form-fitting dress was a rich billiard green, as if in unwitting tribute to Ramsey's profession, and maybe if she hadn't accessorized the gear to death with accents of an identical midnight blue the outfit might have passed for classy. For that matter, after encountering on the boardwalk countless old bags wrapped in fake leopard-skin coats and dragging yappy little dogs, Irina was able to see her mother as a beacon of tastefulness in comparison.

Irina opted for a salad. Raisa made do with two tiny toast points laced with salmon caviar. Ramsey ordered pickled herring, lamb-and-rice soup, a refill of the bread basket, chicken Kiev, and a beer. Raisa often enjoyed watching other people gorge themselves, but the injustice of this conspicuous consumption would grate. Ramsey ate like a pig and Ramsey wasn't fat.

He asked respectfully about her history as a ballerina, allowing Raisa to drop, *again,* that it was getting pregnant with Irina that had brought her professional dance career to a close. When he inquired after her teaching, she vented her disgust that these days American children had no discipline, no tolerance for pain, and no capacity to forgo a Ho-Ho in the service of art.

"You find anyone to play *snookers* with?" she said, as one might ask a five-year-old if he had found a little friend to play marbles.

"After playing four tournaments near back-to-back," he said levelly, "winning one and making the finals in three, I reckon I can take a few days off from *snookers.*"

No pick-up.

After downing his third beer and virtually throwing his Platinum MasterCard at the poor waiter, Ramsey announced that he'd an errand to run. Since his reputation as a gentleman on the circuit was not entirely a pose, he did remember to fold his napkin, place his fork tines-down across his plate, and wish Raisa a pleasant afternoon. Nevertheless, he steamed off in what was, to Irina, a state of undisguised fury.

"Your *husband,*" said Raisa in his wake. "He have nice table manners."

That damning-with-faint-praise was all the comment that Raisa deigned to pass for the remainder of the day on her daughter's choice of mate, though Ramsey's absence that afternoon provided ample opportunity to express approval or share private reservations. Raisa may have been forced into retirement as a dancer at twenty-one by the horrifying burgeoning of her first child, but she was still a performer to the core, and dramatic pronouncements would be squandered on an audience of one.

❖ ❖ ❖

Ramsey returned wearing the composed determination that Irina recognized from tournaments. He took his wife and mother-in-law out to dinner at a swank (if garish) restaurant on the Avenue. Raisa ordered generously for herself, which Irina knew better than to take as a good sign. The point of each dish was that her mother wouldn't—the conceit ran, couldn't—finish it.

Raisa regaled Ramsey with tales of his wife's artistically precocious childhood. A mother was supposed to brag like this to a new son-in-law, but maybe that's what made Irina uncomfortable with the hard sell. Raisa was following protocol. She seemed less proud of her daughter than proud of herself for being proud. Besides, Irina would have been powerfully more touched had her mother dwelt instead on her substantial achievements as a grown-up.

By the main course—of her cutlet, Raisa would eat three bites—the conversation curled. *"Nu, rasskazheetye,"* she said. "How you two meet?"

"I used to collaborate with Ramsey's first wife," said Irina.

"Bozhe." Raisa raised her eyebrows. "As Americans say, *the plot thickens."*

Good Lord, she used an article. Irina wanted to pin a ribbon on her mother's chest. "No, Mama, the plot's not that thick. When Ramsey was married to Jude, we were only friends. Lawrence and I used to dine with them a couple of times a year."

Unfortunately, Irina's introduction of the L-word granted Raisa implicit permission to use it too. *"Tak,"* she said, *"Rumsee*—you and Lawrence friends?"

"We were friends," said Ramsey tolerantly.

"But no more," said Raisa.

"No, you couldn't say just now we're best mates."

"And Irina"—Raisa's gaze shuttled between them—"how Lawrence do? He sad?"

"Lawrence," Irina borrowed from that anguishing cup of coffee in Borough, "is *managing.*"

Ramsey looked at his wife. As she'd ostensibly not seen Lawrence since she left him, shouldn't she have said she had no idea? Caught in the middle, Irina was irked. She might have willingly answered her mother's questions in private this afternoon, but in private they'd have meant something else.

"But how this come about?" Raisa pried. "You have dinner, two couples, and then, just like that, you marry man across table?"

"Mama, look. One night Lawrence was out of town, and Ramsey was divorced. We got together as friends, and it was perfectly innocent. Except that we fell in love. I wasn't looking for it, and neither was he. Falling in love isn't something that you decide to do, any more than you decide on the weather. It descends on you, like a hurricane."

Alas, Irina's set piece was tainted with a hint of talking herself into something. The question of whether you were responsible for your own feelings—whether emotions were bombardments to which you were helplessly subjected or contrivances with which you were actively complicit—tortured her on a daily basis. Are they something you suffer, or something you make? You can control what you do, but can you control what you feel? Did she choose to fall in love with Ramsey Acton? And should desire have indeed thundered from the heavens like a "hurricane," given that the subsequent downpour had rained upon Lawrence a grievous injustice, in that theoretical universe whereby she could choose, would she have opted to forgo it?

"Ten years ago," said Raisa, "you say you fall in love with Lawrence. What happen?"

"I don't know what happened." Even with Ramsey beside her, Irina sagged. "And I do still love Lawrence—in a way . . ."

"So, when this new love fall from sky. You walk out, next day? Go marry *Rumsee*?"

"No, Mama, I am an adult, and we obviously had to think about it."

"How long you do this—*thinking*?" A reflexive generational disapproval may have battled appreciative amazement that her plain, underconfident daughter had mustered the pluck and sex appeal for adultery.

"Not that long." Irina folded her arms. "Mama, I know I said I was in love with Lawrence, and I was. I still think he's a wonderful man, and I won't hear a word against him. Still, what's between me and Ramsey is different."

"How different?"

"We're *closer*."

"*Da, ya vidyela*," Raisa said dryly. *Yes, so I've seen.*

"Obviously, Mama—" With a hand gesture of exasperation, Irina knocked over her wine glass. Ramsey's signature Chateau Neuf du Pape Rorschached over the white tablecloth. Her cheeks burned to match the stain. "Oh—nothing's changed, I'm still a klutz!"

"You're no such thing, pet!" Ramsey patted and covered the spill with his napkin without seeming to make a fuss, then refilled her wine glass to the brim. Finding no one with whom to share it, Raisa's pitying smirk floated in space.

"As I was saying, Mama," Irina recovered, darting a grateful glance at her husband, "obviously falling in love with Ramsey was the most wonderful thing that's ever happened to me. But I wouldn't want you to get the wrong idea. Leaving Lawrence was incredibly painful, not only for him but for me. This isn't some flighty little whim of mine."

Irina should not have had to say any of that, and as soon as it was out of her mouth she felt humiliated. Somehow whenever you're obliged to swear that a romance isn't "a flighty little whim," a flighty little whim is exactly what it appears.

"Yes," said Raisa, putting down her fork summarily; she saved grammatical English for special occasions: "I'm sure it was very unpleasant."

Maybe the problem was exclusive to her mother, but Irina suspected not. That is, maybe for any parent the hardest prerogative to grant grown children isn't the right to be treated like real professionals, with their own homes and the respect of important people, but the right to annex adult *feelings*. You'd have grown too habituated to consoling weepy moppets who are "in love" with the boy in the front row, while certain in the knowledge that next week they would be equally smitten by the boy in back. Raisa still spoke of her marriage to Irina's father as a tragedy of Tolstoyan proportions, while the droll story of their meeting—broke, Raisa was playing a bit part in a B-movie called *Tiny Dancer*, in which Charles was supposed to coach her on her Russian accent—was straight out of Chekhov. But it wouldn't come naturally to accord a little girl with buck teeth, inordinately attached to the worn-down stumps of her Crayola-64, the capacity for heartache on the same epic scale. So there was likely no rendition of the Ramsey–Lawrence triangle that wouldn't, to Raisa, sound tinny, trite, and dubious. When Irina put forward that leaving Lawrence had been "painful," Raisa could only hear "It was sort of awkward and Lawrence said mean things to me." When Irina said that falling head over heels for Ramsey was "the most wonderful thing that had ever happened to her," Raisa could only hear "He takes me out to dinner, and he has a pretty face." And now that Irina had asserted in womanhood that she'd "fallen in love" with more than one man, her mother would revoke her provisional licence, itself only granted begrudgingly after years of her loyalty to Lawrence, to have ever properly "loved," the way real grown-ups love, anyone in her life.

After paying the hefty bill, Ramsey was fuming, whispering in Irina's ear on the way out of the restaurant, "Your mum is *rude*." He clarified later that he was referring to her having ordered such an array of delicacies only to have the better part of every course swept away. While he didn't care about the money, somewhere in the affected finickiness lurked ingratitude: "Like chucking it back in my face!" But Irina thought at the time that he was referring instead to her mother's having put them both on the spot like that, trying to uncloak a sleazy, duplicitous affair as the provenance of all this *happiness*.

Yet there was just enough truth in that charge to make Irina pensive on the walk home. Back in 1988, once Lawrence had moved into West 104th Street, Irina had visited her mother in Brighton Beach to break the news that she had finally met "the love of her life." She remembered employing the shopworn phrase without self-consciousness, and meaning it with all her heart. The scene had engendered a rare sweetness between mother and daughter, even if it did take years for Raisa to credit the extravagant claim, and to achieve a reluctant (if now unfortunately tenacious) fondness for Lawrence herself. But that is not an announcement you can make twice. As splendid a man as Irina believed fiercely she'd shown up with the night before, a shabbiness, a sheepishness, had contaminated the introduction, and retroactively sullied as well that erstwhile precious memory from 1988. Irina told herself that these days people married two or three times as a matter of course, and to have a second great love was hardly incredible. But she was, at core, a romantic of an archaic cast. While she loved Ramsey, she did not, quite, love their story.

❖ ❖ ❖

That night Ramsey and Irina cozied in her old bedroom with the Hennessy XO, trying to keep their voices low. "Well, it seems safe to say,"

Irina observed resignedly, "that you two aren't getting on like a house afire."

"I don't give a monkey's how she treats me—"

"Nonsense," said Irina. "Of course you do."

"Good on you, I reckon I do. I never been treated like more of a waster in my life. If that bird says *snookers* one more time I've half a mind to sock her in the gob."

"Well, Ramsey, most Americans—never mind Russians—know next to nothing about snooker, and have no idea the kind of status you enjoy in the UK. My mother is full of pretensions and in a lot of ways she's a total fraud, but I'm pretty sure she's not faking on this point: She'd never heard of snooker."

"She's still never heard of snooker."

"That may be. But no matter how much you regale people with 'In this other country, people who do this for a living are cultural icons,' none of that sinks in when it doesn't connect with their own experience. I could *tell* you about how handsome and revered John F. Kennedy was, but if you'd flat-out never heard of him, you couldn't possibly grasp what it meant when he was assassinated, not one bit."

"Who's John F. Kennedy?" His deadpan lately was flawless.

She biffed him. "Stop it."

"But never mind me. I cannot stick watching you scurry round the house, rushing to put the furniture legs in them special dents in the carpet, snatching up my water glass before I'm even finished and washing and drying and putting it back in its special place in the cupboard. I hook my jacket on a chair downstairs, and ten seconds later I look round and it's disappeared. It'd be bad enough if it was her, but it was you! Why humour the bird? You play up to these daft bints and you just make them worse! If it was my own mum, I'd be flinging my suitcase full of gear all round the sitting room and filthifying as many dishes as possible, just so's I can leave them crusty on the counter. And mind, pet, before I'm through here I'll not only be grottying up the crockery, but chucking it!"

"I thought you were a *snookers* player, and now you want to play *bowls.*"

By turns wry, then confiding, their quiet debrief was so amicable that Irina let her guard down. Just about the time she was inclined to introduce her old bedroom to the depravity of adulthood, Ramsey raised, *casually*—

just what did she mean tonight that she "still loved" Lawrence Trainer, "in a way"?

"In a way," said Irina warily, knowing better than to add any new words because, no matter what they were, they would inevitably dig her deeper. "What I said."

"I marry you," he said, and Irina's heart fell to the very floor, for she knew that voice, and he may have sounded moderate and reasonable and just, well, *interested* in a little *clarification*, but it was telltale, like the sound of an engine turning over once and dying and then once again and dying, but there was petrol in that tank and he was *just getting started*. "We're out with your mum. Who I just met the day before. And you natter on to her. In front of your husband. About how you *love* another bloke?"

"*In a way*, I said. I was very clear, not in the way I love you. I was obviously talking about a feeling that I'm not ashamed of and that doesn't threaten you in the slightest. Otherwise, why would I talk about it when you're sitting right there?"

If the astute, objective side of Irina were hovering over the room watching this unfold, that good angel would have shouted, "SHUT UP!" For the worst thing she could do when these ructions got under way was to explain herself. To feed the flames. To add *more words*. But Irina was among other things polite. They were having a conversation, which seemed to oblige her to say things in return, even as she knew that every time she opened her mouth she breathed accelerant, and she'd be better off sealing it with duct tape.

Ramsey was already gearing up. "Why didn't you stop and think how *humiliating* that is to your husband? In front of your mum! Who I'm meeting for the first bleeding time!"

"I don't see what's wrong with my saying that, when the feeling I'm talking about is round and warm and safe. I lived with Lawrence for almost ten years. You wouldn't expect me to feel nothing for him, would you? I mean, God forbid that you and I should ever split up, but in the terrible event that we did, would you want me to come out the other side and feel nothing for you? Absolutely nothing?"

"There now, you see? Five minutes into this carry-on, and you're leaving me!"

"I didn't say anything about leaving you, it was just theoretical—"

"And not only do I have to sit there listening to my own wife coo about how she *loves* this other bloke, but I'm to take another bite of kabob while she swoons—*again*, I might add—how he's 'a wonderful man' who she 'won't hear a word against'?"

It went on for *hours*. While Irina tried to keep her own voice to a hoarse whisper, Ramsey's sotto voce hadn't lasted two sentences, and in no time he was giving Raisa—whose bedroom was across the hall—a performance whose building bombast a ballerina with a soft spot for Tchaikovsky would have to admire. Whether she would continue to admire it at two, three, and four in the morning was another matter. "Would you please keep your voice down!" Irina would plead, her throat raw from screaming in a whisper. "She can hear every word you're saying! How do you think this makes me look? Makes us look?" But Irina's imprecations only inflamed him, so that back comes, full-voice, "What do I care what that dried-up twat thinks? Why do you? Is that all you can think about, keeping up appearances? When I put my heart on the line with you? Stuff what your mum thinks, I'm talking about what's, to me anyway, a matter of life and death!"

The light behind the curtains was beginning to grey—and the bottle of Hennessy XO beginning to wane—by the time Irina collapsed on the bed and turned her back. The sun might be rising, but her head had gone black, and she no longer cared if her mother could hear her sobbing from across the hall. "You promised me," she said, before sinking to a bleak sleep. "You *promised* me."

❖ ❖ ❖

When Irina dragged herself downstairs after two hours' sleep she found her mother whisking a sponge around counters that were already clean, in a spirit of exceptional smugness. "*Dobroye utro, milaya!*" she cried gaily. "*S Rozhdyestrom tebya!*"

"Yeah, Merry Christmas to you, too," said Irina heavily. God, cheerfulness could be a form of assault.

"Sleep well?" The English was pointed.

Peering through the slits of her swollen eyelids, Irina briefly met her mother's eyes. "Not especially."

That was as close as they came to mention of the discordant palaver that must have kept Raisa from sleeping at all; she'd already worked out at the bar, and the royal-blue carpet in the front room showed the slashes of fresh, feverish hoovering, perhaps to remove Ramsey's offending indentations. Nevertheless, last night's quarrel was written all over Irina's face, which was puffy and bleached. Her eyes were still red, and as she drooped over her coffee to let the steam condense on her face, her forehead clenched in a dull throb. She had a hangover, but of a particular kind. Ramsey had drunk almost all of the cognac, but Irina had had lavish opportunity in the last year to establish that, between crying and drinking, anguish was the far more ravaging the next morning. Her eyes were burning, her muscles stiff; her skin was tight, her saliva thick.

Yet Ramsey trotted down looking perfectly chipper. She'd no idea how he could kill half a bottle of cognac and not appear the worse for wear. Maybe a knack for metabolizing eighty-proof was one of the many talents that suited him to snooker.

Sometime during that two hours of sleep, he must have nudged the bedding out from under her and worked off her clothes, for she'd woken this morning naked, covered, and embraced head to toe by a warm, beautiful, affectionate man whose touch revealed that if they'd simply done this last night, touched instead of talked, they might have skipped that whole folderol and arisen well rested for Christmas to boot. When now he knelt beside her chair to fix her with those soft grey-blue eyes and kiss her lingeringly on the mouth, she was infused with a gush of gratitude, made no less powerful for her recognition that it was perverse. Being thankful to a man who'd made her cry because he was no longer making her cry duplicated the syndrome that Lawrence deplored in relation to IRA godfather Gerry Adams—lauded by his own prime minister and promoted as a candidate for the Nobel Peace Prize because he was *no longer* blowing the British Isles to kingdom come. Though Ramsey would never hit her, Irina worried that this was exactly what kept battered wives coming back for more: an addictive gratefulness that it's over, a tenderness made precious for the very fact of having been so long withheld, and by the by, what public-service adverts for help-lines on TV never care to mention, the sex. This morning's had been top-drawer.

Accordingly, when Ramsey stood she held on to his hand, using it to pull herself up. Raisa could disapprove of groping all she liked, but Irina stood in her husband's arms and pressed her cheek to his chest not only because she needed the contact like a drug, but also to establish, firmly, that whatever her mother may have overheard, they had made up. Unfortunately, Raisa would have seen a thing or two over sixty-four years, including, in this neighbourhood, more than one battered wife. When she looked over at the two wrapped in a clutch, her expression only ratcheted up another notch of knowing smugness, as if all this turnabout lovey-dovey merely confirmed the same devastating verdict she had reached conclusively at two

Irina faced the rest of the day with dread. Post-apocalypse on Victoria Park Road, she and Ramsey would have required nothing more of each other than unremitting physical contact, keeping a leg in a lap or a hand on a knee as they sipped rejuvenating coffee, intertwining fingers as they ventured for a quiet, shaky amble through the park, kept short as one would curtail the walks of cripples or convalescents. They would tender tiny favours or presents, Ramsey slipping off to return with an untried brand of hot sauce, while Irina matted the poster from the China Open to hang with the others downstairs. But today no delicate, mutually considerate ritual for the restoration of normal affections would present itself. It had to be fucking Christmas. Any time now, Tatyana and family would burst in with the fixings for a huge dinner at whose prospect Irina's stomach lurched in revulsion. She wasn't up to this. She wasn't up to this at all.

❖ ❖ ❖

As Irina had explained to Ramsey on the plane, until Tatyana was about twenty, she'd striven to become the reincarnation of their mother. Six years younger and not, like a certain someone, conceived in resentment, she seemed to have inherited all the fluidity and flexibility of which Irina had been cheated, and made a model ballet student. With rounder cheeks, more symmetrical features, and straight, even front teeth, of the two girls Tatyana was the more conventionally pretty. Though she wasn't as tall as Raisa and had come by a more substantial bone structure from their father, she fought biology with some success by consuming so little that in comparison even Raisa seemed a healthy eater. The regime grew only more punishing after she began to grow breasts—protuberances, in ballet terms, against the law. She was admitted to a prestigious dance school in Manhattan, and Irina supposed that, if she were to let go of a competition over long ago, the story was sad. Tatyana had worked fantastically hard. And she did get impressively far, including a recital at Lincoln Center. But she was a little too short, and never able to starve off those hated mammaries to the satisfaction of the countless companies that never called her back after auditions. Tatyana's crushing disappointment alerted Irina to the secondary tier of gifted also-rans that lined most of the arts with grief. Especially rarefied fields with few slots at the top fostered a whole cohort of talented people who worked very, very hard and who were very, very good, who deserved to be rewarded for their astonishing effort and achievement, and wouldn't be.

Tatyana was also an object lesson in what happens to perfectionists who register with finality that they are labouring toward the unachievable. It's an all-or-nothing mind-set, and, almost gleefully, Tatyana chose nothing. Still commuting to Hunter, Irina was home the night her sister announced that she'd quit, and would never forget watching that tiny girl prepare herself a massive plate of spaghetti. Their mother was horrified, but Irina thought it was glorious, half a pound of pasta slipping strand by strand down that painfully slender throat. Tatyana had wrested victory from the totality of her defeat, overthrowing not only her mother but herself.

She proceeded to renounce not only dance and hunger, but worldly ambition of any description. She wanted a husband, and she got one, within the year—a nice-looking second-generation Russian from the neighbourhood, who worked construction. She wanted kids, and she got those, too—now ten and twelve. She wanted all the bagels, birthday cake, and borscht that she had denied herself for two decades, and had been making up for lost time ever since. Irina had always felt a little sorry for Tatyana's husband, Dmitri, a quiet man with an air of bewilderment. His wife had leapt the species barrier—from bird, to cow.

You'd expect the younger girl's fall from grace to alienate their mother's affections. Rather: whereas first Tatyana flattered by imitation, now she flattered by contrast, and was thus seamlessly stitched up as the daughter closer to her mother's heart.

Irina supposed that Tatyana was probably happier having turned her back on dance, as many people would probably be happier if they stopped torturing themselves with the American obligation to have a "dream." Yet these perfectionist types never change their stripes altogether, and Tatyana had embraced domesticity with the same extremity as she had ballet. She was eternally quilting, canning, baking, upholstering, and knitting sweaters that nobody needed. Her officious conduct of mother-hood gave off that whiff of defensive self-righteousness characteristic of contemporary stay-at-home moms. She was stifling, fussy, and overprotective, for if children were to redeem her existence, they would redeem it with a vengeance.

Today's celebration was bound to be classic: her sister would completely take over, and bustle in with an overkill of presents, side dishes, wreaths, and dopey little hats. It would have been more efficient by half had they all simply gone over to Tatyana's rather than having her cart all the dinner things here, but she'd lately conceived a mawkish sentimentality about "Christmas at home," at curious odds with their upbringing of third-degrees over an unwashed water glass and plate-by-plate disinheritance of that cobalt china.

Tatyana would have been briefed on the phone—she and Raisa spoke without fail every day—so when she soldiered up the walk laden with carrier bags she wouldn't have done a double-take on encountering Ramsey, smoking on the stoop. Immediately drafted into toting foil-covered dishes and peerlessly wrapped packages, he schlepped in silence without complaint, but his expression evidenced a growing how-did-I-get-here? dismay.

Irina helped slip dishes into the fridge, aghast to discover that her sister had made an authentic *kulebiaka,* decorated with a bramble of holly leaves and berries made of dough; the complex salmon-mush encased in pastry took the better part of a day to prepare. Her personal view that a nice salmon fillet artfully underdone and sauced not only took a fraction of the time but tasted better by a yard she kept tactfully to herself.

"Irina, I was blown away by your news," Tatyana whispered in the shelter of the refrigerator door. "Mama may be scandalized, but I think your having finally left Lawrence is fantastic. I couldn't say so while you two were together, but honestly, I found him insufferable. So condescending! He treated me with *scorn,* just because I don't publish in the *Wall Street Journal* and happen to make a mean Charlotte Russe. Such a know-it-all! Always going on about some impenetrable whathaveyou in Afghanistan, when really, who cares?"

"I can see why you wouldn't share his interests," said Irina cautiously. "But when he went on like that, it was because he was genuinely excited about the topic."

"*Chush,*" Tatyana dismissed. "He was a show-off. And he was cold. You're Russian. You need to be with someone who has soul."

Irina had to watch what she said, after last night, and spoke under her breath. "I don't think Lawrence was—is, since he's not dead—I don't think he's cold." (In point of fact, Irina said instead, *Ya nye dumayu shto on kholodny,* not taking any chances.)

"Come on, you don't have to defend him anymore! He treated you like a child. Telling you what to do all the time, never letting you finish a sentence. And he didn't seem to have the least understanding of what it means to be an artist."

"He never encouraged me to be pretentious, if that's what you mean." Though it should have been heartening to garner support for her rash switcheroo, her sister's unsuspected dislike for Lawrence was surprisingly hurtful.

"I haven't had a chance to talk to him yet, but Ramsey seems very nice."

"Yes, well," said Irina, "a lot of people think that when they first meet him."

"He *is* nice, isn't he? You married him!"

"Of course!" Irina backpedalled. Though if "nice" covered keeping your wife up until six with monotonous, unrelenting accusations mortifyingly audible to her mother, the label didn't mean much.

Once the *pirozhki* were browned in the oven, the two sisters, from a childhood of collusion in such matters, immediately washed and dried the pan, frantically whisked crumbs from the counter, and picked the odd flake of crust off the floor with a wetted forefinger, ensuring that none of these remnants clung to the trap of the sink. When they brought the little meat pies to the parlour on a tray, Tatyana's two kids were perched rigidly on the edges of their seats. Subdued and overfed, the kids didn't dare to scuff their shoes against the carpet or knock the chair legs with their heels in the fidgeting of normal children. As Raisa asked about their schoolwork, they received each question with the seized, mind-blank terror of a six-syllable word in a spelling bee.

Dmitri had already broken out the bottle of frozen vodka that, however requisite at any Russian feast, Irina would not personally have selected for her husband's breakfast. Moreover, Ramsey and Dmitri's extensive parsing of the comparative merits of Stolichnaya, Absolut, and Grey Goose played to an impression whose seeds Ramsey had already mischievously sown with his mother-in-law. He was surely dying for a fag, which would drive him to knock back those shots with edgy rapidity.

After Tatyana foisted plates of *pirozhki* on everyone but Raisa, she

303

settled next to Ramsey, who promptly beelined to the one subject that the rest of the family took pains to avoid. "Irina said you was a dancer, and then turned your back on the whole kit."

"That's right," said Tatyana tightly, fussing with a crust.

"She said as well you was dead talented."

"Well, that was decent of her. But I obviously wasn't talented enough."

Most people would have seen a veritable sign blinking by then, SORE POINT! SORE POINT! and moved quickly elsewhere. But snooker banter excepted, Ramsey had little time for empty chitchat, and ploughed determinedly on. "I didn't get the idea that was the problem. Bristols, wunnit?"

"Cockney rhyming slang," Irina provided at a distance. "Bristol Cities equals titties."

"I suppose if I were really ambitious," said Tatyana aloofly, "I could have had them surgically reduced."

"But how does it feel now you let it go? Ever kick yourself? How you should have tried harder?"

"No, come to think of it," said Tatyana, turning fully toward Ramsey at last and putting down her *pirozhok*. "When I gave up ballet, a tremendous weight lifted from me, and everything suddenly seemed relaxing and simple. I love the arts, but if you look at what the arts themselves celebrate, it's often the sweetness of ordinary life. Mealtimes and children and sunsets on the boardwalk. So it stands to reason that if there's any point to the arts, then your life itself is the most important artwork of all . . ."

Irina marvelled from across the room as, egged on by Ramsey, Tatyana went on at fervid length. Christ, she usually blithered about renovations to their en suite bathroom. Finally she must have caught herself at seeming impolite, though it was clearly an effort to relinquish the limelight.

"But Ramsey," she said. "Tell me more about yourself. My mother says you're a professional pool hustler?"

"You could say that," he said, saluting the absurd thumbnail with another shot.

"Oh, you could not," said Irina, crossing to their chairs. "Cut it out."

"I think it sounds exciting!" said Tatyana breathlessly. "You know, sort of underworld—shadowy and dark."

"If you've been getting the lowdown from Mama, you don't mean *shadowy,* you mean *shady.* Which Ramsey is not. Look, *my dear,* I wish you would—"

"The wife wants me to announce straight-out how I'm *famous.* She don't seem to twig that your proper celebrity never ponces round some punter's sitting room and declares how bleeding *famous* he is. She wants me to sound like a prat."

"What's a *prat*?" peeped Nadya, the ten-year-old.

"A pillock," Ramsey explained. "A wanker. A complete and utter doughnut."

"How do you sound like a *donut*?" asked Nadya. "They don't make any noise!"

"Oh, yes they do!" cried Ramsey, reaching over to swoop the little girl out of her chair before she knew what hit her, dangling her over his head. "They say, 'Oi, I'm a top-sixteen *snookers* player, mate, you better treat me like I'm important!' "

A shock wave went through the room—unaccustomed to the intrusion of a little *life*—as Ramsey twirled the girl overhead so that her legs spun out, coming perilously close to the samovar. Nadya laughed—a sound that, from Nadya, Irina may never have heard before. Irina smiled; she knew what it was like with those long fingers braced around your ribcage, dangling two feet off the floor. It occurred to her wistfully that Ramsey would make a good father.

But the boisterousness was bound to read to her mother only as proof that Ramsey was getting drunk. Which, come to think of it, he was.

"Right, you lot," Ramsey announced to the kids, taking charge. "Let's us open a few prezzies, hey?" Before anyone could stop him—the initiative was literally *out of order,* for in the McGovern tradition they did not unwrap gifts until after the meal—Ramsey had reached for a box under the tree and thrown it to the boy. Looking about himself for permission but on the spot, Sasha began to nervously peel off each piece of tape one by one.

"Fucking hell!" cried Ramsey. "Sasha my lad, what po-faced tosser taught you to open parcels like that? Your sister wants to know what's a *prat,* well that's how a *prat* goes at a prezzy. You're meant to rip the thing to shite!"

Not yet apprised that this family always smoothed and refolded wrapping paper for reuse next year, Ramsey proceeded to demonstrate, until Sasha got into the spirit and together they shredded the glossy

305

paper and threw it in the air. Alas, in his abandon, Sasha knocked one of the bowls of sour cream off a side table, and it landed sour-cream-side-down on the royal-blue carpet.

"Never you mind that, mate," said Ramsey, scooping the sour cream into the bowl and sucking the side of his hand.

Tatyana was already streaking to the kitchen, shouting with unconvincing gaiety, "I'll get it, Mama, don't worry! It'll come right up!"

"*Sod* the sour cream, love!" said Ramsey, pulling a silk handkerchief from his pocket and soaking it with vodka to give the stain a cursory wipe. When Tatyana beavered back with a host of sponges and spot-removers, Ramsey rolled his eyes, clearly not worried that Raisa would notice. She noticed.

The present Sasha had unwrapped was from Ramsey, a Sony PlayStation and a copy of Sony's "World Championship Snooker 1999" video game. Since the software included the entire tour's calendar of ranked events—starting with the Grand Prix and concluding, of course, with the World—Ramsey had just given Irina's family an animated guide to his whole life. Although Sasha and his sister seemed delighted with the PlayStation, they huddled over their only video game in crestfallen befuddlement. Frowning at the box in his lap, Sasha whined, "What's *snooker*?"—thereby unwittingly announcing the whole visit's running theme.

"*Snooker*"—Ramsey knelt at his chair—"is the *best game* in the *whole world.*"

"Nobody at my school plays that," Sasha said sulkily. "I've never heard of it."

"Bloody hell," Ramsey muttered. After standing and pouring himself another shot, he turned back to the kids with the hyperactive desperation of a children's TV presenter confronting an unusually sullen audience. "Right, we can start with a song, hey? Fancy learning a new song? Whilst we get this bugger up and running? *Snooker loopy nuts are we! / Me and him and them and me . . . !*"

The fact that the kids merely cowered encouraged Ramsey to belt out his Christmas carol of choice at an even higher volume. "*For the yellow, green, brown, blue, pink, and black!*" As instruction booklets and connection cables spread at the pace of potato blight across the carpet, Tatyana frantically stuffed scraps of wrapping paper and cellophane into a carrier bag from the kitchen. "*We're all snooker loopy . . . !*"

"Irina."

Raisa's summons was quiet. But for Irina it had a distinctive timbre that would pierce the roar of throng—recalling as it did the countless glasses of milk she had spilled as a girl, the vases she had shattered.

Standing from her throne-like chair, Raisa continued, "*Pazhalysta, uymi svoiyevo muzha.*"

"I doubt I could control my husband even if I wanted to."

"*Snooker loopy nuts are we . . . !*"

"*Irina, ya dumayu shto nam nado pogovorit.*"

Mother and daughter repairing the short distance to the kitchen was a formal exercise in privacy only; everyone in the parlour was bound to hear anything above a murmur. As for Raisa's discreet switch to Russian, even the children were fluent, and if she feigned to spare Ramsey's feelings she knew full well that he was sure to demand an account, and that her elder daughter would soon occupy the no-win position of either injuring her husband or lying to him.

"It is only two in the afternoon," said Raisa *po-russki*. Though the translation that Irina would later provide Ramsey would be heavily edited, she would try to get across that, in Russian, Raisa was acidly articulate. "And that man is already drunk."

"It's Christmas, Mama," said Irina, conceding to Russian as well.

"He has been drinking nonstop since he arrived here. Believe me, in Brighton Beach you develop an eye for it. This is not an inability to take 'stress' "—she used the English fad word—"due to meeting his new in-laws. This is not making a special exception for the holidays. That man is a lush."

They stood with the kitchen table between them, Raisa's hands resting with their bright red nail polish on the back of the end chair; Irina gripped the chair opposite.

"He rarely drinks during the day, and he ordinarily holds his liquor very well—"

"Too much is too much, and no one holds it 'well.' " (*With a load of balls and a snooker cuuuuuue!* pierced the kitchen from the parlour.) "Irina, I have tried to hold my tongue and to respect the fact that—at least you claim to have married him. But I cannot understand what possessed you. Lawrence, as far as I could tell, was very good to you. He was faithful, thrifty, and considerate. I didn't always understand what he was working on, but it was obvious to me that he did—whatever it was—

that he worked very hard. He was abstemious. He would never have crawled onto the floor singing silly songs with a bottle of vodka."

"I can see how Ramsey might not be making the best impression, but you won't let him. You've made no attempt to get to know him—"

"*I don't need to,*" Raisa announced. "I know the type. I recognized what he was the moment he walked in the door."

"Oh?" asked Irina archly. "What type is that?"

"He is a taker," said Raisa readily. "He will get away with as much as you let him, and then a little bit more. Inside, he is a bundle of self-indulgence and childish desires and bad habits. The fact that all this selfishness and greediness and vice is cloaked in charm makes it all the more dangerous. Men like that don't last, and men like that take you down with them."

"I'm amazed you've garnered so much insight into my husband, given that you've hardly talked to him."

"I could tell you a great deal," said Raisa, rearing her shoulders with her trademark imperiousness. "Not that I expect that you want to hear it. Can you imagine that a man like that will be faithful? Oh, this sort can turn up the magic like a spigot—or like a *thermostat.* They can seem so *interested,* so *caring.* You saw what he did with Tatyana. You saw her light up. The poor girl runs herself ragged for her family, and no one ever pays her that kind of attention—"

"What kind of attention?"

"You know exactly what kind of attention. Of course she melted. It sickened me to watch. Don't you think he turns on the same *oh, you're so fascinating and beautiful* with other women behind your back?"

"No, I don't." Irina wanted badly to charge, but didn't dare, that Raisa seemed mostly affronted that Ramsey had declined to turn that "kind of attention" on his mother-in-law.

"Honestly, Irina, what were you thinking?" Raisa relinquished the chair and began to roam, with the same air of *just getting started* that had made the bottom of Irina's stomach drop out the night before. "Were you thinking? Or did you let what's under your skirt get away with you? Oh, I grant he's not a bad-looking man. But do you think even that face will last, assuming that you don't get tired of it first? He is dissipated, and too old for you. Even if they stick around, men like that die on you, and leave you to get old on your own with no money."

"He's only five years older than I am!"

"When he starts to fall apart, what will you have left? A drunk in your bed, and debt collectors at your door!"

"I *told you*. Ramsey has plenty of money!"

"*For now*. I have seen the way he throws it around. Just like your father! They have holes in their pockets, and for a few days it is one big party! And then you wake up one morning and they need to borrow a dollar to buy the newspaper."

"You know, this *refusal* of yours to grasp how highly he's regarded in Britain is sheer obstinacy! Ramsey Acton is a *world-renowned snooker player*!"

"*Snookers player!*" Raisa practically spit. "And that voice of his. The way he talks. So low-class. I don't know how you can stand it."

"I love the way he talks. It has flavour!"

"My English may not be very good, but even I can tell that he talks from the gutter!" Raisa had begun to wave her hands, as if conducting her beloved Tchaikovsky. "I ought not have to tell you things like this, at your age. Marriage is practical. It is not romance only. In this way, I made a terrible mistake myself, and I cannot bear to see you repeat it! Lawrence was not rich, but he made a regular wage—"

"Leaving aside that Ramsey *is* rich, why does everything for you have to do with money?"

"I am not talking about money alone! Marriage is an alliance. I do not mean that it is like forming a corporation. I am not as cynical as you think. It is more like an alliance between countries—meaning that it should be to your mutual advantage! You pool your resources—"

"See? More *money*!"

"*Not* more money. The most important resources you pool are the strengths of your characters. But if you insist on seeing what I tell you as all to do with a cold, businesslike perspective on marriage, then very well: *character is a commodity*. Lawrence was steadfast. He had principle, determination, and discipline! Lawrence would have taken care of you for the rest of your life. Lawrence was responsible, and that man you've run off with is a scoundrel!" Ergo, Irina had just traded gold futures for pork bellies.

"You don't know him at all!" Irina was trying ferociously not to cry.

"Irina, I do know what I'm talking about! Your father was beguiling. He was handsome. He was funny, with the many different voices. At the beginning, he treated me to the high life. But Charles was a weak man, an indulgent man, who never planned for the future. All he cared about was having a good time, today."

"Yes, as a matter of fact, Ramsey and I do have a wonderful time together, *today,* not that you'd understand what that means—"

"Oh, I have seen your *wonderful time.* In the parlour drunk on the floor in front of the children, there is your *wonderful time*—"

"And yes, I do find him attractive, more attractive than any man I've ever met. But he's also very generous, and very kind—"

"*Kind?* This is what I hear last night? This was kindness?"

Irina bowed her head. "All right. The relationship is—volatile. But that's because there's so much fire in it—"

"He berated you! I may not have understood all the words—he uses so many ugly-sounding ones that I do not even wish to learn—but I recognized that tone of voice. I tell you, I never allowed your father to speak to me like that. You know he and I had our differences, but there was a line he knew he could never cross."

"He crossed plenty of lines, including having affairs with every script girl and moon-eyed extra he could get his hands on as soon as he escaped this house. But that's not Ramsey's fault! Papa has nothing to do with Ramsey!"

"You change the subject because you are uncomfortable with it, yes? You want to remind me about those floozies, because you don't want to talk about last night!" Raisa towered behind her daughter, who had turned her back. "He is abusive! Have you no pride? What I hear from across the hall, it sounded like every other house on this street. One more husband, drunk and shouting, with no class, no self-respect, and most of all no respect for his wife."

"Look," said Irina, turning back around. She had often dreamt of standing up to her mother, and it was about time at forty-three, but in fantasy she was never shaking. "What are you saying? That I should get a divorce? Because you know him better after he's crossed your threshold once than I do after knowing him for seven years?"

"If you had an ounce of sense in your head, you would run back to Lawrence and beg his forgiveness. Tell him that you had one of those middle-aged—what do Americans call them, some kind of attack. That you know you have been foolish, but you would please like to come back!"

Irina looked at her mother in dull disconnect. If anyone had pride in buckets, it was Raisa, which meant that she would never rescind her judgment, no matter how many years of monogamous, temperate devotion she might ultimately witness from *Rumsee Achtun*. Though she and her mother had battled over a host of trivia—last year it was over the fact that Irina had dabbed her mouth with her linen napkin during the borscht course, when she *thought* that's what the damned thing was for—previous confrontations were tiffs. This was not a tiff. This was a rift. In English, the words sounded alike, but the consequences could not be more contrasting.

Irina threw up her hands. "I'm sorry you don't like him."

She turned heel, as her mother cried at her back, "I cannot watch a tragedy unfold before my eyes and keep silent!" Apparently she didn't share her daughter's view that there was nothing more to say.

◆ ◆ ◆

Now that the show trial was finally over in the kitchen, Tatyana rushed past Irina in the hallway, whispering, "The *kulebiaka*!" Oh, dear. That's what that smell was.

Back in the parlour, the company's guilty expressions confirmed that the off-camera dressing-down had successfully secured the audience that Raisa required. Only Ramsey seemed oblivious, as captivated by "World Snooker Championship 1999" as the kids were bored by it. But her mother's aggressive, accusatory tone would have translated, Russian or no, and the frequency with which "Lawrence" had punctuated his mother-in-law's harangue and "Ramsey" cropped up in his wife's defensive retorts would have left the subject matter anything but opaque.

As Irina stooped to put an arm around his shoulders, Ramsey kept his gaze trained on the TV. "This gizmo's right sophisticated, pet. Back-spin, side-spin . . . And the sound effects are the business! They even got the interruption of the odd mobile."

On the television, she recognized the avatar clearing the table as a Looney Tunes incarnation of her own husband. Clad in his pearl waistcoat, Cyber Ramsey was severe and unsmiling, in contrast to the zany, hyperactive character hunched rabidly over the controls. The animators had emphasized the long lines in her husband's face and greyed his hair; alas, the younger gaming set perceived him as a wizened old coot.

Worst of all for Ramsey's ulterior purposes, the likeness simply wasn't good. Thus Raisa strode haughtily back into the room and glanced contemptuously at the screen. Her son-in-law had given the children a toy for Christmas only to hog it himself, and all she saw sidling around a big green table was an anonymous cartoon.

"Hey," said Ramsey, "one of the brilliant things about a visit home for Christmas is opportunity for a nice mother–daughter *chat.*"

At *chat,* the crack of a ball rang from the game, as a recording of Dennis Taylor marvelled, "Now, that's a long deep screw from Ramsey Acton!" But Raisa gave no indication of having discerned his name in the commentary, and shot Ramsey an icy smile. "I see Irina only one time each year now she live in England. And so many changes this year, *da*? We have much to talk about."

He pulled Irina with him to a stand and slipped an arm around her waist. "Glad to hear it. Good you got that over with. 'Cause"—he downed a shot with his free hand—"we got other places to be, do you know what I mean? Irina, pet, could you nip up and pack our bags? I booked us into the Plaza, and check-in's before six or we could lose the room."

Meeting Ramsey's eyes, Irina read clearly, *It's her or me.* The choice was hardly difficult at the age of forty-three, and she leapt upstairs to throw their luggage together, in a state of curious jubilation. The seditious notion that there were other places to stay in New York besides this dark, oppressive duplex in Brighton Beach had never entered her head.

When she lugged the bags downstairs, Tatyana met her at the bottom. "Irina," she whispered. "Don't go! At least stay for Christmas dinner. There are *zakuski* in the dining room, including that magnificent caviar that Ramsey bought—it will go marvellously with the blini. I was able to scrape the burnt bits off the *kulebiaka,* and we have a whole roast suckling pig for the main event!"

"I'm sorry, but we can't," said Irina. "You must have heard some of that—or all of it. I can't ask Ramsey to stay where he's not welcome."

"At least try to patch things up a little, or who knows how long the stand-off could last! You know how stubborn Mama is."

"She's not the only one who's stubborn. And I didn't start it. I'm sorry, Tatyana, I know you've gone to an awful lot of trouble to make a beautiful meal. I hope this hasn't ruined it. Try to give the kids a nice Christmas."

"I just want you to know that I don't agree," said Tatyana, placing a hand on her sister's arm. "I think he's wonderful. Dashing, exuberant, funny. I'm infatuated with his accent. He sounds just like Michael Caine! And he obviously adores you. You're very lucky. You two have something incredibly special, and I hope you'll be happy together. I'm sorry, but he just seems to push her buttons about Papa."

When Irina returned to the parlour, Ramsey and Raisa were faced off, Ramsey in his leather jacket, Raisa in her slender red-wool dress whose pads extended her shoulders to the breadth of her adversary's. Tall, wiry, and flinty in bearing, these two were catastrophically alike. If nothing else, they were both prima donnas.

"Ready, pet?" Ramsey asked, slipping his hands under Irina's arms and raising her high off the floor, then sliding her body down his in slow motion back to the carpet; the lift and controlled set-down were almost pointedly balletic. Her laughter was loose. Relinquishing any desire to please was so relaxing that she w. ndered why she didn't give up on the futile project more often.

"I so sorry you have to leave," Raisa told Ramsey.

"Well, I don't get much time off this season, and—not to seem ungrateful for your *hospitality,* Mum—I ain't spending the whole holiday worrying about whether my chair's in them special dents in the carpet. Ta!"

Taking a ready Gauloise from behind his ear, Ramsey turned with his fag dangling unlit from his lips while Irina said softly, "Bye, Mama," kissing her hastily on the cheek. As he reached for his bag, Ramsey exclaimed, "Blimey, almost forgot!" in the tone of having done no such thing. Raisa was not the only one in this house with a sense of theatre. He rooted through his jacket pocket, and tossed Raisa a set of keys. "Happy Christmas! It's in that multilevel round the corner. I bought you a car."

As he tucked a parking-lot ticket into the breast pocket of her dress, Raisa's face would have looked no less stricken had Ramsey *socked her in the gob.* As they left the house, Irina's mind reeled with several certainties: that whatever model awaited her mother in that garage, it was aggressively, pugnaciously classy; that it was aggressively, pugnaciously costly; that— Raisa having not dropped word-one about wanting a car—aside from brute expenditure, the gesture was designed to signify absolutely nothing; that her mother would never, ever thank Ramsey for such an extravagant present; and that she would never give it back.

❖ ❖ ❖

Once they disembarked from the taxi on 59th Street, there proceeded the most delightful Christmas of Irina's life. After Ramsey threw clothes onto the furniture of their opulent room because he could, and went around jacking up the thermostat and jerking chairs goofily out of their depressions in the carpet, they knocked back with a bottle of champagne to watch *It's a Wonderful Life* naked under the spread. Thereafter, they dressed to the nines, and headed to the Oak Bar for a little more champagne and oysters on the half shell. Rather than opt for the hotel's conventional Christmas dinner, they celebrated release from heavy fare like *pirozhki* and salmon in charred pastry by preferring plump Gulf shrimp with fresh horseradish and crunchy patty pans. Irina regaled Ramsey with a bitterly comic translation of the scene with her mother in the kitchen, and segued to a long reflection about her father. As one of those rare Christmas presents that you actually adore, for the entire evening Ramsey never once mentioned *snooker*.

Back upstairs by one a.m., Ramsey drew out his Discman and asked her to dance.

"Oh, I can't," said Irina. "Really, I'm awkward and I have no sense of time and I'd probably break a lamp. Ask Mama."

"I reckon I'll not ask your mum another bloody thing in my life. Get your bum over here."

"Ramsey, no! I've had too much to drink, and I'd just embarrass myself."

Undeterred, Ramsey put on John Coltrane's "Giant Steps," and drafted her into a jig. Though at first she couldn't stop laughing, at length she allowed the exercise to glide from farce to festival. All her life she had spurned school sock-hops, and fled to the kitchen when party hosts cleared a space by the stereo. Through the 80s, when the very granite of Manhattan trembled from gyrating clubs, Irina had preferred quiet dates at bistros. At weddings, she was wont to pinion a nearby guest with earnest conversation like pinning his hand to the table with a steak knife, in desperation to avoid being hauled to the floor. She couldn't dance, she hated to dance, she did not know how.

Yet in their Plaza hotel room, no one was watching but Ramsey, who, last night aside, really *was* kind, and would never hold her tentative first efforts up to ridicule. He himself was uninhibited, careering with a wacky devil-may-care that granted his partner permission to try any ludicrous move in return. He twirled his forefingers in the droll circles of a Motown chorus, jagged a raised knee with a hip that looked dislocated, unfurled her from his clasp only to roll her back again like a curled piece of paper,

314

and most of all, never let her go. Adopting an eclecticism that would have appalled the likes of Raisa and Tatyana, they mixed up jitterbug shimmies, disco turns, tango thrusts, rock-and-roll boogie, and even, in a nod to the nightmare they had jettisoned that afternoon, the odd *arabesque*. As their DJ, Ramsey followed with Duke Ellington and Sonny Rollins, moved on to Glenn Miller, threw in a dash of R&B with Captain Beefheart, and rounded up with a salacious Sly and the Family Stone at a volume that made Irina grateful the walls of the Plaza were bank-vault thick. Something about the common rhythm they had already discovered in bed translated to the floor beside it, and by the time Ramsey had slipped into the Discman his last selection, a garnish of modernity in Ice-T, Irina was beginning to wonder if as a rule of thumb you shouldn't so much look to marry your perfect fuck as your perfect dance partner—although there was no harm in marrying both.

▣ chapter eight ▣

This year, it was Irina who reminded Lawrence of Ramsey's birthday, and Lawrence who dragged his feet. He was awfully busy. Due to some old coincidence, did they have to get together with Ramsey Acton every 6th of July until the end of time?

"Are you saying you want to *drop* him?" she asked incredulously.

"Nothing as active as that," Lawrence said. "Just not pick him up again."

"Not picking him up again *is* the way you drop people."

"But he can be a little tedious, can't he? The only thing he knows how to talk about is snooker."

"You used to love talking about snooker!"

Lawrence shrugged. "Maybe I've said all I've got to say." He pretended to go back to reading. Irina stood before his couch until he glanced wearily up from the page. "Why do you look horrified?"

"We've known him for years. Is that the way it's going to be with me? Suddenly that's it, *do svidanya*, because you've *said all you've got to say*?" Irina had an anguished apprehension that this was indeed what happened to some couples, and that the experience of simply running out of script could come upon you with no warning.

"I'm discussing Ramsey's birthday, and suddenly you're shrieking about my leaving you or something. Dial it back."

"We have a friendship. He has every reason to believe that we care about him. And Ramsey is a nice man."

"Oh, who's not *nice*."

"You're not, at the moment."

316

"Jesus, last year I had to put a gun to your head to even call the guy!"

True, last year she had met Ramsey in Lawrence's stead, to maintain his romance with a snooker celeb, but the evening had turned into one long *Speak for yourself, John*. After a few months of tug-of-war Lawrence had lost ownership of Ramsey Acton, decisively so in Bournemouth. Be it Ramsey or Russia, Lawrence required superior if not sole possession or he wasn't interested. Thus his veto of another birthday dinner translated: *If I can't have Ramsey, then you can't, either.* But she would not completely relinquish the man, who had become like those two or three sneaked cigarettes a week—rationed in cautious quantities, perfectly harmless.

"That's right," said Irina, "and *you* said that if I didn't ring him he'd be hurt."

"Finally over your own dead body you make a date, then tell me later you two caroused all night and got stoned off your heads."

She'd hoped he'd forgotten. "That's not what I said."

"Now I suggest we skip the birthday thing this year, and you go bananas."

"I'm not going bananas. I'm saying we should be considerate. It would cost us one night. I'd do all the cooking—"

"And I'll buy the entire case of wine the guy will go through in *one night*. Or morning, more like it."

"I could tell him that you have to get up early to work."

"Don't bother. To Ramsey, getting up in the morning—at all, much less to work—is an alien concept. He'd hang on to four , as usual."

"You used to like him."

"Yeah, well, sometimes I just go off people."

"I know." There was a dolefulness in her voice that he didn't notice.

Yet after all that, once Irina did ring Ramsey, he had other plans. Did she remember his telling her about the Ooty Club, in India? He referred to their evening in Bournemouth as if it were a long time ago. Of course, she assured him. Well, he was going on a hadj. She was surprised that he knew the word. A pilgrimage, she said. Yes, he said. He would be gone for most of July. A visit to a single snooker table wouldn't consume a whole month, and she wondered if he was drawn to the subcontinent, like so many Westerners, in a mystic, searching way. Well, have a lovely trip, she said. The call was so short, his voice so distant, that she rang off perplexed at how close she'd felt

317

to him last year. Yet it crossed her mind that he might have arranged to be abroad for his birthday on purpose.

She was bereft the rest of the day. Abandoning the tradition broke a spell of sorts, and Ramsey would have known that. Lawrence would be delighted. Now there would be no obligation to see Ramsey next July, or the many Julys thereafter.

■ ■ ■

It was an ordinary difference of opinion, but later the memory from that autumn would stand out. Before they got ready for bed, Lawrence had grown heated about the impeachment proceedings under way in the US Congress.

"I thought you hated Clinton," she said.

"He's a smarm," said Lawrence. "A megalomaniac with no principles other than the eternal elevation of William Jefferson Clinton. *But.* He is smart."

"Good God, you never say that about anybody, and now when you do it's about someone who's done something incredibly stupid."

"Fooling around with that cow was *ill-advised,* but politically meaningless."

"Lying isn't politically meaningless."

"It is when it's about sex."

"Oh, you're not going to say that, are you? Not *all men lie about sex.*"

"Well, they do!"

"Do *you*?"

Lawrence reared back. "Of course not!"

"And why is it only men who are supposed to lie about sex? If it's such an intrinsically mendacious subject, why don't all women lie about it, too?"

"They probably do!"

"So do you think *I* lie about sex?"

"Not really."

"Not really?"

"Not at all!"

"So what makes you and me so special?"

"Irina, we're talking in bland generalities."

"I'm not. You are. So I'm asking you: what makes us so special?"

"Because we have . . . some sense of decency, I guess. A good relationship. Though that doesn't mean we wouldn't cut each other a little slack."

"What kind of slack?"

"I don't know, like if I watch a woman walk down the street who has nice gams, I wouldn't expect you to take my head off."

"But we're not talking about checking out some woman's legs. We're talking about feeling her up and coming all over her and then claiming self-righteously over and over that you did no such thing!"

"Okay! I wouldn't expect to be cut that much slack."

"Why apply a higher standard of behaviour to ourselves than we do to the president?"

"Why are you suddenly so prudish? Who cares if Clinton jerks off on some intern's dress, so long as he doesn't accidentally press The Button while he's getting his rocks off?"

"I'm not a prude, because sex wasn't the subject. The subject was lying."

"About sex."

"About anything. Back in February, Clinton stared straight into the camera, looking me, who voted for him, in the eye. And he said, without blinking, 'I did not have sexual relations with—that woman—Ms. Lewinsky.' *Bozhe moi,* the little pauses, as if he couldn't even remember her name. I felt personally insulted."

"So he didn't handle it well. That shouldn't be an impeachable offence. This campaign the Republicans are on, it's sheer opportunism, and abuse of the Constitution."

"You really don't think it's important, do you? That he's stonewalled on this thing for the better part of a year?"

"No, I don't. I think it's important that he ordered missile strikes on Sudan and Afghanistan, and I think it's important, unfortunately, that he missed Osama bin Laden."

Irina didn't recognize the name, but wasn't in the mood to play up to his expertise. "All that matters is the big worthy work that men do. Whether they lie through their teeth and the way they treat their wives is trivial."

"I didn't say that, but we were talking about politics and not what we think of Clinton as a person. As a person, okay, he's a creep. But he doesn't deserve to be kicked out of office for shoving his cigar up Monica's box. Waste of a good cigar, in my opinion, which maybe should be impeachable." Along with most American males at the time,

319

Lawrence found Clinton's most egregious offence that of poor taste. Monica was fat, homely, and dumb, and the president of the United States could have done better.

Irina plopped into her chair. "Oh, I guess I wouldn't have him impeached, either. But I would see him divorced. And that's not going to happen. Hillary's worse than he is. All that *vast right-wing conspiracy* rubbish, after they'd obviously been scheming for days. Then she'll pretend to be all shocked and hurt if he ever comes clean, and she'll always stick to her story. They're not lovers, they're a cabal—it's the Clintons who are a conspiracy. They make backroom deals, little pacts and tradeoffs, for their mutual self-promotion. I guess that's one way of doing things, but for a marriage it's awfully bloodless."

There Irina stopped. Her depiction sounded a disturbing echo.

▣ ▣ ▣

In all, Lawrence had been testy ever since returning from Russia in June, and the prospect of a Brighton Beach Christmas didn't improve his demeanour.

"I know your relationship with your mother is difficult," said Lawrence, the train to Heathrow once more stalled between stations. "But I want you to make me a promise."

"Shoot," said Irina.

"Promise that you won't pick a fight with her."

"She's the one who does the picking!"

"Don't rise to the bait, then. This trip is trying enough without yet another catfight. That thing about the napkin last year was ridiculous."

"What's the point of *having* a napkin, if you can't use it to dab your mouth?"

"She was right, beet juice stains. Not that I give a shit, it was pricey linen. But let's not hash that out again. It was boring enough the first time." He'd always been a tease, but lately his barbs weren't funny.

Of course, every couple went through periods when they were closer, then farther apart, right? Lawrence was obviously under pressure at work, and she shouldn't have made him squander his brief holiday on her family. And after snaking for an hour through the check-in queue at BA, anyone would be cantankerous. It was a miracle they were still able to joke in duty-free about buying Raisa a two-pound Toblerone before settling on a slim bottle of fino sherry—on special.

320

Boarded, Lawrence immediately booted his laptop, though he'd have to shut it off again before takeoff. Not in the mood to read, Irina reflected wistfully on the days when taking an airplane was more adventure than ordeal—though she still managed to marshal that absurd sense of anticipation of a roundly inedible meal. She wanted to ask Lawrence to talk to her, but that would mean lining up something to talk about. There *was* something to talk about, but she couldn't quite name it to herself, and flailing attempts to get at it were bound to make his mood even worse.

So she focused instead on what to order from the beverage cart. She rather fancied a glass of red wine, but it was only four-thirty a.m., and Lawrence wouldn't approve of drinking in the afternoon. Indeed, as the plane inched through the takeoff queue, the amount of energy she lavished on wine versus goody-goody juice was preposterous. Thank God that no one could glimpse inside her head, this ostensible artist obsessing over a miniature of Beaujolais. Imagine if other people could hear what you were thinking, and what drastically different estimations of one another you might make in that case. Would the discovery that everyone else on the plane was preoccupied with what kind of free booze they would order prove comforting or depressing?

By the time the cart juddered to their seats, her thoughts had moved on to why she was so afraid to defy Lawrence's displeasure. It wasn't her fault that his mother was an alcoholic, the label itself a puzzle; on visits to Las Vegas Irina's de facto mother-in-law had downed two or three drinks, but nothing to worry about. Might his mother be less a drunk than her son a killjoy?

Lawrence ordered seltzer. Irina asked for tomato juice.

After the meal, an amorous couple in the middle seats opposite began going at it under the minimal cover of an airline blanket. Low grunts and moans were punctuated by stifled giggles. The blanket writhed, and for periods of time a head would disappear beneath it. This same couple did not share Lawrence's abhorrence of drinking in the afternoon, and had been requesting their plane fare's worth in vodka miniatures since takeoff.

"Jesus Christ," Lawrence muttered, loud enough to be heard. "Get a room."

Irina didn't care for that expression—hip in timbre, puritanical in intent. Why was it any skin off Lawrence's nose if a couple of kids couldn't keep their hands off each other? He wasn't Muslim or anything. She could see being amused, or fascinated, a little bored since you'd seen it before, or even charmed, but not, absent religious objections, offended.

Yet Lawrence's disgust knew no bounds. "Better push the button for the flight attendant, Irina. See if she's got a Durex. While she's at it, have her bring me a barf bag."

"Lawrence!" Irina whispered. "They're not doing any harm, and they can hear you!"

"Or maybe ask for a fistful of Finlandias," he continued, jacking up the volume. "Another couple of rounds, and he won't know his cock from his elbow. Then *maybe* we'd be able to watch the movie."

"You're such a jerk."

"I'm not a jerk," he corrected. "I'm an *asshole.* Calling an accredited asshole a run-of-the-mill *jerk* is like forgetting to call an MBE *sir.*"

"*Sir Asshole,* then," she said. "Shut up!"

When they settled into *The Full Monty,* the grappling in the middle seats subsided just as Irina identified the feeling the exhibition had stirred. She wasn't amused exactly, or fascinated, certainly not bored, and decidedly not offended. All right, maybe she was a little charmed. But most of all, she was jealous.

◻ ◻ ◻

Once the door flew open, Raisa paused a theatrical beat—that they might take in her stunning outfit—before throwing her arms wide and proceeding with the usual smacking and grasping of shoulders that Irina didn't buy for a minute. In her mother's embrace, she stiffened.

"*Dobro pozhalovat!*" Raisa effused. "*Ya tak rada vas vidyet! Pozhaluysta prokhoditye, prokhoditye!*"

"Man," said Lawrence. "That's one drop-dead dress, Raisa! After the last year's wardrobe, I'm always waiting to see if you'll top yourself!"

Irina rolled a quiet eye. The line was typical. With Raisa, Lawrence liked to have his cake and make fun of it, too.

They bundled the luggage upstairs, packed the clothes into drawers, and buried the bags out of sight. Just because it was their room didn't mean that Raisa wouldn't chafe at a dropped sock. Lawrence brought the sherry downstairs, but declined when Raisa offered to open it; she looked pleased, as if he'd passed a test. He proceeded to admire her hairstyle, to admire her fitness, to admire the Christmas tree. Irina's mother had absolutely no idea the kind of irreverent, caustic man she lived with; honestly, it was almost as if Raisa had never met Lawrence. If Irina were her mother, she'd be wondering what on earth her daughter saw in this earnest lickspittle.

Raisa left to get tea. Lawrence perched on red velveteen; he looked uncomfortable, keeping that shelf from ramming into his neck, but he knew better than to move the chair. When Raisa returned, he leapt to take the tray.

"Your tea service is dynamite," said Lawrence. "Must be worth something."

Raisa beamed. Irina shook her head. Given its transparency, she was always amazed that flattery worked. And it wasn't only her mother who was gullible on this point. It worked with *everybody*.

"*Da*," said Raisa. "Such shame. Creamer and sugar bowl some of only pieces left of china my mother cart from Soviet Union in trunk. Heirloom, from her mother. For years, our family envy of other Russians in Paris, who have nothing from old country! Most unusual cobalt blue, I never see anywhere else. Like colour in stained-glass window!"

Lawrence had heard about the cobalt china A MILLION TIMES. At last he chimed in sympathetically, "Too bad. I heard Charles threw it at you, one plate at a time."

Sanitized! Irina had said that they threw it at *each other*.

Well trained, Lawrence poured a round, while Irina studied the sideboard's crowning samovar, which had likewise survived the war in her grandmother's mythic trunk. If a glorified teakettle, and far too laborious to use, the great bulbous brass urn was handsome, and she'd always coveted the samovar a little; it carried off the same haughty bearing as its mistress, and seemed to constitute the seat of power in this house. The chances of her inheriting the thing were scant. Tatyana's name was written all over it.

"*Tak*, Lawrence. What you work on now?"

"Well, you remember that I spent a month this spring in Russia. You wouldn't believe Moscow these days. Restaurants, hotels, boutiques . . . The semicriminal elite has money to burn, but the proles are in bad shape. The begging and public drunkenness are terrible. Did you know that in Russia, beer is classified as a soft drink?"

As they were treated to a mini-lecture on the state of the erstwhile Evil Empire, Raisa folded her hands in rapt fascination. He loved being the authority—so let him. Nevertheless, in a just world they would both be updating her mother about the country that Raisa had left behind, rather than those two bonding their hearts out while Irina played with her tea ball.

◫ ◫ ◫

Your dress is a knockout!" Irina whispered in her old bedroom. *"Sure 'nuff, you look in great shape!* Lawrence Lawrensovich, you are shameless."

"What's shameless is she eats it up," Lawrence said quietly. "I've asked her where she got that samovar a dozen times. She never remembers telling me."

"Why should she? She rabbits on about that samovar to everybody."

"The rest may be horseshit, but she does look pretty damned good for sixty-four."

Irina had still not recuperated from the fit of ravenousness that hit her over the summer, and coming home was having the predictable psychic effect. "I knew it," she said, looking at herself critically in the mirror. "My mother always makes me feel fat."

Lawrence said lightly, "You haven't gained that much weight."

It was the first time he'd acknowledged that she'd gained any.

◫ ◫ ◫

While Irina was huddled over her coffee the next morning, Lawrence strode into the kitchen in moist sweats, exuding the boisterous self-right-eousness particular to people who launch barbarically into the cold in trainers out of a dead sleep. "Well, that must have been close to six miles!" he said, still breathing hard.

Irina frowned. Detesting the exercise nut, she treasured his modera-tion. "You wouldn't usually do more than four."

"Eh. Doesn't hurt sometimes to push it."

"Lawrence, you want breakfast?" asked Raisa, still in her leotard. "Eggs? Black bread?"

"Nah. Just coffee, thanks."

The warmth of the coffee glass cupped in both hands didn't pene-trate the gloves, so Irina clapped her palms to get the blood running.

"You make your point, Irina, you can stop dramatics with your hands," said her mother, in English for Lawrence's benefit. He'd convinced her that he remembered nothing of his university Russian, the better to eavesdrop on her asides. As a result, he knew exactly what Raisa thought of his dress sense.

"I'm not being dramatic, I'm trying to get them warm. You always think I'm having you on, but I do have a condition—"

"Every American have *condition*. Big competition, who have more *conditions*. No American ever say, 'My hands cold.' Has to have fancy name."

"Yeah, you have to join a group," said Lawrence. "With confessional meetings and a Web page."

"Are you telling me," Irina charged her partner, "that Raynaud's is all in my head?"

"You get up in morning, and *exercise*, Irina, you stay warm all day!"

"She's right," said Lawrence. "If you started the day with a few calisthenics, you'd probably stimulate your circulation."

"If I started the day with *turning up the thermostat*, I'd stimulate it a lot more."

"Irina, you should see gas bill!"

"But it's bloody *Christmas Eve!*"

Lawrence shot a warning look across her bow: *You promised.* "Actually, the price of natural gas has been escalating pretty steeply. New exploration hasn't yielded much, and even the reserves in the North Sea are drying up."

"Once in a while," said Irina, "it would be nice not to address the whole state of the world as if we're all on *60 Minutes*, but one modestly sized house, on a single morning, which is Christmas Eve, and the woman you love is cold."

"Okay, one small house," Lawrence conceded. "It makes more sense to conserve body heat with a sweater than to warm your entire environment."

"Nip in air keep you awake, make you keep moving!" As if to demonstrate, Raisa was rushing about the kitchen, creating a remarkable to and fro with the storage of a single clean spoon.

"Damn right," he agreed ferociously. "Overheated houses put me to sleep."

■ ■ ■

As they strolled the Avenue under the el after coffee, Lawrence gave her a cajoling shake of the shoulder. "Hey! Why are you so grumpy?"

"You never take my side. I always feel ganged up on, and it's *my* mother."

"I'm just trying to keep the peace."

"What's so great about peace?"

"Actually, that question sometimes comes up in conflict studies. Peace is a little dull. It always presses the existential question of, you know, what's the point, what are you trying to achieve, not only as an individual, but as a country."

"So how do people in *conflict studies* resolve this peace-sucks problem?"

"Same way as any sane man visiting his mother-in-law: It beats the alternative."

Lawrence loved Brighton Beach, for he was naturally stimulated by externals—not a bad thing, really, for inward spelunking into family dynamics was claustrophobic, whereas the outside world that lay before them was as vast as their appetite for it. After all, her own work entailed meticulously deconstructing the lush fluctuation of colour in a single leaf, or discerning the complexity of its lines as seen lolling backwards from a side view. There was simply so much to *look at* in the most commonplace vista that to spend any time at all dithering over thermostats or napkins seemed a waste. She had always valued the way Lawrence helped to pull her into the very world that she would feign to draw.

So Irina shed her sulk, and poked with him into shops, pleased that the visit to Moscow had made him braver about chatting up clerks in Russian. They considered getting some caviar for a Christmas treat, but it was exorbitant. So they partook of the pleasures on offer that were free, the spectacle of ex-Soviets on the boardwalk. Burly men in their seventies bared sagging chests to an overcast December sky and strode stoically into the icy shallows. Teenage girls paraded fluffy white fur coats that looked to have been made from poodles. A dishevelled character rummaged bins for bottles, which he would upend to drain their last drizzles of beer, vodka, or wine down his gullet.

When they met Raisa at Café Volna, Lawrence greeted her with the usual, "That dress is *killing*!" He would only order a salad, despite Irina's derision that he "ate lunch like a girl." Goaded by her mother's remark that she was looking "healthy," Irina defiantly ordered pickled herring, lamb-and-rice soup, chicken Kiev, and a *beer*.

When Raisa asked dutifully after her daughter's illustrations, Irina admitted that she was feeling uninspired. Needing to "knock herself for six," she might take Lawrence's advice and investigate computer graphics. But the quality of her mother's attention was merely patient.

"*Skazhi*, Lawrence. You think you stay in London much longer?"

"Blue Sky is a good place for me right now. I could see putting in several more years."

"Since when?" said Irina. "I thought you were keen to get a post with the Council on Foreign Relations in New York."

"I've had a change of heart. In London, I can take advantage of the special relationship."

"What *special relationship*? With whom?"

"Between Britain and the US, you moron. It's a standard expression."

"Don't call me a moron."

"Irina, I call everyone a moron."

"Except me. Not ever."

"All right! I'm sorry! Jesus Christ. I just mean, if I stay in Britain I'm ideally situated to keep a policy hand in both the States and Europe."

"Bloody hell, when were you going to tell me?"

"I just told you."

Watching the show, Raisa submitted to Lawrence from the sidelines, "You know, longer she stay in UK, Irina change how she talk, *da*? She use expressions I no hear in New York. And even way she say words. Every year, more differences."

"Yeah, I know," Lawrence groaned. "On the plane, she ordered a to*mah*to juice."

Since she'd ordered the to*mah*to juice to pander to his paranoia about his mother who didn't even really *have* a drinking problem, it was rich to get stick for it. "When you grow up bilingual," said Irina, "language seems less fixed. Besides, I think British lingo is *a bit of all right*." She managed to deliver the expression with almost no consonants.

Lawrence folded his arms. "To the contrary, growing up as a second-generation Russian-American gave you an identity problem. Making matters worse, you were a social reject as a kid because of your buck teeth, so as an adult you bend over backwards to fit in."

Irina's cheeks burnt. "How long have you thought that?"

"Approximately forever. But this faux Brit-speak is wrong-headed. You're trying to please, and it backfires. You invite contempt. Brits want you to talk like an American, because that's what you are. When you ask for to*mah*to juice, you come across like a suck-up who has no self-respect.

327

I wish you'd get that through your head, because other Americans think that to*mah*to shit is pretentious. You sound like a pompous ass."

"Excuse me," said Irina. "*You*, of all people, are taking me to task for 'trying to please'? After you've just told my mother that you like her dress three times?"

His expression blackened. "I do like your mother's dress, and I don't see anything wrong with saying so." He looked at his watch, and left a twenty on the table. "I've got some errands to run in the city. I'll see you guys for dinner." Like that, he was gone.

"Lawrence is under a lot of pressure at work," Irina apologized; for months, the hackneyed explanation had circled in her head like a fly.

Raisa switched to Russian. "Lawrence is a good man. He is thrifty, and considerate. He makes a regular wage. He works hard. He is disciplined about alcohol. He is not like the men around here, all lazy drunks who can't keep a penny in their pockets. I never see him raise a hand to you. Maybe you should be careful."

"*I* should be careful? He berated me!"

"Sometimes a woman must look the other way. Not take issue with every little thing. And he's a man. He has his pride. What you said, about his complimenting my dress. You embarrassed him."

"But he embarrassed me! That crack about my teeth—"

"This is what I mean." Raisa squeezed her daughter's arm. "You look the other way. You rise above. It isn't weak. It's grown-up. All men are little children. So the woman cannot afford to be a little child, too, or your home turns into a kindergarten."

"Lawrence hasn't been himself lately. When he went to Russia, I was jealous. I wanted to go too. I wasn't very nice about it. He may still be angry at me over that."

"I am sure you are right. That will pass. Just take my advice, for once? You look the other way, you rise above, about the small things. And then if something ever comes along that is big, you know how, and are already in the habit."

◼ ◻ ◼

Lawrence returned late afternoon, mumbling something about Christmas shopping, though he wasn't carrying any packages. He offered to take everyone out to dinner at the usual garish Russian restaurant on the

Avenue. When they went upstairs to get ready, Irina stopped him in the hallway.

"I'm sorry about what I said at Café Volna. I didn't mean to put you on the spot about being obsequious with my mother. Or I did mean to, but I shouldn't have. You just hurt my feelings. I had no idea that the way I talk gets on your nerves. I don't think it's all *trying to fit in*. I pick up a few British expressions because I like them."

"Oh, forget it. No big deal." Lawrence detested this kind of talk.

"I seem to be getting on your nerves a lot."

"No, you're not."

Well. So much for that.

"Will you kiss me?"

Lawrence looked at her blankly, as if she had asked him to stand on his head. He shrugged. "Okay." One kiss, tight-lipped and brief.

"No, really kiss me."

The full-bore kiss was foreign, but exciting for that, as if she were trysting with an illicit lover, and it was a tremendous relief. For a woman, barring one other point of entry that Irina found unpalatable, venturing into the moist, vulnerable cavern of a man's mouth was her only route to getting *inside*. When Irina opened her eyes, she caught her mother's gaze at the end of the hallway, shining with approval.

▫ ▫ ▫

At dinner, mindful that Lawrence was paying, Raisa ordered only a main course. She asked what Irina and Lawrence did for fun in London, and Lawrence told her about taking Irina to her first snooker tournament last year. When Raisa didn't recognize the word, he treated her to a detailed description, talking up how enormous the table was, and how many shots ahead you had to plan. She acted enthralled, asking loads of questions with the usual pumped-up enthusiasm. He explained that they knew one of the players, considered the consummate gentleman of the sport; he said their friend was a real celebrity in the UK, who was consequently very wealthy and took them out to lavish dinners a couple of times a year. Maybe it was the mention of money, since for once she seemed sincerely impressed.

"The ethos is courteous, civilized, maybe most of all elegant," Irina contributed.

"Your friend Zeetos, he snappy dresser?"

Irina smiled. "No, his name is Ramsey. *The ethos* means the overall atmosphere and set of values. Still—courteous, civilized, elegant? He has kind of a down-market accent, but actually, that describes Ramsey pretty well."

"This *Rumsee*—he handsome man, *da*?"

"I guess," said Irina, as if she'd never considered the question before. "And maybe you could call him a snappy dresser. Tasteful anyway. He's very graceful, and tells wonderful stories." She'd said more than she'd intended to, but for some reason whenever the subject of Ramsey arose she didn't want to let it go. She added emphatically, "And he *really* likes Lawrence. I can't help but find Ramsey a little boring, since I'm not that big of a snooker fan. But those two are best mates—I mean, best friends. They trade snooker anecdotes for *hours*. I hardly get a word in edge-wise."

"You sure managed last time," Lawrence muttered.

"He sound just my type. Maybe I visit you in UK, you introduce me to this rich, famous *snooker* player, *da*? Fix up your old mama?"

Maybe it was the image of Ramsey and her mother hitting the town hand-in-hand that drove Irina to drink, but her hand overshot the glass and splashed four ounces of the cheapest red on the list all over the white tablecloth. "Oh, nothing's changed!" she cried, flustered. "I'm still a klutz!"

"You can say that again!" said Lawrence. "For Pete's sake, Irina, what a mess!" Mopping the wine with his napkin, he made the cleanup seem an enormous bother, moving the salt and pepper, candle, and flower vase. "She's always been like this, right?"

"*Pravda*," her mother agreed with a collusive sigh.

"In London, I pour her cabernet into sippy cups."

She hadn't knocked over a glass for years. They were splitting a single bottle; humiliated, Irina rued having wasted a measure of wine she now sorely required.

"When you go to Russia," asked Raisa over coffee, "who you go with?"

"Oh, it was a whole group," said Lawrence. "From Blue Sky."

"These all men? With no wifes? Sound lonely, for whole month. Such shame that Irina could no come with you."

Why did she ever tell her mother *anything*? "It was a business trip, Mama. And I had my own work to do."

"It wasn't all men. One fellow was a woman—well, that sounds incongruous—research fellow, I mean." He added gratuitously, "She's kind of annoying, actually."

"Irina tell me you work very hard these days."

"Afraid so. The American State Department has commissioned a survey on terrorism around the world, and it's a huge project."

"When you get home?"

"Oh, it's getting to be about nine at night."

"This make very long day. And no so long to spend with Irina, *da*?"

"She's used to it."

"*Nu . . . mozhet byt,* she should get no used to it."

"I don't mind," said Irina. "Lawrence is ambitious. I won't help him by nagging."

Raisa switched to Russian, and what she said translated roughly, "When I told you this afternoon that you should overlook the little things, I didn't mean that you should overlook everything, yes?"

Well, if Lawrence didn't understand that, Irina didn't, either.

◘ ▣ ▣

"Man," said Lawrence quietly, flopping onto their bed that night. "How'd you like our friend *Zeetos*? Tell me she doesn't get shit like that wrong on purpose. In fact, contriving to be underestimated is strategy. I've started to theorize that your mother's English is secretly the match of H. L. Mencken's. She just wants to entice you into saying stuff you think she can't understand so you'll blow your cover."

"That's what you do around her with Russian," said Irina, taking off her blouse.

"You'd think that bag of bones could make a few inroads on her plate when she only ordered one course. What a loon! I swear she sneaks down to stuff her face with those Pepperidge Farm cookies when nobody's looking. Otherwise she'd be dead."

"No, a subsistence diet slows your metabolism to a crawl."

"So is that what you're doing? Keeping your *metabolism* up? I've never seen you eat so much in one day."

Irina clutched her blouse to her chest. "I hate being browbeaten, even tacitly, and maybe my rebellion went a little far today. But you'd rather starve to impress her. Every time we come back from Brighton Beach you've dropped three pounds."

"Is this more riding me for 'trying to please'? Because those that's-a-nice-dress-Mrs.-Cleavers are a *joke*. A joke for your benefit, so you're supposed to get it."

"Of course I know you're playing a game. But then you're incredibly mean behind her back, and I wish you'd stop it."

"Would you *keep your voice down*?" he whispered. "This morning I was taking her part too much. Now I'm too mean to the broad. Which is it?"

"It's the combination I don't like. It's hypocritical."

"You know, I'm starting to wonder if on the tube I should have made you promise not to pick a fight with *me*."

"I'm not trying to pick a fight—"

"Then *don't*. Your mother's just across the hall, and if we're up till all hours having a shouting match we make ourselves look bad. Now, brush your teeth."

Maybe because he was working such long hours, for the last six months the frequency with which they'd been having sex had dropped—nothing precipitous, perhaps by one less night a week, still roughly sating Irina's erotic appetite. But satisfying a need to come is one of a host of purposes the activity serves, a surprisingly minor one. Especially in the established relationship, its most vital function is reassurance. So once they were in bed and Irina reached around with a beseeching stroke of his hip, only for Lawrence to mumble something about jet lag and doze off, she was more than disappointed. She was nervous.

▫ ▫ ▫

Since the night before they had neither fought nor fucked, Lawrence and Irina began Christmas Day well rested.

"*Dobroye utro milye!*" Raisa cried gaily. "*S Rozhdestvom vas!*"

Returned from another overkill run, Lawrence wiped the bottom of his coffee glass and set it on a saucer. In the early days, Irina had been grateful for the way he fell into lockstep with her mother's lunatic sense of order. But there was nothing like the parental imprimatur to put the kibosh on your attraction to a man, and this morning his scurrying to wash and dry and put away the coffee glass before it was even cold was irritating.

"Irina," said Raisa with a pretence of lightness. "I mention this before, *da*? When you take shower, you drain soap dish and dry. You leave soap in puddle, it turn to jelly. Lawrence very good about this. Sometimes you forget."

Irina trudged back upstairs to drain the stupid soap dish, and then convened with Lawrence in their bedroom to wrap presents.

Right before they'd left for New York, Lawrence realized that in Moscow he'd neglected to pick up anything for Raisa. "Oh, dear," Irina had worried. "And you've been to the *motherland*. I'm afraid she'll be offended." Tentatively, she suggested that maybe the most diplomatic thing to do was to give her mother the Rostov choker.

It's funny how you can make an offer in all sincerity, and still be crushed when you're taken up on it. On the heels of her proposal, Irina hoped frantically that Lawrence would insist she keep his gift, Raisa's sensitivities be damned. Instead he commended her quick thinking, and promised to find her a replacement in due course.

She didn't want a replacement. Her very ingratitude on first receiving the present had guaranteed that her about-face before that taxi on Trinity Street would be total, and her attachment to the jewellery was now improvidently fierce. Thus when they spread their presents on the bed beside a pile of refolded wrapping paper from last year, Irina opened the attractive Twinings tea tin she'd found for the necklace and gazed inside possessively. "Do you still want me to give her the choker?"

"I wasn't the one who wanted to give it to her, you did. But yes, why not?"

"I only thought . . . Well, you said you went shopping yesterday. I thought you might have found something else to give her instead."

"No, I didn't. I didn't find much of anything. It was Christmas Eve, and a goat-fuck. If you were expecting me to buy something different, you should have said so."

"Oh, that's okay," she said forlornly, and wrapped the tin herself.

When she heard Tatyana arrive *en famille*, Irina trotted downstairs to greet them in the foyer. Tatyana dropped her carrier bags and opened her ample arms to enfold her only sibling. "Welcome back! I'm so thrilled to see you! I've been looking forward to this for weeks! And look at you, you're looking *fabulous*!" Tatyana gave Lawrence an equally hearty hug. Thankfully, she had no idea that he thought she was an idiot.

While the sisters unloaded the food in the kitchen, Tatyana extolled, "From what I hear, Lawrence is doing *sensationally* in London! A neighbour of mine brought by a copy of the *Wall Street Journal* last month, and if it wasn't Lawrence's byline on the op-ed page, big as life! I was so impressed! And there I was, just piddling around in the kitchen over another Charlotte Russe. It must be awfully stimulating, living with someone who's so *learned*."

"Stimulating is one word for it," said Irina quietly, stashing the blini.

"Well, aren't you just busting with pride?"

"Lawrence can be . . . a bit of a know-it-all. A bit of a show-off, intellectually." She spoke under her breath. In the parlour, he was already rattling off the complications of Afghanistan to Dmitri. "This think-tank job may not have been great for his character. He's become chronically condescending."

"*Chepukha*," Tatyana dismissed. "He always treats you with respect. And he goes on about politics with such feeling! I find that kind of passion in a man terribly attractive."

Irina gave up. There was nothing more frustrating than venturing criticism of someone you were supposed to esteem, and getting no uptake whatsoever. She was left twisting in the wind, sounding like a bitch.

So they retreated to territory that should have been safe, although cookery was also a minefield. Both sisters were cooks, but of radically contrasting types. Irina was prone to experiment; Tatyana followed recipes to the letter. Irina pushed flavours to their limit—never adding a clove of garlic but the whole bulb; Tatyana specialized in elaborate concoctions with lashes of cream and butter that were classically artful but lacked counterpoint. Irina found Russian cuisine dumpy; Tatyana enthusiastically reproduced their culinary heritage with tasteless authenticity. Where Irina was all very slam-bam (Tatyana would say careless), throwing dishes together with fistfuls of this and that in the confidence that all would work out in the end—which it *did*—Tatyana levelled exact half-teaspoons of cinnamon with a table knife. As far as Irina was concerned, in the kitchen she dashed off Kandinskys, while her sister dabbed paint-by-numbers. Since they'd had terrible rows in the past—Irina would add so much lemon zest to a birch-log icing that it was "ruined"—she settled on the most neutral substance she could think of.

"I don't understand this fad for salt mills," said Irina, fetching the shakers for the *zakuski* table. "With pepper, a mill makes a huge difference. But freshly ground salt?"

"Yes, you're right, the flavour's identical!" Tatyana agreed ardently.

"Though you might get something textural out of the variations in the size of the grains, don't you think? For example, I do like that shardy, crystalline quality of Maldon."

"Or how about *grey* salt!" Irina rejoined. "It has this marvellous mineral bite . . . !"

While mutually forceful feelings on these subjects allowed for much-needed *bonding,* once they brought out the *pirozhki* and Lawrence had moved on to a conclusion to thirty years of brutal sectarian warfare in Ulster, Irina felt girly.

Despite her professed appetite for learned discourse, Tatyana nipped Northern Ireland right in the bud. In no time she was regaling the company with the travails of redecorating their en suite bathroom, despairing that contractors tracked plaster everywhere. When Lawrence quizzed her earnestly about the pattern of wallpaper she'd chosen, then about the tiles, the toilet, and the taps, Tatyana responded in heartfelt detail, blissfully unaware that his encouraging comments were savage: "Little trumpets or little boats—that must be really hard to decide! . . . I can't imagine the upheaval! How do you manage? . . . Yes, that's the modern-day quandary—those silent flushers are civilized, but they just don't get the job done!"

Weary of his game with Tatyana, Lawrence tried to teach her two kids the bar trick of propping a coaster half off the table, flipping it up, and catching it in a single motion; they found his flawless repetition of the trick mesmerizing, though neither seemed to have the knack. His patience with adults was thin; with kids it was limitless. It occurred to Irina wistfully that Lawrence would make a good father.

Alas, just when Sasha was getting the hang of it, he knocked a bowl of sour cream onto the carpet. Lawrence streaked to the kitchen and returned with an armload of sponges and spot-removers, feverishly expunging the stain. He admonished the kids, "Maybe we'd better not try the coaster trick around all your grandmother's beautiful things."

Thus it was back to adult conversation. Irina asked Dmitri about his construction business and didn't care, Tatyana asked Irina about her illustrations and didn't care, Raisa asked the children about their school-work and didn't care, and Lawrence, stuck in the corner with Tatyana, was ultimately reduced to asking more questions about her bathroom absent the spirit of sly send-up that had made the first set marginally entertaining. Everyone complimented the *pirozhki,* while Irina thought they didn't have nearly enough onion, or enough anything, and tasted mostly like dried-out hamburger.

So this was *peace*—which, according to their resident conflict studies expert, "beat the alternative." No one got into an argument. No one said anything insulting. No one broke into rowdy song or raised a voice. While they were provided tiny lace-edged napkins with their appetizers, Irina excused herself to wipe her greasy hands on a paper towel just to be on the safe side.

Yet once she returned, her frustration was building in combustible quantities. She was reminded of being gussied up in a pert pink dress and patent-leather pumps after church as a girl, having to hang around the house forever waiting for some hunk of meat to overcook, scolded the while that though she had to keep on the scratchy dress for Sunday lunch, she wasn't allowed to draw pictures because she might get crayon on her outfit. What was the point of growing up if you didn't earn yourself escape from Sunday Lunch Syndrome? It may have been the twenty-fifth of December, but Irina was not a practising Christian, and it should have been *within her gift,* as Lawrence would say, to demote the holiday to just another day of the week if she chose. *Why* would she inexorably volunteer to shuttle dishes back and forth for an extravagant *zakuski* array that she didn't even want? *Why* was she obliged to converse politely about Tatyana's PTA work when she was not remotely interested? For years she had whispered dark vows about how when *she* was a grown-up *she* wouldn't ruin half of every weekend trying to keep stains off her uncomfortable clothes and talking about the boring old *PTA*. Here she had finally clawed her way to adulthood, only to willingly shackle herself once more to other people's hopelessly crap idea of a good time. Why didn't she and Lawrence check into a hotel, order champagne and oysters, and fuck like bunnies? She was forty-three years old—*why couldn't she go and colour?*

Irina sidled over to Dmitri, even if he always seemed a little tongue-tied, because of the lot he looked the most companionably glum. Moreover, to ease himself through the occasion, with the excuse of good ethnic form, he had broken out the frosty bottle of vodka that he'd slipped into Tatyana's cooler. He wasn't knocking back shots like a Cossack; nevertheless, inroads had been made.

"Would you mind if I had some?"

"*Da, konyeshno,* Irina, let me get you a glass."

Bang, Lawrence's black look was Pavlovian. It was *two in the afternoon*. But rather than suddenly demur that she preferred to*mah*to juice after all, she smiled encouragingly as he filled the glass to the brim, and toasted brightly to Lawrence, *"Za tvoye zdorovye!"* Then she drained the whole pour in one cold, glorious gulp like a *real Russian*.

If the *pirozhki* were only teasers for the grand *zakuski* course to come, Irina was already full. The day before, being bullied to starve herself had driven her to overeat; being bullied to stuff herself had the corresponding effect of putting her off her dinner. She did help Tatyana lay out the *zakuski* in the dining room—herring and black bread, blini with smoked salmon, pickled beets, "poor man's caviar" made of eggplant, hard-boiled eggs, cucumber salad, and that enormous *kulebiaka* (which, its decorative pastry delicately browned, did look splendid)—but bustled dishes about as cover for not eating them. In sufficient quantity food grows repulsive, and all Irina could see when she looked at that groaning board was an oppressive array of leftovers. Aversion to the buffet made her second and third vodkas fiendishly effective.

Once the main course was laid out—the whole roasted suckling pig on a bed of kasha, braised red cabbage, grated-potato pudding, and string beans with walnut sauce—Irina merely snitched a bit of crackling from the pork to go with her wine.

In such abundance, a meal is less a feast than a mugging. The company staggered back to the parlour as if bashed on the head. Even Tatyana agreed that they might take a breather before dessert, and open their presents.

The vodka had been primly whisked away before dinner, but the bottle was easily located in the freezer, and now seductively cold. As she returned to the parlour with her bracer, Irina's face flushed with the high colour of Christmas cheer. When the polite one-at-a-time unwrapping began, the extra shot helped to drown her sorrow when she handed off their present to her mother. Raisa put the choker on, and Irina purred about how well it suited her; much was made of Lawrence's having brought the gift from Moscow. For once Raisa's effusion evinced a trace of sincerity. But watching the choker leave her own life with finality pierced Irina with a grief all out of proportion to the scale of the loss—a monumental mournfulness that she herself did not quite understand, even as a lump formed in her throat at the very point where the enamelwork once had rested. Grim consolation, presumably she might inherit it when Raisa was dead.

The abundance of the other gifts, however well-meaning, engendered that all-this-trouble-and-money-for-what? deflation of the average American Christmas. Tatyana's heavy package for Irina contained a set of massive homemade candles that the kids had helped to cast; Irina's foreign residence was an abstraction to her sister, and it would never have occurred to Tatyana that now she would have to drag ten pounds' worth of gaudy paraffin back to the UK in zip-strained luggage. Lawrence got two ties, when he hardly ever wore them; Raisa a synthetic shawl, a lumpy sweater, and some cheap costume jewellery from the children, appurtenances all destined for a bottom drawer. Since one compulsively buys people the last thing they need, Tatyana received mostly food. Nearly *everyone* had given Dmitri aftershave; the boxed bottles that collected at his feet, two of the same brand, were an embarrassment. Likewise Raisa persisted in purchasing her grandchildren toys designed for younger kids—the label on the doll for ten-year-old Nadya specified "For Ages 4–7"—and children never interpret such slips as ignorance, but as calculated insult.

Towards the last, Irina shyly handed Lawrence an envelope, from which he pulled a postcard-size drawing. He frowned at first, and she was hurt that he didn't seem to recognize it, for she'd gone to some effort replicating the illustration in miniature.

"It's the arrival of the Crimson Traveller," she explained, "the first version, for *Seeing Red*. I told you, it was an odd man out, and in the end I couldn't use it and had to draw the panel again. I framed the original for you. It didn't make any sense to bring all that glass to New York . . . so I made you that little reproduction. You liked the picture so much, remember? You said the style was—*bonkers*."

"Oh, yeah . . ." he said foggily.

"I thought you might like to hang it in your office."

"Sure, that's a great idea!" he said, and kissed her cheek. But his enthusiasm felt pumped, like her mother's, and she was still not convinced that he remembered the illustration at all. Moreover, her gift may have been a tad perverse. The unruly sensation that had taken hold of her when she scrawled that alarming panel had derived from a place that Lawrence had no vested interest in her choosing to revisit.

In turn, Lawrence fetched his own present from under the tree, and Irina's heart leapt when she saw that it was small. *That's* why he'd gone shopping yesterday! If they would still give her mother the choker, he was determined to compensate her loss with a necklace equally lovely on this very day. He was so kind!

Inside the package was a set of keys.

"Merry Christmas! I bought you a car."

As she stared at the keys in dumbfounded silence, he went on. "Well, us a car, but I'll still walk to work, so you can have it during the day. So you can shop at the bigger Tesco on Old Kent Road, and not drag bags from Elephant and Castle. It's nothing flashy, a used Ford Capri, but the 1995 model was rated highly in *Consumer Reports* . . ."

It would be impolitic to submit that she really wasn't bothered about lugging bags from Elephant and Castle. Even a used car was a major financial undertaking, what with the insurance, petrol, and parking, and the present smacked of executive decision. It was nice to be surprised, but she might have preferred to be consulted. After she kissed him in thanks—and he mumbled, "Whoa, don't light a match near your mouth!"—Irina grew further perturbed over the fact that she'd never dropped word one about wanting a car. Thus even more than high-handedness the gift smacked of brute expenditure, as a substitute for something more precious, if not in the fiscal sense.

Aside from the choker, tendered with regret, was there to be no present this Christmas that didn't fall flat? She'd expected at least the Discman they'd bought the children to go down a treat. But Tatyana had whispered in the kitchen that the kids had been campaigning for a Sony PlayStation for months, and the platform was too costly; by the time Sasha unwrapped the Discman, the blanket under the tree was denuded, and it was crushingly apparent that no one had obliged. Sensing his letdown, Irina talked up the accompanying Alanis Morissette album, *Jagged Little Pill*, helping Sasha to fit it into the portable CD player while Tatyana laid out dessert—just in case there was anyone left in the family who didn't yet want to throw up.

Oh, Alanis Morissette was probably more up Irina's alley than Sasha's, who at twelve would be tepid on music by a girl. But Morissette's go-it-alone fuck-you suited her mood at the moment. With the wrapping stashed for next year, booty stacked beside each chair, the carpet was clear. In a wild departure from her wallflower past—if only to shuck the pervasive disappointment with which the room was imbued, and to court a sensation of lightness after being surrounded by all that food—Irina began to dance.

She was unable to entice Sasha to join her—he was at an awkward age, and shy—much less could she tempt spoilsport Lawrence to become her *partner* in the sense that the previous generation would have meant. But never mind them. What a waste all these years, to have ceded such an exhilarating pastime to her mother and sister, when for both it was primarily a source of suffering. True, she was a *tad* unsteady on her feet. Unschooled, and lacking even the latent muscle memory of a raucous youth, Irina jigged the parlour in an eclectic style, snatching moves from disco, jitterbug, and boogie. She sang along with the lyrics loudly enough to drown Lawrence's grumbling on the sidelines, "Irina, you're making a fool of yourself." Mischievously, to punctuate one wailing refrain she extended a leg backwards into an arabesque.

And knocked over the samovar.

"Lawrence," said Raisa in that spilt-milk voice over which, in defiance of the standard axiom, Irina had cried plenty as a girl. "*Pozhaluysta.* Could you control my daughter?"

He could. And he did.

❖ chapter nine ❖

If in the previous year Irina had gloriously overthrown the tyranny of her own stinting, purposeful nature, in the year following she tried strenuously to reinstate the same strict, diligent woman whom she had once come to resent. As in most revolutions, creating chaos is a cinch, restoring order thereafter an undertaking both dreary and monumental. But however oppressive one's own character can become, long enough as someone else, you begin to miss it.

She had instigated a similar revolution in tenth grade. The summer before, her braces had been removed. When she smiled, her front teeth no longer shelved grotesquely over her lower lip, and the most agreeable-looking people smiled right back. Little by little she had learned to hold her head high, to stroll from her hips, and to meet the gazes of upperclassmen with the brazen challenge of a budding vamp. Yet this revelation was destined to unfold in slow motion, for only that moment on the sixth of July when she leaned into Ramsey Acton and this handsome desirable kissed her back was the process of realizing she was no longer an eyesore complete.

Since childhood pariahs often court compensatory approval from adults, Irina had always been a straight-A student. But now the cool people with low-slung jeans, long hair, and miasmic Indian cottons that had bled in the wash were enticing her to their basement stairwells, where they proffered joints as tight, slender, and tapered as Ramsey's cue. She experimented wickedly with skipping class. Trading on her upstanding reputation with an embarrassed mumble to teachers about getting her period, she got away with it, too.

But there came a time to pay the piper. Towards the end of sophomore year, her art teacher was organizing a field trip to the Museum of Modern Art, and qualification for the privilege required meeting a minimum academic standard. Voice steeped in disappointment, Mrs. Bennington had announced to the whole class that Irina McGovern's grades were too low for her to qualify. As one, her classmates turned in amazement towards this hitherto goody-two-shoes, and whatever shred of street cred her newly disreputable GPA may have garnered failed to compensate for the shame. What had she done? Who was this tearaway fuckup, where once sat an honours student? Irina had bartered her dignity for fun.

Thus her experience that January had an unpleasantly familiar texture. It had been mortifying enough for the straight-A student to ask Puffin for an extension. And while technically she'd met the deadline, deep down inside she knew those drawings were not "hasty." They were terrible.

Across the occupations, plenty of established professionals pass off the shoddiest work imaginable and are sometimes lauded for it. After all, most of the world doesn't know the difference between the rare blaze of true genius and the derivative manufacture of the rank hack. But just her luck, Irina's editor on *The Miss Ability Act* had to have integrity, which despite its noble reputation is a ghastly quality when you find yourself on its receiving end. On their return from Brighton Beach, Irina knew she was in trouble when she got not a phone call or e-mail, but a letter. In two terrifyingly short sentences, her editor informed her that another illustrator had been assigned to the project. The drawings were "unacceptable." She heard the word in Mrs. Bennington's voice.

In fact, while the editor had been terse, the Mrs. Bennington in her head went on at some length. *Admit it,* she scolded. *On an average day, you don't get out of bed until noon; you go through half a pack of cigarettes and never less than a full bottle of wine. You read a newspaper at best once a week. Even during occasional erotic respites, you spend a disproportionate amount of your leisure time—assuming you have any other kind of time—thinking about sex. The only scrawls in your diary run, "Preston, RA v Ebdon, best of 13"—the landmarks of another person's occupation. You had six extra months to complete one project, and you botched it. You are even more dissolute than your husband, who at least— haven't you noticed?—still meets his obligations.*

The rejection was, as everyone seemed to say so incessantly those days, "a wake-up call." That very night, Irina laid down the law. No, she would not come with Ramsey to the Benson & Hedges Masters. No, she would not come with him to the Regal Scottish Open. She had to stay home and work. Morosely, Ramsey acceded. They both knew that an era had closed. She would come to miss it.

Thereafter, like most wives in this game, Irina accepted her fate as a snooker widow. Ramsey would return between tournaments when he could, but for weeks at a go Irina was pledged to knock about the four floors of Victoria Park Road on her lonesome.

The half-hearted feelers she put out to authors were unavailing, and Puffin was a burnt bridge. For years she'd relied on Lawrence to pursue the side of her occupation that she detested, begging for more work. Too, she'd always depended on the structure and intent of someone else's narrative for inspiration; in this sense, Irina really wasn't an artist, but a natural illustrator. So perhaps the answer wasn't to find another writer, whose plots were so frequently predictable and preachy, but to become one. Plenty of illustrators composed the text as well, and at least writing her own tale on spec would obviate any more of these humiliating e-mails.

In Irina's girlhood, one of her favorite dolls had a long, full skirt. When it was upright in one direction, the hair was tousled brown yarn, the dress a dark floral print. When it was upended, the skirt flipped over the brunette's head to reveal a blonde-haired alter ego, with a dress of light blue plaid.

Irina conceived a storybook that flipped like that doll. On the front was the cover of one tale, on the back, upended, the cover of a second. The first story would proceed on the right-hand page, with captions at the bottom, while on the left was the second story upside down. Both stories would involve the same hero. Both stories would start at the same juncture in the hero's childhood. But the tales would proceed differently, depending on how the protagonist resolved his initial dilemma. As for subject matter, once Irina arrived at it, she could only laugh.

For eighteen months Irina had been watching bright refractive spheres streak across a lush green backdrop framed by mahogany rails. These images cropped up in her dreams, and she often saw primary-coloured orbs when she closed her eyes. The pictures had got *inside*. She'd meant to be escaping from it, but in the end it made inexorable sense that the plot of her first illustrator-authored storybook would have everything to do with *snooker*:

Martin is a prodigy at snooker from the instant he is tall enough to see over the table. But his parents believe that snooker clubs are dens of iniquity (or however you get across the concept of depravity to small children who are not supposed to know what it is, and most decidedly do). They are adamant that he not neglect his studies, because they want him to go to university, like his father. They forbid him to go near a snooker table. But Martin is already more accomplished at snooker than many of the grown-ups at his local. And he loves to play snooker more than any other thing. What is Martin to do?

In one story, Martin defies his parents. He skips school to play snooker. He gets better and better, and sometimes makes the grown-ups very angry, because they don't like being beaten by an upstart little boy. Since Martin seems bright, his parents don't understand why his marks at school are so poor. Finally when a neighbour congratulates them on their son's winning a junior tournament, they realize that the boy has flown in the face of their wishes. They inform him that if he does not turn his back on snooker, he will have to leave home. Martin feels he has no choice, and is now good enough at snooker to make money at it. Still, he misses his parents, and the pain that they are no longer speaking to him never seems to go away.

Martin becomes a famous snooker player. He earns scads of money. He has many adventures. He makes lots of friends, even if people who play snooker are not always very smart, and sometimes they are a little boring. For that matter, sometimes Martin himself is a little boring, because he doesn't really know very much about anything besides snooker. He neglected his schoolwork, and never went to university. There are good things and bad things about his life. It can get lonely, even if strangers often wave to him on the street. Once in a while even he gets a little tired of snooker. But it is still a wonderful game, and there is only so tired you can get of something you do very well. There are many peak moments. Since even people who are very, very good are not always going to be the very, very best, Martin never quite wins the World Championship, but that is all right. (This healthy note of realism was probably influenced by Casper's *Sacked Race*.) He's sorry that he hasn't been close to his parents, who have never forgiven him for defying their authority. But when he looks back on his life, Martin realizes that he has spent his time doing something that he loves and that, to him at least, is beautiful.

But if you flip the book over, the story proceeds very differently—or so it seems at first. At the crossroads, Martin decides to obey his parents. They are older than he is, and must know best. He is sorry to let snooker go, and at first he misses it badly, but he bears down on his studies, always does his homework, and brings home report cards with perfect marks. The things he learns are very interesting. The same knack that he displayed on the snooker table makes him excel at certain subjects at school. He is skilful at geometry. He is brilliant at calculating angles, and grasping mathematical relationships between objects. When he goes to university, he studies astronomy. Now instead of contemplating small red orbs on a field of green, he studies fiery planets on a field of black, but sometimes when photographs come back from exploratory missions to Mars or Venus the pictures are not so different from the ones you see when lining up a red with the corner pocket.

Martin becomes an astronaut. (Whether this was a credible career trajectory, Irina wasn't bothered; in a children's book you're granted wiggle room.) There are good and bad things about his life. His parents are proud of him, but he is often out in space for years at a time, and he gets lonely. Sometimes, even though to other people being an astronaut must seem exciting, it's a little bit boring, checking the instruments day after day. Once in a while staring off into the stars he wonders what it would have been like if he'd played snooker instead. But he knows that sometimes you make a choice, and you live with the consequences, the nice bits and the not-so-nice. He is lucky to experience many peak moments. He loves taking off in a rocket, and landing with a splash in the ocean. He even comes close to winning a Nobel Prize, and though in the end it goes to someone else, that is all right. Because when he looks back on his life, Martin realizes that he has spent his time doing something that he loves and that, to him at least, is beautiful.

Once Irina got down to the illustrations, she forgot all about envying Ramsey his long, boozy nights in bars, and stopped worrying about other women. Fatalistically she assumed that if he loved her he'd keep his pants zipped; besides, she knew in her bones that on this point her mother was wrong. While a few more pieces of furniture were still required to kit out the house, Irina was now contented to live without them. She often stayed up working late, and even fixing a sandwich was irritating. She drank less. She cut back on smoking.

Most of Irina's previous work had specialized in carefully gradated, blended colouration and luxurious, Rembrandt-like fluctuation of hues—which took great time and care, and was one reason those "hasty" drawings had been noticeably deficient. The new illustrations were anything but careless. Yet with these new images she discovered the hard line and the bold contrast. Forms didn't blend into the field, but fiercely stood their ground, brilliant red balls looming against a pulsating green backdrop. Because the story line focused on what Martin did professionally rather than on interpersonal drama, she designed each panel with no human figures; his parents were off the page, casting shadows over green carpet like cues over brightly lit baize. This absence of figures, and strong solids—the balls, the cue, the rails, the racks—meant she could draw on the resources of Russian constructivism, cubism, and abstract expressionism, and to imply the hurtling of objects through space she added dashes of futurism as well. As for medium, it was not the message, and she reached for whatever chalk, coloured pencil, charcoal, or tube of acrylic would deliver the desired effect, and sometimes to achieve a perfectly hard line or bold blare of a single colour she glued on razor-bladed swatches of glossy paper from adverts in *Snooker Scene*.

For the astronaut story, the style was identical. The planets looked like snooker balls, the stars like constellations of reds by the baulk cushion. Even Martin's geometry homework resembled diagrams of complex four-cushion plays in *Snooker Scene*. Though she didn't attend a single one of Ramsey's tournaments for the rest of the season—not even the World—she felt more intimate with his occupation than ever before. It was always this way, that by drawing something she came to own it.

Irina kept the project under wraps. When Ramsey returned home between tournaments, he was forbidden to enter her studio on the top floor, and she chafed at the distraction of his incessant tiddles on her door. In fact, he began to get on her nerves.

For one thing, Ramsey was a festival of intestinal complaints. This is the sort of thing you never learn about a man until you live with him, but he was wont to spend up to an hour at a time in the loo with the door closed, sometimes three or four times a day; the mysteries he concealed therein she supposed she was better off spared. And vague colonic discomfort was only the beginning. He was getting tendonitis in his left arm. His lower back ached. He had a strange pain in his kidney—or was it his gall bladder?—which she dismissed privately as gas.

To Irina's despair, just when she was getting rolling with the new illustrations, Ramsey cancelled his trip to Asia in March because of a head cold. You would think the poor man had come down with bubonic plague. Lying abed sipping hot toddies, Ramsey posited that this was no "common" cold and might be pneumonia, or Legionnaire's disease. Since his symptoms came down to a runny nose and a dry, forced-sounding cough, Irina proposed that maybe he was suffering the effects of too many Gauloises.

Irina was ordinarily a willing nurse, and went about fetching him toddies and tea, hankies and toast. But Ramsey made a demanding patient, and his instincts to play up his suffering made her sympathy come less easily than it might have had he evidenced some minimal measure of stoicism. So when she caught the cold as well, she stiff-upper-lipped it, going briskly about her day in the hopes of demonstrating a sturdier approach to illness. Alas, she merely convinced him that he had a far more lethal dose of what ailed them, while she must have pretty well "fought the bastard off."

Fortunately, while the rest of Ramsey's body languished at death's door, one part of his anatomy was hale as ever. Separations stored up explosive sexual appetite, sparing them the sating or boredom that always threatens with too much of a good thing. The fire that ran in her veins with Ramsey in bed lit a match to the pages upstairs, and the balls and planets in her illustrations pulsed with an energy that, had anyone understood where it came from, could have got her arrested for trading in kiddie porn.

Miraculously surviving his head cold and back on the tour, Ramsey continued to phone home every night, but the calls often went funny. Irina was convinced that he was primarily jealous of a pile of paper. But big surprise, all their scrappy calls regarded Lawrence. Irina had slipped off to see Ramsey for months, had she not? Irina had lied to Lawrence, had she not? Her loss of moral standing was apparently permanent. For Ramsey was dead sure that she was seeing Lawrence on the sly while he was gone.

Which she was.

But she wasn't carrying on with her ex in any sordid sense. They met for innocent cups of coffee. For them both, to rescue a postapocalyptic warmth was to redeem their decade's investment as not having been sunk in a junk bond. Behold, they did like each other, even once the worst had come to pass. Why, there were afternoons when she met him for a cappuccino near Blue Sky that she forgot for moments at a go that they had ever broken up. He still talked about Kosovo, as he would have back in the day. Their only acrimonious meeting was the one in which he pointed out that he shouldn't have had to learn she was married from Clive Everton on TV.

Her gratitude for what seemed a tentative forgiveness—as witnessed by his willingness to see her at all—was boundless. She had done the worst thing that it was possible to do to a person, in her view, and he would still sit across from her, ask after her work, even ask about the very scoundrel for whom she'd forsaken him. In his staunch loyalty to the prodigal, Lawrence was like fathers are supposed to be, and never are.

As he had the first time they met officially as exes, Lawrence still trained his gaze forty-five degrees from her face, allowing her to study him in wonderment without her contemplation being observed. At such times it came to her that he was a good man. That she was lucky to have known him, luckier to have known his love, and perhaps foolish to have risked everything a woman could ever dream of for everything and a little bit more.

Through this period she developed one other habit that she didn't disclose to her husband, which didn't involve Lawrence exactly. On occasional weekdays, with Lawrence sure to be at work, Irina would take a long walk south. Quietly, since she still had the keys (Lawrence may have let her keep them simply to spare himself the embarrassment of asking for them back) she would ease into the building on Trinity Street, and slip into her old flat. While she couldn't help but notice anything changed or lying about, she told herself she wasn't spying, for that was not her intent. She didn't poke through Lawrence's post or open his laptop. Sometimes she simply stood in the middle of the living room for minutes, or walked down the hall, glancing into the kitchen at the long rows of fading spices, touching the prints of Miró and Rothko, amazed that this diorama of her former life remained so intact that she could physically walk around in the past. Other times she sat in her old rust-coloured armchair, glancing up at the drapes she had sewn, perhaps perusing the *Daily Telegraph* left on the green marble coffee table from that morning—though she was careful to remember its folding and orientation, and to replace it exactly as it had lain. She smoothed the rumples from her chair before departing, and since Lawrence never said anything, she supposed she was successful in making her presence unfelt.

It was a curious pastime. But on Victoria Park Road, she was surrounded by snooker posters and snooker trophies and snooker magazines. On these surreptitious trips to Borough Irina wasn't really visiting Lawrence, but herself.

Meanwhile, Irina and her mother had still not spoken, and the impasse was now sufficiently entrenched that Irina couldn't imagine what advent might dislodge it. While silence technically took no time at all, she was surprised to discover how draining it was on a daily basis. She and her mother were not-speaking in an active sense that required a great deal of energy, and Irina lost more than one night's sleep tossing over whether the next time she saw her mother would be in an open casket. But the only way of making up to the woman would be to give ground on her cruel reading of Ramsey. Irina was at least able to keep tabs on the family through Tatyana, who seemed to enjoy her role as secret interlocutor. Irina fed her titbits about Ramsey's lucrative winnings and his rock-solid fidelity, but Tatyana liked to play both sides, and Irina could never be sure if her notes in bottles ever washed up on Brooklyn's shore. Irina made every attempt to simply write her mother off, but Raisa would promptly write herself back on again, like graffiti sandblasted away by public authorities that promptly reappears the next day. Thus Irina was confronted with the maddening tenacity of the blood tie. Oh, you didn't have to love each other; indeed, you could revile each other. But the one thing apparently not in your power was to demote a member of your family to the *unimportant*.

In her solitude, it came as a shock to register that she had been utterly neglecting her friends. Now that she'd finally remembered them, like that last item on your grocery list that you dash back for while someone holds your place in the checkout queue, Irina wouldn't have blamed any of them for huffing, "Oh, hubby's off on tour, *now* you want to have dinner, when before we were expendable? No, thank you!" Fortunately, most of Irina's friends had been around the romantic block, and regarded friendship holidays during which you restored or ruined your life as par for the course.

Yet these revivals of friendships were skewed. Last summer, she and Ramsey had gone over to Betsy and Leo's for dinner. While superficially the occasion was a success—polite, solicitous; their hosts had gone to lengths over the food—in retrospect it was a disaster. Betsy liked Lawrence. Betsy missed Lawrence, and Betsy probably held it against Irina, just a little, that now when she had her friend over to dinner she didn't get two for the price of one. She may also have felt wounded by the fact that Irina had failed to follow that advice not to "shoot her wad" on a "fancy, shiny gadget" that wouldn't last, and clearly thought Irina had lost leave of her senses. Leo had held forth about the state of the music industry, but neither of them had even passing interest in snooker; Ramsey's returning discourse on the rise of the attacking over the strategic game met an earnest attentiveness wildly at odds with Betsy's casual social brutality when she was being herself. Both parties vowed on parting that they must do this again soon, didn't mean it, and hadn't.

Thus Irina decided, daily, to ring Betsy *tomorrow*. She shied from the disapproval, the incomprehension, and especially the diplomacy, which from Betsy would feel so unnatural. For that matter, a whole cadre of companions clearly regarded Irina's running off with a snooker player as an attack of short-sighted intoxication that would end in tears. This whole pro-Lawrence contingent came in for short shrift. Melanie, by contrast, belonged to an opposing constellation of friends, who finally let fly that they had never been able to abide Lawrence, and who lauded Irina's departure as the bravest, most life-affirming gesture she'd ever made. Somehow the latter group's company proved the more pleasant to keep.

This year Irina was genuinely sorry when once more Ramsey failed to win the World. Worse, this year he was knocked out in the very first round, which (alas) brought him home earlier than usual. Militantly, for the months of May and June, when he was footloose and at her disposal, she completely ignored him during the day. She was closing on a finished draft.

Working flat-out, she met her private deadline with only a day to spare. For Ramsey's forty-ninth birthday in July she led him upstairs, ushering him into the room from which he had been banished since January.

He slowly turned the drawings; intended for reduction, each sheet was two feet by three. At first his silence made her nervous, and she worried that he didn't like them, or resented her incursion into his territory. Her fears were allayed by the dumbstruck expression on his face. He wasn't talking because he was afraid to say anything lame. At last he must have resigned himself that he talked the way he talked. Turning the last panel of the astronaut story, he said solemnly, "This is fucking brilliant."

That would do nicely.

They had a simple dinner at Best of India that night. After heaping the drawings with still more praise, Ramsey ventured, "I hate to sound thick as a post, since I know the story's for nippers. But what's it mean?"

"The idea is that you don't have only one destiny. Younger and younger, kids are pressed to decide what they want to do with their lives, as if everything hinges on one decision. But whichever direction you go, there are going to be upsides and downsides. You're dealing with a set of trade-offs, and not one perfect course in comparison to which all the others are crap. The idea is to take the pressure off. Martin gets to express many of the same talents in each story, but in different ways. There are varying advantages and disadvantages to each competing future. But I didn't want to have one bad future and one good. In both, everything is all right, really. Everything is all right."

Ramsey asked plaintively, "In the snooker story—why couldn't he win the World?"

Irina laughed. "Because that would undermine my thesis. Snooker isn't his sole destiny, even if it works out in many regards very well. And you don't have to win the World to be a great snooker player, right?"

"Bollocks!" he said with a laugh, and clinked her glass.

❖ ❖ ❖

Despite the lesson of the tale itself, "everything was all right" for Irina only after protracted tribulations. For months, she e-mailed JPEGs from publisher to publisher. More than one UK editor admired the work, but cited its production costs as too high. Moreover, she hadn't a hope in hell of selling American editors on the idea, when it required explaining upfront as she had to her mother that no, *snooker* was not a card game. It began to look as if the fruit of her fevered endeavour would never see the light of day.

Since misfortunes arrive in clumps—if misfortune this turn of the wheel could be counted—during the begging-bowl period of that autumn, Irina got pregnant. It's true that, acting on some vague notion about giving her body a rest, when Ramsey was to be away for three weeks for the LG Cup she'd gone off the pill. Knocked out in the second round, he'd come home unexpectedly, and they'd used condoms. Well, one night excepted . . . From the day she'd lost her virginity with Chris, she'd always found penis-in-a-Baggie sex repellent. But for pity's sake, she was forty-four! Hardly a goddess of fertility, and they'd only been lazy that one time! On the other hand, for a child to proceed from all that fucking had about it a genetic inevitability. A kid, after all, was the point.

She first suspected that one of the tadpoles that had been straining to swim the channel had finally plunged home two days after Ramsey left for the UK Championship. As she trotted up and down the stairs, her breasts ached. When they grew only more swollen and tender, Irina took a home pregnancy test. Before she ever had the chance, per the directions, to balance the plastic white wand upright on the counter, a solid line in its window formed the unambivalent slash of a "Do Not Enter" sign. The fact that now of all times Ramsey wasn't at her side vivified the style of motherhood that lay before her.

Unless Ramsey quit the tour for keeps, for two-thirds of the year Irina would be a de facto single parent. She would get up for night feedings all by herself. She would lie abed with a child at her breast watching bad late-night TV. She'd shop alone for clothes and baby food, struggling to fit a pushchair into the Jaguar. Ramsey would ring from time to time and ask her to put the baby on, and throw the child joyfully over his head on little visits, but for the most part she could look forward to little or no assistance from a father in *Bangkok*. He might take to parenthood as entertainment. Yet Ramsey was not responsible. He'd be the kind of father who rocked up with flashy toys but never came home with nappy-rash cream. All the aspects of parenthood that were a drag would land in her lap. The kid would resent Meanie Disciplinarian Mommy and idolize Indulgent Hardly-Ever-Home Dad, world-renowned snooker star—for Irina knew from experience with her own father that children reliably favour the parent in shorter supply.

So she was touched, and amazed, and wondrous; she was also realistic. Nevertheless, the prospect of scraping her beloved's baby into the bin like table scraps was intolerable.

As Irina battled for footing, she hated the idea of telling Ramsey on the phone, and procrastinated—though as a consequence the calls they did have were halting and false. She was afraid that he'd be put out. He'd never talked up having a family, nor rued having sired no children with Jude. He might regard the pregnancy as an inconvenience or worse, and she worried that he'd no longer be attracted to her as she grew large.

Her delay was fortuitous. Towards the end of the UK Championship, she began to bleed. Numbly she checked into hospital for a D and C. She only told him when it was over.

Of course, she knew what he'd say: He was terribly sorry not to be with her during such an upsetting ordeal, and he promised to come home soon. But surely nature knew best. She was a little old to become a new mother; though he'd be careful not to injure her pride, he'd point out gently that she'd have given birth at forty-five. Taking a pregnancy to term might have been too hard on her, which her body had recognized. Wouldn't the chance of birth defects have been awfully high? Why, often when you miscarry, it's because there's something wrong with the baby, and that's why your system rejects it. And they hadn't really been prepared at this stage of the game to raise a child, had they? Who would have grown to be a teenager with elderly parents. Of course, if they'd married twenty years earlier . . . But they hadn't, had they? So maybe they'd been spared an agonizing choice. All this may have been true, but Irina was in no mood to hear it. She recoiled from the prospect of her husband's unspoken but palpable relief.

Ramsey surprised her. He said none of that, not even the part about being sorry not to be with her and coming home, though he would later upbraid himself for not doing so. At the time, all he could do was cry.

❖ ❖ ❖

Seeking the standard compensation of the childless career woman, Irina did finally locate a small concern in London called Snake's Head that was so taken with her snooker book that they would assume the costs of production, even if the advance on offer was risibly small.

Frame and Match was published in September of 2000 to little fanfare. The company tried to capitalize on the fact that the author was married to Ramsey Acton, but hadn't the publicity budget to leverage the advantage. Reviews were appreciative but few. The print run was low, the cover price high, and Irina's survey of Waterstone's and WHSmith confirmed that only a handful had made it to the chains. But somehow, *everything was all right*. She had her ten author's copies, which she doled out discerningly, to Betsy, to Tatyana, and—with reluctance—to her mother by post, a peace gesture of sorts. Irina wasn't famous and she wasn't raking in royalties; she hadn't *won the world*. But she had spent her time doing something that she loved and that, to Irina at least, was beautiful.

◘ chapter nine ◘

The niggling sensation of something being wrong or changed that had plagued Irina since Lawrence's return from Russia gradually subsided. If he was hard on her for getting plastered at Christmas and denting her mother's samovar, Lawrence had a powerful sense of decorum, and his dressing-down in such circumstances was only to be expected—as well as his insistence that they personally lug the thing into a local metalsmith and pay for the repair. Should indeed something have altered, the mind is merciful in such matters, and often cannot recall what it does not have. That period of subtle perturbation had been peculiar, like repeatedly detecting a flicker in the periphery of her vision, yet when she turned to stare directly where she thought something had moved, the vista stood stock-still. Thereafter, the very memory of sensing something amiss, too, blessedly evanesced, and her version of events became that everything was fine, everything had always been fine, and she had never thought otherwise.

One was perpetually subjected to tales of "obsessive love" in cinema: the kind of romance in which you lose yourself in the other, flooding over your own boundaries to mingle indistinguishably with the oncoming waves from an opposite shore. Irina had no idea how such people ever got anything done—earned their keep, paid the bills, and shopped for dinner; in fact, you never saw them doing anything of the kind in movies. Too, the "consuming passion" was always portrayed as mutually destructive, as proceeding inexorably toward private Armageddon.

In any event, Irina and Lawrence had embraced an alternative romantic model, one that mightn't have made for riveting movies, but did make for a fruitful life. Lives. Separate, fruitful lives. Having no interest in "losing himself" in her or at all, Lawrence regarded the project in which they were engaged—and it was a project—as one of helping each other to become the finest discrete individuals as they could manage.

Lawrence called her to her responsible, competent, professional self. Last June, she had delivered the portfolio for *The Miss Ability Act* well before deadline; each panel was exactingly wrought. While not knocked-on-butt agog, her editor had been firmly pleased and admiring. Known as reliable and meticulous, Irina remained in the good graces of one more company, and they were glad to offer her another contract for a small book already under way with another author—thanks to Lawrence's productive nagging to always keep her eye on the next project.

Because Irina hadn't the background to be of use to Lawrence in his research on the Tamil Tigers, she helped him in return by cheerfully assuming the everyday burden of shopping and cooking. In fact, when he took her aside the January after they returned from Brighton Beach— confiding that he'd just as soon pick up lunch around Blue Sky, and spare her sending him off to work with a sandwich—she'd felt strangely hurt. The prepared meats section of the supermarket had occasioned a queer pang ever since.

To Lawrence's credit, the boost of his professional profile since the Good Friday Agreement last year spurred him to bolster Irina's prominence in equal measure. He did not want a humble, subservient helpmeet who merely made sure that they never ran out of milk. The amount of time he dedicated to getting her up to speed in computer graphics was stupendous. As a belated Christmas present that she actually wanted, he bought her a new Apple, better for graphics than a PC, and all the necessary software.

Meantime, Irina had been powwowing on another matter with Betsy for months. (She and Betsy had grown close—in contrast to Melanie, a lively but high-strung actress whose vivacity could turn acrid on a dime, and around whom Irina had always to remember to be a bit careful. Melanie's bitter quip about what a homebody she'd become under Lawrence's thumb sent a chill through the friendship for keeps.) Irina was, after all, a *children's* book illustrator. In Betsy's view, the one sure formula for "going forward" as a couple was to have a child. Now, there were no guarantees, at forty-four. But Irina wouldn't be manipulated once more by Lawrence's shrugging relationship to all the things in life that actually mattered. With his passive acquiescence, she tossed her pills into the medicine cabinet like throwing dice, then tried to put the matter from her mind. She would get on with her work, take supplements of folic acid, and see what happened.

◼ ◻ ◼

It was Lawrence's idea that after mastering the new software she consider authoring her own book. He decried the weak material she was forced to illustrate; if she couldn't do better, she wouldn't do worse. Fortified by his faith in her, Irina took the plunge.

In girlhood, one of her favorite toys was her Etch A Sketch. As Irina recalled, when you were painstaking enough, and your sister didn't come along and shake your picture upside-down out of sheer meanness, it was possible to improve on crude outlines, and pattern or even blacken whole solids. A trip to Woolworth's confirmed that the classic toy was still in production, so the allusion wouldn't be lost on modern-day children.

It took many hours and calls to cybergeeks referred by friends, but eventually Irina got her software to approximate the line quality of an Etch A Sketch with staggering exactitude. Having perfected the technique at the keyboard, Irina set about drafting a story line to go with it:

A little boy named Ivan has a best friend called Spencer. The two boys do everything together—build tree houses, go skateboarding, try to best each other in sack races. At school, they are so famously inseparable that their teachers insist on seating them rows apart, to prevent the two from whispering during lessons. But Ivan's mother always knows to pour two glasses of milk after school, and slice two apples (which the upscale parents who bought these books would prefer to cookies), since Spencer was sure to come over every afternoon to play. Spencer is brainy, and often helps Ivan with his homework. After the work is done, they learn to make popcorn all by themselves—though on their first try, they forget the pot lid, and kernels fly all over the kitchen. Later the tale of the popcorn sailing through the room and landing in their hair, floating little white boats in the dishwater, becomes a story they love to retell on camping trips in the tent when it's raining.

But one day when Spencer is home sick, and Ivan is sorrowfully on his lonesome at school, Ivan meets another boy at recess. The new boy, Aaron, is tall, witty, and clever, as well as gifted at kickball. He seems to like Ivan especially much. Soon Ivan is having such a good time with his new friend that he forgets all about missing Spencer, and asks if Aaron would like to come over to his house after school.

Ivan's mother is surprised to see a different boy turn up with her son, but there is no telling about childhood friendships, so she serves them milk and fruit with no questions asked. Aaron and Ivan go outside to skateboard, and it turns out that Aaron knows all kinds of tricks that Ivan has never learned before. The truth is, Ivan is having even more fun with Aaron than he ever did with Spencer, quite.

Suddenly Ivan looks up to find Spencer staring forlornly through the open gate of the backyard, where Aaron is teaching Ivan to do flips. Spencer must have started to feel better, and his mother had let him come over to play. Ivan will never forget the look on Spencer's face before the boy turns and runs away.

That night, Ivan feels terrible. He can't eat his dinner. He can't sleep, and tosses and turns until daylight. He keeps seeing the desolate expression on Spencer's face, and remembering all the games they played together, all the homework that Ivan would never have been able to get right if it weren't for Spencer's help. And then he remembers the afternoon of the lidless popcorn, and bursts into tears.

The next day at recess, Ivan pulls Aaron aside. Ivan confesses that he really likes Aaron, and thinks he's the greatest skateboarder he's ever seen. But Ivan already has a best friend. His old best friend may not be as good at skateboarding, and maybe they get a little bored with each other some afternoons, but that's the way it is when you know somebody really well. Ivan says that Aaron will have to find someone else to play with, because he doesn't want to feel as bad as he did last night ever again.

But that is not the end of the story. A few weeks later Aaron *does* find another boy to play with, and in an afternoon they become best friends—the very best. In fact, they, too, are inseparable. And the name of Aaron's new best friend is Spencer.

That night, Ivan feels terrible.

□ □ □

When she showed the story to Lawrence, he was appreciative, but he had a problem with the ending. "Why don't you just stop there?" he asked, pointing to where Ivan tells Aaron to find another playmate. "Lop off the rest, and you've got a solid, simple, unified story about loyalty whose point any kid could get."

"But I don't want it to be too simple," she objected.

"It's a children's book!"

"The biggest mistake children's book authors make is writing down to their audience. Kids are short. That doesn't mean they're stupid."

"But that ending fucks everything up!"

"Fucked-up sounds realistic to me."

"Look, up to that penultimate point, you're saying basically, stick by old ties—and we'll leave aside for a sec the fact that you can have more than one friend."

"You can only have one *best* friend, as any schoolchild knows. A huge proportion of the drama in childhood is all about who fills that slot, and who gets booted out."

"But as is, the moral of this story is that the protagonist was a sap, and should have run off with the new kid when he had the chance. Like, screw old ties, it's a Darwinian world out there, every man for himself."

"That's one way of reading it," she said coolly. "The other slant you could put on it is that Ivan feels terrible in both instances, and your author never tells you in which he feels worse. In fact, the suggestion is—since the wording is identical—that between betraying and being betrayed, the anguish may be a toss-up."

"There is no way that any kid is going to get that," Lawrence insisted.

"There is no way that any kid is *not* going to get that," Irina countered.

Lawrence took umbrage that she resisted his editorial advice, but Irina stuck to her guns on the ending, and then got down to the illustrations. Drawing with a mouse admittedly inserted a sense of remove, but the computer was no less engaging than paint or pencils, in its way. She especially enjoyed drawing wonky fluffs of popcorn, the judder of the line imparting a sense of explosion. Though she did miss colour, the black-and-white format enabled her to concentrate on the expressiveness of the figures—the slim, attenuated grace of Aaron, the wide-eyed, despondent close-up of Spencer's stricken face when he believes that in a single day he's been replaced. Because to accurately reflect the nature of an Etch A Sketch drawing the line could never lift, depicting isolated elements like eyes and shirt buttons was technically challenging. Once she was satisfied with a picture, she surrounded the illustration with the red frame of the toy, adding two white knobs on the bottom.

The work was well under way when Lawrence came home one night in March looking alarmingly pale. He admitted that he'd felt "a little weird" all day, but had soldiered through to nightfall at Blue Sky. She knew something was terribly wrong when he couldn't make a dent in their popcorn. Not long thereafter, he slipped off and closed the loo door, though the sound of violent retching escaped its cracks. The next day, a Saturday, Lawrence propped himself in front of his computer to work on a paper about the guerrilla war in Nepal. At regular intervals, he would scuttle to the loo, quietly brush his teeth, and return to the keyboard.

Lawrence made an exasperating patient. For a solid fortnight, he dragged himself out of bed at seven, dressed for work, and stared down a cup of coffee that clearly turned his stomach. Then it would be left to Irina to take the coffee away, fix a cup of weak tea and piece of unbuttered toast, and put him back to bed. Though he was dropping an alarming amount of weight, he perpetually urged her to return to her project, and apologized for the distraction of his "stupid little virus." Yet when towards the end of his convalescence she too came down with a touch of something—just a mild sore throat and runny nose—Lawrence, still shaky and off-colour, fetched pillows, hankies, and hot lemon drinks, even braving the ghastly Elephant & Castle for novels and lozenges. For Pete's sake, he was the only man she'd ever met on whom she would have urged *more* self-pity.

❏ ❏ ❏

The fact that she finished her project on Ramsey's birthday—his forty-ninth, she calculated—wasn't altogether coincidental. Oh, she hadn't proposed to Lawrence that they try to resume their old tradition; goodness, they hadn't seen Ramsey since Bournemouth nearly two years before, and there comes a point where you put off getting in touch out of sheer embarrassment that for far too long you have put off getting in touch. Besides, last year Ramsey himself had let them off the hook. But because the sixth of July remained a powerful marker in her mind, it made a fitting private deadline, of whose significance Lawrence was agreeably unaware when she unveiled the illustrations that night.

"It's fucking brilliant!" Lawrence announced when he had finished leafing through her printouts. Alas, he could not resist adding, "I still think that ending is off. But you're only going to listen to an editor, who will tell you the same thing."

Despite his reservations, Lawrence dedicated himself to seeing *Ivan and the Terribles* celebrated in the world of commerce with a determination that put her supportive trips to Tesco in the shade. He declared that it was high time she replaced her mousy, small-time agent with heavy-hitting representation, and did exhaustive Internet research on which influential British agents had lucrative sales in the US. He "helped" her design—i.e., put together himself—a professional-looking submission package, including a CD of both the *Ivan* illustrations and digital photos of previous work, a polished CV, and confident cover letter. Her studio grew stacked with identical manila envelopes, all neatly addressed with printed labels and pasted with proper postage. She may have been a tad uneasy with his taking over so completely; at once, his efforts on her account moved her more than she could say.

Meanwhile, six months had elapsed since Irina had ceased to stop by the clinic in Bermondsey to pick up new packets of pills, and yet her periods proceeded to make her feel heavy and churlish in perfect cycle with the moon. Thus that autumn she prevailed upon Lawrence to see his GP, and got a checkup herself. Irina's blood-work confirmed that for a woman her age her hormone levels were splendid. But when his GP rang, her partner grunted through the call with a gruffness that even for Lawrence seemed impolite.

"Well, that's it, then," he said when he hung up. "Low sperm count." He sank onto the sofa. He didn't turn on the television, though it was time for the news.

Irina sat beside him, and tucked a lock behind his ear. "It's really hopeless?"

"Seems like!" he said. "You know, I've read that male potency in the West may be plummeting because of widespread use of oral contraception. You girls pop all these pills and then pee them away, and the estrogen gets into the water supply."

Irina smiled. "Are you saying that it's *my* fault?"

"Well, it's nobody's *fault,* is it?" he said ferociously.

"This really bothers you, doesn't it? Even though, on the kid business, I sensed you were on the fence."

Lawrence stood up. "Well, it's probably better this way, isn't it? You're forty-four. Pregnancy would be hard on you, and at your age the chances of birth defects soar. Maybe if we'd gotten on this a long time ago . . . But Jesus, by the time the kid entered college, we'd be drawing social security. Besides, with me at Blue Sky weekdays, you'd do most of the work, and that wouldn't be fair. Your career would suffer."

Though she sympathized with his sense of having been unmanned, Irina was struggling with her own disappointment, and sour-grapes wasn't helping. "No, I know you. Between weekends and evenings, you'd find a way to pull your weight and then some. Look at the way you nurse me when I don't feel well, or how you're helping me with *Ivan*. You're chronically responsible. You'd be up at four, crooning and rocking and feeding the baby breast-expressed bottles from the refrigerator so I could get some sleep."

Lawrence shoved his hands in his pockets and looked to the floor. "Yeah, probably." Glancing up, he seemed to remember her. "Did you have your heart set on this?"

"Oh, we'd left it so late, I couldn't afford to count on it. I've just had this feeling that something more needs to *happen*. We just keep going on and on and . . ." She shrugged.

"Lots of other things can happen," he said, though the promise sounded ominous. "Still, I'm sorry."

"You know," she said tentatively, "we might think about alternatives."

"Adoption?"

"That's more of a crapshoot than I'm ready for. I meant—maybe in vitro."

"If my jizz is firing blanks, it's not going to hit a bull's-eye in a petri dish, either."

"No, obviously it would have to be someone else's." She avoided the word *sperm*.

"A bank?" Lawrence wouldn't use the word himself. "That's still half crapshoot. Who's to say the donor's not a serial killer?"

"I was more thinking that maybe we could ask—someone we know."

"Like *who*?"

Irina looked away. "No one comes to mind, off the top of my head . . ."

Lawrence thrust his face into her line of vision. "*Someone we know,* and you wouldn't need in vitro, would you?"

"Lawrence! I wouldn't do that."

"*However* some other guy's spunk gets up there, are you seriously proposing that I constantly bump into *someone we know* and he knows and I know that he's the real father of my kid? Use your head! How would you feel if you had to raise a son or daughter that was, I don't know, mine and Betsy's?"

She smiled. "Could do worse."

"Forget it. Forget the whole fucked-up thing. If it's not clean, I'm not interested." *If it's not mine, I'm not interested*—a running theme.

Irina did forget it. Lawrence had violent convictions about what a man did and did not do. Of course, borrowing a cup of sugar from next door would never have worked, emotionally at least. But for once Irina despaired of her partner's rigidity, his strict notions of manliness, which now constrained her life as well. Because physically? Maybe a woman knows these things. Maybe a woman can tell. She had a gut instinct that the first donor prospect who popped into her head would have been a perfect match. It would have worked. In vitro or otherwise, it would have worked—the very first try.

◻ ◻ ◻

So they sought the standard compensation for a childless career woman, and lo, in short order three prestigious agents were eager to take Irina on. The basis on which she selected the winning representative surprised her; it was out of character.

Irina had been frugal her whole life. Her mother was obsessed with money, and as a girl she'd coloured her crayons to nubs. Granted that Lawrence now made a decent wage, but she had never believed that his money was her money quite, and she felt self-conscious that with her stingy illustration advances she couldn't completely cover her half of the rent. Shopping in thrift stores, buying their furniture at Oxfam, was one way of contributing to the family coffers.

Yet there was a meanness to this outlook, a reluctance to spend the currency of life itself. Unrelenting penny-pinching precluded bursts of you-only-live-once abandon, as well as the fuck-it thrill particular to costly purchases that are foolhardy. It sobered Irina to realize the degree to which she allowed parsimony to control her decisions, on both the large scale and the small. When she had offered to pay her own way to Russia, had she really been serious, or did she make the gesture only knowing full well that Lawrence didn't want her along? For that matter, they were a hop, skip, and a jump from the Continent, yet she never urged Lawrence to take holidays in Rome or Venice, because it was *too expensive*. When was the last time she'd bought herself a new dress? Not a new old dress, a new new dress? She couldn't remember. They now had this Ford Capri, but she still did most of the shopping on foot, to save on petrol. At Tesco, she'd always get the yellow-tag mangetout, despite having a yen for French green beans—which were *too expensive*. If bargain-hunting afforded a scheming little pleasure, were there not also pleasures in extravagance—in obliviously blowing £200 on a single night out?

The first agent was nice. The second agent seemed in uncanny accord with her artistic sensibility. The third agent promised that *Ivan* would sell for pots of money.

Bingo.

Pitching simultaneously to Britain and the States, Irina's new agent put the book up for auction, and between the two markets Irina's Etch A Sketch project brought in $125,000. Irina took Lawrence out to dinner at Club Gascon, and though they didn't quite manage to squander £200 on five courses with matching wines, they came damned close.

Thus they were in festive form for Christmas in Brighton Beach again. This time there were no fights about the heating or napkins or soap dishes, much less any drunken displays of abandon that knocked over the samovar, and when familial gatherings proceed with unerring smoothness and conviviality, they can also seem profoundly pointless. On the plane home, Irina fantasized about what kind of climactic quarrel she could pick with her mother that might issue in a merciful era of not-speaking. Some concocted impasse would save so much bother, including those newsy international phone calls placed with dutiful regularity every month. Still, the visit had its gratifying side. Tatyana had fallen all over herself hugging and squeezing and declaring for no reason at all that she "simply adored her big sister," of whom she was "incredibly proud," which meant that inside she was seethingly jealous.

Ivan and the Terribles was published in September of 2000 to great fanfare on both sides of the Atlantic. Its publicity budget was generous, and if the reviews were less so, large adverts in the New York and London *Times* more than made up for critical nitpicking. The print run was enormous, the cover price widely discounted, and Irina's survey of Waterstone's and WHSmith confirmed that stacks had made it into the chains. Decry "selling out" as you may, there was a variety of selling out—of copies—whose stigma Irina would gladly assume. No one was going to tell her that those piles of red-framed glossy hardbacks on Waterstone's front tables weren't *beautiful*.

❖ chapter ten ❖

Irina told herself she could use the constitutional, but her heels down Grove Road rang with the same self-deceit of afternoon clips into the bedroom on the pretext of stowing a pair of socks, when her real intention was to masturbate. If she was walking all the way down to Borough, chances were high that she would indulge her secret vice.

The morning's mild late-April weather was overcast, yet she felt oddly dogged by a shadow, a darkness at her back. She'd allowed plenty of time for this adventure—the tube ride home, then a late-afternoon train to Sheffield from St. Pancras. As for the vice, though it was Saturday she'd assurance by e-mail that Lawrence was safely at a conference in Dubai. So the drag on her spirits must be the impending World final tomorrow. Ramsey had once more got his hopes up, and if he went down in this one, that would make eight championship finals that he'd reached and lost. He'd turned fifty last summer, and if he didn't prevail in the 2001 he might never get a chance at that title again.

More honestly, the dread may have been of going to another *snooker* tournament, period—smiling idiotically beside Ramsey as the supportive little wife. It would be one thing were Ramsey ever obliged to play the supportive little husband. But aside from her sparsely populated book launch at Foyle's last September—for which, Snake's Head being strapped, Ramsey had bought the wine—he'd had little experience of what it felt like to be invisible.

Her attendance at tournaments was now a constant bone of contention. That first season during which he'd kept her tucked in tow Ramsey had taken more titles than in the ten years previous, culminating in making his seventh final at the Crucible. Yet the following two tours, with her company at best sporadic, his ranking had nosedived. His reduced status at Match-Makers translated into the loss of perks like limo service, and while he may not have cared much about limos in and of themselves, he did care about what they meant. Worse, dropping from the Top 16 required this giant among men to play qualifiers to gain entry to tournaments whose trophies had decorated his basement snooker hall, which was, he said, like having to ring the doorbell of your own house.

So Ramsey had concluded that Irina's presence made all the difference, and pressured her at every turn to come along. She'd insisted that she was a woman with her own career and not his lucky rabbit's-foot. She didn't ever want to get bored with snooker (that was the politic formulation), and that meant only going to see him play when she felt like it (okay, basically never). Oh, his expectation that she attend the final tomorrow was more than reasonable, and it had been ungenerous of her to watch yesterday's semi at home on TV—and "watch" only loosely speaking, since the match was really just on in the background while she e-mailed Lawrence about Dubai.

Crossing London Bridge to Borough High Street was bittersweet, passing Borough Market a sharp reminder of how little she cooked these days. But then, maybe all those pies had been a waste of time. She couldn't say.

The instant that she slid her old key in the lock and slipped into the flat, something felt changed. The air smelt more fragrant. A saucy black beret decked the coat rack.

The living room at first glance seemed unaltered, until her eye lit indignantly on a muddy-brown Lissitzky, which had replaced the Miró. Lawrence, buy new art prints? On the table lay the *Independent,* a paper that he ridiculed as shrill. Where, pray tell, was the *Telegraph*?

Padding uneasily down the hall, Irina poked her head into her former studio, long ago converted to Lawrence's study. Now, in the space where her drawing table once sat, was a second desk, and not of the Oxfam ilk that Irina favoured but brand-new. Further reconnaissance turned up a clatter of makeup on her dresser—gaudy lipsticks that Irina herself eschewed—and in the loo, mango-blueberry shampoo.

Lawrence used Head & Shoulders.

It was in the kitchen that Irina began to frown. To her consternation, her long rows of spice jars had been reduced to a few crude standards like premixed Italian seasoning and dehydrated parsley. Some twenty popcorn seasonings, several like Old Bay and Stubb's Barbeque Spice Rub toted from New York, had vanished wholesale. The larder had also been culled, her dark sesame paste, rose water, and pomegranate molasses replaced with soup mixes, instant gravy granules, and bottled Bolognaise. The seal was broken on Irina's massive rainy-day jar of Spanish anchovies in olive oil; she shouldn't betray her presence here, but the amount of self-control it took to keep from putting that big beautiful jar sternly in the refrigerator was stupendous.

Irina's pulse accelerated. Clearly any moment now the door could open, even with Lawrence in Dubai. It would have been wise to skedaddle, but she had come all the way from the East End to bathe in the light of her old life streaming through those eight-foot windows. So instead she contrived a plausible alibi—"Terribly sorry to have startled you; I'm Lawrence's ex, Irina, just dropping by to pick up a—pair of shoes!"—and settled into her rust-coloured armchair to contemplate this revolutionary state of affairs.

Jealousy under the circumstances was preposterous. Irina was the one who'd walked out, and if Lawrence had found a hand to hold a full three and a half years later, that was not only his right but his due. Presumably this turn of events might lift the burden of guilt that still weighed heavily when she conjured his lonely life. She continued to feel responsible for Lawrence; it was always hard to slip in here and not leave broccoli in the fridge. Yet she was not so selfish as to keep Lawrence eternally at her beck for occasional cups of coffee. While she was a little hurt that he'd not seen fit to inform her of a new woman in his life, technically it was none of her business. Nevertheless, when poking about the flat she'd felt for all the world like a little bear who cries, "Who's been sleeping in my bed?" and "Who's been eating my porridge?"

After an hour of reverie, Irina bestirred herself, and drew on her jacket. Maybe she'd be cured for good of this perverse pastime, now that Goldilocks might come barging in unannounced at any moment. Cautious to maintain her alibi all the way to the pavement, she rustled into her old wardrobe for a pair of pumps—shoved to the back, behind a line of whorish stilettos.

She scurried downstairs and pulled the front door closed. Yet at the very point that she should have been able to breathe a sigh of relief, her heart stopped.

On the kerb, Ramsey stood propped against his opalescent-green Jaguar XKE, smoking a cigarette. The snapshot unerringly duplicated his appearance at her doorstep on his forty-seventh birthday—once again, leaning but perfectly straight, Ramsey himself resembled a cue stick set against the car—except that when he retrieved her for sushi that summer those cool, contemplative inhalations had been mesmerizing, while just now the same tableau made her want to throw up.

"What are you doing here?" she asked in a strangled voice.

"Funny, that. I was about to ask you the same thing." There was no gracious ushering to the passenger seat, but a quick jerk of his head in its direction. "Get in."

Irina hung back. "I know how this looks. But he's not up there. I could show you."

"Away from the table, I don't fancy playing games. Your man hiding in the cupboard, or nipping out the back?"

"Ramsey, please! Go upstairs with me! Let me show you that no one's there!"

"You humiliated me enough for one day, *ducky*, and I'll not have this argy-bargy on the Queen's highway. *Get in*." He flipped his fag into the gutter, where it joined several other fresh butts, swung into the driver's seat, and pushed open the passenger door. Glumly, Irina complied.

The Jaguar ploughed from the kerb, Ramsey's flinty gaze trained forward. He looked torturously attractive—slender wrists extending from the leather jacket as he gripped the wheel, the facets of his face all the more chiselled for being set in rigid fury. It was always like this, when he cut himself off from her, that she longed for him, physically longed for him, and she had to stop herself from slipping her hand into the taut, hot hollow of his inner thigh. Cutting her eyes nervously towards the driver's seat, she thought in dull helplessness, *I will always want to fuck him.*

Indeed, at that moment she was visited by the disconcerting vision of having got divorced, perhaps over the very sort of gross misunderstanding now under way in this car, and then running into her ex-husband by chance at a bar. She knew with perfect certainty that even with years of hostile impasse intervening, she would no sooner lay eyes on this gangly, achingly well-proportioned snooker player—pretending aloofness no doubt, feigning indifference to her arrival, pulling on a Gauloise and laughing collusively with his mates—than she would want to fuck him.

Snugged forlornly apart in her bucket seat, Irina was reminded of one of her most dog-eared sexual fantasies, if hardly the stuff of Germaine Greer: getting down on her knees before those tall, neat black jeans and begging him, begging him please would he let her suck him off. Surely fantasies of self-abasement, while commonplace, were *unhealthy,* but that's what she would do in that bar. She could see herself, perhaps not having crossed paths with the man for a decade, during which no cards, no e-mails, and no calls, falling to the floor and imploring him, would he please take it out, could she see it one more time, could she touch it and suck it and make it hard. Here all this time she'd been anxious over Betsy's old admonishment that sexual infatuation never lasts, but no one had warned her against the equally wretched alternative whereby come what may you couldn't get shed of the fixation, and it stuck to your fingers like tar.

"Where are we going?" she asked after several awful minutes of silence.

"Sheffield," he said. "In case you forgot, which it seems you have done, I'm playing the championship final tomorrow."

"But I haven't packed a bag." She looked at the plastic holdall in her lap, wondering how she'd explain the shoes.

"Worse things happen at sea," he said sourly.

"I seem to recall getting it in the neck a few years back for not packing a bag."

"Bournemouth, ducky, was a mere difference of opinion. I'll show you getting it in the neck."

Irina closed her eyes. "How did you know I was there?"

"I followed you, didn't I?"

She turned to him in incredulity. "You're supposed to be in Sheffield. You came all the way down to London to lurk outside your own door, and follow your wife, wherever she happened to be going? What if I'd been going to Safeway? Wouldn't that have dug up a lot of dirt—scandal, she's still buying yellow-tag vegetables! My God! Do you distrust me that much?"

"Turns out I don't distrust you near enough."

"It's not easy to tail a pedestrian in a car. Are you that lazy, or did you like the challenge?"

"Look, I drive down to give you a lift up to Sheffield, so you don't have to take the train. It's meant to be a surprise. Just when I rock up, I see you leave the house. So I'm—curious, like."

369

"You weren't curious. You were paranoid."

"Paranoia, darling, is fear what ain't warranted. In this case, seems not."

"Ramsey. *I am not having an affair with Lawrence.*" The assertion sat there uselessly, like the shoes in her lap, which didn't even match her outfit.

"Just saying the same thing over and over don't make it so."

"I've only said it once. And I'm only going to say it once, too." Irina had a sick feeling that she'd repeat herself plenty by the time this was through.

"Fair enough. What was you doing in his flat, then? Having tea?"

Irina glanced defeatedly at the shoes; she'd never fob off on Ramsey the implausible excuse she'd concocted for Goldilocks. Besides, maybe, just maybe, this was an opportunity for her husband to understand her better. "I go there . . . once in a while. When Lawrence won't be home. I like to . . . walk around. I sit in my old chair. Sometimes I read the paper. That's all."

As an argumentative tool the truth was overrated. Ramsey grunted *Uh-huh* with disgust, as if she might have made more of an effort. "And why would you do that, then?"

She gazed out the window. "I love you, but—sometimes I feel a tug. Of my old life. Almost as if it's still running alongside this one. It's not that I exactly regret leaving Lawrence, but I can't help but wonder what it would have been like if I'd stayed. You and I have a wonderful life together. But it's fractious, you have to admit . . . You're gone for weeks, and then when you're home we keep bizarre hours and drink too much . . . So there are things about life with Lawrence that I miss. The order. The simplicity. The peace. I like to visit. It connects me with my past, and makes me feel more like myself."

"His dick in your cunt must make you *feel like yourself* as well."

Irina pressed two fingers to her forehead. "As for what else I miss, Lawrence never said ugly things like that to me, ever."

"Should have, shouldn't he? Wasn't you messing about with me?"

"So now I'm just a slag. Because I fell in love with you."

"You don't *exactly* regret leaving Anorak Man. Now, there's reassurance a bloke can well hold on to." As Ramsey took out his wrath on his fellow drivers, for once Irina wasn't relaxed by faith that his snooker skills transferred to the road. Suddenly small coloured balls bore no resemblance to two-ton vehicles whatsoever.

"Look," she said, "I know my explanation sounded strange. But you're in the final tomorrow. For the sake of your own concentration, you have to put this aside—"

"How considerate. For *my* sake, I'm to sweep the fact you're shagging another bloke right under the carpet."

"I *am* being considerate, you idiot! Isn't winning the World what you've worked toward since you were seven? You don't need all this aggro! You need a *nice meal,* and a *pleasant evening with your wife,* and a *good sleep.*"

Alas, the harmonious scenario could not have sounded more far-fetched.

❖ ❖ ❖

"Your man," whispered in Irina's ear once she had hastily settled in the Crucible's guest section, "has looked in better nick."

She shot a sharp glance over her shoulder at Jack Lance. "He's here, isn't he."

"By a whisker. You wouldn't think, now, that a geezer with a ranking of thirty-two would play quite so fast and loose with a championship final. Had us all on tenterhooks, he did. Whiff of the prima donna, sashaying in here with thirty seconds to spare. And fancy, without even bothering to comb his hair."

"Ramsey's *ablutions,*" she said stiffly, facing forward again, "ran a little behind."

"Had a pretty hard night of it yourself, love, from the looks of you." Jack's breath was hot on the nape of her neck.

"Thank you for your concern." She hated Jack Lance. It wasn't just that he was greasy and hated her, too. When Ramsey slipped from the Top 16, all the little gestures of flowers and champagne and room-service sushi were cut off with the same abruptness with which a smile would drop from the manager's face. Now that, in defiance of anyone's expectation, Ramsey Acton was back in the final, Jack was once again brownnosing up a storm, as if he hadn't given Ramsey the bum's rush for two solid years. Although the manager had a point—for every twenty minutes, late-comers were docked a frame—it was only thanks to Irina's shaking and fetching and phoning, *Jack,* that Ramsey's inert body wasn't still cutting a diagonal across their hotel mattress.

Lights down. To rousing acclaim, the MC introduced Ronnie

O'Sullivan: the heir apparent, the bête noire. Though the dickie-bow rule had now been relaxed, O'Sullivan had respectfully donned one anyway, along with a traditional white shirt and black waistcoat; he had traded the ponytail of his bad-boy youth for a cropped, conservative cut. After taking the cure in posh adult summer camps, he'd not even coldcocked any WPBSA officials for a couple of years. Striding to his chair, at the ripe old age of twenty-five Ronnie exuded a new seriousness, his demure smile to the crowd flashing the turned leaf of a Reformed Character.

When the MC introduced his opponent, Ramsey Acton also appeared a changed man, but in the only manner that a player with a lifelong reputation for grace, sportsmanship, and stately deportment could transform: for the worse. His bow tie slanted at a seasick angle, and unfortunately a heavily starched white shirt holds not only planes but creases. Unshaven stubble glinted in the stage lights. Before locating his chair, Ramsey stood with a slight weave squinting at the crowd, as if astonished to find himself in a snooker tournament when he thought he was on the way to the launderette.

Irina put a hand to her head. The night before, he'd ordered a bottle of Remy from room service, and over her protests dialled for a second around sunrise. She'd been petrified that he'd be hungover for the final, but hadn't thought to worry about an eventuality far more dire: that he would still be drunk.

Snooker was rife with the myth of drink, but myth it was. Even Alex Higgins, who famously performed three sheets to the wind, had never exactly benefited from not being able to see the cue ball. More, however larger-than-life the legendary Hurricane's inebriated lurchings about the table may have sounded in recounting, at the time those sessions must have fostered in his audience only an embarrassed cringe. Ramsey himself had never bought into that bunk about booze begetting inspiration, claiming that Higgins underachieved his whole career for the very fact of playing rat-arsed.

Irina did not understand why Ramsey kept groping about his person, nor did she understand when instead of beginning the frame he shuffled over to confer with the referee. Much less did she understand when the ref announced, "Frame, Ronnie O'Sullivan," when neither player had taken a shot.

Jack slipped out, returning to whisper furiously, "Your man forgot his chalk."

"So?" she whispered back. "Couldn't someone lend him some?"

"That's not the point. It's a penalty. One frame. One whole bloody frame."

Starting one down without O'Sullivan having potted a single miserable red, Ramsey took the first break-off. He clutched the rail to steady himself, and the wild stroke failed to contact the white altogether. Previously in pin-drop form, the crowd rumbled in astonishment, drawing a stern "Settle down, please!" from the ref.

Was Ramsey's disreputable condition all his wife's fault? From their arrival in Sheffield Irina had tried to get it through his thick skull that for her to carry on with the very man she'd left for Ramsey would make no sense. After a triathlon of weeping and screaming and barricading in the loo, punctuated by door-rapping reprimands from hotel management and wall-pounding from next-door guests, *finally* he had seemed to believe her, but by then it was morning. Though he'd dressed for the final with time to spare, the arc of falling out to falling in again was still not complete, and they'd clutched into bed—hence the unkempt condition of Ramsey's gear. She'd hoped fucking would make him feel better, but now that the results were on display before millions of BBC viewers it seemed that their desperate morning grapple had further exhausted the man. Besides, there's a big universe out there that is beyond fault, in which whoever is to blame is of no consequence—in which all that matters is what happens.

What happened was awful.

For O'Sullivan's part, his opponent's reek of eighty-proof may have objectified the less estimable moments of his own career. Likewise Ramsey's missing sitters that the poor bastard would have potted the first time he picked up a cue at age seven might have reminded Ronnie of frames he himself had thrown away in fits of petulant defeatism. Perhaps he was aghast at having a mirror held up to his younger self, or to the dishevelled has-been he, too, might become on rounding fifty. In any event, the more carelessly Swish banged balls every which way except in the pockets, the more meticulously the Rocket cleaned up the mess that Ramsey had left behind. Indeed, the spectacle was gastronomic, like watching a clumsy restaurant patron litter his setting with dinner-roll crusts, and a nimble waiter arrive between courses with one of those clever scrapers to politely clear the table of every crumb.

Familiar from previous tournaments, the eight fans whose black

T-shirts spelled out G-O-R-A-M-S-E-Y had ebulliently stationed themselves in a middle row at the start of the match. After the interval, the A, M, S, and E never returned. G-O-R-Y passed comment on a massacre.

When the afternoon session concluded with Ramsey whitewashed eight–nil, Irina rose from her seat only to have Jack admonish her, "Done enough damage for one day, love. You let me at him first." She stewed just long enough for Jack to report back that "his royal highness" was refusing to open his dressing-room door. Sure enough, when Irina herself pleaded and cajoled, the lock remained bolted, the only sound from behind the clinking of glass. She retired disconsolately to their hotel room.

When she hunched back into her seat for the evening session, Jack wasn't speaking to her, which she supposed was a blessing. While the Crucible crackled with electricity, the audience didn't display the excitement generated by the impending grand contest between two greats of the game so much as the bawdy leering and elbow-jabbing that precedes a striptease.

Ramsey did deliver a song and dance. Since he'd been barricaded in his dressing room for hours, the fact that his hair remained wild, his chin scraggly, his clothing so crumpled that it might have been used to scrub the floor bespoke the same wilful up-yours for which Alex Higgins had made a reputation twenty years before.

For that matter, Irina had seen the videos, and the antics on stage studiedly duplicated Alex's most egregious displays of shit-faced contempt. When sitting out, Ramsey slouched with legs extended and feet splayed, his face washing with waves of boredom or annoyance. At the table, he indulged the splashy trick shots that he'd exhibited at the Ooty Club. Many of these four- and five-cushion spectaculars did indeed pot the object ball, but he'd have given no consideration to position thereafter, and the flamboyance reliably netted a single point. Rather than try to disguise his condition, Ramsey flaunted it, negotiating from table to chair with an exaggerated sway, and knocking back the liquid in his Highland Spring bottle with gasping gusto, as if it held something far more invigorating than mineral water.

While the afternoon session had been painful—fundamentally, Ramsey could not play—the evening one was mortifying. Irina had seen her husband's game slip out of kilter; *she had never seen him rude.*

Yet once O'Sullivan was up ten frames to nil, Ramsey grumbled something like "Poncy wanker!" Whatever he said, it drew a caution, and any more "ungentlemanly conduct" risked expulsion from the match. After O'Sullivan accomplished a remarkable break of 133, Ramsey didn't quietly tap the edge of the table, snooker's equivalent of tipping one's hat, but rolled his eyes. Since O'Sullivan responded with table manners that would have wowed Amy Vanderbilt—nobly calling a foul on himself after double-hitting the cue ball—the two opponents had perfectly exchanged roles, as if Ramsey were ceding not only the final, but his soul. Higgins had defied the courteous conventions of the sport from arrogance; Ramsey would only defy them from self-loathing.

Of the chaps in black T-shirts, only G and O made an appearance. After the interval, they had taken their own advice and gone.

The carnival concluded, she knocked gently on Ramsey's dressing room. This time he opened the door. He was still unkempt, but his face, ashen and lined, was sombre. For all the theatrics with the Highland Spring bottle, it had surely contained no more than water.

Ramsey said nothing. He let her wrap her arms around his rumpled waistcoat, and draped his own lifelessly around her back. She put her palm to his cheek, and assured him she'd be right back; she informed the reporters outside the door that Mr. Acton was *indisposed,* and there would be no postsession interviews. When she returned, Ramsey was still standing motionless in his dressing room. She fetched his coat from the couch, and held it out; he stuffed his arms numbly into the sleeves. There was something sinister about the fact that on the way to the limo, as she fended off thrust microphones, Ramsey put up not a word of ritual protest that even his wife was forbidden to lay a hand on the lovely Denise. But had she not remembered to pick up his cue herself, he'd have left it behind on the floor.

Alas, the charade was not yet over. The final of the World Championship is best of thirty-five frames, a marathon traditionally played over four sessions and two days. That Sunday night, Ramsey allowed himself to be fed in their room, woodenly lifting the fork to his mouth like a grave-digger's spade. He drank no alcohol, and plenty of water. He continued to say nothing. He got ten hours' sleep, clutching Irina like a pillow, after which he showered, shaved, and ate a fortifying breakfast that he didn't appear to taste. Methodically he donned his black trousers, white shirt, and pearl-coloured waistcoat, all freshly cleaned and pressed by the hotel. His dickiebow was perfectly horizontal.

When he walked on stage for the afternoon session, no trace remained of his Alex Higgins impersonation of the previous night. His bearing was dignified, his comportment polite. The fact was that he played extremely well, more than holding his own by the interval at three frames to one.

But the day before Ronnie O'Sullivan had made Crucible history by winning the first sixteen frames on the bounce. He needed only two frames out of the next nineteen to clinch the title. Of course, technically Ramsey could still win the championship. But before the interval he had lost the single frame that he could afford to, meaning that he would now have to take fifteen frames straight to prevail. Even in the most celebrated dark-horse victory in snooker, the legendary World final of 1985, the terrier Dennis Taylor had never lagged behind the purportedly unbeatable Steve Davis by more than eight frames.

When the players emerged for the second half of the session, Irina could imagine the commentary that must have run on the BBC: grudging admiration from Clive Everton, who would have been deeply affronted by Ramsey Acton's poor sportsmanship the day before, conceding that this afternoon Swish was "showing plenty of bottle." Ramsey did not go quietly. His form was exquisite, his breaks substantial. There were no self-destructive bouts of braggadocio at the sacrifice of position. His safeties were calibrated, his snookers fiendish. He took three more frames in a row. He would give these fine people who paid money to see him an excellent show.

But Ramsey was fifty years old. He was no longer quite the player he once was, and he had never been superhuman. In the session's final frame, he barely missed a fantastically difficult yellow, and let Ronnie in. O'Sullivan cleared the table. Ramsey's firm concessionary handshake, his sustained locking of eyes during which he even managed a smile, delivered a congratulations for Ronnie O'Sullivan's first World Championship title that seemed as heartfelt as anyone could ask for. He was far too much of a pro to blub on camera, but his wife was close enough to detect that his eyes glistened.

Though Ramsey Acton had defended his honour with a short-of-humiliating final score of eighteen-six, there would be no fourth session; ticket-holders for the evening performance could apply for free passes next year. So inexorable was this result that for the Monday afternoon session Jack Lance had not even bothered to come.

❖ ❖ ❖

Thus the splendid news that Irina received within a fortnight of their return to Victoria Park Road could have been better timed. To her amazement, a jubilant call from Snake's Head informed her that *Frame and Match* had just been short-listed for the prestigious Lewis Carroll Medal, an international award for children's literature renowned for moving copies with its distinctively embossed gold sticker on the cover. She hadn't a clue how her obscure volume had ever come to the attention of the judges, for half of its modest print run of two thousand had already been returned by January. The sheer unexpectedness of her good fortune would have buoyed her all the more under ordinary circumstances.

These were no ordinary circumstances. Ramsey would hardly eat. He slept long hours, and took afternoon naps. He still burrowed into snooker biographies, and read *Snooker Scene* cover to cover, but when he did so he scowled. He disappeared for hours at a time to his table in the basement, firmly closing the door behind him, and lending his wife an unease of a piece with her *what is he* doing *in there?* when he locked himself for ages in the loo. On the one occasion that she'd bridged the battlements to bring him to the phone, she discovered him sprawled on the floor, surrounded by rails and bolts, with a crazed look on his face. "Jack has an exhibition match lined up, if you're interested," she said, and he quipped without looking up, "Already made an exhibition of myself, didn't I?" In response to her puzzlement over why one end of the table was disassembled, he mumbled something like, "Too much rebound. Table's unplayable." It had been a little like coming upon Jack Nicholson typing "All work and no play" thousands of times in *The Shining*, and she'd left him to it.

So rather than race down the stairs and pound on the basement door exuberantly demanding admission, Irina rested the receiver in its cradle and returned to the series of black-and-white still-lifes she'd been doodling in rapidographs. The little smile rising over her notebook was all she permitted herself in celebration.

Once she'd sat on the news for a week—the moment never seemed right—she had to admit that she was dreading its delivery, and that she resented dreading it. Ramsey conducted his whole occupational life in the limelight. Even as runner-up at the Crucible he'd earned almost £150,000; he may have rued the fact, but his performance had been on TV. Now with one light in her own life she felt compelled to hide it under a bushel.

However, the medal's organizers were anxious to arrange a date for the prize-giving dinner at which all short-listed candidates could be present, and were proposing one of several evenings in September, before which she and her spouse would be flown to New York and put up in a hotel. She had to give them an answer, including whether Ramsey would like to go. So during an arbitrary and until that point lacklustre dinner at Best of India in latter May (the brown-rice-and-vegetable rule guaranteed that they ate out virtually every night), Irina unveiled her godsend.

Feigning that the news had come in that very day tainted her cheerful astonishment with a hint of falseness. Hastily, too, she appended that of course she didn't expect to win—as, she supposed, she didn't—although being short-listed might sell "a few" extra copies. After all, she said, the scope of the Lewis Carroll Medal may have been "international," but it hailed from Manhattan; the likelihood of its being awarded to a book about a sport that Americans didn't know from Parcheesi was negligible.

Ramsey kissed her across the table, nipped next door to the off-licence for a bottle of plonk champagne, and returned to propose that they schedule a fabulously expensive dinner some other night to celebrate. Nevertheless, when she explained why *Frame and Match* would never win, he agreed—lighting into another bitter riff on the gobsmacking ignorance of snooker that he'd encountered in Brighton Beach. He assured her that of course he'd accompany her to the ceremony in September—provided it did not interfere with the Royal Scottish Open. After only a few minutes, their discussion of her good fortune gave way to talk of which tournaments Ramsey would enter next season.

As the week proceeded and blended into the next, they did go out to dinner numerous times, but never officially to acknowledge her short-listing, and somehow the promised occasion never quite materialized.

❖ ❖ ❖

Although while dressing for the reception in the Pierre Hotel on Fifth Avenue Irina was understandably nervous, the scale of her anxiety seemed disproportionate. Over and over she had recited to herself that it was enough to be nominated, and indeed she knew in her gut that *Frame and Match* would never clinch the Lewis Carroll. Clapping and smiling and acting implausibly exhilarated on someone else's account was bound to be an ordeal, but one short and survivable. So the source of her fretfulness while she wrestled with her unruly hair had little to do with girding for defeat.

By happy or unhappy coincidence, depending on your perspective, this very week Lawrence Trainer was scheduled to be in New York—for some dreary conference called "The Growth of Global Civil Society." He had long been her greatest supporter, and the four years that had elapsed since they'd parted had surely transformed him from jilted lover to comrade. He'd sounded so thrilled for her when she e-mailed him news of the Lewis Carroll in May (Ramsey's being home all the time had precluded confiding cups of coffee near Blue Sky for the entire summer). Besides, this was her party, and it was her right. So she'd invited Lawrence to come tonight, and he'd accepted.

Irina might have stuck by the decision without regrets had she informed Ramsey well in advance that Lawrence was coming to the awards dinner and brooked no argument, or even given Ramsey the illusion of being consulted on the matter before she issued the invite. But no. Every night in August when she'd considered raising the attendance of her "comrade" with Ramsey, she'd felt sick to her stomach—though not quite as sick as she felt now, with the reception to start in half an hour, and Ramsey in for a big surprise.

To make matters worse, one of the other five short-listed authors was his ex-wife.

"That's a right skimpy dress, pet," said Ramsey behind her as she messed in the vanity's mirror. "The hem's not two inches from your fanny."

"Badger me enough, and I'll tuck it around my waist."

He ran a finger into her cleavage. "You planning some sort of jacket?"

"That's right," said Irina. Her application of eyeliner was so unsteady that she looked like Boris Karloff. "I spent two hundred quid on this thing, so of course I'm going to cover it up with a large burlap sack."

"No, you're going to swan into that do downstairs half-starkers, and every tosser in the room will want to fuck you."

"You used to like it when I looked sexy." Lord, did nothing ever change? He reminded her of *Lawrence*.

"I love it when you look sexy—shut in a cupboard with a padlock."

She turned from the mirror as he was slipping on his jacket and said, "Wow!" She'd grown inured to his snooker gear, but rarely saw him in a proper tuxedo. "You're the one belongs locked in a closet."

It would take many more compliments than that to placate her husband. For all the hotel rooms they'd shared, this was the first time they'd ever checked in under his wife's name. He'd bristled when the porter called him "Mr. McGovern," and his abrupt anonymity on arrival in JFK yesterday had put his nose out of joint. On opening *Ramsey Acton*'s passport, the immigration agent hadn't raised an eyebrow, and his "Welcome to the United States" was the same bored greeting that he shovelled at every other tourist in the queue.

"If you don't stop pacing like that," she said, "we're going to be dunned for leaving runnels in the carpet. Are you edgy about seeing Jude?"

"Not particularly. Though with you tricked out like that, I reckon she'll be jealous."

"Why? She divorced you."

"Birds don't like it when you fancy their discards. Like when you rustle round in somebody's rubbish and pull out a right serviceable knickknack. Suddenly they get to thinking, *Oi, give that back! That's a right serviceable knickknack!*"

"I worry that Jude assumes we were carrying on while you were still with her."

"So?" Ramsey slid his palms into the hollows of her hipbones. "Let her."

❖ ❖ ❖

So powerfully was Irina distracted by the impending arrival of Lawrence Trainer that she'd given little thought to Jude Hartford, whose path she'd not crossed since their falling-out five years ago. As she and Ramsey descended in the gilt elevator, an encounter with the woman was imminent. Most people would field an uncomfortable reunion of this nature by rising above—extending limp congratulations for being short-listed, making no allusion to previous unpleasantness nor even to the incongruous fact that Jude and Ramsey used to be married, and presenting a united front of seamless connubial contentment. But since social awkwardness always brought out in Irina that bizarre confessional incontinence, chances were she would within minutes blurt that Ramsey was irrationally jealous, had probably started to drink too much, and picked fights at the drop of a hat—all to a woman sure to use any unattractive intelligence to smear Irina behind her back.

Clutching Ramsey's hand, Irina entered the events room to mark Jude's presence at the far end by the drinks table—though in that floor-length ivory kaftan the woman might easily be mistaken for a refreshments tent. When Jude turned with a swirl toward the entranceway, her outsized expression of astonished joy took a fraction of a moment to arrange itself. Like Lawrence of Arabia leading the charge on Aqaba, Jude flapped across the room with her arms extended wide, and as the dervish advanced, Irina feared the expression on her own face was one of horror.

"Darling!" Jude smothered her ex-friend in a shimmer of upscale synthetic. "And don't you look *divine!*" Irina's "You, too!" was weak. Billows of fabric failed to disguise the fact that Jude had put on weight. Yet she still emanated that distinctive hysteria—a desperation for a fineness of life that, like a gnat, was only surer to elude her the more frantically she snatched after it. "And Ramsey. You dear man!" Jude brought his forehead to her lips as if delivering a blessing. "*Jude,*" he replied. As if that said it all.

A tall, squarish character ambled from behind. He exuded a languorous cannot-be-bothered-to-try-to-please that generally correlates with having money. When Jude introduced Duncan Winderwood grandly as the "tenant of my affections," he said in a plummy accent, "I'm so *terribly* pleased to make your acquaintance," employing that pro forma aristocratic graciousness meant less to make you feel loved than to ram down your throat how civilized he was. Irina instinctively disliked him, and she could tell that he didn't care. Being British, Duncan was the one man in the room who would almost certainly recognize Ramsey Acton, but his interaction with her husband was brief and bland.

"Isn't this a coincidence," Irina submitted aimlessly. "About the Lewis Carroll."

"Pish and tosh! To be honest, it *isn't* a coincidence!" Jude cried, laughing through the sentence. "Talent will out, don't you think? *Talent will out!*" She seemed to have forgotten all about having impugned Irina's work as "flat" and "lifeless."

"There's no way mine will win," said Irina. "The subject matter is too obscure." When Ramsey shifted at her side, she appended quickly, "For Americans, I mean."

"To be honest, I *did* think your illustrating a book about snooker was good for a giggle," said Jude. "Didn't you used to think snooker was a big bore?"

"I've gotten—a lot more interested," said Irina faintly.

"I suppose you haven't had much choice!"

"You made a choice, I recollect," Ramsey intruded brutally. "To rubbish my profession at every opportunity."

"I think what Ramsey's trying to say," said Irina, "is that we all need a drink."

Fortified with a glass of red that was tempting fate with all that white sailcloth, Jude exclaimed, "I was simply floored when I read you two had got married!"

"It was certainly a surprise to *us*," said Irina forcefully. "I hope you don't mind."

"Mind! To be quite honest, maybe back in the day we should have switched places at the dinner table and saved us all a pack of trouble!" Jude's conversational tic was beginning to wear, even if *to be honest* had spread like genital herpes among the British bourgeoisie. Much as its counterpart plague among the young—*D'ya know what I mean?*—conveyed a persistent and often justifiable insecurity about an ability to speak English, the repeated insertion of *to be honest* seemed to imply that unless otherwise apprised you could safely assume that the speaker was lying.

"Ramsey, you old dog," she continued. "I worried that I missed something in the *Guardian* social pages about a big shindig. Not that you look a year over forty-nine, sweetie, but didn't you turn fifty last year? I pictured you letting out the Savoy with the haut monde."

"We didn't fancy a lot of fuss." His delivery was grim. For his fiftieth the summer before, Irina had taken Ramsey's admonishments that he "didn't fancy a lot of fuss" at face value, and repeated the homemade sushi spread that had so overwhelmed him in 1995. His eyes had continually darted beyond the candlelight, as if a hundred well-wishers would soon spring from the shadows. It emerged that she hadn't read his signals correctly—*no* apparently meaning *no* only in cases of date rape.

The hall was growing packed, and the event's organizers pulled both couples away to meet the foundation directors, journalists, and judges. Although Irina read apology in the judges' eyes (sorry, but we didn't vote for you), they did all heap praises on *Frame and Match*, talking up the vibrancy of the colours, the freshness of her material . . . Starved of serious approbation for most of her career, Irina was perplexingly deaf to the tributes. Compliments were empty calories, like popcorn.

She explained to the group that the lipstick-red, the lemony yellow, and the creamy green merely duplicated snooker balls as faithfully as she knew how. "As a matter of fact," she added, "snooker first took off in the UK as a spectator sport because of the advent of colour television. The BBC needed programming that was literally colourful. So the show *Pot Black* was born, the players became national celebrities, and what started as a haphazard, mostly amateur game got organized into rankings and tournaments and high-stakes purses."

Jude's expression was pitying: *Oh, my poor darling, you* have *had an earful.*

"Ramsey"—Irina pulled him forward—"was on *Pot Black* all the time!" Alas, she only put him on the spot. The group could follow up with no better than, "So you're a snooker player!" and Ramsey could return with no better than, "Yeah." Silence.

In the midst of this conversational maw, Lawrence made his entrance.

Obviously, Irina might as well have invited a suicide bomber from the West Bank, or the Mask of the Red Death. But the moment she met Lawrence's deep-set brown eyes from across the room, they flushed with a warmth that put out of mind, however temporarily, the scale of her mistake. Ramsey's grey-blue irises could wash oceanic, as available as open water, but something about their very colour gave them also the terrifying capacity to go cold. Yet despite the scorn that often issued from Lawrence's mouth, it was in the nature of that particular shade of umber that his eyes could express a limited set of emotions: tenderness, gratitude, injury, and need. When they lived together she had often chafed at the shabbiness of his dress; now those familiar dark Dockers and the threadbare button-down with no tie made her smile. In fact, everything about Lawrence that once vexed her now entranced her instead. She loved his fundamental humility, at such odds with his intellectual bluster as The Expert. She loved his slumped, unassuming posture. She loved the fact that at an occasion of this nature he could always be relied upon to hold up his end of things; you could throw Lawrence into any social pool, and he would swim. She loved his rigidity and discipline, all just a cover for a raging terror of the gluttony, intemperance, and sloth that would surely ensue should he ever step off the straight and narrow. She loved that Lawrence Trainer was truly able to be "happy for" another person's good fortune, and his demeanour as he advanced glowed with his present happiness for hers. Lastly, while she may long before have lost touch with the urge to tear off his clothes, she still loved his face. She loved his carved, haunted, beautiful face.

It was a toss-up whether Ramsey would find the more unforgivable her invitation to Lawrence in the first place, or her expression when he walked in. Either way, when she glanced at her husband, Ramsey's eyes had made ready use of their capacity to go cold.

Lawrence diffidently pecked her cheek. "Congratulations!"

"Thank you," she said. Ramsey put his left arm around her shoulders and pulled her tight, his hand mashing her upper arm. "Ramsey? Lawrence happened to be in town, and so I asked him to come."

"*Happened* to be in town. Ain't that lucky."

"Hey, Ramsey!" Lawrence heartily shook Ramsey's free hand. "No hard feelings. Really, it's great to see you."

"Anorak Man," said Ramsey. With Irina, the epithet had morphed to caustic slur, a token of his refusal to dignify her former partner with a proper name; to Lawrence's face, the handle inevitably resumed a measure of the affection with which it had first been coined. But Ramsey didn't *want* to feel any of his old fondness for Lawrence. Even less did he wish to confront the awful truth that Lawrence Trainer was a nice man.

"Hey, congratulations on making it to the final in Sheffield this year!" said Lawrence. "What does that make, eight?"

"You should know." Ramsey could hardly talk, so furious was he to be having this conversation at all. "You're the boffin."

This mashing business with Ramsey's left hand had grown actively unpleasant. "Lawrence, let me get you your *one* glass of wine," said Irina, discreetly disengaging from her husband's clasp. In science fiction, when parallel universes collide, the molecular integrity of the whole world is often imperilled, and now she knew why.

"Listen," said Lawrence quietly beside the bar service. With twenty feet separating the two men, the atomic particles of the room settled again. "I checked out your competition at Barnes and Noble. Man, you're a shoo-in! Those other entries totally suck! I mean, get a load of that piece of shit that Jude wrote—and now that I get a look at her, *load* is the word. When I came across the title, I bust a gut!"

In *Children of Size*, a chunky little girl is smitten by a boy at school, and to win his favour she goes on all manner of diets. Hungry all the time, the once cheerful protagonist grows peevish. The *tenant of her affections* finally bewails that he had been smitten with her as well, until she became so unpleasant. Behold, he likes a bit of heft. The little girl learns to eat sensibly and to love her own body, even if she would never be thin—happy ending.

"You know, Ramsey didn't seem too thrilled I showed up," said Lawrence. "I could just have a quick drink and go. I don't want to ruin the evening for you. It's your night."

"*Davay gavoreet po-russki, ladno?*" she asked, and continued in hushed Russian. "Yes, it's my night. Which means I should be able to have you here if I want to. And you belong here. You kept me going in illustration through some tough years. Please don't go. Please?"

"I'll stay if you want me to," he assured her. "But why is he still so touchy, after all this time?" Lawrence's Russian was surprisingly fluid.

"*Mozhet byt potomy shto on vidit shto yavsyo yeshcho tebya lyublu.*"

Embarrassed, Lawrence switched to English again. "You only love me in a way. Maybe you should tell him I'm getting married. That might make him feel better."

Irina cocked her head. "Would I be making that up?"

Lawrence said softly, "*Nyet.*"

Irina glanced at her toes before looking up again. "Congratulations. I guess that's good news." She shouldn't have appended the *I guess*, but she couldn't help it.

"*Da, na samom dele,*" he said fervently. "Very good news. I hope you don't feel bad that you and I, that we never— We didn't get married but maybe we should have, and this time around I'm going to do it right."

"Lawrence Trainer!" shrieked the refreshments tent. "Look at the pair of you, like old times! Why, our old foursome is back! Just a tad mixed up, that's all."

"Hi, Jude," said Lawrence wearily. He could never stand Jude Hartford.

Jude introduced Duncan, and the toff went into his somnambulant spiel about how absolutely inexpressibly thrilling it was to meet yet another guest about whom he didn't give a damn. Without missing a beat Lawrence returned, "Indeed, frightfully, frightfully delightful to make your acquaintance as well, old bean," getting the geezer's accent to a tee.

For the first time at the reception, something stirred in those muddy eyes, and Duncan seemed to wake up.

"I say," said Duncan. "Taking the piss, are we?"

"Got that right," said Lawrence flatly, and turned away.

"I adore you," Irina whispered.

"You used to," said Lawrence lightly. "And why not? I'm adorable." Something had loosened in him—it was no longer difficult for him to see her—and Irina realized that he had finally let her go.

❖ ❖ ❖

For the sit-down dinner in the adjoining room, the Lewis Carroll contestants and their escorts were seated together at a large round front table. Just her luck, Irina's place card was positioned between Ramsey and *Duncan*. Lawrence was sitting at another table nearby, and Irina kept him wistfully in the corner of her eye, noting how readily he engaged the guests on his either side in heated conversation. Politics, no doubt—Nepal, Chechnya, who knows. Funny, she'd once been irked by the way he took over socially; now she was charmed to bits.

When she asked after the nature of his work, Duncan said that he "dabbled in a few investments," ergo he and the Queen had divvied up the better part of England between them. Irina said, "I can't say I've ever been very interested in finance," to which he replied, "Makes the world go round, my dear," and she snapped, "Not mine." There is nothing quite so icy as two people being patronizing to each other, and Irina, usually a good conversational soldier, concluded abruptly that life was too short.

But Ramsey wasn't providing much by way of salvation. His bearing was stony. His wine glass was drained, and she wished the waiters weren't so attentive to refills. She'd married a man who detested small-talk, and who never felt at ease outside the rarefied world of snooker, but Ramsey's fish-out-of-water performance this evening was extreme even by the minimal social standards she had learned to apply to him. Well before her Great Sin was revealed with the arrival of a certain someone, he had barely spoken to a soul, and so far this was like navigating a formal dinner with a houseplant.

"I hate it when they prepare this sort of starter with that dollop of *mayonnaise*."

Ramsey stared her down with dull incredulity.

"The salmon terrine's not bad," she said helplessly, "if you scrape it off."

A waiter whisked away Ramsey's starter untouched. When he proceeded to ignore his main course as well, eyes cut toward him askance.

"Not touching your dinner," she whispered. "It's a little embarrassing."

"*I* am embarrassing *you*?" he muttered bitterly.

To ruin her own evening, she would have to ask. "Okay. What's wrong?"

"You humiliated me."

The rest of the table having written the pair off as standoffish or bashful, with luck she could bury the tiff beneath their chatter. "I'd have thought your wife being nominated for a prestigious award would have made you feel proud instead. My mistake."

"You made a mistake, all right. Count on it." With a raised eyebrow, a waiter cleared off his untouched plate, while a second topped up Ramsey's wine.

"May I hazard a guess that this hunger strike has something to do with my having invited Lawrence?"

"What do *you* think?"

As the waiters cleared the rest of the table, Irina accidentally caught Jude's eye. In any fantasies about a chance encounter like this evening's, Irina had conjured a gentle display of how perfectly suited she and Ramsey were for each other, how hopelessly in love. This is what it looks like, she would have liked to imply, when Ramsey Acton has found the right woman: he is relaxed, jubilant, sometimes hilarious, and physically exquisite. In this sense, though only in this sense, would Irina have enjoyed making Jude Hartford jealous. But presently Jude's eyes stabbed instead with supercilious pity. This was not a revolutionary Ramsey, a centred, self-possessed, celebrative man who had truly learned, if late in life, to *squeeze the orange*; this was a Ramsey that Jude knew all too well. Indeed, her face glowed with the smug relief of having successfully passed along the Old Maid in a game of cards.

The proceedings on the dais got under way, the director of the Lewis Carroll Foundation presenting each entry with a brief bio-graphy of the authors and illustrators. As Irina's book was introduced, Ramsey continued to mutter furiously that it was "bad enough" that she had asked Anorak Man to a public dinner, but that it was especially outrageous to have the "shambolic state of his marriage" paraded before his ex-wife. As Ramsey leaned into her ear, his head blocked her view of the projections of *Frame and Match*.

"Lawrence was a big booster of my career," she whispered; it was increasingly impossible to disguise the fact that they were having a row. "It's appropriate for him to be here."

"*Appropriate*," Ramsey mumbled, "is you showing up at a do with your husband, full stop. And how'd you like your man having a go at me over the World final?"

"He wasn't *having a go,* he congratulated you for getting so far!"

As the foundation director had asked for the envelope, Ramsey's harsh whisper was so close to her ear that it hurt. "He was rubbing my nose in them first two sessions, all wink-wink like, *I saw you fall flat on your arse, I watched you get stuffed—*"

"Please stop!" She'd been holding it back for the last hour, like sticking her finger in a dike, but the floodwaters were now too high, and despite herself Irina began to cry.

"I saw your face tonight," Ramsey continued, undeterred. "All soft and wobbly. The secret rabbiting in Russian. You're still in love with him! You're still in love with the bloke, and our marriage is a laugh!"

The audience burst into applause, and then rose for a standing ovation. Wiping her eyes hastily, Irina struggled from her chair and tugged Ramsey up with her, though she had missed the announcement of the winner altogether. It was a little ugly, but she prayed that the victor wasn't Jude, and was guiltily relieved when she saw Jude applauding with everyone else. Irina's own clapping was fatigued. While she had previously dreaded having to feign joy on another contestant's account, now she really was glad—that this cataclysmic occasion would soon be over. Nevertheless, the ovation did seem to be going on an odiously long time, and as she glanced around the table all the other candidates were applauding, too, and mouthing things at her that she didn't understand. Finally the applause died down; while a few elderly guests resumed their seats, everyone else remained standing. Well, let them, but Irina was wrung out, and led the way by plopping back into her chair.

"Ms. McGovern," said the director, and the audience emitted an uneasy chuckle. "As we understand it, no one else has been nominated to accept the medal in your place."

Irina's face burned, her body needling head to toe. She looked in a panic around the table to make sure that she hadn't misunderstood, and everyone nodded encouragingly and smiled. She edged unsteadily from her chair and meekly climbed the stairs. The beaming officiator looped her neck with a golden disc the size of an all-day sucker.

"Th-thank you," Irina stuttered too close to the mic, and it buzzed. Her mind was a blank, or almost. That is, there was only one person she wanted to thank. Only one person who had supported her through the long lean years of no prizes. One person who had always urged her to believe in her talent, who had marvelled at the drawings in her studio at the end of his own hard day. And of all those gathered here, there was only one person whom she had better *not* thank if she knew what was good for her. All right, but she would not, absolutely would not thank instead the man who had just single-handedly destroyed this occasion, and as a consequence left it at thank you, period, and stumbled away.

❖ ❖ ❖

In the flurry of handshaking that followed, Lawrence hung humbly back. When he finally took his turn in the receiving line, he tried first to simply shake her hand like the others, but Irina was having none of that, and hugged him close. While she hoped that her reddened, puffy eyes would be mistaken for having wept tears of joy, when they disengaged he took a hard look at her face; he hadn't lived with her for nearly a decade for nothing. Squaring up to Ramsey, who was propped at her side with all the animation of an umbrella stand, Lawrence may not have grabbed Ramsey's lapels, but his aggressive stance seemed to indicate that he'd thought about it.

"If you don't treat her right," said Lawrence through his teeth, "so help me God, I will punch your lights out." With a graze of Irina's temple, he was gone.

A touching bit of chivalry, but it would cost her.

❖ ❖ ❖

"You're drunk," said Irina in the elevator. "We will not talk about this now."

"That so. And when will my princess deign to resume our chat?"

"If we have to continue this disagreeable exchange, we will not do so until we get back to London. Until then I don't care what you say, I will not participate."

Irina was true to her word. She was stoically deaf to Ramsey's multiple attempts to get a rise out of her, and the only sounds she emitted in their hotel room were the *pock* of dental floss and rasp of her toothbrush. She tugged off her dress, unrolled her tights, and crawled into bed. As she reached for the light, Ramsey asked plaintively, "Not even going to say good-night, pet?" The crisp flip of the switch spoke for her. Slumber had always been out of the question when matters between them were the slightest bit out of whack, but tonight she dropped to sleep like plunging from a tall building to the pavement.

For the following Monday, Irina had arranged to meet her sister for coffee, and when she left the room Ramsey was still sleeping off however many bottles of wine had substituted for a roast beef dinner. The hasty tête-à-tête was meant to make up for the fact that not only her mother but Tatyana had given the Lewis Carroll dinner a miss, explaining that their mother would regard her attendance as taking her sister's side. By the time they met in a Broadway Starbucks, Irina was only grateful for Tatyana's absence the night before. Her sister was an unreliable ally, and would have savoured relating Ramsey's drunken distemper to their mother, since it seemed to confirm everything Raisa had intuited the instant she met the man.

"You don't look so hot," said Tatyana after the usual bear-hug. "Considering that I read in the *Times* this morning that you won."

"Well, as they say, winning isn't everything." Irina would have to suppress her impulse to confide; the scuttlebutt would get back to Brighton Beach. "It's a bit of a letdown, is all I mean. To get what you've always wanted."

"Wouldn't it have been more of a letdown to lose?"

"Oh, probably. Make mine a cappuccino? And a muffin. I'm starving."

While Tatyana fetched sustenance, Irina considered that the person she really wanted to confide in was Lawrence; the fact that he was at large in this very city right now was a torture. Anyway, what did it matter. She would have to live without his counsel indefinitely now.

"Got a little gossip," said Irina brightly. "Lawrence is getting married."

"You don't say! Who to?"

Irina frowned. "Gosh. I forgot to ask."

"Pretty low-quality gossip, big sister. How do you feel about it?"

Irina took a deep breath. "I'm happy for him. *Very* happy."

"Are you sure? You don't sound that happy."

"Oh . . . I guess there's something sad about it," Irina allowed cautiously, the gross understatement turning this heart-to-heart to farce. "So final. The absolute end of an era. Whoever it is, she's very lucky."

"How did you find out?"

"Lawrence came last night. I invited him, since he was in New York anyway."

"Wasn't that awfully awkward?"

"Oh, not at all," Irina said heartily. "Ramsey is so socially adept, and we're all grown-ups. In fact, Ramsey seemed glad to see Lawrence, and grateful on my account that he made an appearance. They've always liked each other. In no time, those two were nattering on about snooker, just like the old days."

"So how's it going, with you and Ramsey?"

"Fine," said Irina flatly—and then decided, so long as she was lying, to do so with panache. "He was over the moon when I won the medal last night. Couldn't stop singing my praises to other people. I was abashed. I tried to remind him that it was déclassé to brag about your own spouse, but he was so proud that he wouldn't listen. He's vowed to paint the town red when we get home." And wouldn't he, in a sense.

When they parted, after an update on Dmitri, Raisa, and the kids, Tatyana cocked her head. "I still don't get it. You're in love, you won a big prize—and you look at death's door. Your face is harrowed."

"It's just makeup. I wore eyeliner last night and slept on it. Makes my eyes look ghoulish."

"Get some cold cream, then!"

"I'll do that," Irina mumbled, though fairly sure that the darkness her sister had detected would not readily rub off.

◆ ◆ ◆

By the time Irina returned to the Pierre late afternoon, Ramsey had showered and packed. He seemed to have got with the programme, and said no more than she did—i.e., nothing. Meeting her eyes, his own flashed with undiminished anger. She absolutely refused to feel attracted to him. As she took refuge in the officious logistics of checkout, the clench of her jaw gave her a headache. In the taxi to JFK, the departure lounge of Terminal 4, and the cabin of the 747, they continued to observe the protocol of speaking only necessities to the driver and flight attendants, and not a word to each other. By the time they tucked back into the Jaguar at Heathrow's long-term

391

parking at ten London time the next day, muteness had grown habitual, and almost relaxing.

Irina's signal to stop for milk on the way home proved fortuitous. Once she closed the door on Victoria Park Road behind her, it would not open again for a solid two days.

❖ ❖ ❖

"I'm still waiting for my apology," she announced in the hall, back to the door.

Ramsey dropped his carry-on from a greater height than seemed necessary. "A bird could grow grey waiting for the likes of that. And when do I get mine?"

"When hell freezes"—she clipped past him to the kitchen to store the milk in the fridge—"and pigs fly."

In retrospect, the dispute may have turned into such a marathon because it departed from orthodox form. Customarily, Ramsey made an accusation; Irina defended herself; Ramsey made the accusation again. The sheer monotony ensured that even Ramsey would finally get bored. But this time, Irina took the initiative, and fired the opening volley herself.

"*Who do you think you are?*" Hands on hips, she had located the deepest register in a voice that was always husky. As Ramsey drew up to his full six-three in the kitchen doorway, chin at a pugnacious tilt, she was glad for the two-inch boost of her high heels. "I have spent *hours,* and *hours,* and *hours* listening to you despair about how underappreciated you are, about how no one gives you credit for originating the 'attacking game' that's now become standard practice among younger players. About the awful injustice of how little money you won in the early days, when the purses were minuscule, and now these upstarts walk off with a hundred grand just for making it to the semis. About how terrible it is that *Snooker Scene* hasn't done a profile of you in ten years. I've gone to tournament after tournament—and all you can remember is the matches I missed. But do we *ever* sit at dinner and talk about my disappointments? No! I worked my ass off for *Frame and Match.* I was paid a pittance for it, and the print run and distribution were abysmal. But have you heard me keening every night about how underappreciated I am? Have you had to listen to me moan on and on about the fact that I've toiled my whole life in relative obscurity? No! So *finally,* for the *first time ever,* something good happens to me, I get a little credit, one day in the sun. I ask you to come with me to celebrate something that I've achieved, and you sabotage the whole event! Whispering all that poison in my ear, and refusing to eat anything while drinking like a fish? Bickering even through the announcement of the winner so I can't even hear it, and at the very moment I should have been feeling on top of the world I feel like a fool? It was an act of vandalism! The oldest power-play in the book, too—*Don't get uppity, bitch, because no matter how famous you get, I can always make your life hell.* You didn't care that I was short-listed, and you didn't care that I won! *All* you cared about was the fact I'd invited Lawrence, who had every right to be there, and whom I had every right to invite! And if that offended you, frankly, my dear, *I don't give a damn.* Sunday night had *nothing to do with you.* A concept that is obviously alien. Everything has to be about you, you vain, narcissistic bastard! Well, Sunday night was supposed to be about *me.*"

It was, in snooker terms, a spectacular clearance, but unfortunately this occasion would prove their personal World final, and she had only taken one frame. Just like Sheffield's, this match was slated for two days and two nights, and Irina hadn't the stamina to keep sinking the same angry reds over and over again. There was no getting around the fact that Ramsey was the real pro at this game, and was far more accustomed to keeping his composure while his opponent got in all manner of splendid shots, confident that one slip or rerack would let him back in. As she caught her breath by the fridge, Ramsey took his cue for his own visit.

"*Fair play,*" he said. "But why's your *day in the sun* got to be my own day in the shade? You totally ignored me! At the tournaments where my own wife *stoops* to show up, I introduce you round, I fetch you a drink, I keep my arm around you, don't I. I never wiggle out from under, like, *Don't touch me, you animal!* for all the world to see—"

"You were *hurting* my arm! And I had other people to talk to. For a single evening, you were not the centre of my universe, and that's what you couldn't stick!"

"—Least of all have I ever asked along some other bird what I used to fancy, and to be honest still fancy like mad, hovering off in the corner, speaking our own private language, having a laugh at what a waster you are!"

Later, at this point Irina's recollection would begin to fragment. Bits and pieces: Apparently Lawrence had always been lurking in the background as the real *tenant of her affections*. Ramsey refused to believe that Lawrence "just happened" to be in town, and was sure that the predator had flown all the way from London to impress her. Anorak Man, in this version of events, had for years been lying in wait, ready to pounce the moment relations with her husband showed signs of strain. And what was this about "hoping Jude didn't mind" that she and Ramsey had married? Was their marriage something to apologize for, to be ashamed of? Her hug with Lawrence after the award ceremony converted to "throwing herself into his arms." Lawrence's "bracing" Ramsey after the ceremony developed over the course of a day into "issuing that death threat." He'd thought he'd found enduring love, and now he found himself party to the same "second-rate, two-timing rubbish" that everyone else settled for, in preference to which he'd rather be by himself. As for convincing Ramsey that when he caught her outside the flat in Borough Lawrence was actually in Dubai, Irina was sent decisively back to square one, and rerunning the entire palaver from Sheffield must have absorbed at least three or four hours on Tuesday night. Over the course of those two days Ramsey assembled a veritable retrospective of her transgressions in the post-birthday world: arranging "appointment TV" to ogle Lawrence on the news, "declaring her love for Anorak Man" in front of her mother, "running him down" to other players in Preston— all the way back to *You should have packed a bag*.

Throughout, Irina refused to play her trump card: that, Ramsey's raving fantasies to the contrary, Lawrence was getting married. The news still ached, and it was private. She would not violate the personally sacred by flinging it like a rolling pin.

Meanwhile, the house on Victoria Park Road might as well have twisted into the sky like Dorothy's, and nothing from the rest of the world so much as sailed past the windows. She wasn't about to launch out for a *Daily Telegraph,* and turning on the television under the circumstances would have been an act of inflammatory hostility the proceedings could ill afford. Likewise checking e-mail was out of the question, even if Irina yearned to click through the host of congratulations surely hovering in cyberspace. The telephone rang around three on Tuesday, and for some reason continued to do so at regular intervals for the rest of the afternoon, but picking up the phone mid–spousal harangue was hardly politic, and more than once when the ringing resumed, Irina, in tears, wasn't fit to answer. By early that evening she jerked the receiver off the hook to shut the bloody thing up.

Since it is the beginnings and endings of most great sporting events that one remembers, Irina later retained her most coherent memory of the last frame.

It was coming up on dawn of Thursday morning, and if there is always something queasy about that indeterminate time of day, like coffee lightened with skimmed milk, the dull greying through the cracks in the curtains was especially sickening when it signalled the close of a second sleepless night, following on the one before, during which Irina had only dozed on the plane. To say she was hallucinating with exhaustion would overplay the matter, but she was certainly losing sight of what purpose all this verbal laying waste was meant to serve.

Ramsey had sunk into one of his maudlin phases. He had given her everything, his whole being, saving nothing out for himself. He had even sacrificed what meant most to him in all the whole world, the championship final—

"What do you mean?" said Irina, lifting her head blearily from the kitchen table. "How do you figure that?"

"I catch you shagging Anorak Man the day before, I'm not going to play proper snooker, am I. It's a wonder I knew which way round to point the cue."

"Yes, it's a wonder, since you were stinking drunk!" So many times had Irina repeated her explanation about having only been "visiting herself" that Saturday in Borough that it had come to sound absurd to her own ears, and she had learned to skip it.

"I was blind with grief, pet. Them first two sessions, all I could see is you and Anorak Man, groping in that bed upstairs—"

"After a bottle and a half of Remy, you couldn't see your hand in front of your face! Can we get this straight? Are you *seriously* holding me accountable for that fiasco in Sheffield?"

Ramsey glared with matching incredulity. "What, or who, drove me to drink? Are you *seriously* not holding *yourself* accountable for the biggest public disgrace of my life? Ducky, you are dead lucky your Ramsey Acton is a forgiving man!"

It was amazing that after all this time Irina could still marshal the energy for outrage, but they do not make adrenaline for nothing. Moreover, he had released from embargo all that she had not let fly back in May.

"You disgraced yourself! And furthermore, you disgraced me! Do you think it was easy for me to watch my own husband stagger around the table unable to get a ball within two feet of a pocket? The while looking like a dog's dinner—clothes crumpled, hair like a dish mop? All those rude remarks you made to O'Sullivan—I wanted to crawl in a hole and die! Forgiveness—I have ladled you forgiveness in buckets!"

"In the charmed universe where I had a loyal wife what didn't mess about with another bloke the day before, I'd have wiped the floor with that wally O'Sullivan, no two ways about it!"

"In the *charmed universe* where you took your own wife's word, maybe you would have won the final. But I will not take responsibility for your mistrust!"

"I handed you my trophy on a plate. And mind, ducky, you'd not have won that sodding medal in New York, if it wasn't for me."

Irina's mouth gaped. "Not only did I lose your trophy for you—but you won my medal for me. How does that work?"

"I gave you snooker. No snooker, no *Frame and Match*, and no poncy medal, neither." *Neever.*

"You *gave me* snooker? Well, can I please give it *back*? Because I am *sick* of snooker, sick to *death* of snooker, I'm sick of the very word *snooker*, and if I never saw another snooker match in my entire life I would face east and kiss the floor!"

Ramsey turned white. He stood and cornered on his heel, marching to the basement door. She first assumed that he had fled to his lair to escape his own violent impulses. But violence comes in as many flavours as ice cream, and within the minute he emerged carrying Denise. With nauseous deliberateness, Ramsey propped a foot on a kitchen chair, and cracked his cue of thirty-three years across its back.

❖ ❖ ❖

The murder of Irina's rival had the one merit of releasing all the tension from the room. The very air seemed to slacken, the ticking of the clock over the Aga cooker to grow more sluggish. The sun had risen, its streams through the curtains mockingly bright.

Irina dragged from her chair to make coffee, wincing as the grinder let loose its banshee wail, as if mourning the demise of a fellow inanimate object. She discovered that they were out of milk.

"I can't drink straight espresso on an empty stomach," she said leadenly. "I'm going to head out for a few things. Do you want anything?"

The halves of his splintered cue clutched in each hand, Ramsey shook his head. Thank heavens he made no bid to come along.

When Irina walked outside into the crisp morning air, she went into shock that there *was* an outside. Yet it wasn't the great outdoors that produced this sense of relief, but getting away from Ramsey.

When she checked out at Safeway, the familiar clerk didn't meet her eyes. Par for the course in commercial exchanges these days—so it was more curious that, after gathering herself, the clerk *did* meet Irina's eyes, soulfully full-bore. She placed the change in Irina's hand with solemnity, the way one pressed a coin into a child's moist outstretched palm in the days when kids were still awed by a quarter. "Cor," said the girl, "I'm awful sorry, like. I reckon I don't know what else to say."

Baffled, Irina didn't know what else to say, either. Perhaps the change was incorrect, but she'd already plunged it into the pile in her pocket. How badly could she have been cheated if she'd only given the girl a pound? She shrugged, and a mutter of "No harm done" seemed to cover the bases. Or it should have, but the peculiar look the girl shot her in return was piercing.

The open-air market on Roman Road was already under way, and Irina was in no hurry to return to the kitchen where Ramsey would be still holding the two halves of his life in each hand. So she headed for her regular vegetable seller, and picked out some runner beans. Smiling at the merchant, she thought her face might crack; her lips hadn't curved upward for days.

When Irina had first strolled Roman Road on Ramsey's arm, locals were cool; the East Enders were resentful about ceding the neighbourhood's national treasure to an American. But she didn't trade on her status, and gradually they had seemed to warm. Nevertheless, when she presented her basket of produce to the beefy man behind the cart, he, too, looked her searchingly in the eyes with an intensity that was unnerving. "Blimey," he said. "Terrible thing, innit?"

Maybe there'd been an accident or fire nearby, but honestly she was so depleted, so underslept, and so increasingly tortured by the implications of that splintered stick of ash back in the kitchen, that she hadn't the energy to care about some strangers' misfortune. It wasn't pretty, but on days like this the whole world could go to hell and she couldn't be bothered. *No harm done* wouldn't work this time, so she settled for a neutral *mmm*.

"Here now, you take that," said the vegetable seller, selecting three enormous navel oranges and putting them in her bag.

"Oh, but you needn't—"

He added an avocado. She thanked him, and though she'd been pleased with herself for gaining acceptance in the area, she hadn't realized her progress had been so considerable as to extend to free fruit. Touched, she had ambled halfway back down the road before, as an afterthought, she ducked into a newsagent to pick up a *Telegraph*.

Standing before the row of broadsheets, Irina, already pale, went paler. It is possible she began to weave; she certainly felt faint, though not from lack of sleep.

Catatonic at the kitchen table, Ramsey still clutched his shattered cue. In silence, she slid the stack of newspapers onto the table, pushing his ashtray slagged with cigarette butts out of the way. In the photo on the uppermost front page, angled gray beams resembled the ashy fag-ends in close-up. Irina bowed her head. Tears—the only ones worth shedding amid a septic tank of wastewater spilled these last two days—spattered the photograph.

"I have never—" Her breath caught. "I have never—" She tried again. "I have never been *so ashamed*."

▣ chapter ten ▣

It was at Irina's urging that she and Lawrence watched the 2001 championship final between Ramsey and Ronnie O'Sullivan, for her partner's romance with snooker seemed permanently to have waned. Granted, they'd not seen Ramsey for three and a half years, and he probably qualified as no more than someone they used to know. As they watched the first evening session, she wondered if Ramsey had found another woman yet, and couldn't shake the hope, both absurd and unkind, that he hadn't. Ramsey had become a funny mental dependency, as if another life were running alongside this one, perhaps no better or worse but certainly different, and she liked to reach out and touch it from time to time, like dipping her hand into the river from a canoe.

Ramsey was, as ever, impeccably turned out—closely shaven, not a hair out of place, his gear pressed, his pert dickie bow in perfect parallel with the floor. The loutish-featured O'Sullivan may have been touted as a Reformed Character, but even in biddably traditional attire couldn't help but look in comparison like a slob. Ramsey's motions at the table were sure, smooth, and steady, and while they both played fast, Ramsey seemed brisk, O'Sullivan impatient. Ramsey sank superb pots, but never at the sacrifice of position, whereas Ronnie couldn't resist spectacular shots designed to impress that netted him a single point. Though O'Sullivan was never overtly rude, the older player's exquisite deportment—Ramsey always tapped the rail appreciatively whenever his opponent had racked up a fine clearance—seemed to drive the younger man to a contrasting churlishness. In his chair, the Rocket slouched, allowing his expression to wash with boredom or annoyance. He spent one of Ramsey's more stylish clearances with a towel draped over his face—presumably to retain concentration, but more likely to keep from having to watch. Though Clive Everton observed that Ramsey's ranking had progressively deteriorated over the last three years, Irina had a gut sense that their old friend had finally arrived at his day in the sun.

"I think he's going to win," Irina predicted at the end of the first night, with Ramsey up ten frames to six. For Irina, the commercial success of *Ivan and the Terribles* had issued in a sumptuous era of well-wishing and optimism on others' accounts.

"No way," said Lawrence, whose brief newscast celebrity around the Good Friday Agreement had effected no such transformation. "The poor bastard's cursed. And how old is the guy now? Has to be past fifty. It's over."

The bookies agreed with Lawrence, and before the final had put the odds of Ramsey's victory at eight to one. Yet Ramsey held his lead the next afternoon, and went into the fourth session fourteen frames to ten.

She cajoled Lawrence into watching the last session together the following night. O'Sullivan wasn't being a baby for once, and as Everton said "dug down deep"; before the interval, he narrowed Ramsey's advantage to fifteen–thirteen. Not conventionally engaged by sport of any description, Irina was now so excited that she couldn't sit still, bouncing up from her armchair to pace the carpet with leonine restiveness. Once the score notched to sixteen–fifteen, and then drew even at sixteen apiece, she became so agitated that the game was almost too painful to watch.

"What's with you?" asked Lawrence from his sofa. "It's only a snooker match."

"Time was you'd never have said *only* a snooker match, *milyi*. Besides, this is electrifying as personal drama. Ramsey must have been playing this game for over thirty years. It's his life's dream to win this tournament. Now he's within two frames . . . One frame! It's seventeen–sixteen! Can you believe this?"

Irina was literally jumping up and down, and the television audience was doing the same. Ramsey's boosters may have reduced in number over the years, but every snooker fan knew the story of Ramsey the Runner-Up. Like Lawrence, most accepted the myth that he could never win this title, that he was cursed. The prospect of Swish breaking the spell, like Sleeping Beauty discovering the alarm clock, produced a groundswell of

400

exhilaration even among the members of the audience wearing "Rotherham for the Rocket!" T-shirts.

Along with the crowd, Irina groaned and covered her face with her hands when Ramsey missed an easy red, and let O'Sullivan in. This was exactly the kind of sudden, inexplicable lapse under pressure that had lost him six finals before. As O'Sullivan cleaned up to level the match again, Lawrence chided, "I'm telling you, Ramsey can't do it. Something in him must not want to. His whole identity is wrapped around being this not-quite. If he ever took the championship, he'd wake up the next morning having no idea who he was. Just you watch. He'll botch it."

"Wanna bet?" said Irina. "A thousand dollars."

"Get out."

"*One large.*" That ample advance on *Ivan and the Terribles*, with another six-figure contract in the pipeline, was teaching her the heady joys of profligacy.

"Okay!" said Lawrence. "But you'll be sorry."

Irina was already not sorry. Even if Ramsey did bollix the deciding frame, marshalling such fierce belief in their old friend felt splendid, and seemed to improve his karmic odds.

"Now, that is *unfortunate!*" intoned Clive Everton. O'Sullivan was feeling the pressure himself, and his heavy-handed break-off had left a red available to the corner pocket. He sulked back to his chair, where it was best he got comfortable, for Ramsey not only potted that red, but proceeded to pick its little friends off the pack as if denuding a cluster of grapes on a summer afternoon.

For the spectator, there are two kinds of sportsmen: those you trust, and those you don't. It is likely the divide correlates with whether the sportsman trusts himself, but in any event watching a player in whom you have imperfect faith fosters anxiety. Watching the kind who has it, whatever *it* is, and knows he has it, is relaxing. Indeed, certain characters so consistently engender an unswerving confidence in their audience that all the tension leaves the game, and they attain a reputation as dull. Given his history, Irina would have classified Ramsey Acton, in this situation, as the kind of player who made you nervous.

Yet with $1,000 riding on his performance, as the break built to forty, forty-one, forty-eight, Irina resumed a comfortable loll in her armchair. As he approached the magic number at which O'Sullivan would need snookers, her apprehension should have been building unbearably; yet at sixty-four, sixty-five, and seventy-two Irina felt only more languidly at her ease. At seventy-three, Ramsey needed one more colour to have victory assured, and he potted it. Just like that. Just as she knew he would. It was the easiest grand she'd ever trousered.

The crowd clapped wildly. Irina smiled serenely at Lawrence. The referee hushed the audience. Its result may have been conclusive, but the frame wasn't over.

"I say," said Clive Everton. "Ramsey Acton may have a chance at a 147!"

Snooker's Holy Grail, unusual at the practice table and supremely rare under tournament conditions, a 147, or *maximum*, is the highest score it is possible to rack up on a single break. Indeed, Ramsey had played off the black for the entire visit so far, and meanwhile the remaining reds were spread like a whore's legs. Thus Ramsey Acton purled around the table with the luxuriousness of having already won, and once he exceeded 100 the audience went bananas. O'Sullivan's fans had forsaken their idol wholesale; the largely working-class crowd had abandoned the sport's hushed, courtly conceit and reverted to type. The referee seemed to have resigned himself that hounding this rough-and-tumble rabble into silence would be like trying to shove a pit bull into a dress. Oh, a 147 was just icing on the cake; it wasn't necessary. But then, neither was snooker.

When the last black went in to complete the maximum, the crowd erupted, and the cheers and catcalls lasted two or three minutes. The news had been dominated for months by awful public barbecues to eradicate foot-and-mouth disease, whole herds crisping on hillsides while stalwart Yorkshire farmers wept like babies and rural suicides mounted; how rarely these days did anything lovely air on television.

"I wonder if it isn't a little bit of a letdown," Irina mused. "Getting just what you've always wanted."

"Losing would be more of a letdown," said Lawrence. "Ask me. I just lost a thousand bucks."

"Donate it to the charity of your choice. There must be some fund for retired snooker players down on their luck. . . . Look at him! It's so touching. He's not blubbing, and he's doing a good job of holding them back—but I swear he has tears in his eyes."

Academically, she recognized how important it would be for Ramsey to have a woman with whom to share the crowning achievement of his career. But when in the hubbub following the trophy presentation no

402

lithe, glowing little number threw her arms around that lean racehorse neck, Irina was privately pleased.

◫ ◫ ◫

The attainment of any life's dream was doubtless seeded with an insidious emptiness, a now-what? sensation sufficiently unpleasant as to induce a retarded nostalgia for the days when you were still tantalized by what you thought you wanted. Yet Ramsey surely preferred contending with the fact that the silver urn he clutched that night at the Crucible was just a cold, useless hunk of metal to the alternative whereby the useless hunk of metal belonged to someone else. In kind, even if in the moment the accolade might feel no more rewarding than the "moon ring" at the bottom of Cap'n Crunch, Irina herself had always yearned to win a prize. The longing felt childish. It was childish. In fact, it was the very grade-school nature of the yen—like Spacer's pining to win a blue ribbon in his sack race—that made it so tenacious.

So when the call came in from her editor at Transworld an afternoon in latter May informing her that *Ivan and the Terribles* had been short-listed for the Lewis Carroll Medal, Irina acted like a ten-year-old. She twirled around her studio. She cried, "Oh, rah, rah, rah!" and did not care if the neighbours could hear. But none of this gallivanting was doing it for her; the experience still wasn't quite *happening*. The news would only arrive in a profound sense once she delivered it to Lawrence.

The telephone seemed wasteful. She grabbed her jacket, and flew out the door. On the way to Blue Sky, her stride grew so long and light that for short distances she broke into a run. In the lobby of Churchill House, she begged the receptionist not to forewarn her "husband" of her presence—everyone here thought they were married—because she wanted to surprise him.

She surprised him. The door to his office was closed, but no de facto wife should have to knock.

Something wasn't quite right. Surely those two ought to have been sitting on either side of his desk, or contemplating his computer screen. Even if they were conferring together on the couch, shouldn't there be papers? Although it wasn't that the duo was too cozy; by the time she got the heavy door open, they were sitting bizarrely far apart.

"What are you doing here?" asked Lawrence in a strangled voice.

"Funny," said Irina lightly. "I was about to ask the same thing about *Bethany*."

"Oh, just consulting about work stuff," said Bethany brightly, standing and smoothing her tiny skirt. "It would bore you. Ta, *Yasha!*" With a blazing smile at Irina, the little tart swished out the door.

Irina had arrived with wonderful news. In willing that its delivery *would be* wonderful, she struck out the last sixty seconds in her head with a dark line of Magic Marker, like one of those redacted manuscripts of declassified documents issued to satisfy Freedom of Information requests. She even deleted the fact that *Bethany* had a special name for Lawrence—a Russian diminutive for a middle name with which Bethany had no reason to be acquainted. Bethany and Lawrence were colleagues. These people were surely in and out of each other's offices all the time.

Given the cheerful nature of her errand, she even managed to put out of mind her running grudge over the fact that the illustration from *Seeing Red* that she'd framed in glass for Lawrence's Christmas present two and a half years ago was still propped against the wall—though she had lugged it here herself. Blue Sky was fussy about not putting holes in the plaster, and Lawrence had never got round to asking the housekeeping staff to run a wire from the cornice.

So she told him. He hugged her, and proposed a fabulously expensive dinner to celebrate that very night. He declared his utter confidence that she would win. Only in his arms did the honour come home.

▩ ▩ ▩

Although while dressing for the reception in the Pierre Hotel on Fifth Avenue Irina was understandably nervous, the scale of her anxiety seemed disproportionate. Try as she might to protect herself from getting her hopes up, she knew in her gut that *Ivan and the Terribles* would clinch this prize. So the source of her fretfulness while she wrestled with her unruly hair had little to do with girding for defeat.

By unhappy coincidence, Jude Hartford was also short-listed for the Lewis Carroll. Ever since Irina had spotted her name in the *Telegraph* article about the award she'd been trying to fashion an attitude with which to confront the woman. Curiously, Irina couldn't cite a single romantic breakup over which she still harboured strong feelings of any kind—be they good-riddance or good wishes. By contrast, the rare friendship that had blown up in her face left a jagged edge that for years later she could still run her tongue over like a broken tooth. Friendships aren't supposed to take on the apocalyptic structure of romance; like old soldiers, they might fade away, but never die. Breakups like the one Irina went through with Jude, replete with the harsh words and total renunciations of a lovers' quarrel, defied the natural order. Mortal clashes between friends have about them a savage gratuitousness; romantic partings, in retrospect, a soothing quality of the inevitable. Thus Irina's umbrage even after five years still felt raw.

"Hey, that is one hot dress," said Lawrence.

Irina bit her lip. "You don't think it's too short?"

"Hell, no. You've got a whole two inches before the hem hits crotch."

"It's more low-cut than I realized in the store. Maybe I should wear that little black jacket."

"Don't. You look sexy."

Irina was surprised; he'd usually say *cute*. "I thought it makes you uneasy when I look sexy."

"That's a load of horseshit. Where'd you get that idea?"

"You don't like it when I dress up."

"I don't like it when *I* have to dress up."

"Speaking of which . . ." She gave the familiar dark Dockers and threadbare button-down with no tie a disparaging once-over. He was such a handsome man if he just stood up straight and made an effort! "I hate to break it to you, but I think most of the men will be wearing tuxes."

"Well, I'll be sure to feel sorry for them, then. Are you edgy about seeing Jude?"

"A little," she admitted. "I haven't a clue what to say to her."

"Tell her to go fuck herself. Tell her that you're more talented than she is, and smarter than she is, and that you're incredibly relieved not to have to listen to her tired liberal bromides at dinner anymore. Tell her that you're going to win tonight, and that *The Love Diet* is the most pathetic piece of PC crap you've ever seen. Just because she can't keep her hands off the Twinkies doesn't mean that every pork-wad kid in the country should *lu-u-v* themselves, and that it's okay to be overweight."

"Actually, the book is practically Atkins for eight-year-olds. But thanks for your diplomatic advice." Lawrence had a way of siding with Irina in such extremity that he drove her to her own adversary's defence.

Indeed, Lawrence hadn't read the competition carefully. Jude's storybook was about a chunky little girl who grows so smitten by a boy at school that she cannot eat. Never a worthy object for her affections, the little boy is unremittingly chilly and difficult. Yet meantime the protagonist slims down so in her lovelorn state that every other boy in her class is stuck on her—happy ending.

■ ▣ ■

Trailing apprehensively behind Lawrence, Irina entered the events room to mark Jude's presence at the far end by the drinks table—in a form-fitting evening dress, looking amazingly svelte. But it wasn't sighting Jude that hit her midsection like a right hook.

The sensation recalled Irina's real-life version of Jude's little storybook. In junior high school before her braces came off, she would often walk into the cafeteria and spot the handsome student-council president, on whom she'd had a torturous crush for three years straight. She'd sit nearby but never at the same table, straining to overhear his conversation while feeling so self-conscious of her own that she could barely ask her girlfriend what she thought of the tuna-melt. In those days, it was rational to be anxious—of drawing attention to herself; of not drawing attention to herself. Yet at forty-six, she could not put her finger on why this unexpected apparition in the Pierre Hotel would likewise stab her stomach to the point of nausea. In any event, that tall, tuxedoed gentleman at Jude Hartford's side was none other than Ramsey Acton.

As she and Lawrence advanced, neither of their old friends seemed to notice them, so intently were they engaged with each other in hushed, urgent-sounding tones. Ramsey's hand on Jude's arm confirmed that they'd got back together. Irina felt a curious little sag.

Jude looked up with a distracted, harried expression. "Oh, hi there!" Her delivery was aerated as ever, but her eyes were vacant. They did the whole cheek-kissing thing; pecking Ramsey, Irina lingered to inhale.

"Just like old times!" Irina said with nervous gaiety. "Our old foursome is back."

"Yes, it's quite a coincidence," said Jude aimlessly.

"Well, maybe it isn't," said Irina, straining to be generous. "Maybe it's just talent—both being talented . . . You know, cream rising to the top." She hated herself for acting as if all that acrimony had never happened. But the twist of Jude's face implied that she truly couldn't recall the ugliness of their last encounter, being much more absorbed by some misery in the present.

"Call me prejudiced," said Lawrence, "but I think *Ivan and the Terribles* is fantastic." He gripped Irina's waist.

In turn, Ramsey slid an arm around Jude's shoulder, which he massaged with his left hand as if kneading a dry, resistant mass of pasta dough. Jude had never seemed very sensual—she was too tense, too highly strung—and didn't appear to be enjoying the attentions. He had beautiful hands. Irina thought, *What a waste.*

"So, you two"—she nodded at the couple—"are giving it another go?"

Jude managed an anaemic smile. "Authors are prone to sequels."

"Not a promising analogy, pet," Ramsey chided. "Your average sequel is never near as good as the original."

"To be honest," Jude said with that faintly hysterical laugh, rearranging her stance in such a way as to shuck Ramsey's arm, "having a hard time topping your own success is generally only a problem when you had a success to begin with!"

Irina was not sure what they had walked in on, and tried to turn to a neutral subject. "I've missed our birthday dinners," she told Ramsey.

"I have as well," he said with feeling. "And didn't you miss a corker last summer."

"I pulled out all the stops for Ramsey's fiftieth," said Jude. "Hired a room in the Savoy. Invited the whole snooker crowd, and not a few of the haut monde. To be quite honest, it was terribly dear! But everyone—everyone *else*—said it was the occasion of the year."

"I don't fancy a lot of fuss," Ramsey muttered.

"Yes, sweetie," said Jude with a pressed-lip smile. "Several thousand quid later, I got that message loud and clear."

"Hey, Ramsey!" said Lawrence, clapping the snooker player's shoulder. "Congratulations on winning the championship!"

"Cheers, mate," said Ramsey lightly.

"Lawrence and I watched the final on the BBC," said Irina, omitting the fact that Lawrence had lobbied for *CSI* instead. "It was wonderful. And finishing with a 147!"

"Don't happen every day," he conceded. "Shame our friend Jude here had to wash her hair."

"I had *previous commitments*!" said Jude with exasperation.

"You didn't *go*?" asked Irina in astonishment.

"I'd have been there if I could have been. Though to be honest, snooker's never been my cup of tea."

"Oh, I've only gotten more interested!" said Irina passionately.

"It's a bit different when you've not much choice."

Now a bona fide fan, Irina was mystified how Jude could hook up with a snooker pro and be so wearied by the sport. If *she* were with Ramsey Acton, she'd go to every match! But Irina had resolved to be gracious. "By the way, Jude—congratulations yourself!"

"Sorry?" Jude seemed to have forgotten why she was here.

"For being short-listed for the Lewis Carroll, of course."

"Oh, that!" Jude said absently. "Well, mine can't possibly win."

"Why not?"

"Just a presentiment." Jude looked worn out. Round patches of rouge stood out like tiddlywinks; underneath her cheeks were surely drawn. "Yours, though. It has a proper chance. The illustrations are very clever."

Clever was a mile from *good,* its connotations cold and empty, and the conflict from five years ago came back in a rush.

"I see you've moved on to computer graphics," Jude added.

"That's right," said Irina coolly. "The book's sold surprisingly well."

"Yes," said Jude with returning coolness. "It would."

"I think we all need a drink," said Irina.

As they filtered toward the wine, she fell into step with Ramsey, and drew him aside. "After all you told me at Omen," she said quietly, "I'm surprised you're back with Jude."

"At my age, I'm too knackered to make a new mistake. It's easier to make the same one."

"But are things all right between you two?" Just as in Bournemouth four years before, they fell into a ready collusion. "She seems—jumpy."

"You mean, she's acting like a right cow. This spot of good fortune—well, success don't always have an improving effect on people."

"You should know. You must feel so satisfied. Finally winning that title."

"Remember what else I told you that night?" He knocked back his wine in a gulp. "*I'm never satisfied.* Get one thing you want, and it clears the way to seeing what else you're missing."

She met his eyes. "And what would that be?"

He looked back, but didn't answer. "You know, something tells me you're going to win this medal tonight."

He really shouldn't have said such a thing to Jude's competition. "I bet you've told the same thing to every girl on the short-list, you cad!"

He didn't smile. "I'm no womanizer. You should know better."

Their locked gazes had grown uncomfortable, but if she broke eye contact now she'd seem a coward. "Have you read *Ivan*?"

"I read it."

"Did you understand it?"

"I understood it." As if to demonstrate as much, he didn't deliver his next sentence as a non sequitur. "Irina, me and Jude's planning to get remarried."

Irina glanced at her toes before looking up again. "I guess that's very good news." She shouldn't have appended the *I guess,* but she couldn't help it.

"Leastways, maybe I'll get the house in Spain back," he said, but the effort at leavening failed. "And you're married anyway, more or less. What else is a bloke to do? I reckon you're greedy, pet. Like to have your cake, and make eyes at it as well."

It was the closest either had come to acknowledging that temptation on his forty-seventh birthday, and the moment was so ungainly that Irina was grateful for the intrusion behind her. "Irina Galina!" Only one person in the world pronounced that double-barrel without irony, and Irina turned to hug her mother with much fanfare.

"*Pozdravlyayu tebya!*" Though Raisa congratulated her daughter, her plunging crimson gown indicated a little confusion as to which member of the family was the star of the hour. "*A eto shtoza krasavets?*"

"The *handsome man* is Ramsey Acton, an old friend of mine. You remember, Lawrence and I mentioned him a while ago. The snooker player."

Irina was pulled away to meet the judges and press, and left her mother pulling the whole Passionate Russian Number on Ramsey, her hands gesticulating so broadly that she might easily have upended a passing platter of shrimp toast. Putting on a great show of fascination with snooker, Raisa laid on the Slavic accent with a trowel. As a ghastly alternative future flashed before her eyes, Irina was suddenly grateful that Ramsey was engaged.

Thereafter, Irina found herself adjacent to an aristocratic man whose aura of being at sea stirred her compassion. She asked what had brought him here.

"I happened to be in New York for a board meeting, and Jude Hartford asked me to attend," he said in a plummy British accent. "But the lady's barely said two words to me. And that snooker chap she's with—bloody rude!"

"Ramsey, rude?" said Irina incredulously. "You must have misunderstood."

"I fear I understood all too well, madam. Good-night, my dear. And good luck."

A nice man, but his story didn't add up; Ramsey was the most polite, considerate man on earth. To wit, he caught Irina's ear again. "I met your sister," he said. "Bird rabbited on—"

"Now, how can a bird *rabbit*?"

"You're a prig, you are," he said affectionately. "Bird *banged* on—that better?" (One grew inured to glottal stops in London, but back in the States his *that be-ah?* was charming.) "About how she was 'only a housewife and mum,' different to her sister who's all famous and such. Never heard a bird so humble on the one hand, and so hacked off as well. And out of nowhere your woman starts waffling about how you was never cut out to be a mum yourself. How all you care about is your work, and larking about foreign countries, and if you was to have a sprog you'd leave it hanging upside down with marbles in its nose while you had to go and paint another daisy. Quite a sodding earful, that."

"What did you say?"

"What do you figure? That you was warm, and decent, and smart, and I reckoned you'd make a blinding mum. That got her to shut it."

Irina laughed, and said without thinking, "I adore you!" as they were all called into dinner.

■ ■ ■

At the large round table at the front, Irina and Lawrence were seated together, but Ramsey and Jude's place cards were on the far opposite side. Irina had no idea how Lawrence did it; normal people would start the conversational ball rolling with something anodyne like, "I hate it when they prepare this sort of starter with that dollop of *mayonnaise*!" Yet in no time he had involved most of the table in a heated discussion of the new Bush administration. Ramsey wasn't fussed about politics, period, so it didn't strike her as peculiar that his bearing was stony. But she did find it noteworthy that Jude Hartford, *Guardian* subscriber and Old Labour zealot, said nothing.

For hotel fare, the roast beef was impressively rare, and delicious. So it was a shame that Ramsey must have been feeling unwell; he wasn't touching his dinner.

While the opposite couple's refusal to engage with the rest of the table made them seem standoffish, Ramsey had an excuse. He was a snooker player at a literary gathering, a fish out of water, and naturally a little shy. Jude was in her element, and should have been acting as interlocutor. What a difficult woman! Poor Ramsey. Irina hoped he knew what he was doing, patching things up with Jude.

After the waiters cleared the table and the foundation director introduced each entrant with slides, Jude began whispering in Ramsey's ear. Oh, for pity's sake! The woman sits out the entire dinner not saying word one, and finally starts talking at the very point it's time to shut up. Presumably Ramsey hadn't any choice but to respond, though he'd surely be abashed about conversing during the director's speech. If this were a snooker match, a referee would have ejected Jude from the hall.

Once the slides from *Ivan and the Terribles* flashed on screen, Irina grew irate. She'd been looking forward to this occasion for months, and Jude's carry-on was distracting. As the red-framed Etch A Sketch compositions were projected, Irina and Lawrence looked at each other and shook their heads. It was astounding that Jude would choose this of all junctures to pick a fight. Ramsey must have been mortified! He whispered in return, probably imploring her to please take up her grievance another time—although any admonishments along these lines were unavailing. More astonishing still, when Jude's illustrator's drawings for *The Love Diet* followed, she didn't even look at the screen, much less bother to listen to an admiring précis of her own book.

The director requested the envelope. Lawrence clasped Irina's hand, squeezing with the tight, moist grip of a child's at the dentist. So compelling was the anxiety in his face—that carved, haunted, beautiful face—that Irina spent what they both prayed would be her moment of triumph looking not up at the podium but in Lawrence's eyes.

So convinced had she been of prevailing in this contest that her ears played tricks on her, and at first she could have sworn that she heard her own name distorted with a crackle of static through the PA. But the identity of the victor was written unmistakably across Lawrence's face, which suddenly drained of blood and collapsed in a heap like a wet towel.

It was the oddest thing. Though she had been foolish to get her hopes up, and thereby set herself up for a fall, Irina felt fine. Her smile at

Lawrence was beatific. Like Jesus taking on the sins of the world, Lawrence seemed to have assumed the full weight of her disappointment. Her most immediate concern was for his own consolation, and she kissed his hand quickly before letting go, that they might both applaud the winner. Winner? Whatever the papers might say tomorrow, Irina McGovern had won this evening. For as she rose from her chair to join the standing ovation, she could not imagine any prize greater than the one she had won thirteen years earlier on West 104th Street.

Jude had struggled to her feet, and was clapping, feebly, along with everyone else. Surely she understood that you weren't supposed to applaud yourself? She looked confused, and at length did stop patting her hands together like limp flippers, but only to plop to her chair. Mouthing *Congratulations!* and *Go on!*, Irina met her old friend's eyes, and was surprised to find them swollen and red. It was queer, feeling sorry for the only person at this table who had just pocketed $50,000 and the proceeds from selling perhaps one hundred thousand extra copies of her last book.

Prodded by the director, Jude finally reported for duty as if skulking to the principal's office. Her acceptance speech bordered on incompetent. While she did remember to thank Ramsey, to whom she wasn't even married anymore, and with a shit-eating profuseness at that, she forgot to commend her illustrator or to thank the judges. She had a dazed, unfocused quality, as if surprised to find herself at an award ceremony when she had thought she was headed for the launderette. Usually so flamboyant and excitable, she mumbled sheepishly to the podium, as if she wished that this event were already over and that everyone would go away. If this was to pass for one of the best days of Jude's life, Irina would hate to see the lousy ones.

When the formal folderol was dispatched, Lawrence gave Irina a hug. "I'm really sorry," he mumbled in her ear. "Your book was miles better, and it should have won."

On drawing apart, Irina, unlike the victor, was dry-eyed and cheerful. "Thank you. I know you think so, and that's medal enough for me."

He studied her, disconcerted. "You really don't seem that upset."

"I'm not. It was still exciting to be nominated, and I love you." What a rare business: once in a blue moon to get your priorities straight.

"Oh, you poor dear!" cried Tatyana, squeezing Irina so tightly that she couldn't breathe. "You must feel simply wretched!"

"I sure judges already regret their choice," said Raisa regally. "That speech your friend give—*ochen plokho*. You win, you do better."

One of the judges approached her in the throng. The earnest middle-aged woman's tender, concerned manner recalled Mrs. Bennington, her tenth-grade art teacher. "The foundation doesn't award silver medals," she said with a hand on Irina's arm. "But you should know, dear, that you were the runner-up. The voting was very close."

"I appreciate that. But I'm afraid maybe I should have taken my partner's advice." Irina glanced up at him with a smile. "Lawrence thought strongly that I should have kept the ending simpler. Just stick-by-old-friends, without the extra twist. I was awfully bloody-minded about it. But I'm inexperienced as an author; I'm really just an illustrator."

"No, no!" said the judge. "I thought your ending was wonderfully enigmatic, and very true. Our problem was with the illustrations, I'm afraid."

"Oh! The Etch A Sketch thing . . . ?"

"The concept was delightful. And your technical execution was accomplished. But we weren't happy with the computer-generated images. They were a little clinical—like the difference between an LP and a CD. If you had reproduced drawings on a real Etch A Sketch, dear, it's possible that you'd have won."

"It's all my fault," said Lawrence morosely when the woman was gone. "I was the one who pushed you to try the computer."

"Don't be silly. It should have, but using a real Etch A Sketch never occurred to me. Hilarious, really. I was a genius at Etch A Sketch when I was eight years old."

They stood in the queue to congratulate Jude, who still looked less as if she'd just won a prestigious award than as if she'd just drawn the Old Maid in a game of cards. Upstairs in their room, they had Consolation Sex, which, if Irina was still facing the wall, wasn't half bad, and she even managed to persuade Lawrence to keep the light on. For one of the evening's losers, she was absurdly content, and fell vertiginously to sleep as if plunging from a tall building to the pavement.

◻ ◻ ◻

While Lawrence shifted their bags the next day to the cheaper Upper West Side hotel provided by his upcoming conference on "global civil society," Irina met Tatyana at a Broadway Starbucks.

"You look pretty jovial," said Tatyana after another sympathetic bear-hug. "Considering that you lost."

"Well, as they say, winning isn't everything!" Irina said brightly.

413

While Tatyana fetched their coffees, Irina suffered from a funny pining to talk to Lawrence, though they'd only parted an hour before. This yearning for his company in the middle of the day used to be a constant plague when he went off for work, and she missed it. These last few years, being separated had grown too easy. Her flush of gratitude last night had revived the sharper feelings of an earlier era, when the sound of his key in their front-door lock made her heart leap.

"Got a little gossip," she said when Tatyana returned. "Which you might share with Mama, to warn her off. That tall, thin chap she took such a shine to last night? He's getting married."

"Ooh, she'll be very put out!" Tatyana laughed. "She's a dreadful flirt of course, with any man. But I haven't seen her that entranced for ages. On the train home, I heard all about how *elegant* he was, how *graceful*, how she loved his accent. If you want to know the truth—maybe he did British accents back in the day—I think something about that guy reminded her of Papa. And she couldn't stop going on about—what was it—*snookers* . . . ?"

"Snooker. But you tell her he's taken," said Irina flatly. Honestly, the prospect of Raisa courting Ramsey Acton—much less the other way around—made her want to hurl.

After Tatyana brought her sister up to speed with news of the family, she rounded on last night's ceremony. "You must be *so* disappointed. Coming all the way to New York, only to have to applaud for someone else. And she's a friend of yours, right? Or was? I wonder if that doesn't make it worse."

Irina shrugged. "Jude can have it. That award sure didn't seem to make her very happy. And Lawrence was so devastated when it wasn't me that—I almost felt as if I'd won. Even at the reception, he couldn't stop singing my praises to other people. I tried to remind him that it was déclassé to brag about your own partner, but he was so proud that he wouldn't listen. It hit me over the head last night—that I already had exactly what I've always wanted: a smart, funny, loyal, handsome man."

When they were parting, Tatyana cocked her head. "I still don't get it. You just missed out on this huge prize. But you're *glowing*!" She seemed annoyed.

▣ ▣ ▣

Irina's revelatory gratitude for what she had in the first place was sadly short-lived. For if she ordinarily took for granted the architecture of her

414

personal life, even more so did she take for granted the literal architecture of the city from which she hailed. Granted, history lends itself to the conclusion that pause is rare, that any respite is as merciful as it's bound to be brief, that the very nature of existence is unstable and it is therefore best to be prepared for just about any catastrophe lurking right around the corner on any arbitrary morning. Thus the only real surprise should be those single sunny awakenings on which there is no surprise. Yet in defiance of all we know in theory, it remains common psychic practice to assume that world affairs will keep bumbling along the way they've been doing, much as from day to day Galileo himself would have persistently perceived the spinning globe on which we hurtle as standing still.

Thus what Irina would later rehearse about that Tuesday morning with weak room-service coffee in the Hotel Esplanade was its regularness. The *before* by its nature never feels like before. Irina was out of bed for forty-five minutes while September 11, 2001, was still just another date on the calendar, and had no way of knowing how precious they were.

Accordingly, she would squander them on feeling peeved that Lawrence had insisted on getting up so early, when she'd have liked to sleep in. The unexpected exhilaration of Sunday night had subsided, and it was beginning to sink in that she'd lost the Lewis Carroll. There would be no headlong rush to buy her book at Barnes & Noble, no embossed medallions feverishly applied to remaining stock, no "Lewis Carroll winner" in succeeding flap-copy bios. It was unlikely that she'd have a chance at such an imprimatur again, and abruptly there seemed little to look forward to. No wonder Ramsey had been so frustrated with his status as perpetual also-ran. Americans in particular made such a stark distinction between winning and losing, no matter how close you got—didn't that judge say that she missed by a hair?—that runner-up and nobody blurred to the same thing.

Lawrence's despair on her account had peaked, and was no longer quite so moving. At their dinner at Fiorello's last night, she had enjoyed his reprise on Jude's crummy book (which, having skimmed it, he now decried as a Bible for anorexics), along with a riff on what a pill the woman was, how appalling was her acceptance speech (his imitation was hilarious), and how insane Ramsey must be to ask for a second dose. But this morning Lawrence was once more buried in his laptop; his mind had clearly moved on to the presentation he'd to give tomorrow about Chechnya. Uneager to see her mother that night, she worried that Raisa would only take the news of Ramsey's engagement as a challenge; her head swam with the nightmare of her mother rocking up with loads of luggage in Borough, insisting they get that lovely snooker player round for dinner. Her own brush with Ramsey at the Pierre vibrated in Irina's head like a plucked guitar string. Despite her epiphany about having in Lawrence everything she'd always wanted, it pained her that her parallel-universe fancy man, The Chap She Almost Kissed, was getting remarried. The Esplanade was dumpier than the Pierre, with none of the shoe-shine sponges and aromatherapy face-wash frippery that Irina would never use but compulsively slipped into her carry-on, and it made her feel like a chump to pay five dollars for a small bottled water.

"Huh," Lawrence grunted over the screen, as she gazed out at West End Avenue feeling sorry for herself. "AOL says a plane ran into the World Trade Center."

"Well, that sounds careless," said Irina irritably. "I know those pilots in private planes sometimes get off course, but Jesus, the Trade Center is bigger than a breadbox. You'd think maybe he'd turn wheel before busting into it. The sky is clear as crystal, too!"

Over Irina's objections—she hated the yammer of television in the morning; it made her feel dirty—Mr. Newshound had to see it for himself. He mumbled something about finding a local station, but the building was smoking on CNN.

"Oh my God, that hole is huge!" said Irina in consternation, shoving her coffee aside and walking closer to the screen. "Lawrence, that could take *years* to fix. What a pain in the arse! It's the kind of repair that will have Wall Street covered in that depressing scaffolding over sidewalks forever—"

"Looks too big to be a private plane. I wonder if it was a commercial . . . ? That's hard to believe. What pilot could be such a moron?"

"That fire looks terrible. If people were already at work—!"

"Shsh! I want to hear this."

But at the very moment that Lawrence shushed her, the commentator stopped talking. The camera veered to the other tower, and though this same footage would replay all day, and all week, and sporadically through as many years to come as years remained with video technology, there was a first time, and it was different.

"Lawrence, what's happening?" Irina shrieked. "Two freak accidents in the same morning, the coincidence is impossible!"

"It's not a coincidence," said Lawrence levelly. "It's terrorism."

The most proximate "terrorists" to London were those IRA goons who ran about hugger-mugger in balaclavas, and frankly looked ridiculous. Though she had never said so outright, since the sentiment might sound hurtful, hitherto Lawrence's professional speciality had always about it an almost comical little-boy quality.

"But who would do such a thing?" she screeched. "This is insane! What's the point?"

The CNN commentators and "experts" hastily contacted down the line would soon cast a wide net regarding the identity of the culprits, from white supremacists to Saddam Hussein. But Lawrence didn't hesitate. "It's Osama bin Laden."

"Oh, who's *that*?" She was furious.

"He was linked to the first Trade Center bombing, the USS *Cole,* and the embassy bombings in East Africa. You haven't been paying attention."

Under ordinary circumstances, Irina might have taken offence. But she did not. He was right. She hadn't been paying attention.

She didn't even mind when he told her to shut up. She shut up. He turned up the volume. Two other planes were reported hijacked. One of them ploughed into the Pentagon. The fourth crashed in Pennsylvania. For the first time in history, every single airplane in the United States was ordered to ground. Irina and Lawrence remained standing. All of her interjections were obvious: *This is awful.* It was already apparent that for some time to come whatever you said would sound dumb. But the events of that morning had already grown so eclipsing, and in comparison the two of them and what they said and thought so small, that it was almost as if they didn't exist at all. Thus Irina had no opportunity to rue the fact that she had ever wasted a moment's anguish on some trinket called the Lewis Carroll Medal, because as bodies began to drop from upper floors, the award, her entire career in illustration, her frustrations with her sexually competitive mother, and her seditious attraction to Ramsey Acton withered so rapidly that these once monumental matters never even had the chance to seem puny. They simply vanished.

Much as it's worth recalling that for whole years of World War II no one knew whether Hitler might win, it would soon behoove Americans to remember that for a few hours on that eleventh of September no one knew if more planes might be out there, if the White House or the Empire State Building might be next, if the very government were about to topple or the island of Manhattan to upend into the sea. Now that the spinning globe on which we hurtle was clearly not standing still, anything could happen, and anything did.

As the tower shrank from the sky like a dusty, stepped-on accordion, for the first time in her life Irina knew the true meaning of *horror*. In a few thick seconds, a skyscraper that had prowed the tip of Manhattan since her adolescence and that she had never much cared for was no more. It hadn't seemed to fall down so much as evaporate. In fact, the empty shifting billows defied the rules of physics, whereby energy is neither created nor destroyed. The erection of that 107-storey tower had required a great deal of energy, and all that energy had been destroyed.

Identical twins often enjoy the same bond of long-married couples, and one half of the pair will languish when the other dies. Within the hour, perhaps the second tower followed suit out of sorrow—sitting with an eerie grace beside its sister as if giving up. Just as when the news came in that Diana had died in a Paris tunnel and Irina rued having so callously fired adjectives like *vapid* and *saccharine* at the poor woman while she was still alive, Irina wished with frantic superstition to take back every casually unkind slur she had ever uttered about the World Trade Center— her dismissals of the gaudy lobbies, her comparisons of its unimaginative commercial dimensions to a giant two-for-one offer on boxes of Colgate. It was as if someone had been listening and she hadn't meant, no, no, she hadn't meant that she would just as soon it went away. Maybe it was less important to like something than to be used to it.

Lawrence put an arm around her shoulder while Irina cried. They were tears of another order than she had shed before—over her ineptitude at ballet as a child, jeers of "donkey face" in junior high, the falling-out with Jude, her loneliness while Lawrence was away. In retrospect, it was perplexing that she had ever wept on these measly occasions of distress, when all along full-scale tragedy—the malignant, sickening history of the human race— had been unfolding just beyond her doorstep. On CNN, one commentator after another was already saying that nothing would ever be the same again. But it would be. Too many things had already happened after which nothing should have been the same again. This was not the first time people had done something hideous, and it wouldn't be the last.

Today of all days it should have been possible to weep the whole day through, but it wasn't. The fact that she had sobbed for entire evenings at a go over the loss of one boyfriend yet now found it too demanding to whimper over the loss of multitudes for more than two or three minutes was just one of those ugly facts about herself that Irina would have to live with.

After blowing her nose, she rang her mother. No answer. "The whole world's coming to an end," Irina despaired over the receiver, "and what do you want to bet that Mama is *exercising*."

It seemed lunatic to keep watching events on television that were occurring eight miles south. "I have to see it with my own eyes, Lawrence. To make it real."

"None of the trains are running. And they must have blocked off downtown. You're not going to get anywhere near it."

"Please?" She took his hand. "Walk with me?"

So they made a pilgrimage, a hadj—threading down into Riverside Park, where on the walkway by the Hudson the curvature of the island obscured what lay smouldering at its tip. Only when they trudged to the end of the pier at 72nd Street was it possible to see the white cloud rising, a bland puff at this distance, but real enough. Irina associated disaster with clamour, yet no sound emitted from the park but unearthly quiet, oblivious birds, the odd shuffle of feet as they were joined gradually by other New Yorkers, making the same numb trek. Few people spoke, and then only in murmurs. Everyone was polite, orderly, even down the West Side bikeway, commonly the scene of mean-spirited competition between cyclists, in-line skaters, and prams. In defiance of urban convention, strangers met one another's eyes. For the first time in her memory this felt like a unified city, a single place, and while much reference was made to its *communities*, the experience of feeling a part of one was rare.

"I think I owe you an apology," said Irina softly in the West 50s. Aside from the occasional race of emergency vehicles, the West Side Highway to their left, ordinarily bumper-to-bumper in midtown, was deserted, Mad Max. "Your work—I may not have thought it was very important."

"That's all right," said Lawrence, who had never let go of her hand. "Sometimes I forget it's important myself."

They were not stopped until West Houston Street, where a police cordon was drawn. A large, respectful crowd had gathered in silence. The air stung with an acrid smell of burnt rubber and nickel, and the bikeway railings were collecting a fine, baptismal ash. Hands to their sides, everyone faced the funeral pyre rising in the distance, paying homage for perhaps five minutes, then turning quiet heel. Irina and Lawrence bore witness for their five minutes, and ceded their places to others.

On the way back uptown, they walked inland. Even when the subways began working again around five, neither made a bid to get on. You did not make pilgrimages by turnstile. In Times Square, with no traffic, they trudged up the middle of Seventh Avenue. The digital ticker overhead streamed, U.S. ATTACKED . . . HIJACKED JETS DESTROY TWIN TOWERS AND HIT PENTAGON . . . Bits of flotsam caught by the wind swirled over the empty roadway like the aftermath of a frenzied New Year's Eve, after the ball has dropped, and the whole city is hungover. A few restaurants had opened, although any establishments that looked Middle Eastern had their shutters drawn tight.

"I hate to sound petty," said Irina at Columbus Circle. "But if it had to happen—I'm glad we're in New York. If we were back in Britain, I'd feel left out."

"Well, I guess that is a little petty," he admitted. "But what's not petty now?"

"I'll tell you what's not petty," she said, stopping to turn him towards her. They were impeding the entrance to Central Park, but surrounding pedestrians were deferential, and gave them berth. Irina put her hands on either side of his face, and kissed him. Her cheeks tracked once more with purely private tears, but they were without shame.

❖ chapter eleven ❖

After she and Ramsey had gone at it hammer-and-tongs while oblivious to the single most catastrophic historical event in their lifetimes, Irina's revulsion produced one positive side effect: her vow that she and Ramsey would never, ever fight again. Even Ramsey, for whom the newspaper only properly began in the sports pages, was nearly as sobered, and the promise she extracted to reform seemed sincere.

For Irina, the penalty levied for such a gross sense of disproportion was banishment. From frequent phone calls with Tatyana, Irina inferred that in New York an insidious competition was already under way over ownership: who had loved ones die, who had escaped from the Trade Center just in time, who happened to be downtown that morning, who had seen the towers fall live rather than merely watched them on TV, who was having asthmatic attacks from bad air on 19th Street instead of breathing easy on the safe, unaffected Upper West Side. All the way out in Brighton Beach, and having missed even the first televised collapse of the towers altogether while picking up a few things on the Avenue, Tatyana's local standing was little more privileged than it would have been in Idaho. Thus she seemed to enjoy regaling her sister with tales of shut-down subway lines, describing the eerie occupied atmosphere of Manhattan, with police and National Guard troops on every corner like an African republic after a military coup. Only in comparison to an expatriate an ocean away on 9/11 could she play up her position as an insider.

For the attack would never belong to Irina. Not one whit. Her right to an opinion about what kind of structure might be erected in the World Trade Center's place, or about the retaliatory invasion of Afghanistan, had been rescinded, and whenever such subjects arose in conversation she grew subdued. The cataclysm itself morphed into a personal reprimand, a disaster contrived to remind Irina Galina McGovern in particular of how dreadfully the outside world could go off the rails when your back was turned. It was certainly a reminder that there *was* an outside world, and forever linked in her mind with private disgrace. She even battled a lunatic superstition that had she not been bickering behind closed doors, had she been reading the newspaper, focusing on what mattered, her very attentiveness would have pinned those towers to the sky.

That morning, Irina had accused Ramsey of "sabotage" in the Pierre Hotel; in truth, they were both guilty of planting bombs under their own car. Humbly they agreed with each other that to mar the perhaps twenty, at most thirty years remaining to them as a couple by going at each other's throats was wasteful in the extreme, and after September 13, 2001, neither could be too kind, too tender, too sweet.

Ramsey took Denise in to a man in the City, meant to be a miracle worker with snooker cues. But after a £2,500 repair job, Ramsey said he might as well have launched into the back garden and torn a branch from a tree. He searched far and wide, and spent several thousand pounds on a variety of flashy substitutes. Yet just as in romance, he did not need five not-quites, but one true love; he could no more replace Denise than Irina herself. He withdrew from the LG Cup, then the UK Championship, and for the first time began to contemplate retirement from the game.

Irina was torn. She relished neither dogging him around the tour, nor waiting out still more nine-month seasons as a snooker widow in the East End. But she hated the idea of his bowing out on such a sour note, that vulgar, drunken final at the Crucible. At only forty-six and on the heels of winning the Lewis Carroll, Irina had no intention of retiring herself, and she was nervous that Ramsey's pottering about with no structure to his day would put them at odds. He was already interrupting all the time, "Where's my black jumper?" while she was scribbling feverishly to meet a deadline. She worried that without snooker he would be lost, and that something vital in her own heart might die as well. She had fallen in love with Ramsey Acton, world-famous snooker star. Ramsey Acton, former snooker star, didn't have the same ring.

They did conduct many a languid evening exploring what avenues Ramsey could pursue after hanging up his cue—commentating for the

BBC, doing advertisements for a sponsor, starting a snooker camp for the underprivileged, writing his memoirs. Yet she knew in her bones that Ramsey would never start a snooker camp, or anything else. In retirement, he would flip disaffectedly through *Snooker Scene,* glower disaffectedly at tournaments on television, and otherwise prop glaze-eyed before *How Clean Is Your House*?

Nevertheless, there would be advantages. Putting out of mind the Ooty Club Rule—to wit, Ramsey was exclusively interested in travel to places that had something to do with snooker—Irina supposed that they could make profitable use of his ample winnings and see the world. Were he not on tour for most of the year, they could finally enjoy a home life—the simple pleasures of coffee and *Daily Telegraph*s, clean windows and daffodils, cabernet and *Newsnight*.

On into the winter, entertaining his options became a full-time occupation in itself. Consuming the present with fanciful futures was an adolescent pastime, unseemly for a man of fifty-one. He knew perfectly well that he was not going to buy an organic farm, or move to South America.

Meanwhile, since neurosis is like a gas, and will expand to fill whatever space it is provided, Ramsey the footloose became an even more flamboyant hypochondriac. Lately his complaint had migrated from a vague unease about his bowels to the fact that it took too long to pee. He was starting to get up out of bed two or three times a night to evacuate his bladder, and was forever moaning about lower-back pain, or stiffness in his upper thighs. Nary a day went by that he did not declare himself nonspecifically "off-form," though getting him to describe what precisely he meant by that, where did it hurt, was he constipated, was like quizzing a child of three.

Well, everyone had their quirks, and Irina could abide Ramsey's. She'd known for years that he had a nervous, scrutinizing relationship to his body—some ghastly terminal illness was always lurking around the corner—and frankly, she had a hard time taking his dithers about his health seriously so long as he continued to smoke. As Ramsey varied his phantom ailments, Irina varied her response. Sometimes she humoured his every pang and groan; lately she was more in the mood to ignore them.

It was all manageable. Working on a new illustration project, Irina could afford his interruptions upstairs; eager for busywork, her husband ran most of the errands. Filling time with virtually nothing was a talent, and Ramsey appeared to have the knack. A leisurely, companionable vista seemed to open up before them, but for one blot on the landscape.

After 9/11 and that ghastly set-to, they'd both been shell-shocked, and it was natural for their sex life to have subsided. But by October or so, surely a regular schedule of intimacies might have resumed. After all, through the worst of their fractiousness, the one thing they'd always been good at was fucking.

Yet lately Ramsey seemed rarely inclined to do more than wrap his body around her back. The fit, as ever, was delectable, but there were alternative configurations that fit pretty bloody well, too, in which Ramsey evinced decreasing interest. One night in November they did put it together, but, as if having found it dark and scary in there, his dick shrank shyly and withdrew exhaustedly to surface. On another, they must have tried for half an hour, but repeatedly stuffing in his spongy penis recalled the first time that Irina had tried to insert a Tampax as a teenager, and didn't realize that you were supposed to keep the soft cotton braced inside the cardboard sheath. On a few evenings thereafter she tacitly pressed the matter, sliding her fingers down his smooth, flat stomach, only to find—well, it was like reaching into an open jar of pickles that hadn't been refrigerated. "Just ain't happening, pet," he would mumble, and after a reassuring squeeze she'd let him be.

Maybe like two sticks rubbing together they'd become too dependent on friction to ignite, and enforced tranquillity couldn't light their fire. To get nostalgic for screaming matches seemed foolish, but she hadn't meant to throw out the baby-making with the bathwater. Alternatively, maybe, despite his cheerful declarations that closing the door on snooker for good would be "a relief," at the prospect of retirement he was depressed, perhaps clinically so. Impotence—a word she ducked—was a classic symptom.

She preferred either theory to the third: that Betsy was right. That you couldn't "keep it." That their continual desperation to get their hands on each other having lasted over four years made them lucky, but that all relationships eventually trace the same arc: sex settles down to something nice and plain, familiar and, on many a night, sneakily too much bother. Her disappointment was soul-destroying. What was the point of leaving Lawrence and wreaking all that havoc, only to end up where she started?

424

But in that case, she and Ramsey were fatally out of sync. She still wanted him, with an intensity that was becoming obsessive. When Ramsey made runs to Safeway, she was getting into the bad habit of hurriedly, frantically masturbating in her studio while he was gone. Her fantasies were vivid, verbal, and various, but had one thing in common: they were always, without fail, about her own husband.

◆ ◆ ◆

So it was tacky, but before she embarrassed him by raising the issue at dinner, or sought therapeutic redress, Irina sought re-dress, period. For Valentine's Day, surely there'd be no harm in trying the racy-underwear gambit. Something visually fresh might stir him, and at the least they might find the new gear a laugh.

Along with half the men in London it seemed, she ventured into Agent Provocateur, to find that lingerie had come a long way from the scratchy red lace and garters displayed in the sex shops along Christopher Street in her youth. Some of the teddies were tasteful, the bras comely but not uncomfortable, and at length she had a fabulous time. At checkout, her haul came to an appalling £312.16, but what the hell. Ramsey was rich.

"I'm sorry, madam, but your card has been declined."

Pinkening, Irina fought the impulse to announce that she was no bankrupt, thank you very much; that her husband was a sportsman of international renown who had earned millions . . . when the saleswoman wouldn't believe her and didn't care.

"Oh," she said. "Maybe my husband forgot to . . . or there's been a computer error. Please, take this one."

To Irina's mortification, the Visa and Switch were also declined, and the queue behind her, in the Valentine's Day rush, was curling down the aisle. The only other plastic at her disposal was Lawrence's MasterCard, still jointly in both their names, whose expiration date did not arrive until next month. Putting a charge from Agent Provocateur on Lawrence's bill was beyond the pale. "If you could put that aside for me," she mumbled, "I'll come back with cash." Primly, the saleswoman slid under the counter the pile of beautifully beribboned boxes, her jaded expression betraying a scepticism that this deadbeat would ever return to retrieve them. She was right.

Bearing no gifts with which to bare gifts, Irina returned to Victoria

Park Road in a state of suspension. There was an explanation, some temporary financial snafu. She found Ramsey in the kitchen affixing a tip to one of those new cues, each of which had cost in the range of £1,000. Just now, she wished that he would firmly declare his retirement, rather than merely withdrawing from tournaments one by one—in which case there would be no purpose to gluing that tiny circle of felt so meticulously to the tip of a stick good for little more than an impromptu flagpole.

"Where you been, love?" he said, and she said, "Shopping." "Don't see no packages," he observed, and she said, "Nope." He left to pee, and when he returned he proposed, "Valentine's Day, innit? Reckon it's time we hit that place in Smithfield you're always on about, and reclaim it from Anorak Man."

"Club Gascon could run us three hundred quid, knowing your taste in wine." She suggested evenly, "I think we should eat in."

"Hey, you only live once!"

"In terms of pricey dinners, we've lived several times." Although eager for assurance that a pile of cheques simply never made it into the post, Irina was uneasy. "Ramsey . . . Is there any reason you know of that your credit cards might be declined?"

Ramsey pared the sides of the tip intently with a razor blade. "They might be under a mite bit of strain, like."

"Why would that be?" she asked calmly, though there are varieties of calm that border on insanity; she had begun to tremble. "Do you need to transfer some funds?"

"You could say that. Like, from some other git's to my own."

She had to sit down. "What are you telling me?"

He examined the ferrule critically; he'd nicked the brass. "I'm not well clear on the big picture—dosh bores the bollocks off me, to be honest—but it seems I'm a tad skint."

"You're *broke*?"

"That'd be more of an American expression."

It was a strange experience, to start to hyperventilate while merely sitting in a chair. "I don't think this is the time to explore colloquial niceties. Ramsey, would you stop fussing with that cue and talk to me!"

He put the cue down and looked at her, and she could see that he was clearer on the *big picture* than he let on.

"According to your Web page," said Irina, "you have lifetime earnings of over four million pounds. *Where is it?*"

426

Ramsey shrugged. "Jude took me for a fair whack. And ducky, you got any idea what a doddle it is to run through a few million pounds?"

"Don't *ducky* me! You promised. We're not duckying anymore, full stop."

They sat across from each other and breathed.

"You won 150 grand for the final in Sheffield." They would not fight, she was not going to fight, but her throat had tightened and her lungs hurt. "You bought those cues, got Denise repaired—or embalmed, since it merely allowed for a proper burial. We've been out to eat. But we can't have run through £150,000 in the last nine months."

"I put a flutter on the results of the final."

"Your own final? Is that legal?"

"Long as you don't wager on the other bloke, there's no rule against it. I bet on myself. Reckoned it showed confidence. And at eight-to-one, I'd have made a packet."

"Why, how much did you bet?"

"Hundred."

As it registered that he did not mean £100 but £100,000, Irina's face burned so hot that stuck into the Easy-Bake oven of her childhood it would have browned a cake. "You never told me you had a gambling problem."

"Never said it was a problem."

"It is now."

"Rubbish. Just what Clive Everton would call *unfortunate.*"

"When Everton says *unfortunate,* he usually means *stupid.*" Not only was the observation lifted tactlessly from Lawrence, but it surely qualified as hurling invective, and she took it back. "I'm sorry. That just came out. I don't want to have a row." The adrenaline had peaked in her bloodstream, and left her weak. "Why didn't you tell me that you were in financial trouble?"

"Didn't want you to worry, did I? *Love* spending money on you, pet."

It was time to take over as the grown-up. Which Irina had not hitherto been acting. She didn't know anything about his finances, because she'd never asked. She'd been playing the girl. Like Ramsey himself, she'd bought hook, line, and sinker into the classic delusion of the nouveau riche: that a lot of money is tantamount to an infinite amount of money.

"Isn't this a strange time to consider retiring, then? You haven't played a tournament this season."

"One of the reasons I been giving the tour a miss is dosh, pet," he said softly. "Eats, motor, and kip—the circuit's not free. None of them new cues shoot better than a barge pole. I don't at least make the quarters, the first rounds dig us deeper in a hole."

"I wish you'd *told* me! . . . Still—there's no need to panic. This house is worth a fortune on today's market. We can take out a mortgage."

Ramsey frowned. "Are you meant to take out three?"

"I thought you owned this place free and clear!" More breathing. "Okay." More breathing. "But that means you're not just broke," she put together. "And with the credit cards maxed out as well . . . You're in debt."

"That'd be one way of putting it."

"You have another way of putting it?"

"Not particularly."

"Where are you going?"

"Take a slash."

"You just went a few minutes ago."

"Tea," he said, though she doubted it; the cognac was on the counter. When he returned, he walked as if ninety years old, clutching his lower back. "Off-form," he muttered.

When you plug one escape route in a system under pressure, it tends to spring a leak somewhere else; at last, full-fledged exasperation infused her voice. "Would you *please* go see a doctor? Either get whatever's ailing you seen to, or shut up!"

Ramsey raised his hands. "Fair enough!"

"I assume you do at least have health insurance?"

"Mmm. Seems to me that private policy was one of the first things to go."

"For Pete's sake. Well, there's still the NHS. You have a GP?"

"Not registered."

"You're a hypochondriac, and you don't even have a doctor?" She'd never before used the word to his face.

His expression blackened. "My plumbing's acting up, not my head. And I don't fancy doctors."

"When was the last time you had a checkup?"

"Couldn't say," he said warily.

"You're over fifty. You're supposed to be getting a colonoscopy, and I don't know what else. I'll find you a GP tomorrow. We'll get you registered, and make an appointment for a full overhaul. You must have paid a fortune in taxes. Might as well get something out of them."

Thus officiously Irina took charge, and good luck to her ever giving it back.

❖ ❖ ❖

Irina met with Ramsey's accountant—thereby incurring another expense that they apparently could not afford—and got the grim lowdown. Ramsey had a few tucked-away investments that hadn't matured, but it was probably worth sacrificing some interest to reduce that confiscatory credit-card debt. Meanwhile, to keep up with mortgage payments and daily expenses, they would have to live on Irina's income, such as it was.

Irina's private savings were generous for a nest egg, but minimal for a livelihood. Ramsey's standing obligations were so crushing that the $50,000 from the Lewis Carroll seemed suddenly spare change. As for the giddy royalty cheques supposedly sure to follow, her new publisher in the States had found sales of *Frame and Match* disappointing. Apparently even that gold embossed sticker couldn't browbeat Americans into buying a book about *snooker*. She wouldn't receive the first half of her next advance until she delivered the goods. Ramsey had treated her to the life of Riley for almost five years, and she couldn't defensibly resent covering the household expenses for a while. Still, she wished someone had warned her at the time that the bills for all that champagne and sushi would ultimately fall in her own lap. They'd wasted so much money!

Between suddenly having neither professional nor purchasing power, Ramsey must have felt unmanned. He couldn't stand having his wife pay for everything, but he had no choice; thus he capitulated to a childlike dependency across the board. Mindful that in many respects she'd been acting like a little princess, now Irina did everything. She gave the housekeeper notice, and once-overed the house from top to bottom herself. When she announced that they were not, end of story, eating out, and further that the ashram routine was out the window, he didn't put up resistance. Yet the new regime did require her to cook every meal, and, since she was choosy about ingredients, to do most of the shopping. All of which put her behind on the new illustrations, their only immediate prospect of income. So helpless had Ramsey become that he wouldn't even go to the appointment with his new GP by himself, though it was only a standard checkup. The GP was bound to certify him as fit as a fiddle, but at least an official verdict that there was nothing wrong with him would oblige Ramsey to stifle the bellyaching when they had bigger problems right now than his imaginary disorders.

Sitting in the stark waiting room of their local East End clinic, Irina surveyed the other patients—Bangladeshis on one side, whites on the other, the latter either gaunt or overweight. Indigenous East Enders gawked back; nods and elbows in adjacent sides signalled recognition of their local snooker star. She hated being a snob, but it was hard not to share the locals' dismay that the man who graced their television screens several times a year obtained his medical care from the grotty old National Health Service along with everyone else.

His name came up, and she told him to be brave, already sounding like his mother. Ramsey hated having blood drawn; well, who didn't. With a little wave, he disappeared down the pea-green hall, and she had an odd, momentary presentiment of waving good-bye, not to Ramsey for a few minutes, but to a taking for granted of something beautifully unconscious and simple that might never walk back into the waiting room again. Studying the digital readout advising patients to be sure to tell their doctors when treatments actually worked in order to "keep up morale," Irina cursed herself for not having brought a book.

He was gone a long time. When he finally returned, shirt cuffs unbuttoned, leather jacket in hand trailing a sleeve on the floor, Ramsey wore an expression whose particular shade of seriousness she had never seen before. She'd sometimes given him a hard time about being such a whinger. But with that look on his face, Irina was reminded of the glib 60s graffiti, EVEN PARANOIDS HAVE REAL ENEMIES. The corollary stood to reason that even hypochondriacs get sick.

❖ ❖ ❖

"I'd thought you weren't attracted to me anymore," she said.

They'd instinctively descended to the basement snooker hall, where Ramsey felt most at home. Yet they huddled on the leather sofa with an incongruous refugee quality, like asylum seekers in their own house. Beneath the conical light over the snooker table, the baize glowed once more like a verdant pasture for a picnic, but it had more the look of grass that's greener on the other side. The field lay physically before them, but the serenity it vivified belonged to the past.

"But it's that you can't, isn't it? Why didn't you tell me?" All this time it was what Ramsey *hadn't* been complaining about that should have concerned her.

"Figured it might get better. And I was scared."

"Denial's not just a river in Egypt?" The hackneyed wisecrack wasn't funny; already, jokes came hard. Even Ramsey's *It's my prostrate*—he was not that illiterate; he knew the difference—had fallen flat.

"It seems so unfair," she said. "Why couldn't it be a little patch of something suspicious on your shoulder blade? It's as if someone up there is gunning for us. Hitting literally *below the belt*."

"Can't say I ever been persuaded that you always kill the thing you love, but sure as fuck somebody's going to."

"But it's not definite. You need more tests."

"Yeah," he said hopelessly. "But when that Paki stuck his finger up my bum, his face went queer. Geezer didn't look happy."

"You shouldn't call him a Paki, I guess," she said dully. It wasn't *attractive,* but the large numbers of Third World doctors that now stocked the NHS drew universal mistrust, on the arguably unfounded presumption that they weren't well trained. "When do the lab results come in?"

"Dunno."

"Meantime, how are we going to do anything? I can't imagine making dinner, and not only tonight, but ever. Eventually we'll starve. And forget drawing dopey little pictures. How do people manage in such circumstances? How is it that you don't trip over hundreds of people on any given day who've simply flopped down on the sidewalk? There's your *prostrate cancer*." Suddenly a door had opened onto the anguish that had surrounded every side of this charmed house for years, and she realized that until now her life had been exceptionally pleasant. It would have been nice to notice.

❖ ❖ ❖

Irina recovered her culinary powers—in fact, she was so anxious to do for Ramsey that he objected she was going to make him fat—and otherwise occupied much of the next several days reading medical pages on the Internet. The upside of this research was that it gave her something to do, the downside that it made her sick.

The assertion on each of these Web sites that virtually every man will come down with some form of prostate cancer sooner or later was reassuring, though just because the malady was common shouldn't make it ipso facto any more palatable. Every therapy described, and they were legion, posted encouraging success rates, but also a list of possible side effects. Though these varied in specifics and severity, a pattern began to emerge: pelvic pain, mild urinary urgency, scrotal swelling, *impotence*. Infection around incision, postoperative bleeding, incontinence, *impotence*. Blood in urine, burning sensation in lower scrotum, difficulty in urination, *impotence*. Diarrhoea, rectal irritation, nausea, *impotence*.

It would not do to feel sorry for herself, though she hoped it was not reprehensible that she might feel sorry for Ramsey and Irina the couple. In the days she was agonizing over whether to part with Lawrence, she'd thought a lot about sex, about whether it was important. In choosing Ramsey, she had clearly concluded that sex was *very* important. Now it was time to revisit the question, and for the sake of her husband, herself, and their future happiness try to conclude instead that they could live without it.

Well, of course they could live without it. Despite the great cultural to-do over the matter, it didn't take very long, did it; it didn't occupy much of the day. Its gratification was fleeting. It was merely an exercise in putting one thing inside of another, and a woman could experience the same sensation, more or less, by other means. As for emotional deprivation, maybe she'd have been more anguished if something along the lines of Alex Higgins's throat cancer prevented them from kissing. She could still fall into his mouth like sky-diving in the dark; they could still interlock into an inscrutable coffee-table puzzle in the morning. They could still dine together (if no longer in a restaurant . . .), and hold hands on the way to the cinema. Ramsey was no less handsome, and she would still melt unexpectedly when glancing across the rim of her coffee cup. Why, veritably all of life's smorgasbord was still spread before them, and to fixate on the removal of one tasty dish from the table seemed churlish in the extreme.

Be that as it may . . . if fucking didn't take very long, something about the diversion benefited the rest of the day. While she was resourceful enough to counterfeit the sensation, she didn't *want* it by other means. Indeed, when Ramsey moved to pleasure her these nights, she gently dissuaded his hand, for the prospect of getting off while her husband stayed put was no more appealing than the idea of going on a romantic island holiday all by herself and sending postcards. Since his checkup, even kissing had subtly transformed. Oh, any number of times of an afternoon she was accustomed to reaching for his lips and going no

432

farther. Yet now kissing was a reminder of constraint—not of what they might do, but of what they could not. Even in private, Irina installed a moratorium. Cat's-away shenanigans in her studio while Ramsey made runs to Safeway suddenly seemed like cheating, like sneaking bars of chocolate when your spouse was on a diet. If Ramsey was doing without, Irina would do without. In all, it was a small sacrifice—wasn't it? It should have been. It really should have been. Alas, the fact that it should have been didn't mean it was.

Yet while any wife would naturally ponder the matter, the intensity with which she brooded over the prospect of everlasting celibacy was suspect. Perhaps she seized on her husband's incapacity in bed to distract her from what could prove another pending impotence, of a more ultimate sort.

❖ ❖ ❖

"Of course, it's natural for your imagination to run away with you," said Irina as they walked to the clinic to which Ramsey had at last been summoned. "But most of what I've read on these Web pages has been comforting. Even if you have it, so long as it's at a reasonably early stage, the chances of a complete recovery are high. They've come a long way with this stuff, and there's a huge range of different treatments. Granted, they all come with a little—discomfort—but most of that is temporary."

"*Most of that*," said Ramsey, who'd not come near the computer. "What bit's not temporary?"

The, ah, *pattern* that Irina had detected in sets of side effects she had kept to herself. "There's really no point in talking about this until we're sure that anything is wrong."

"But you was just talking about it."

"I'm nervous. Motor-mouthing. It's not helpful, I'm sorry."

Cherry blossoms in bloom, Victoria Park was viciously beautiful. Clasped in her own, Ramsey's hand, usually so dry from cue chalk, was sweating. "Irina," he said softly, "they're pretty much gonna cut my dick off. Ain't that right?"

"Shh."

As they sat again in the waiting room, Irina was mystified why she had ever been anxious about anything else. She marvelled how she could ever have worried whether Ramsey would win a mere snooker match, or have lost ten minutes' sleep over a cheap bauble like the Lewis Carroll.

It was inconceivable that she had repeatedly dithered over an editor's reaction to a few inconsequent drawings, and the fact that she had devoted an iota of concern to whether a stain came out in the wash seemed beyond preposterous, indeed profane. But then, maybe none of that had ever qualified as *anxiety*. Maybe in the end choosing the wrong colour blue for a backdrop, losing cheques in the post, and dropping an irreplaceable button from your favourite shirt down a storm drain were all just forms of entertainment.

Once they seated themselves before the Asian's desk—who wasn't Pakistani after all, but Indian—Irina didn't like it that Dr. Saleh spent a long moment looking down at Ramsey's file before raising his head. She didn't like it one bit.

"Mr. Acton," the small brown man began. "I am referring you to an oncologist at Guy's and St. Thomas's."

"Excuse me," said Irina, flushed with fury. "Is that your idea of how to tell my husband that he has cancer? That he's being 'referred to an *oncologist*'?"

"It is one way," Dr. Saleh said warily.

"Ramsey is a snooker player. I doubt he even knows that word!"

"Mrs. Acton," he said quietly. "I am not the enemy."

"I'm sorry," she said. But she wanted to stay angry. As soon as she let go of the rage she started to cry.

Remaining stoical, Ramsey stroked her hair. Bankruptcy may have inspired him to childishness, but the likelihood of major illness had had the opposite effect. Since his checkup, he had been sombre, serious, and adult. "But you can tell us something," he said; *summat,* even his pronunciation made her ache. "You're not going to shift us to some other bloke and keep shtum."

"Your PSA test indicates highly elevated prostatic acid in your blood. Your oncologist will order more tests to establish to what extent—but your urine test did not turn up an alternative explanation for these results. So it is very likely that the malignancy has metastasized. . . . You *are* familiar with this word?"

"You mean it's probably in the lymph nodes," Irina intervened heavily. "Or even in the bones. You mean this may be stage three. Or even four. Already."

"We must not leap to conclusions without more tests. But this is a possibility, yes." He remembered to add, "I am very sorry."

"What about the biopsy?" asked Irina; taking charge had become a habit. "What's the Gleason grade?"

The doctor's head tilted. "You have been reading about this subject, madam?"

Irina shrugged. "Internet . . ." She had no idea if medical folks were exasperated by the overnight online experts barging into their offices, confident that they know more than GPs, or if doctors were grateful not to have to explain everything from scratch.

In any event, professionals often take refuge in plain fact, and the doctor's answer was unadorned. "The Gleason grade is five."

Irina slumped, gut-punched.

"What's that, pet?"

She kicked herself for not bringing Ramsey up to speed before this appointment. But she hadn't wanted to frighten him. And she hadn't wanted any of this to be true. "It means," she said, trailing a finger along the tender skin at the corner of his eye, "that the cancer is very aggressive."

"Well, the scale's one to ten, innit? Five can't be that crap."

"No, sweetheart," she said with a broken smile. "The scale is one to five."

"So you can see why it is very important that you act on this referral immediately," said Dr. Saleh.

"I know that this isn't your job," said Irina, who had gone from belligerent to beseeching in the course of five minutes. "But could you give us some idea of the kind of therapy an oncologist is apt to recommend?"

"Cryotherapy—"

"We've tried that," she said wryly. "It isn't working."

Blank. Foreigner. Didn't get it. "Both cryotherapy and brachytherapy are only options if the cancer has not spread much beyond the prostate. If a lymph-node biopsy is positive, a prostatectomy will not be recommended, either."

Irina felt a stab of stupid, selfish relief. The chances of permanent impotence following a radical prostatectomy were 80 percent.

"Hormone therapy, radiation, chemotherapy, perhaps some combination. Your doctor will decide."

Someone had to ask this, and she admired him for daring to bring it up. "Meanwhile," asked Ramsey, "what about shagging?"

"You will not harm yourself, " said Dr. Saleh carefully, "if you find that you are able."

"I realize it doesn't matter now," said Irina. "But is there any reason? Something he did wrong? Ramsey's a little young, isn't he? Statistically?" Too late she caught herself; if she was fishing for smoking as a catalyst, the impulse was to blame Ramsey, which was not very nice.

"Statistics are a general guide only. In medicine, all things happen under the sun. Or in this case," Saleh said, and made his one attempt at a joke, "perhaps not under the sun. It is not proven for certain, but there does seem to be a link between increased rates of prostate cancer and lack of vitamin D."

Forcing a smile, she stroked Ramsey's cheek, still milky from a life indoors. "Too much snooker, then?"

"No such thing, pet." They rose to leave.

❖ ❖ ❖

Philosophically, Irina believed in Britain's National Health Service. It was a fine idea, that all medical provision be free at point of care, although critics, surprisingly few considering the size of the National Insurance levy on the average payslip, were quick to point out that the service was anything but free. Yet however sterling in theory, in practice the NHS was chronically underfunded. Its waiting lists for treatment were infamously and sometimes fatally long. Scandalous cases made headlines in which cancer patients had the wrong breast removed, the wrong kidney, the wrong leg. In public hospitals, the superbug MRSA was killing twelve hundred patients a year. A full third of the NHS budget was dedicated to paying off malpractice suits. It may have sounded horrid, but once they dragged from Dr. Saleh's office Irina no longer cared about sounding horrid, or being horrid: the NHS was fine for *other people.*

Thus for the tests that would establish the baseline of Ramsey's condition, Irina insisted on going private. At least they didn't have to wait. She shepherded Ramsey to get a second PSA test and prostate biopsy, to cover the possibility that the NHS labs had been playing silly buggers with his samples and those of some unfortunate who was truly sick, and the whole business was another inside-pages mistake. Once an independent lab stubbornly, maliciously produced the same findings, a private oncologist ordered a computer tomography X-ray, a radio nuclide bone scan, a lymph-node biopsy, and an MRI. But by giving in to the American impulse to buy *the best*, Irina fell under the sway of the deeper motivation that drove many of her countrymen to exhaust their reserves for the same purpose. She did not want to buy the best of tests. She wanted to buy the best results.

In which case, her money was wasted—and a great deal of money that was. After extinguishing the greater part of her savings, Irina had to concede that they would have to return, tail between legs, to the NHS. Since many National Health doctors augment their incomes with private patients, after a hair-tearing delay the system coincidentally shuttled them back to the very same oncologist whom they'd seen privately, and who was at least—oh, God, something about mortal illness exposed what a terrible person you were, and apparently had been all along—white. "So," he said wryly on their return, "back with the proles."

It was as Dr. Saleh had foretold. This Dr. Dimbleby recommended hormone therapy in combination with radiation, and chemo if and when—it was usually when—hormone therapy grew ineffective. Burdensomely clued up on the side effects of these gruesome treatments, Irina suppressed her dread in Dimbleby's office by reciting the we're-really-gonna-fight-this and I-know-you're-no-quitter resolutions that she must have learned from a host of made-for-TV movies, films that seemed to confuse a life-threatening illness with a come-from-behind election campaign by the Conservative opposition. Yet Ramsey himself asked quietly if maybe one option was not for him to simply go home and let nature take its course, since if the disease didn't kill him, the cure surely would. He seemed under no illusion that hormone therapy bore the least resemblance to last year's brave Tory challenge to an entrenched Labour majority. Moreover, he appeared strangely resistant to the notion that, in addition to being poked and prodded and needled, losing his ability to be a real man with his wife, feeling increasingly *off form* and facing the prospect of feeling far worse in the days to come, he was now expected to marshal his little remaining energy to grandstand on the stump and shout rousing slogans to the faithful as if spearheading a get-out-the-vote drive.

When Irina expressed frustration that Ramsey wasn't joining in her refrain of *we're gonna fight this,* the oncologist, who had a mischievous side, intervened. "Contrary to common perceptions," he said, "extensive studies have compared patients who are determined and optimistic versus others who, quote, *give up.* Surprisingly, demeanour makes no statistically significant difference in survival or recovery rates."

Thus brandishing a sword at the heavens or tossing it into the Thames was no more than a matter of whim.

❖ ❖ ❖

After the batteries of tests and his humble resumption of his place at the back of the NHS queue, Ramsey was not scheduled to begin his treatments until nearly his fifty-second birthday. Assured that a few days would not make any difference, Irina appealed privately to Dimbleby to delay the first round of antiandrogen drugs and relentless radiation therapy until after the sixth of July.

However disreputable their finances, one night back at Omen or another sumptuous spread of homemade sushi would not have broken the bank. But Irina didn't like to repeat herself.

That evening, she lit two candles on the big wooden kitchen table, otherwise barren. It stayed light so late in July that she had waited until eleven p.m., at which point in the candles' golden glow she flourished a great silver tray before Ramsey's place. On the tray, in the very middle, lay a single bright blue pill.

Ramsey looked from his minimalist entrée, like a serving on *The Jetsons,* to his wife. "This what I think it is?"

"Dimbleby said there'd be no harm done, and it might be worth a try. He also said that after you start these treatments . . . you're likely to want to 'concentrate on getting well.' "

"Meaning, I'll feel like a dog's dinner," Ramsey translated.

"Well, you know doctors."

"They're liars."

"They're *understated.* You game?"

"Lady, I'm game if it means using lolly sticks for a splint."

She poured him a goblet of his favorite sauvignon blanc—£30 a bottle, and the last in the rack. He toasted, "Here's mud in your eye—or something a bit more untoward," and knocked back the pill.

They sipped, and waited. Put in mind of the story, Irina told him about getting hold of a batch of magic mushrooms back in high school through a dubious source. She and her friend Terri had sat at Terri's kitchen table on an evening when her parents were out. They poured hot water over the shrivelled brown twists, and after a few minutes downed a cup each of the bitter, lukewarm tea. Then they sat, just like this, looking at the yellow walls, staring down the paint and waiting for the colour to change, for the letters of the crocheted bless this happy home to dance, for the refrigerator to hum show tunes. Too late to turn back from a slight anecdote whose resolution she now realized boded analogously ill, Irina said, well, nothing happened. But, she added, in the expectant interim between chugging that foul brew and resigning themselves that Irina had bought nothing more mind-altering than dried shiitakes from Chinatown, lo, the colour of the walls had vibrated without help, the yellow paint pulsing exuberantly in the mellow lantern light. The cliché in crochet was already dancing, and the refrigerator hum, that deep thrumming reassurance that all was well, constituted a show tune of a kind. The mushrooms were duff, but Terri's kitchen was a revelation, and each visit to that room thereafter had filled Irina with narcotic joy.

Meantime, it was like that, with Ramsey's face: a revelation, with or without the middle-aged magic mushrooms. She kissed him. She said, "It doesn't matter if it doesn't work."

"I know," he said, and they finished the wine. "But I think it's working."

They slipped down to the snooker hall. Ramsey switched on the light over the table; this evening the baize invited them to picnic again. The scarlet, canary, and beryl-green balls naturally psychedelic, the triangle gleamed with the secret of Terri's kitchen: that the visual world courses with psilocybin of its own accord. Promoting bygone tournaments in Malaysia, Hong Kong, and Bingen am Rhein, Ramsey's glassed snooker posters framed the fact that he had led a fine life. It was new, and unwelcome, to begin to think of his achievements as finite and finished, but better to marvel at a job well done than to fall once more into the trap of obsessing, like his fans, over the only tournament that he'd never won. As Ramsey slowly unbuttoned her shirt, Irina grappled with the thought: *This is it? These last five paltry years, this is it?* Funny how you're always waiting for your life to begin, like staring down those walls in Terri's kitchen and waiting for them to seem beautiful when they already were. You can spend an awfully long time anticipating the arrival of what you've had all along, like finger-drumming for a delivery from FedEx while the package sits patiently unopened outside the door.

They undressed each other in a leisurely fashion. Ramsey's finely muscled abdomen flickered like a school of small fish, and his penis was what she'd once thought of as its normal size. "You know, we used to go for months," she said, running a finger over her old friend, "and I'd never see it any smaller. I imagined that you walked down the street with this—baseball bat."

"I did," he said. "Them weeks we was apart, in hotels on the road— I done *terrible things* to you in my head."

". . . Do you feel all right?"

"I feel better," he said, moving against her, "than *all right.*"

Not wanting to tax him, Irina began to roll on top, but Ramsey was having none of that. "No, pet. I'm fucking you like a man tonight, make no mistake."

Irina was glad. She enjoyed his towering overhead; she liked the view. It had been long enough for that protective amnesia to move in, since you don't miss what you can't remember; when he first pierced through to that aching spot at the top, her eyes widened in surprise.

"Irina?" Ramsey so rarely used her name—as if it belonged to her old life with Lawrence, or perhaps to Lawrence himself. "I'm sorry about—" *Shh,* she hushed, but he pressed on. "I'm sorry about the rows. I'm so in love with you, but I've not always known—"

Ahh.

"—how to go about it."

"By and large," she whispered, "especially *large*—you've gone about it very well indeed." If the thought came to her that sex with Ramsey should always have been like this, the thought rebounded that it had been.

"You're dead decent, pet. But I been a proper toe-rag, I have. I just hope that—whenever—you find it in your heart to forgive me."

It would not do to say so outright, but they both knew that this was the last time. Then again, presumably for everyone there came a point that you did everything for the last time. Tie your shoes. Look at your watch.

❖ ❖ ❖

Ramsey may have been a baby about head colds or constipation, but he accepted real suffering with manful stoicism—as if for years he had been getting all the whining out of his system in preparation for facing true disaster without complaint. The radiation treatments, five days a week for two solid months, gave him a painful rash on his perineum, induced bouts of diarrhoea, and so debilitated him that on return from the hospital he would take to bed. Nausea being more or less constant, the meals she served him there—whose delicate seasoning did not come naturally—

often went untouched. He would have been dropping weight, were it not for the androgen-blockage treatment, which made him puffy. Testosterone, apparently, fed the cancer, but it had its uses, didn't it; under the influence of drugs intended to choke the hormone's supply, Ramsey no longer slipped a hand up her thigh. His physique softened. The tiny fishes of abdominal muscles swam away. The subtle mounds of his chest filled to small breasts. The sharp, defined lines of his body began to blur, much as the keen cookie-cutter features of a gingerbread man loll and spread when you slide the cold dough into the oven.

One perverse advantage to the long hours Ramsey languished in a half-sleep upstairs: Irina could now arrange to see Lawrence if she liked without detection. It was a freedom she'd gladly have abdicated, but the urge to speak with him was strong. The very fact that after all they'd been through the two were still miraculously on speaking terms seemed to promise recovery beyond the worst of traumas, if not to dangle the possibility of eternal life.

They met in late August in a Starbucks on the Strand near his office. Ramsey had just finished one of his last radiation treatments, and would not be cognizant for hours. She and Lawrence had e-mailed each other over the months, but it had been nearly a year since they'd met at the Pierre Hotel. She registered a little shock; she'd forgotten what he looked like.

Lawrence's shock may have been the greater, and he made no effort to disguise it. *"Irina Galina!"* he cried nostalgically. "You look fucking awful."

Irina glanced at her hands, their dirty nails jagged, the skin newly striated with fine parallel lines. "Ramsey looks worse."

"Are you eating anything?"

Apathetically, Irina had noticed the last time she bathed that her breastbone was prominent, and the skin over her stomach had slackened; she was old enough now that it was starting to crenellate. "I pick at the dinners I make for Ramsey that he's too sick to eat, but you can understand why I might not have the appetite for polishing them off."

"You're so gaunt! You can't take care of him if you don't take care of yourself."

Homilies. "I assure you that I'm not the one you should be feeling sorry for."

"What's his attitude like? Because if you really resolve to buck it, mind-set can make a huge—"

"His oncologist says to the contrary. You can apparently be as dismal and fatalistic as you want, and negativity has no effect whatsoever on the outcome."

Lawrence frowned. He was a great believer in the power of will, his own being prodigious. "I don't know about that. I wouldn't take one doctor's—"

"Just because you don't like the idea," she cut him off, "doesn't make it a lie. And if you think about it, expecting someone who's in agony to get out the pom-poms and cheerlead for the team is a little unreasonable. That said, he keeps his chin up. When it's not sunken flat on his chest. He sleeps a lot."

"What's the prognosis?"

She shrugged. "We can't get a straight answer. And it doesn't matter what they tell us; all that matters is what happens. He'll probably do chemo over the winter."

"Hair loss . . . more nausea . . . all that?"

"*All that.*"

"I guess he's not playing much snooker."

"Funnily enough, when his energy rises, he does. He says it relaxes him. And for the first time since he was a kid, he can play for fun —for the sheer pleasure of watching the balls go in, for that cracking, glassy resonance when they meet. And with nothing riding on his game anymore, he doesn't beat himself up when he's *off form.*"

Ramsey's condition was such a vortex that she had to be mindful about discussing only her own concerns. "But you must tell me—how's the marriage?" In an e-mail, she had made up for the faux pas of not asking the woman's name in New York.

"It's different. From you and me. More . . . tempestuous, if you know what I mean."

She smiled. "I'm afraid I *do* know what you mean. Do you prefer that? Or would you rather have back that peaceable, ongoing thing we had? Quiet. Warm. The clockwork day. The passion turned to simmer and unspoken. It wasn't so terrible, you know. Anything but."

"Apples and oranges."

"True, but there are points in life that you have to decide whether to eat an apple or an orange."

Lawrence squirmed. "I guess I'm not into looking backwards."

"I am. I go back to certain junctures and what-might-have-been my heart out."

"Waste of time."

"Probably," she agreed cheerfully.

"You know, even if . . . the worst happens. At least you'll be well provided for."

The financial situation Irina had nimbly edited from her correspondence. "Not exactly," she admitted. "Ramsey's broke."

"That's impossible!"

"All those restaurant bills he picked up when the four of us went out? Just multiply that devil-may-care by several thousand times."

"How are you managing?"

"Not very well. I used up most of my savings on private medical care. And for the last six months, I've had to put illustration on ice."

Lawrence couldn't bear to hear of misfortunes that he could not ameliorate in a practical fashion—he was a *doer*—and his eyes lit before she could stop him. "Well, let me help you! I could spare ten grand no problem, probably even twenty! It wouldn't even need to be a loan. You could have it."

She put a hand on his arm. "No, I couldn't. That's incredibly sweet, but Ramsey wouldn't hear of it, and neither would I. Don't worry. I've other resources."

When they parted, Irina said, "Maybe I shouldn't, but sometimes I miss you. Your steadfastness, your solidity. That's not too traitorous, is it?"

"Nah," said Lawrence. He added a bit too lightly, "Hey, sometimes I miss you, too! Rhubarb-cream pie, and piles of chilies."

"You miss my *cooking*?"

"Better than being glad to get away from it. And I didn't mean that's all I miss. But yeah—I do miss your cooking. If you don't mind. You're one of these women who takes care of people. I didn't realize it until recently, but all women aren't like that."

Irina idled down the Strand, bemused. All those years she'd thought Lawrence was taking care of her.

❖ ❖ ❖

As for the *other resources* Irina put off making the call, but another mortgage payment was around the corner. She punched in the digits so slowly—7 . . . 1 . . . —that the system cut her off, and she had to start again.

"Mama?" Her voice was piping. "It's Irina. . . . Listen, I know we've had our differences, but Ramsey is very sick. . . . Yes, I thought she would have told you. But what she doesn't know is that we're having some— money troubles. . . . Mama, *please* don't I-told-you-so, this isn't the time! . . . Yes, we do still have the house, and I guess, on my own account, I could give it up, but Ramsey—he's so ill—and he loves this place—I can't do that to him right now. So I was wondering—do you still have the car? . . . I'm sorry to have to ask, but I'd like you to sell it."

❖ ❖ ❖

By February, all anyone else could talk about was an impending war with Iraq, but Irina was contending with another invasion, and with weapons of mass destruction that had thus far proved far more manifest than Saddam Hussein's. When Ramsey was confined to bed after chemo treatments, it had become an art, and a discipline, to continue to discern beneath the bloat the fierce lines and narrow contours of the face she had fallen in love with. He no longer grew the stubble that had abraded her chin back in the day and betrayed her waywardness to Lawrence; turned the brownish-yellow of ancient parchment, the skin even on his arms and legs was now baby-smooth and hairless. Yet from the slight white wisps remaining on his scalp, she could infer a full, raging head of hair, as with an elegant line drawing she could imply mass with a few pencil strokes. As the months had worn on, the project had grown palaeontological—with only partial impressions in a great bland slab from which to reconstruct a rising pterodactyl. When he was too weak to get up she had learned to manipulate his bedpan without embarrassment, reminding herself that we're all leaky vessels of blood and shit and piss, if we manage to disguise that fact for as long as possible behind a locked bathroom door.

Perhaps the hardest loss to accept was minor, or seemingly: the crème brûlée aroma that once wafted so enticingly from the base of his neck, that round, wholesome cloud of baking custard. As if the ramekin had been left in the oven on high, now the custard had curdled; the sugar had burnt. The drugs leeched off his skin with an acrid reek, and although when she kissed him the flavour was still sweet, it was sickeningly so.

Befogged by pain medication, he never seemed to forget who she was, but he could grow hazy on other details. One day last week he had flailed out of bed, convinced that he'd only half an hour to make it to Wembley to play the Masters or he'd be disqualified. (For the delusional, he was astute; that week the Masters was indeed under way in North London, leading Irina to conclude that the snooker circuit was hardwired deep in Ramsey's brain.) So this one afternoon stood out. His grey-blue eyes no longer flecked with white caps, but calmed to clear, penetrable pools. He was weak but lucid, and the minutes at a go when she could truly talk to mission control had grown dear.

"Love?" he said, taking her hand as she sat on the edge of the bed. His metacarpus was papery, and poppled with premature liver spots. "There's something I need to tell you before I can't tell you nothing."

She loved the way he talked: tell you *nuffink*. "Okay, but don't strain yourself."

Defying her caution, he struggled to sit up, and she helped him arrange the pillows. "I owe you an apology, pet."

"If it's about the rows—"

"It's not about the rows. I been powerful selfish. Back when I first took you to Omen on my birthday"—*burfday*—"I ought to have paid the bill and drove you home."

"And not kissed me over your snooker table? But that's one of the most wonderful memories of my life!"

"I know I been jealous of Anorak Man," he ploughed on. "But not 'cause you been a slag. You been a good wife. I reckon in my gut I always knew you never shagged the bloke once we was married. But I still been so jealous I could taste it like metal in the mouth, like I was sucking on a 50p."

"But I left Lawrence for you. Why has that never been enough?"

"'Cause you shouldn't have done," he said. "'Cause I know you made a mistake. You'd have been better off with Anorak Man and no two ways about it."

"Oh, rubbish! The pain meds have gone to your head."

"Don't contradict me, woman. I've not been able to say this before, 'cause it fucks me up like. But there's one upside to this checking-out palaver—"

She tried to protest, but he raised his hand. His strength was not likely to last, and she should probably let him talk.

"I can say the truth." The *troof*. "I'm a waster, pet. About all I could ever offer you was my dick, which you seemed to fancy for reasons I could never rightly understand, and now it's about as sexy as a mealy banger on cold mash. What's worse, I burnt through all the dosh, and I'll be leaving you nothing but bills and a house in hock. I can't even leave you a World Championship trophy, 'cause you was right: I disgraced you at the Crucible. It was all my fault—what you said around 9/11, and you was bang on. But the trouble wasn't just the drink, pet. It wasn't just the Remy. My problem's that I love you too much, too much to stick. So much that I done a terrible thing, pet.

"Taking you off of Anorak Man was the biggest sin I ever done in my whole sodding life. I could see you was good together. And he was dead sound. Helped you with your work and such like, where I don't know children's book editors from pork pie. He'd have took care of you, pet, and he's clever, cleverer than me by a pole. He makes them political jokes I never get. Not even bad to look at, if you like that sort of thing. Always treats me proper as well, complimenting my game, keeping up with stats like my centuries and that. To thank him, I nick his bird—the bird he loves more than the world, even if he's not always brilliant at showing it. But I got to have you for myself, 'cause I'm a selfish git. If there's any St. Whose-it sitting up at them pearly gates, that'll be the first thing out of the geezer's mouth: Why'd you take Irina? Why'd you take Irina from Anorak Man, you tosspot? How could you ruin that beautiful bird's life?"

The soliloquy having exhausted him, he sagged down the pillows. She patted the sweat from his brow with a washcloth, and fed him a sip of water.

"Now, don't you think that determination is up to me?"

"No," said Ramsey staunchly. "Never met a bird who knows what's good for her."

"Is that so? Still, I get to take my turn, don't I? And meanwhile, you *shut it*. Okay?" He grunted.

"First of all, screw all that *pearly gates* tripe when you're still here. But maybe you're right, that there are things we can say now that would have been harder before. Now, I grant you: Lawrence *is* 'dead sound.' I've never made any bones about the fact that Lawrence treated me wonderfully well, and I know that's been a burden for you. It would have been so much easier if he beat me or drank or philandered, and then I'd have been purely grateful to escape. I confess that I haven't been purely grateful. You say that your greatest sin was taking me from Lawrence. Well, the greatest sin in my life was leaving him, and in truth

446

I've never been quite the same person since. I've never thought of myself quite as highly again. I loved Lawrence; I know this isn't easy for you to hear, but I still love Lawrence, although in a way that really shouldn't make you jealous.

"On the other hand? If I didn't kiss you over that snooker table, I'd never have known the highlights of my life. And it wasn't only that one kiss, either; it was all the kisses. There have been single moments of kissing you, and fucking you . . . And in case you think it's only that inexplicably attractive dick of yours, single moments like watching you saunter toward me on that stage in Purbeck Hall, slinging your black leather jacket . . . Seeing you sink a far red with the white tight on the cushion when Clive Everton has just announced that the shot is impossible . . . Hearing you duet with Ken Doherty through all five verses of 'Snooker Loopy' . . . Catching the look on my mother's face when you flipped her those car keys in Brighton Beach . . . Dancing to Charlie Parker in the Plaza . . . Well, they're worth, as you would say, the *whole kit*. The rows, the lonely nights with you in Bangkok, the fact that we suddenly don't have any money. I'm not sure I've the right to say it was worth hurting Lawrence's feelings so grievously, but it's only wised me up to think of myself in a less flattering way—as a normal, flawed, inconsistent woman instead of a saint. Those moments, they were even worth—this. I still hope that you can make it through, my sweet, and that all these dreadful treatments are the worst of it. But even if you don't. I'd still kiss you on your forty-seventh birthday. Knowing what I know, I'd still lean into your arms and kiss you over that snooker table, and willingly take the consequences, good and bad."

Somewhere far too early in her monologue, he had fallen asleep.

▣ chapter eleven ▣

In the penumbra of 9/11, everything seemed stupid. Dinner seemed stupid, and buying more kitchen towels seemed stupid. Hoovering seemed stupid. Illustration seemed stupid. Remembering that on Monday nights *ER* came on at ten o'clock seemed stupid, although they still remembered. Accordingly, a heavy, effortful sensation attended the pettiest of enterprises; indeed, the pettier the task, the more onerous its completion.

Only one thing did not shrivel into one of those mummified orts under the stove so inconsequential that even the mice ignore it, and that was Lawrence's work. It may have seemed ever so slightly stupid to Irina before, but no more. He was a bit embarrassed to make good on his offhand assertion in Tas some years ago that "someone might as well cash in" on calamities that have already happened. But Lawrence had effectively been playing the same lottery combination for years, and finally his number had come up. Terrorism was no longer a tiresome sideline. Lawrence's speciality had streaked to the top of the international agenda in the same number of seconds it had taken for those towers to come down.

Their claim on 9/11 was modest, and shared by millions of New Yorkers. They had merely been in the city at the time, and uptown at that; neither had lost family or friends. Yet gradually Lawrence asserted ownership. He had put in the spadework on this issue while most of his colleagues had dismissed terrorism as a longstanding bore, and had earned his share of what were, however appallingly, substantial occupational rewards.

Overnight, Lawrence was much in demand. He was pulled onto the same circuit of news programmes that had solicited his expertise after the Good Friday Agreement, only this time he was waxing eloquent about a subject of worldwide concern, and not merely about a peace agreement in the back of beyond. The *Wall Street Journal* and the *New York Times* commissioned op-eds. Simon & Schuster signed him for a book about "new" versus "old" terrorism, which paid a six-figure advance. He got a raise at Blue Sky, suddenly nervous of losing him.

Thus by early 2003 Lawrence and Irina were amply provided for, and their two-bedroom rental began to feel cramped. Despite the runaway property market—in five years, London property values had doubled—Irina proposed that they buy a house. She pointed out that you could still get a few decent deals around Ramsey's neighbourhood of Hackney and Mile End.

Lawrence's noncommittal response echoed his reaction to her proposal that they get married six years before. His reaching for the very same phrases—*I guess so, If you want, I'm not especially bothered either way*—did not seem coincidental. These days anyone could opt out of a flimsy old wedding licence, and meantime a fisherman's eight-foot-square shack in Suffolk, with one toilet and no bath, was now listing for £250,000. Thus in contemporary urban life, mutual investment in property *was* marriage—real marriage, the binding, frightening, complicated kind that precluded ready escape. No wonder Lawrence squirmed. But for pity's sake, they'd been together for nearly fifteen years. He might stop hedging his bets.

◻ ◻ ◻

It was the morning of Valentine's Day, an occasion they'd got in the habit of acknowledging with no more than "Happy Valentine's Day!" and a peck. A bad habit, and Irina had resolved in advance to do better this year.

Grabbing his overcoat, Lawrence hurried to the door, and she stopped him. "Don't wear that sports jacket. You forgot, it has that grease stain on the lapel." When he protested that he didn't care, she insisted. "If I take it in today, I can get it back from the cleaners in time for your interview with *Dispatches*, and it's your favourite for TV. Besides, you're BMOC at Blue Sky now, and have no business looking like a slob."

"No!" he said with a ferocity that took her aback. "I'm in a hurry, forget it! I'll wear something else for *Dispatches*!"

"Lawrence!" Hands on hips, she was flummoxed. "I'm offering to take your jacket to the cleaners, which is a *favour*, remember? And that stain is very obvious. Just switch it for the blue one, which will look fine with that shirt."

Standing in the hallway, he looked cornered, though why her offer to clean his jacket would make him feel hounded was beyond her. He removed the offending item with the slow, funereal motions with which he might have draped it across the glassy-eyed face of a pedestrian who'd been fatally run over. Even when she took it from him, he held on to it a little longer, and they almost ripped a seam.

On a whim admittedly trite, Irina went shopping at Anne Summers that morning. The idea was really more of a joke (if, it transpired, a pricey joke) than a serious bid to spice up their sex life, whose routine was now so ritualized that the introduction of any new element would be as revolutionary as Vatican II. Brusque sorts like Lawrence dismissed risqué undergarments as *Rocky Horror* camp. Still, she nursed a tiny hope that the black satin teddy might turn him on. To this day, she had no idea what *did* turn him on. One thing was sure: if he did get off on sexy lingerie, he'd never have told her.

Debating whether to keep it wrapped in the box or to surprise him by wearing it to bed, Irina checked the sports jacket for spare change or stray business cards, and was about to head off to the cleaners when she encountered a lump in the inside pocket.

A mobile phone.

An ordinary enough discovery, except for the fact that to her knowledge Lawrence didn't own a mobile phone. He had certainly never given her the number. And they'd discussed the matter. While they could afford them, Irina regarded spending as akin to voting, and she resented the exorbitant UK price plans; British children were squandering such a large proportion of their meagre resources on mobiles that chocolate sales had slumped. Since they were both easily contacted by landline, Lawrence had seemed in accord, so much so that she first assumed that he'd picked up someone else's mobile left behind at some meeting, intending to return it.

To confirm as much, she turned the set on and pressed the button. *Bethany.*

Lacking a surname, presumably the listing was first for beginning with *B*. But as she pressed the tab, she found only six more numbers entered into the permanent memory: Club Gascon, Irina, National Liberal Club, Omen, Ritz, Royal Horseguards Hotel.

Heart pounding, she scrolled up to the *B* entry, and hit send.

"*Yasha!* But why are you—?"

END.

Irina spent the rest of the afternoon in a state of suspension. There was an explanation, some temporary professional exigency that required this phone, perhaps provided by Blue Sky. She distracted herself by puzzling over the listing of Omen, the strange coincidence, and the inconsistency: Lawrence detested Japanese food. Her mind idled to her theory that the cuisine had latterly grown so popular for being light, and thus beloved of women for lunch.

On return home, earlier than usual, Lawrence was boisterous. "Hey, sorry I forgot this morning—happy Valentine's Day!" His smack on the lips rebounded like a basketball. Her diffident father greeted his daughter with a similar springy terror, as if at any moment the cops would burst from the bushes and arrest him for incest. "I thought we could call Club Gascon, and ask if they have a cancellation."

When she pointed out that he had therefore not planned the occasion in advance, he admitted that making a reservation had slipped his mind.

"A night at Club Gascon could run us 150 quid," she said unenthusiastically.

"Hey, you only live once! And I thought that tight fist of yours had loosened up."

It had. The financial objection was disingenuous. Since finding Club Gascon listed on that mobile, which exuded an alien, Kryptonite weakening in the pocket of her cardigan, she didn't feel that their favourite special-occasion restaurant belonged to them anymore. "I've already thawed the chicken," she said.

He didn't press it. Club Gascon having cancellations on Valentine's Day was a farcical notion anyway, unless some other woman in this city had also found a mysterious mobile in her partner's sports jacket. Lawrence busied himself, tossing junk mail, studying the TV listings, dusting the dining table, though that was her job. He commonly came home fagged, tight-lipped, and terse. Yet washing dishes, he delivered a rapid nonstop monologue about the Bush administration's maladroit alienation of prospective UN allies on Iraq, whose invasion Lawrence both deplored and seemed to be looking forward to. Then he dropped airily, "Take in my jacket?" She said yes. "Thanks! You don't have to pick it up. I'll do it."

"That won't be necessary," she said, and she caught him sneaking a long look at her face as the water ran. But it was only when she said, "Mind if we skip popcorn tonight? I'm not in the mood," that his eyes flecked with alarm. *They always had popcorn.* Its seasoning maybe—Thai 7-Spice or American Barbeque—but the bowlful itself in front of the news had never been a question of mood.

Keeping her own counsel through dinner, Irina knew she should have just come out and asked him about the phone; the longer she delayed putting the question, the more malignant it seemed to grow. But dread is a mighty discouragement, and after cleanup she even let him tune in the Masters.

Though she'd grown into an avid snooker fan, this last season Ramsey Acton had been mysteriously absent from the circuit, and her fascination with the game had waned. She wasn't familiar with the players in this match, and felt no investment in who won. She had no idea why they were watching this. Or rather, she did.

Yet tonight, Lawrence was glued to the screen. When she interrupted with a comment on Paul Hunter's girly hairstyle, he brushed her off. "Would you *please*?"

"Please *what*?"

"Just—keep it down, so I can follow this!"

"You said a few years ago that you'd had it with this game," said Irina. "Since when did you get so involved in a snooker match again?"

"Americans say *snooker*!" he exclaimed, rhyming the word with *looker*. "I'm sick to death of this pretentious wannabe Brit-speak! You're a Yank just like me, and an American doesn't watch *snoooooooooooooooooooker*!"

The *OOO*s rang through the room. Irina fluctuated between injured, angry, and stunned. Gravely, she rose from her armchair, and switched off the set.

"Look, I'm sorry I used that tone of voice," Lawrence backpedalled. "I've had a hard day, that's all."

Irina kept her back to him, bracing her hands on either corner of the TV. "I've had a hard day, too," she said quietly.

"Come on!" he cried from the couch, resorting to the boisterousness

452

with which he had first burst into the flat. "Turn it back on, and I promise I won't be such a jerk."

She turned around, blocking the black set, forcing him as she might have years before to look at his woman of an evening instead of that screen. "Lawrence. Why have you never told me you have a mobile, or given me the number?"

His face churned. That was the point, before he said a word, that he broke her heart. The contortion of those muscles paraded a *decision* over whether to tell her the truth. Once he finally spoke, Lawrence's opting for the honesty route didn't nearly compensate for the fact that candour had been a choice. For an alternative direction to have beckoned, it was probably well trod.

"I guess," he frowned, "we have to talk."

Irina sank into her armchair, and cursed herself. Had she kept silent, she might have won another precious day or two of normal life. Clearly that normal life was not really so normal, and hadn't been for some time, but if lying to your partner was anathema, lying to yourself was bliss.

"You mean," she said, and it really wasn't fair that she was the one who had to say it, "about *Bethany.*"

"Yeah," he croaked.

It had always been a joke. Putting the woman's name in italics, speaking it with that droll hint of sarcasm. The jealousy had been a game. She'd been jealous for fun, because it made Lawrence seem more attractive; it hadn't been *serious.* Because Bethany—well, *Bethany*—the little vixen was too OBVIOUS, wasn't she? But then, if an Islamic iconoclast is going to make war with the West, he's not going to blow up a Rotary Club in Nebraska, is he? He's going to knock down the World Trade Center. An African monomaniac isn't going to hold free and fair elections; he's going to rig the ballot and then declare himself president for life. It's what made the world such a bore really, the plodding predictability of it all, the fact that appearances, alas, are rarely deceiving, so that when your partner works with an attractive woman who wears scandalously short skirts and flirts with him shamelessly, that's the one he'll have an affair with, *dummy,* for you ignore *the obvious* at your peril.

The burden of these scenes isn't only their banality, but your obligation to solicit all the information that you don't want to know. "How long," she said, "has this been going on?"

453

Again his face kneaded with that awful *deciding*. He might have allowed, "Only a few weeks," and got away with it, but Lawrence did seem to have registered that for him to have come clean on *the main thing* only to fudge the details would make this conversation utterly futile. "It's hard to say . . ." he stalled.

"I realize it's hard to *say*," she countered. "I doubt it's hard to *calculate*."

He continued to train his gaze at a right angle to her chair. "Five years," he said. "Or a little under."

Irina looked at Lawrence blankly. She had no idea who he was.

The few moments that followed were misleadingly silent, for in that time a low rumble in her core built to that notorious roar of an oncoming train that fleeing onlookers had described during the fall of the twin towers. Irina was abashed at the analogy, surely a vain misappropriation of national tragedy, but the sensation of implosion was still akin. After all, she had dully marvelled watching CNN that September morning at how effortlessly over the course of a few seconds a great feat of engineering, the labour of many years, a tribute to tireless devotion and even love, had been laid to waste. Likewise, the alliance in this living room had taken even longer to forge, and was equally a labour of love, yet was just as readily annihilated. If your own life is a self-contained city, then Lawrence was a tower at the prow of her island. With Lawrence felled—or the myth of Lawrence, as she had understood him only moments ago—her skyline was suddenly levelled and more plain. Certainly the feeling in this chair in the rubble of her personal apocalypse recalled that everything-is-stupid aftermath of 9/11, save that even on September 11 there had been one thing, one solitary thing, that hadn't seemed stupid. Now that, too, was bagatelle.

"Why?" Another obligation, but because the question had to do with the inner workings of a total stranger, she was not sure that she cared.

"Well, I *could say*—"

She stopped him. "Mention versus use."

His face was ploughed into itself. "I don't know."

"You must have thought about it." She was calm, albeit dead calm, sails slackened.

"Sometimes. Others, not at all. I keep things—separate. You know, I—"

"Oh, God, you're not going to say *compartmentalize*, are you?"

"Uh—not anymore!" She didn't smile. "I guess I didn't like this feeling, like I was this regulation think-tank wonk, and, you know, solid, steadfast . . . a good doobie, a good soldier . . . I had the urge to be—bad."

"It would have been easier on me if you'd just sneaked a couple of cigarettes," she said dryly. In retrospect, her own dirty secret seemed hilariously, bitterly small.

He raised an eyebrow. "I've known about that, you know. Your breath . . ."

"You know I sneak two fags a week, and I'm oblivious to your having an affair for five years. What does that make me but a *moron.*"

"No, it makes me careful. I wasn't dropping clues, hoping to be found out. I've dreaded hurting you. I've gone to lengths not to."

"I'm supposed to feel flattered? That you cheated *well*? Because going to *lengths* not to hurt me is not fucking some other woman at all." She had claimed that fabled *moral high ground,* but the air was thin up here, the landscape bleak, the company nonexistent. The moral high ground was a lonely steppe. She might have preferred a grottier lowland, slumming in the mud with everyone else.

"Well, obviously," he said, staring at his hands.

There was no need to try to make him feel any more ashamed; she regretted that *lengths* remark, as if both she and Lawrence were ganging up on him. "Is that it?" she asked gently. "You were tired of being a choir boy?"

"I felt—packaged. Boxed up, to other people, to myself. To you, even. I know this whole thing isn't like me. And I've racked my brains over that. But I came to the conclusion that doing something that wasn't like me was part of what drove me to it. I wanted to do something outrageous."

"But what you've done—are doing—isn't outrageous. It's commonplace."

"It hasn't felt," he admitted, "commonplace."

The assertion came with pictures, and she winced.

"I guess I wanted something that was mine," he added.

All of Russia wasn't enough? "I was yours."

"Something private."

"You mean secret."

"All right. Secret. Still, I don't totally understand it," he puzzled. "I love you."

455

"What about Bethany?" The woman had earned her way out of italics.

"I don't know."

"Do you *tell* her that you love her?"

"Sometimes," he said warily. "But only in—certain circumstances."

"In those—*certain circumstances*. With me. Has it been that crap?"

"No, it's been fine!"

"A pretty feeble adjective for fucking the love of your life."

"Look, I don't want to rub your nose in it. And you're a great-looking woman, in addition to being a fantastic cook and an incredibly talented artist—"

"Don't," she said. "I don't know why, but the longer you go on like that, the more it sounds insulting."

"The point is, with, um— Well, it's different."

"It's hotter."

"That'd be one way of putting it."

"You have another way of putting it?"

"Not particularly," he said glumly.

Irina was not sure if the impulse behind her next question was to understand, or to hurt herself. Nor was she sure why she might want to hurt herself, or what she had done that should be punished. "Do you kiss her?" she whispered.

"What kind of question is that?"

"The kind I want an answer to."

Flustered, he said, "Well, what do you think?"

"Because you don't kiss me."

"Oh, I do, too!" he objected.

"Pecks don't count. You haven't really kissed me in years. So you kiss her instead. I think that hurts me more. I might be able to forgive you for fucking her a thousand times. I'm not sure I can forgive you for kissing her once."

She might have kept looking the other way, slipping the mobile quietly back into his jacket when she brought it back from the cleaners. Now, presumably, they had to do something. Which seemed wasteful. This was all about sex, yes? In all, it was a small transgression—wasn't it? It should have been. It really should have been. Alas, the fact that it should have been didn't mean it was.

"I wish I could admonish you with what a loser she is," Irina proceeded leadenly; none of what she was about to say was in her interests. "How she's feckless, or uneducated, or dumb. How you two have nothing in common. How you're used to being around people who care about the world and who actually read the newspaper, so with some airheaded bimbo with Nautilus-tightened deltoids you'll get bored. How this is clearly some harebrained infatuation that won't last five minutes—when it's already lasted five years. Because none of that's so, is it? She's smart. She speaks six languages. She has a doctorate. Since she's riding the same terrorism wave as you are, I assume her career is going great guns. You two have everything in common—more, I suppose, than we do. I've appreciated when you try to explain your research to me, and you make a credible show of caring what I think. But we can't really get into it, all that intellectual sparring and meeting of mi..ds. I'm an illustrator. Icing on the cake, you have the hots for her. You're perfectly suited."

Meanwhile, Lawrence had dropped his chin, and shed two discreet tears—one for her, and one for him. "I'm sorry," he said. "I had what I wanted more than anything in the world, and I messed it up."

She studied him. When he'd returned from that conference in Sarajevo, and she had the night before declined that very other life of which Lawrence had for the last five years been so generously availing himself, she had conjectured that the journey toward true intimacy was a deconstruction— a progressive discovery of the Other as not-you, of how little you understood your partner, an *un*knowing. Yet however often she may have challenged the kind of constraining generalizations that Lawrence now averred *packaged* and *boxed* him—that he was "kind" or "confident" or "regimented"—the one cornerstone of his character that she had never tried to dig up was that Lawrence James Trainer was loyal. In theory, then, they were now closer than they had ever been, because the process of unknowing was complete.

◻ ◻ ◻

It might have seemed odd to outsiders, but they slept together that night. Wearing clothes would have made a weird situation weirder, so they took them off—though somehow the surprise black-satin teddy no longer seemed *appropriate*. Irina drew Lawrence, Total Stranger, to her breast and stroked his hair. According to script, she should have been seething. Yet she couldn't find the anger, and she looked for it long enough to conclude that it wasn't there. She felt sorry for him. A peculiar but at length fortuitous choice. As it turned out, feeling sorry for Lawrence would prove a fleeting privilege, and she'd have all the time in the world to feel sorry for herself.

When they woke that morning, she wondered if the anger might be lying in wait, and she would rise in a single motion to rail at Lawrence as he cowered in the bedsheets, screeching like a harridan possessed. But the rage wouldn't come. She didn't scream about how many lies he had told her, or pry masochistically into the methods of his subterfuge. She padded numbly to make coffee. She felt diminished, frightened, and defeated. More and more the whole sorry business felt obscurely her fault. Since Lawrence thought it was his fault, they shuffled the flat in mutual apology—deferent, solicitous. Lawrence didn't care for any toast.

On impulse, she saw him off for work downstairs, all the way to the pavement. They hugged. As she watched him slouch towards Borough High Street, Irina realized that, from the red flag of that mobile phone onwards, she had yet to cry. But once Lawrence reached the light and turned to give her another hangdog wave, she remembered that simple sequence from a few years before, when she'd run after him in the rain in socks, to hand off his trench coat, his ham sandwich—a memory sweet for its very ordinariness, a rare slice of *normal life* that she'd savoured like pie. So when she lifted her hand to wave back, she could only manage to raise it waist-high, the strength required to bring it to her chest having failed her. The fingers waggled weakly, while the features of her face ran like ink in the rain. It wasn't raining this morning, but it should have been. Because Lawrence never came back.

◼ ◼ ◼

Irina slipped into the train, and miraculously got a seat. It was only six-thirty p.m. and for an eight p.m. engagement she had allowed too much time. Though there was always the Northern Line, which had a way of vacuuming the fat from your schedule like liposuction. Voilà, between London Bridge and Monument the train stuttered to a halt, its quiescent passengers no more startled than by the fact that on one more night the sun had set.

The nature of her errand might be considered rash, although people who have nothing to lose may have lost, along with everything else, the capacity to be rash. True, she could have waited for a proper night's sleep, but there was no telling when that might next be, and the very irrationality of her urgency helped to drive it.

The evening before, she had gone through the standard paces because she hadn't known what else to do with herself. She'd made dinner. The time came and went for Lawrence's traditional arrival from work. By nine p.m., she returned the chicken breasts, stuffed with ricotta and wild-boar pancetta, to the fridge. She checked the answering machine, in case he'd rung while she was taking out the rubbish. Finally she thought to retrieve her e-mail, and the message from his office address was brief: "I don't know how to say I'm sorry in a way that makes any difference. You have every right to be mad. I guess I won't be coming home. Maybe we both need some time to think." Considering to whose flat he had doubtless repaired, she didn't imagine that he'd be doing a lot of thinking.

She sat in her rust-coloured armchair. She didn't drink. She didn't eat. She didn't play Shawn Colvin. She sat.

All night, she hunted feverishly for her fury. For *five years* Lawrence had been fucking the daylights out of his sassy, know-it-all colleague behind her back, and she did indeed have "every right to be mad." Anger is protective; it holds the darker emotions at bay. Yet dejection and despair were bound to penetrate any feeble bramble of wrath, like intruders in Doc Martens crushing a narrow skirting of blackberry bushes around an unlocked house.

On a lone thin wick did a flame of fury flicker, and she stared into it as if mesmerized by one lit candle on a cake.

Ramsey's forty-seventh birthday. That Gethsemane over his snooker table. She'd said no, hadn't she? She'd averted her face, and fled to the loo, where she stared herself down in the mirror. So why hadn't Lawrence done likewise? Why couldn't Lawrence have confronted the same fork in the road, seen the harm that lay left, and determinedly chosen the right? And now look. She'd cheated herself for a fool's rectitude. The electricity she'd felt with Ramsey that night, and revisited in tiny, jaw-juddering jolts at Bournemouth, the Pierre Hotel, had been like jamming two fingers into a live socket. But she'd denied herself. And for what?

She must have dozed a couple of hours around dawn. She woke in the chair with a start; there seemed no time to lose. Might those two have waited, to give themselves time to think? Besides, Jude was the sort who would want a big production, even the second time around, and that took many months of planning. Maybe it wasn't too late. Digging out the number, she moved with the jagged haste of Dustin Hoffman at the end of *The Graduate*. Only after dialling did she realize that he might be playing the Masters in North London this week, and would need his sleep.

"It's Irina," she said, her clarifying "Irina McGovern" a token of the fact that they hardly knew each other. She realized that she risked sounding like a nut, but among the many things she no longer cared about was sounding like a nut. "Have you gotten married?"

A bleary pause; she had woken him up. "Now that you mention it, I don't seem to have got round to it."

In the rush of relief, she had to sit down. "I'd like to see you." After *fair enough, lemme get me diary,* she cut him off. "How about tonight?"

When he named a venue convenient for himself—Best of India on Roman Road—she was disappointed. Any restaurant that "finally," as he remarked, had a liquor licence was a dump. She had hoped for a reprise of Omen, that she might return to her own fork in the road and turn left. Likewise, her heart fell when he suggested that they meet at the restaurant; she was no longer worthy of retrieval in his Jaguar. "I'd give you a lift," he added, "but I flogged the motor." She was consternated. *Sold* that 1965 classic? Since the XKE was a part of her private landscape, he might have asked—much as when a tree splays on either side of a property line, you get permission from your neighbour before you fell it.

Well, she wasn't about to take the Ford Capri, little more than a four-year parking problem, and a gesture in retrospect intended to buy her off. So here she sat on the Northern Line, under the river, in the same navy blue skirt she'd worn to Omen, cursing herself for tossing the white blouse with the tear in the collar into the bin.

It was February, not summertime, and as she emerged from the Central Line at Mile End the wind whipped, biting. That luscious July in 1997, the sky had been lambent until after ten; now, nearing eight, it had been pitch dark for three hours. That magical birthday—Oxo Tower to the left, Tower Bridge to the right, the dome of St. Paul's catching the light up ahead—the vista of the Thames out the open window of the Jaguar had spread a picture-postcard reminder of how lucky she was to live in one of the most dramatic cities in the world. Yet the area around the Mile End tube stop was grungy, cluttered with rancid-smelling fried chicken joints, low-lit, and vaguely threatening. Traffic was heavy, the pedestrian signals short; aggressive drivers careered through the crosswalk, inches from her shoes. By two blocks up Grove Road, her gloved hands had grown cadaverously cold.

The restaurant was drafty, and chintz of old Christmas tinsel still scalloped the cornice. Though she was a few minutes late, Ramsey, usually so punctual, was not yet in evidence. She took a seat, banging her hands together, and ordered a glass of house red, on so little sleep sure to go straight to her head. It had done just that by the time she'd nearly drained the glass, the door tinkled, and Ramsey sidled in at half-past.

She was immediately struck that he looked off-colour, almost yellow, and little remained of his hair. Some men lost it all at once, she supposed—though she was astonished that he'd gained weight. Oh, he wasn't paunchy, but his face was bloated and blurred. Unless the light was playing tricks with the folds of his shirt, he'd grown those little breasts of the overindulgent. Heavy drinking? Once renowned for the swift, fluid grace of his break-building, presently Ramsey walked with a faint geriatric creak; he was still graceful, but painfully slow. "Sorry I'm late," he apologized, kissing her cheek; his lips were chapped, his breath disagreeably sweet. "I'd an appointment that set me back."

The wine eased cutting to the chase. "You said on the phone that you hadn't gotten married. Or yet, anyway. Is that still on?"

"No," he said. "Jude studied on it hard. What she'd have to be up for. I give the bird credit for knowing her limits. And I'd well rather she backed out when she did than get halfway in and then decide she couldn't stick it."

"You make marrying you sound like such a trial." Irina smiled teasingly. "Is it really that bad?"

"Make no mistake." His return tease was minor-key.

"Well, I'm sorry it didn't work out." She dispatched the last few drops of acrid wine. "Actually, I take that back. I'm not sorry at all." She banged the glass down like a gauntlet, and looked him in the eye.

The grey-blue irises were overcast, his gaze distant. In his remoteness, Ramsey looked very wise, but in a way that made wisdom seem not altogether pleasant. A wise person, for example, doesn't believe that he has to pick up any old gauntlet just because somebody flopped it on his table, and he said nothing. Self-consciously, she scanned the meagre wine list. He let her take the initiative, and she ordered a merlot.

"So how's Anorak Man keeping?"

"I wouldn't know. Lawrence left for work yesterday morning, and never came home."

461

"That don't sound like the bloke!" The energy of the exclamation seemed to cost him, and he sagged.

"Yes, well. Lawrence seems taken lately with acting out of character."

"You worried, pet? Rung the Met?"

"There'd be no point to telling Missing Persons. I've a pretty good idea where he is."

The wine was uncorked with ridiculous flourish for a bottle that probably sold for £3 on the High Street, and Irina ran out of appetite for being coy. "He confessed two nights ago that he's been having an affair with a colleague for nearly five years. He's made himself scarce because he's ashamed of himself. And maybe because he's more in love with her than he admits. Or in lust, and I guess close up it's hard to tell the difference."

"So sorry, love," he said, and unlike her sorrow on his account, readily retracted, he did sound truly, deeply sorry. "Must be powerful hard on you."

It was hard on her. Though she had gone about arranging this meeting with fierce, hysterical determination, the image of Lawrence on the corner of Borough High Street waving good-bye, perhaps for the last time, was starting to intrude torturously on this interlude. Beneath the bloat, Irina could still discern the fierce lines and narrow contours of the face she'd once been dying to kiss. Yet his rumpled cotton shirt was misbuttoned, and he'd neglected a belt. Rather than arrive in that entrancing black leather jacket, he had bundled in wearing, of all things, a faded blue *anorak*. Unable to quite plug into the high voltage that had thrummed between them at Omen, she suffered from an awkward, groping sensation, as if clattering the thick brass bars of a three-prong blindly against a socket cover in the dark.

Eating didn't much appeal, but she was grateful for the ritual of ordering a meal. She reflexively ordered a vindaloo, he a chicken tikka; not at her most diplomatic, she muttered something about the dish not really being Indian at all but a British invention, and awfully bland.

"Only grub here I can stick. I don't fancy self-torture."

"You don't like *chilies*?" she said with amazement, and tossed off without thinking, "As a couple, you and I would be hopelessly incompatible."

"You reckon?" he said, with a returning lightness that got her hopes up.

The food arrived, in all its irrelevancy. Ramsey was barely touching his wine; maybe he'd realized it was time to cut down. Meantime, with the comings and goings of patrons, the restaurant heating system couldn't keep up, and Irina kneaded her hands together in a gesture that must have made her appear even more anxious than she was. They looked at each other over the steaming ramekins, and it seemed to hit them at once: for the first time since they'd met, they were both free.

"Your hands . . . ?" he asked. Her mumble about having a "condition" was incoherent, but she did manage to get across that they were cold. He moved the dishes aside, and reached forward, sliding his long, dry, tapered fingers slowly from the tips of her fingers to her palms, then wrapping them around the oysters below the thumbs. That was when it happened: the three prongs stopped rattling on the plastic cover, slipped cleanly into the socket, and hit the mains.

"You're on the rebound, pet," he murmured. His hands never stopped kneading, smoothing, squeezing, fingers sliding along the vulnerable undersides of her wrists. Should the effortless, inventive choreography of their hands be any indicator, they might make lovely partners on a dance floor. "Or after one day, I'd call it more of a ricochet."

"It hasn't been only a day," she said. Her hands were warmer now, slithering into valleys and slipping under overhangs like twin skates undulating across an ocean floor. "You remember when we went to Omen on your birthday, and we went back to your house? There was a moment over your snooker table, when you were teaching me to brace the cue. I've never been sure if you were aware of it. I was dying to kiss you. But I wanted to be good. I didn't want to hurt Lawrence, or mess up my life. So I didn't, and ran to the loo. Now—when I look back on that moment, I think I made a mistake."

His fingers ceased to circle the knobs of her knuckles, and gravely stilled. When she tried to slide her own hands up over his veiny metacarpi, he pinned them to the table; the skates had swum into a lobster trap. It was past time for him to say something.

"If it's truly over with Jude?" she carried on in the silence, like Wile E. Coyote churning off a cliff into thin air. As a rule, cartoon characters only fall when they look down, so she didn't. "I'd like to come home with you."

With a last light squeeze, Ramsey's hands withdrew.

Irina thought she might cry out. The current cut off so abruptly that the lights of the shabby restaurant should have gone dark. The power outage set off the same implosion in her midsection as Lawrence's admission night before last, and she couldn't take two terrorist attacks in as many days.

"I'd be no use to you," he said heavily. "You're a beautiful bird. You could do better."

"Now, don't you think that determination is up to me?"

"No," said Ramsey staunchly. "Never met a bird who knows what's good for her."

She looked down at her vindaloo, forming a layer of congealed grease. "It was all in my head, wasn't it? I thought it was mutual. I thought you wanted to kiss me, too."

To salvage her pride, he should have begged to differ, even if he had to lie. Instead he said, "At my snooker table all them years ago? You didn't make a mistake. But I did, didn't I? I ought to have paid the bill at Omen and drove you home."

"To the contrary," she said. "That night was one of the highlights of my life."

"Look, pet." He looked pained. She now felt badly, having so misapprehended the situation, and embarrassed him like this. Too little sleep and too much anguish had addled her judgment. "You're better off with Anorak Man and no two ways about it."

"All very well," she said, defeated. "Except that *Anorak Man* doesn't seem to think he's better off with me."

"My own advice, for what it's worth, is you two patch things up. For donkey's years I seen you was good together. I reckon what you just discovered is hard to square, 'cause when I was about the bloke was always dead sound. He can help you with your work and such like, where I don't know children's book editors from pork pie. He's took care of you, pet, and he's clever, cleverer than me by a pole. He makes them political jokes I never get. Not half bad to look at. Always treats me proper as well, keeping up with stats like my centuries and that. Far as I could ever figure he loves you more than the world, even if he's not always brilliant at showing it."

"No, he apparently hasn't been brilliant at showing it for the last five years," she said wearily. "So that's very sweet, your pushing me back on Lawrence as an act of noble self-sacrifice. But I would really rather you just take the compliment." So long as she had already humiliated herself,

464

she might as well go all the way. "I think I could fall in love with you. I think I almost did, on your birthday. Even if you're not interested, that's nice, isn't it? I'd at least like you to feel flattered."

Ramsey took his time, tapping out and lighting a fag. "It's dead nice," he said, his tone as drained as his complexion. "I'm flattered, I am. But I'm a waster, pet. And about as sexy as a mealy banger on cold mash."

"I don't know about that."

"I do," he said softly, spewing smoke. "I know about that."

"You seem to think so highly of Lawrence," she said, trying to control the quaver in her voice. She'd put Ramsey in such an untenably awkward position that it really wouldn't do to cry. "And I may know you only so well. But I do know this much: you'd never have betrayed me, like Lawrence. You'd never have deserted me."

"You reckon?" he said sceptically, tapping an ash into his chicken tikka. "I wager you'd have said the same thing about Anorak Man, three days ago."

"Maybe," she begrudged.

"Besides, sunshine," he added quietly, touching her forehead. "There's different sorts of betrayal. And, love, all manner of desertions."

The waiter asked if there was something wrong with their orders, and they demurred that they just weren't hungry; he cleared the dishes and brought the bill. Though Ramsey would ordinarily whisk it up right away, the tab stayed untouched on the table. "Here, let me," said Irina, reaching for it. "You've taken me out so many times."

"I might just take you up on that," he said sheepishly.

The tension was gone. If she'd made a fool of herself, so be it, and now they were able to sip the wine and catch up like the old friends they would apparently remain. She bummed a Gauloise. "It occurred to me after I rang this morning that you might be playing in the Masters this week," she said. "But I haven't seen you on the BBC once this season. Have I missed something?"

"Missed the fact I retired. It was Jude's idea, though I could see the merit. Go out on a high note, swan off into the sunset with that Crucible trophy. She'd notions about me commentating, or flogging some product on the telly. Can't say I got the energy of late . . . But I could sure use the fees. Fact is, I'm a bit skint."

"*You?* Short of money?"

He sighed. "I ain't *husbanded my resources,* as they say. Jude, you know, she's bloody high upkeep, and somehow that $50,000 she won in New York never made an appearance. So with all the travel in style to Spain and that, my winnings from the Crucible burnt up like autumn leaves by the end of the year.

"But it's queer," he mused. "Talk about the way your mind keeps coming back to some turning point, like that moment of yours over my snooker table? I been known to place the odd wager on my own matches, see. And I was *this close*"—he held his thumb and fore-finger a quarter-inch apart—"to putting my last hundred grand on a flutter in that 2001 final. But me and Jude'd started up again by then, and that woman—well, you know how she feels about snooker. I figure she did a number on my head. I just couldn't quite get up the confidence that I'd win. I got so far as to picking up the phone, but put it down again. Jesus wept! Would have cleaned up, at eight-to-one. I'd be taking you out tonight to the poshest joint in town, after trousering eight hundred grand."

They walked together in silence to the end of Roman Road, where Irina would turn left towards the tube. It was depressing, the evening being yet so young that she needn't worry about making the last train.

Putting a hand on each of her shoulders, he turned her into the orange of the streetlight. "Irina, that night of my birthday"—*burfday*—"it wasn't all in your head. But *timing is everything.*"

It is late. After eight p.m., or even nine. With no need to greet her returning warrior, no nightly obligation to provide freshly popped corn, pink pork escalopes, broccoli with orange sauce, she needn't cut short her rambling constitutionals. These lunatic walkabouts have reached ever further afield these last two months—through Green, St. James, and Hyde Parks, on to Regent's or, today, all the way to Hampstead Heath. She has traipsed without respite for five hours, and will return to Borough fatigued. Wearing herself out is the idea. Then, in those first weeks, wandering the city in an abstemious stupor had been purely about keeping herself from the liquor cabinet, the wine, the packet of fags she no longer has to hide.

She is wearing the faded blue polo neck. A faint golden ghost still haunts the left breast. She refuses to toss the shirt in the rag bag. Lawrence had scrubbed at the curry stain for ten minutes with pre-treatment over the sink. She has every reason to have soured on such memories. But who could wring acrimony from any partner, ex or otherwise, having laboured to rescue a tattered top because he loves it, or loves it because he loves her? Once loved her. As for the pretty red scarf at her neck, it was a present from Indonesia, which he brought back after a conference in Jakarta. While doubtless he'd been on the junket with *her*, she cannot shred it in a rage. To the contrary, the trove of this and every other gift that populates the flat, freshly finite, has grown more precious.

As she trudges the last leg home along the Thames, the lights of the South Bank across the river glimmer with the Shakespeare and Pinter that Lawrence would never make time for. Unencumbered by a workaholic, she could now attend all the theatre that she likes. She doesn't like. Climbing the slope of Blackfriars Bridge, she feels Hampstead Heath in her knees. Why, she's walked fifteen miles today, if not twenty.

A waste of time. She should be getting started on the new illustrations. The commercial success of Ivan has increased the pressure to produce—and isn't that the way. Not long ago, no one gave two hoots about Irina McGovern's next children's book, and she'd have given her right arm to be in the position she's in today. Now that she has the audience, she wishes it would go away. If Ramsey's humiliating thanks-but-no-thanks when she threw herself at the poor man in February is any guide, there must be some rule of the universe that says, "All right, you can have what you want, but not while you still want it." Circumstances reversed, Lawrence would take refuge in his work—in its dryness, its coldness, its dullness even. Yet she isn't able to bury herself blindly in a drawing in the same spirit. The darkest, most morbid of artwork still draws on a vitality that she cannot rouse.

Nearing the flat, she surveys the heavy postindustrial neighbourhood with its Victorian remnants of red brick. She searches for her former sense of satisfied ownership, of having annexed a brave new world far from Brighton Beach, where her mother makes her feel clumsy and plain. Instead she feels like a foreigner again, and wonders what she's doing here. It was Lawrence's job at Blue Sky that had brought them to Britain. Now rather than savour the flavourful local expressions—"a bit of a dust-up"; "that knocks the competition into a cocked hat"—Britain just seems like any old somewhere else, somewhere she doesn't belong. The city is awash with Americans anyway, and, latterly, with nouveau riche Russians on package holidays, who speak in a savvy, post-Soviet slang she can't decipher. She doesn't feel special. Worse, she feels abandoned, as if having deplaned during a layover, only for the flight to take off without her. Maybe shipping back to the US would keep at bay this confusing sensation she has almost nightly: an overweening ache to go "home" when she's already there.

At the door of the flat, she fumbles with her keys. The stairwell's timer-light is out. She hasn't been on top of things lately; she never remembers to ring the management company during office hours. The flat too is dark. Lately she keeps the drapes drawn during the day. She gropes for the switch. It is killingly silent. Ironically, she had joined her neighbours in a ten-year campaign to have Trinity Street gated down the middle to block through traffic. A shortcut to a major route south, the narrow, historic road had choked bumper-to-bumper during rush hours. For years, she had railed from these windows at the drivers, who were loud and rude. Within days of Lawrence's departure, Southwark Council had come through. Now that she has what she wished for, the stillness outside is oppressive. She misses the rev of engines and irritable honk of horns, which might have provided a reassuring sense of human bustle nearby.

To the surprise of her former self, she turns on the TV. After battling Lawrence for years over telly OD, now she, too, keeps it yammering the whole night through. Well, television is a creditable substitute for heavy traffic, and she's not going to play Scrabble alone.

BBC2 announces the upcoming broadcast of the World Snooker Championship in Sheffield. She hastens to change the channel. She won't torture herself. It's not only that Ramsey has retired.

He rang up not long after her botched propositioning of the poor fellow at Best of India, to make sure that she was all right. She suggested, awkwardly, that maybe they could be friends. Grown-ups don't usually tender friendship so baldly, and she'd sounded like little Ivan in her own unaward-winning book. Ramsey hemmed and hawed. Finally he must have feared that he was hurting her feelings, and came clean.

She apologized for not noticing in the restaurant, because she had been too absorbed in her own devastation. Now that she has stopped by Hackney several times, she finds that Ramsey's illness provides them a common quality of convalescence—if she is to indulge the conceit that Ramsey is getting better. Some afternoons she intersects with visiting snooker stars. Stephen Hendry and, more surprisingly, Ronnie O'Sullivan are especially attentive, and she feels sheepish about ever having dismissed Hendry as boring, or O'Sullivan as uncouth. In person, Hendry has a sly sense of humour, O'Sullivan a heart. She brings the odd shepherd's pie or rice pudding, which she doubts that Ramsey eats. They are not close enough—yet, anyway—for her to help him with what he really requires: sponge baths, or assistance with the bedpan. Of course, he does have a day nurse from the NHS, a terribly possessive middle-aged Irishwoman who is obviously a snooker fan, and who is always trying to get visitors to cut it short. Upstairs, she teases Ramsey that the nurse fancies him like mad. Frail and preternaturally aged, he finds the joke much funnier than she intends. Despite the sadness of it all, she is relieved to have found someone else to care for. When he urges her to go live her own life, she assures him that he is doing her the favour, and she means it.

Mercifully, the electricity has never returned; the prongs no longer even clatter against the socket. Timing is everything.

On her own account, she has resolved to eat proper meals with vegetables. Yet so far by the time she gnaws through some crackers and cheese, she can't get it together to steam broccoli. (After these insane walkabouts, she's losing weight. But if she's honest, she makes up for plenty of lost calories with alcohol.) As she stands over the cutting board to catch the crumbs, her eyes roam the rows of spices beside the stove: juniper berries, wild thyme, onion seeds. Now that she has no one to cook for, the spices will stale. The oils in the exotic condiments will go rancid—aubergine pickle, Thai satay.

The time may come soon that she'll have to go through all this crap, because the flat is too large and dear for a single tenant. A second month in a row, on April 1 the rent was quietly deducted from Lawrence's current account. She can't allow him to keep paying her expenses if he doesn't live here. He should have cancelled all the direct debits weeks ago—the TV licence, the council tax bill. She resolves, weakly, to pay him back. Nevertheless, a gnawing anxiety of her abrupt single life is money. Maybe it's a girl thing. She has salted away £50,000 of her own. But no nest-egg could be large enough to make her feel as safe as she did for fifteen years, most of them *with little in the bank—yet with a strong, capable, resourceful man as her protector.*

She has learned the hard way that there is no safety. That there never was any safety. So it is the illusion of safety that she misses, nothing more. Ruefully, she conjures what has long been her touchstone, the apotheosis of refuge—that tent holding its own against the elements in Talbot Park when she was fourteen. In the end, it was a token of false security, really, of the dangers of ever allowing yourself to imagine that you'll be okay. Because she should have sealed the seams. By three , the tiny drops along the stitching had joined to streams. A dark line of waterlog was crawling from the feet of their sleeping bags predatorily towards the necks, and the girls got cold. Shaking and drenched, they had huddled down the muddy path to a pay phone outside the office, which was closed. But now there was no one to ring, like Sarah's mother, to take her home.

She uncorks a Montepulciano. She will dispatch the bottle by self-deceivingly small measures. Thank God the vodka is finished. She has not allowed herself to replace it. She flops into the rust-coloured armchair. She has yet, after more than two months, to splay on his green sofa. She lights a fag, her third of the day, one of the dubious privileges of solitude. She is free to kill herself by degrees without being hounded. But she misses his castigation. The voice in her own head is tinnier, and merely whispers that she will quit altogether "soon" or "next month." During those first few weeks, she got up to a pack a day. She didn't care. She has clawed that back to half. Still, the carpet has begun to exude the telltale reek of a smoker's lair. A real smoker.

The drags are contemplative. It's nice here. But she despairs that she made all the decorating decisions herself, which leaves her surrounded with only her own purchases, her own tastes. He lived so lightly here. Rather than feel tormented by numerous reminders, she wishes that he'd left more behind. His coffee glass—she bought even that. His clothes—stowed; she would have to open drawers and wardrobes to go looking for her own sadness. There had been some laundry, but that was tenderly folded weeks ago, and now if she presses those flannel shirts to her face they smell only of Persil.

She did come across the electric clippers last week, recalling the only time she cut his hair. There is something sensual about cutting a man's hair, intimate, animal, like a chimpanzee's grooming of burrs from the coat of her mate. She'd gloried so in the project that he grew impatient. The cut came out too short in the front, and he'd announced peremptorily that next time it was back to the Algerian barber on Long Lane. The clippers were an emblem, therefore, of a failed experiment, and of an afternoon on which he'd not been kind. So it didn't make a lot of sense to have switched on the appliance, to have gripped the vibrating column—it stirred her like a sexual aid—but you could apparently wax nostalgic about bad memories. It hadn't made a lot of sense, either, when she'd bowed her head onto his small oak desk— he'd taken his computer with him that morning; he had known that he wasn't coming back. Resting her forehead on the wood, the way Muslims touch the floor when they pray, she'd petted that desk like a dog. But then, it was very late, and that was before she'd run out of vodka.

If she knows she should be angry, outrage would further wear her out. Besides, she does not for a moment believe that Lawrence delighted in his subterfuge. He may well have revulsed himself, but in so doing he had also interested himself—in himself—and fascination was much more likely Lawrence's downfall than delight. Moreover, a sense of complicity in her fate has done nothing but compound. Granted, on a few evenings she'd made an effort to shift the programme in bed. She'd made that bid or two to get him to make love to her while looking her square in the eye. She'd asked him about his fantasies. But she hadn't tried very hard. She'd been afraid, though of what? She'd been lazy. So she can't get up a head of steam over that tart at Blue Sky. If it hadn't been Bethany Anders, it would have been some secretarial floozy who wasn't as smart. Because as it transpired, Lawrence didn't like fucking turned to the wall any more than she did. As it transpired, Lawrence had missed kissing, too. His pursuit of Bethany made Lawrence seem less virtuous, but more ambitious.

Simply vanishing like that had been brutal, and she should be angry about that, too. Still, he did ring up soon after, to apologize. And she understands. Lawrence may have toyed with being "bad." But he is at core a staunchly moral person. Ergo, the one thing he cannot bear is being in the wrong. He might be able to face her. He cannot face himself. It is his sole cowardice.

Irina thinks a lot about what she feels. By her third glass and fifth fag, Lawrence's more practical conventions commend themselves. Pretty soon she will have to nip all this feeling in the bud, and start deciding what to do.

Another slab of Port Salut. Of course, the most sensible solution to feeling peckish this time of night would be popcorn. Even for the slightly drunk, the high-fibre, low-fat snack would take five minutes to fix. Scores of seasonings beckon from the spice rack. But she tried going through the motions once. Blossomed like a wedding bouquet, the untouched bowlful made her cry. There are four unopened bags of kernels in the cupboard, and at some point she'll throw them away.

Unsteadily, she turns off the tube, chains the door, turns down the heat. These small rituals and even brushing her teeth she no longer takes for granted. Only recently has she not woken to unwashed highball glasses and smeary knives in the sink, her teeth furred, the whole flat chidingly toasty, the heat having run full-blast all night. The self-control required to get herself to bed, and once in, to get out again, she has had to rebuild from scratch, like a stroke victim relearning the words weather and pail.

Under the winter duvet, now too hot, she considers masturbating, but declines. She doesn't know what to fantasize about anymore. And this is crazy, but the unfathomable, half-painful sensation of sexual arousal now seems faintly evil.

She flips a few pages of Ian McEwan's Atonement, and registers nothing. Par for the course, and clinching today's perfect score of zero accomplishments from morning to night. That arduous walk to Hampstead Heath was not only fruitless, but visually blighted: she kept mistaking a curled brown leaf for excrement, white flowers in a meadow for trash. Following on such an unproductive afternoon, she should be disgusted with herself. But she is not. She is well pleased. By hook or by crook, one more day is over.

chapter twelve

"I just met Ramsey's parents for the first time," said Irina, twirling the stem of her wine glass. "They were nice—very British and civilized. But I'll tell you what was hilarious: they don't talk like Ramsey at all. None of this South London *d'ya fink?* and *baffroom* and *I kant do it, neever.* Perfectly BBC. His father is a history professor at Goldsmiths College, and could practically stand in for Paxman."

"So was Ramsey's accent put on?"

"Oh, I don't think so, not put on. Learned, is all."

"Yeah," said Lawrence. "I bet it doesn't help you in snooker, with *the lads,* to sound like Jeremy Paxman."

"Still, what's heartbreaking?" she said. "I bet it would have meant a hell of a lot more to Ramsey if they'd skipped his funeral, and come to one World Championship final."

Their storied restaurant so enticingly around the corner from the church, Irina and Lawrence had slipped off after the service for a quick drink at Club Gascon. Otherwise Lawrence would have melted away, since some things don't change; he still hated social occasions of any description. So she'd been unable to cajole him into attending the big memorial do later that afternoon.

"Are you sure?" she'd pressed. "Stephen Hendry, Ronnie O'Sullivan, John Parrott—all the snooker stars will be there."

"Nah," he'd said. "I'm not family or a close friend; I'd just feel uncomfortable." It had been nice of him to come to the funeral, though. Ramsey would have been touched.

"What do you think's behind all that?" he wondered. "The parental standoff?"

"Oh, I guess they warned him if he dropped out of school and pursued this absurd snooker lark he'd ruin his life. Then he ends up on TV for thirty years. Some people just can't stand to be wrong. You should know. You're not that different."

"Hey, did you get a load of Jude?"

Irina laughed. The sensation was such a relief that it also served as a reminder that she hadn't been doing much laughing for quite some time. "I know! God, what a drama queen! All that sobbing and flopping about! Anyone looking on would have thought she was the widow, and not an ex he divorced eight years ago."

"She's a pill," said Lawrence, with a viciousness that used to bother her so much, and now seemed strangely sweet. "Using somebody's death as an occasion to draw attention to yourself is totally low-rent. Hey, do you want something to eat?"

"With the memorial thing . . . We don't have time, but thanks."

He squinted. "You're too thin."

"Well. You can imagine, with everything . . . You know, the last several months . . . Baking rhubarb-cream pies hasn't been at the top of my agenda."

"I guess you've had a pretty hard time."

"Yup," she said. "I have."

Of course, this week she'd been ragged. For the living, death is thievery, and she'd suffered a householder's outrage just as surely as if someone had busted in and stolen her stereo. But there were respites. Just now she felt tranquil, reflective. There was something to this mortality business. It made life seem so big and sad and strange. Funny, how the most glaring fact staring you in the face from the cot had a tendency to slip the mind. For most of her life, she'd had to drag it out for contemplation from time to time as a discipline, the fact that everybody dies. So funerals were an opportunity of sorts, sitting you in the pew to face the music. Too, she was so happy to see Lawrence. They'd not met for such a long time. The feeling between them had an unexpected repose, an improbable ease.

"Ramsey," said Lawrence. "He was all right."

"Ramsey," said Irina, "was what I would call a *lovely man*. You're what I would call a *fine man*."

"Oh, I don't know how fine," he said, looking away.

"No, you are," she insisted firmly. "A *fine man*. An interesting distinction, don't you think?"

"So what do women prefer? For their men to be *fine*? Or *luuuuvly*?"

"Oh, whichever a woman ends up with, she'll wonder if she wouldn't rather have the other."

"I'm afraid I said a few things about Ramsey along the way that I feel bad about now."

"You had your reasons." She patted his hand. "Don't worry about it."

Touching him, however briefly, felt foreign, yet this was a man with whom she had had sexual intercourse for years. But when you split, you rammed intimacy into reverse. She'd seen him pee thousands of times, but now if he went into the loo and it was just the two of them, she bet he'd close the door.

"I don't know if I've ever admitted this to you outright," said Irina. "I've always wanted you to think of me as ambitious—you know, a serious professional and all. And I do—or I used to, and I suppose I will again—enjoy what I do, and try to do it well. But the truth is, there's only one thing I've ever really wanted more than anything else, and it isn't professional success. I could live without that. The only thing I can't live without is a man. That must sound dreadful, out in the open! But at the risk of sounding gormless, I wanted true love that lasts. I think even growing old could be interesting so long as I got to do it alongside someone else. I wanted companionship. Maybe not to the last dying breath; someone has to go first. But at least into my seventies? The thing is—I thought that was a modest ambition. I thought setting my sights that low, I had some chance of getting what I wanted. And now even with so meagre a goal, I've failed it. I can bear being on my own, don't misunderstand me. It's *okay*. But I didn't think I was asking that much, Lawrence. Especially since I was willing to make a compact with the universe that I'd sacrifice everything else for it—money, fame, prestige; saving the world, finding a cure for cancer. So I feel cheated. All I asked was to stroll into the sunset with a hand to hold, and I'm denied even that."

Lawrence had been through his own trial by fire, and the annealed version was more thoughtful. He stroked his chin. "Maybe it *isn't* a modest ambition. Maybe you were asking for the moon."

She smiled. She liked him.

"Besides," he added, "just because a relationship doesn't last forever, doesn't see you to your seventies or to until you croak, doesn't make it meaningless. If it did, then everything would mean squat. What lasts forever? Nothing and nobody. Look at us. I think we had a damned good stretch together. That's more 'companionship' than most people get."

She took only the tiniest sip of white wine. It was midafternoon, the memorial do was bound to be boozy, and she'd been trying to keep a lid on her drinking. "You know, the last few days it's preyed on me. On average, women outlive men by six or seven years, right? Of course, it's the last thing you think about when you're falling in love. But for a woman—one of the most important things you choose when you pick a mate is *whom you'll help die.*"

"I won't need any help," he said with a grin.

"Oh, yes you will. And I hope you get it." She fought back the urge to light a cigarette. Submitting to Lawrence's scowling disapproval might have been nostalgic, but she was trying to keep a lid on the fags, too. "What I just told you. About wanting a partner above all else. Is that a girl thing?"

"*Nah,*" Lawrence dismissed with a sweep of his hand. "Men just won't admit it."

"Thank you. I've always felt a little bad about it. Weak."

"It's a good weakness," he said heartily. For Lawrence to conceive of any weakness as "good," he must really have changed. "It's the nicest thing about you."

In truth, she had also felt bad for quite a while about failing her own high-flown romantic notions. For years she had loved Lawrence Trainer and Ramsey Acton at the same time. That had seemed to cast suspicion on the integrity of both affections, leaving each dilute. But perhaps instead she was doubly blessed, and her passion hadn't been divided in half, but multiplied by two. After all, it had always been frustrating: if you put the two of them together—Lawrence's discipline, intellect, and self-control, Ramsey's eroticism, spontaneity, and abandon—you'd have the perfect man.

"I've sometimes wondered whether it really matters all that much, whom you choose to live with, or to marry," she mused. "After all, there's something wrong with everybody, isn't there? Ultimately, we all *settle.*"

"Oh, *it matters,*" he snorted readily.

"I should have asked you before. How's it going with *Bethany*?" The italics were for old times' sake.

He raised his eyebrows, then dropped them in defeat. "Not great."

"I'm sorry." She surprised herself with the sincerity of her regret.

"She sort of—moved out."

"*Sort of.*"

"She thinks I'm stodgy."

"You are stodgy. It's adorable. You'll be a grumpy, irascible old man."

"I'm already grumpy and irascible."

"So you're precocious."

Reluctantly, she signalled for the bill; she had to get going. The memorial gathering was all the way down in Clapham, at Rackers, Ramsey's old snooker club. As they idled out the door, Irina asked, "How's the terrorism biz?"

"You read the papers," he said. "Thriving. How about you? Anything on the docket?"

"Oh, I've been thinking about moving back to the States. Leaving the ghosts behind."

"Doesn't always work," he said lightly. "Ghosts sometimes follow you. I've been thinking about moving back to the States myself."

Out in the summer air, in Smithfield Square, she treated herself to a good look at Lawrence—from some residual embarrassment, they hadn't quite gazed at each other directly during this whole encounter—and took the measure of her feelings. She loved him, but that wasn't good enough. The word *love* was required to cover such a range of emotions that it almost meant nothing at all. Since the love we distil for each beloved conforms to such a specific, rarefied recipe, with varying soupçons of resentment, pity, or lust, and sometimes even pinches of dislike, you really needed as many different words for the feeling as there were people whom you cared for in your life.

This love was unusually round. She loved all of Lawrence, as he was —including his harshness with other people, his bad posture, his dependency on television, a pernicious emptiness that all those years together she'd never been able to fill. At once, she sensed a slackening. Romantic love is a taut rope, and in some respects a fight, for you are always thrashing against, if not the beloved per se, your own undignified enslavement to someone else. It was possible that a different kind of love awaits, once you've called the tug-of-war a draw—one that's loose and kind and safe, a love that's relaxing and quiet and easy, like leaning back with a tall vodka-and-tonic and putting your feet up on a porch rail after an exhausting afternoon of sport. Yet it was equally possible that by at last embracing Lawrence in his entirety, by no longer battling the many shortcomings she would fix, by no longer being infuriated by the numerous regards in which he failed an ideal, she had given him up.

"I don't know why I have an urge to tell you about this, it was such a long time ago," she said at last. The silence had been making him nervous, and if she didn't head him off he was sure to start chattering about al-Qaeda. "But do you remember when you were away at that conference in Sarajevo? You pushed me to have dinner with Ramsey on his birthday, and I didn't want to go."

"Yeah, dimly. And?"

"There was a moment, that night. I was overcome with the desire to kiss him. That may sound like a small temptation, but it wasn't. I hadn't been given to kissing other men, or even wanting to kiss them. In fact, I had the unshakable conviction, at that juncture, that I was facing, strangely, the biggest decision of my life. Does that sound crazy? It's haunted me ever since."

"Well. Did you make the right choice?"

"Yes," she determined, with a little frown. "I think so."

about the book

Writing *The Post-Birthday World*

ALTHOUGH THE structure of *The Post-Birthday World* should be self-evident, the occasional reader fails to register the concept—in which case this novel is confusing, exasperating, and pointless. No harm done in spelling it out, then: Ensconced in a long-term and hitherto contented relationship, at the end of the first chapter my protagonist Irina is alarmingly drawn to kissing another man. Thereafter, the narrative splits into two parallel universes: the one in which she gave into temptation, and the one in which she remained faithful to her partner and demurred. Thus after a single first chapter we have two Chapter 2s, and Chapter 3s, etc., until the final chapter concludes both stories at once. Neither storyline is intended to be any more real, or more of a fantasy, than the other.

The purpose of this structure is not simply to play literary games. Because in the strand of the novel in which Irina kisses this other man she will end up marrying him, hinging the book on this single decision allows me to explore the implications, large and small, of whom we fall in love with. I'm as fascinated with the contrast between going to the supermarket with one man versus another as I am in the difference our selection of partner makes to our careers.

Hence this is not merely a novel about choice, about how weird it is that single decisions can have such enormous repercussions. It's about the repercussions of a particular decision. Surely it's time we admit it, men and women both: that we agonize more about romantic love than about global warming. So—what difference does it make, if we pick the man or woman behind curtain #1 or curtain #2?

The answer the book delivers, insofar as it delivers one, is: some. Frustrating, huh?

For I was not interested in writing a novel about the Good Man vs. the Bad Man, which would be flat, and would leave the reader nothing to do. Instead, like *We Need to Talk About Kevin* before it, *Post-Birthday* is what I call participatory fiction. You are presented with Irina's two departing futures, and the end of the novel throws Irina's original quandary right back in your lap. OK, now you know the results. So which man would you choose? Fully informed of the consequences, you're Irina at the end of that first chapter. Do you kiss the guy, or not?

Neither Lawrence nor Ramsey is a paragon. Lawrence is set in his ways, sometimes, as Irina notes, "a little bossy," sexually fearful, and disciplined and frugal to the point of killjoy. Yet he is also supportive of her career, smart, ambitious, and, in his own way, very tender. On the other hand, while Ramsey may be flamboyant, sexy, extravagant, and emotionally expressive, he is also jealous, unstable, inclined to pick fights, fiscally irresponsible, and undereducated. While of course I hope that these characters live and breathe on the page as singular creations, I also hope that they stand in for classic archetypes that most women will recognize: Mr. Reliable vs. Mr. Exciting. Since there are forms of excitement that we could all live without, the preferable mate is anything but obvious.

The two romantic prospects in this novel are flawed, because romantic prospects are always flawed in real life. The tongue-in-cheek epigraph, "Nobody's perfect—KNOWN FACT" may be reductive, but in practice we all have to come to terms with our lover's shortcomings if we're going to have a lover at all. Although this perspective is anti-courtly love (that old-fashioned view that there is only one person out there who is meant for you), I do not believe it is pessimistic. If nothing else, having to make do with imperfect partners reprieves us from having to be perfect, too.

Weighing the merits of one sort of relationship against another is hardly the province of women alone, and happily a host of men have told me how much they enjoyed this novel. But one question

Post-Birthday raises is particular to women: is Irina's driving desire to find enduring love antifeminist?

Of course, anyone can have a career and love both; these goals are not zero-sum. Nevertheless, I would describe Irina's willingness to admit that she wants "a man" above all else as *post*-feminist. After having achieved a satisfying work life, women these days can come full circle: oh, I see. I want love *even* more than—or certainly as much as—a successful career. There is a liberation in the embrace of romantic desire, and in the refusal to feel ashamed of its power.

A special note about Lawrence, who was sometimes thumb-nailed in even admiring reviews as "boring." However understandable, the adjective offends me. Sure, he's a bit staid. But Lawrence and Irina have the kind of relationship that many of us end up with when it lasts. The erotic fire may have subsided, but you enjoy each other's company, and you're still delighted when your partner walks in the door. This steady, companionable, often ritualized relationship is rarely portrayed in fiction with any depth or respect. Yet I believe it has a poetry, a beauty, and a profundity that I tried to do justice. Their quiet lives may appear humdrum to others, but the subjective experience of such couples is not *boring*.

When asked whether I personally fancy Lawrence or Ramsey, I am always coy. I adore them both. As with the central question in *Kevin*—did the boy become a killer because his mother didn't love him, or is Kevin evil—there is no right answer. Or rather, the right answer is up to you.

Pleasingly, readers seem to divide straight down the middle regarding which man they prefer, and sometimes get into marvelous fights over the matter. Moreover, the nicest thing about this novel for me is the way it spurs readers to tell their own stories. So punters will come up to me at signings to confide, "I left a Lawrence for a Ramsey, and it was a disaster!" I eat this stuff up. Tell me more! Like most members of my profession, I'm an incurable voyeur.

Lionel Shriver, 2015